THE LAST WITNESS

Praise for *Past Imperfect*

'Matthews maintains the suspense . . . an engrossing odyssey into
the seamy side of a world that is near, yet sometimes seems so far.
Compulsive reading' *The Times*

'Impressive . . . strong characterization and a relentless race against
time to avert the worst carry the reader along the thick pages of
this psychological and legal thriller with a difference' *Time Out*

'Intriguing thriller [with a] . . . dogged and sexy French detective.
Treat yourself' *Prima*

'One of the most compelling novels I've read . . . an ambitious and
big novel which will keep you enthralled to its last page'
Cork Examiner

'Shows that he is already a novelist of real accomplishment . . .
keep[s] the reader irresistibly gripped . . . [an] exhilarating,
picaresque sweep of plot' amazon.co.uk

'Matthews delivers one of the best debut thrillers in years, brave,
ambitious and remorselessly entertaining. *Past Imperfect* is a stormer'
Dublin Evening Herald

'This intelligent, captivating thriller marks a fine debut'
Ipswich Evening Star

About the Author

As well as being a novelist, John Matthews is an experienced journalist, editor and publishing consultant – though following the success of *Past Imperfect*, which became an international best-seller, he now devotes most of his time to writing novels. He lives in Surrey with his wife and son.

THE LAST WITNESS

John Matthews

MICHAEL JOSEPH
LONDON

MICHAEL JOSEPH

Published by the Penguin Group

Penguin Books Ltd, 27 Wrights Lane, London w8 5tz, England

Penguin Putnam Inc., 375 Hudson Street, New York, New York 10014, USA

Penguin Books Australia Ltd, Ringwood, Victoria, Australia

Penguin Books Canada Ltd, 10 Alcorn Avenue, Toronto, Ontario, Canada m4v 3b2

Penguin Books India (P) Ltd, 11 Community Centre,

Panchsheel Park, New Delhi – 110 017, India

Penguin Books (NZ) Ltd, Cnr Rosedale and Airborne Roads,

Albany, Auckland, New Zealand

Penguin Books (South Africa) (Pty) Ltd, 5 Watkins Street,

Denver Ext 4, Johannesburg 2094, South Africa

Penguin Books Ltd, Registered Offices: Harmondsworth, Middlesex, England

First published 2001

Set in 11.5/13.5 pt Monotype Bembo

Typeset by Rowland Phototypesetting Ltd, Bury St Edmunds, Suffolk

Printed in England by Clays Ltd, St Ives plc

A CIP catalogue record for this book is available from the British Library

ISBN 0–7181–4411–2

Acknowledgements

My thanks goes to all those who helped me with research, but in particular to NORCAP for information on adoption searches, and the RCMP in Montreal for throwing valuable light on the inner workings of their Criminal Intelligence Unit. And, once again, my thanks to all those at PFD and Michael Joseph/Penguin for their tireless commitment and support.

To my mother.
And to my wife, son, and all the family and friends
who have remained true and constant
through the years, good or bad.

Prologue

April 4th, Montreal, Canada

There are times when all hope seems lost. When every precept and foundation previously held as true seems to have been torn down or to have faded into insignificance, and all that surrounds and lies ahead is grey desolation. And while those feelings may not last long, perhaps only moments, when they hit they are all-consuming, they form a high, impenetrable wall beyond which nothing else can be seen.

Elena Waldren was gripped by such dark contemplation, darker than she'd ever known before, as she sat parked in Montreal's Rue St-Urbain, thousands of miles from her home in Dorset, on probably the most important quest of her forty-five years, her passenger a ten-year-old Romanian girl who at one time had been as close as her own daughter, yet had become practically a stranger the past two years. She shook her head; that was part of the problem right there. But she couldn't keep them all under her wing for ever.

She'd pulled in hurriedly to the side, and the afternoon traffic flowed past, becoming heavier now towards the rush hour. Rain pattered against her windscreen, slanting slightly with a fresh breeze off the St Lawrence. Elena remained oblivious to everything beyond her own thoughts, her head buried in the crook of her right arm braced against the steering wheel.

How could she have been so wrong about everything? She'd always thought she'd seen so much, lived so many rollercoaster troughs and peaks, that there could be few surprises left; the one advantage of the over-forties. And now in only two days, half of her past had been completely rewritten.

'Are you okay?' Lorena asked.

'Yes . . . I just need a minute. I'll be fine.' Fine? The police wire had been out for a while now, probably since their trail through France, and no doubt soon her face would be on TV news bulletins. And for what? Her own quest now at a dead end, and the danger that had led her to take such drastic action and drag young Lorena on this odyssey was probably imagined – as so many people kept telling her all along. For the first time Elena woke up to just how much she was out of her depth: she was just an aid worker from a backwater Dorset village home shared with her pipe-smoking, unassuming husband and two children; running the gauntlet with police across two continents was far removed from any past experience she could draw upon.

But at least she now knew his name: Georges Donatien. Twenty-nine years, and she'd missed him by only days. Never to be seen again. Cruel fate. All she had, or would ever have, was his name on a scrap of paper and the few brief reminiscent stories from the Donatiens.

'*Georges*. Georges Donatien.' She whispered the name almost as an incantation, as if that might suddenly bring a clearer image to mind beyond the few stark, smiling photos she'd scanned at the Donatiens'. Something to help fill that twenty-nine-year void. She felt nothing now but cold and empty, and she braced her head firmer into her arm to quell her body's trembling. Tears were close, but she swallowed hard, biting them back. Half of it imagined or not, Lorena had been through enough not to have to see her now so distressed.

She took a fresh breath and sighed it out. It would probably have been just as bad if she had met him, started to sow the first seeds of attachment, only for him then to be taken brutally away. Either way, the pain now would have been the same.

She started to shake off her dark mood and lift her head – but Lorena's muttered 'Ele!' and her sudden awareness of a figure by the car, made her look up sharper: brown uniform, one hand by the gun holster, the other reaching out.

The RCMP officer tapped at her window, signalling for her to wind it down.

1

February 11th, Montreal, Canada

'Two minutes over now. He's late.'

'Don't worry, he'll show.' Michel Chenouda sounded confident, but inside it was just one more worry to stack with the mountain of others that had built excruciatingly over the last hour of the set-up.

Four of his RCMP team were with him on the second floor of the warehouse overlooking the St Lawrence dockside, the other three in an unmarked car around the corner, and dead centre in their night-sight binoculars' frame was their mark Tony Savard, waiting for Roman Lacaille and his men. It was −7°C that night and Savard's breath showed heavy on the air. Three years' tracking in the shadows of the Lacailles, Montreal's leading crime family, and now hopefully, finally, Michel would nail them.

The Lacailles had put up a strong legitimate business front over recent years, but Chenouda was convinced they were secretly behind eastern Canada's largest drug supply network. Then eleven months ago, with the murder of Eric Leduc, one of the network's key men, he had the confirmation he wanted: Roman Lacaille was responsible for the murder, had pulled the trigger himself in a fit of rage. They heard it first from the car's driver when pressured over a vice bust; but he refused to officially testify and finger Roman Lacaille, and five months later he was dead. A 'boating' accident. That left only two other witnesses: Tony Savard and Georges Donatien. But Donatien was too much 'family' for them to hope he'd testify, so they'd piled on the pressure with Savard: if he didn't come forward, he'd be next to go. Finally Savard cut a deal.

The only problem was that unlike Donatien – who was in the back of the car when Leduc was shot – Savard was standing outside the car on watch. He hadn't seen Roman Lacaille actually pull the trigger. There was also the problem of Roman Lacaille's likely plea of self-defence.

The plan now was therefore a meeting with Roman Lacaille to discuss general business, and almost jokingly, by the way, Savard would comment about the mess of cleaning up after Leduc. 'Couldn't you have shot him out of the car? We were still finding bits of him there two days later.'

Once Roman Lacaille opened up about the shooting, Savard would then press a bit about the gun on the floor not being Leduc's normal piece to try and break his self-defence story, and they'd get it all on tape. Enough hopefully to . . .

'*Attends!* Something's happening. Vehicle approaching . . . fast! But it's not Lacaille's Beamer, it's a black van. Stopping. Back doors opening . . . two men getting out. Something's wrong. They're wearing ski masks!' Chac, his closest aide in the RCMP, was main lookout. Chac moved quickly aside and let Michel Chenouda look through the binoculars.

Michel watched as a startled Tony Savard was bundled into the back of the van, looking sharply over his shoulder; a silent plea for help. He reached for the radio mike.

'Move now! Two men have just grabbed Savard. Black Chevy Venture. No sign of Lacaille, and we're not even sure it's his men. So get close so that you're ready to cut in on them when I say.' Michel had switched to English for the command. The driver, Mark, was only three years up from Ottawa, and Michel liked to use English with those for whom, like him, French was a second language. Now more than ever: he couldn't risk even a split-second delay for the driver to understand.

As the back-up car swung into view, a faint night mist swirling opaque in its beam, the van was already heading off. A gap of maybe eighty yards between them, Michel estimated, but closing quickly with the car having gained momentum. Sixty yards, fifty . . .

But as they came to the end of the warehouse block and the first intersection, Michel watched in horror a large double trailer cut suddenly across just after the van had passed. The squad car braked hard and slewed to an angle, stopping just yards short.

They beeped, flashed their lights and shouted furiously, but the truck driver simply lifted his palms and shouted back in defensive protest. Only when badges were frantically waved and their cherry siren was put on the roof and fired up, did he start moving; though even then only slowly. The van was long gone.

At that moment, Savard's voice came over clearly on sound. '*Jesus!* What's happening . . . what's going on?'

Only silence returned. Nobody answered.

Michel watched the screen-finder dot recede rapidly out of the dockside, continuing straight for a moment before bleeping and flashing at a tangent. 'They've turned off either at Lafontaine or Ontario, heading east,' he hissed into the radio mike. 'Looks like they're headed downtown. We're going to cut across and back you up.'

Michel grabbed the screen-finder and directed two of his men to come with him, the other to stay with Chac. They took the stairs at a flying run, two and three at a time. Michel's heart pounded hard and heavy, almost in time with the screen dot. His breath rasped short; he carried more weight than he'd have liked, and at moments like this it told.

Michel took the passenger seat, and the youngest of them, a lanky, twenty-nine-year-old Montreal Anglophone named Phil Reeves, drove. His heavier, twelve years older, bulldog-expressioned Quebecois partner, Maury Legault, sat in the back. In age, build and countenance, Michel was practically a hybrid between them. Except that in certain lights and at certain angles, his high cheekbones and the slight almond slope of his dark brown eyes gave away his Mohawk ancestry. But now as they sped off and he caught his own reflection briefly in the side window, he looked as hangdog as Maury. Defeated. Three years' work funnelled now into only frantic minutes, and it was all fast slipping away.

Michel watched the dot move deeper. As they approached Lafontaine, he could tell that the van was now on Ontario, the next cross street. He raised Chac on the radio phone.

'Anything on sound?'

'Nothing significant. Some rustling and movement, traffic sounds in the background, but no voices. Nothing since Savard asked "what's happ –"'

Even over the radio mike, Michel heard what had stopped Chac mid-sentence: a faint background crunching and a strangled, guttural *'Merde!'* followed by some indiscernible mumbling from Savard. At that same instant, the screen-finder dot disappeared.

'No, *no* . . . please no.' Michel closed his eyes as he made the breathless plea. He swallowed hard, fearing the worst with his next question: 'Have you still got sound, Chac?'

'Yeah . . . still there. Heavier rustling now, and Savard's breathing's more laboured. Now he's coughing . . . or sounds like him. The others wouldn't come over that clearly.'

Michel slowly let out his breath and opened his eyes again. Thank God, at least they still had that. The directional signal had been in

Savard's watch, the wire — because they knew Savard was likely to be searched vigorously by Lacaille — was sewn discreetly into his coat lapel.

'They've obviously only smashed his watch. Let's just pray they don't find the sound bug.' But he knew it was practically worthless unless Savard's captors actually spoke, gave some clue of where they were headed. 'Link me in directly to the wire, Chac. We're running blind here. Maybe I'll be able to pick up something from background traffic and city sounds.'

As soon as the wire feed came over the radio, Michel turned it up. The hiss of static and faint rustling filled the car. Michel immersed himself in it, blotting out completely the surrounding traffic noise as Phil sped along Rue Ontario. After a moment he could pick out the rise and fall of Tony Savard's breathing. A faint cough, a swallow. Then a few seconds later Savard's voice came over, loud and distorted.

'Where are we going? I can't see nothing with this hood on.'

Michel clenched a fist tight. Savard was trying to tell them what he could. No answer returned.

Michel homed in on background sounds beyond Savard's breathing: traffic drone, a horn beeping, a faint distant siren wail. Michel turned the radio down. He couldn't hear the siren himself from outside, which worried him. It meant that they weren't anywhere close to Savard.

Michel patched in to the other car. 'Mark, can you hear a siren from where you are?'

Moment's pause, then: 'No, nothing here.'

'We've lost directional, but we've still got wire sound. Any fix on where they're headed from where you are?'

'We followed what you last gave us, east on Ontario. But no sign of them. They gained a good half mile when the truck blocked us. They could be anywhere.'

'Okay. I'll let you know if we pick up anything useful on the wire.'

Back to Savard's breathing. The siren had now faded from the background. Then after a moment in gruff Quebecois, the first comment from Savard's captors.

'Where's our drugs money, Tony?'

'*Quoi?* . . . What drugs money? I don't know nothing about that. I was there for a meet with Roman Lacaille.'

'Don't know the man personally. Now, again — where's our money, Tony?'

'*I don't know* . . . don't know what you're . . .'

Chac's voice crashed in. 'More action here. Roman Lacaille's Beamer's just rolled up. He's getting out with another man, bold as you like . . . looking around.'

Michel's heart sank. Whatever was going to happen with Savard in the van, Lacaille was distancing himself from it. *'I turned up as arranged, but he'd already gone. And half a dozen RCMPs know it couldn't have been me, because they were watching me through binoculars.'*

'Now he's lifting his arms in a "where is he?" gesture.'

Michel could picture Lacaille gloating as he made the gesture. He closed his eyes and solemnly nodded. 'Okay. Nothing we can do with him, though. And he knows it. Put me back to the wire.' Staying with Lacaille wasn't productive.

'. . . last time. Where is it, Tony?'

'I told you . . . I don't even know what you're talking about.'

A marked pause, background traffic drone returning, Savard's breathing laboured, expectant. Then finally: 'Well . . . if he's not going to talk.'

Michel tried to discern what was happening from the next sounds: heavier rustling, movement closer to Savard, then a guttural *'Espèce d'enculé!* What the fu . . . *uuugh*,' receding quickly into two more grunts and heavier breathing from Savard, now raspier, more nasal. Michel guessed that Savard's mouth had been bound. The rustling and movement faded, then after a second a fresh voice came from the front.

'*Bon.* So, where are we going to do this?'

'I thought St-Norbert.'

'No, not good. The car park there's only five storeys. He might survive the drop. Could still be alive and talking when he hits the deck.'

Michel's hopes leapt: some fix on where they were headed at last! But at the same time the reason for the binding became clear, and he felt for Savard: they knew he'd start shouting and screaming at their new turn in conversation. Michel could hear Savard hyperventilating with fear, muffled grunts mixed with rapid nasal wheezing.

'So where would you suggest?'

'Place Philips car park. Eight floors, straight down. He won't survive that.'

Savard's grunting and wheezing was almost out of control, combined now with some shifting around and thudding. He was obviously writhing in protest, the only movement he was left with.

7

Michel wished that he could reach out and hug and reassure Savard: *Don't worry. We know where they're headed now. We'll get to them before they can throw you.*

Phil turned and dropped two blocks down to René Lévesque to make better time heading into the city centre, and Michel alerted Mark on the radio phone. 'We just got it on the wire that that's where they're headed.'

'Ste-Catherine entrance or Philips?'

'We don't know. You take Ste-Catherine, we'll take Philips.'

Silence again. Only the sound over the wire of Savard's muffled breathing as Phil floored it through the night-time streets, touching seventy.

Within the cocoon of darkness of the hood, Savard's terror had reached a peak. He'd found breathing difficult with the restriction of the hood as it was, had felt his own hot breath bouncing back at him; but now with something bound tight around his mouth over the outside, pushing the cloth in, it was practically impossible. With each breath the cloth felt as if it was sucking in, gagging him, and the binding had also pulled the hood tight against his nose. Upon hearing he'd be thrown, he'd writhed and banged about; partly in fear, partly in vain hope of catching the attention of cars or people they passed. But as the blood pounding through his head hit a hot white crescendo and he felt nauseous and almost blacked out, he stopped. He reminded himself of the wire. They'd handled him roughly bundling him into the van and tying his hands and feet, but he was pretty sure it was still there. Michel had no doubt heard where they were headed.

But with two entrances and five sections to the car park, what were the chances of Michel and his men getting to him in time? They could already be two minutes behind as it was and could easily lose another couple of minutes finding the right section of car park. It would do him little good if Michel caught up with his captors *after* he was thrown.

The night-time streets flashed by Michel's window, with most cars pulling hurriedly over with the sound of their approaching siren. But half the time Michel kept his eyes closed, immersing himself deeper into the sounds on the wire: Savard's fractured breathing falling almost in time with his own rapid pulse, feeling himself almost there alongside Savard to will home the message: *We'll be there, don't worry. We'll be there to stop them.*

It took only just over three minutes before they hit the Place Philips entrance and started up. Mark had radioed in twenty seconds before as he entered on Ste-Catherine Street, and was now winding furiously up towards the third floor. At Michel's instruction, they'd both killed their sirens for the last few hundred yards of approach. Michel didn't want Savard's captors suddenly taking fright and shifting him somewhere else.

As Phil swung into the fifth floor, Michel heard over the wire the van stopping, a door opening, closing. Then the van's back doors opening.

'Okay. Should be good here.'

'Yeah.'

Savard's breathing again started to become more rapid, frantic. Brief writhing and thudding, and then some rustling and short muffled grunts from Savard. Michel pictured him being lifted out.

Michel clutched tight at the radio mike. Mark should be near the top now. 'We've just heard the van stop – they're taking Savard out. See anything from where you are?'

'We're just coming on to the eighth now.' Brief background squeal of tyres, then: 'No . . . nothing on this first stretch.'

Michel drummed the flat of his left hand against the dashboard as they sped along the sixth and swung into the ramp for the seventh. *'Come on! . . .'*

Savard felt himself being carried away from the van, heard his carriers' short shuffling footsteps, but they were crunching slightly, as if they had crêpe soles? Then, after a few yards, they paused and his back was partly rested on the thighs of the man behind.

'Okay, one last chance, Tony . . .'

Savard felt the binding around his mouth being untied and pulled free. His breathing eased a bit without the constriction.

'Where's our money?'

'I told you, I don't . . . *I don't know,*' he gasped. '*Please*, you've got to believe me.'

Phil squealed up the last part of the ramp to the eighth. Michel's eyes darted rapidly around as the car straightened and sped along. He couldn't see anything immediately, no sign of the van or Savard being carried. He pointed. 'Maybe in the next section.' Then, into the mike: 'Anything where you are?'

'No, nothing. We've already checked two sections. One more to go.'

Michel's hand drummed the dashboard more frantically as Phil

9

swung into the next section. From the voices over the wire, he knew there were probably only seconds left.

'We haven't got to believe anything, Tony. Last chance . . .'

'Fuck's sake, guys . . . I *really* don't know,' Savard spluttered. 'If I did, don't you think I'd tell you?'

A second's silence, then the other man's voice. 'Let's get him closer to the edge. He's not going to talk.'

Faint rustling and movement, repeated mumbled protests from Savard, then: 'We'll not clear this rail unless we swing him.'

'Yeah . . .'

Savard lost it then, his protests and shouts of *'No!'* hit screaming pitch as Michel imagined him being swung.

Mark's voice came over the radio phone. 'Nothing here. We've searched every corner.'

'Okay.' Phil had just turned into the last section and Michel's eyes scanned wildly around. Savard's screaming filled his head. He had to be somewhere here, *somewhere* . . . Suddenly his rapid dashboard drumming changed to a sharp slap. 'Stop! Stop the car now! *Stop!*'

Phil screeched to a halt and Michel immediately swung his door open, listening.

'. . . Two. On the count of three.' The words were all but drowned out by Savard's raucous screaming.

Michel could hear everything clearly over the wire, but from the surrounding car-park sounds there was nothing. Yet Savard was screaming loud enough to be heard two blocks away. He didn't even trouble to check with Mark; he'd have heard it from Mark's section from where he was. Michel's heart sank, a chill running through him. Savard was nowhere nearby, he'd been taken somewhere else. There was nothing they could do to save him.

'. . . *Three!*'

Savard had already pictured clearly in his mind the eight-floor drop, and his final scream as he was swung high for the last time rattled his throat raw. And then he was sailing free, his mind spinning fast-reel frames within the hood's darkness to match his sensation of falling, his scream echoing down through the floors – praying that mercifully he'd black out halfway down – gaining momentum ever faster, faster, *until* . . . but the ground hit earlier than he expected. Maybe no more than a few yards. And it felt soft, his fall dampened by a cushioning of snow. His screaming faltered into nervous, staccato exhalations; he hardly dared believe that he was still alive.

'That's just a practice run, Tony. If you don't tell us where the money is, we're going to do it for real.'

Savard swallowed hard. The terror was quickly back. He wished now they *had* killed him. He couldn't face going through the knife-edge fear and anticipation a second time.

He was shaking uncontrollably, his voice quavering. 'Jesus, guys . . . *Jesusss.* I told you, I don't know.'

'No more chances, Tony. This is it . . .'

Savard felt himself being lifted again. 'No! No! . . . *No!'*

Michel could hardly bear to listen any more, knowing with certainty that there was nothing they could do to help. But the voices gripped him in almost morbid fascination – though now he was homing in more on background sounds: stillness, virtual silence. No traffic or background city drone. They should have picked up on that earlier when Savard was lifted from the van! If they had, they might have known they were wasting their time at Place Philips, might have been able to . . .

'We haven't got time to move him somewhere else to do this. I reckon we should finish it here.'

'I don't know . . .' Brief hesitation from the other man, then resign-edly on a faint sigh: *'D'accord.* I suppose you're right. No point in dragging it out. He's not going to talk.'

Savard felt himself being put back down on the ground. He was confused. Weren't they in a high building somewhere? But then there wouldn't be snow on the ground at Place Philips car park – which also explained why Michel and his men hadn't caught up with him. For the first time Savard also tuned in to the virtual silence around. Where *was* he?

Michel could almost feel Savard's surprise coming across in waves with his screaming having subsided into rapid, fractured breathing. From background sounds, Michel judged they were outside the city by at least a few miles; a deserted field or some wasteground perhaps. Lacaille had duped them at every turn, had probably known about the wire and had set up a cassette in the van with the drone of city traffic to throw them. But then how had they replicated the ramps for Savard not to realize he wasn't winding up through the levels of a car park?

Michel could picture the guns being taken out, the silencers attached, and he closed his eyes. Of all the moments Savard had protested and screamed in fear, now it would be justified; yet Savard merely continued to breathe heavily, like some confused, trapped animal. It seemed both ironic and unfair that his last moment should end like this.

And as the gun shots finally came, two in quick succession and another seconds later, Michel did Savard's screaming for him. 'No . . . *Nooo!*' His eyes scrunched tight, his bellowing plea reverberated through the cavernous car park. And as its echo died, all that was left was the sound over the wire of footsteps crunching on snow, receding quickly away from Savard's body.

2

Elena flicked through the report in her lap as Nadine Moore wended through the Dorset lanes. A weak sun threw dappled light through the trees, and at intervals Nadine glanced across and pointed at the file, prompting.

'That's the last interview with the Ryalls, there. Eleven months ago. Two months later the official adoption order was made and we were out of the picture.'

'And no alerts since?' Elena asked. 'Nothing to raise concern?'

'That would normally only come up through Lorena's school or GP. But no, nothing.' Nadine forced a tight smile after a second. 'But, anyway, it seems you're the one she first turns to for help.'

'Seems so.' Elena nodded and mirrored Nadine's smile. She looked again at the file, flicking back a page.

The call had come through at almost 1 a.m. Lorena's voice had been hushed, and Elena got a picture of her sneaking in the call while the rest of the house was asleep. 'Sorry to disturb you, Elena. But something troubles me here. And I didn't know who else to phone.'

Lorena's English had improved tenfold in the fifteen months since she'd last seen her. 'It's no trouble at all. Now tell me – what's the problem?'

'It's Mr Ryall. He comes to my bedroom late at night, and I . . . I don't feel comfortable.'

'In what way?'

'I'm not sure.' A heavy swallow from Lorena, her breath coming short. 'Perhaps I shouldn't have called. I'm sorry.'

Elena reassured her that she'd done the right thing, then pressed if Ryall was actually touching or interfering with her. A long silence, too long, before Lorena's uncertain 'No'. Then: 'I don't know', and something incoherent in Romanian, Lorena's voice quavering before she finally lapsed into muted sobbing. Seconds later she hung up.

Elena didn't sleep well afterwards, contemplated phoning back or actually jumping in the car and heading to the Ryalls'. But Lorena's obvious fear of disturbing the house and her own concern that breaking procedure could upset progress, *if* anything was happening, held her in check.

She phoned social services first thing in the morning. She received the call back from Nadine Moore forty minutes later that Lorena had requested she also be at the interview. 'She says she'll feel more comfortable talking about it with you there.'

Elena had only met Nadine Moore once before, when she'd taken over Lorena's case halfway through the final adoption assessment year. Nadine was a bright-eyed twenty-eight-year-old with crinkly brown hair framing round wire-frame glasses. Strong contrast to her older, more matronly predecessor who often spoke in tired, condescending tones, as if long ago she'd developed the style to deal with errant parents and found it difficult to switch off. Maybe in another ten years all the verve and optimism would be knocked out of Nadine as well.

Elena herself might at one time have been described as matronly, but her hectic schedule the last years with the aid agency – jumping aboard last-minute flights or supply trucks headed for Bucharest or Bosnia – had rapidly burned off the pounds. Now she looked more like a trim, mid-forties Jackie O, the first touches of pepper showing in her dark hair. In looks – though decidedly not in temperament or in her outlook on life – she'd taken more after her Cypriot father than her English mother.

Elena buried herself back in the report. The final assessment findings told her little beyond what she already knew about the Ryalls from when they'd started the whole process in Bucharest. Cameron Thomas Ryall, fifty-two, founder and head of CTR Micro-Tech, married to Nicola Anne Ryall, forty-four, housewife by occupation, for the past fourteen years, his second marriage. No children of their own, though Mr Ryall has a son, Michael, now twenty-eight, from his first marriage. One previously adopted daughter, Mikaya, originally from Cambodia. Mikaya was now nineteen and at university.

Well-established businessman. Comfortable and secure home environment. One-career household (prospective mother always at home). Previous successful history with adoption. Ryall had collected star points at every turn, and perhaps, Elena reflected, he'd known that all along – Lorena's adoption planned with the same skilled precision as his last takeover bid. The only thing which might have gone against Ryall was the high-flying nature of his business. But his main plant and HQ was only eight miles away, by far the area's largest 'green field' industrial enterprise and nearby Chelborne's largest employer. Not only had Ryall avoided the absentee-father label of so many high-powered executives, he'd also gained the final cream topping of local champion of the people.

'You still feel quite close to her, don't you?' Nadine was looking across with a slightly pained, quizzical expression. She'd purposely sidestepped 'feel responsible for'; it might make it sound like a forced obligation. 'How long did you know her in Bucharest?'

'There was a gap in the middle – but twenty months altogether.' Elena nodded. 'And yes, I suppose I do.' They were all special to her in some way. All eighteen children between the three orphanages in Romania, now all settled in new homes, hopefully safe and secure, around Britain. But how to explain that Lorena had stood out, struck an even more poignant chord than the rest? A natural closeness and affinity you feel with a particular child, yet you can't pinpoint exactly why? Or perhaps part of it was due to what Lorena had suffered after the first orphanage closed and her eleven months living rough on the streets, one of Bucharest's 'sewer children', before re-emerging. Elena still partly blamed herself for that.

But what Elena couldn't open up about was why this current alert set off so many personal alarm bells after what had happened with her own father. She'd buried that so deep for so long that she'd probably never be bold enough to share that with anyone.

Elena looked up as Nadine swung into the Ryalls' driveway. An impenetrable rhododendron hedge ten foot high spread out each side of double wrought-iron black gates almost as high.

Local champion of the people. Any move against Ryall wouldn't be popular, *if* anything was happening. But Elena prayed that it was all a false alarm first and foremost for Lorena's benefit. She pushed away the thought that it was also partly for herself as abruptly as it had struck. Possible failure with one of the eighteen just wasn't an option.

Nadine got out of the car and buzzed the security intercom by the gate.

Elena felt the walls and barriers go up as they went deeper into the Ryall house.

They were ushered into a large open entrance hallway, then on through a narrow, walnut-panelled passage, by the Ryalls' maid, who – according to Nadine's report – also doubled as a cook and was at the house daytimes four days a week. Cameron Ryall maintained it was important not only that they should have time together privately, as a family, but also that they shouldn't become reliant on a house-keeper to the extent that she might become viewed as a surrogate mother by Lorena. 'She'll have enough trouble adapting to one new mother without any such confusion.'

Ryall certainly knew how to score the points. Elena bit at her lip. She should avoid slipping into prior judgement; it wouldn't help her have a clear view now. Ryall might have been sincere.

Through half-open doors as they went along, Elena got a glimpse of a large oak kitchen and another room with a piano and some books, games and toys stacked to one side. The centrepiece, though, was the room they were led into: a high-ceilinged drawing room some thirty-five foot square. Overlooking was a book-lined gallery, and the walnut-panel theme had been continued, with a painting displayed on each panel. Elena recognized two originals by Thornhill, the Dorset landscape artist, but on the far wall to their left were more modern works, out of keeping with the Edwardian house: two abstracts Elena didn't recognize, then a Chagall and a Seurat. They weren't close enough for her to tell if they were original or not.

The maid asked if they wanted tea or coffee. They both chose coffee: Nadine white, Elena black.

The few minutes with her out of the room preparing – the only sound the remote clink and clatter of china – were tense. They didn't speak. There was only one thing now on their minds, and it wasn't a conversation they could risk being overheard.

Their eyes were naturally drawn to the oversized picture window at the end of the room. At least twelve-foot high and gothic-arched, it provided a dramatic view over the pool and the gardens beyond. Flowerbeds and linking paths flanked one side, and the lawn tabled steadily down so that they could see clearly over the bordering rhodo-dendron hedge towards the sweep of Swanage Bay. The wind was steady, and a succession of distant white-caps were just discernible dancing through the sea haze. Approaching the house from the car, they'd clearly heard the ebb and surge of the sea, but now it was deadly silent: muted through eighteen-inch-thick stone walls and double-glazing.

As if on cue, the Ryalls walked in just before the coffees were brought through. Eager smiles and handshakes all round. Cameron Ryall looked keenly at Elena as he held her hand a second longer.

'Nice to see you again. Last time we met was –'

Elena filled the gap: 'Cerneit orphanage, Bucharest.'

'Yes, yes, of course. Must be almost two years now.'

They sat down. The awkward silence settled again for a moment, and as Nadine opened by explaining the reason for her visit now – that Lorena had confided in a schoolfriend about some worries and concerns at home – the Ryalls' countenances quickly became solemn.

This had been the final game-plan agreed with Lorena: Lorena hadn't wanted it known that she'd phoned directly about any worries. Elena was watching Cameron Ryall's expression closely: no visible flinching, just his eyes darkening a shade. Graver concern.

'As explained, we do have to follow these things up.' Nadine took a quick sip of coffee. 'So, after speaking to you, I would like ten or fifteen minutes alone with Lorena. If that's okay?'

'Yes, of course,' Cameron Ryall said. He sat forward, forearms resting on his thighs; a picture of eager compliance.

Nicola Ryall nodded her concurrence, eyes quickly downcast. Who would be taking the lead became painfully clear. Standard role positioning between them, or had she been coached? 'This could be delicate: leave it to me.'

When Nadine had phoned and made the appointment with Nicola Ryall, Nicola hadn't made it clear whether Mr Ryall would also be present. The meeting had been arranged for 4 p.m., just after Lorena returned from school. Cameron Ryall obviously considered it important enough to leave early and let his global conglomerate run itself for a couple of hours – or perhaps he had hidden reasons for concern? Elena pushed the thought back again.

Cameron Ryall was stocky, his dark-brown hair heavily greying at the sides, and, apart from a few extra pounds, looked very much the same as when she'd last seen him. His most startling feature was his dark blue eyes, which in certain lights, depending on their dilation, appeared almost black.

He was dressed casually in dark green rugby shirt and jeans; the soft-edged, caring parent. When she'd first met him at the orphanage, he was wearing an oversized parka, as if he was a war-zone journalist. Then later at the Bucharest adoption agency, a dark grey suit and tie. Man for all seasons.

Nicola was a slim, attractive blonde, but her hair was cut short and she was wearing a small-check plaid skirt and plain cream blouse, as if she was trying to appear more prim, reserved and country-setish. Or perhaps this was more of her husband's stage management: 'Less glamour will give the impression of less self-interest. You'll come across as more motherly.'

Nadine opened up her folder on her knees, pen poised. She glanced down briefly at some typewritten notes before turning to a blank page and looking back at the Ryalls.

'Now, has Lorena mentioned anything to you recently about something troubling her?'

The Ryalls looked at each other briefly. Cameron Ryall answered with a slight shrug.

'No, not that we can think of.'

'Anything at all?' Nadine pressed. 'However small and irrelevant it might have seemed at the time?'

Nicola Ryall's expression lifted, as if a fresh thought had suddenly struck. 'Well, she did complain not long ago about problems with some schoolwork. History, I think it was . . .'

'Yes, yes,' Cameron Ryall quickly picked up. 'Her spoken English is quite good now, but she still has problems with written English. And for history she has to do a fair few essays.' He forced a weak smile. 'She finds them something of a struggle.'

Nadine started on the rest of her checklist: progress with other subjects? Friends at school, and how was Lorena settling in generally? Outside friends and interests? Lorena was settling in fairly well, no problems with other subjects that the Ryalls could think of. A few friends made at school, only one from outside that they knew of. After a moment, Elena partly faded it out. Nadine had prewarned that, with much of it routine questioning, she'd be largely redundant until they talked to Lorena. She was there to comfort and reassure Lorena, nothing more.

Cameron Ryall answered politely and methodically, his wife providing only sporadic input. Eagerness to allay any concern was the general tone; no hint of defensiveness or agitation that Elena could pick up on.

Elena got up and walked towards the picture window. It wasn't so much her redundancy but frustration that suddenly settled hard. Left to her own devices, she'd have bulldozed in with a chain of direct, awkward questions and by now had the Ryalls pinned in the corner. But that wasn't, as she knew from past, often tedious, experience, how the social services worked.

Procedure. Questions had to be open, devoid of angle. 'Subjects must have the opportunity to volunteer information without undue prompt or influence.'

Elena looked out over the gardens and pool. With the winter light fast dying and a chill wind, it looked inhospitable. She recalled two photos Lorena had sent with a short note five months back: one of her in the pool with an oversized beach ball in bright sunshine, the other of her blowing out the candles at her April birthday party with a few friends – probably taken in the breakfast or dining room. Happy days with her new family. Few signs now of a child's joyful activity, thought Elena; the atmosphere in the house was flat and sterile. Pretty much like Nadine's interview technique.

The softly-softly approach might work with some, but Elena doubted it would with Cameron Ryall. She remembered from the first adoption report that he'd been a practising barrister for three years before going into business. With now almost thirty years of hard-edged trading under his belt, he could run rings round the Nadines of this world.

But then Nadine had told her that probably little would be revealed until they spoke to Lorena directly, and then if anything looked suspicious she would hit the Ryalls with bigger guns at a second interview. Perhaps her attachment to Lorena was making her *too* anxious for a quick solution, which was no doubt why Nadine had reminded her so pointedly to stay in the background with the Ryalls, 'however angry and indignant you might feel. And after the initial introductions with Lorena and putting her at ease, leave everything to me.'

Her husband Gordon, too, had tried to calm her crusading spirit when she'd told him about the meeting with the Ryalls. 'It may all come to nothing, you don't know yet. And even if something *is* happening, it's not your problem any more, it's the social services'. You did your bit by caring for those children until they found homes. You can't be expected to stay responsible for them all for ever.'

But that was the problem, she *did* still feel responsible for them all. And in that moment, she felt a strong pang of guilt that in twelve years of marriage, she'd never told Gordon why. She'd never told him the full story about her father. Perhaps he was right, it would all come to nothing, and she would never have to tell him. It would stay her secret, as it had done already for over half her life.

★

'No, no. There's no problem.'

'Are you sure?' Nadine let out a slow breath. 'This is quite important. It's why we're here.'

A brief hesitation from Lorena, but it was quickly brushed aside. 'No, really. Everything's fine. I was worrying for nothing.'

They were in the music and playroom they'd passed earlier. Lorena had been ushered in from her room by the maid, then they'd been left alone, the door closed.

There had been a tense moment towards the end of interviewing the Ryalls when Nadine had asked a similar question: 'Moving closer to home, is there anything here troubling Lorena that you can think of?' Elena had turned from the window and moved a few paces back towards the Ryalls, focusing intensely and staring almost straight through them – not sure whether she was still looking for tell-tale signs or was hoping to unnerve them. Cameron Ryall had answered the same as Lorena, though without any hesitation.

Lorena appeared to have grown almost two inches since Elena had last seen her, was now close to five foot. Her hair was long and straight and somewhere between light-brown and corn, with just a hint of red in certain lights. Her eyes were a large and expressive grey-green with a sprinkling of pale-green flecks. In a few years, she would no doubt pass for a stunning pre-pubescent cat-walk model, and perhaps that had partly contributed: because she was so pretty, it was easy to believe the worst about Cameron Ryall. Elena tried to detach herself from that thought, but it was difficult.

Lorena's English was near-perfect, though still with a distinct Eastern European accent, its edges now smoothed by a gentle Dorset lilt. The combination was quite cute and endearing.

They'd hugged enthusiastically on greeting, and Elena felt reluctant to part, clinging on to Lorena's hands a moment longer as Lorena asked if she got the photos, and she in turn commented that Lorena had grown and asked how she was. But it became quickly, painfully obvious that there were few safe footholds without getting to the business at hand, so Elena made the introductions and offered some encouragement – 'Nadine's here to help you. Just tell her everything in your own words, in your own time' – then let Nadine take over.

Nadine started with the softer ground covered earlier with the Ryalls – friends at school or from outside, how she was settling in generally, problems with her history essays – before zeroing in with questions about problems at home. But it seemed to have served little purpose; Lorena was still edgy, ill at ease.

Nadine was uncertain whether to ease back and circle slowly in again, or to be more direct. She glanced at Elena, whose frustration and impatience were painfully evident. The risk with a direct blast was that Lorena could clam up completely; but there was probably little to lose, she certainly wasn't getting anywhere with the soft approach.

'When you phoned Elena, you mentioned that Mr Ryall was coming to your bedside late at night, and that this disturbed you. Why did this disturb you?'

'It just did, that's all.' Lorena looked down for a second. 'He used to come to read me bedtime stories, but I told him I was too old for that now.'

'But has he still continued to come?'

'Yes, but less now. Now it's more for when I have the dreams than to read me stories.'

'The dreams?'

'Yes, I . . .' Lorena glanced towards Elena. 'I used to have bad dreams that I was underground, trapped . . . couldn't breathe.' She put one hand up dramatically to her throat. 'They stopped, but not long ago, maybe six or seven months, they came back again.'

Elena could see that Nadine was still grappling for a full picture, and cut in. 'Lorena lived rough with other children on the streets of Bucharest for almost a year after the first orphanage closed. In the winter, to keep warm, this often meant them making their beds and sleeping underground in the sewers. For a while afterwards at the second orphanage, before she came to England, she was plagued by nightmares about that.'

'I see.' Nadine nodded. 'And when Mr Ryall comes to your bedside over those dreams, does anything happen? Anything that might disturb you?'

Lorena's brow knitted. 'In what way?'

Nadine swallowed imperceptibly and continued staring steadily at Lorena. 'Has there ever been any physical contact?'

Lorena blinked slowly, absorbing the weight of the question. 'No, well . . . only him soothing me, stroking my head, you know, to calm me.'

'Nothing else?'

Lorena shook her head. 'No, nothing.'

Elena remembered many a night soothing Lorena's brow at the Cerneit orphanage, and now Cameron Ryall had taken her place. Elena noticed the dark, fearful shadows return to Lorena's eyes with talk about the dreams, but did something else lie behind those shadows? Natural discomfort of a young woman fast growing up with a man visiting her bedroom late at night, or was something more worrying going on? Was this a safe and secure loving home – everything Lorena had always dreamed of and more – or a gilded prison?

Lorena would have grown up quicker than most, Elena reminded herself: she'd have had to think and act like an adult just to survive on the streets of Bucharest. She'd had so little real childhood. And perhaps, as a result, she just couldn't relate to the Cinderella and pink ribbons images Cameron Ryall was trying to sell with his bedtime stories. She was keen to embrace adulthood fast so that she could blot out her childhood completely; kid herself it never happened. Maybe it was the only way she felt she could be truly happy. Certainly it would explain a lot.

'How often do you have these nightmares now?' Nadine asked.

'Sometimes I'll have none for two weeks or so. Then two or three might come one night after the other.'

'And is it always Mr Ryall that comes to see to you, or does Mrs Ryall sometimes come?'

Lorena shook her head. 'It's usually him. She usually only comes to me when he's away somewhere on a trip.'

'And does Mr Ryall visit your room late for any other reason now apart from the dreams? Does he read you some stories still?'

'No, no stories any more. But sometimes he comes to my room just to talk – you know, asking about schoolwork, how I'm getting on. Things like that.'

'Does that happen often?'

Lorena shrugged. 'Mainly when he's been away somewhere and hasn't seen me for a few days. Apart from that, not much.'

Nadine asked a few more questions, trying to get it clear just how often Mr Ryall visited her room late at night. One way or another, Ryall managed to visit at least once a week, sometimes twice.

'How about when Mr Ryall is around you at other times? Do you feel comfortable then?'

'Yes, it's . . . it's okay.' A flicker of uncertainty for a second, then Lorena shrugged nonchalantly. 'No problems.'

'And Mrs Ryall? You get on well with her?'

'Yes.'

'You never feel uncomfortable around her at any time?'

'No.' Lorena smiled faintly, as if the question was slightly ridiculous.

Elena watched Lorena intently throughout the exchange. The atmosphere in the room became tenser with each question, and Elena's emotions were seriously divided. A chink of uncertainty in Lorena's eyes and she'd feel like screaming: 'Stop shying away, covering up! If you don't say something, speak up, we can't help you. You'll stay trapped here at Ryall's mercy.' But when Lorena appeared sure-footed and confident, it would hit that other part of her that wanted desperately to believe that nothing was happening; though maybe she too was selectively erasing, unwilling to accept any possible horrors after what Lorena had suffered in Romania.

Nadine took a fresh breath. 'So, more or less, all of your problems stem from your discomfort with Mr Ryall coming to your bed late at night now that you're older. Is that about it?' Nadine tapped her pen on her folder as she waited for Lorena's answer.

Lorena merely nodded, chewing lightly at her bottom lip.

'So, if and when you have these bad dreams, if we ask that Mrs Ryall comes to you rather than Mr Ryall – I suppose that would solve your problem?'

'I suppose it would.' Lorena fluttered her eyes down in submission for a second before looking up again. Embarrassment at having wasted their time, or still holding back on something? It was difficult to tell.

'We'll see what we can do.' Though Nadine didn't know where she'd even start: she could hardly reproach Ryall for showing due care and concern for Lorena. And telling Ryall that he couldn't tuck his beloved daughter in bed after a few days away would be even more absurd. She pressed one last time, if nothing else to save later criticism from Elena that she might not have been thorough. 'And are you absolutely sure there's nothing else troubling you concerning Mr Ryall – either connected with him coming to your room late at night, or otherwise?'

Lorena's eyes flickered, as if she was searching for something that was just out of reach. 'No, no . . . there's nothing. That's it.'

But by the way Lorena looked fleetingly back towards the closed door, as if towards the Ryalls in the drawing room beyond, Elena knew in that instant that something was wrong. Cameron Ryall had coached Lorena, or for some reason she was covering up for him.

★

Savard's body was found at 5.43 a.m., only yards from the taxiway of an old abandoned airfield two miles south of Longueuil, an area used by the man who discovered the body when he'd arrived for the early-morning training of his greyhound.

The first police arrived at 6.18 a.m., and within twenty minutes had been joined by two more squad cars, forensics and a meat wagon. The call to Michel Chenouda came through just after 6 a.m., disturbing him from barely two hours' sleep. He'd spent till 1 a.m. with his team backtracking and trawling some likely spots for Savard, and sleep had been difficult in coming; Savard's voice on tape and the images that went with it had kept him turning uneasily.

Michel arrived minutes after the meat wagon. The first dawn light had only just started to break, so Michel had a torch with him. The flashes from photos being snapped of Savard's body cut starkly through the near-darkness, competing with the flashing beacon on a nearby squad car. The only other light was from torchlight playing and the headlamps of two vehicles, one pulled close to Savard's body.

Three of the police squad and everyone from forensics, Michel knew. One of the homicide sergeants, Lucien Feutre, looked up as he approached.

'Michel.' Brief smile that fell into a shrug and stern grimace. 'Rough break. I'm sorry.'

'Yeah. I know.' Michel nodded dolefully, looking around. 'Thanks.'

Savard's body was illuminated by the headlamps, blue-spray body-outline markings already made in the snow – so Michel played his torchlight mainly to each side.

'Who found him?'

Feutre glanced back and pointed with one thumb. 'Guy over there. He was walking his dog. Want to speak with him?'

Michel looked at the figure at the back of the milling activity, who had probably been questioned a while ago and wished now he hadn't found the body and subjected himself to fifty minutes of standing around in the cold. His greyhound looked equally bored, tongue lolling as it looked to one side.

'No, no, it's okay.' Normally, he would have had a chain of questions, and a hundred more for forensics: how many shots? Time of attack? How did he get here? But he knew practically everything from the wire tape.

He played his torchlight around again as Feutre went over to tell

24

the man he could go. He picked out quickly the repetitive circles of tyre tracks, but it took a moment more to find the main thing he was looking for: a ramp made up of packed snow thirty yards away; sharp slope one side, gradual, almost imperceptible decline, the other. They hit the sharp side on each loop, and Savard gets the sensation they're rising up through the car park.

His gaze swung back to the main circle of light and Savard's body. It was curled almost in foetal position, a dusting of snow from a fresh fall overnight covering it. The hood, pulled back to the crown for photo identification, was dark blue, and Savard's hands had been tied in front with rope. There were a number of other small things he could have clarified at this point, but he also knew now why he was shying from asking the questions: each answer would bring back Savard's screams too vividly when they'd only just stopped ringing in his ears. He would read the reports later and make a few calls; some distance at least.

An Arctic wind whipped across the flat expanse of grass and over-grown taxiway. Michel felt it cut through him like an icy hatchet, taking his breath away. His eyes watered.

He took one last lingering look at Savard's body and slowly closed his eyes. They'd obviously headed due south straight over the Jacques Cartier Bridge rather than downtown. Roman and Jean-Paul Lacaille had played them for mugs at every turn: the finder smashed, the wire left in place and traffic sounds played; the snow ramp. Savard was already practically dead as they'd watched him through binoculars waiting for Roman Lacaille – only they hadn't known it.

You'll be safe. We'll be watching every moment, guarding your back. Weeks of meetings before Savard was finally confident enough to go ahead. 'Don't worry, nothing will happen to you,' they'd assured. Yet Savard had died like a trussed chicken, his final moments filled with terror.

Michel was doubly determined to nail the Lacailles, but now only one witness remained: Georges Donatien. And Donatien was practically family, engaged to marry Jean-Paul Lacaille's only daughter, Simone, the apple of his eye.

Michel opened his eyes again, taking in the horror of what had happened to Savard in an effort to will himself on; but already he knew it was an almost hopeless quest. They'd have to move mountains to get Georges Donatien to testify.

3

This was Georges Donatien's favourite time of day, that hushed, suspended moment just as the morning rays broke through; especially given who was lying beside him and what they'd been doing.

Simone. He admired her for a moment in the soft first light, the long sweep of her olive-brown back, her wavy black hair in disarray and spilling over one shoulder. He gently traced down her spine with two fingers. The trick, as always, was to touch her so lightly that she wouldn't awaken. He pulled the sheets lower to give his hand freer range, then continued tracing down, down, until he reached the cleft of her buttocks. He felt a subtle tremor run through her body, her subconscious registering that it liked what he was doing, but hopefully not enough to make her stir. Not yet.

He held his hand motionless and held his breath too, suddenly conscious of his own heartbeat in the lull, until her tremoring subsided. Then he started tracing slowly back up the ridge of her spine. If he was really careful, sometimes he could spin it out for a few minutes. Tracing delicately, as light as spider's feet, up and down, each time being more daring, going lower, deeper between the cleft of her buttocks, feeling the heat there and her slight dampness from the night before. Or was that just from now? Revelling in her faint trembling, almost seeing the goosebumps rise as the first light hit her body, pausing again breathlessly like a frightened schoolboy each time she looked close to . . .

She groaned throatily and moved one leg. He waited a few seconds after the groan had died, but with one leg now pushed wide, he felt drawn to go still lower rather than higher. Her heat and moisture pulled him in like a magnet, and he couldn't resist pushing his luck that extra inch by probing gently with one finger. She groaned again, he froze . . . and was about to pull his hand away when her leg shifted back again, trapping him, and the groan became a soft purr.

'Uuhhhm . . . *c'est bon.*' She rolled towards him, bringing her left leg up so that it rested on his thigh. She smiled at him and blinked. 'Good morning.'

'Good morning.' Georges smiled back tightly.

One of her hands traced deftly down his stomach, and she watched his expression closely as she gripped him and started gently stroking.

A short hiss of pleasure, his eyes closed for a second before shaking it quickly off and glancing towards the alarm clock. 7.22 a.m. Georges started mentally totting up the time for coffee, shower, dressing and driving the six miles to Cartier-Ville.

'Look, Simone, I don't have time for this now. I've got an eight-thirty breakfast meeting with your father. I won't make it if we fool around.'

'If you can't handle the beast, you shouldn't wake the beast.' She pouted challengingly, still stroking.

'Who said that?'

'I don't know.' She shrugged. 'Voltaire, maybe Rabelais.'

'Sounds more like Cousteau to me.'

Another small shrug, then she quickly ducked down and started kissing down his stomach.

He tensed. 'No, Simone, *no*. It's nice, too nice . . . but I really don't have time now.'

She paid no attention, kept kissing down, and a light shudder ran up from his calves and through his body as he felt her take him into her mouth.

He surrendered to it for a moment before starting to protest again. 'Pleasssse, Simone, not now . . . I just don't – '

The ringing phone startled them both. She broke off, looking at it accusingly. Georges squinted at the call-monitor display.

'It's your father!' He pulled away from her and lunged for the phone. 'Yes?'

'Georges . . . Jean-Paul. Sorry to disturb you. But I forgot to ask when we last spoke – did everything go okay with the revised plans from the architect?'

'Yes, they did, and I've got them with me.' The main reason for their urgent meeting now. Georges had been away five days in Puerto Vallarta to oversee Jean-Paul's new investments there: twenty-seven-hole golf course with integral development of two hotels, a casino, and 214 'greenside' bungalows and villas. The rounding-off of Jean-Paul's Mexican portfolio, which already included three hotels, a marina development, another casino and four clubs between Cancun and Puerto Vallarta. But delays had threatened this latest project when one of the hotels hit a survey problem.

'No problems now?' Jean-Paul confirmed.

'No. Everything's fine now. I . . . eerrr.' Georges bit his lip. Simone had reached out and was stroking him again. He shook his head and frowned at her. She smiled back challengingly and continued stroking, moving her mouth so teasingly close that he could feel her hot breath on him. Her tongue snaked out, and he shook his head more wildly, silently mouthing, *'No!'* He hastily cleared his throat. 'Err . . . I made sure I was there this time for the survey. There's nothing now to stop it being passed.'

'That's good.' A second's silence from Jean-Paul as he absorbed this, or perhaps he was distracted with something else his end. Then: 'Are you okay?'

'Yes, fine . . . *fine.*' Beads of sweat popped on his forehead. He watched in horror Simone's mouth move closer, lips pouting. 'Touch of bad throat, that's all.' Brief wry smile. He spoke in quick bursts, still fearful of what was coming. 'Probably the sudden change in temperature.'

She held him in limbo a second longer, mouth poised – but finally, at just an inch away, she blew a kiss, smiled lasciviously and pulled back again.

Simone was enjoying this, he thought. Pretty much a continuation of the rest of their relationship: her fighting for his attention over and above her father. At times she was impossible; but perhaps, at twenty-three, six years his junior, she was still allowed to be. Being born into one of Montreal's wealthiest families hadn't helped, especially with a father so keen to indulge her; not only to compensate for her losing her mother Claire when she was only eight, but also no doubt for the many unseen horrors being played out behind the scenes while she was growing up. Jean-Paul Lacaille had made sure that his only daughter's childhood was sugar-coated.

'I'd better go,' Georges said as he watched Simone straddle him, panicking about what she might do next while her father was still on the phone. 'Get everything ready for our meeting.'

'Yeah, okay,' Jean-Paul mumbled distractedly. Then his voice came back sharply, sudden afterthought. 'Oh, one more thing. Have you seen this morning's news yet?'

'No, not yet.' *I've been too busy in bed with your daughter.* He could feel Simone's heat pressing hard against him. She reached for him, started stroking again. He could tell from her sly smile what she was about to do. He prayed that Jean-Paul would sign off quickly.

'There was an item on about Tony Savard.' Jean-Paul sighed heavily. 'He was killed last night. His body was found in the early hours this morning.'

'Oh, I see.' That killed it instantly. Simone wouldn't be able to do much with him now, regardless of effort.

'Now I know this falls outside what I originally brought you in to be concerned with. But given the background with Savard, I think it's something we should discuss.'

'I agree.' Georges felt numb, cold, and found it hard to free either clear thoughts or speech.

Simone rolled off and curled to one side, frowning: but it wasn't a look of spoilt petulance, more of concern. Warmth, compassion, *joie de vivre*, sharp wit: all the traits that over the sixteen months of their relationship had made him fall more deeply in love with her, when he'd finally dug beneath the preconception – guided as much by his own staunch work ethic and views about her cosseted life, as by reality – that she was spoilt.

But, for a moment, he wished that spoilt Simone was back. He could kid himself that life was still just a playful tug-of-war between her and her father. He could forget what Jean-Paul had just said about Savard, and could ignore Simone's look of concern, mirroring the panic that must have swept across his own face as he contemplated the chain of nightmare problems that Savard's death could ignite. He just hoped his first assumption was wrong.

The fat man took the first photo as the couple came out of the apartment.

They leant into each other a few paces from the building, a quick parting kiss, and the girl ran just ahead. He followed their movements with a quick burst on the camera's motor drive. They were an attractive young couple, the girl with long, wavy black hair, the man close to six foot and athletic-looking with dark-brown hair cut short in a spiky crew-cut, and dressed well in a light grey suit and black Crombie. Though the fat man knew, from old photos he'd spied in the man's apartment, that when his hair was longer it also waved slightly, and that the suit – from the many he'd flicked through in his wardrobe – was no doubt Armani or Yves Saint-Laurent. They say that people are attracted to those with similar features, and certainly there were some similarities between the two: large brown eyes, his perhaps slightly more hooded than hers, but both with the same olive-skin tones, hinting at a Mediterranean or Latin background.

She got into a bright turquoise Fiat sports coupé parked just in front, while he went through a side door towards the garage. The fat man took another few snaps as she looked around and pulled out, then a minute later some of the man as the automatic garage doors opened and his grey Lexus edged out.

Simone Lacaille and Georges Donatien, Montreal's golden couple, seen at all the right parties and openings – and a few of the wrong ones – and regularly photographed, his own snapshots aside.

The apartment building was in the fashionable Westmount district, and its penthouses – of which Donatien's was one – had luxurious split-level atrium living rooms affording breathtaking views over the city and the St Lawrence. After thoroughly searching the apartment eight months back, the fat man had stood for a moment admiring the view, breath misting the atrium glass, contemplating ruefully just how far out of reach such an apartment was on his RCMP policeman's salary.

By now he knew everything about them, their every move. She stayed over at Donatien's two or three times a week, but *always* the first night after he'd been away on a business trip. She would head to Lachaine & Roy on Rue St-Jacques, one of Montreal's leading advertising agencies, where she was an accounts manager. Her father didn't have shares in the company – he was careful not to be overt with his influence on her career, she would rebel – but he did have interests in two of its major accounts. Donatien, first day back, would head downtown to the Lacaille company office on Côte du Beaver Hall, or to the Lacaille residence in Cartier-Ville.

The one and only apartment search all those months back had been at the request of Michel Chenouda, his immediate boss and closest RCMP confidant. They'd worked together as partners when Michel had first arrived from Toronto, but within the year the fat man'd left the RCMP after a bungled vice bust led to an attempted hit on one of his key drug informants, and went into private investigation. Technically, he was still private when he'd let himself into Donatien's apartment; Michel had already smoothed the way for him rejoining the RCMP, and all the papers were rubber-stamped, but the break-in was ten days before he was handed his badge and gun. No doubt Michel would have loved to have the apartment searched again now, but for the risk: he wouldn't involve a badged officer, and there were no other private gumshoes Michel would trust with something like that.

He'd been a keen amateur photographer in his late teens, and private work had given him the opportunity to hone his skills. The mountain of photos he'd taken of the Lacailles over the past eighteen months Michel would rigorously scan for tell-tale signs – Simone Lacaille's engagement ring when it first appeared, new contacts of Roman or Jean-Paul Lacaille not recognized from past file photos – and he'd meanwhile be looking at artistic merit: light, angle, composition.

Now, with Michel's wake-up call at 6.30 a.m., more photos. 'They've just found Savard's body. I'm here with forensics. Donatien is the only one left now – we'll need to shadow him closer than ever.' Michel was on his mobile and sounded slightly out of breath.

The fat man was worried that it was becoming an obsession. The reason for the obsession he understood, but still it worried him. A dozen or so more photos to add to a file of hundreds, and probably now enough box files of paperwork to fill a truck.

He let out a heavy exhalation as he started up, checked his mirror and pulled out. Perhaps it was the familiarity of the routine, or perhaps his preoccupation with getting back to the station in time to develop the photos before his meeting with Michel – but he didn't notice the man parked fifty yards behind, who had pulled up just as he was taking his second stream of photos.

'Chac! Chac! Good stuff. Good stuff!' Michel hailed as he watched the fat man pin five fresh photos from his morning's effort on the corkboard.

The C was soft, so the uninformed often made the mistake that the nickname had an English derivation from the fact that the man was built like a shack. But it had come from his habit of saying *'Chacun son goût'*. He'd originally been known as 'Chacun', then finally just 'Chac'.

Eighteen photos already covered the corkboard, providing a quick-glance profile of the Lacailles and anyone vital connected to them.

Michel stood studying them from two yards back, then threw a quick eye over the others and back again, as if measuring how they slotted into the whole picture.

'So, still very much in love,' he said.

'Looks that way.'

Michel leant in closer, studying finer detail in the photos. What had he been hoping for? Some small sign of cracks in their relationship, so it might be easier to get Donatien to testify against the Lacailles. After all, she was only in her early twenties, impetuous, strong-willed, and probably wasn't yet settled emotionally. Before Donatien she'd had a chain of boyfriends, seemed to change them every other month.

Michel shook his head as he studied the look on Simone's face kissing Donatien goodbye. Wishful thinking. Their relationship had held solid for sixteen months, and looked stronger now than ever.

But the photo he was finally drawn to most was of Donatien just as Simone headed away. Perhaps business hadn't gone smoothly in Mexico, but Michel doubted that was it: the expression of concern suddenly gripping Donatien looked too heavy, severe. Donatien knew about Savard.

'When's the wedding planned?' Michel asked.

'Early July – the eighth.'

Michel nodded thoughtfully, still scanning the photos. He already knew the date off by heart, but a changed date might hint of some cooling off. He was getting desperate.

They'd all be there, Michel reflected: slim, dapper Jean-Paul, his mid-brown hair greying heavily in sweeps at each side, but still looking younger than his fifty-one years. His mother Lillian, seventy-four, who now spent more time at the family's holiday residence in Martinique than in Montreal. She was deeply religious and her permanent tan, designer clothes and henna-tinted grey hair at times seemed vain, superficial affectations at odds with her firm-rooted nature, with all revolving around the church and family; but she looked well, and her age showed only with her slightly matronly bulk and resultantly slowed gait. Simone's younger brother Raphaël, fifteen, now in 6th Grade at Montreal's top Catholic school, St Francis, where he shone in art and literature; but to his father's concern he was poor at maths, showed little promise for business, and spent his every spare moment roller-blading or, in the winter, snowboarding.

They looked like any other new-moneyed Montreal family, probably more upper-middle than top-drawer – until you got to the photos of Roman and the Lacaille family's key enforcer, Frank Massenat, so often in Roman's shadow. Then the underlying menace of the family became evident.

Roman was four years younger than Jean-Paul and, while only two inches smaller at five-eight, looked shorter still due to his broadness and bulk. While Jean-Paul had been on the tennis court or jogging,

Roman had been in the gym pumping iron or pummelling a punchbag until he was ready to drop. He was known as 'The Bull', not just due to his build, but because of his habit of keeping his head low while looking up at people, swaying it slightly as he weighed their words; a motion that would become more pronounced if he started to doubt or didn't like what they were saying. He reminded people of a bull measuring a matador for attack – and there had been many horror stories of Roman striking out swiftly and unpredictably, head first, ending any potential argument or fight by caving in his opponent's face.

Head and shoulders above Roman, Frank Massenat was a giant. Seven years earlier, when he first joined the Lacailles, he was at the peak of physical condition, but a diet of salami and pastrami rolls, beer and rich cream sauce meals had steadily piled on the pounds, so that now he looked like a big lumbering bear with a pot belly. With his eyes heavily bagged and his jowls, he seemed almost ten years older than his thirty-four years.

In contrast, Jon Larsen, the family's *consigliere* for almost twenty years, would fit in well in a family wedding snap. Close to sixty, slim, now mostly bald with only a ring of grey hair, he could easily have passed for an uncle or perhaps Jean-Paul's older brother.

Michel's gaze swung back to the photos of Jean-Paul. In the end, Jean-Paul always absorbed him most – not only because as head of the organization he warranted the main attention – but because Michel never could quite work him out. At least with Roman and Frank, what you saw, you got.

Michel was a keen modern-jazz fan, and he remembered once being surprised on seeing Jean-Paul Lacaille at the city's main jazz club, Biddle's, on Rue Aylmer. He later learnt that, indeed, Jean-Paul was a strong jazz aficionado, particularly of the new Latin jazz. Michel found it hard to equate in his mind this urbane, charming persona, now also presumably with good musical tastes, with what he knew to be the cold-hearted, brutal reality. Here was a man who, as easily as he smiled and nodded along with his guests in the jazz club, could with the same curt nod signal that a man be brutalized or his life taken. The two just didn't sit comfortably together – though charming, smiling, socialite Jean-Paul was the image being pushed more and more these past few years, as he tried to convince everyone that he'd turned his back on crime and had become 'legit'. Michel didn't believe it for a minute.

Three photos Michel had purposely pinned to one side of the main spread. The three main losses of the Lacaille family: Pascal, Jean-Paul and Roman's younger brother, shot dead five years before at the age of thirty-six, the tragic end result of a feud with the rival Cacchione family; their father, Jean-Pierre, dead fourteen months later, many said of a broken rather than failed heart – Pascal had been his favourite; then just three years ago, Jean-Paul's second wife Stephanie after a long battle with breast cancer. The Lacailles had seen their fair share of tragedy these past years, reflected Michel; but even that Jean-Paul had sought to turn to advantage. He'd held up Pascal's death like a banner as the main reason behind his decision to move the family away from crime. Jean-Paul was a consummate audience player, would have made a good politician.

Michel rubbed his eyes. 'When do you hope to hear from Arnaiz?'

'Within a few hours. Certainly before lunch.' Chac forced a tight smile. 'Hopefully he might have something interesting this time.'

Michel nodded, but he doubted it. Chac was just trying to lift his spirits after the calamity with Savard. On the last five trips by Donatien to Mexico – the trips to Cuba they hadn't monitored – Enrique Arnaiz had turned up nothing. Arnaiz was a private investigator Chac had dug up from his old card file. The *federalis* wouldn't get involved unless or until Donatien was seen with known drug associates or other criminals – so each time Arnaiz would have Donatien followed and those he met with photographed for comparison with *federali* files. Michel wasn't hopeful of anything turning up this time either.

That was the other conundrum. 'What do you think, Chac? Is Donatien what Jean-Paul keeps selling him as, the golden boy making good on his shiny new leaf as a legitimate businessman – or are his hands dirty along with the rest of them?'

Though the question had been posed before, with Savard gone Chac knew that it was now far more significant. He weighed his answer carefully. 'On the surface at least he looks clean, however much that goes against the grain with the Lacailles' past form. But from our point of view, I suppose it's best if he is clean. If he's in with the rest of them all the way, we'll never get him to testify.'

'That's true.' Michel's voice was flat, nonchalant. He took a fresh breath. 'Now all we've got to do is get him to turn his back on the love of his life and betray her entire family.'

'Yeah, that's all,' Chac agreed drolly. Then, after a few seconds' uneasy silence: 'One thing we never did work out was what Donatien was doing in the car the night Leduc was shot. The only time it looked like he might be getting his hands dirty.'

'No, that we never did.' Michel continued staring contemplatively at the spread of photos, as if they might magically provide the answer, and after a moment Chac left him alone with the Lacaille family and his thoughts.

He worked quickly and efficiently through the penthouse.

He found a ventilation grille in the main en-suite bathroom to take one bug, the hollow base of a table lamp in the dining room another. Then he paused, hard pushed for good places for the others: a lot of flat, smooth surfaces, minimalist furniture and decor.

In the end he cut a tiny hole in the fabric beneath the main sofa and tucked a bug far to one side with one finger, did the same under the beds in all three bedrooms, then removed and clipped back a kitchen cabinet plinth to conceal the final room bug. The phone bugs, one in the drawing room and one in the main bedroom, he put in place last.

Carlo Funicelli stood for a moment in the middle of the apartment, looking from one extremity to the other, wondering whether he'd left any dead sound areas. The guest bathroom and maybe the first yards of entrance corridor. Hopefully not too many vital meaningful conversations would take place there.

Funicelli headed out and grabbed the lift. The doorman gave him the same curt, disinterested nod as when he'd walked in; as he did with anyone who had a key and seemed to know where they were going.

From his pre-break-in briefing, the keys had come courtesy of Simone Lacaille. Donatien was too careful with his set. But she had a spare set to let herself in for when he was working late on a night she was due to come over; she might start preparing dinner for them or, if he'd been away for a few days, often she'd restock the fridge. Love. But she was careless with her set, often left it lying around. She regularly spent weekends at the Lacaille family home, particularly when her father arranged get-togethers, and it had been easy for Roman to grab the keys for a few hours to have them copied.

An hour and a half before the designated time for him to call, Funicelli headed downtown and killed it having coffee and window-browsing in the underground Place Ville-Marie complex. It was too cold in the city to spend any length of time above ground. He called from a phone booth there rather than on his mobile, as instructed.

'Yeah. City desk.' Roman Lacaille's voice answering had a slight echo to it. He was leaning on the bar in their Sherbrooke club, a cavernous basement thirty yards square spread before him. The bar staff had all left long before the first twilight, as had the bar manager, Azy, after helping him go through the night's till receipts, and the cleaners had just twenty minutes ago shut the door behind them. He was on his own.

'It's done. The place is live and kicking,' Funicelli said.

'When? When can we listen in?' Roman's tone was pushy, impatient.

'Now. It's already rolling. The receiving monitor's set up only a few blocks away. Anything more than a ten-decibel sound and it'll kick in, the tape will start rolling.'

'Great work. Give the Indian a cigar.' Roman smiled. His pet names for Chenouda: Sitting Bull or Last of the Mohicans. He knew the last thing Chenouda would be getting right now was a cigar, unless he was bending over to receive it. With the Savard fiasco, maybe he should rename him Sitting Duck. 'I'd like to go see the set-up some-time, listen in. Probably best one evening. More action.' Roman chuckled.

'Yeah, sure. When?'

They arranged it for two evenings' time, when Simone was next due to stay over, and signed off.

Roman looked thoughtfully at the club around him after hanging up. At night it would be a sea of lithe, writhing naked bodies under wildly rotating crimson and blue penlight spots, heavy male hands eagerly reaching out to slip ten- and twenty-dollar bills into tangas or garters.

Upmarket lap-dancing club, the last bastion of the Lacaille family's past criminal empire. Five years back, they'd had associations with a chain of downtown and Lavalle clip joints and massage parlours rolling in big bucks. This now was the furthest Jean-Paul had decreed they should go with the flesh trade. But it was less drastic at least than his moves away from every other area – drugs, racketeering, loan-sharking, fencing; in those, he hadn't even kept a foot in the door.

So after a decade and a half of making sure all of that ran and ran smoothly, this is what Roman was left with: counting the takings in a pussy club. Oh sure, they'd just opened another smaller one in Lavalle and then there were the two nightclubs and the restaurants. But it hardly compensated.

This squeaky-clean crusade might suit Jean-Paul, but little thought had been given to anyone else, especially him. But then, Jean-Paul never had given him much thought; a tradition no doubt passed down from their father, Jean-Pierre. Pascal and Jean-Paul had always been his favourites. Now with Jean-Paul it was always Raphaël, Simone, Jon Larsen, roughly in that order, or, more recently, Donatien. The new golden boy.

They all no doubt looked upon him as just a dumb ox, a muscle-headed old-school moustache Pete, and becoming more of a dinosaur by the day with Jean-Paul's new business direction. Redundant.

Most of his life he'd spent in Jean-Paul's shadow, but no more. He had more street-smarts than the lot of them put together, and the time to make his play couldn't be riper. Though everything with Savard had gone well, half of it had been laid in his lap by the RCMP. The next stage with Donatien wouldn't be so easy.

The pressure mounted steadily through the day.

Just before lunch, Maury Legault put his head round Michel's door with the news that they'd found the van used with Savard, left abandoned in a St-Hubert side street.

Maury was tentative, hesitant, as he passed on the information – even though Michel had made it clear first thing to the entire squad room that it should be the prime focus of their efforts. 'No let up until we see a breakthrough.'

But then interruptions had been few throughout the morning, as if people were apprehensive about entering the inner sanctum of his office with its photo-montage homage to the Lacailles. And when he did venture out, the normal frantic hubbub of the squad room would noticeably subside and a few eyes would be averted and look down, suddenly absorbed with paperwork. It was as if he'd had a close relative die, not an informant.

'Was it the original registration?' he asked Maury.

No, the plates had been switched. 'The original to match the chassis number was reported stolen in the early hours yesterday morning. We pulled it up just minutes ago on the bulletin board.'

Pretty much as Michel had expected. Maury informed him that forensics and two mechanics were going over the van with a fine-tooth comb, but Michel wasn't holding his breath. One of the Lacaille past

37

enterprises had been an auto-chop shop. They knew how to make sure a vehicle was left clean.

Three hours later Maury came back with the news that it looked like it had been steam- and chemically cleaned.

Michel simply nodded and cast his eyes down, numbed more by a pervading lethargy at the thought that this would be the pattern at every turn than his lack of surprise. And partly by lack of sleep. He hadn't slept well the night before the Savard sting operation, turning over in his mind all manner of scenarios; now only two hours last night. He felt ragged.

Trying desperately to avoid his department head, Chief Inspector Pelletier, hadn't helped. He already knew what was coming. Pelletier had left him alone the first few hours of the day: respect for Savard or the dead case? But then Pelletier obviously thought sufficient mourning time had passed, so that Michel could explain, clearly and succinctly, how everything could have fallen apart so disastrously.

The calls, one just before lunch and another early afternoon, came from Maggie Laberge, Pelletier's PA, through Christine Hébert, one of two constables on the open squad-room message desk. Always protocol and distance with Pelletier.

Michel had parried the first call by passing the message through Hébert that he knew what it was about, but he was still busy gaining vital information to be able to give Pelletier the full picture. With the second call, he spoke directly to Laberge and sold her more of the same: 'We're close to breakthrough on a couple of key things. Each extra second I spend close on top of everything right now is vital. Hopefully things should free up in an hour or two.'

Soon after, Chac'd informed him that yet again Arnaiz in Mexico hadn't turned up anything suspicious on Donatien; then Maury came in with the news about the steam-cleaning. Each extra hour he delayed only made the picture worse, not better. Screw-up of the year, and any hope of redemption was fast disappearing with each extra head that appeared at his door or fresh file slapped on his desk.

Early forensic findings had been the biggest body blow. Some blood had been found under the fingernails of Savard's right hand. The hope had been that Savard might have clawed the neck or face of one of his abductors, or even through their clothing as he frantically grappled at their arms when they swung him. But the report concluded that it was Savard's own blood. The first shot had struck his chest, and he'd put one hand up defensively to the wound before the final two shots came: one to the neck, one to his head. The report made chilling reading, brought Savard's screams back too vividly.

Just before signing off, almost as a by-the-way, Laberge informed him that they had to liaise on time because Pelletier wanted Tom Maitland, Crown attorney, to also be present at the meeting. Michel knew what that meant. While Pelletier might justifiably reach the conclusion that a potentially prosecutable case now looked out of reach, it would carry more weight with Maitland's legal-eagle view-point at his side.

Michel knew then why he was delaying: not so much for a fresh lead to salvage something from last night's disaster – the past track record with the Lacailles had long ago made him cynical – but because he was desperately seeking an angle to convince them, and himself, there was still mileage left in the case. If he presented Donatien – soon to become part of the Lacaille family – as his only remaining hope, they'd kill the case straight away.

He took a hasty sip of his sixth coffee of the day, trying to clear his thoughts and focus. But no ready answers came.

The only light relief of the day came when Chac responded gruffly, 'Well, they can suck my dick', when he'd explained his pending dilemma with Pelletier and Maitland, his fear that they'd now want to hastily close the Lacaille file.

'Is that because you've already asked everyone else and they've said no?'

Chac beamed broadly, despite the barb. And Michel realized then how impossibly intense he'd been all morning. The pall hovering over the squad room each time he opened the door was not just in respect of Savard's death, but also of the possibly dead case and his feared reaction. Chac was simply glad to see a chink of his old self resurface.

But the mood died quickly as Chac reminded him that even if he convinced Pelletier to keep the case open, at best it would only give him a few months' grace. 'Once Donatien is married, it's game over. And Roman Lacaille knows it.'

Michel's desk phone started ringing. He looked through the glass screen towards the squad room. Christine Hébert was looking over at him, pointing to the receiver.

No doubt Laberge chasing for Pelletier again. A film of sweat broke on his forehead. He couldn't delay any more. What would he say? Maybe bluff for now, say that they had reliable inside information that Donatien would soon about-turn and testify. That at least might give him a week or two's grace to either make good on that claim or come up with something else.

The seed of the idea was still only half-formed as he picked up the receiver at the end of the third ring. 'Yes?'

'It's your wife, Sandra,' Hébert said.

He was caught off guard for a second. 'Oh . . . right. Put her through.' She rarely phoned him. Hébert never termed her 'ex', despite it now being four years they'd been parted.

Then, with her first words, 'Michel, you said four o'clock and it's already four-twenty', he came up sharply from his chair, suddenly remembering.

'Oh, Jesus, yeah . . . I'm right there.' Basketball championship with a rival school with his son Benjamin, now nine years old.

'If you couldn't make it or it was somehow awkward, you should have said so earlier. He's been looking forward so much to −'

'I know, I know. I'm there, I tell you. I'll be with you in under ten.'

'It's not often that he has things like this. What happened?'

'Something came up, that's all.' He didn't want to be specific or shield behind the dramatics of the past eighteen hours: *the biggest case of my career has just gone down in flames*. Besides, she'd heard it all before. The stake-outs that ran hours over, the last-minute suspects and late-night emergencies. The steady stream of late nights crawling into bed and so little quality time with her and the children that had finally led to the collapse of their marriage. She'd moved to Montreal so that she could have her mother's help with babysitting while she went back out to work. He followed ten months later so that he could be nearer his children, but history was repeating itself. Chac had always claimed that his absorption with the Lacailles was partly to fill the void from losing his family, and perhaps he was right. He looked thoughtfully at his desk photo of Benjamin and young Angèle, only six, against the overbearing backdrop montage of the Lacailles. Certainly, in the last twenty-four hours, his family hadn't got a look-in. 'It's completely my fault, I'm sorry. But I'm leaving right now.'

He hung up swiftly before Sandra could draw breath to grill him more. He grabbed his coat and was halfway across the squad room as Hébert waved frantically at him.

'It's Maggie Laberge again. Wondering whether −'

He held one hand up. 'I'll call her back from my car. Ten minutes, no more.'

A bit more time to refine what he was going to say. He thought of little else as he sped through the traffic. How would he know if Donatien was likely to turn turtle and testify? Their only feed from within the Lacaille camp was Azy Ménard, bar manager at their nightclub on Rue Sherbrooke. Was it likely Donatien would confide directly in him? No. He'd have to think of a credible go-between to be able to sell the story.

He tapped his fingers on the wheel as he hit a small tailback of traffic at the first stop light on Ste-Catherine. The rush hour was starting; it was going to take him a little longer. Snow flecked with dark-grey slush was banked over the kerbs each side, and the exhaust outflows of the cars ahead showed heavy in the freezing air.

Chac's words spun back . . . *a few months?* The same was true for Roman Lacaille. What would he do? Just bide his time, knowing that soon he'd be home dry anyway? Or was he determined to rid himself of every last witness to that night with Leduc?

4

'Is there nothing else we can do?' Elena pressed.

'Not at this stage, I'm afraid.' Nadine Moore let out a tired breath at the other end of the phone. 'I've been in touch with Lorena's school and GP, told them to let me know if anything appears untoward with Lorena. Physical indications obviously from her doctor, but from the school all they can look out for are mood swings or problems with her work.'

'And they didn't tell you of anything they'd noticed already?'

'No. I'd have phoned you straight away if there was any news. I know how anxious you are.' With the silence from the other end, Nadine added, 'As you said, it was just a momentary look. You could well be wrong – it could be nothing.'

'No.' Elena shook her head. 'I know Lorena too well. There's something wrong.'

'Maybe it was just concern about the fuss caused by our visit. She started to think about what might be said to her after we left.'

'I don't know.' Elena felt herself wavering, but only for a second. She reminded herself that she'd only seen that look on Lorena's face twice before: once when she was recalling some nights in the sewer waking up with rats crawling over her; the second time with the threat of the second orphanage closing when she'd dreaded having to go back to the streets again. Elena knew the difference between fear and concern with Lorena. She was aware of a presence behind her and glanced over her shoulder. Gordon hovered by the door to his study. With a taut half-smile he turned back in and she pulled her attention back to Nadine. More emphatically: 'No. It's more than that, I know.'

Nadine exhaled loudly. Practically a replay of their conversation after leaving the Ryalls yesterday, and now it was painfully evident that she wasn't easily going to dispel Elena's worries, imagined or otherwise. But there was little else she could do. As it was, she'd stretched as far as she dare go: telling Ryall that he should avoid visits to Lorena's room late at night had been like tiptoeing through broken glass. Cushioning the reproach – 'It's just one of those things with girls at her age. They become very secretive and self-conscious. You weren't to know' – had done little to ease Ryall's pained, incredulous expression.

'With Ryall not visiting her room any more, hopefully that should put pay to any problems. *If* there were problems originally.'

'Yes, hopefully.' Elena didn't feel convinced. Doubt still nagged at her. But she sensed that Nadine's position was starting to become entrenched; little would be gained by pressing. She elicited a promise from Nadine to let her know the moment anything new came up, and signed off.

Yet it wasn't just Nadine that was doubtful. When she'd recounted everything to Gordon the night before, he'd wondered whether she might be reading too much into it all. Now that tight smile when he'd heard her pressing Nadine.

She pondered whether to broach the issue again with him – she'd hoped at least for support from Gordon, if nothing else, so as to not feel so isolated with her concerns – but from his voice trailing through from his office, she could tell that he was on the phone.

She went back to her upstairs studio to do more painting. Time to allow her mood to settle, her thoughts to focus. Her painting helped with that. Brush-stroke therapy.

She'd spent much of the last month painting version three of the chine – the steep wooded ravine leading to the sea – which their house overlooked. Version one had been a standard landscape view that she wasn't happy with. Gordon had prompted: 'What is it that you most like about the chine, that you find magical?' She'd admitted that it was the feeling of secrecy and being protected once deep inside it, with the open sea at its end representing freedom. Yet as she would move closer to the sea and hear its rushing surge, that also came to represent all the volatility and madness out there; what she was perhaps hiding away from. 'In the chine I feel safe, as if it's a haven.' 'Then paint that,' Gordon had suggested.

Good, solid, dependable Gordon, sometimes infuriatingly laid-back with his slow, pedantic deliberations – but always intuitive. The voice of reason in a storm. Probably why now his support was so important to her.

Her second attempt had too much contrast between the darkness of the chine and the harsh light of the sea horizon beyond. This time she was trying to capture some warmth and texture, some detail and depth to the trees and foliage, the faint chinks of light reflecting off the brook trickling through. She'd taken three photos in the summer as a guide, but she knew the chine so well she could practically paint it blindfold.

Her style of painting was conventional landscape with a hint of impressionist, but became unconventional through its use of layering – the habit of building the oils in layers employed by the Old Masters. It had been originally due to the expense of canvas, and therefore the need to repaint over old paintings or the false starts of works in progress. For Elena, it afforded the luxury of being able to paint over her errors until she reached perfection. She considered herself not that good an artist – despite two local exhibitions and one at a small Notting Hill gallery when they were in London – and so for her the layering became in part a device behind which she could shield her lack of ability. Nobody would ever know.

The one thing she shared with the Old Masters was the rich texture and depth she gained through the many layers. But as now she carefully dabbed and stroked, she found herself becoming increasingly agitated rather than relaxed. Her hand started to shake on the brush. The therapy this time wasn't working.

Elena could only catch a glimpse of sea beyond the far ridge of the chine, a heavy grey-blue almost merging with the mist and cloud. Quite different from the Ryalls' broad sea panorama seven miles up the coast – but Elena couldn't help imagining Lorena looking from her bedroom window at the same dull, brooding sea, wondering if anything was happening or whether she'd been left alone and forgotten.

'You don't think I should pursue it, do you?' Elena looked at Gordon directly as she toyed with the last of her dessert.

She'd tried to broach the subject twice earlier: the first time Shelley McGurran, her boss at the agency, had phoned; the second time her daughter, Katine, had walked into the kitchen halfway through them talking while she was preparing dinner.

They'd let the children leave the table early to watch TV with their desserts; they were now out of earshot in the adjoining lounge.

'It's not that I think you're wrong. Your suspicions may very well be right – something *is* happening.' Gordon gave a small shrug. 'After all, you know Lorena better than most. It's just that from your position there's little you can do – you're out of the loop now. And if, as you say, social services can't do anything, you're just going to get frustrated trying to pursue it.'

Elena held Gordon's gaze for a second. Obviously her two false starts earlier had given him time to prepare: he'd chosen the route of lesser confrontation, not wanting a heated debate over whether or not her suspicions might be right.

'But if social services can't or won't help her – who else is there to help her? Who else does she know in this town?'

'I know, I know.' Gordon held one hand up, sighing, as if exasperated that despite his efforts he'd still hit a confrontational wall. 'I think you're right to try. But unless you budge social services to your way of thinking, how far are you going to get? Even if you convince them something is happening – regardless of it being based only on a hunch over a worried look from Lorena – they'll still need something concrete to be able to pursue it.'

As always, the voice of reason. But as much as she knew that, annoyingly, Gordon was probably right – what hit her strongest, as with the many times he'd been right before, was his smug, know-it-all overtone, which would usually draw out her instinctive rebelliousness. Though through twelve years of marriage she'd learnt to curb her worst traits, so all that resulted now was her lightly chewing her bottom lip as she looked back down at her dessert.

Sudden awkwardness with the silence; when she lifted her head she glanced through the open archway to the lounge. Christos, twelve, their eldest by three years, was pointing to something on the TV and making a comment to Katine, who was just out of view.

Elena shook her head. 'I mean, my God, she's only eighteen months older than our Katine. If anything is happening, she must feel so . . . so helpless. And vulnerable.'

Gordon reached across the table and clasped her hand. 'Maybe they'll hit on something through her school or GP.'

Elena smiled back tightly. Gordon had aimed to reassure, but it had backfired as a sharp reminder that those were their only hopes. If nothing came to light, Lorena would be quickly forgotten, consigned to some social services 'dead file' cabinet – no doubt larger than any other.

After a second, Gordon asked, 'What was it with Shelley?'

Elena faltered slightly with the shift in topic before refocusing. 'Oh . . . it was about the next supply consignment. It's almost ready – five or six days. I'll ride with it to Bucharest, stay maybe a week between the two orphanages, then catch a flight to Sarajevo.'

Gordon nodded. Europe's child-neglect hot-spots that had been Elena's roster the past four years: Romania, Bosnia, Chechnya – where they'd adopted Katine eighteen months before Elena joined the agency. In fact, the main driving force behind her joining: *'We were able to help Katine. But she's just one child out of thousands in the same position. If I can, I'd like to be able to help more children like Katine.'* Anything from two to four weeks away on each round-trip tour, then two or three weeks back in the UK helping Shelley McGurran organize the next aid consignment.

'How are things now at the Cerneit?' Gordon asked. He knew from Elena's recent conversations that the Cerneit was one of their most troubled orphanages.

'We've managed to cut down on the two or three to a bed – but now every inch of floor space is littered with mattresses. You can hardly get a foot between. And just when we got the hepatitis under control, there was an outbreak of scurvy.'

'What from?'

'We sent over a large consignment of porridge oats last time. But they went mad with it, gave it to the children for breakfast, lunch and dinner – weren't sensible enough to balance it out with fresh fruit and veg.' She shook her head, half smiling in disbelief. 'They said they didn't realize and, besides, they claimed to be short on cash for food the last couple of months: a problem with the boiler had forced them to spend more on building maintenance and take it out of the food budget.'

Gordon looked down for a second – the point he'd been circling towards was now within grasp – before looking back up meaningfully. 'That's the other thing with this now. If there is a problem with Lorena – what do you do? Just turn your back on all those hundreds of other children who need your help?'

'That's unfair and you know it,' Elena protested. 'This is just a one-off. It's not as if it's the sort of thing that happens every day.'

'The point I'm trying to make, Elena, is where do you draw the line? You've become a surrogate mother to a lot of these children and it's great that you've become so close to so many of them. But you can't be a mother to the world. At some stage you've got to let go, let someone else take the responsibility. You can only stretch yourself so far.'

'This is different. And, as I said, unlikely to happen again.' Elena flickered her eyes to one side, towards the children in the next room. Gordon was right, but she didn't want him to see he'd hit a painful raw nerve. Feeling his eyes still on her, she added, 'This isn't just about my past closeness to Lorena, or perhaps me reading too much into the worried look in her eyes. It's also the atmosphere in the house and with the Ryalls that tells me something is wrong.'

'In what way?'

'Well . . .' She struggled for the right words. 'Tense to say the least – which perhaps you'd expect given the nature of our visit. But I couldn't help feeling that something was being hidden. And Cameron Ryall came across as a complete control guru.'

'Isn't that also what you'd expect from someone in his position?' Cameron Ryall's status warranted only sidebars in the financial pages of the national press, but locally he was big news: Chelborne's Bill Gates.

Elena shook her head. 'No, it went beyond that. Nicola Ryall had obviously been primed, but I got the strong feeling that she was actually afraid of him. As she sat there, hardly daring to answer or interject, all I got was a picture of my mother sat there in a similar position.'

'Oh, right.' Gordon exhaled, a slightly defeated sigh. So now finally they were getting to the root of the problem: her father.

Gordon looked down awkwardly, toying with the rim of his wine glass. Just when he thought that finally her father's shadow had gone from her life, inevitably it would rise again, like a phantom. The all-controlling figurehead who had guided – or would a better word be destroyed? – so much of her life. Whose hand could be seen in practically every major step or decision she'd ever made – forcing her to have an abortion when she became pregnant at sixteen, and then the growing gap between them finally leading to years of rebellion: leaving home early, the bedsits and hippie communes, protest marches and 'discovery' trips to India and Marrakesh, where she'd ended up living for two years; days where the edges became increasingly blurred in a euphoric haze of dope and dabbling with LSD – before she woke up to the fact that she wasn't just rebelling against everything her father stood for, but was also punishing herself.

Eleven years she'd spent pursuing 'alternative' lifestyles; they'd met three years after her return from Marrakesh when she was working in her uncle Christos' import business, and they'd married ten months later. Their adopted boy they'd named after her uncle, who – though Elena would be reluctant to admit it – everyone else saw as partly filling her need for a father figure, but one that understood her, loved her. Christos was also what she would have named her aborted child had it been a boy. Then later her desire for another adopted child, a girl, and the resultant urge for her to do more for other orphaned children.

But hers wasn't the only life she'd felt had been scarred by her father's over-dominance. She blamed him also for the suicide of her younger brother, Andreos, who had knuckled under her father's influence, yet in the end felt he'd not only betrayed what he truly wanted to do but, regardless, would never have been able to live up to his father's demanding expectations. Andreos opted out in the most dramatic way possible.

Her father had died five years before, but the scars still ran so deep that she'd refused to attend the funeral. But more than anyone else in her family, Gordon felt that she'd kept her father's memory alive with her every action through the years, and now his ghost was back again in the shape of Cameron Ryall's dominance over Nicola Ryall and Lorena.

Certainly, on the surface at least, there were similarities with Ryall: her father had parlayed a 1950s Greek Cypriot trading company into Britain's ninth largest merchant bank. But any link between them, real or imagined, only returned Gordon full circle to one of his first concerns.

'Has it struck you that the reminder of your father might be making you read too much into it all, seeing demons where they don't exist? You see the surface signs with Ryall, then fill in the gaps to suit.'

Elena shook her head vigorously. 'No, no. It's more than that with Ryall.'

'Like what?'

Elena stared back levelly. As much as she'd carefully skirted around the issue, it was back squarely in her lap. But she could never tell Gordon what had really happened with her father: too many years now she'd spent not only telling the lie, but living it. She reached across and touched Gordon's hand.

'There were a lot of things I never talked about with my father. Nothing significant, just small things, which is probably why they hardly seemed worth mentioning. You know, it's like when you know someone's unbalanced way before they start wildly swinging an axe.' She looked down briefly at the table for inspiration. 'You see it first in the tense way they grip a coffee cup, or their reaction to someone saying something out of place or wearing something they don't like. Small things. And it's things like that I see now between Ryall and his wife. It's . . . it's hard to put my finger on. Maybe no more than a hunch. And maybe you're right – that hunch could well be wrong.'

Gordon held her gaze for a moment before she glanced away. He could tell that she was deeply troubled, and while the analogy made sense, her finishing on the note of so casually casting off her previous concerns made him suspicious. He took a fresh sip of wine, and suddenly the uneasy thought hit him like a thunderbolt.

'My God . . . don't tell me your father was molesting you?'

Elena threw her head back and laughed out loud at the suggestion. She subdued it quickly. 'No, no. My father might have been a monster in every other way . . . but he wasn't molesting me.'

Gordon raised his glass and smiled. 'Now you've got *me* at it. Seeing demons where they don't exist.'

Elena was glad of the light relief to suddenly dead-end their conversation. But her half-smile as she raised her glass to clink with Gordon's also conveniently shielded the bitter irony: what in fact had happened with her father was in many ways far, far worse.

Elena became increasingly agitated as she counted down the days to her going away.

Clinging to the hope that Nadine would call with fresh news from Lorena's school or GP, or that Lorena herself would phone again. But, as Gordon had pointed out when he'd picked up on her agitation, 'Surely best if she doesn't call. At least one sign that Ryall is doing what he's been told and is keeping away from her room. Or that her first call was a false alarm.'

But the comment only made her focus more on why she remained uneasy: the abject fear she'd read in Lorena's face in that brief moment. She was concerned that if the problem with Ryall resurfaced, Lorena might be too frightened to raise the alarm again. Also, she was Lorena's only possible ally, yet now she was leaving. Deserting her.

The last day was particularly tense. She thought of putting in a last-minute call to Nadine, then wavered against the idea before finally going ahead, only to discover that Nadine was out on visits and unavailable. Then work and final arrangements took over – checking rosters and schedules, last-second calls to synchronize their journey over – and she was headed for a midnight shuttle in a van loaded to the brim, leading the way for the main two-ton supply truck behind.

The long drive gave her time to think again about Lorena, probably too much, and at one point her driver, Nick – twenty-eight, square-jawed, who looked like he'd stepped from a jeans advert despite his years of wild debauchery as a roadie – asked her what was wrong.

'One of the kids I placed with an English family a couple of years back. I'm worried about her.'

'Is she ill, or just a bad family?'

Elena smiled tautly at the 'just', as if it was a far lesser worry than illness. She didn't want to go into detail with Nick. 'That's what we don't know yet. We're hoping she's mistaken.'

Nick half shrugged, sensing Elena's reluctance to elaborate. 'Hope it works out.'

'Thanks. Me too.' She looked to one side, losing herself momentarily in the darkness of the endless line of fir trees bordering the autobahn.

One of Nick's favourite Ry Cooder tracks was playing on the CD, and he turned it up a notch. With the repetitive scenery Elena found herself slipping into catnaps and their small talk didn't return for a while, with Nick by then alternating with some of Elena's favourites: Santana and Peter Green-era Fleetwood Mac.

When they arrived in Bucharest, the hectic turn of events pushed all thoughts of Lorena into the background. A seven-year-old boy at the Cerneit orphanage with a prolonged headache and eye strain was finally diagnosed as having meningitis. Two more suspected cases were discovered over the next few hours, and Elena was caught up in a maelstrom of activity: treatment for the three cases and organizing vaccines for the remaining children, with frantic calls back to London for wired funds to cover it all.

The boy's condition worsened on the third night, and she kept up a bedside vigil for five hours holding his hand and praying that they wouldn't lose him. It struck her then: Gordon was right. These children needed her, this is where her main focus had to be. She didn't have time, nor the mental or emotional space, to be divided on two fronts.

The boy rallied well the next morning and Elena headed off with Nick, a day behind schedule, to the orphanage in Brasov. As they approached the Carpathian mountains, dusk was falling. They looked dark and foreboding at the best of times, often shrouded with mist, ideal fodder for the shadowy myths and legends surrounding them.

But staring into the rising wall of darkness with the last dusk light as a pale trim, Elena was suddenly gripped by recall of the chine – the one and only time she'd taken Lorena there on a day out to introduce her to the area before she settled in with the Ryalls.

She'd taken Lorena to see her home, then they'd gone down the steep wooded bank into the chine. As they'd reached the bottom of the chine and the darkness of the ravine and the dense foliage above enshrouded them, she'd gripped Lorena's arm tight and asked her to listen. 'Listen?'

It was eerily silent and cool, and after a moment of them standing stock still, they could pick out the sound of the brook running gently through the bottom of the chine towards the sea.

'You hear that?' she prompted. 'It's magical down here, isn't it? Like some secret hideaway from the rest of the world.'

Lorena hadn't answered, and at first Elena thought the trembling where she gripped Lorena's arm was because of the coolness of the chine. But the shaking became rapidly worse and Lorena murmured tremulously, 'I don't like it down here . . . Please let's go. The darkness, the water, it . . .'

Lorena lurched forward, practically dragging Elena, and within a few paces they'd hit a run. They followed the bottom of the chine close to the running brook, bursting through the branches and foliage as they ran frantically, breathlessly, towards the light of the sea horizon ahead. Lorena's increasingly laboured breath started lapsing into strangled sobs. Their legs pumped hard and their lungs ached with their rasping breath – but the light never seemed to get closer. The dark, dense foliage remained all-enveloping, suffocating, the light at the end still distant, out of reach, except for a single shaft which seemed to burn through, intensify, as if trying to . . .

'What . . . ?' Elena sat up, startled.

'Are you okay?' Nick repeated.

Elena shielded her eyes from the searing headlamps of an oncoming truck. She'd fallen asleep; it was now pitch dark. Catching up after her vigil with the boy last night.

It took her a second to adjust back to her surroundings. She and Lorena had in fact burst through to the light of the open beach quite quickly, their breathlessness lost on the fresh sea breeze, and Elena had hugged Lorena tight and kissed the tears from her cheek, muttering,

'I'm sorry, I'm sorry.' She hadn't realized that the chine might remind Lorena of her sewer days.

Suddenly the image of Lorena standing alone at her bedroom window, deserted, came back to her. Despite Gordon's wise words and her own rationalizing of the past days, she couldn't help wondering if that was what Lorena wanted from her now: to once again help her out of the darkness towards the light.

But when eleven days later Gordon called to tell her that Lorena had phoned again, it threw her into turmoil. Whether because she had once again become absorbed in the plight of the orphaned children, or was clinging to the rationalization that nothing was happening or, even if it was, that it was no longer her problem – Elena wasn't sure. But part of her wasn't surprised at the call, and she wondered why she hadn't trusted her instincts, why she'd allowed herself to so easily get pulled with the flow.

'She said that Ryall stayed away from her room for a while, but now he'd started coming back. And that she needed help. No doubt *your* help.'

Slightly numbed, Elena said simply, 'I suppose I'd better call Nadine Moore again.'

A few seconds' silence with only the faint static-line hiss, then Gordon asked, 'When are you heading back?'

'I'm not sure yet. I'll call you later today when I know.' She'd decide after she'd spoken to Nadine Moore whether to fly back straight away or wait out the five days left of her trip. 'And Gordon, I . . .'

'Yes?'

'It's okay.' She bit lightly at her bottom lip. 'It doesn't matter. I'll see you soon, anyway.' It just didn't feel right pouring out her heart over this faint, static-charged line; even though the distance, and not having to face him, might have made it easier. And perhaps when she got home, having harboured the secret now for so many years, it still wouldn't feel right.

Signing off, Elena found that she was trembling. She knew now why she'd so readily clung to rationalization, and it had little to do with refusing to accept the worst after everything Lorena had already been through in her troubled past. It had to do with her own past – the wall of lies she'd so carefully constructed throughout her life, to Gordon and everyone else, but most importantly to herself. What lay at the core of their adopting Christos and Katine and her decision to work with strife-torn, orphaned children. She'd feared from the outset that this incident with Lorena might open up the wound in her psyche, and part of her, despite her raw instincts, had tried to push the portent away. Now, having to face it square-on meant admitting that the founding principles of over half her life had been wrong. There was nothing left to stop the wall crumbling.

5

One single incident now threatening so much. Practically everything he'd planned and worked towards these past five years. It hardly seemed believable. Jean-Paul Lacaille shook his head as he looked through the long french windows towards the courtyard. The windows were almost twice his height, in keeping with the spacious, high-ceilinged room: one of four sets along its thirty-eight-foot length.

At the room's centre was a long baroque-style table and fourteen Louis XIV chairs. The 'power room' where practically every key decision of the Lacaille family had been made over the past three decades.

When his father had bought the house in '65, the courtyard had been enclosed only on three sides, overlooking a formal Italianate garden. But with their growing family – three generations of Lacailles under one roof at the same time and increasing workload at home – they'd finally added a fourth wing, with an office, pool and gym opposite the stable block. The catalyst for the addition, though, had been their battle with the Cacchiones: the fourth wing completely enclosed the courtyard, made it more of a compound. But none of their precautions was to help save Pascal; he'd been the last they'd thought Cacchione would target.

The house had originally been built in the 1920s by a timber and minerals baron, a small-scale Versailles Palace to properly reflect his new-found wealth and status. His father's route to its grand portals had started with cigarette and contraband smuggling during the Second World War off the Tyrrhenian coast of Corsica. A rival Union Corse Mafia member gained territorial advantage by paying heavier bribes to his local Bastia mayor, and his father felt it was time to move on. He arrived in Montreal in March 1953. The city was wide open then, ripe for docks and construction-union racketeering. Numbers, clubs, loan-sharking and prostitution followed. With hedged construction bids, his father had earned millions out of the '64 Olympics alone. Then soon after came narcotics.

Like so many old-school Mafiosi and Union Corse, his father initially tried to steer clear of narcotics, considering it a dirty, dishonourable enterprise; but in the end the profits were too large to ignore. By the early 70s, the Lacaille family were one of Canada's largest drug suppliers, second only to the Toronto-based Cacchione family.

Relationships with old-man Arnaldo Cacchione were reasonable, at least not too strained: violence was minimal, usually meted out to those who broke the rules from within their respective camps, or the rising number of small outside gangs trying to muscle in on their territory. But when young Gianni Cacchione took over the reins, things changed: he was ambitious, territorially aggressive, and a showdown with the Cacchiones became inevitable. A couple of minor soldiers were lost on each side, then a Cacchione family cousin, before finally the retaliatory hit on Pascal.

Quiet, unassuming Pascal. Always playing backgammon or jazz guitar, or with his nose in a book – if not the company's accounts, then anything from a Victor Hugo classic to the latest American hot seller – his tastes were wide and eclectic. If it weren't for the family business, maybe he'd have had more time to establish his music career, his first and main passion. And of all of them, he'd had the least to do with the business, never got involved in the muscle or enforcement side, only its balance sheet. That was probably why Cacchione had targeted him: himself, Roman and his father – the most obvious targets – were guarded to the hilt. So they'd picked off Pascal on the side 'as a message'.

The message worked. Nothing was ever the same from that day. His father lacked the stomach to fight on. Pascal had been his favourite, the baby of the family, and worse still he blamed Roman for the hit on the Cacchione cousin that had led to the retaliation with Pascal. Internal family wrangling was intense.

Watching his father's clawing sorrow and increasing frailty over the following months was what finally steered Jean-Paul towards his momentous decision to try and move the family away from crime. In the lull, they'd lost the main advantage and the best territories to Cacchione in any case. They could make as much by being enterprising in other ways: the stock market, construction, more casinos and clubs. Roman was against the idea, but with still the shadow of a finger pointing at him over Pascal's death, his protests weren't forceful.

Jean-Paul gained the main support from family *consigliere*, Jon

Larsen, who pointed out that to achieve their aim, they'd need a keen financial eye on board. Two months of head-hunting by Larsen, and the name Georges Donatien was proposed: one of the youngest and hottest rising investment portfolio managers with Banque du Québec. Donatien had just turned in the best past-year performance on pension-fund portfolios: an impressive 34 per cent. But it took ten months of cat-and-mouse courting to finally get Donatien aboard, by which time it was too late for his father.

Jean-Paul's quest had by then become a burning ambition, with the final seal of it being practically a deathbed promise to his father: 'I'll clean this business from top to bottom, you'll see. What happened with Pascal will never be allowed to happen again.'

But it had come from the heart. All he could picture in that moment was himself, twenty years on, mourning the death of his own son, Raphaël. They had all the money in the world. Yet so much of their lives was spent looking over their shoulders and worrying about the safety and welfare of family. It was no way to live.

His father had smiled indulgently. 'A noble quest, and one that hasn't been achieved before, as far as I know. But you seem determined – I'm sure you will succeed.' Marked contrast to the previously aired doubts and concerns that as much as he might wish to escape the past, 'The past will never allow you that escape.'

His father had become increasingly morose and maudlin in his fading months, contemplating that a 'sins of the father' retribution had been visited on Pascal. Jean-Paul couldn't help reflecting on the messy chain of events with Leduc, now bouncing back in their laps with Tony Savard's murder.

Jean-Paul took a deep breath and looked up to where two pigeons tried to nestle into the roof gables. An early-morning winter mist hung low, obscuring half of the green-copper Versailles roof, vapoured body heat and breath rising up from the stables towards it. How much of this grand edifice had been built on spilled blood and shattered lives over the years? The room where Raphaël had been born, or where they'd celebrated Simone's first communion and clinked glasses over numerous birthdays, weddings and anniversaries? Or the rooms where his father and Stephanie had been laid to rest, or Raphaël's bedroom, covered with pop and rollerblading posters like any other fifteen-year-old's? Or this room now where counsel had been held on lives to be spared or lost?

Perhaps his father had been right: however hard they tried, they never would be able to escape the past. And maybe they simply didn't deserve to ever be able to.

'So how would you read it, Georges?' Jean-Paul asked.

They were sat at one end of the long dining table, Georges and Jon Larsen either side of Jean-Paul at the head, and the mood was tense.

'I would go more or less with Jon's view,' Georges said.

'More or less?' Jean-Paul raised one hand as if whisking air. 'Have we missed something? How might you differ?'

They'd spent the first twenty minutes of the meeting discussing business – his round trip to Mexico and Cuba, building schedules there, shares and investment portfolio performance, last quarter's figures for the clubs and casinos – before turning to the subject of Tony Savard's murder.

Georges chose his words carefully. The Lacaille family's past battles with the Cacchiones had made this a brittle subject. 'I agree with Jon that it's most likely the Cacchiones are behind it. But we shouldn't overlook the possibility of a rising group of independents or bikers trying to play us and the Cacchiones off against each other. Not only do they divert attention, meanwhile they take advantage of the resulting vacuum.'

Jean-Paul nodded sagely for a second, then shrugged. 'But we're no longer involved in crime. We don't pose a threat.'

'No. But since the incident with Leduc, the police for one believe that we're still heavily involved. And if that's a clear advantage for the Cacchiones, then it's an advantage for others too.'

'Except for one thing,' Jon Larsen offered. 'Gianni Cacchione would have to try and divert the blame in any case because of his situation with Medeiros. And this whole drama with the RCMP probably came about as a by-product of that. A happy accident.'

Round in circles. They'd tossed the same subject around probably more than any other at this table the past few years. Just when they were making good progress with their new direction, it would rise up again to drag them back.

The most likely scenario they'd hit upon was that Gianni Cacchione had put Leduc in the frame to divert suspicion from his own continued drug dealing. With the Lacailles pulling back from drug dealing and crime in general, Cacchione had eagerly filled the void. But fourteen months later he had a run-in with his supplier Carlos Medeiros, head of Colombia's leading drug cartel. Medeiros accused Cacchione of shafting him out of $11 million over the previous seven shipments, and promptly cut off supplies. Cacchione tried other suppliers in Colombia and Mexico, but Medeiros had either co-territorial or distribution arrangements with them, and word had already spread: Cacchione was widely blackballed.

A number of independents had sprung up, some of them no doubt genuine; but Medeiros began to suspect that Cacchione was still behind the biggest new player, and supplies were threatened again. At that point, Eric Leduc – a Lacaille family lieutenant who helped Roman out with security for their local clubs – suddenly came into the picture as linked with this rising lead drug network. Worse still, they heard on the grapevine that Leduc had become the subject of an RCMP investigation. The police believed that the Lacailles' new 'legitimate business only' direction was just a front; that secretly they were still involved in crime and running drugs, with Leduc as their frontman.

Jean-Paul was horrified. He was certain that Cacchione was behind setting up Leduc primarily to throw Medeiros off the scent; but this had also resulted in putting the Lacailles under the spotlight with the RCMP. Cacchione must have been laughing up his sleeve.

They decided to get to Leduc's bank accounts before the RCMP. The accounts' movements were complex, and so purely through necessity – their original set-in-stone policy was that Georges would never get involved in anything linked to their past criminal activity – Georges was called on to quiz Leduc. Roman rode shotgun purely to provide psychological pressure with the silent threat of muscle should Leduc decide not to be cooperative, and Leduc was allowed to nominate one batsman of his own: he chose Tony Savard. The only other person present that fateful night was the driver, Steve Tremblay, a doorman from one of their downtown clubs, who was outside the car, smoking and swapping stories with Savard when Leduc was shot. The police saw Leduc's death as confirmation of their involvement in drugs, the result of their desperation to bury the traces. Now with Savard, further confirmation: the spotlight would be on them all the more.

'We've invested so much time thinking Gianni Cacchione is behind it all,' Georges commented. 'And while that's still the most likely option, we shouldn't shut out all other possibilities. We could find ourselves blindsided if something else suddenly comes up.'

'I know, I know.' Jean-Paul rubbed his forehead. 'Truth to tell, I should never have sent you along to confront Leduc in the first place.' Their ten-month cat-and-mouse game to finally get Georges aboard had been mainly laying strong reassurance that he'd only be involved in 'clean' business. Georges even stipulated that he would never get involved in any laundering: 'The money has to be cleaned before I get to it. If I'm meant to be a clean trader, then let's start how we mean to continue.' Yet despite all their determination that Georges should never get roped into the past-crime side of their business, by default it had now become the topic *du jour* at every other meeting.

'You weren't to know it would end so badly,' Georges said. 'And besides, who else could you have trusted to pick through Leduc's accounts?'

'I suppose so.' Jean-Paul smiled tightly. It offered little consolation. Hearing Georges even talk about the problem was a sour reminder of just how far they'd been dragged off course. Dragged back to the past. Jean-Paul turned to Jon Larsen. 'What are the police saying?'

'Three shots, the final one to the head. Professional hit, probably connected with Savard's criminal activities. And that he was under investigation – no doubt part of their purge against us, though that part I'm assuming.' Larsen glanced at the notepad before him. 'Oh, and they're looking for a black van – a Chevy Venture that they suspect might be connected. Apart from that, nothing. I'll do some digging, but we might not get much more than that.'

Jean-Paul nodded. Chenouda's group handling of the investigation against them was tight-knit and secretive. Little of any value leaked out from RCMP headquarters.

'And what's Roman's view?' Larsen asked.

'I only spoke to him briefly on the phone, but he's pretty sure Cacchione's behind it.' Jean-Paul tilted his head and shrugged. 'Apparently, after the mess with Leduc, Savard confided in him that he was concerned that because Savard was a friend of Leduc's, Cacchione might worry that he had been privy to secrets about Cacchione's drug network. That wasn't the case, but Savard feared that Cacchione might believe it to be so.'

Larsen asked, 'Do you think Cacchione might have been also responsible for Steve Tremblay's death?'

'Maybe,' Jean-Paul conceded. Until now, they'd had no reason to believe that the death of the car driver was anything other than what it appeared: a boating accident. Now he was beginning to wonder.

Georges looked down for a second. Was it just family allegiances and respect for Jean-Paul that stopped anyone airing the other possible option: that with the increasing RCMP investigation, Roman might be keen to bury all traces of that fateful night. Or was he worried simply because of what he knew about that night that nobody else at this table knew? He could hardly scorn those allegiances, when it was exactly that which had made him shy away from telling all to Jean-Paul in the first place. Yet now that one lie – or at least not telling *all* the truth – was becoming dangerously compounded.

Jean-Paul misread his look of concern. 'If it's Cacchione's intention to target others from that night, you and Roman will have to be extra vigilant. I'll talk to Roman about stepping up security.'

Great, thought Georges. So now his future health would rest in Roman's hands, yet he'd cut himself off from being able to tell anyone why he didn't feel entirely comfortable about that. 'Okay,' he said meekly.

'This whole affair with Leduc has been messy, and unfortunately could get messier still,' Jean-Paul said with resignation. 'But I'm determined that it won't be allowed to hold us back or in any way affect our new direction. I think the two of you appreciate more than most how important that is to me.'

As Jean-Paul came on to discussing with Jon Larsen their most recent problem of fresh licensing pressure with two clubs – which they feared was all part of the general RCMP Lacaille-family purge – Georges suddenly felt strangely remote from their conversation; the stranger, perhaps, he'd always been. The weight and grandeur of the room pressed in as it had done at that first meeting with Jean-Paul and Jon Larsen: the rococo-edged ceilings and pillars; the rich red drapes tied with gold brocade; the high-backed Louis XIV chairs; the collection of family photos on a long side table with priceless ormolu clocks interspersed – an altar to time–family continuum; the ornate cherub statue by Houdon, who apparently had also made statues of Voltaire and George Washington. Georges had been struck as he'd first walked into the room with the feeling that Jean-Paul might see himself as a modern-day Napoleon.

But over those initial few meetings, Georges started to see the other side of Jean-Paul: a warm, caring family man with noble – if venturesome and foolish – hopes and aims. An image that was keenly massaged by Jon Larsen in heart-to-hearts straight after those meetings: 'No doubt you've read and heard all the dark stories – rumoured or otherwise. But don't worry – I'll be first to make sure that Jean-Paul keeps to his promise that all that side of the Lacaille family is now history. Jean-Paul's one of the fairest men I've worked for, and I've worked for a few in my time. Otherwise I just wouldn't have stayed around this long.'

A hard-bitten corporate lawyer for thirteen years before joining Jean-Paul, Jon Larsen perhaps saw in Georges a kindred spirit: a fellow exile from the business world. And whether through that or not, Georges did find himself bonding closer with him than anyone else in the extended Lacaille family. Larsen was now in his late fifties, with a strong resemblance to Mr Magoo – except that what little ring of hair Larsen had left was kept brush-cut short – and all too often Georges found they shared the same thoughts and views. Over the past three years, they'd swapped many truths and confidences. Except one.

But it wasn't Larsen's pep talks that had finally convinced him to join the fold; nor Jean-Paul's firm promise that all the money would be cleaned before he started work with it; nor their offer to almost double his existing $280,000 p.a. earnings with Banque du Québec, with additional share bonuses in the Lacailles' many businesses.

What finally had decided him was that Jean-Paul's quest had touched his heart. After their fifth or sixth meeting, Georges couldn't remember now, Jean-Paul sat him down with a large brandy and told him about the family background that had forged in his heart and soul the desire for this new direction: how Pascal's death had destroyed their father; how he and Pascal had played together as children and Pascal in his teenage years talked about becoming a musician or writer; how Jean-Paul himself had strongly related to that, because secretly he'd dreamed of becoming an architect or designer before the family business sucked him in. Jean-Paul had then pointed to the picture of his son Raphaël on the side table. 'He's only twelve now, and perhaps his dreams aren't fully formed yet and he's still talking about being a train driver or an astronaut – but I don't want him to end up the same as Pascal.'

In that moment, Georges hadn't seen a crime don, but the frightened teenager who'd buried his dreams, then later his younger brother, both in the name of familial duty – yet now was frantically grappling with whether he'd be able to turn back the tide before it claimed another generation.

Georges had phoned back within the week to tell Jean-Paul that he'd join him. And from that point the quest rapidly became a crusade: not just for Jean-Paul to prove to himself that it could be done, or for Georges as a money-man the challenge to try and match the sort of high returns previously notched up from crime – but because their aims had started to attract keen outside interest. Four other leading crime families – most notable among them Jean-Paul's close friends and past crime allies, the Giacomelli family of Chicago – were eager to see Jean-Paul fare well: after all, if he succeeded it could provide a useful blueprint for them. Others were more sceptical, saying that it had never been done before simply because it *couldn't* be done. Lacaille was trying for the impossible.

Suddenly their quest had become a cause célèbre. Bets were being taken each side on whether they would win or lose. And it hit Georges then just how monumental the stakes were: succeed and he not only provided the salvation Jean-Paul so badly craved, but they also might show the path for countless crime families to follow; fail, and it was back to the dark ages.

And now Roman's rash action that one night, compounded by his own lie, could bring down the whole deck of cards. The crushing weight of it all was almost too much to bear.

Georges laid his right hand flat and firm on the table to stop it from trembling. His attention was pulled sharply back by the mention of Roman.

'We could go around in circles speculating on how this whole mess might have been avoided if Roman had just grabbed Leduc's gun from him or pushed his gun arm to one side. But it could just as easily have gone wrong the other way.' Jean-Paul turned one palm towards Georges, his eyes softening. 'Either yourself or Roman could have been shot. Regardless of the unfortunate repercussions now, it was self-defence. So we have to stick together on this.'

'Yes, we do,' Jon Larsen agreed; a tone of resigned compliance.

But Georges noted that Jon Larsen's eyes stayed fixed mostly on him, perhaps picking up on his consternation or his slight flinch at the mention of 'self-defence'. Georges wondered how much longer he could hold out alone bearing the burden of his knowledge; or whether simply too much had flowed beneath the bridge for him now to be able to tell anyone.

★

Michel Chenouda knew that he shouldn't have risked the lie practically as soon as the words were out.

'How long before they have firm identification?' Chief Inspector Pelletier asked.

'Nine or ten hours is their best estimate. But it could take as long as twenty-four hours.' Michel fought to keep any hesitancy out of his voice. 'The quality on CCTV photos is low, so there's a lot of gaps for them to fill in. I'll check with them as soon as we're finished.'

'And they're pretty confident of being able to lift something positive?' Maitland confirmed.

'Yes, yes.' Michel doodled absently on a pad. 'So they told me at the last count.' The truth was far removed: the department dealing with photo enhancement, T104, adjoining forensics, had told him the shadows looked too heavy for a decent identity lift. They'd do their best, 'But don't hold your breath.' But with every other lead dead and Pelletier and Maitland not in the least enlivened by his hopes of getting Georges Donatien to testify, despite his efforts to play up the option – he felt as if everything was rapidly closing in on him. That Pelletier and Maitland had practically decided beforehand that they'd be presiding over the case's funeral, and Michel's explanations and defences were treated merely as eulogies. There was much head shaking from Pelletier about the manpower and cost of the case so far, with Maitland throwing in his bit about the difficulty of resurrecting any workable legal structure: 'Even if Donatien is as hopeful an option as you make out, don't forget he's your *last* witness. There's no possibility of his testimony being corroborated. With Savard alive, at least there was the hope that Donatien – facing a probably heavy sentence for being an accomplice to murder – might well have turned Crown evidence and corroborated his story.'

Michel sensed that if he didn't come up with something dramatic fast, they might close the file there and then. Although late the previous night he'd come up with the idea of checking CCTV cameras on likely routes from the dockside, they hadn't hit on any possible matches until just an hour before the meeting. Michel painted it as brightly as he could and threw it into the impatient jaws of Pelletier and Maitland to hopefully stop them in their tracks. It appeared to be working. So far.

'Which camera did you catch them on?' Pelletier asked.

'Heading south over Jacques Cartier Bridge. They'd fooled us that they'd headed downtown, in which case we might have caught them on some of the larger building cameras. But we suspect they headed straight over Jacques Cartier. The camera picks them up practically flat on when they're about fifty yards away.'

'Any possibles that spring to mind from what you can see now on the photo?' Pelletier asked.

'No, nothing yet. The shadows are too dark, but hopefully, when they're lightened, features will become clearer.'

The room fell silent again. Michel felt the same tension return as when he'd first realized everything was fast slipping away and Pelletier was ready to close the case. But everything was still hanging by a thread; Pelletier looked only partially swayed.

The table they sat around accommodated eight and had been carved from one single piece of teak, according to Pelletier. The 'chopping board', as it was known in the squad room. Casual day-to-day progress meetings took place in Pelletier's adjoining office. But if you were asked into the meeting-room annexe, inevitably it was for something serious: a reprimand, an internal inquiry, a suspension or a badge that had to be handed over, a case file to be closed. As Crown attorney, Maitland was usually present when a final nod was needed on the legal guillotine, and the two made a strange contrast: Pelletier was heavy-set and bullish with a ruddy complexion, as if his blood pressure was threatening to erupt. Maitland was slim, tall and angular and, with his long nose and thinning hair, had a hawkish air, a dash of contrast provided by his pale, wan complexion; combined with his reputation for killing cases on often annoyingly small points of law, this had earned him the nickname 'The Undertaker'.

Pelletier was at the head of the table with Maitland in the next place down to his right, with then a seat gap between him and Michel. Suitable distance. The muted drone of traffic from twelve floors down on Boulevard Dorchester strained to rise through the thick plate windows and be heard above the faint swish of the air vents and the flicking of papers.

Pelletier was distracted for a moment by Maitland looking back through his file for something. 'So either late tonight or at the latest by midday tomorrow before we know for sure if we've got something that will give us a positive ID?' he confirmed, glancing towards Maitland as if his approval was also needed for any delay. But Maitland was still head down in his file.

'Yes,' Michel said, looking expectantly at the two of them. He tapped lightly on the table to ease tension as Maitland continued flicking through, until he realized the tapping was almost in time with his pulse and stopped.

Maitland kept one finger in place as a marker in the file as he finally looked up. Pronounced freckles or the early onset of liver spots showed on the back of his hands. 'I see from your notes that Donatien's marriage to Simone Lacaille is planned for early July.'

'Yes. The weekend after Canada Day.'

'Three and a half months.' Maitland glanced at his file again and pouted thoughtfully. 'So. If we get an ID, what happens to your plans with Donatien?'

Michel was thrown. He thought his suggestions about Donatien had been killed. He held one hand out towards Maitland. 'I didn't think you saw Donatien as a possibility.'

'Before, no. But if we can get a positive ID on the van passenger and, as you suspect, this in turn leads back to Roman Lacaille – we've got the same situation we had before with Savard. Corroborated testimony.'

'You don't think Donatien's testimony would be good enough on its own?' Michel realized he might be hinting at his doubts about getting an ID match, and added, 'Or the van passenger's?'

'They're not necessarily interdependent.' Maitland forced a tired expression, as if he was explaining something to an errant child. 'With Donatien we get Lacaille on murdering Leduc. With the van passenger, we get Lacaille on arranging Savard's murder. It's just that from what you've said, I don't see much hope of us getting Donatien to testify. He's already practically family, and about to become even more so with his impending marriage. Unless we can somehow bring extra pressure to bear. The possibility of something else against Roman Lacaille which might bring out the whole business with Leduc could be what we need to tip the balance on Donatien's testifying.'

'I see.' Michel nodded thoughtfully. Except that with hopes of ID slimmer than he'd made out, it would probably all fold back in on him, and he'd lose the possibility of Donatien at the same time. At most he might have earned himself a day's grace on them closing the file.

Pelletier, sensing that Michel seemed more morose than he should, offered: 'Sounds like something of a plan at least. *If* we get an ID.'

'Yes,' Michel agreed hastily, snapping himself out of it. 'It does.' Be thankful, he told himself: when he'd walked in he'd been fighting for minutes; now he had a full day. He'd come out of the execution room still alive: practically a first. Something in what Maitland had said played at the back of his mind, but any clear focus was out of reach; all his thoughts were on how he might turn his one-day reprieve into two or even three days.

Michel's heartbeat reached panic level within minutes of leaving the conference room. A fleeting look in Maitland's eye as Pelletier wrapped up the proceedings that warned him that Maitland might have picked up on his own uncertainty and discomfort. Perhaps he should have come across as bolder and more enthusiastic when he'd confirmed with Pelletier that, indeed, he'd let them know the minute there was news from T104 on the image enhancement. And the reminder of T104 quickened his step now as he made his way along the corridor. He punched the lift call button brusquely, then twice more after a few seconds.

It was vital he got down to T104 before Maitland decided to put in a progress call. Otherwise the game was up straight away. The lift to his right finally pinged. He tapped his fingers impatiently against its side wall as he rode down, and by the time he hit the first-floor corridor he was practically breaking into a run, the rapid clip of his step echoing on the tiled floor.

He deflected a couple of greetings with brief nods and 'hi's before reaching T104 two doors from the end of the corridor. He spotted Yves Denault, head of T104, a few desks down, leaning over a computer with one of his assistants.

On a wall-chart behind Denault's desk were computer-printed insignias of every known Hell's Angel and Rock Machine chapter in the province. Drug distribution in Quebec normally followed a pattern. The Colombians made the main shipment deals with the local Mafia, who then organized distribution with the bikers: from there it hit Quebec's bars, clubs and cafés. The Lacailles were the only Union Corse-based family operating in Canada; their counterparts invariably had Sicilian or Neapolitan Mafia roots.

Michel explained the dilemma to Denault, that he'd played things up a bit with Pelletier and Maitland. 'So if they call, either be non-committal or, if you can, play it up the same. We can always let them down later.' He shook his head and gave his best harried look to Denault's raised eyebrow. 'Sorry, Yves. I just need that extra time right now.'

'It's okay, no problem.' A slow blink of acceptance. 'I understand.

It might come up better than I thought anyway. It's too early to tell.'

Michel gently patted Yves' shoulder in thanks and made his way back up to his office.

The Lacailles' photos stared down defiantly at him as he sat at his desk and eased out his breath, and he yanked his attention to his own family photos. Young Benjamin had looked over and smiled radiantly at him from the basketball court within a minute of him arriving. He wondered if the boy noticed how late he was, and whether Sandra would make sure to let him know that his father had almost forgotten, that if it wasn't for her call he might not have shown up at all. It still seemed important for her to score points off him with the kids. Perhaps because she'd been the one to push for the split, she seized on every opportunity to support her case: see, your father shows up either late or never. No time left for us after his work. Same as always.

On the only occasion Benjamin had asked how he felt about his mother, at Christmas a few months back, he'd been caught off guard and answered, 'I loved her, of course.'

'And now?'

He'd only had time to think about it for a minute. 'I still do.' And the spontaneous rush of feeling that flooded back brought a lump to his throat. If he'd had more time to think about it, he might have answered more diplomatically: 'I'm still very fond of her, of course.' And suddenly seeing young Benjamin's eyes struggling to comprehend, he'd added hastily, 'But I made some silly mistakes. Maybe she'll forgive me, one day.'

Benjamin's awkward turning away to stare vacantly at the floor told him that she probably wouldn't. She was still too busy using his back as a dart board, while all he could do was make a chump of himself by saying he still loved her.

Michel's desk light blinked. He picked the phone up, and within minutes was immersed back in the hectic cycle of the other cases *du jour* demanding his attention – a leading drug distribution biker up for his preliminary hearing on attempted murder the next day; a truckload of smuggled Winstons pulled up going through the Kahnawake Indian reservation – but none of it really sparked his interest. Only one thing he wanted to know now. He checked through computer files and fended the calls off numbly, mechanically, until Yves' call forty minutes later. He felt a momentary hope at the sound of his voice. Maybe something had broken. 'How goes it?'

'Nothing yet. We've filled in two strong areas of shadow, but working at these sizes it's going to take a while. It's still too early to tell.'

Michel knew the process well from numerous previous photo lifts. They worked at fifteen to twenty times' magnification, filled in the dots and patches, then pulled it back down to see how much definition had improved.

Fresh breath from Yves. 'But I thought I'd let you know that you were right about Maitland checking up. Or rather it was that asshole Campion who phoned through, keen to know how close we were. I said that we were hopeful, but would know more by late morning, early afternoon tomorrow.'

'Thanks, Yves.' So his twenty-four-hour reprieve was secure. For now. Assistant Crown attorney Campion's eagerness to step into Maitland's shoes sooner rather than later had made him something of a departmental joke: pathetically fawning with Maitland, trying to adopt an air of ruthless efficiency and pontification with everyone else, and failing miserably, he was known either as 'asskiss' or '*le petit Napoléon*'.

'Did he ask many questions?' Michel asked.

'A couple – but nothing significant. Don't worry, I covered it well. He went off satisfied.'

'Satisfied' and Campion didn't sit well together. Michel could hardly remember him smiling; just a nervous tic which passed as the trace of a grimace and faded quickly.

Yves signed off with the promise of phoning as soon as he knew something – though that call didn't come through till the evening, almost three hours after Michel had headed for home. He'd dozed off in front of the TV and the ringing phone woke him abruptly.

Yves' voice at the other end was excitable, slightly breathless. 'We changed directions slightly, and we hit on something. We weren't getting anywhere fast with that first frame, we'd pulled it up and down four times and the shadows still obscured too much. So we started looking at other frames.' Yves paused, as if allowing Michel to catch up.

Michel blinked absently at the TV images ahead, but he was awake and sharply tuned from Yves' first sentence. He gave an encouraging 'Right'.

'At first we thought the frames further away would be too far for anything clear, and on those closer the angle of vision would be too sharp. But we decided to run through them anyway, and on part of the more distant sequence we suddenly hit gold. The passenger leans forward, only for a second, to get something off the dashboard – but it's enough to lift his face clear of any shadows. It's a more distant shot, a bit more grain – but with virtually no shadows I think we've got chances of an ID from it.'

'When will you know for sure?'

'An hour. Two max.'

On TV an all-day Quebec news channel was playing, with the next three days' regional weather in a bottom band of sun, cloud and snow symbols. The building had cable, and between the English and French channels the total was forty-seven. Forty-seven channels and nothing on; Michel had flicked through practically all of them before settling for news and weather. He felt excited by Yves' words, but for some reason the images still numbed him, in the same way that they'd pushed him towards sleep shortly after dinner.

Or maybe it was now conditioning; each time he'd become wrapped up with a possible breakthrough, he'd been let down. Neutral positioning was safer: the free-fall if it all came to nothing was less.

Yves promised to call back when there was more news, and Michel prompted that if it took longer than Yves expected, he should still call, 'No matter what the time'.

The silence after hanging up brought home the tension of expectancy all the harder. An hour or two more to know if the case lived or died. The image changes from the TV flickered across the subdued lighting of his apartment, pushed the photo snaps through his mind: Donatien, Jean-Paul, Roman . . . then Tony Savard's terrified face, pleading for his life. An image to match the screams on tape.

Michel stood up abruptly, started pacing to ease his tension. At least here, at home, he was surrounded only by family photos. Angèle blowing out the candles on her fourth birthday cake. Benjamin with his first bike. The whole family together in St Lucia, photographed by an obliging hotel waiter; five years ago now, a year before the split. Michel grimaced tightly. Happier times; it seemed remarkable how suddenly his life had changed.

He lifted his gaze from the photos and looked through the window on to the street. A two-bedroom loft apartment on Rue St-Sépulce in the Old Town – the extra bedroom had squeezed him with the mortgage and taxes. His original intention with buying in the area, shortly after the decree nisi, was to enjoy a town-bachelor pad and the life that went with it. But then he realized that opting for only one bedroom would mean that Benjamin and Angèle would have to sleep on put-up beds in the lounge on the alternate weekends they stayed over. It would be viewed as an entirely selfish move by Sandra, an extra dart in his back. So he pushed himself for the extra room for the kids' sake.

Outside a light dusting of snow lay on the street, which was quiet, almost deserted; only the brake lights of a single car edging slowly down towards the riverside. In the summer the area would be a frenzy of activity, tourists ambling at all times of the day or night among the narrow cobblestone streets, rollerbladers and cyclists along the riverside promenades, the cafés of Place Jacques Cartier where he'd treat the children to dinner and ice cream while they watched the changing scenes of musicians, mimes and milling street activity. Summer in Old Montreal with their father. Some fond memories at least.

Michel liked this old part of town; in architecture the surrounding streets could be turn-of-the-century Paris, a surviving enclave against the skyscraper canyons of downtown. One small spot of Europe among square-block architecture that defined practically every city for thousands of miles to the Pacific. And it all started here, thought Michel, looking across the street to the floodlit stone-wall flank of the Basilique de Notre-Dame, Montreal's first church.

Michel shook his head. In a few months, as the surrounding streets were humming with summer life, Georges Donatien and Simone Lacaille would be married there. Not the wedding chapel behind where most well-placed Montrealites got married and which was good enough for Pelletier's own daughter two years back, no. Simone and Georges were Montreal's golden couple; they'd be married where Celine Dion was married or not at all. And the RCMP, as with every major crime family wedding, would be mingling with the crowds on the pavement and in Place des Armes, taking snaps. More photos for his wall.

Except that by then there'd be no reason for any more photos for his wall; all chances of getting Donatien to testify would have been long lost. In fact, in only an hour or two he might know it was all over, if . . .

Michel stopped himself, looking keenly towards Notre-Dame. Maitland's words suddenly spun back: '*I don't see much hope of getting Donatien to testify. He's already practically family, and about to become even more so with his impending marriage. Unless we can somehow bring extra pressure to bear . . .*'

70

Michel became aware that his hands were balled tight in fists at his sides. He willed himself to relax, eased out his breath slowly, unclenched his hands. With Yves' fresh hopes of a photo ID, it suddenly hit him that he now had an opportunity to press Donatien that might not arise again. Even if Yves finally came up with nothing, he could probably milk it to good effect for twenty-four or even forty-eight hours.

Michel turned to the phone. He needed to share this with someone, and if he remembered right Chac was on duty roster until midnight. He smiled to himself as the phone rang out. Chac would comment that he must be crazy pulling in Donatien for questioning, and then he'd calmly explain.

6

Cameron Ryall looked from the dining-room window as their car approached up the drive; much the same position he'd stood in when they'd first visited. Except that now he was angry.

Angry at himself, angry at young Lorena, or at this new social worker and the 'save all the world's children' aid worker who had no doubt wound her up into action in the first place – Lorena's 'friend'. Ryall's anger spun and bounced wildly in his head without firm direction; he wasn't anywhere near calm enough to focus it on any one thing.

Classical music played softly in the background – Vivaldi's 'Allegro from Spring' – but it did little to introduce an air of calm. The blood still rushed through his head a beat too fast and his hands trembled slightly, and so he had to forcibly will that calm, close his eyes and take deep breaths, repeat to himself, 'You mustn't let them see that you're troubled. Take control. *Control.*'

He felt strangely giddy, as if through that lack of control – as on the few occasions he could recall it happening before, if only for seconds or minutes that passed like laboured hours in which he'd bounce, at lightning speed, every possible angle – he'd been cut adrift from all good sense and purpose. He rallied every nerve and fibre of his body hard against it now.

His wife Nicola was even more agitated, though through fear rather than anger. She hadn't wanted to face them a second time; she'd barely weathered the ordeal of their first visit and had asked him to beg off her presence now with the excuse of a crushing migraine or flu. At least that might tie in with the reason why he'd again visited Lorena's room: 'Sorry. My wife's still sleeping off the bug.' But that might skirt too close to the truth and invite the questions: is she ill often? Is she regularly under prescription from the doctor for anything? Does she suffer from depression? Her secret drawers of valium, prozac, amphetamines and sleeping tablets – prescription or otherwise – or the hidden bottles of gin, which so often pushed her into a stupored haze that made her take to her bed early. And, besides, it was more vital now that they put on a united front. He'd told Nicola that she'd just have to compose herself. She had to be there beside him.

Ryall took a deep breath. But his salvation would be with Lorena. He was angry that now she'd called them twice, but in the end she'd never betray him. Betray their secret. Because, in the end, there was no secret that she could recall. No memory of bad things happening; just wild imaginings. And once those imaginings were finally put to the test and brushed aside, the abiding image left was that he was a good father; a trusting, responsible, caring father who had raised two children not his own and done it well. A prominent, well-respected local citizen who gave generously to local charities, particularly those involved with children's welfare. He could almost imagine the heads shaking in local village-shops if, heaven forbid, news of this outrage ever leaked out: 'Surely not? Mr Ryall's such a nice, caring, generous man.' God, they had some nerve to put him through this.

The car was beyond his angle of vision now, but he heard it stop and its doors open, close. A steady breeze swayed the trees and rhododendron hedge, and white caps danced in the bay ahead.

He was guilty only of loving Lorena more than he should, but was that wrong? And he'd protected her from the rest; her mind was blanked to it. No. Lorena would never betray him. But he had to ensure that it all ended here, now, because with repeated visits Nicola would surely crack. He closed his eyes tight for a second – *never betray him, never* – and had just started to feel the first waves of calm descend as the door bell rang. He turned off the Vivaldi and went to answer it.

'So. The nights that Mr Ryall came again to your room were last Thursday and . . .' Nadine Moore's pen poised over her pad. 'When was the other?'

'Three or four days before that . . .' Lorena's eyes flickered: trying for precise recall, or troubled at the memory? It was difficult to tell. 'I can't remember exactly.'

They were in the same music/playroom as before, and between Nadine's questions the pauses were long, the silences heavy. Nadine's pen could be clearly heard scratching across the paper. She seemed to be making more notes than before.

Elena sat to one side and slightly behind Nadine, and after the initial hellos had said nothing throughout. Again, Nadine settled Lorena into the mood with general questions about how school and home life had been since their last visit, before circling around to the key point of her adoptive father's repeated visits to her room.

'And why did he come to your room on those occasions?' Nadine looked up at Lorena pointedly each time her scribbling ended. 'Was it because you had more bad dreams?'

'No, not on the first occasion.' Lorena shook her head. 'He noticed that I was troubled about something at school. He was worried that I might be being bullied – but it was nothing, just a bit of an argument with a couple of other girls. We only talked about it a bit at supper, so he came to my room later to talk some more.'

'And on the second occasion?'

Lorena cast her eyes down. 'Yes. That time it was a bad dream. It was very late too, I . . .' She looked as if she might continue, but then the thought went or she decided against it.

Nadine took the opportunity to make another note, then asked, 'On either occasion, did Mr Ryall offer any explanation for why he'd come to your room rather than Mrs Ryall?'

'The first time, no. We were talking about the school problem earlier, so perhaps he just thought it normal that we continue talking later.' She shrugged. 'He didn't need to explain.' Lorena paused, as if allowing for Nadine to make another note. But Nadine kept on looking at her expectantly. She continued. 'The second time he mentioned that Nicola wasn't well. She'd gone to bed early, you see . . . and it was very late then.'

'What sort of time?'

'One or two o'clock . . . I'm not sure. I'd lost track a bit with sleeping and then the nightmare.'

Elena noticed Lorena's hands clutching and playing with the hem of her T-shirt. Kikambala Beach Club, Mombasa, from a beach holiday the previous Easter. After a lifetime of uncertainty, the girl now with supposedly everything. But Elena could read the underlying signs; she'd seen the same shadows in Lorena's eyes before. Lorena was as uncertain and fearful now as she was back in those dark orphanage days.

'And on that first visit to your room,' Nadine pressed on, 'though nothing was mentioned directly by your father – how was Mrs Ryall that night?'

Lorena had to think for a moment. 'I don't think she was very well then either. She'd had a bad cold for four or five days, maybe even a week . . . and one night she went to bed even before me.'

'And what time do you go to bed?'

'Nine to nine-thirty in the week. Ten at the weekend.'

Elena's hand clenched tight in her lap. So far everything was tying in with what Cameron Ryall had said in their twenty-minute pre-session with the Ryalls: *'I wouldn't have gone to Lorena's room at all if my wife hadn't been incapacitated on both occasions. She was down with the flu and took to her bed early for most of the week.'* But maybe something would come out now, Elena thought, as Nadine came on to what had actually happened with Ryall on those visits.

Lorena looked troubled, her eyelids fluttered as if she was trying to focus on an indefinable object slightly to one side on the floor.

Nadine prompted, 'It's okay, take your time . . . starting with the first visit. What happened then?'

Finally: 'That first time, not much, really.' She took a deep breath. 'We talked about the problem at school and I kept telling him it was nothing. I was eager for him to go, you see. But it took a while before he was finally convinced . . . and then he reached out and stroked my brow, saying, "You'd tell me if something was wrong, or if this happens again, wouldn't you?" ' Lorena looked directly at Nadine and then quickly down again. 'I answered, "Yes, of course" . . . but I think he sensed I was nervous about him touching me, and he quickly took the hand away.'

'Now – and this you should think carefully about, Lorena – did Mr Ryall touch you anywhere else on the body that night?'

'No,' Lorena answered quickly, though hesitantly.

Nadine kept on looking at her directly for a moment before the next question, even though Lorena engaged eye contact only briefly. 'And did Mr Ryall stay in your room for long after that?'

'No. He left almost straight away then.'

'I see.' Nadine looked down finally and made some more notes.

Elena shared Nadine's disappointment in that moment. But she also sensed a deft, purposeful circling in by Nadine and, unconsciously, she found herself sitting forward, expectant, as she came on to Ryall's second room visit. More had apparently happened then.

'Did he soothe your brow again on that occasion?'

'No. He shook me gently out of the dream by my shoulder.' Lorena crossed her chest with her right hand to her left shoulder. 'Then he held me by the hand, or maybe the wrist – I can't remember exactly – and told me, "It's okay . . . *it's okay.*" '

The room fell deadly silent, both of them wrapped up in the

explanation, anticipating the revelation of what Ryall did next. But Lorena trailed off then, and Nadine had to prompt, 'Then what?'

'Everything wasn't too clear then . . .' Lorena shook her head helplessly. 'Except in the dream.'

'The dream?' Nadine asked incredulously. 'What, another dream?'

'Yes, yes . . . But it was different this time,' Lorena struggled to explain, sensing mounting doubt from Nadine. 'This time it wasn't like before with me trapped in the sewers, in the darkness . . . This time Mr Ryall was touching me, his hand going lower down my body, still saying, "It's okay . . . *it's okay.*" Trying to comfort me.'

Elena noticed that Nadine seemed taken aback by the plea in Lorena's voice that the dream was somehow significant, when very obviously she was thinking just the opposite. Nadine held up one hand: a stop sign. 'Let me get this clear. Did Mr Ryall at any time touch you like this outside of the dream? Were you at any point – if only for a minute – awake when any of this happened?'

'I don't know . . . I . . .' Lorena was flustered by Nadine's newly assertive tone.

Elena felt for Lorena: she was only a child, and bad dreams had been associated with so much of the sorting and filing of her troubled past. It was probably difficult for her to grasp how anyone else wouldn't attach the same importance to them. She was clutching again at the hem of her T-shirt, though this time Elena noticed her hands were shaking. Finally: 'No, I . . . I can't remember being awake when this happened.'

Nadine looked round briefly at Elena. A 'we won't get anywhere with this' expression. She pressed Lorena again. 'This is important . . . think hard.'

Lorena's eyes flickered, again searching for elusive clarity – but again nothing slotted into place. 'I'm sorry . . . I'm sorry. I don't think I was awake then.'

'Don't think?'

Lorena closed her eyes for a second as she reluctantly let loose the last strand. 'I'm pretty sure I wasn't . . .' She swallowed hard. 'I'm sorry.'

The furthest Lorena was likely to go towards denial, but it was enough: there was simply no angle left from which they could claw back. Elena could see it all slipping away. Nadine's shoulders sagged, her pen suddenly frozen. After all, there was only one thing left to write: CASE CLOSED. Elena felt suddenly despair at the thought that it might all end here. She decided to intervene.

'Lorena, this is twice now you've called us. But if all of this is happening only in your dreams, we just can't help you.'

'But sometimes it seems so . . . *so real*,' Lorena protested. 'As if it is actually happening. And it frightens me. I told you – I don't want him to come to my room any more.' She shook her head in annoyance, as if throwing the blame back to them.

'We told Mr Ryall to stay away from your room,' Nadine offered. 'But on these two occasions your mother was ill. I'm sure he'd have stayed away otherwise, so it shouldn't be a big problem.' Nadine chewed at her lip, and Elena read the thought that could have been voiced: But what to do when Mrs Ryall is ill again?

Elena felt a twinge of panic. It seemed wrong for it to all end like this now, as if they'd hardly tried at all. She pictured Nicola Ryall sat with her hands clasped tight together, saying even less than the last time. Her mood nervous, agitated. Everything had tied in so neatly: her illness, then Ryall mentioning that he was sure it was all just in Lorena's imagination, possibly linked to her continuing problem with nightmares. *'It's probably all just a call for attention. I assure you nothing untoward is actually happening.'* Now both statements seemed to have been supported.

Nadine sighed. 'Elena is right in that we can't do much with what we have.' She forced a reassuring smile that came across more thinly than she'd have probably liked. 'But at least if all of this is only in your mind, we have the comfort that nothing is really happening. You're not at risk.'

Elena bit at her bottom lip. Her own mother had also stayed silent, afraid to go against her father. The same obdurate, dogmatic grip in which he'd held nearly all the family. *So real.* Elena wondered if Lorena was trying to tell them without really telling them. The dreams were a safe midground. 'If something's happening, you've got to tell us,' she implored. 'Has Mr Ryall been talking to you, telling you not to say anything?'

Lorena's brow knitted and her lips parted as if she was about to speak. Nadine wheeled around on Elena, staring daggers: a 'that's strictly off limits' look. 'You don't have to answer that,' she warned Lorena. But Lorena had already lost whatever thread was there, her eyes shifting uncomfortably for a moment before looking down.

'I'm sorry,' Elena said. 'She just seems so confused, and I suppose I'm scrambling for reasons why.'

A fresh breath and Nadine continued winding things down, asking

Lorena calmly if, while they were still there, there was anything else she wanted to mention. A second's thought, and Lorena shook her head – but Elena could still see the uncertain shadows in her eyes, and she reminded herself how troubled Lorena must have been to call her now twice. The intense concern that had made her race back early from Bosnia for this meeting now. Running breathlessly through the chine with Lorena, trying desperately to get her out of the darkness and into the light. *Into the light.* Only in her mind. Confused. She leapt for the only remaining door she could see still partly open.

'If this is all only in Lorena's mind, perhaps, as Mr Ryall suggests, even linked to her continuing problem with nightmares – surely at least we should request psychiatric assessment.'

'That's true.' Nadine contemplated Elena levelly. 'But we just don't have enough for such an order with what we have now. We could only make the request – it would be left up to the Ryalls to decide.' This was said as if Nadine doubted strongly that the Ryalls would comply.

'I understand.' Elena nodded indulgently. She leant in close to Nadine and lowered her voice so that Lorena wouldn't hear. 'But if we sold the psychiatric assessment to the Ryalls on the grounds of it being linked to Lorena's continuing problem with bad dreams, he'd have little reason to object. After all, it's the dreams, he keeps complaining, that are dragging him to her room late at night.' Elena smiled slyly. 'If he does object, it's going to look highly suspicious.'

Nadine held her gaze a second longer. Nadine resisted matching her smile, but Elena caught a faint tell-tale glimmer in her eyes.

Nadine turned back to Lorena, who looked vaguely perplexed with their secret exchange. Nadine's eyes softened, her voice dropping a note, mildly grave. 'Would you like that, Lorena? To see someone professional who could help you – if your parents agree to it?'

Lorena's eyes darted from Nadine to Elena, as if seeking consent. Elena smiled tightly with a faint nod. 'Yes . . . yes, I suppose so,' Lorena said finally. 'If you think it will help.'

'Yes, I do.' Nadine made a brief last note on her pad and drew a hasty slanted line across. 'Let's just hope your parents share that view.'

Lorena blinked slowly with a barely audible 'Thank you', but she was looking more at Elena than Nadine. Elena acknowledged with a nod and smile. But the fact that they were giving Ryall a run for his money – he wasn't getting it all his own way – was a small consolation.

If Ryall said no to the psychiatric assessment, they'd be back to square one. Worse still, they'd know then that almost certainly Ryall was keen to keep something hidden, yet they'd be powerless to do any more about it.

7

In the dream everything seemed a fraction slower than Georges recalled it happening in real life.

He was firing question after question at Eric Leduc, mostly relating to a list of bank deposits and withdrawals from an account in a false name that they'd traced back to him – funds that Jean-Paul suspected were derived from cocaine trafficking.

Leduc was directly to his right in the back seat, Roman on the other side. Fifteen yards away from the car, out of earshot, Tony Savard and the car's driver, Steve Tremblay, paced and shuffled around smoking and swapping small talk, glancing back occasionally to the car to keep tabs on progress.

Leduc was nervous, his eyes darting from Georges to Roman with each question. Fear of Roman's intervention should he answer wrongly. But there was almost an acquiescence there, as if he was asking silent permission for each answer. Although generally Leduc was stumbling, evasive: answers of any real substance were few. And with each duck and manoeuvre from Leduc, Roman's fury rose another notch.

Though Georges was turned away from Roman for most of the time, he could sense that silent fury building through Roman's right leg, shaking increasingly despite one hand gripped tight on his knee to try and quell it. Roman's glare in the fleeting moments Georges did look round spoke volumes: his jaw was set tight, his teeth grinding together with each 'I don't know' or 'That part of it wasn't anything to do with me' from Leduc. The growing tension had become like a powder keg in the back of the car: Roman's agitation, Leduc's panic with his eyes shifting uneasily with each fresh question – Georges should have known that it would explode at any second.

At one point Roman reached across and grabbed Leduc brusquely by the lapel. 'Come on, you fuck, give. You know a lot more than you're telling.'

'I know, I know.' Leduc held his hands up defensively. His eyes were darting almost out of control. He smiled hesitantly. 'But I've got something that will hopefully clarify everything.'

Roman held Leduc's gaze steadily for a moment. He let go of Leduc's lapel slowly, reluctantly.

A tiny pulse pumped at Leduc's left temple. A trickle of sweat ran down his neck from behind his ear.

A brief relief in tension, and then it happened. Everything slipped, the images tilted and seemed suddenly more distant, hazy. Suspended, almost frozen flicker-frames that would stay with them for ever.

Leduc reached down for something – they caught a quick glimpse of it, a black object tucked into his ankle sock – though it wasn't quite clear at first what it was. But Roman was already reaching for his gun inside his jacket; it was out practically in the same motion, pointing. Two shots were fired: both through Leduc's heart before he'd hardly lifted the object clear from his sock.

Then, as Leduc flew back against the side window, blood erupting from his chest, the object fell from his hand and they saw what it was: a black notebook.

Roman's eyes were raw panic. 'I thought it was a gun. I thought it was a gun.'

Leduc's blood was everywhere: splattered against the window behind, splashed on the roof, on the windscreen, a heavy gout on Georges' chest and lap, and sticky and warm on the seat where he gripped tight for some reality with one hand.

Roman's expression quickly changed; his eyebrows knitted together, pleading. 'Christ's sake, don't tell Jean-Paul how I fucked up. It's gotta be our secret. Believe me, I thought . . .'

Roman's next actions were fast, almost a card sharp's sleight-of-hand, because Savard and Tremblay were heading frantically towards the car: Roman flipped a gun from a strap by his right ankle on to the floor by Leduc, grabbed the notebook and tucked it into his inside pocket.

Roman stared hard again at Georges. 'You with me on this?'

'Do I have much choice?' Georges looked at the newly placed gun on the floor and Roman. Savard and Tremblay were only yards away, almost upon the car. Georges eased out a long breath and closed his eyes momentarily in submission, nodding hastily. 'Yeah, yeah. I'm with you.'

Then everything suddenly slipped another notch; part of it was more hazy, surreal, yet his senses seemed more finely tuned. He felt every small motion, every tic of expression from Roman, like a ponderous, heavy heartbeat.

Savard and Tremblay were no longer there, it was just Roman and him alone with Leduc's body.

Roman's eyes were piercing straight through him. 'I don't believe you. I don't trust you. You're gonna betray me.'

'No, no, I won't. It's okay. I'm with you on it.'

Roman's gun rose to point at him. His eyes burnt with intent. 'If not now, then at some stage you'll betray me. I know it.'

Leduc's blood was already congealing, sticky everywhere he touched, the stench from his body waste overpowering in the confined space. 'No, no. I won't betray you. I swear.'

'Georges . . . Georges? Are you okay?'

The gun levelled at his face, a sardonic smile creasing one corner of Roman's mouth as he started to pull the trigger. *'One day . . .* And I just can't risk that . . .' He could feel Roman's hand on his shoulder, even though Roman's free arm appeared to be at his side . . .

'No, no . . . I promise, I . . .'

He jolted sharply upright a second before the bullet hit, bathed in sweat, Simone's face above him blurring slowly into vision, her hand gently stroking his shoulder.

'You okay?' She watched his eyes focus on her and leant forward and kissed him lightly on one cheek. 'You were shaking the bed a lot, calling out.'

'I know, I know. I'm sorry.' He cradled his forehead for a second and then ruffled his hair with his hand, orientating himself. They were at his place and it was still dark outside. He glanced at the bedside clock: 5.12 a.m. 'Just a dream.' He stated the obvious, as if that might brush it all quickly away.

'Anything interesting? Terri Hatcher got your head trapped between her thighs? Or maybe Roseanne, if it was a nightmare?'

'Nothing so exciting.' He gave a light snigger, which subsided into a shiver that ran through his body. 'That night with Leduc coming back to haunt me.' He shook his head wearily. 'And it's not the first time.'

'Oh, I see.' Simone glanced down awkwardly. She looked up slowly after a second, met his eyes steadily. 'You know, Papa never really talks about business with me. But he's mentioned that incident to me twice now. I know that he feels badly about it, feels that he should never have sent you along.'

'I know.' He nodded and gently clasped her hand. Now it was his turn to feel a stab of guilt: her father was still shouldering the blame and meanwhile he was continuing to shield the truth from him. It was Jean-Paul he was betraying, not Roman; betraying the trust Jean-Paul had long placed in him. He owed Roman little or nothing.

He ran his hand up her arm and gently stroked her shoulder. He bit at his bottom lip as he met her gaze. 'Look. There was something that happened that night with Roman and Leduc. Something that I never . . .' And then he was reminded of why he'd gone along with Roman and said nothing: the newcomer to the fold driving a wedge between two brothers who'd worked the family business together harmoniously for so many years. His allegiance to Jean-Paul was balanced against the family code of silence and not ratting. He didn't want to be the messenger of bad tidings, the reason for any rift. On the one occasion since that Roman had broached the subject, he'd commented, 'I won't tell Jean-Paul. But *you* should – you owe it to him.' Simone was staring at him expectantly and he stumbled into 'I never obviously have come to terms with it. So maybe that's why it keeps replaying in my dreams. The gun firing, Leduc's body tossed back like a rag dummy. His blood was everywhere . . . *everywhere*. I can still feel it sticky against my skin sometimes when I sweat at night.'

'You poor thing.' Simone lightly stroked his brow, then traced one finger down one cheek and across his top lip. He closed his eyes and she leant forward and kissed where her finger had been, her tongue gently probing. It became a long, deep, sensuous kiss that made his mind flee all else for a moment. And as she finally broke away, she said teasingly with a faint smile, 'There's only one thing you should feel sticky against your skin', and started planting butterfly kisses slowly down his body.

She pushed him back with the gentle but firm press of her fingertips and he surrendered to her soft kisses and caresses as he lay flat on his back, his eyes gradually adjusting to the dark and forming images in the faint street light that filtered up to play across the ceiling.

Savard had brusquely swung open the car door only seconds after he'd finally submitted to Roman, 'Yeah, yeah. I'm with you.'

Leduc's body slumped back with the opening door and was half supported by Savard's thigh. Savard's eyes shifted haphazardly, trying to extract some sense from the scene of the carnage.

'He had a gun, a gun,' Roman protested, waving his own weapon towards the offending object on the floor.

Savard had his own gun out, but it was held loosely, didn't pose a threat. Savard's eyes darted between Roman and the gun on the floor. 'I thought you searched him.'

'I did, but it was in his ankle sock.'

Savard's eyes rested finally on Georges, as if for confirmation. And after a second Georges nodded numbly and cast his eyes down.

From that moment on, the die was cast, immovable; and now that he'd kept up the same pretence, the same lie, for so long, an extra impenetrable layer of concrete had been added.

Georges blinked to shift the ceiling images, a slow tear welling in the corner of one eye as Simone started to make love to him. She trusted him, as did Jean-Paul. But Georges just couldn't see any way out of it.

The tape operator, Carlo Funicelli, sat up as fresh sounds started the tape rolling again. A Calabrian Italian who ran an audio and electronics shop in St-Léonard, he supplemented his income by fencing goods and the occasional specialist bugging job like this one. The tape was on sound activation, and as he glanced at the clock – 5.11 a.m. – he realized he must have dozed for over four hours.

'Georges . . . Georges? Are you okay?'

'No, no . . . I promise, I . . .'

'You okay?' Some faint rustling. 'You were shaking the bed a lot, calling out.'

'I know, I know. I'm sorry.' More rustling and movement. 'Just a dream . . .'

Funicelli sat back, relaxing. Nothing exciting, no dramatics. He thought at first they might be shouting or arguing with each other, something of a first. Some chink in their relationship that Roman would have been happy to hear about.

Roman had told him what to listen out for: any tension or arguments, any sign of cracks on which he could build. And any calls from Donatien to other girls which might be suspect. But Donatien had made only three calls to women, all work-related, no underlying sexual signals, and, overall, his relationship with Simone Lacaille appeared rock solid. In fact, all they seemed to do when Simone came over was cook, eat dinner and screw. Some inconsequential small talk interspersed before and during dinner, then within half-an-hour – you could almost set your watch by it – the small talk would peter out and they'd head for the shower and bed.

That part had made it fun listening. Funicelli had found himself unconsciously rubbing his crotch during their last heated session five hours earlier. He wished now that they'd set up a video as well; he might have been able to sell the tapes to some porn hack to put on the Internet along with Pamela and Tommy Lee.

He bristled, sitting up a bit sharper at Donatien's mention of a gun firing and Leduc's blood being everywhere, then gradually settled back. Scuttlebutt was thick and fast with the increased RCMP heat, but Roman had given him the main bones of the incident: 'Leduc got frisky, pulled a gun, so had to be taken out. And unfortunately Donatien was there at the time. Too much for his delicate banker sensitivities.'

No fresh, startling revelations now that Funicelli could discern. Donatien even paused at one point, as if undecided about talking about it at all. But still not the sort of tape to have fall into RCMP hands. He'd give it to Roman in the morning.

He reached out to the recorder, deciding to replay the section in case he'd missed something – then paused, his finger hovering over the stop button as the next sounds came over: Simone Lacaille gently kissing down Donatien's body. Funicelli knew what was coming next. He pulled his hand back and braced it on his thigh. A faint film of perspiration glowed on his brow in the yellow light from a side lamp. He'd wait for them to finish, then replay the section.

Michel hovered over the computer screen as the images came up: one face on, two profiles, one full length showing height against a calibrated measuring strip.

'Not sure,' Michel said. 'Go back to Venegas. Let's have another look.'

The same format of four shots scrolled down for Enrique Venegas. Yves Denault had phoned through finally just after 11 p.m. that he had a reasonable lift – but give him till early morning and it would be in far better shape. Michel had got in at 6 a.m. and within an hour they'd raised five possible matches. Now they'd worked it down to just two: Steve Turcotte and Enrique Venegas.

Michel's money was on Venegas. Turcotte's hair colour and the shape of his eyes more or less matched, but there was a broadness to the bridge of Turcotte's nose that didn't quite fit the CCTV-frame lift. Unless Yves had somehow narrowed the nose when filling in the grain and shadow.

Michel held up the 10 × 8 CCTV-frame enlargement next to

Venegas' computer mug shots, his eyes jumping rapidly between the two, comparing.

'I think it's Venegas,' he said on the back of an exhalation that carried finality. 'The nose, the hairline, the eyes. Only the mouth and part of the jaw line, where it starts losing definition, we can't be sure of.'

Yves nodded. 'I would concur. I myself thought it was Venegas, and we took a quick poll between us and forensics: five out of six thought it was Venegas too. The other reserved judgement, didn't want to swear between the two.'

'Okay. Okay.' Michel lightly shook the 10 × 8 and flicked its top corner with the back of one finger. 'Enrique Venegas it is.'

He thanked Yves and went back up to his office. He accessed the full file for Venegas from his computer and checked the date of last update: almost two years. He buzzed through to Christine Hébert, gave her Venegas' file reference and Social Security number, and asked her to come back to him pronto with Venegas' current address.

He drummed his fingers lightly on his desk top as he hung up, as if trying to catch the flow and rhythm with which everything should happen. Timing would be essential. They'd have to pull in Donatien at practically the same time as Venegas for the plan to work. He picked up the phone again and buzzed Chac to prime him that they'd come up with an ID match. 'Enrique Venegas.'

'When do we roll?'

'Soon. I'm waiting for his current address confirmation, then we're all set.' Michel checked his watch. 'As long as Venegas hasn't moved too far out of town, we should be on his doorstep not long after eight.'

'What's the team split?' Chac enquired.

'You take Phil Reeves and three armed constables for back-up for Venegas. He could be armed, and we'll need reasonable show. I'll just go with Maury for Donatien. We don't expect any resistance or trouble there.'

'Will you go to Donatien's apartment?'

'No, we'll head to the Lacaille offices on Côte du Beaver Hall, flash our badges as he approaches the door. He might already be there – a lot of mornings he makes an early start.' Through his glass screen, Christine was deep into a phone conversation with one finger pointed towards her computer screen, as if checking a specific detail. She didn't look towards or acknowledge him. 'I'll let you know the second we've got a green light on Venegas' current address.'

86

In the lull after hanging up, Michel felt the tension of expectancy grip him again, so decided to kill time by scrolling down through the rest of Venegas' file while keeping half an eye on Christine in the back-field of his vision.

One truck hijacking eleven years ago, Crown failed to prosecute. Attempted murder eight years ago, five years served by Venegas in Orsainville Prison. At least two other hits attributed to Venegas, neither of them pursued due to lack of evidence.

Michel scrolled down through the attempted-murder case and double-clicked on the hyper-text heading: *Trial transcript*. Eighty-four pages of it between the English and the French. Michel found himself rolling rapidly through the pages, skimming sentences, only half paying attention – until one paragraph caught his eye: *'Four months before the alleged final shooting in which you attempted to take Gérard Fortin's life, Mr Fortin claims that you and another man, Michael Trapani, abducted him. That you pulled up in a van with blacked-out windows, put a sack over his head, and drove off.'*

'That's baloney.'

'You deny it?'

'Certainly.'

'A conversation then ensued between yourself and Mr Trapani as to which high building you intended to throw Mr Fortin from, clearly designed to frighten Mr Fortin in the extreme. Except that in the end, after you'd swung him several times and Mr Fortin was convinced he was about to die, you dropped him unharmed in a farmer's field.'

'Don't recall it. Sorry.'

'Mr Fortin was then told, "That was a practice run. If Mr Cacchione doesn't have his money by the end of the month, we do it for real."'

'Sorry, sorry. Still don't strike no chord.'

'And this apparently is a popular method used by the Cacchiones – and others – to enforce payment from those who might have welshed on drug or other debts. It leaves absolutely no marks on the body, no sign that they've been threatened or intimidated.'

'Sounds good to me, and I'll try to remember it for future reference. But you got the wrong man.'

The transcript simply related what was said and Michel had to imagine the rest: the muted chuckle from the jury and gallery at Venegas' jibes and protests, and the Crown attorney holding firm to his ground as he steamrollered over them.

'And because Fortin was finally unable to pay, that is why you returned

four months later with another accomplice, Anthony Orozco, to accomplish what you had previously threatened to carry out . . .'

Michel's blood ran cold. The method was well known to him, popular four or five years back more than now – but seeing Venegas' name linked directly to such an abduction completed the circle. If there was any remaining doubt that Venegas was involved with Savard, now it had gone.

Two minutes later Christine came through with Venegas' address, and Michel noted it down – 'Rue Messier, one block south of St-Joseph' – while still scanning through the salient details of the Fortin case: two shots to the chest, one to the head. But the head shot had deflected off Fortin's cheekbone and through the front of his face just below his right eye. Fortin had been lucky. He lasted six years before another bullet, probably ordered by Cacchione, succeeded where the other had failed and removed half of his skull. This time, case unproven.

Roman was with Frank Massenat at Santoriello's, his favourite café just off of Rue Ste-Catherine. For his money they served the best espresso in town and had fourteen choices of pancake toppings.

He was diving into a stack of five with maple syrup, crushed walnuts and cream with a sprinkling of nutmeg for his breakfast when Carlo Funicelli walked in. A half-drunk cup of espresso was at his right hand in a cup almost large enough to be a soup bowl, his second refill. Massenat was making good progress with demolishing a large French stick sandwich of pastrami and Brie.

All these two seemed to do was eat, thought Funicelli; or was it just that their meeting places were inevitably cafés and restaurants.

Funicelli passed the cassette tape across. 'Last night's offering.'

Roman dabbed at the corner of his mouth with his napkin. 'Anything interesting?'

'No. She came over again last night, but it was pretty much as usual. Cook. Eat. Talk. Screw.'

'So, no signs of trouble between them? No complaints from him that his goody-two-shoes suburban family might not be too keen on him marrying into a high-profile crime family? Or from her that his dick's too small and she's concerned about them having a long-lasting satisfying relationship?' Roman smiled and nudged Massenat. It was like Johnny Carson and Ed McMahon, except that Massenat was a beat slow in responding with a laugh.

Roman's style of humour was brash and gauche, but sometimes it hit the mark because in part it became self-parody and also a welcome relief from the other side of his character: the stormy mood swings and violent temper.

Funicelli risked only a tentative smile – you never knew when that mood might change – as he shook his head. 'No such luck.'

Roman's smile slowly subsided to a quizzical frown. 'And no calls to or from any other girls?'

'No.'

Roman looked at Funicelli and Massenat. 'You know, this guy ain't human.' He thought of his own hectic love life: Marie, his main girlfriend, a thirty-two-year-old from the right side of Outremont whose husband had died in a car smash four years ago, he dated primarily to keep up appearances and please his mother. Marie was classy, well-bred and, most importantly for his mother, her family were deeply religious and hailed from the Corsican village only thirty miles from that of his mother's family. Marie he took to all family engagements and high-profile functions. But for sex, excitement and wild nights, he had two club girls in tow: one of them, Viana, from their Rue Sherbrooke club partly due to him feeding her increasingly expensive cocaine habit; and then there was that beautiful Malaysian girl with a body like a fourteen-year-old Russian gymnast's at a Lavalle massage parlour he visited now and then.

'Not of this world, not of this world.' Roman took a scoop of pancake and washed it down with a slurp of coffee. 'He's got tossed salad instead of testosterone. I don't believe in all this perfect nineties-man shit. He's gotta have a dark secret somewhere.' The words were slightly muffled and slurred with his mouthful of food. He dabbed again with his napkin and pointed at Funicelli. 'You'll see, you'll see. Mark my words. It's just . . .'

His mobile started ringing in his inside pocket. He took it out, looking down at some invisible object just beyond his plate, as if Funicelli and Massenat had suddenly ceased to be present. '. . . a matter of time. Yeah?'

Roman recognized the voice at the other end straight away, but he caught only brief bursts from the garbled, breathless sentences: '. . . in the van that night . . . they're moving in now . . . you should warn him . . .'

'Whoa, whoa. Slow down. Which van? *Who's* moving in?'

'I don't want to use names on a mobile line. All I can say is the guy in the front passenger seat that night, they picked him up from a security camera and ID'd him. They're moving in on him any minute.'

Venegas! An icy claw gripped Roman's stomach. 'Any minute? How long has he got exactly?'

'They're checking for his current address right now. They could be on his doorstep in anything from fifteen to twenty minutes. Less, if they trust it to a local squad car.'

Roman doubted that they would, but he'd still have to step lively. 'Okay. Thanks.' He picked up his napkin and threw it over his half-finished plate in disgust. It was also a signal that he'd finished. He waved and called out to the waitress. 'Hey, hey. *L'addition*. Let's settle here.'

The waitress came over and flicked back through her pad. Roman's face became a study in battling muscle contortions as she summarized what they'd had. 'And did your friend have anything?' She looked at Funicelli.

'No, he didn't.' Roman slapped down a $20 note and stood up in the same motion. 'Keep the change.' Which raised only a meek smile from the waitress, unsure whether the $5 tip compensated for the attitude.

Massenat looked at the third of a stick roll in his hand, then finally decided to take it with him. Funicelli lagged a few paces behind as Roman hustled quickly towards his BMW parked down the street, a sleek black series 7. The air outside was fresh, but for one of the first times that year it was above zero. The first hint that spring might not be far away. At eight paces from the car, Roman pressed the remote key and the BMW briefly beeped and flashed its accord.

The rush and panic of Roman's departure reminded Funicelli that there was one thing he'd forgotten to mention. 'About the tape. There's one thing on it . . .'

Roman wheeled around on him impatiently. 'What?'

'There's one point where Donatien mentions that night with Leduc.'

Roman looked agitated, his eyes darting uncomfortably, though Funicelli wasn't sure how much of that was due to the call just past. 'Why didn't you tell me before?'

'I was about to — but then you had that call . . .' Funicelli swallowed hard. Roman's eyes burnt straight through him. He wished now he hadn't mentioned anything, just let Roman hear it for himself. 'But it was nothing . . . just a stupid dream from Donatien and him mentioning how the incident still troubled him sometimes. But apart from that nothing.' Funicelli reached out to put a reassuring hand on Roman's shoulder, then decided against it. Roman's powder-keg eyes warned that one touch might set him off. 'There was nothing beyond what you already told me. Believe me. Nothing to worry about.'

Roman's eyes continued to dart frantically and search his, and looked about to settle when another voice came from behind: 'Got some change?'

Roman turned sharply. Confronting him was a tramp with wild hair and a Grizzly Adams beard, though it was difficult to tell if the beard was white-streaked from frost and sun-bleaching, or from dried food and vomit. Roman sneered and leant away from the tramp, catching the first mingled stench of cheap wine, stale body odour and vomit.

He felt suddenly as if his brains were frying, too many random signals hitting him at once. Maybe only minutes to save Venegas from the clutches of the police, Donatien mentioning Leduc and Funicelli trying to tell him it was *nothing*, and now this bum in his face enveloping his best camel hair in street-stench and vomit breath. It was like some fucking conspiracy.

'A dime or a dollar, it don't matter. Whatever you can spare.'

Roman saw red, a fireburst burning through the back of his skull. 'Get away from me, you fuckin' bum.' He swung out hard against the tramp's left shoulder, a half-push, half-rabbit punch.

The tramp flew back and hit the building wall behind solidly, his head flung back and connecting with a thud. He looked dazed, startled, and his knees started crumpling.

Roman moved in and cocked his right fist to hit him again. Massenat was quickly behind him, clasping one arm firmly around his chest.

'Come on, Roman. Come on.'

An elderly couple who'd just come out of the *dépanneur* across the street were looking over curiously at the commotion.

Roman's chest rose and fell heavily against Massenat's restraining arm, his eyes still glaring at the tramp. 'You fuckin' asshole. Didn't nobody tell you it's still winter?' In summer they were out in force along Rue Ste-Catherine. They seemed to be hitting the streets earlier each year; perhaps this one had even staked out his car, smelling money. 'Go back to your fucking cave for another month. It's too fuckin' early to be out begging, yer hear?'

Massenat clutched his arm firmer around him. 'Come on, come on.'

Roman finally, reluctantly, shifted his eyes from the tramp and Massenat lifted his arm free. Massenat was right: the tramp wasn't the problem, it was the situation now with Donatien and Venegas. A sense of everything, at the click of a finger, fast closing in on him. *Jesus.* He probably wouldn't even have time now to get to Venegas before the RCMP. He'd pull up in his Beamer only to find a police welcoming committee ready to pull him in as well.

Roman glanced towards his car, then at Funicelli. 'What you driving these days?'

Funicelli shrugged. What was this? Not content with working out his frustrations on the tramp, now it was time for unsubtle put-downs? 'Chevy Cavalier. Why?'

'It's okay, nothing.' Roman shook his head. 'Just a thought.' He just couldn't risk driving out to Venegas' house now, regardless. His only hope was to phone Venegas to warn him.

He took his address book from his inside pocket and started looking through. His hands trembled as he turned the pages: the aftermath of the run-in with the tramp, or the fact that within minutes his fate could be sealed? If they had Venegas on camera, they had enough to put Venegas away for life; the temptation to do a deal would be intense.

Roman leafed through the pages more frantically, starting to wonder now if he'd ever put Venegas' number in his book.

8

'811 to 839 . . . Just crossing du Parc. We should be on St-Denis any minute.'

'Read you, 811. We're on St-Denis already, heading south towards the St-Joseph junction . . . only about nine or ten blocks away. We're to wait at the St-Joseph junction, is that correct?'

'Yeah, copy. Don't proceed into St-Joseph until we're there.'

Michel listened to the 800-waveband progress of the cars heading towards Enrique Venegas. He was in his RCMP standard-issue Ford Taurus with Maury Legault as they waited for Georges Donatien to arrive at his Côte du Beaver Hall office.

Maury was busy making the point that his own divorce was worse than Michel's, or indeed anyone else's in the squad room, that the knives still out for him from his wife were longer and sharper. 'You know what she told the children last week? That I used to beat her. I never hit her even once. Once when she threw a saucepan at me, I grabbed her arm to stop her throwing another, but that was it. I *never* hit her.' Maury shook his head morosely.

Michel nodded and sympathized at the right moments, but along with most male members of his squad, he'd heard it all from Maury before and, by extension, it struck him as a sad reflection on the high failure rate of department marriages, if this was all it now came down to: bittersweet trumping. My divorce was worse than yours. And so, hearing some movement at last over the 800 network came as a welcome relief.

'Where is he?' Michel looked at his watch: 8.16 a.m., when normally Donatien was in sharply at 8.00 a.m. He'd found himself becoming increasingly agitated as Maury spoke, not sure if it was the worn topic, the wait for things to start happening over the radio, or Donatien not showing up yet. Surely he hadn't gone out again to the Cartier-Ville mansion; he'd been there for a morning meeting only two days ago. Maybe he had a breakfast meeting somewhere else.

'This guy she's with now is a minor-league hockey player. St Laurent Icebreakers or some such shit.' Maury sneered in disbelief. 'She tells the kids I hit her, and meanwhile she's hooked up with a fucking hockey player. I think she's lost the plot somewhere, been watching too many of his . . .'

'Maury!' Michel held one hand up. He was about to add, 'I need to concentrate a while', but at that moment the radio came alive again – so he just made a chopping motion with his raised hand.

'. . . *811. We're at junction of St-Joseph now, and waiting. As instructed.'*

'*Copy. We're just crossing the Rue Rachel junction. Should be with you in under two minutes.'*

The voices over the radio reminded Michel of the night chasing Savard. He closed his eyes for a second. *Please God,* let us keep a safe grip on this one. He knew he'd been lucky to even get this second chance; there wouldn't be another.

'There he is,' Maury commented, and Michel opened his eyes to see Donatien's Lexus swing into the underground car park.

'Okay, showtime.' Michel put on a headset with a small receiver and earpiece on one side, so that he could still monitor progress while with Donatien. A mouthpiece snaked around, and he could patch in and speak by pressing a button on the receiver. But the arrangement was that he'd just listen in, unless something pressing called for his input. He'd be too busy with Donatien.

They flashed their badges at the foyer reception guard and Michel announced, 'We'll be going up to the sixteenth floor. Santoine International.' It was a statement, not a request.

The guard held up his hands, the normal signing-in procedure immediately waived. 'Sure, sure.' He swivelled one palm towards the lifts and forced a smile beyond his concern.

They got into a lift within seconds; no others had gone up from the basement, so they'd wait for Donatien to come out on the sixteenth floor.

'*839 . . . We see you now. We'll turn here into St-Joseph and wait for you to pull behind before proceeding.'*

'*Copy.'* Brief static pause, then: '*Just one perp, huh?'*

'*Yeah. But he'll have a weapon, and he knows how to use it. So due caution, and follow my lead to the letter.'*

Michel closed his eyes and let out a slow breath as the lift rose, trying to ease the tension. Always the way: hours with nothing happening, then too much happening all at once. But there had been no choice but to move on both of them at the same time: once Venegas was in custody, news would travel fast and the Lacaille ranks close tight.

Chac's voice was on 811 with Phil Reeves driving. They'd have had to wait twenty minutes to assemble an armed back-up squad at Dorchester Boulevard, the quickest option had been to pull a patrol in from Mount Royal and then meet up at the St-Joseph junction.

Turning in to St-Joseph, they were only three hundred yards from Venegas' front door. Michel felt his pulse racing with anticipation.

The lift doors opened. The corridor was quiet as they stepped out: only faint strains of activity from an office at the far end. They both looked back expectantly at the floor indicators.

'Here we are, Rue Messier. As I say, follow my lead . . . should be about a hundred yards down, apartment block on the left. We'll stop about thirty yards short so your car's not visible.'

'Copy . . . okay.'

Chac's car was unmarked, the back-up a blue-and-white: no point in forewarning Venegas.

The lift to their far right pinged. Two conversing women in their thirties got off first, followed by Donatien. The women gave Michel and Maury a brief glance, no doubt in response to their acute attention to the lift's occupants – then headed swiftly and primly in the opposite direction to Santoine International.

Donatien paused after two steps, looking them over, assessing. But Michel waited another second for the women to have faded from earshot. 'Monsieur Donatien, Georges Donatien. Staff Sergeant Michel Chenouda, RCMP Criminal Intelligence.' He flashed his badge. 'There are some matters we'd like to discuss with you concerning the Lacailles.'

A slight flinch from Donatien, then his eyes darted past them to his office and quickly back again.

Through Michel's earpiece, the sound of car doors opening, closing. *Footsteps picking up pace on concrete, quickly joined by two or three more sets.* Michel pulled his attention sharply back. 'Ah . . . I don't think this is something we could do here. Some of it's quite sensitive information that I don't think you'd like your staff overhearing. And it also involves me playing a tape to you – which is all set up back at the station.' Michel held one arm out towards the lifts.

Donatien's brow knitted. 'Am I under arrest?'

'No, no. Not at all,' Michel assured. *The hum of a lift rising, faint shuffling. Chac's voice: 'I'll knock, and me and Phil will stand to one side, our guns with safeties off but still holstered. You three stand a yard behind, but face-on with guns drawn and pointed with a clear bead on the opening door.'* 'It's just some information that we need to pass on, but we believe it could be vitally important.' Michel paused, looking down for a second as if to add suitable gravity to his next words. 'We're concerned about your future welfare and safety. We believe you could be in danger.'

'Concerned about my safety?' Donatien shook his head and smiled crookedly; but Michel picked up the underlying strain in his voice, the tone slightly higher. He'd hit a nerve. 'That's very gratifying, Inspect –'

'Staff Sergeant.'

'Staff Sergeant Chenouda. But I think you know the rules. Before I can even think of speaking to you, I have to have my lawyer present.'

Lift door opening. Muted, rapid footsteps along a carpeted corridor. Chac's breathing heavier, expectant. But the only thing Michel had control over now was Donatien, and it was fast slipping away. His mouth was suddenly dry; he moistened his lips with his tongue.

'That's your prerogative, sir. But I only have clearance to play the tape concerned to *you*. It's considered privileged information, and we'd have to seriously review how playing it to a lawyer – particularly an *organization* lawyer – might later affect our case.' *Doorbell ringing, then three sharp raps.* Michel's palms were sweating, his nerves as taut as piano wire. Handling the two at the same time was a nightmare. 'You might also consider how letting an organization lawyer overhear the tape might affect your own position. And safety.'

It was all there between the lines, thought Georges. 'And this tape concerns the Lacailles, you say?'

'Yes . . . that's correct.' *Brief pause and then another buzz and sharp rapping.* Michel bit at his bottom lip. But at least Donatien was starting to waver.

Georges weighed his options: if he called Perrault, the Lacaille family lawyer, Roman would know about it in seconds flat. If he called an independent lawyer, that in itself would look suspicious, as if he had something to hide. The Lacaille tentacles reached too far for comfort with city law firms; he couldn't be sure of using one that would go undiscovered. He could just say no to Chenouda, but then he'd never find out about the tape or the supposed danger he was in. Chenouda had played him well; he had his interest piqued, and knew it. The only thing that struck a strange chord was Chenouda's radio headset complete with mouthpiece. It was obvious from Chenouda's eye contact breaking off at moments and his split-second delay with some responses, that he was at the same time listening in to something.

Georges chuckled lightly, partly a release of tension. 'What is this?' He pointed to the headset. 'You auditioning as one of Madonna's backing singers?'

Michel forced a wry smile. 'Something like that.' He had Donatien hooked, he could tell. He didn't feel inclined to ease off the pressure by slipping into weak banter.

Door opening. Chac announcing himself and asking for Enrique Venegas. 'I have a warrant here for his arrest.'

'He's not here.' A woman's voice. 'You just missed him.'

'How long ago did he leave?'

'Ten or twelve minutes ago.'

Georges watched Chenouda's eyes flicker as he listened in. What was it? Was somebody at HQ instructing him? If he mentions a lawyer, say this. If he's obstructive, say that. He noticed Chenouda's eyes cloud after a moment, look worried.

'I don't know,' Georges said. 'I think if I'm going to come in with you, it's something I've got to think over for a while.'

Michel was gripped with panic. His heart had sunk upon hearing that they'd missed Venegas, and now it was sky-diving again. *Shit.* Now he could lose Donatien as well. But he knew that pressing harder would be the wrong play. Nothing left but to ease off, take a step back.

Michel shrugged. 'That's up to you. Our information has it that Roman wants to move fast on this. But if you want to delay and run the risk, fine. You probably know Roman better than me.' He turned to look at the lift lights.

Maury, who had stayed silent throughout, forced an apologetic smile and shrugged as Donatien's eyes fell on him.

'We still have to check and see, you understand . . .'

'Yeah . . . okay . . . okay.' The woman sounded hesitant, uncertain for a second. Then the jostling and rustling of them moving around the apartment. Michel's heart pounded hard. *Please God*, find Venegas hidden in a back room! And now he was playing Russian roulette with Donatien as well. His legs felt weak, unsteady. He could feel Donatien's eyes on him, almost feel his mind frantically hammering: Savard dead, but just how far was Roman prepared to go? And what exactly *was* on that tape?

'What's that sound from behind the door at the end?'

'That's nothing . . . nothing . . .'

But the woman sounded nervous, her voice tremulous, and Michel's heart pounded almost in time with Chac's laboured breathing as Chac moved towards the door, opening it . . .

'Only my daughter.'

Sound of a radio playing. 'Yeah, I see . . . okay.' A young girl's mumbled response which Michel couldn't discern. Michel's nerves eased.

The lift to the far left was the first to arrive. Four people got out, gave the assembled group a cursory glance, then moved off, three in one direction, one in the other. The back of Michel's neck ached with tension. Come on, Donatien, don't slip away from me as well. And he was about to turn and add something to try and retrieve the situation when Donatien finally spoke.

'If I come down to you without a lawyer, you appreciate I'm not going to answer any questions.'

'You don't have to,' Michel assured. 'We'll simply play you the tape and tell you why we think you're in danger. If you have any comment on that, fine.'

Maury leapt across as the lift doors started closing and they sprang quickly open again.

They stood as an awkward tableau for a moment with Maury half in, half out. Then finally Donatien nodded.

'Okay, okay . . . how long will we be?'

'An hour or so, no more.' Michel held Donatien's gaze steady, trying to keep any flinch from his eyes. He knew it was a lie: once Donatien was in his grasp, he'd be lucky to get out this side of nightfall.

After a moment a resigned nod and another 'Okay' from Donatien, and Michel held one arm out like a bellboy.

'She's telling the truth, Michel. He's not here.'

It was the first time Chac had addressed him directly. Michel felt any last vestiges of hope slip away, his heart sinking again, this time in tune with the lift's fall.

Michel pressed the receiver's button. 'How long does she think he's gone for?'

Chac asked and Michel heard the woman reply that he hadn't said. 'But he packed and took with him a large kitbag – if that's any clue.'

'You hear that?' Chac confirmed.

'Yeah.'

'Any suggestions?'

'Probably. But let me come back to you in a couple of minutes.' He had an idea forming, but he'd prefer to air it out of earshot of

Donatien. He'd wait for Maury to put Donatien inside the car and hold back outside a moment to talk with Chac.

With the silent lull following and Michel's expression thoughtful, almost morose, as the doors opened, Donatien asked, 'Something wrong?'

Michel smiled wanly. 'Yeah. I just heard Madonna gave the spot to someone else.'

Within ten minutes of Michel calling Chac back with his thoughts about Venegas, Chac called Dorchester Boulevard HQ to put out a general alert for Roman Lacaille's black series 7 BMW.

The alert hit first all squad cars on Montreal Island, Montérégie, Laval, Laurentides and Lanaudière, then minutes later was spread to up-province Quebec.

Venegas' sudden departure might have been purely coincidence, but if he had somehow got warning that he was being moved in on, Michel was betting good money that Roman Lacaille was involved. 'Check his usual haunts, and if there's no luck put out an alert for his Beamer. It's distinctive, can't be too difficult to track down.'

No news had fed back by the time Michel led Donatien into a private room. Setting up the tape and having Donatien brought a coffee killed another eight minutes, but still nothing. Michel's unease returned. It promised to be a tense session, but knowing that Venegas was loose out there somewhere added an extra edge. If anything broke, he was going to be excusing himself a fair few times from the interview room; part of the key was not letting Donatien know the state of play with Venegas.

The other thing pressing hard now on Michel, an increasing leaden cloak of suspicion that seeped like cold rain through every muscle, making him shudder, was that if Venegas had received a warning – which then might also explain how Roman Lacaille knew that Savard was in with them – then just who in his department could be the leak?

Roman Lacaille held his speed steady at 65 mph on Highway 40 towards Trois Rivières and Quebec City.

'Where is this cabin?' Venegas asked, glancing briefly up as he retuned the radio, the Montreal easy-listening FM station they'd had on beginning to crackle and fade.

'About eighty miles north. Lac Shawinigan, just beyond Trois

Rivières. In the summer it gets busy, but this time of year it'll be deserted. It's ideal.'

'Is it a family cabin?' Venegas raised an eyebrow. 'I mean, is it going to be an option they might easily jump for?'

'What, you think I'm stupid?' Roman waved one hand off the wheel as if with another quick flick he might just slap Venegas. 'It's a friend of a friend's. They ain't going to trace it in a hurry.'

Venegas had always unsettled Roman. The product of a Sicilian mother and Venezuelan father, he had tight-knit curls and thick lips which might have been sensuous if they weren't so out of place with his button-bead dark eyes. But then he hadn't chosen Venegas for his companionship but for his reputation as an ice-veined hit man – which made Roman all the more unsettled now thinking of what lay ahead. Venegas had put on a baseball cap to hide his trademark curls and shield part of his face; obviously he was concerned that photos might already be out on the wire.

Venegas looked across hopefully from beneath the cap's peak as Stevie Wonder's 'I Just Called to Say I Love You' came on. 'Is that okay?'

Roman shrugged. 'Yeah. It'll do.' The other brief flash choices had been Waylon Jennings, some hip-hop and a religious programme; but most of all the changing sound bursts grated on Roman's nerves, given everything else swimming around in his mind.

Getting Venegas away had been frantic: his phone call to immediately warn Venegas, then Venegas packing a bag and getting clear with probably only minutes to spare before the RCMP arrived at his door. At Roman's instruction, he'd walked two blocks from his apartment and grabbed a cab to a Boulevard St-Laurent café, where Roman caught up with him ten minutes later. Venegas threw his kitbag in the back seat and they sped north.

The first few miles, particularly crossing the Anuntsic Bridge, had been the worst. The tension tightened his nerves until the pulse throbbing at his temples ached. Even now he was tense and watchful of patrol cars and his speed: several cars passed doing 70 mph or more, but just as many were going slower. He wanted to be as nondescript as possible among the traffic flow.

Venegas was looking out thoughtfully over the snowbound landscape. 'Is the cabin heated?'

'Yeah, there's a wood-burning stove. And apparently there should be plenty of chopped logs at the side.' Roman looked at him. 'But anyway, you're not going to be stopping there long. Ten days, two weeks for the heat to die down, time too to get a false passport – and then you'll be gone.'

'Do you know where to yet?'

'Martinique – I know a few places there. Or maybe Yucatan or Cuba; we've been doing some business there recently.' Roman shrugged. 'I haven't completely decided yet.' He was making it up as he went along. He knew that Venegas wasn't going to make it any further than eighty miles north. But he was becoming increasingly anxious as the miles rolled by knowing that Venegas was armed to the teeth: a semi-automatic in his kitbag and a 9 mm in his inside pocket. He had asked what Venegas was carrying by the way, as if he might make up any shortfall. Roman had two guns with him: a .44 in his inside pocket and a .38 in the glove compartment.

'Martinique sounds nice,' Venegas said absently.

'Yeah,' Roman agreed. He welcomed the light conversation to ease his nerves; it might also help Venegas chill out. Venegas had noticeably calmed since the first frantic half-hour of their drive, but at moments his gun hand was still skitterish – clenching and unclenching on his knee or starting to move towards his jacket when the occasional car passed too close. Roman could do with relaxing that hand a notch more. 'Our mom goes down there regularly. She gets any browner and picks up any more patois, she'll be a native.'

'How long would I have to stay away?'

'Could be a while. Eighteen months, maybe more, for something like this to blow over.'

'Beaches good down there?' Venegas asked, thinking ahead to swaying palms and white sand when nothing but snow rolled past their windows.

'Yeah, real good. Mom stays in the south of the island, at Le Diamant, and there's a beach there that . . .'

Roman broke off abruptly, noticing for the first time the squad car hanging four cars back.

'Something wrong?' Venegas asked as Roman's eyes flickered repeatedly to his rear-view mirror.

'Blue-and-white. But whatever you do, don't look round.' Roman noticed Venegas' gun hand, which had slowly relaxed with the tropic-isle talk, clench tight and tense again on his thigh. 'Hopefully won't be a problem.'

'I thought you said your plan would work.' Venegas stared stonily ahead.

'I thought it would.' But as the squad car moved up closer to only two cars behind, Roman had his doubts. He could picture them checking the registration, then they'd drive up just behind and the siren would wind up for them to pull over. Venegas' gun hand sneaked inside his jacket.

'For fuck's sake.' Roman fired Venegas a warning glare. 'They'll have a pump-action pointed at the back of our heads before they even step out.' He glanced back to his mirror to see the squad car ease up just behind.

'We've got to do something.' Venegas' eyes shifted frantically, at one point towards his kitbag in the back with the semi-automatic. 'Can't just let them take me like this.'

Roman started sweating, trying to weigh up the squad car and what Venegas might do next. Still no siren as yet. 'Don't even think about it,' he hissed under his breath, as if the car behind might hear. 'Why do you think they're hanging back? They're radioing for back-up. Even if they decide to pull us over on their own, the cavalry will be here before your gun's even stopped smoking.'

Roman's jaw tensed as the squad car pulled out from behind and started edging up alongside. Roman wasn't sure whether to keep staring straight ahead or glance over as you might with any car that passed close. Venegas' face too was a tense, frozen study, now turned slightly away – but at least his gun hand had moved away from his jacket and was rested back on his thigh. The squad car pulled directly level, and Roman finally went in-between and cast a brief sideways glance, hardly shifting his head. But the passenger-seat officer took little notice of them; he seemed wrapped up talking to the driver.

They eased by in only seconds – though for Roman, expecting the siren to suddenly wind up or another officer to pop up from the back seat and point a pump-action through the window at them, it felt like torturous minutes – and then they were past.

Roman didn't speak again until they were thirty yards clear.

'See, told you.' He let out a long, slow breath. 'My plan with switching cars worked.'

Roman Lacaille's black BMW had been stopped eighteen minutes earlier on Boulevard Viau, en route to Carlo Funicelli's shop in St-Léonard.

Frank Massenat was driving as three squad cars converged – two from behind, having raised the siren to push them over, and another, seconds later, from the opposite direction.

Five guns were trained on Massenat and Funicelli while they were summarily searched, facing away, hands on the roof of the car. No guns were found: Massenat knew that even a simple carrying violation could get him six months. And when their names were found not to match those of the alert, the lead constable put in a call to Dorchester Boulevard.

Chac came on within a minute, and fired a chain of questions relayed through the constable.

'Where's Roman Lacaille now, and why are you driving his car?'

Frank Massenat answered that he didn't know where Roman was; he only had the car because it had to go to a garage later. 'It's playing up. Ticking noises from the engine.'

'What's Roman driving now?'

'I don't know. He said he was going to hire a car.'

'Where from?'

'*Pardon.* Don't know that either.'

Chac didn't believe any of it for a minute, but there was nothing he could do. He instructed the constable to let them go, then headed for the interview room to tell Michel the bad news.

Venegas' photo came up on the small TV at the back of the counter by a display of sweets, and Roman tried not to look too interested as the cashier totted up the last of the groceries in his basket. Morning news on TQS, one of the main Quebec TV stations; the sound was on low and Roman could hardly pick out what was being said.

He'd turned off the freeway for Lac Shawinigan and stopped at the first gas station with adjoining store to pick up groceries for Venegas' stay. Venegas wouldn't be needing any of it – it would all end up in his own kitchen cupboards – but it was important to keep up the illusion, not give him any reason to become suspicious or tense. For the same reason he'd made the journey alone. Frank Massenat in the back seat might have sent the signal that it was a one-way trip.

'Fifty-eight dollars forty. *Merci.*'

The news had moved on to a light-plane crash near Jonquière as Roman paid and got his change.

His breath showed on the cold air as he made his way out to the car. He wondered whether to say anything to Venegas about the news flash, but decided against it. It would only make him edgy and tense again. He'd only just managed to get Venegas' nerves settled back to anything near normal, twenty minutes after the patrol car had passed them. Venegas was starting to think of two week's quiet rest in a log cabin, then off to Martinique. Keep him thinking that way.

'There.' Roman dumped the bags on the back seat, started up and pulled out. 'Should keep you going for a while.' He gave a brief glance in the rear-view mirror before joining the road. The front of the car had been facing away from oncoming traffic; even if someone had paid heed to the news flash, Roman doubted they'd have noticed.

'What did you get?' Venegas asked.

'Coffee, bread, some burgers, tuna, a few tins of salmon.' Roman waved one hand theatrically and smiled. 'You want fresh fish, just cut a hole in the ice and put a line down.'

'You're kidding?' Venegas fired back only a half, sly smile, and Roman wasn't sure whether he was questioning that there was fish there, or found the image of himself as a backwoodsman unlikely. He reminded himself not to get testy. Keep Venegas relaxed.

'Sure. Plenty of fish down there, winter and summer. Just cut a hole, smile down at 'em, and they're leaping up out at you already.' Roman beamed.

'Yeah, sure.' Venegas sounded unconvinced as he looked away, blandly surveying the passing scenery.

If that's what it took, playing the oaf, thought Roman, then fine. Venegas was more relaxed than he'd seen him all journey. 'A couple of summers ago, even Franky had a try and caught some fish. One look from him you think would scare them away. You know what we call him?' Roman looked across. A sign flashed past: Lac Shawinigan, 8 miles. Venegas shrugged and smiled back weakly. Roman chuckled. 'Franky-stein. All he needs is a bolt through the neck . . .'

Roman kept the banter up on and off for the next few miles, Venegas providing the occasional comment and grimace, and his jaw started to ache with the effort of forcing a smile beyond the tension drawing his nerves increasingly taut as they got closer to Lac Shawinigan. Roman felt as if his nervous system was plugged in directly to every minute detail: the thrum of the wheels on the road; Venegas' slow blink as he surveyed the snowbound landscape; Venegas' left hand moving up . . . past his jacket to rub his nose as he turned to Roman.

'You're going to a lot of trouble with all this for me,' Venegas said.

With the silent lull after the chain of banter, Roman wondered whether Venegas had picked up on his tension. 'Nooo . . . no problem.' He pushed an easy smile and waved one hand from the wheel. 'The fix you're in is directly as a result of you doing something special for me. It's down to me to put right, no question.' He stared the message home, keen to reassure Venegas; but he couldn't discern any wariness in Venegas' eyes. He looked back sharply to the road. The turn-off for Lac Shawinigan showed fifty yards ahead.

He slowed, indicated – though no traffic was approaching and only a single car was just visible a quarter of a mile behind – and swung in, gripping the wheel firm to stop his hands from shaking. A rough track; in the summer it was bumpy, but now thick snow had levelled it out. No tyre tracks: nobody had been down here in recent hours.

'Which cabin is it?' Venegas asked.

Roman was thrown for a second. The one and only time he'd visited three years back it had been summer, the tree foliage thick; now foliage was sparse and the ice-bound lake and the cabins were visible through the trees. 'Oh, uh . . . the third on the right,' he guessed. He remembered only it was on the right, but wasn't sure whether it was the third or fourth cabin. It hardly mattered: Venegas wouldn't be making it that far.

The cabin belonged to a friend of Frank Massenat and his one visit had been to thrash out a drug deal with the head of the bikers, Roubilliard. He wouldn't have risked bringing Venegas out to a Lacaille family cabin. But now, following Venegas' gaze towards the lake and the cabins, he saw something that worried him, what looked like smoke rising from the fifth cabin along . . . *Someone was out here!* Then it was lost behind some trees as he came up to the car park spread out on their right. No vehicles there.

Roman swung in. 'See . . . Told you. Nobody around this time of year. You won't see anyone now till the end of April, May.' But he was still wondering about that smoke, eager to get another glimpse. A line of fir trees bordered the edge of the car park and the first ten yards of pathway towards the lake; he'd have to wait until they walked past them.

Roman got out and opened the back door. Venegas opened the other side and took out his kitbag, but reaching in for the grocery bags Roman paused: with both hands full, he'd be at a distinct disadvantage, especially if Venegas carried his kitbag in his left hand with his gun hand free.

'Something wrong?' Venegas asked.

'Uh . . . yeah.' Roman quickly thought of how to even the balance. 'Last time after a long break the padlock was all rusty – we couldn't get the key in. We might need something to break it. Hold that for me, would yer?' He handed one grocery bag to Venegas and put the other under his arm as he went around and opened the trunk – he just hoped Funicelli had a tyre lever. After a bit of rustling around he found the toolbag tucked in on the left. He took out the lever and shut the trunk.

Roman's mouth was dry, his nerves racing uncontrollably. He could easily have pulled his gun on Venegas before grabbing the tyre lever, but still he needed to know about that smoke. He couldn't risk it if someone was by the lake.

Their feet crunched on fresh snow: no previous footsteps either that Roman could discern. The path ran for about forty yards to the lakeside. Between the fir trees, he caught flash glimpses of the cabins, but he just couldn't tell if it was smoke or only mist rising.

Venegas hunched and made a mock shiver. 'Colder than the city here.'

'Yeah,' Roman agreed blandly: *but not half as cold as where you're going*.

For some reason, Venegas had fallen in half a step behind him. Perhaps he had picked up on his vibes, was being wary – or was he just letting him lead the way? But the motion of dropping the tyre lever *and* swivelling around would give Venegas too much of an advantage. He needed to get Venegas in front and somehow distracted. Roman's heart thudded hard and fast, marking almost a double time to his crunching footsteps.

They cleared the fir trees and there was a clear view of the cabins again. But still Roman couldn't tell if it was smoke or mist – which suddenly struck him could be turned into an opportunity. He slowed his step and fell back. 'Is that smoke I can see rising over there? Fifth cabin along? Or just mist? I mean, if someone else is down here, you shouldn't be here.'

Venegas moved ahead of him and peered at the cabin. 'No, I . . . I don't think so – it's not smoke. Looks like mist rising to me.'

Roman tensed himself to pull his gun. 'Are you sure?'

Venegas squinted his eyes more intensely towards the cabin. 'Yeah . . . sure. You can see where the sun's coming through a gap in the trees and hitting the roof and . . .'

Venegas heard the tyre lever hit the snow and turned to see Roman's

.44 pulled and pointed at him. Roman's grocery bag followed the lever. Venegas let out a sneering half-laugh of disbelief on a burst exhalation. 'What is this?'

Roman waved the gun. 'Drop the groceries and your bag and keep your hands above shoulder level.' Venegas met his gaze steadily, defiantly for a second, as if he was measuring his options. Roman waved again with his gun and Venegas finally dropped the groceries and his kitbag.

Roman moved in quickly, took Venegas' 9 mm from his inside pocket and grabbed the kitbag. 'Thanks. I'll take the AK too.' He tucked the 9 mm inside the kitbag and prodded the air with his gun. 'Now let's move on down to the lakeside.'

With another sneering half-snort and a resigned shrug, Venegas turned and started walking ahead. Roman kept three paces behind.

After a moment, Venegas remarked, 'What, you getting me all the way out here was just to shoot me?' He said this as if all the small puzzle pieces of their journey out had at last slotted into place. Or did Roman detect a faint note of hope and clinging disbelief in the voice?

'No, I'm not going to shoot you, as it happens.' Which was true, he wasn't. 'You're just going fishing.'

Silence, only their footsteps crunching on snow as Venegas struggled to make sense of this. He finally decided to disregard it as a bluff. 'Come on, Roman. What happened to Martinique?' He half turned; his eyes pleaded, but his voice carried a partly joking tone, as if he knew he was clutching at straws.

'Tickets were too expensive.' Roman fired a trite half-smile. 'And my mother said she didn't want to see you there.'

A few more paces, and the inevitability dawned on Venegas. Roman saw his shoulders visibly sag. He started to get desperate. 'For fuck's sake, Roman. Come on . . .' His voice was shaky with mounting nerves, the words spluttering slightly. 'You know I wouldn't talk.'

'Temptations are huge these days. Especially with the sort of plea deals going to nail people like me and Jean-Paul. Sorry.'

Silence again. Both of them tuned into every small sound from the surrounding woodland and the lake: the faint scurrying, fifty yards to their right, as a bird flew from a bush; the cawing of a crow in the distance.

Roman's nerves had steadied a bit after their wild hammering just before pulling the gun, but still he was tense. Lightning-speed reflexes were one of Venegas' traits. Roman reminded himself not to get too close.

They reached the edge of the lake and Venegas turned. He was noticeably trembling; Roman wasn't sure whether from the cold or because of what was about to happen.

'Please, Roman . . . you don't have to do this. Your secret with Savard's safe with me.' His voice was cracking, almost on the edge of tears.

'It sure is. Because the secret's staying here with you. Forever frozen.' Roman smiled drolly and made a sharp prod with the gun. 'Now let's go for a walk on the lake.'

Venegas looked down and around apprehensively.

Roman prompted, 'Don't worry, the ice's thick – it'll hold you. And I'll be walking right with you to keep you company.'

Another air stab with the gun, and Venegas finally, reluctantly, started heading out. Roman dropped the kitbag and followed, keeping a clear four paces behind.

Venegas' eyes continued darting for options – or perhaps he was unsure that the ice wouldn't give way at any second. His gaze eventually settled on the lake-shore cabins.

'You know, I think that *is* smoke coming from that cabin.'

'I don't think so.' Roman didn't even trouble to look; he wasn't going to risk taking his eyes off Venegas for a second. 'I think it's just you blowing smoke.'

The lake was only half a mile wide, but its fourteen-mile length snaked out of sight in both directions; there was a strong river run-off at one end which made its currents lethal. They could feel the wind whip harder as they went deeper out, shifting the thin layer of snow on the ice in flurries.

At sixty yards from the shore, Roman announced, 'This'll do.'

Venegas turned. 'What now?' His breath's vapour was heavy on the air with the walk and his rising panic; though his eyes were curiously dull, as if part of him had accepted what was going to happen. 'I thought you said you weren't going to shoot me.'

'I'm not.' Roman allowed himself a last-second gloating that Venegas still hadn't worked out what was planned for him, then slowly lowered the gun and eased off a shot by Venegas' feet. A burst of snow and ice sprayed up.

'What the fuuuu . . .' Venegas jumped a step to the right like an off-balance flamenco dancer.

Roman fired the next shot the other side and this time heard the ice crack. Another quick shot a yard behind, and with a louder crack Roman watched in satisfaction as a block four foot square broke away. Venegas leapt back in horror from the shifting mass, his eyes registering only then what Roman intended.

Roman smiled, easing off a quick shot just behind where Venegas had leapt to. Another loud ice-crack and leap from Venegas. This is fun, thought Roman: like *Riverdance* with bullets.

He fired another shot two foot behind and the crack spread further, the ice block Venegas was standing on threatening to break away. The panic on Venegas' face was absolute and he tried to leap clear again – but the sudden thrust of his push-off snapped the last resistance and the block broke free.

Venegas toppled and fell, but with the momentum of his lunge he managed to grip on to the rim of the ice bordering the hole; he was submerged only from the chest down.

The shock of the water hit him like an ice truck. As he frantically scrambled to pull his body out, Roman fired another shot two foot beyond his fingers. A crack, but not enough, so Roman fired again just behind.

Ice and snow erupted and the block snapped away. Venegas slipped sideways and tumbled completely under, his arms flailing in the water. His head bobbed back up quickly, and he managed finally to get a few fingers' grip on the next solid ice edge.

Roman became frantic. He had only two bullets left. It had seemed a good idea at first, making it look like a straightforward drowning rather than a hit; now he began to wonder. But he could see that strong currents were dragging at Venegas; he was struggling to keep grip and his face was purple from cold and the effort.

Roman fired again, and there was an impressive spray of snow and ice, but to his consternation the ice held firm. Roman's heart pumped wildly. He'd have to get in close to make this last bullet count, and Venegas' pleading, frantic eyes lifted towards him as he moved in – Venegas knew this was the *coup de grâce*.

A large chunk of ice was blown clean away with the shot, and Venegas went with it, his body dragged quickly under by the current.

A suspended moment with only flat water and no Venegas, the faint echo of the shot still reverberating – and Roman was about to turn away when he saw one hand clutch out and grip the ice. He stared back desperately towards the shore and Venegas' kitbag. Too far – Venegas would have pulled himself back up by the time he got back with a fresh gun.

Only one thing for it, he would have to kick Venegas' hand away – but he couldn't risk having all his weight close to the edge, so he rushed in and scrambled out almost flat, kicking out in the same motion.

Venegas' hand held firm, so he kicked again. It was knocked free – but then in horror Roman noticed Venegas' other hand rise up almost instantly to grip on. And something else in that instant that took his breath away, made his blood run cold: a cracking noise as a yard-long split appeared to one side of where he was lying: any sudden movement and the whole ice-block would split away! He lay inert for a few seconds, his chest rising and falling hard as fear and panic gripped him. And at that moment – an almost surreal apparition – Venegas' face loomed below him, wild cod-eyes staring up. Then Roman focused and realized that his shuffling around had cleared a patch of snow and he could see straight through the ice.

Their eyes locked for a second – Venegas perhaps surprised at seeing Roman there so close, or wondering why Roman looked as panicked and afraid as him. But at least now he could fully measure Venegas' dilemma: the current was tugging at him ruthlessly, so that he was pushed up almost horizontal under the ice, with one hand gripped on hard trying to pull him back.

Venegas surely couldn't last much longer like that, and Roman wondered whether he should just lie still and watch the last bubbles leave his mouth, or take the risk and kick out again to finish him straight away.

Venegas made the decision for him by making one last frantic pull back towards the hole – his body shifted over a foot beneath the ice as Roman kicked out once, twice, and Venegas' grip was finally jolted free. Roman smiled and waved as Venegas' body drifted back past him, unsure whether Venegas' bewildered, watery focus was able to fix on him or not – and then Roman's smile quickly faded as another crack sounded in the ice.

He scrambled desperately, only just managing to slide his torso on to the solid ice edge beyond as the block beneath him broke loose, his legs from the thigh down dipping into the icy water. For one terrible moment he thought that Venegas might see his legs dangling in and grab hold, and he slithered forward breathlessly until his whole body was clear of the water and supported on the ice.

He rolled over, his breath rasping hard with exertion and the adrenalin rush, and a laugh suddenly broke free – not quite sure if it was Venegas' expression as he'd drifted past or his own close escape that he found so amusing. A steady, raucous laugh that was made to falter only by his fight to regain breath; as the sole sound to break the eerie silence of the desolate surroundings – all the birds had fled the nearby trees with the gunfire – it sounded ominous and out of place. A lone victory cry.

9

'I know.' Elena shielded her other ear from the drone and throb of the ferry engine as she spoke into her mobile. 'But if this meeting goes well now, there's no reason why I shouldn't head out there anyway tomorrow or the day after.'

She was on the short ferry hop between Studland and Sandbanks. On the line was Shelley McGurran in the aid agency's London office.

'You don't have to,' Shelley commented. 'Sarah was happy riding shotgun with the shipment, and she should be quite capable by now. They're not going to be in Bucharest in any case until late tomorrow night.'

'That's why I suggested leaving tomorrow or the day after – to tie in.'

Shelley sighed faintly. 'Really, Elena – it doesn't need two of you. If it did, I'd be the first to say. Besides, with Sarah not around I could do with your help here with a bit of PR and fundraising.' In spite of her fourteen years in London, Shelley still had a warm Dublin lilt, almost tailor-made for this task now: reassurance.

Elena fell silent for a second. 'Are you sure she's up to it?'

Shelley sighed again. 'Who knows? Hopefully, yes. But if not – she's got to learn sometime. Don't forget, your first trip out you were thrown in the deep end too.'

'That's true.' A small agency of only fourteen, including drivers, their grand designs were led more by ever-shifting dramas and emergencies than by careful planning. An endless cycle of phone calls and paperwork for fundraising and to organize goods and shipments, with planned calendar dates constantly hopscotched according to which emergency suddenly screamed loudest. That was part of Elena's concern now: that her own private drama with Lorena was just one problem too many, a feather to tip over their already precariously balanced apple-cart. Somebody was having to cover for her. And so, despite Shelley's assurances, she felt she just had to offer to make good.

Everything had gone quiet for over a week, and then came the call from Nadine Moore: her supervisor, Barbara Edelston, had requested a meeting at which Elena's presence was also required 'in order to make a full and accurate assessment'. Nadine related this with questioning parody, as if stung that her own presence at the meeting and her report requesting the assessment, filed straight after their last meeting with Lorena, weren't on their own enough. Elena didn't want to get drawn into departmental sensitivities, so merely asked why the delay. Possibly consultation with a relevant external party, such as a psychiatrist, Nadine aired, but she wasn't sure.

Elena glanced at her watch. She'd missed the earlier ferry she'd hoped to catch, but she should still just make it on time; perhaps a few minutes late at most.

'You can catch up with Viorel and the others next time,' Shelley said.

'Yeah, right.' Viorel was the seven-year-old boy with meningitis whose brow she'd mopped half the night before he pulled back from the brink. Elena knew that Shelley meant well, was only trying to put her mind at rest, but it also served as a reminder: they need us too, desperately. Whether from the throbbing of the ferry, or the fact that the coming meeting would likely decide Lorena's fate, make or break – she felt suddenly nervous. She shook off a faint shiver.

'Don't feel guilty,' Shelley said, as if picking up on the vibes. 'Look upon this with Lorena as aftercare. If we're going to spend our lives in the hope that these children will finally find safe, secure homes, only to find they're still in danger – then we're all wasting our time.' Shelley drew a laboured breath. 'I mean it, Elena – go for it. And all the other worn clichés that apply: give no quarter, take no prisoners . . .' Shelley's suddenly lighter tone trailed off as Elena watched the ferry ramp ahead swing down.

'Thanks.' Maybe Shelley was just trying to make her feel good, but there was no time left for debate. Car engines were starting in readiness to move off. 'I'll phone you straight afterwards – let you know how it went.'

Barbara Edelston was early fifties with light brown hair cut short and a matronly build. She was less severe and stern than Elena had feared and even smiled at reasonable intervals, though this couldn't be construed as overfriendliness; it was a vaguely condescending smile, as if she was merely humouring the less informed.

Edelston also played an extremely close hand. Elena couldn't get any indication which way it might swing from her opening ten minutes, in which she confirmed the basic points of Nadine's report: reasons for first alert, times of the two visits, parties present at each. The only hopeful spark was Edelston commenting that 'Ms Moore's report indeed pushes a strong and convincing case for psychiatric assessment for Lorena.'

Only a couple of questions had so far had involved Elena, but now Edelston turned to her. 'When did you first meet Lorena?'

'Just over four years ago – February, ninety-five. She was at the orphanage at Cimpeni.' A sea of children and distressed, pleading faces, but Elena still vividly recalled Lorena's large grey-green eyes cutting through the mass. A strangely serene gaze, given the surrounding mayhem.

'And did she in any way show signs of being mentally disturbed then?'

'You mean, was she having bad dreams?' Elena felt it important to confine the definition. When they'd first arrived at Cimpeni, some children had suffered such extremes of deprivation, chained to beds or kept in basement rooms without light for months, that all they could do was rock back and forth and groan. Lorena had been one of the more hopeful cases. Elena shook her head. 'No, she was quite alert when I first met her. Given the appalling conditions, she'd coped well – and there were no bad dreams then that I knew of.'

Edelston had Nadine's report open on the desk before her, with her own notepad at the side. She looked at them briefly, as if for a prompt. 'So, when did the dreams first occur?'

'Not long after the Cimpeni orphanage closed and her eleven months rough on the streets of Bucharest. You see, in the winter they slept mainly in the sewers to keep warm.' Elena looked down for a second, one hand clutched tight at the memory. 'We blamed ourselves a lot for that . . .' Elena covered the details quickly: their not reading the signs earlier that a local developer was after the building; the hasty shipping out of the children to 'temporary shelter', a run-down hospital on the outskirts of Bucharest. 'But it was a clearing house for so many other orphanages and fresh children off the street that overcrowding was intense, and food and care were non-existent. A single nurse used to act as daytime warden only, and would just lock the children in and leave them to their own devices at night. It took us ten days to mobilize to get out there; but on one of those nights, two days before we arrived, almost forty of the children broke out, believing – and probably rightly so – that their chances of fending for themselves on the street were better.' Elena looked at Edelston steadily, taking the opportunity to drive home the silent plea: look what she's already been through, don't let her suffer any more now. 'Lorena was one of those children, and I didn't see her again until she showed up at Bucharest's Cerneit orphanage – where we're also very involved with aid provision. It was shortly after then that her bad dreams started.'

Edelston made a one-line note before looking up again. 'Did she have any psychiatric counselling at that time, or indeed at any time before the Ryalls made their adoption approach?'

'No, she didn't. It was hardly Frazier country. We . . .' Elena cut herself short. The question struck her as somewhat ridiculous. They'd had enough problems keeping the children alive, let alone delving into their psyches. But she might come across as condescending, which would then harm their chances. She tempered her tone. 'Well . . . there were nearly always pressing medical emergencies, and resources were tight.'

'I see.' Edelston looked uncertain for a second as to where to head next. 'So, the implication is that had the resources been there, Lorena would probably have received psychiatric counselling at that stage.' She barely waited for the mute nod from Elena. 'And so, when the Ryalls first met her in Bucharest to start the adoption process – who, without doubt, would have had such resources and also had a strong vested interest in Lorena's mental stability from the outset – was psychiatric assessment recommended then?'

'No, it wasn't.' Elena's voice faded off and she fired a brief sideways glance at Nadine. It was a valid point: why request assessment only now, when apparently the problems with Lorena's dreams were even worse when she first met the Ryalls. Just before walking in the room, she'd been hit with the first positive rush that surely there was strong hope: why else would Edelston ask her along? If it'd been Edelston's intention to dismiss the request out of hand, then surely she'd have just had the meeting with Nadine alone and let her pass on the bad tidings. Less confrontation. Now, as Elena felt the first serious assault on that hope, Edelston's every gesture began to grate. But Elena reminded herself that this could be Lorena's last chance, and she was damned if she was going to let it be washed away with a few ingratiating smiles, curt, efficient pen strokes, and now an annoying raised eyebrow that looked more smugly challenging than questioning. She could almost still feel Lorena quaking in her grasp as they ran . . . *the light at the end of the chine remaining distant, out of reach.*

Elena drew fresh breath. 'I think that with many an adopted child of Lorena's age, there's an acceptance that there will be some psychological scars from their past, given what often leads to them being orphaned: the death of their parents or abuse by them, or abandonment at birth; with all those years to dwell on the fact that, unlike other children, they don't have or live with their parents, aren't part of a family. With Romanian children, the terrible hardship and deprivation of the orphanages have been so widely publicized, that that acceptance becomes even stronger. Parents know and accept that they might be taking on emotionally damaged goods: as long as the children are physically healthy and have easy, big smiles, they tend to look no further than that.'

The eyebrow was lowered and Elena forced a tired sigh. 'I think the hope is always that when the children are given a better life, all of the emotional problems attached to their past will happily fade into the background. And with Lorena, that indeed was the case for the first year or so. It's the fact that the dreams and memories of her troubled background have resurged after so long, and the circumstances in which they've come back – Mr Ryall visiting her room – that's now given cause for concern.'

'I know, I know. I understand that.' Edelston nodded eagerly and turned her right palm towards them. 'Miss Moore's report has made a very clear and strong case for that, as I mentioned. But I think the background you've given me is also useful. What I wanted to make sure of is that real opportunities for psychiatric assessment hadn't been ignored out of hand before, and weren't being brought up now merely as a ruse to dig deeper into this problem of Mr Ryall visiting Lorena's room – when on the surface it appears nothing is really happening there: just a young girl's growing awkwardness with an adult male visiting what she increasingly sees as her private space, her bedroom, with the rest manufactured purely in her dreams.'

'I think the main reason for the assessment is that we really need to separate the two,' Nadine offered; 'see where Lorena's dreams end and reality begins. Probably nothing is happening, but analysis would allow Lorena to also see that. She could lay her fears to rest and sleep easy.'

'I see. Is that what you feel?' Edelston smiled primly. 'Remind me to dig out your psychiatric diploma – it must have slipped out of your file.' As Nadine looked down submissively, blushing, Edelston saw Elena's rising outrage and held one hand up. 'I'm sorry, that was uncalled for. But I think it's important to steer clear of amateur analysis. Now, I'm quite prepared to approve assessment if I think it's warranted and, as I said before, there's no ulterior motive. The question is, are you both firmly of a mind, without reservation, that that is the case?'

Elena was caught off guard by the sharp turn-around. A sudden glimmer of light back again. 'Yes . . . uh, of course. This is all about Lorena's welfare, nothing else.'

Nadine, regaining her feet from her put-down, was slower to respond. 'Yes, absolutely.' She gestured with one hand. 'As I put in my report.'

'So this has absolutely nothing to do with trying to dig up something on Mr Ryall because you've failed to uncover anything through conventional methods?'

Edelston was looking at the two of them keenly and Elena heard faint alarm bells. Obviously Edelston'd had contact with Ryall and he'd aired his concerns. But if they simply stood their ground, surely they'd still win the day? 'No. We're interested only in Lorena turning her back once and for all on her bad dreams.' Elena's tone was firm, resolute. 'Which is a psychiatrist's territory, not ours. And hopefully any worries she has about Mr Ryall will evaporate at the same time.'

Nadine was more hesitant, sensing that her supervisor was on the scent of something, and gave only a nod.

Edelston continued looking at them pointedly and a thin, smug smile appeared, as if she'd just corralled two errant children after a long chase. 'I'm glad you're both so sure about the worthiness of your intentions.' Edelston reached to a side-drawer and took out a small cassette recorder. 'Because after hearing this, I'm afraid I'm far from convinced.' With a momentary hover of her finger for emphasis, she pressed Play.

'Elena is right in that we can't do much with what we have. But at least if all of this is only in your mind, we have the comfort that nothing is really happening. You're not at risk.'

Elena felt her stomach dip as if a trap door had opened. Ryall had taped their last session! Her legs weakened and she felt dizzy, a misty cloud at the back of her eyes threatening blackout.

'At this point you both appear to have given up the ghost,' Edelston prompted. 'And then comes the fight back.' Her eyes settled steadfastly on Elena.

'If something's happening, you've got to tell us. Has Mr Ryall been talking to you, telling you not to say anything?'

'You don't have to answer that.'

'I'm sorry. She just seems so confused, and I suppose I'm scrambling for reasons why.'

Marked pause and then a tired inhalation from Nadine. *'Before we go – is there anything else you'd like to discuss with us, Lorena? Anything which you think might help us . . .'*

Barely audible *'No . . . it's okay'* from Lorena, and Edelston talked over the rest of Nadine's winding down: 'Noble early attempt, but no rule broken so far . . . and at this stage we're back on track . . . until we get to . . .' Edelston held one hand up like a conductor.

Even without the elaborate cue, Elena knew what was coming. She closed her eyes, surrendering the last faint light of the chine as the cloud thickened, making her temples ache. And Lorena was no longer with her but back at her bedroom window, looking out over a grey, misty sea: lost, forlorn. Elena felt herself sway slightly in the self-imposed darkness, nausea rising.

'If this is all only in Lorena's mind, perhaps, as Mr Ryall suggests, even linked to her continuing problem with nightmares – surely at least we should request psychiatric assessment.'

'That's true. But we just don't have enough for such an order with what we have now. We could only make the request – it would be left up to the Ryalls to decide.'

'I understand. But if we sold the psychiatric assessment to the Ryalls on the grounds of it being linked to Lorena's continuing problem with bad dreams, he'd have little reason to object. After all, it's the dreams, he keeps complaining, that are dragging him to her room late at night. If he does object, it's going to look highly suspicious . . .'

Elena felt the last vestiges of hope fall away. She wanted to reach out to Lorena, explain: 'We tried to help you . . . but in the end our own eagerness let you down. I'm sorry.' But there wouldn't even be that chance; after this, they'd be barred from all contact with her.

Edelston's expression was challenging, one eyebrow sharply arched. 'So . . . no ulterior motive, you claim?'

Elena didn't respond; she just looked down, embarrassed, as on tape Nadine pushed the idea of assessment to Lorena. Their position was untenable, no possible footholds from which they could bounce back. Ryall had won the day. There was nothing more they could say that would save Lorena from his grip. And from now on she'd never even get close to knowing what went on beyond his high gates: she'd be lucky if she ever got to see Lorena again.

Roman slotted in the cassette tape.

He hadn't got the chance to play the tape earlier with all the panic with Venegas, and only remembered now as he hit the freeway fourteen miles south of Lac Shawinigan. He'd planned originally to dump Venegas' kitbag in a rubbish tip in Lavalle, but then become anxious about carrying it all the way back to the city: what if the police had worked out the car switch and he was stopped on the way? In the end he ran back from the shore and threw the kitbag through the hole in the ice.

His nerves were still racing now with it all, his hand shaking as he fed in the cassette. The voices were indistinct at first, could barely be heard above the engine and the thrum of the wheels. He turned the sound up a bit, then realized it was just the rustling of the bedsheets and Donatien mumbling. He picked out only *'No . . . It's okay . . . I'm with you . . .'* and the rest was lost. Then Simone's voice came crashing in loudly: *'Georges . . . Georges. Are you okay?'* Roman turned it back down a fraction.

'No, no . . . I promise, I . . .'

'You okay? You were shaking the bed a lot, calling out.'

'I know, I know. I'm sorry . . .'

Funicelli had told him that the worrying part came just after Donatien broke out of his dream. Nothing significant so far. He started to get impatient listening through their banter about Terri Hatcher and Roseanne and Simone's comments about her father, and he was about to wind the tape further on when the words hit: *'Look. There was something that happened that night with Roman and Leduc. Something that I've never . . .'*

Roman's hand pulled back again, his shake now more pronounced. He realized that he'd swayed slightly from his lane when an overtaking truck blasted its air-horn from behind. He straightened up.

'I never obviously have come to terms with. So maybe that's why it keeps replaying in my dreams. The gun firing, Leduc's body tossed back like a rag dummy. His blood was everywhere . . . everywhere. I can still feel it sticky against my skin sometimes at night.'

'You poor thing . . . There's only one thing you should feel sticky against your skin at night . . .'

At the sound of rustling sheets and kissing, Roman stopped the tape and hastily rewound. Funicelli was right to have alerted him, but it wasn't Donatien talking about that night with Leduc that was most worrying – it was what *wasn't* said. Roman found the section again and hit Play:

'. . . *that happened that night with Roman and Leduc. Something that I've never . . .*'

It was all there in the silence between the words: Donatien was about to tell Simone, then suddenly had a change of heart.

'*I never obviously have come to terms . . .*'

Roman stopped, rewound, played it again, homing in on the silence in between: a siren wailed its way through the city in the background, a faint rustle of sheets . . . but Roman was tuned in solely to what Donatien's thoughts might have been in those few seconds.

He replayed the section again twice straight away, then once more just as he hit the outskirts of Montreal. There remained little doubt: Donatien had been only a second away from telling all. He'd been lucky this time, but what about next time and the time after that?

A weak, hazy afternoon sun flickered through the stanchions of the Anuntsic Bridge as he drove across, picking out a faint film of sweat on his forehead. The burden of that night obviously weighed heavy on Donatien, and at some stage he was bound to break. The problem was that 'accidents' had run their course, and he couldn't get near making a move on Donatien without Jean-Paul's consent. How in hell was he going to convince Jean-Paul that his golden boy needed to be taken out?

'*No, for God's sake, noooo . . .*' Savard's scream rattled the recorder's small speaker.

'*Three!*'

Georges closed his eyes as he imagined Savard being thrown from the building, sailing free . . . but hadn't newscasts said that Savard was shot? Maybe it was one of those cases where the police withheld information so that they knew when they had the right suspect. A soft thud came a second later, followed by another voice.

'*That's just a practice run, Tony. If you don't tell us where the money is, we're going to do it for real.*'

Chenouda was staring at him keenly. His eyes had hardly left him throughout the tape playing, but there were selected moments, like now, when he pressed home a special message: *it's not just that they killed Savard; look at the mental torture they put him through.*

They'd locked horns earlier when it came over on the tape that Roman's BMW had pulled up only a moment after the van with Savard had sped off, and Chenouda had stressed the significance.

'See. Clever. He shows up late, knowing that it will already have gone down – and has the cheek to hold his arms up in a "where is he?" gesture. He knows he's on camera, so at the same time he gets an automatic alibi.'

Georges protested that just because Roman was there didn't necessarily mean he had anything to do with Savard's murder.

'Then tell me: who else knew about the meet to be able to set up a bushwhack like this?'

Georges didn't have any ready answers, and fell silent again through the rest of the tape. The sirens, the tension of the chase, the sound of voices jumping back and forth between Savard's abductors and the police network, within minutes had Georges' nerves ragged. He tried to keep a poker face throughout, not let his emotions be too apparent, but it was difficult. The ruse of Savard being thrown from a high building was frightening beyond belief, and now the clawing tension towards the finale: Savard's abductors discussing whether or not to move Savard before finally deciding to do it there. Then the ominously expectant, time-frozen silence with the guns being taken out, with Georges suddenly aware of every small sound in the squad room: Chenouda's shallow breathing, his partner, Maury, scratching a doodle lightly on a pad, a clock ticking on the far wall. As the three shots finally came with Chenouda's scream of 'Noooo!', Georges physically jolted.

Chenouda swallowed slowly, though he waited a moment more for the footsteps crunching on snow to fully recede before he pressed Stop. His eyes were still fixed keenly on Georges.

'Quite a boy, your Roman.'

'He's not my favourite person either.' Georges' voice was slightly hoarse as he struggled to regain composure; his stomach was in knots and his hammering nerves seemed to have robbed his breath. 'But that still doesn't mean he was involved with something like this.' It was a bluff: his doubts about Roman were rising hard and fast, but the last person he wanted to share that with was Chenouda. All he wanted to do was get free and clear from this claustrophobic interview room so that he could bring some clarity to his wildly churning thoughts. 'Look. I've listened to your tape – as promised. Can I go now?'

Michel didn't answer, he just continued staring straight through him, a faint smile appearing at the corner of his mouth, as if he could read the bluff. After a second he stood up, started pacing. 'There was a specific reason why Savard was there that night to meet with Roman. You see, we could have gone with what we already had: Savard claiming that Roman shot Leduc, with you there beside him at the time. But Savard wasn't actually in the car when it happened, and then too we'd have had the problem of winning over Roman's likely plea of self-defence. Chances were we wouldn't have been able to nail him. Roman claimed that Leduc had a gun, you see. It was there on the car floor by the time Savard reached the car.' Michel kept on looking hard at Donatien from the end of the table. 'But then you'd know all about that – you were right there with him when it happened.'

Georges shook his head. 'You know I'm not saying anything without a lawyer present – that was our arrangement.' He glanced towards Maury for support. Maury had stopped doodling and started making notes. Not that there'd be much to note: Georges had no intention of saying anything.

They were around a bare pine table – minimalist Ikea to match the modern Spartan lines of Dorchester Boulevard. An informal interview, so it had been agreed at the outset that it wouldn't be taped. Georges was relieved also that there were no wall mirrors; nobody was looking in from another room.

Michel rested his hands on the end of the table. 'The main purpose of the meeting that night was for Savard to draw Roman out on the issue of the gun, try and break his self-defence cover. You see, Savard was pretty sure Leduc didn't have a gun with him.'

Georges looked down, hopefully hiding his flinch and the shadow that crossed his eyes in that second. Chenouda's gaze was penetrating, unsettling; he could feel it searing through, probably reading volumes into his reaction.

'Then again, you'd probably know that too,' Michel aired, 'since you were right there beside him.'

Georges was on his feet, his chair grating back abruptly. 'Lawyer, lawyer, Chenouda – or I'm walking.'

Michel ignored the protest, barrelled on. 'And you know why Savard was sure Leduc didn't have a gun? Because as Leduc got into his car for them to go to the meeting, Savard saw what was in his ankle sock: it was a notebook, not a gun. A black notebook.'

Georges wished now he hadn't stood up; his legs felt suddenly weak, unsteady. 'Is that so?' he challenged, but his tremulous tone defeated any intended bravado. Chenouda wasn't fooled for a minute. He not only knew, but seemed pretty sure of his ground that Georges knew too; it was unnerving.

'The other thing is – that gun on the floor?' Michel's voice rose questioningly. 'Smith & Wesson 6900. Savard couldn't remember Leduc ever carrying a gun of that type. But it was one of Roman's favourites for a compact second gun.'

Georges shook off a faint shudder as Chenouda's glare burnt through him. He should never have come along; he'd walked into a lion's den, a trap. He sat down and let out a tired, worn sigh. 'I want to leave. This isn't what we agreed I was here for. I was just to listen to your tape – you apparently had some warning about the danger I was in – and that was it.'

'Oh yes – your warning.' Michel swept one hand out dramatically. 'Do you really think Roman's going to let you live after the trouble he's gone to getting rid of every other witness to that night? And you pose far more of a threat than Tremblay or Savard. They could only put Roman there – you were right beside him.' Michel stared the message home. 'You're the only one to know that it was cold-blooded murder rather than self-defence.'

Georges cradled his head in one hand, massaging his temples. There was a lot of merit in what Chenouda said; in fact, too much merit, adding ballast to the silent demons that had been gripping him since that night with Leduc. But he didn't want Chenouda to know that he'd hit a nerve and risk falling deeper into his trap. He wanted to be somewhere at least a few blocks away over fresh coffee, or perhaps a shot of something stronger, to be able to examine, alone, what he really thought. He didn't even trouble to look up this time. 'You've played the tape, you've issued your warning – can I go now?' A worn, flat tone.

'Can I go now? . . . Can I go now?' Michel mimicked. 'You're a fucking stuck record.' He waved a hand to one side. 'Sure, be my guest. Go out there and let Roman kill you.'

Georges looked at Chenouda and Maury, hardly believing he was being allowed to go so soon, before getting uncertainly to his feet. 'I'm not convinced Roman had anything to do with Savard's death. So I'm afraid I just don't see the danger the same way you do.'

'Not convinced?' Michel raised an acute eyebrow. 'I thought you bankers were meant to be sharp guys. Oh, and I forgot –' He put one hand up, a stopping motion. 'Pretty soon we're going to know for sure whether Roman had anything to do with Savard or not. Which was actually the other reason why I asked you in right now.' Michel drew fresh breath and explained about Venegas being ID'd from a Jacques Cartier Bridge camera; he was being sought as they spoke. Michel glanced at his watch: almost an hour since they'd gone to Venegas' apartment, twenty minutes since they pulled up Massenat in Roman's BMW. Chac and his team were now parked within eyesight of Venegas' apartment entrance and a province-wide alert was out. How much longer before Venegas showed up? 'We expect him to be pulled in any minute.'

Georges sat slowly down again. 'So if you've got him – what do you need with me?'

'What I need is for you to see this as your last opportunity. With Roman fingered by Venegas, he'll likely go down for Savard *and* Leduc – because without one there isn't motive for the other. And we've got Savard on record putting you right beside Roman when it happened. So the minute we cuff Venegas – you're just one beat away from going down for accomplice to murder.' Michel stared the threat home, seeing the alarm rise in Donatien's eyes before he became uncomfortable and averted his gaze. 'Unless, that is, you give us your account first. Now's your chance. Maybe your *only* chance.'

Georges ruffled his hair brusquely before looking back directly at Chenouda. 'We're into lawyer territory again. And we agreed at the outset I wouldn't be answering anything where I might need a lawyer.'

Michel ignored the protest. He sensed that he was close to breaking Donatien. Just one more turn of the screw. 'I might be wrong – but I don't think you'd have willingly gone along with Roman knowing that he was about to murder Leduc. That isn't your role in the Lacaille organization. And witness to self-defence is not even a misdemeanour. But with you staying quiet, it's starting to look more and more like it was murder.' Michel held one hand out, an invitation. 'If you come clean, I'll make sure you don't even see a cell door. But if not . . .' Michel waved the same hand towards more uncertain, worrying alternatives.

Georges felt the small room closing in on him tighter. His pulse was racing and there was a constriction in his throat making swallowing difficult. He couldn't believe how quickly everything had been turned around on him. An hour ago he'd been heading to his office, now he was only a step away from a jail cell. Depending on what move he made next.

Michel felt the conflicts tugging at Donatien like raw electricity in the air; he was close to the brink. Just one more push should do it. 'You need to share this with someone for another reason, Georges. Every minute you keep this secret to yourself, you pose a threat to Roman. While he can't breathe easy, how much longer do you think he's going to let you breathe? With the secret out, that problem goes too. You get rid of the death threat and the jail cell in one.'

Georges had to admit, that was tempting: no more double game with Jean-Paul or wondering what Roman might do next, no more dreams in the middle of the night with Leduc's blood sticky against his skin, no more . . . He suddenly stopped: *Jean-Paul!* His main anxiety all along had been his guilt over not telling Jean-Paul, and this would just constitute further betrayal. He owed Chenouda the same as Roman: nothing!

Georges shook his head. 'If this was just about Roman, fine. But I work for Jean-Paul, not Roman.' Georges felt the escape rope firmly in his grasp, his nerves easing a fraction. 'I would never do anything to betray the trust Jean-Paul has put in me, and believe me, it's reciprocated. Even if I did have reason to fear Roman, he wouldn't be able to make a move on me without sanction from Jean-Paul. Which won't be forthcoming – now or at any time. So while I appreciate your concern about my safety – thank you, but it's misplaced.' Georges forced a hesitant smile.

Michel's jaw tightened. At times he could look upon Donatien as the business innocent caught up in the Lacaille wolves' den; at others, like now, he was the smooth, smug money-launderer hiding the Lacaille dirty millions and laughing up his sleeve at the RCMP. And when that view held sway it angered him all the more because, unlike Jean-Paul and Roman, Donatien had had a choice: he was outside of their world and had a highly paid, respectable job with a bank. He could have simply turned his back.

Michel sneered thinly. 'Jean-Paul and Roman have worked side by side now for over twenty years. They've been through hell and high water together, buried both their father and their younger brother in the name of a crime empire that's survived now two generations. If it comes to the crunch and that's threatened, do you really think Jean-Paul's going to take your side against Roman's just because you've turned some good trade these past few years and you're shacked up with his daughter?'

'We're to be married, in case you haven't heard.' Georges' tone was indignant. 'But where all your theories fall apart is that they're not even involved in crime any more.'

'You expect me to believe that? The bikers are still getting their supplies to distribute. It's business as usual. And a lot of the old Lacaille contact names, like Leduc, keep cropping up.'

'It's Cacchione, or a new independent. Maybe even more than one.'

Chenouda's sneer was back. 'You and I both know that Medeiros won't go near Cacchione. And he wouldn't trust these levels of transaction to some new kids on the block. He's dealing with old friends; and with Cacchione out of the picture, that leaves only the Lacaille family.'

'You don't get it, do you? That's what me being brought in was all about. To make money from legitimate enterprise so that they didn't need crime. After Pascal was shot, everything . . .' Georges faltered, his voice trailing off. He was getting drawn out by Chenouda, heading into areas he shouldn't be talking about. 'Look – we've covered much more here than we agreed. I've got to go.' He stood up and smiled tightly. 'Earn some more legitimate money.'

Michel shrugged. 'Yeah, sure. Cool your heels for a while in one of our cells while we pick up Venegas – then you're free to go.'

'*What?*' Georges' voice was strained with incredulity. 'You said before I could go straight away.'

'Oh, did I say that? You know, that's the problem with not running a tape. You never can keep track from one moment to the next.' Michel's voice was heavy with sarcasm; then his tone suddenly became low, threatening. 'You must be kidding. You know now we're on to Venegas. As soon as you walk out of here, you could put a call through to Roman and ruin our operation. And if you want to call a lawyer, fine – he'll only tell you the same: that under Section 450 we're allowed to hold someone up to twelve hours when an active operation might be threatened.'

'You bastard, Chenouda.' Georges glared. 'You knew all the time you were going to do this. You planned it.'

Michel moved in closer. 'No. I pulled you in to save your neck from Roman – which you don't seem to appreciate. And also because this is your last chance to save yourself from a charge of accomplice to murder. Once we've pulled in Venegas, that chance has gone. So now you've got some free time to contemplate the wisdom of talking or not.'

Georges met Chenouda's hard stare evenly. The nerves were back somersaulting in his stomach and tightening his throat, and his first instinct was to continue fighting back. But the rollercoaster ride of the last half-hour had drained him and the situation seemed almost too surreal for comment, so that all that came out in the end was 'This is ridiculous' huffed on a weak exhalation. 'So when do you expect to be picking up Venegas?'

Michel turned away slightly. 'A half-hour. Maybe an hour or two. Who knows?'

Georges' shoulders slumped at the prospect of possibly hours in a cell. 'You knew it all the time,' he hissed. 'You knew that –'

'We don't have time for this now,' Michel cut in brusquely, holding one hand up. 'I've got an operation in progress to get back to. All I can say again is, use the time wisely to rethink whether it's worth taking an accomplice-to-murder rap for the Lacailles.' He stared the weight of the message home one last time, but he still couldn't tell if he'd made any headway.

He told Donatien again about his right to a lawyer, but Donatien merely fired back defiantly, 'If I'm not going to talk, what's the point?' before Maury led him away.

Michel sat down slowly in the silence of the interview room. The exchange had exhausted him. Hopefully some time in a cell would weaken Donatien's resolve; he'd get a taste of what the next few years might be like if the chips fell the wrong way for him, and crumble.

The confrontation had given him the measure of Donatien, but still he wasn't sure: the business innocent, or the smooth money-launderer? Maybe the next few hours with Donatien within arm's reach in the cells below would help provide some clarity for both of them.

Elena stared into the churning water over the ferry rail.

A faint mist obscured landfall at the far end of Poole harbour and the open sea at her back. The short ferry hop had come to symbolize freedom for them, escape from all the madness of the world outside; but now it felt as if they'd merely been escaping reality and the veil had finally been lifted on what a waste half her life had been.

Elena had protested to Edelston that surely the fact alone that Ryall had taped their last meeting showed his guilt. Edelston didn't agree.

Ryall suspected that Lorena was being led and cajoled into admitting something that just hadn't happened, that was purely in her dreams, and the tape had borne out that concern.

Elena had launched one last desperate assault. 'That's what we'd hoped for in recommending psychiatric assessment. It would have separated the dreams from the reality and cleared up any doubt once and for all.'

'That's as may be. But due to your overeagerness and overstepping the mark, that chance, I'm afraid, has gone.'

She shook her head. Nothing more she could do for Lorena; unsure now whether the leaden weight on her shoulders was because she felt she was to blame, or because she felt redundant and helpless. But was it too late to save herself?

When she'd first made the ferry hop, she'd been with her parents and younger brother. She'd been only eight years old and imagined that she was sailing away to a magical, mystical land; that the short strip of sea separated them from an entirely different world – which became all the more magical when she discovered the chine. They'd been on the beach and she'd gone deep inside, out of sight, and she'd lost track of time, wrapped in its cool, shaded embrace, sitting by the gently running brook while a squirrel eating a berry on a nearby branch looked at her curiously. She'd been gone for over forty minutes and her parents had scolded her when she'd emerged. They'd been frantically looking for her, worried that she might have drowned. Her father's anger was strongest, and finally it boiled over. He lashed out with an increasingly hard flurry of smacks on her backside before her mother intervened. It was just one of many volcanic eruptions of her father's constantly stern, bubbling temperament, which she and her brother spent half their lives in fear of ever provoking.

The first time she'd made the ferry journey with Gordon had been thirteen years earlier. They'd been going out together for only three months, and after that first trip made the habit of coming down every spare weekend in the summer months. Gordon was working in London in the City at the time, and for him the short ferry hop symbolized escape from the mad cut and thrust of the finance markets that consumed him all week. A year after they were married, they'd bought a weekend cottage in Chelborne, only two miles from where they now lived.

Then six years ago came Gordon's heart attack and his decision to leave the City and move to the area permanently. They put out requests with local estate agents, and details of the house overlooking the chine came through their letterbox four months later. They stayed in the weekend cottage while improvements were made; Gordon started a small investment brokerage business based from home, handling a select few old clients and some local new ones, and she also shifted half her London workload to a home desk and computer. When she wasn't on a plane or truck bound for Eastern Europe, she spent most of her time on the phone, so it hardly mattered whether she was in London or Dorset.

Gordon's income was more than halved, but their London house sale had left them with a healthy financial cushion. Most importantly, Gordon felt happier, less stressed, and they both had more quality time to spend with the children.

Elena shook her head. Each stage in their lives appeared so carefully planned and mapped out – except that half of it had been a lie throughout. And she'd lived that lie now for so long that she could never bring herself to tell Gordon; it would cut him to the quick, bring on another heart attack. No, this was a quest she'd have to make alone, in secret.

'Christos Georgallis . . .' She muttered the name almost as an incantation under her breath, quickly swallowed by the steady breeze swirling into Poole harbour. Twenty-nine years? She wondered where he was now. She had so much to tell him: that in reality she'd never stopped thinking about him; that she'd always loved him, and that she was sorry, sorry . . . *sorry*. She clenched her eyes tight as the tears welled. Oh my God, she was sorry.

But she wondered first and foremost if she'd ever be able to find him. Knowing how intent her father had been on burying him for ever out of sight and reach, probably not.

10

'You called earlier?' Roman hunched his collar up tight. The chill of the icy wind outside penetrated the thin glass of the telephone booth. His caller's usual booth two blocks from RCMP HQ had come up on his call monitor at home.

'Yes, I did.' The voice at the other end was flat, bland. The caller didn't make the point that it had been three times or give any hint now as to why things were so urgent. It'd been arranged at the outset that Roman was only to be called at home in an emergency, and nothing potentially incriminating should ever pass between them over the line.

'You can call me back on this number.' Roman read out the call booth number.

'Yeah . . . fine.'

The line went dead, and Roman stamped his feet and blew in his hands as he waited for the call back. It took a moment longer than usual.

'I've started using the booth a block further away from home – just in case they've cottoned on to me using the nearest booth,' his caller explained.

'Okay – where's the fire? What's happened?' Roman's tone was impatient, the wait in the cold and the cloak-and-dagger routine adding to his edginess.

'It's Donatien. He was at our HQ today, being questioned by Chenouda . . .'

Roman felt the cold grip him even tighter as the details came out, what few he was able to extract with a chain of increasingly staccato questions: What time? How long for? What was said?

Minutes later he was speeding towards the lap-dancing club on Rue Sherbrooke. He'd kept Funicelli's car, not wanting the hassle of being stopped and quizzed by the RCMP. He swung in wildly as he approached, screeching to a halt and slamming the car door. So far he'd taken out his anger and frustration only on inanimate objects – slapping the kiosk glass after hanging up, banging one fist repeatedly against the steering wheel as he drove – but he swore that if the club doorman or any of the staff said the wrong thing, he'd lay them flat in one.

But it was all smiles, nods and cordial greetings as he made his way through: *'Bonsoir, Monsieur Lacaille. Ça va?'*

Azy, the head barman, fired him a broad Caribbean grin as he perched on a bar stool.

'What'll it be, bossman?' To Azy, everyone was man, my man, or bossman, according to status.

Roman leant both arms heavily on the counter and let out an exaggerated huffed sigh. Azy's smile was hard to resist, but all Roman could muster was a weak grimace. 'Usual fucking poison. A triple.' He looked around. 'No Gérard then, tonight?' The rotating manager between their three clubs and restaurant, Gérard was there at most two nights a week.

'No. He said he'd come by about nine tomorrow night.' Azy lifted out a bottle without giving it a glance and poured a third of a large balloon of Hine. 'Celebrating something?' he enquired.

'Celebrating?' Roman cocked a quizzical eyebrow. He raised the glass, took the first slug. 'Nah. Just something to break the ice.' He smirked to himself at the image of Venegas sliding away beneath the ice. The only thing to have gone right all day. 'It's ass-freezing weather out there.'

Azy missed any hidden significance and held the same half-smile as he put back the bottle, the lights and mirrors behind picking out his blue eyes. The product of a Jamaican father and Quebecois mother, he'd been hired for his astute customer handling, and his familiarity with practically every known cocktail from Maine to Shanghai. Just turned thirty, with dreadlocks dangling around his coffee-toned broad cheekbones like a dead spider, and clothes that were always hip and stylish, he was popular with the girls: he was usually their first choice to confide in if there were problems, in or outside the club.

Roman swivelled round and surveyed the room: Amy, Chantelle, Janine, Lucy, then a new girl he didn't recognize, but he was looking mainly for Viana – finally picking her out in the subdued lighting of a far corner, dancing for a customer. He'd wait until she was finished, then call her over. Just after nine-thirty the club was almost half full: not bad for a weekday.

Celebration? He'd thought originally of coming down here for a quick victory drink after Venegas. The warm glow of a drink in his stomach and some warm pussy in his lap would have reminded him too how good it was to be alive after his own close escape. But after the call he'd just had, it was simply somewhere with loud music and writhing bodies to help drown the madness of the day.

Three hours? Three fucking hours? He'd asked the question twice in disbelief when told how long Donatien had spent at RCMP HQ. His contact tried to reassure him that he didn't think anything dramatic had been said, otherwise he'd have probably heard about it by now – but he'd let him know more tomorrow.

Three hours? Not much said? Huh! Who was he kidding? In that time Donatien could have spilled every last detail about the Lacaille family, including all their shoe sizes – and no doubt that night with Leduc would have been the first topic in the frame.

Roman eased his collar as he felt a sudden rush of heat to his face and neck. They could be on their way to him in a squad car any time now. Or maybe they were still working on final strategy and backroom legal paperwork? But if it involved checking with Crown prosecution, surely his contact would have heard by now? He took a couple of hasty slugs, then knocked back the rest in one and ordered another triple.

The first hint of concern tempered Azy's smile as he poured, realizing that Roman was on overdrive: normally he'd nurse a single brandy for almost an hour.

Roman hit the refill a bit slower; he still had a third of it left to swirl around in the bottom of the glass after fifteen minutes, his jaw working ever tighter as he watched Viana continue dancing for the same man one song after the next. The guy was hogging her half the night; when was *he* going to get a look in? Roman raised an acknowledging hand and gave a brief smile at one point when he thought she'd looked over, but with the darkness of the club it was difficult to tell if she'd seen him or not.

As the next song started, Prince's 'Kiss', and she went into another routine of writhes and grinds, Roman swallowed the last of his drink. That was it. He was going to tell the guy to move on and try some other pussy. But two steps from the bar stool he noticed her wriggling back into her tanga. Next came her short, tight black satin skirt, pulled up her thighs excruciatingly slowly. It was a reverse strip.

Azy's voice came from behind. 'Guy comes by twice a week. Same routine every time – eight or nine songs, finishing how it started. And always with Viana.'

'Yeah. Whatever does it for you.' Roman perched back on the bar stool. 'Hit me with another big one meanwhile, and whatever Viana wants.'

Azy was getting seriously worried now. He'd never seen Roman drink so hard and fast, but there was something bubbling beneath his slightly glazed eyes that warned him not to say anything. Just pour. Smile. What he was paid to do: customers often took him for some sort of social counsellor, but as long as *he* never got the roles confused.

Viana pecked her client on the cheek as she took his money, then made her way over, firing a warm smile as she got closer.

'Sorry, Romy. Some of these guys just seem to want to have the monopoly.'

'Yeah, yeah. Whatever.' Roman didn't want to think about sharing her. He held a hand to one side. 'I've had one of those days. I need some serious attention here.'

They moved about six yards to the side of the bar, the nearest subdued-lit area. Viana took a quick sip of her coke as they sat. The rule for the girls was soft drinks only, except for the last hour when they could drink either vodka or champagne: neither smelt on the breath. Viana moistened her lips as she set the glass down, and spread her legs suggestively, showing a yard of tanned thigh leading to heaven.

'So, Romy – how you been, since . . . since last week?'

'Don't ask. Don't fucking ask.' Roman shook his head quickly, but he found it hard to rip his eyes from one spot: her tanga barely covered her neatly trimmed vulva, and he swore he could see a trace of moisture already there. Or maybe it was sweat from all the dancing?

'You look tired . . . real tired.' She stood up, started swaying to the beat of 'Constant Ariba'. 'Just relax . . . relax.'

Roman felt the ice from the lake and the tightness in his chest from this new problem with Donatien start to melt and ease from his body. Viana's smile, the tease on her lips and in her eyes, her coffee-cream skin glistening with a faint sheen of sweat, seemed to radiate a heat from a yard away that seared straight through him and touched every nerve end. She was gorgeous, an exquisite cocktail of Haitian, Lebanese, French Quebecois and Italian, with crinkly dark hair half-way down her back and soft brown eyes like a bed of autumn leaves; she was by far Roman's favourite of all the girls, despite her cocaine habit which had helped forge their relationship. He'd have chosen her anyway, she was streets ahead of the rest. A natural.

133

Next was the tanga. She bent away from him as she slowly eased it down, then swivelled around and perched herself back on the stool opposite. Leaning back, she scissored her legs high and wide apart and slowly traced her hands from her ankles up. She paused as her hands came within an inch of meeting, as if to make sure Roman's attention was fully on what her hands were framing, before slowly pulling her lips apart to give Roman a glimpse of her pink moistness. Tantalizingly, she slid a finger inside.

Roman shuddered and closed his eyes. A natural.

But as he opened them again, he noticed Viana's previous customer looking over from the bar, his steel-rimmed glasses glinting with the mirrored lights; he seemed vaguely perturbed that Viana was giving someone else such a good show, as if her nine dances with him somehow gave him proprietary rights. He looked like a yuppie banker or account-ant, and suddenly Roman was reminded of Donatien: of how he'd gained strong favour with Jean-Paul so quickly, leaving him on the sidelines of the main thrust and flow of business. Practically out in the cold. He glared back at Steel-rimmed: I'll show you who is in control.

The track changed to 'I'm Every Woman', and Viana turned and leant away from him, bending almost double and reaching back to spread her butt cheeks as she wriggled at him.

'Yeah, that's it, doll . . . spread that smile for me.' But Roman was grinning challengingly towards Steel-rimmed as he reached out and started stroking Viana's thighs.

She didn't protest at first – the club rule was no touching – only a slight frown crossed her face. But as Roman's stroking became more insistent, with one hand rising to lazily trace a finger up the cleft of her butt, she flinched and pulled away.

'Not here, Romy . . . not here.'

'You got that right. At my place you ride my dick like it was going out of style.' Roman said it loud enough to be heard at the bar. Steel-rimmed looked away uncomfortably towards the bottles ahead. Azy too looked perturbed; he'd long suspected they had something going on, but Viana looked distraught at it being broadcast so openly and gauchely. But Azy knew better than to intervene. He kept his head down, studiously cleaning and stacking glasses.

Roman reached out and brusquely grabbed her thigh, pulling her close. 'Come on, stop being so prissy.'

She wriggled and tried to break free. 'No, Roman, no . . . not here.' This time her tone was firmer.

Roman clutched tighter with both hands, keeping his grip. He shook her hard. 'Look I own this fucking club, and I own you. Now just be a good girl and do what you're told . . . Bend for me like you did before.' He glared icily at her, a smile slowly easing as she hesitatingly complied. He could feel her shaking in his grasp, which only added to his excitement. The feeling of control.

Viana's writhing was now more stilted, staccato, as the first clouds of worry crossed her face. This was a different Roman: a fiery, dangerously unstable mood she'd seen a couple of times before, but never directed at her.

Roman smiled contemptuously at Steel-rimmed, who was looking over again. See. I'll show you who is in control. Who's boss. You, Donatien . . . the lot of you. I'll get back what's rightfully mine. He felt the effects of the brandy washing through, making his senses float pleasantly. 'Come on, babe. Spread again,' he murmured dreamily. 'Wide.'

Viana slowly, reluctantly moved her legs further apart, and he ran one finger lazily along her cleft, feeling the warmth and moisture there. Yeah. He'd be back where he should be soon . . . with everything at his fingertips. The sudden sensation that everything around moved in time to his touch: Viana's swaying body, the room and lights around swirling gently, the music pumping almost in rhythm with his own quickening pulse and Viana's trembling. He slipped one finger slowly inside, her heat so feverish it almost burnt.

'Please, Romy . . . please!' Her eyes welled with tears of fear and humiliation.

But her tensing against his finger, increasing the constriction, only heightened his excitement. He pushed more forcefully, working the finger around. Roman glanced over at his audience: Steel-rimmed had already turned away in disgust, but Azy was looking over more keenly and agitatedly, though he then quickly averted his gaze.

'Come on, doll, you know you like it, you . . .' The thought hit him suddenly, caught him mid-breath: Donatien being taken into custody could be just what he was looking for to break golden boy's favour with Jean-Paul! Particularly if Donatien chose not to tell him. All trust would immediately go to the wind. Roman continued working his finger distractedly as his thoughts gelled.

'Please, Romy!' Viana's body shuddered and quaked as her tears flowed freely.

Azy threw down his bar towel and came over. He shrugged and

proffered one palm out towards Viana: a plea for reason. 'Come on, bossman – not like this. The lady's getting upset.'

'What?' Roman tried to rip his thoughts back. If Donatien intended to tell Jean-Paul, the first sign would be with Simone. If he told her, he'd probably tell Jean-Paul. If not . . .

'In private, it's okay.' Azy held both hands out. 'But if you do it here, then the customers start to get ideas. They think they can get away with that sort of thing with all the girls.' Azy injected reason into his voice, but nerves and tension sweated from every pore, his jaw jutting tight as he waited for Roman's fireball temper to spit back at him.

Roman's eyes darted agitatedly between Azy, Viana and the bar – but then he merely nodded and pulled his hands away, raising them in apology. 'You're right . . . you're absolutely right. Sorry.' He glanced hastily at his watch: 10.14 p.m. Funicelli would have had the tape running for over two hours now. There could be something on it already. Perhaps even some indication of what Donatien had spilled to Chenouda. 'Gotta go now. See a friend.' He stood up and slapped a fifty-dollar note on the table for Viana. 'Keep that pussy warm for me, babe. I'll catch you later.' And left a bemused Azy and Viana staring at his back as he scurried out of the club.

Viana dabbed at her tear-stained make-up and thanked Azy for stepping in. And while she sat out the next few songs at the bar, Azy seized the opportunity, having poured a double-shot of vodka in her coke to soothe her nerves and ease her tongue, to find out more about her relationship with Roman.

Azy couldn't make the call until he left the club at almost 2.30 a.m., from a phone booth halfway home.

'I'm sorry to call so late – but you said you wanted to know if I saw Roman.'

'Yeah . . . sure.' Quick throat clearing from the other end as Michel Chenouda sat up in bed, suddenly more alert. 'Go ahead.'

'Well, he came by the club first of all just past nine-thirty.' Azy related Roman's disturbed mood: the heavy drinking, his rough-handling of one of the girls. 'In the end I had to intervene. With the mood he was in, I was expecting trouble, I can tell you. But then he suddenly did a turn-turtle and rushed off, saying he had to see a friend and would be back later.'

A part of Michel relaxed: if Roman was edgy and troubled when he walked in the club, then very likely Venegas still presented a problem. If he'd hidden Venegas away somewhere, he wouldn't have been so troubled. 'We know Roman showed up later, because that's the one and only sighting we got of him.'

'That's right. About an hour and a half ago.'

'And what was he like then?'

'All smiles, relaxed, happy – completely different mood. And drinking moderately this time. He made up with the girl he gave a hard time to earlier, and stayed on to do the take.'

Michel amended his thoughts: perhaps Roman's earlier edginess was because he was waiting for news on Venegas, which had only come in later into the night. But it was all purely supposition: their first sighting of Roman had been just after twelve-thirty when he'd arrived by cab to collect his car from Frank Massenat, who'd picked it up earlier from the garage. Then he'd headed back to the club. But for the rest of the day, except for Azy seeing him at the club, he'd been invisible – which was obviously what he had intended. He could have Venegas holed away practically anywhere by now. They'd had a car parked down the road from Venegas' apartment building, but nothing. All they could do was watch Roman closely for the next few days, keep an all-points alert out for Venegas and hope something broke.

'And was Roman alone each time, or did he meet or talk to anyone else inside?'

'No. He was alone both times. And the only person he spoke to apart from me was the girl.'

Michel ran a hand through his hair and eased a shallow, deflated sigh. Nothing of any real value, except maybe the mood swing. He thanked Azy for the call. 'Anything new comes up, let me know.'

He felt tired and ragged from the day's events; after the news of Roman's sighting, he'd been slow getting to sleep and had grabbed barely forty minutes before Azy's call. He hoped to fall back asleep quickly. But with his mind now active, it was almost another two hours, rapid changing thoughts and images merging with the gentle thrum and hiss of the first street-sweeping trucks, before he was finally able to get to sleep.

11

Two days into her quest and finally Elena felt she was getting somewhere.

'I think we could get to the stage of seeing if there's a match on the name you're searching on the adoption contact register within three or four days.' A hoarse, nasal, female voice from the other end of the phone. Obviously a heavy smoker or suffering from laryngitis from spending her day talking, she sounded like a croaky Southern blues singer, except that she was Welsh: Megan Ellis. 'But the first stage will still be tracking down the birth registration.'

'Well, that's a lot better than the four to six weeks I was quoted by the ACR★ themselves.' A faint sigh of relief muffled by a hasty sip of gin and tonic. She'd hit the bottle heavily on the first frustrating day of searching, but she was doing better today: 2.30 p.m. and it was only her first shot of the day, and this time more because of a possible breakthrough than to drown out the mounting sense of hopelessness of her quest. She'd been told about a small agency in Wales that boasted of being able to trace adoption-separated parties in days rather than the normal weeks; it warranted a minor celebration. Or was it just Dutch courage in case it turned out to be another let-down? 'I'm glad, I'm ecstatic – but why the big time difference?'

'First of all, pure workload at the ACR. They probably wouldn't even get to your application for four or five weeks. The match itself, if there is one, would only take days. Then they write to the child and make it known that contact has been made. It's up to the adopted child to say, "Yes, I'd like to make personal contact with my natural parents." If the child says no or simply doesn't reply, the door's pretty well closed, I'm afraid. The law's very strict on protecting the rights of children given up for adoption.'

'I know.' Pretty much what she knew from her own work and had heard the day before from the ACR and NORCAP.† A hard, bitter

★ Adoption Contact Register
† National Organization for Counselling Adoptees and Parents

pill – if he said at the end that he didn't want to see her – that she'd just have to swallow. At least the first daunting obstacle of the long wait was now out of the way. 'But if a child has asked to be listed on the register, surely there's a high chance they would want contact.'

'True.' Heavy nasal sigh from Megan. 'But don't hold your breath, because that also limits the number of successful matches made. The hit rate is no more than three or four per cent. It relies on *both* parties registering, you see.'

Elena's heart sank. One thing nobody else so far had mentioned. Perhaps as she'd vented her exasperation at the possible six-week wait, they'd thought that telling her the dismal success rate would pile on the disappointment too much. 'Any chance of increasing those odds?'

'Not with the ACR. It's a fixed register, and we go through exactly the same process as them. What you save is the four- or five-week wait at the front end, and we tell you within days if there's a match. But it's still left to them to notify the child – we never get the actual name. That's the straightforward, official way.' Elena heard Megan take a quick pull of a cigarette. 'The other way's not so straightforward, it'll take anything from two days to two weeks, depending how lucky we are – and it costs a bit of money. But the odds are a lot higher: fifty-six per cent is our strike rate so far.'

'How much would it cost?' The money wasn't the concern, just the worry of how to pay anything significant without Gordon finding out.

'Hundred and sixty pounds a day – but he's good, one of the best searchers in the business.'

'I see.' Her income from the aid agency was small and nearly all their main expenses ran through Gordon's account. She could spare six or seven hundred without running short, after that she'd have to think of a crafty way of getting the money from Gordon. 'What would he do for that?'

'First of all he'll sit himself in the family records centre, trawling birth certificates and then adoption records. If we're lucky, he'll find something in only a few days. If not, for instance if he finds the placement agency but they've no longer got records, or the final adopted family he traces have since moved from the address on record, which is often the case, his trawling starts to get more involved and time-consuming: electoral rolls and telephone directories, deed-poll registrations and death certificates. The time can add up, and the money. But the compensation with this method is that if he finds a name and contact address, we put it straight in your hand. You don't have to wait for the child to approve contact. You can phone straight away and say hello.'

A chill ran through Elena at the thought of a voice at the other end of the phone suddenly saying 'hello' after twenty-nine years. But in her mind it wasn't an adult voice as she knew it must now be, but that of a small child, and tears welled with the sharp pang of all those lost years. 'Well . . . I suppose it'll have to be your search man.' Her voice was tremulous and close to breaking, and she cleared her throat, forcing a nervous chuckle. 'Until I run out of money.'

'The other thing you should be aware of is that the large time gap, with us tracing back to the early seventies, will make things more difficult. The law changed dramatically in 1975. Until then, all records relating to a child's placement for adoption were closed by the courts once the adoption order was made. Then, too, we've got the problem that pre '75, a placement agency wasn't necessarily required, and adoptions could be arranged by third parties such as doctors, clergymen or even family members.'

'I understand.' Her heart sank again. Something else to worry about: her father could easily have arranged everything without a placement agency, which would make finding records difficult.

'So . . . the first stage would be tracking down the birth registration.' Faint rustle of papers from the other end. 'Now you say that you don't know the actual registration place, you only have the surname and likely Christian name and, of course, the date of birth. So if you can give those to me . . .'

'Yes, of course, the . . .' Elena was distracted. Faint sound of footsteps filtering through the door of her studio. When she'd last checked on Gordon, he'd been deep into a chain of business calls. Now it sounded like he was starting up the stairs towards her. She'd felt uneasy from the outset doing all this from home, but where else could she have gone? She couldn't realistically have done it from the London agency office; Shelley too knew nothing – *nobody* knew anything except her mother and Uncle Christos. Someone who'd given up their own child wasn't exactly the best qualified to deal with orphaned children. The footsteps receded, Gordon was heading across the downstairs hallway towards the kitchen rather than up the stairs, and her breathing relaxed. 'Sorry . . . just someone I thought wanted me. The surname's Georgallis, or possibly the anglicized version of our family name: George. And the original Christian name chosen was

Christos – though as I say I don't know if that's what was finally put on the birth certificate. And he was born on 15 April 1970.'

'In which area?'

'The actual birthplace was Kilburn, north London, though the family was living at the time in Hampstead.'

'And do you know if it was a hospital or a home birth?'

'No . . . neither of those, I'm afraid. It was a backstreet clinic.' Elena started trembling as she remembered the pale grey walls, the stark instruments and enamel kidney dishes. A frightened schoolgirl being led in by the hand by her father. 'Birth registration wouldn't have been made there, or possibly anywhere in the area. And then maybe not until some time later.'

'I see.' Brief pause, and then the sound of pen on paper continued. 'Now you said at the start that the child's mother was a close relative. Who exactly is that, and what would this child be to you? If it's a sister, for instance, we would still need her approval to search, unless she's since died.'

Elena had kept it at arm's length with every call so far. Having to say it straight out repeatedly would have been too painful. Now, crossing that final barrier to confession, a barrier she'd avoided coming even close to the past almost thirty years, made her trembling run deeper and seem to drain every ounce of spirit and energy from her. She closed her eyes, her voice barely a whisper. 'It's my son I'm looking for. The son that I gave up twenty-nine years ago.'

Over the following few days, Elena's emotions see-sawed wildly.

She cooked for the family that night after instructing Megan, a simple Boeuf Bourguignon, but with Katine's portion set aside before she put in the red wine for the rest of them; the taste was too rich for Katine. Maybe in a few years.

But Elena found herself distracted throughout. She let the meat boil down and catch at one point, then she added too much red wine and overcooked the rice. It wasn't her normal effort.

She'd opened the red wine at the start of cooking and poured glasses for herself liberally. Too liberally by the look of silent reproach fired at her by Gordon as she shrieked and turned down the overboiling rice pot, a bit of wine slopping out of her glass as she lunged.

She almost collided with Christos when she swivelled sharply to drain the pot, then, seconds later, she was at screaming pitch when Katine walked in to show her the latest Mopatop doll.

Then it was a complete about-turn, hugging them both. 'Christos . . . Katine. Sorry . . . so sorry.' Her eyes welled as she straightened, ruffling Christos' hair. New Christos . . . *old* Christos. Replacements that had filled the void in her life – but quickly had become so much more.

Talk was light over dinner. Christos mentioned his school trying to arrange exchange trips to France for the coming Easter and that he'd like to go, and Gordon talked about a local client bitterly disappointed at the drop in his Far Eastern-linked PEP, though Gordon had recommended more of a spread at the outset. Elena said little and Gordon could tell that she was caught up in her own thoughts – at one point missing what Christos had said and having to get him to repeat it – though he waited until they'd finished dinner before he asked, 'What's wrong?'

'Oh, I don't know. I think this whole thing with Lorena has hit me harder than I realized.' Only a half-lie, since that had been the main catalyst. They were in the kitchen and, with the light hum of the dishwasher and the TV on for the kids in the lounge beyond, they couldn't be overheard.

Gordon shook his head and looked down. 'Bad business. I know how you must feel. But you did everything you could.'

'Did I?' She wiped a counter top brusquely with a cloth. 'Looks to me like thanks to my overeagerness, Lorena is now trapped there without us ever being able to help her again. Fine help.'

'You tried, that's the important thing.' Gordon came up and hugged her from behind, kissing her cheek. 'You weren't to know he was so Machiavellian, that he'd go to the lengths of taping your conversation.'

'I know. Perhaps you're right.' She shivered and shrank under his touch. With the duplicitous game she was playing, the secret she'd harboured all these years, she could hardly bear him to touch her. It brought it all too close.

Gordon pulled away with a half-pained expression, a half-smile, and leant over to peck her cheek again. She could tell that he'd picked up on her discomfort, but perhaps he put it down to her abhorrence of Ryall.

'Out of all the children you've seen successfully placed – what, fifty or more – you can't punish yourself so because just one gets lost on the way. It doesn't make it any easier, I know – but you'd almost expect those sort of odds.'

Her shivering became more intense. She closed her eyes. *Just one lost.* 'You're right . . . you're right.' She bit at her lip, fighting back the tears. *For God's sake just go, before I break down completely.*

The next day was even harder, with her starting to expect a call back, and she quickly became restless. She tried to do some painting to occupy her mind, but it was useless. She found she couldn't focus on anything for any length of time. Back once more to agitated pacing, wondering whether Megan's search man would find anything or not. *God*, even if he did, she could be waiting days or even weeks, and the way she felt now was that she could hardly bear to wait minutes more. Another coffee, her fifth of the morning, and finally the build-up of restlessness, as she stared on and off at the dormant phone, made her feel trapped, claustrophobic. She put on her coat and headed out of the house towards the chine.

The air was crisp, heavy clouds moving rapidly on a stiff breeze with only brief breaks of sunshine bursting through. Their garden stretched for almost a hundred yards from the back of the house, mostly gently sloping lawn with a steeper slope for the last ten yards as the descent towards the chine started. As the slope became steeper, the foliage and trees also became denser; there were regular hand-holds as Elena wended her way down the worn path she knew so well. The coordination of her steps and hand-grips was automatic, could have been done blindfold. The trees became thicker, taller, spires reaching hungrily up towards the light at the top of the ridge that hit her in intermittent weak dapples through gaps in the foliage, becoming less frequent as she went deeper.

And suddenly she was there. Her own private place, her cocoon from the world outside. As the path flattened out, the darkness was almost total and she could hear the babble of the stream running through. She closed her eyes and inhaled deeply, enjoying the richly laden smell of damp moss and tree bark mingled with the salt breeze drifting from the sea beyond. Here, everything remained timeless, unchanged; it was exactly as she remembered it when she'd first ventured in at the age of eight.

Eight, fifteen . . . now in his late twenties. All those lost years. She tried to picture what he'd look like now, but again it was the image of a small boy in her mind, running along the beach at the end of the chine, the wind lightly ruffling his hair . . . then as she focused, tried to see him more clearly, she realized the boy was the Christos she had now, a chink of recall from a Cyprus beach holiday when he was five.

She opened her eyes again, her breath showing on the cool air with her heavy exhalation. There was nothing there. No image she could cling to.

He'd been christened, blown out his first birthday candle, grazed his knee, had his first day at school, college, had girlfriends, maybe now was even married and had a family of his own. And she hadn't been there for any of it. Even if the call came through with something and she could find him, all of that would still be lost to her. All she could do was try and fill in the gaps in her mind – but even that small consolation seemed desperately out of reach. There was nothing there. Nothing. Just an empty, aching void.

Her eyes filled, and the tears flooded rapidly over. She dabbed at them, thinking she had it under control, but suddenly her body was convulsed with racking sobs, competing with the trickling of the nearby stream. The tears felt cool against her skin with the breeze, and she rocked gently, muttering, 'Christos . . . Christos. I'm sorry . . . so sorry.'

The wind in the treetops drowned out her voice, which made her plea seem all the more lost, insignificant. She was alone; alone with her secret in the one place where, since childhood, she'd felt she could be alone and secretive. But for one of the first times she no longer felt cocooned and protected, but adrift, vulnerable. The magic was fading. She'd kidded herself all along that she'd chosen it as a sanctuary from the craziness of the world outside, when in reality she'd merely used it to bury the memories of what she'd done; and now she could almost feel them seeping back out of the trees and damp earth to haunt her. *Your only son . . . and you let him go. How could you?*

She shook her head, bit hard at her lip, trying to shake away the silent whispers of recrimination. Maybe as she searched she might get a clearer image of Christos in her mind, something to cling to that would help fill the crushing void inside, and the magic would start to return. She wiped at her tears and started her way slowly back up the steep slope. Her step was heavy, her legs starting to ache only halfway up, and she couldn't help dwelling on the task ahead. Making her way from a place of such long-buried secrets into the open. It wouldn't be easy.

12

'Look, Jean-Paul. I've got to speak with you.'

'I know, you mentioned. But can't it wait till later? You can see how crazy everything is now.' Jean-Paul turned away, pointing over to the far side of the conference room. 'No . . . *No!* The main flower arrangement should go in that corner.' Then he addressed two men laying white cloths on long trestle tables to the side. 'The gravlax should go in the centre, with the canapés around. Then on the next table the side of lamb and the suckling pig . . .'

'I can see . . . I can see.' Roman felt awkward enough with the subject he had to broach, but this army of flower arrangers and caterers hovering around made it all the worse: so many men in one room with female mannerisms and affectations; it wasn't natural. It made him feel uncomfortable, out of place, like a gorilla surrounded by a flock of dancing flamingos.

He'd hoped to speak to Jean-Paul directly upon his return from seeing Art Giacomelli in Chicago. There was a full day spare before preparations started for their mother's birthday party that evening. But Jean-Paul had at the last minute delayed a day, so in the end his only chance was now, in the midst of preparations. Once the party started, there wouldn't be an opportunity; and even if there was, Jean-Paul wouldn't thank him for taking the edge off the celebrations.

Roman touched Jean-Paul's arm. 'It's urgent, Jean-Paul. I don't think this can wait.'

'Right. I see.' Jean-Paul's eyes clouded as he registered for the first time the gravity of Roman's concern. He held one arm out towards the adjoining office. 'Let's go in here.' Then to the caterers: 'I'll be back with you shortly.'

The atmosphere in the fifteen-foot-square room was stuffy, austere: part power-broker, part intellectual. Directly behind Jean-Paul's desk was his diploma in maths and art from the University of Montreal, and a framed thank-you letter from a local politician for Jean-Paul's substantial campaign funds in the late 80s. The far wall was lined with books: Flaubert, Dostoevsky, Voltaire, Joyce, Orwell, Zola, Rand,

Proust . . . Proulx. Jean-Paul the avid reader, whereas Roman had hardly got past *The Three Musketeers*. Roman had always felt uneasy in this room: everything seemed to shout down at him that he was the lightweight brain of the family.

Jean-Paul pressed his fingertips together in a pyramid. 'So . . . tell me.' He opened them out for a second. 'What's the problem?'

As Roman explained about Donatien being taken in for questioning, Jean-Paul's expression darkened. His eyes shifted uncomfortably to some papers at the side before coming back to Roman. 'Are you sure your contact's reliable? That he hasn't made a mistake?'

'No, I'm sure. He's been spot-on every time before. And he works in the same building at Dorchester Boulevard. So it's not the sort of thing he could make a mistake about.' Roman let the information settle a little deeper, enjoying watching Jean-Paul squirm at the thought of golden boy possibly being tainted, before he asked: 'So he hasn't mentioned anything about it to you?'

'No . . . no, he hasn't.' Jean-Paul was still distracted, turning possibilities around in his mind. 'But then I've only just got back . . . and as you can see things have been more than a little hectic.' He gestured towards the adjoining room. 'Maybe it's something he's planning to tell me about later. Maybe too, nothing much happened, so it wasn't worth raising the alarm straight away.'

'And maybe the Pope's dating Sharon Stone.' Roman leant forward, raising a sharp eyebrow. 'He was in there three hours, Jean-Paul. Three fucking hours! The RCMP could know every single financial transaction worth shit and what every one of us has for breakfast.'

Jean-Paul sighed heavily. Maybe Roman was right, but Jean-Paul was also keenly aware of the growing animosity between him and Georges; he needed to be sure this wasn't just Roman axe-grinding for the hell of it. 'We're not involved in crime any more, and Georges wasn't involved either in any of the money-laundering – so what's to tell?' He waved a hand towards Roman. 'This is probably all about that night with Leduc again.'

Roman flinched and sat back. Always the same these days: when it came to the crunch, Jean-Paul invariably sided with golden boy and threw it all back in his lap. 'Three hours, Jean-Paul? What did he do – show them his family snaps?' He shrugged helplessly. 'Even if it was all innocent, you've got to admit – he should have told you.'

'I know, I know.' Jean-Paul nodded solemnly.

Roman could tell that he was starting to teeter. 'And that Leduc incident could easily unravel the wrong way. If they're not convinced it was self-defence, I could go down for twenty. For ordering it, you'd get the same. They've probably been pressing Donatien, saying that they know he was there, but if he turns Crown evidence they'll give him immunity against prosecution as an accomplice. And then with the finances – once they've got the full picture of all the legitimate stuff, how long do you think it's going to take them to trace back to the . . .'

Jean-Paul held a hand up, a priest dispensing a blessing. 'Okay, Roman . . . okay. You've made your point.' His tone was worn, tired. All he could do was defer judgement: there were just too many open interpretations to get out the way first before he'd be convinced that he should mistrust Georges. 'I've pencilled in that I'd phone him about four o'clock before he heads off to get ready for the party, to catch up on business while I was away. I'll leave a few long gaps and pauses, and let's see if he fills them. If not, then we can start worrying.'

Elena grabbed the phone at the start of the second ring.

'He thinks he's found something at last.' Megan's voice at the other end: excited, slightly breathless.

'Where did he find it in the end?'

'Westminster registry.'

'Right. That's great.' Elena too found her breath caught slightly. The first call two days before, only thirty hours after she'd given Megan the go-ahead, had been to say that Terry, her search man, had found nothing in either the Kilburn or Hampstead registries. They'd trawl through the other north London registries before spreading the net wider.

'But before we get too carried away,' Megan continued, 'it's not an exact match. The name he's found is George Georgallis. And the birth date entered is not exactly the same either: it's four days later, 19 April, with the registration itself entered on 23 April. But the certificate is marked "adopted", which is what first made it leap out for Terry.'

Elena was uncertain. Georgallis was a common name among the Cypriot community, and with the few days' difference, it could easily be someone else. Then the thought suddenly hit her: choosing the name George would mean that the family name would continue, regardless of the adopted family name. And she seemed to remember her father having a Greek doctor friend in Pimlico, which would come under Westminster. 'Is it a doctor who made the registration? Is there a name and address given there?'

'Yes, uh . . .' Megan struggled to decipher the scrawled writing. 'Looks like a Doctor Manatis or Maniatis. Charlwood Street, London, SW1.'

'Yeah, that's it. I'm sure . . . I'm sure.' Charlwood Street was Pimlico, if she remembered her London geography: the coincidences were too many. 'Where do we go from here?'

'Well. Underneath "adopted", there's a note of a temporary care order made in the name of Anthony Georgallis . . .'

'Yes . . . that's my father. He thrust a load of papers in front of me only a week after the birth. I hardly even knew what I was signing, I was still so distraught . . .'

'That's okay. You don't need to defend yourself to us, or explain. It's just the more we know, the easier it is when it comes to tracing.' Megan's voice was cool, soothing; as if she'd dealt a thousand times before with mothers who held back the harsher, more painful details. 'Then we've got a note of a court order made some five months later at Highgate Court. That would probably be the next most logical search point.'

Elena felt her trembling start to return. 'I think I know what it says already.' She gripped hard at the edge of the telephone table, trying to brace herself. 'I suffered severe depression soon after signing my baby away and made an attempt to take my own life.' The images were still vivid: the bathroom sliding sideways after she'd taken the pills, her face being slapped hard; but as she tried to focus on her mother's face above her, the bright fluorescent light washed away any definition, searing through her eyes like a hot lance. 'When I recovered, I decided that I just couldn't live with the same sense of loss and guilt for the rest of my life – I wanted my baby back. But my father said that he'd fight me all the way, and he used the attempted suicide to argue that I was unstable and unfit. I didn't even bother to show up in court for the final ruling – it was already a foregone conclusion.'

'I see.'

Despite Megan being battle-hardened and probably having heard every possible story, Elena could swear she heard a faint swallow from the other end.

From downstairs came the muffled tones of Gordon's voice: speaking to another business client while on the other line she unravelled the secrets of the past she'd long held from him. At the local shops the day before, she'd suddenly panicked that Megan might phone while she was out: Gordon would pick it up and, if the wrong thing was said, the secret would be out straight away. But if the trace was successful, she'd have to tell him anyway, and the mounting dread of having to spill all to Gordon hit her in full force.

When no call had come through the rest of that day, she'd almost begun to wish that there would be no trace found; then at least she would never have to tell Gordon. Their lives would continue as before: happy, albeit for her incomplete.

'But that's not the only thing those court papers might show.' Megan's words were suddenly measured, purposeful. 'They might show the family who adopted your son.'

Elena felt a sudden constriction in her chest. She swallowed hard, as if she hadn't heard right and that might clear it. She'd been prepared for weeks or even months of searching, and likely even then nothing at the end of it. It was as if someone had casually told her she had a winning lottery ticket in her coat pocket. It just seemed too easy to trust. 'Are you sure?'

'Not a hundred per cent – but there are strong chances it's registered there, particularly if the adoption was arranged at the same time. We'll know soon enough.'

'How long?'

'Well, normally it can take anything from a few weeks to a few months. But Terry has his ways of speeding things: urgent contact needed because of a serious congenital disorder, rare blood group sharing, things like that. Quite honestly, it's best not to ask. I just leave it to him as to the best and quickest method to get what he wants. Any luck, he should have something within five or six days, certainly within a week.'

In the end it was only four days before Megan called back with some names: Nicholas and Maria Stephanou, and an address in Canterbury, Kent. Terry was checking it out as they spoke. 'Twenty-nine years, so probably they've moved. But at least it's a name and a start point for him to track from.'

Suddenly Elena had a new name to mutter under her breath: George Stephanou. Still it didn't help: no image came to mind for her to cling to. But at least now she felt more alive, full of hope: marked contrast to the doldrums of the past week.

Though later that afternoon she was back again in the doldrums. She'd just left her local corner store after being brought up to date on village goings-on by Mrs Wickens, its shopkeeper of twenty-five years, in her usual shrugging and winking 'yar know what I'm saying' style. Elena's step was lively, brisk – the air was fresh, the sky bright, she was still smiling from Mrs Wickens' stories – everything seemed to be going right at last.

Then Nicola Ryall's dark blue Range Rover drifted by. Lorena was in the back and she saw Elena straight away. Their eyes locked and Lorena swivelled quickly around so that she could continue staring back. Her small hand slowly reached out and touched the inside of the back window, as if she was trying to make invisible contact, and Elena felt a sharp stab of guilt. This past week she'd been consumed with nothing but her own problems, leaving Lorena all but forgotten. The girl's last hope probably now gone of ever getting free from Ryall, and Elena hadn't given her a second thought.

Just before fading from view, Elena thought she saw Lorena silently mouth something. It looked like 'Help me'.

Georges returned with Simone's drink, a Campari and lemon, as the man in the light grey suit with bright floral tie moved away.

'Who's he?' he asked Simone.

'Jacques Delamarle. Local politician, something to do with cultural affairs, if I remember right. My father deals with him now and then because of his heavy contributions to the jazz festival – but he's known him for years. He's an old family friend and also knows Lillian: that's why he's here.'

'No political advantage being sought, then?' Georges raised an eyebrow.

'No. I don't think my father would dare try it here.' Simone smiled and took a sip of her drink. They'd both noticed how over the past year Jean-Paul had increasingly courted political favour. 'If Lillian got even a whiff that he was turning her birthday party into part of his image-bolstering campaign, she'd have his head on a plate next to the suckling pig.' The three-man combo at the end of the room started up again, launching into an upbeat Latin version of 'Besame Mucho', and Simone had to raise her voice slightly. 'He saves all of that for open-house days or business and charity functions.'

There were only about ten people dancing – for the past hour or so most people had seemed keener on eating, drinking and talking, though invariably Lillian and her new 'friend' Max were among the first on the floor. Max was a retired grocer whose expansion plans had peaked at two small Outremont stores and a downtown *dépanneur* before he sold up.

Jean-Paul looked on and smiled graciously, but both Simone and Georges could still read the silent disapproval he was careful to hide. One of Jean-Paul's few character flaws. Normally extremely broad-minded, with little regard for social or class divides, when it came to his mother his class consciousness was suddenly extreme. Nobody was good enough for her.

But Georges was more concerned about something else beneath Jean-Paul's smile, after their earlier conversation. It had started out as a standard business update, but then there'd been a couple of questions as to whether everything was okay and 'Did anything else happen while I was away?' that in retrospect struck him as odd. Not the questions themselves, but the awkward moment's silence straight after Georges had assured that everything was fine.

Probably he was just getting paranoid; he was still rattled after the session with Chenouda and perhaps it had come through in his voice. He'd sounded strained, worried. If Jean-Paul had an inside track with the RCMP, then he'd also know the theory Chenouda was pushing about Leduc and now Savard; he'd have been grilling Roman non-stop since he got back. But things between them seemed to be fine; the smiles and body language were easy and relaxed from the couple of times he'd seen them talk so far.

The only thing he was still unsure of was whether the smiles were easy from Jean-Paul to him, whether . . . *'What . . . ?'*

'I said – so here we are. Stuck in the middle,' Simone repeated. She looked at Jacques Delamarle, then towards Roman and Frank Massenat propped up against the back wall, diving into platefuls of canapés. 'Clowns to the left of us . . . jokers to the right.' Then her brows knitted slightly. 'Are you okay?'

'Yes, fine. Fine.' Georges smiled wanly. Jean-Paul's oddly comical mix at functions: the transition from crime boss to respectable business-man wasn't fully there yet; the past was still mingling with what Jean-Paul hoped was his future.

Roman's Marie was halfway across the room from him talking to two other women, while Jean-Paul's date of choice for the evening, Catherine, was by his side. He'd met her just before Christmas at The Bay's perfume counter while choosing a present for his then girlfriend. In the three years since burying Stephanie, his second wife, he hadn't settled emotionally. Hardly anyone was good enough to match up to her either. Though with each one, Jean-Paul initially had high hopes: he was keen to let it be known that Catherine was not just a platinum blonde, perfume-selling wallflower, she was also doing an evening course in sociology at McGill.

As the song finished, Lillian and Max came over.

'Big day for these two soon,' Lillian said. 'Have you met Max before?' she asked Georges.

Georges held a hand up in greeting at Max and smiled. 'Yes, but only once. Jean-Paul's last Boxing Day open house.' Obviously Lillian had forgotten.

'Maybe we won't be too far behind on the church steps.' Lillian nudged Max. 'Anywhere planned for the honeymoon yet?' Martinique was too hot and humid in July, she informed them without waiting for an answer; so was Mexico. 'Maybe you should head to Europe. Côte d'Azur's nice then, or maybe Italy.'

Simone said that they'd talked about France, but one of those Loire Valley picture-postcard châteaux for the first ten days. 'Then the Med coast with maybe a quick look at Tuscany for the rest of the time.'

She'd barely finished before Lillian, with a quick 'Excuse us', whisked Max back to dance. Jon and Cynthia Larsen moved in from a few yards away, Cynthia asking if they knew where they'd have the reception yet, and would they use the same caterers as today? Impressive spread, but for Cynthia's money – no doubt gained from her current haute cuisine courses to raise the level of her already renowned dinner parties – the rack of lamb was a bit dry and some of the canapé pastry a touch overbaked.

Jon quickly became uninterested and led Georges to one side by the arm. 'What do you reckon on this Cuban thing, then?'

'Well, Jean-Paul mentioned something – but we never really got into it.' Georges gestured towards the end-table spreads. 'Preparations for this I think took over.' Jean-Paul had mentioned at the start of their earlier call that he wanted to talk about increased Cuban investments. But then, after them catching up on events and Jean-Paul asking if everything was okay, they'd never got around to it. Jean-Paul had abruptly signed off, saying that he had two caterers and a party decorator hovering anxiously at his office door. He had to go.

'Right.' Jon looked fazed for only a second, then explained: Arturo Giacomelli was interested in funnelling funds into Cuba. He couldn't do it through the USA, because of the trade embargo. 'But he could do it through Jean-Paul and Canada.'

Georges sucked in his breath. 'We can't handle money for Giaco-melli. It would be back to what Jean-Paul's been fighting so hard to move away from: laundering and trying to play clean with dirty money.'

Jon Larsen held up his free hand. 'We went through all that. This would be totally clean money, straight from the two Vegas casinos.'

'Right.' Georges looked down, pondering it quickly as he took a slug of his beer. 'We'd still have to be careful of not breaching the US embargo. But that wouldn't be a problem if the money was channelled first through Canada and Jean-Paul's side of the Vegas partnerships.'

Jon nodded. 'I think that's one of the options that came up when they discussed it.'

'But I still think it would be safer to run it all through, say, Jean-Paul's Mexico companies first, then on through Cuba.' Georges' thoughts were running double time as he watched Jon Larsen consider the suggestion. Despite the frantic preparations, Jean-Paul had obvi-ously found time to discuss this with Jon in some depth. Georges began to wonder about Jean-Paul's abrupt signing off. Maybe he *had* heard something and was troubled.

Larsen took a sip of his Martini. 'I suppose that's got merit. But we'd have to make sure it was in and out under three months to avoid any tax implications. Then too we should think about –'

'Enough shop talk, I think,' Cynthia cut in. Simone smiled tightly alongside her.

Jon nodded hastily. 'Yeah, yeah. You're right.'

And they stood as an awkward circle for a second before Cynthia commented: 'No ice storms this year, at least.' Then launched into how they'd respectively coped and survived through them last winter.

As Simone explained that it hadn't been too bad – when the power lines started going down they'd all simply headed here to her father's house because he had a generator – Georges was hardly listening. He was looking across and trying to catch Jean-Paul's eye and in return hopefully get that confident, reassuring smile that he knew so well; more vital to him now than ever, because it would tell him that everything was okay.

It wasn't until some time later that he finally managed to elicit that return smile, but by then Georges had run through so many conflicting emotions he was almost past caring. He'd started to drink faster, slugging back two beers and two double Southern Comforts in an effort to lose his worries in the mood and flow of the party. He'd danced with Simone a few times and in the middle of the band's passable rendition of the Beatles' 'And I Love Her', whispered in her ear how much he loved her. He'd thought a couple of times of going over and talking directly to Jean-Paul – maybe he could better discern eye to eye if something was wrong. But Jean-Paul seemed to be endlessly wrapped up talking to other people. He'd just finished a long session with Delamarle when one of Lillian's bridge circle, an elderly surgeon, moved in. Then Jean-Paul's neighbours, a leading realtor and his twenty-years-younger aerobics instructor wife.

At one point Georges caught Roman's eye and could almost swear that Roman had read his consternation: it was a direct, challenging look and there was a faint smile at the corner of Roman's mouth. All Georges could think of was Savard's screams on tape, and he was first to look away. The room felt suddenly as if it was closing in: the beat of the music, Jean-Paul's cold shoulder, Roman staring at him, the rising cacophony of voices all around, a woman just behind breaking into laughter – all of it seemed to spin in his head, make him dizzy.

'Sorry.' He excused himself to Simone and headed to the bathroom, splashing some water on his face as he stared hard in the mirror. Strange how quickly he could become an outcast to the extended Lacaille family, a stranger at this gathering. Marked contrast to the camaraderie when they'd all grouped together under this same roof during the ice storms, playing cards and charades: the Lacaille family and their favoured inner circle against a hostile world outside. Now he too was practically out in the cold, along with the ice sheets.

And it was in that moment, with his frantic, haunted eyes still fixed in the mirror as he dabbed himself dry with a towel, that he finally decided: he couldn't take the burden of this secret any longer. He'd have to tell the truth about that night with Roman and Leduc. He didn't want to tell Jean-Paul directly, that was what he'd been avoiding all along: ratting on one brother to the other. But perhaps he could confide in someone in the middle: Simone or Jon Larsen? Which would be best?

The decision made, he felt as if a burden had been lifted from his shoulders as he emerged. And it was then too that Jean-Paul's smile finally came in return – just after Georges'd whispered in Simone's ear, as Frank Massenat trod on Lillian's foot for the second time during his disastrous attempt at the bossa nova, 'He doesn't need to strong-arm people, he just needs to threaten to dance with them.'

Simone smiled broadly, and as Georges pecked her on the cheek and straightened up, Jean-Paul was smiling over at them. But Georges couldn't tell whether it was directed just at his daughter, or whether it embraced both of them.

'I know that you've already had social services on to you asking about Lorena, Dr Tinsley, but this was something entirely different – more to do with her condition when she first arrived in this country,' Elena elaborated. 'As one of the agency workers involved in her placement here, that was more my neck of the woods.'

'I see. Well, what sort of thing specifically do you want to know?'

Elena could still sense Tinsley's caution on the line. She decided to backtrack a bit, filling in some background about Lorena's sewer days and the severe deprivation in the orphanages. 'She suffered bouts of disturbed dreams in the last orphanage in Bucharest as a result, and I just wondered whether they might have recurred in England.'

'Surely this is more psychiatric or counselling territory, than a physician's.'

'I know. But the nightmares were never so severe that she was recommended for treatment, so this would really be just a general observation on your part.'

'Well . . . I, uh, she never actually complained directly about any dreams that I recall . . . but she did at times seem a bit detached, preoccupied.'

Elena could hear the flicking of some papers in the background; she wasn't sure whether the hesitation was Tinsley showing due caution or just that his attention was only half with her. 'I mean, did she seem troubled? Would you say that she might have been suffering from depression?'

'Depression? A bit of an extreme term for a nine-year-old.' Lightly humouring tone, almost condescending. 'But she was, shall we say, sometimes distant, lost in her own world. I often had to repeat questions. Though I must say I put this largely down to her getting to grips with the language and also getting used to her new environment.'

'Right.' She sensed she'd gone as far as she could about Lorena, but from Nadine's earlier paperwork she'd noted Tinsley's age: fifty-three. 'And the other adopted girl, Mikaya – were you her GP as well?'

'Yes, I was. But I thought –'

'And was there any history of depression or upsets there?' Elena barrelled in quickly with the question, hoping to catch Tinsley off guard. But Tinsley merely continued with his started objection.

'I thought you were only concerned with Lorena – so I don't really see what that has to do with anything.' Defensively questioning.

'Yes, I know. But we're trying to find out if this is just a problem with Lorena. Because if there's been a similar problem of mental detachment and depression with another child, it could be that unconsciously the Ryalls are somehow alienating their adopted children, not fully embracing and accepting them as family.' Elena listened to the shallow fall of Tinsley's breath wondering if he'd go for her story. She felt she was treading on egg-shells; but this was the only plausible story she could think of to get what she wanted. 'As I say, I don't think this is anything the Ryalls would knowingly have done. It's just that children can often be very sensitive – particularly displaced children like these.'

'Look, there was something – but it was absolutely nothing to do with the Ryalls, more to do with a boyfriend.' A brisk, blustery tone, as if Tinsley thought Elena might have heard something and he wanted to ensure she didn't fill in the gaps the wrong way. 'What I can vouch for is that Mr and Mrs Ryall supported Mikaya wholeheartedly and unequivocally throughout the whole matter. Beyond that, I think you should speak to the Ryalls directly or the social services.'

'Yes, yes, certainly. I understand.' My, my, she had touched a nerve. *Boyfriend?* 'You've been very helpful. Thank you.' She bowed out swiftly, getting the distinct impression that if she'd pushed an inch more, Tinsley would have hung up on her.

Elena dialled Nadine Moore's number straight away. She was out, so Elena left her number for a call back. She tapped her fingers impatiently for a second by the phone, then went downstairs to pour a fresh coffee. The first few sips and the aroma made her feel a bit more alert; she hadn't slept well the night before after seeing Lorena.

When by mid-morning there hadn't been any more news from Megan, she'd spent half an hour thinking through tactics before deciding to start on trying to help Lorena. Not sure how far she'd get, and feeling a bit like a frantic juggler given her own dilemma, she asked herself whether she was doing it just because of the lull, killing time so as not to dwell on her own uncertainty. No, she'd have made time regardless. She couldn't have lived with herself knowing she'd simply deserted Lorena at the first obstacle; she had to at least give it one last try.

Gordon was out for a few hours seeing some local clients, so at least the pressure of having him lurking around was gone. Megan and Terry's bill was already up to £830, £300 beyond what she could manage from her own account. She'd made an excuse to Gordon about problems with her car: new disk brakes needed, according to the garage. But what about the next £300, and the one after that? She'd have to either become inventive, or bare all to Gordon. She shook her head: such a momentous secret kept for so long, how could their relationship survive it?

Two hours later she was sat at the back of Chelborne Sands in Nadine Moore's car, the two of them like drug dealers or lovers on a clandestine meet. More secrets.

'It's all there. Everything regarding Mikaya Ryall.' Nadine passed the file across. 'I can only let you read the file, not take it anywhere or copy it. Make notes if you like – but if anyone asks you where you got the information, it wasn't me. Right?'

'Yes . . . of course.' Elena was only half listening as she riffled hungrily through the file. Nadine had protested vehemently before she'd agreed to dig out and share the file, and she'd had to push hard: *'If you're happy with what Ryall did, taping our conversation; and if, despite that, you're satisfied he has nothing at all to hide and everything's all right with Lorena – then fine, don't help me.'* Against her better judgement Nadine had finally relented, though she was still muttering and complaining now that she shouldn't be doing this. 'I must be crazy. I could lose my job if this got out.'

Elena's eyes scanned frantically, leap-frogging for relevant paragraphs. After a moment's strained silence as she read, she slowly looked up, staring blankly ahead. The beach was deep, and winter winds had blown the sand in banks and ridged eddies. On the stronger flurries buffeting the car from the open bay, loose sand was lifted and strewn across the windscreen.

Nadine switched on the wipers to clear it as Elena exhaled slowly; a note of winding down, finality: *Pregnant at fourteen, signs of being sexually active for some time; mystery boyfriend.* It was almost a mirror image of her own background, too close for comfort. A faint involuntary shudder quickly shook away the awkwardness and the similarity: in her own case, there *had* been a boyfriend, but with Mikaya she'd bet anything that he was invented; a ruse to cover up for Ryall. She noted from the file that the boyfriend had never been named. How convenient.

She was suddenly burning with conviction, and angry with herself that but for a chance sighting of Lorena, she might have left her, forgotten, at Ryall's mercy.

She thanked Nadine and headed off with the intention of going straight back home, her fury making her drive faster than normal – but as she was passing Mrs Wickens' store, she decided on impulse to stop. If anyone could fill in the gaps, Mrs Wickens could.

Mrs Wickens nodded sagely. Yes, of course she remembered the whole affair. No, the boyfriend was never named. A few boys that young Mikaya was known to be friendly with were suggested – but she swore it wasn't them. 'She says first of all she couldn't say who it was – then she says she just couldn't remember. Rarl mystery.'

'What does she look like?' Elena asked as an afterthought, about to turn and head off.

'Beautiful girl, stunning. One of the most beautiful Oriental girls I've ever seen.'

Cameron Ryall got the first call from Dr Tinsley late that afternoon. The following two calls notifying him that Mrs Waldren had been asking questions around town came the next day, the last prompting, 'You know, the aid worker who lives with her husband up above the chine', as if for a moment he might not be able to place her.

He'd thought of little else over the weeks spanning the two interviews with Lorena, and now it was all springing back again. Just when over the past week, after the tape and the intervention of Edelston, he'd started finally to relax, thinking it was all over.

His first thought was to contact Edelston to warn her, but then Waldren was a free agent, out of their control. And Waldren's aid agency would likely take no notice.

He seethed and simmered for hours pondering what to do – his attention to the pressing business matters of the day was sparse and often drifted – before finally deciding that he just didn't know enough about Waldren to be able to plan the best way to stop her. In the same way that she was digging about his background, he needed to dig about hers.

He contacted a Chelmsford-based private investigator he knew from his old barrister days, Des Kershaw, whom he'd used just a few years earlier to delve into the private life of a plant manager he suspected of embezzlement. Kershaw was tenacious and thorough: he wouldn't rest until he'd stripped bare every facet of Elena Waldren's background.

The first couple of days, Kershaw uncovered nothing ground-breaking, mostly filling in the shades of the last twelve years of her married life with Gordon Waldren, her work with the aid agency and their two adopted children, Christos and Katine.

One thing at least he had in common with the Waldrens, thought Ryall: adopted children. Kershaw's call had disturbed him halfway through an inspection in the micro-chip section, and he was still slightly breathless from taking off his protective suit. 'Nothing juicy, then, yet? No, right . . . right. Let me know as soon as you've got more . . . *if* there is more.'

Ryall began to worry that nothing worthwhile would come up on Waldren, she was just as she appeared on the outside – the goody-two-shoes aid worker with her two adopted children and finance-broker husband, upper-middle and pristine with her 'champion of downtrodden children' halo – and he'd have to think of other ways of striking back at her, stopping her before she got uncomfortably close.

But Kershaw's increasingly frequent and fervent calls over the following days bit by bit quelled his mounting panic, and when the whole picture became clear he realized that he had more than enough ammunition for his purpose: enough to bury Elena Waldren twice over.

Some of it seemed so unlikely and extreme that he found himself asking Kershaw to repeat segments, pressing if he was sure. Ryall was concerned that Kershaw might have been overkeen to unearth some dirt and had tapped some unreliable sources. But Kershaw was certain of his ground.

'Some of it was hard to find, buried in old articles in local papers from Hampstead and Highgate where the George, previously Georgallis, family used to live – though a couple of incidents managed to warrant small sidebars in the national press. The only word-of-mouth was an old police contact – but I've used him before; he's reliable. And then the rest is pretty much down to court papers: little room for error there. But when you've got the file, if there's anything you're unsure about and want me to check again – just let me know. I'll be happy to oblige.'

There was no need for a call back. Kershaw's report was thorough, detailed and made sober reading. Two drug busts and a third arrest for a Greenham Common anti-nuclear demo that went awry. From the press clippings, most of it appeared to be a rich wild child's rebellion against her establishment father, the founder of what at one stage was

Britain's ninth largest merchant bank. Ryall should have twigged when he first saw the original family name: George. Anthony George, whiz-kid financier of the seventies and eighties.

But it was the earlier problems – the pregnancy at fifteen and giving the child up for adoption, then the attempted suicide and the court's final ruling that she was too unstable, unsuitable as a mother – that was the most damning, especially given her current work. Ryall wondered just how much of her background she'd come clean about with the aid agency, or in the adoption applications for her two children.

Giving up her own child, convicted drug addict, attempted suicide, court-ruled as unsuitable for motherhood: not exactly the best commendations for work with a child-aid agency or to adopt children.

Ryall couldn't resist a wry smile as he penned his covering letters that night to go with copies of Kershaw's file: one to Barbara Edelston, one to Elena Waldren's aid agency – but both to the same effect: that he was still being privately harassed by Waldren over Lorena and, given Waldren's own history, surely she was the last person to be questioning his rights and ethics as an adoptive parent; with an added paragraph to the aid agency venting his surprise that they hadn't more stringently vetted her.

He paused for a moment, wondering whether to send a copy as well to Gordon Waldren, or whether that would be going too far – just how much of her past *had* she told him? – before finally picking up another envelope. She'd been first to draw the battle lines, had been prepared to destroy him. All's fair in love and . . . though this time he didn't bother with a covering note, just slipped a copy of Kershaw's report inside on its own.

He sat back, pleased with his efforts. In the background, Prokofiev's 'Dance of the Knights' played. Fitting battle requiem music. Nicola had gone to bed over an hour before, shortly after Lorena, as usual zonked out on half a bottle of gin and prozac, and suitably unimpressed when he said he had some business to attend to, some letters to write.

Outside, a gusting wind buffeted the high arched windows and the muffled surge of the sea could be heard in the distance – but inside the music filled every corner of the grand room, bouncing back from the windows and vaulted ceiling to the reaches of the gallery library. A resonant sound chamber with just the right balance of absorbent wood: how such music was meant to be heard – with only him at its centre to receive it. He could feel its rhythm and cadences reverberate through his body, rallying his senses, and his spirits rising, soaring. He started waving his hands elaborately to the strident, staccato violin bursts, drawing substance and power from what he'd just done, feeling suddenly master of all that was around: master of this grand room and this house; master of the village and its petty minions, who dutifully passed information back to him; and now master of all those who dared interfere in his life, Elena Waldren and her kind.

He froze for a second, lifting one hand to his right cheek. He swore he could still feel where little Lorena had kissed him. The dutiful 'Good night Daddy' ritual of every night. And every night he could sense too her clinging anxiety as she came close and pressed her lips to his skin, her eyes darting and her small heart hammering as furiously as a humming bird's wings, making the whole ritual all the more angelic, endearing. He had such power over her, yet only a part of her knew how or why.

He looked up, straining his ear to the house upstairs beyond the music, wondering perhaps whether he should make sure Lorena was okay, soothe her brow for a moment: a small victory visit. But he decided in the end to wait a few days: then he could be sure that that victory would be lasting. Nobody would ever trouble them again.

The tears hit Elena as she rounded the bluff beyond Chelborne.

It was one of her favourite views: almost two hundred feet sheer elevation from the sea, with the rolling contours of green hills and pastures spilling gently into the yellow-trimmed expanse of Chelborne Sands and the deep blue of the bay. On days when the sea was wild, like now, she liked it all the more: white caps could be seen stretching out towards the horizon, more lines of conflict and contrast. She'd captured the view twice before on canvas, but still felt she'd missed the key that made her soul soar when she rounded the bluff on a stark, clear day.

The day was clear now, the wind brisk, aftermath of the previous night's gale. But Elena felt nothing but empty, desolate, as she looked out across the sweep of the bay.

'I think that's it . . . I'm afraid. We've hit a stone wall. The chances of ever finding him again now are virtually nil, in Terry's view.' Megan's words of first thing that morning.

She hadn't cried then, just the same empty, gut-voided feeling as now. Terry had discovered that the Stephanous had changed their name by deed poll to Stevens some ten months after the adoption, then simply disappeared off the face of the earth. No forwarding address, nothing on electoral registers or credit files. As with her father, the name was now completely anglicized: George Stevens. Megan and Terry were probably right: with no link traceable to the Stephanous, she'd never find him. *'I'll bury him out of sight and out of reach. You won't find him.'* Her father's words, all these years later, suddenly having crushing resonance. Still a part of her life, despite her fighting so hard to be free from his shadow, was in his grip and control.

Though a few hours later she was far more concerned about Cameron Ryall's control, his influence over much of Chelborne. She'd quickly shaken off her own disappointment: if she couldn't help herself, at least she could still help Lorena. Mrs Wickens' words preyed heavily on her mind: *'One of the most beautiful Oriental girls I've ever seen.'*

Perhaps Ryall hand-picked these girls for their sheer beauty – God knows there were enough of them, an endless sea of children with angelic faces and big eyes that the rest of the world had forgotten. He'd get them into his trust at first, soothe their brows, some seemingly innocent gentle stroking, then would gradually build up until they were thirteen or fourteen, the age Mikaya had been when she became pregnant, and then ... Elena convulsed at the thought. But why didn't they speak out against him? With Lorena, she could understand: she was too young, too frightened, and probably not too much had happened yet; and what had, she'd blanked from her mind.

But Mikaya had been old enough to speak out, especially given the horror of her pregnancy – yet still she'd stayed quiet. What hold was it Ryall had over them?

She realized she couldn't possibly know without finding out more about Mikaya, so she'd headed back into Chelborne. After seeing Mrs Wickens the day before, she'd filled in some gaps at the local dress shop and at the health store. But it was all minor stuff: the school Mikaya went to, what clothes she liked; yes, they knew about the whole messy business with the pregnancy, but no, there wasn't a particular boyfriend they could point to as a likely culprit. 'We haven't seen much of her these past couple of years,' Mrs Frolley at the dress shop finished thoughtfully, 'now that she's away at university.'

But now, when she'd visited Mrs Frolley again to ask 'Which university?' – she'd found her a closed book. 'I'm sorry, I don't know.' Becoming quickly flustered. 'I think I've said more than I should in any case . . . and I'm rather busy now.' Red-faced, she'd scurried away to attend to a customer.

A shop girl at the health store, after going back and checking, informed her that Mrs Boyle was busy stock-taking and couldn't see her – so she'd rested her hopes on the ever-reliable Mrs Wickens.

But Mrs Wickens' reaction had been much the same, albeit delivered as a more open, folksy reprimand. 'When I tell you things, it's in all trust and confidence. I don't expect it to be used in all strange manners.'

Elena tried to appeal to Mrs Wickens' maternal instinct, as she'd raised four children of her own. 'This isn't about any personal conflict I might have with Mr Ryall. It's about the welfare of a young girl who I believe could be under threat. Serious threat.'

Mrs Wickens shook her head. 'I don't believe any of it for a moment. Mr Ryall's a good man. He wouldn't dream of doing anything like that. He's been very good to my Rolly these past years.'

It hit Elena with a jolt in that moment: Mrs Wickens' husband, Roland, worked at Ryall's plant. Given the size of his business in a small village like Chelborne, no doubt numerous villagers – and shopkeepers' relatives – were employed there. After all, Ryall was by far the area's biggest employer. A saving hero to fill the gap after the years of decline in the local fishing industry. Few locals wanted to think badly of him.

A spark of recognition reflected back through Mrs Wickens' eyes, and she turned away with a slight flush, busying herself with rearranging her counter newspaper display. 'Well, you know . . . We each have our own to take care of.'

And it was driving away from Mrs Wickens', rounding the bluff, that the build-up of frustrations and obstacles finally became too much, and the tears hit. She'd been working against the grain, against the impossible, for days and weeks – for decades, if she counted the lost, forgotten time that she'd blanked Christos from her mind, hadn't even troubled to search for him – and only now was that realization hitting her.

Her father's hand reaching across the years to grip her tight, affect her life; and now Ryall's tentacles spreading across Chelborne, blocking, strangling her progress.

The bay ahead became misty and blurred as her eyes swam, and she had to pull over. Maybe that was the key with her painting, that slightly blurred, Monet look – but the thought barely raised a smile at the corner of her mouth, her spirits couldn't be buoyed this time; and she sank deeper down, sobbing uncontrollably. She cried more for the lost years with Christos than for this dead-end now; after all, it'd only taken a week to discover that she would never make good on the twenty-nine years lost. And for Lorena, it was more the sense of frustration and powerlessness than sorrow. She thought she'd broken free of her father's grip years ago, but she'd been fooling herself all along. And now she was facing the same again: another powerful man, and she was unable to prise loose his grasp to be able to help Lorena.

She shook her head, biting back the tears. Maybe Gordon was right: she'd allowed the dividing line between Ryall and her father to become muddied, confused; it wasn't healthy, would only get in the way of her being objective, having a clear view.

Clear view. She wiped again at her eyes, dabbing her cheeks with the back of one hand, and once again the view of the bay ahead was clear. She only wished her troubled thoughts could as easily have been cleared.

After a moment she swung the car out again and continued on down the slow decline towards Chelborne bay, clinging to the one consolation out of the whole mess: at least now her secret would remain forever buried, no reason for its exposure. Her life with Gordon and the children, like the view ahead, would continue much as it had done: bright, untroubled, with few worrying clouds.

13

Jean-Paul turned from Georges as he poured the drink from a decanter on the side cabinet.

'One thing my brother does have good taste in. Brandy.' Jean-Paul brought the glass over to Georges seated towards the end of the long table. Jean-Paul's own glass was already in front of his position at its head. He raised it and smiled. *'Santé!'*

'Yes. Cheers.' Georges savoured its mellow burning as it sank down. An aged Ragnaud-Sabourin that Roman had bought for Jean-Paul at Christmas just past. Georges glanced back towards the door. 'Isn't Jon joining us?'

'No, this is more family talk than business.' Jean-Paul looked directly at Georges for the first time.

'Oh, right.' Georges should have guessed from the late hour and the brandy. A soft, mellow glint to Jean-Paul's eyes, no hostility; but Georges thought he'd picked up a faint underlying concern; it wasn't quite the uncompromising embrace he'd been seeking. 'I thought this might have been about Giacomelli and Cuba. I talked briefly about it with Jon at the party last night.'

'Yes, well . . . we can discuss that maybe tomorrow. Jon didn't have much free time today.' Jean-Paul glanced briefly past Georges' shoulder, his train of thought broken for a second. Then a faint smile creased the corner of his mouth. 'Old man Vito Giacomelli apparently lost a packet down there when Castro took over and all the casinos closed. Art agrees with your assumption that when finally the trade embargoes lift, property prices are going to sky-rocket . . . and I think he's tickled by the idea of making back some of the money the old man lost there. What we've got to do now is turn all of that nostalgic pay-back into a sound business proposition and a clean way of doing it . . . *if* there is one.' Jean-Paul took a swig of brandy and stood up, started pacing. 'As I say, we'll talk more about it when Jon's here.' Fresh breath, and Georges was unsure whether the pacing was Jean-Paul getting his thoughts moving or nervousness and anxiety. 'But in fact it is my recent visit to Art Giacomelli that's prompted this meeting now. You know that Art has been following closely this bid of ours to change the nature of our business, move away from crime and become totally legitimate, clean?'

'Yes, I . . . I know at least that you've confided in him about it more than anyone else. And that he's the crime boss your family has maintained the closest ties with over the years.'

Jean-Paul clasped his brandy glass as if he was praying, then waved one hand expressively. 'This isn't just about old man Vito and my father running liquor and cigarettes across the border in the fifties, or how close our families have been since . . . or even, at the power level, about how that association helped us later with our problem with the Cacchiones . . .' The hand groped emptily at the air for a moment and Georges sensed something difficult was coming. Jean-Paul was normally conversationally fluid, no gaps between his thoughts and words, and yet now he was struggling. 'Art was particularly helpful and supportive when Pascal died.'

Georges just nodded and looked down, sensing it was best not to interrupt the flow. Maybe that was the awkwardness: Pascal's death. All Georges knew of the whole affair, imparted by Jon Larsen – Jean-Paul had never broached the subject directly – was that Giacomelli had intervened to stop the war with the Cacchiones after Pascal was shot. As reputedly America's most powerful crime boss, he had that influence. When Arturo Giacomelli said stop, people stopped.

'Yes, he's interested in how we progress, how successful we are . . . because if it works for us it can work for him and maybe others. A sort of test case if you will.' The hand started moving again. 'But it goes deeper than that . . . a lot of it tied in with Art's thoughts, hopes and ambitions for his own family. Probably you don't know too much about them?'

'Well . . . only that he has a son, Vincent, who works closely with him in the business.'

'Yes, Vincent, dear Vincent, who has given his all to his father . . . yet hardly gets a mention in praise.' Jean-Paul looked sharply, directly at Georges. 'But what you probably didn't know is that Art has another son, Paul, and a daughter, Mia. Okay, Mia has never really come into the frame – she's now at some college doing a fashion photography course, and there's no expectation in any case on women coming into the family business. But what about Paul? He's never in the news like Vincent, because he's not involved in the family business – he's at Annapolis with the Navy – but listening to Art you'd think that Paul was his only son. Paul this, Paul that. Paul could be a Navy commander one day, did you know? He says it with such pride in his voice, as if that was the only thing of real importance to him. Totally ignoring the fact that his other son will one day run a multi-million-dollar crime empire and continue his legacy, each and every day risking a bullet through the head for the privilege. And why, why?' Jean-Paul threw his hand towards Georges as if he was flinging dice. 'Why is he so blinkered, with eyes only for one son?'

'I don't know.' Georges shrugged, easier now that Jean-Paul had found his flow, but still unsure where it was all heading.

'Because he's the son that's managed to escape and make his own way, find some success outside of the family business.' Jean-Paul sat back down and looked thoughtfully into his brandy glass. 'Oh sure, everyone looks at people like Vito and Art as the tough guys, the wise guys – but it never gets any easier. They start tough, no question: confronting longshoremen with bill-hooks and Union strong-arms wielding baseball bats, getting their first blood, then later more killings over turf or to rise up the ranks – some of it hands-on, having to pull a wire through a man's neck – but it never gets any easier.' Jean-Paul relaxed open the hand he'd clenched suddenly tight. 'Because as the money rolls in, their private lives become softer: they move out of their old neighbourhood, buy a house with a pool and a gardener, their wives get their hair done each week and have private fitness and yoga instructors, and their kids go to college and get an education. Suddenly the mean streets where it all started become but a distant memory. And with all that, when they sit back and look around them' – Jean-Paul waved his hand in a half-circle – 'it starts to hit them as ludicrous that they should still fear getting the wrong side of a bullet, still have to look over their shoulders.' The hand pulled back in and Jean-Paul shrugged. 'Sure, they themselves probably accept that fear of a bullet, they've lived with it from day one as part of the package, the "territory". But they start to expect something better for their family. For them, they want that fear gone; they don't want them to have to live the same way they have. That's why Art was so outraged about what happened to Pascal – because Pascal was never really involved in the business; he was just on the fringes doing some bookkeeping. If his music career had been more successful, he wouldn't even have done that. So Art saw him as someone on the edge who *almost* escaped – but never quite made it. Still they got him. Art was outraged because he felt that if they could do that – they were only a step away from yanking Paul from Annapolis and putting a bullet through his head. And the golden rule has always been hands off family outside of the business. That's why when Art intervened with the Cacchiones, the white flag came up so quickly. They'd broken the rules and knew it.' He swilled his brandy and took a quick slug. 'Though by then it was too late for Pascal.'

'I understand.' Georges cast his eyes down for a second. Though it was more the general ethos he understood: he had no idea until now that Giacomelli had taken such a personal interest in Pascal's death because of how it might relate to his own family.

Jean-Paul forced a wan, philosophical smile. 'The only problem is, it's not so simple: fate, circumstance get in the way. Sometimes the kids don't do so well at college, or they show a natural leaning towards the business, or, like Vincent, they start getting into trouble with other things; and the parents think, if they're going to go down that route anyway, they might at least do it professionally, in an organized way. But what starts to form in the parents' minds is a black-and-white yardstick: the successes escape; the failures with little or no choice – despite all the education and privilege heaped on them to keep them away – end up in the family business. That's why Art talks all the time about Paul, with hardly a word for Vincent.'

Georges nodded. He recalled Jean-Paul once consoling Jon Larsen, who was upset that his son had dropped his law studies to pursue a career in palaeontology, telling him that even Carlo Gambino's children hadn't followed him into the business, one of them opting for the radically different, unmacho world of dress design. *'Gambino didn't fight against it, because he knew at heart his children wouldn't be right for it. That's why John Gotti was nurtured to finally take over after Castellano: he came from the same mean streets as Gambino, his edge hadn't been softened by two generations of money and education.'*

'But then you get all the times when it's not so black and white – all the grey areas like Pascal and me, where we end up in the business by default. Pascal because our father found out his bookkeeper was cheating him, and he needed someone he knew he could trust for a while before getting someone new.' Jean-Paul shrugged. 'Though Pascal ended up staying much longer. And me because he feared that Roman wouldn't have the right acumen for the business, or temperament – that he was far too headstrong. And then of course what happened with Pascal ended up supporting that judgement.' He waved his brandy glass. 'You know that my father partly blamed Roman for Pascal?'

'Yes, I know.' They'd touched on the subject before, but never in such depth or so heartfelt. The only emotional plea ever put to him had been when Jean-Paul and Jon Larsen first persuaded him to join the fold, explaining why this bid to clean the business was so vital, so close to the family's heart. It wasn't just a passing whim. And suddenly Georges realized why Jean-Paul was covering it all now: something *was* wrong, was concerning him, and he was testing his loyalty. But was it just a suspicion, or had Jean-Paul heard about Chenouda hauling him in? Which way to play it?

'So hopefully now you can see why cleaning this business is so important, not just to me but so many others like Art Giacomelli. A possible solution for the generations to come, aside from them simply having to step outside of the family business to get their father's approval. Because the problem is not really with them, but with the nature of the business. And the fact that nobody wants to leave a legacy to their children that might end up getting them killed.'

Georges laid one hand flat on the smooth polished table to stop it trembling. *Which way to play it?* Jean-Paul had circled in so well. Georges had always felt the terrible burden of this commitment, the fear of letting Jean-Paul down when he knew how much it all meant personally to him . . . that burden growing by the day with his withheld secret. Then had come the knowledge that their progress was suddenly of interest to other leading crime families, bets and prejudgements were being made on each side; but at least he'd been able to view all that at one step removed from the fray. Now suddenly it was of *personal* interest to Art Giacomelli. He wouldn't just be letting down Jean-Paul, but also America's most powerful crime boss. It was as if Jean-Paul had purposely chosen this factor as the perfect extra pressure to apply. He moved his hand to trace one finger around the base of his brandy glass, his brow creasing: measured concern.

'I knew how important this was to you from the outset, though I must admit I didn't know that it was also something so close to Giacomelli's heart. I thought he was just a good friend and interested observer, nothing more.' He chose his words carefully, sensing that he was tiptoeing through a minefield. 'But my commitment was made on what *I* think about that aim, not anyone else. If I didn't believe wholeheartedly in it and see it as a challenge, I wouldn't have joined you – it's as simple as that. And that commitment remains as strong now as on day one.'

Jean-Paul slowly nodded in understanding. He proffered one palm towards Georges. 'It's just that sometimes it can be difficult joining a family like this. It's easy to feel like an outsider, as if there's nobody you can confide in.'

Confide in. Now there was little doubt remaining. 'Yes . . . I know.' He swallowed hard; his collar felt suddenly tight, a hot flush rising up through his neck to his face. 'And at first, I must admit that was difficult. Particularly given the close relationship you have with Roman: I had the feeling that I might be somehow interfering, coming between you by changing the direction of the business.'

'And now?' Jean-Paul opened out both palms: a priest welcoming confession.

Georges swallowed hard again, a light sweat coming to his brow. It was as if he'd been steadily pushed in a corner with each word-domino played by Jean-Paul. He'd been expecting 'So if you ever feel the need to confide in anyone, don't forget I'm always here for you.' But instead Jean-Paul had done it with just two words; two words as that final feather on the scale to hopefully make him crumble, the burden of his betrayal suddenly too much. But it would be conveniently trite just to blurt everything out and turn turtle on what he'd struggled to avoid all along – setting brother against brother – and it would likely come across as little more than a desperate cheap shot under pressure. And what if he was reading the whole thing wrong, just getting paranoid, and this little heart-to-heart was completely innocent, had simply been prompted by Jean-Paul's recent visit to Giacomelli? But if he said nothing or got the tone wrong, Chenouda's warning could soon hold frighteningly true: Jean-Paul's protection would quickly evaporate and he'd be out in the cold, at Roman's mercy. He traced the same finger back and forth again by his brandy glass – which way to play it? . . . *which way?* – before looking back directly at Jean-Paul, the right words finally in place.

Within twenty-four hours they had all the answers to the information Georges had provided.

Jean-Paul had phoned Roman minutes after Georges' leaving. Roman'd been expecting the call, so after the initial impatient 'So? What did he say?' he merely listened, his breath falling shallow over the line as Jean-Paul ran through Georges' account of events.

Yes, Georges had admitted that he'd been confronted by Chenouda and had to go downtown with him, but he said nothing had happened. 'Chenouda apparently suspects that you had something to do with Savard's death, and he had a tape to play because Savard was wired for sound the night he was abducted. Georges said he only listened to part of the tape before he started screaming for a lawyer. They pumped him some more questions about that night with Leduc, things apparently passed on by Savard – but he claims he said nothing and shouted again for a lawyer. They kept him alone in a holding room for another twenty minutes or so, then let him go.'

'How long did he say they kept him?'

'Just over an hour, maybe an hour and a half.'

'No, it was over three hours. My guy doesn't make mistakes. Donatien isn't telling you the whole picture. And why didn't he tell you all this before?'

'He says that he was nervous about coming between us, has been from day one. He wanted to sit on the information for a few days, perhaps get some advice from Jon Larsen before confiding. Particularly given Chenouda's claim that you had a meeting arranged with Savard the night he was abducted.' Jean-Paul left a marked silence, making clear the gravity of this information.

Roman had known that this could come out and had prepared well; having been caught on a RCMP video, he couldn't deny it. 'Sure, I had a meet with Savard earlier the night he was killed, for which he didn't show. I mentioned to Frank at the time that it was strange, but it wasn't the sort of thing worth troubling you with. Tony was still working protection in Lavalle, and with our club there I'd meet up with him sometimes twice a month.' Roman sensed faint clinging doubt from the pause at the other end. 'Come on! If I'm going to take Tony out, I've got opportunities every day and week to do it quietly, without anyone knowing. You think I'm going to do it knowing that Tony's wired and a pack of Mounties are looking on? No, the Cacchiones are behind it: perhaps they even knew through Savard we had a meet and set it up to make us look bad. And Chenouda's fallen for it, because he's desperate – and so now he puts pressure on our weak spot: Donatien.'

'Could be . . . but I take your point about such an open move.'

Roman sensed the advantage and decided to push a bit more. 'I mean, you know, Donatien is so concerned about not coming between us, and then the first opportunity he does just that – he starts speaking out of school about me.'

'No, he was quite reluctant to talk . . . I had to press him. He kept saying, you really should be talking to Roman about all this, not me.'

'Yeah, well, you're talking to me about it now, and you know what I think – the guy's full of shit.'

They agreed that not much more could be done until Jean-Paul could check with Georges' PA, Jacqueline, just how long he was actually away from the office the morning in question. Roman was sitting the other side of Jean-Paul's desk when the call was made first thing the next morning.

After prompting 'Are you sure?' halfway through, Jean-Paul related pensively that she thought it had been 'about an hour and a half'.

'She's lying, or she's mistaken,' Roman fired back, and in response to Jean-Paul's quizzically raised eyebrow he fell silently thoughtful for a second before coming up with the suggestion of checking with some of Donatien's regular callers.

They came up with six names and split the list between them. Three hadn't called at all that morning; one couldn't remember whether he had or not; but from the remaining two they ascertained that Donatien was out 'about nine-fifteen, nine-twenty', and again at 11.30 a.m.

It could have been two separate occasions that Donatien was out, so they decided to visit the building after office hours and get security to run through the video tapes for that morning. As chairman of Santoine International, Jean-Paul explained to the guard that he feared a breach of security might have taken place. 'Two police officers came that morning and left with Monsieur Donatien. We need to see what time he returned.'

It took almost half an hour to run through the tapes on visual fast-forward. They quickly found the point where Chenouda and another officer entered the building and left with Donatien seventeen minutes later, the timer in the top right corner showing 8.36 a.m. as the guard slowed the tape again. Then came the more tedious trawl for him returning, involving checking the basement garage cameras as well, just in case he'd come back in that way. They finally found what they were looking for: Donatien walking back in through the foyer with a glimpse in the background of the same unmarked grey car he'd left in earlier, the timer now showing 12.09 p.m.; Chenouda wasn't in evidence this time, but judging from the profile of the car's front passenger the accompanying officer was the same as before.

Jean-Paul closed his eyes for a second as the grainy grey images registered. *Three and a half hours!* Georges had lied to him. 'Thanks,' he muttered to the guard.

'You've got to do something about it,' Roman pressed as they walked from the building.

'I know, I know.' Jean-Paul kept up the same brisk pace slightly ahead of Roman, not wanting him to see the pain of betrayal in his eyes, that he was close to tears. 'But this isn't a decision I can take lightly. I need overnight to sleep on it, work out what to do. We'll talk again in the morning.'

Georges looked out over the lights of Montreal from his penthouse: the dark expanse of Mount Royal to his left, a snaking stretch of the St Lawrence to his right – slim ribbons of reflected light punctuating its inky blackness – with the band of downtown lights in between spreading wider and sparser into the distance.

His body was shivering, even though the heating was set at 22°C, his eyes darting, roaming the city's skyscrapers, as if they might provide the answer to his problems and tell him what he should do next. He wished Simone would call back. He was aware that she had a dinner function for a client launch this evening and he'd left two messages now; surely she'd know that he wouldn't have forgotten her meeting and wouldn't be bothering her now unless it was urgent. All she had to do was steal two minutes away. Two minutes.

He relaxed his clenched hands, breathed deeply, tried to ease his tension. He was convinced his salvation now lay with her: to spill all to Jon Larsen wouldn't sit right after his meeting with Jean-Paul, only somebody emotionally close would do; so emotionally close that it wouldn't seem strange sharing with them all the awkward details that he'd shied away from with Jean-Paul.

But what he felt the crushing need for most now was quick action: his explanation to Jean-Paul had only been a halfway house, a stop-gap. And caught on the hop like that, and with Jean-Paul pressing, he'd said much more than he'd have liked. He couldn't admit that he was with Chenouda for three hours given what little he claimed had passed between them; so he'd said only an hour or so and covered himself with a call to Jacqueline at her home straight afterwards.

Maybe he was worrying about nothing. Maybe Jean-Paul would, as he'd suggested, talk to Roman about it, Roman would say something that didn't quite fit, and any shadow of doubt would fall more on Roman than himself. But, as his eyes cannoned between the buildings, measuring the various angles and potential problems, he saw more ways that the chips would fall wrong for him.

Perhaps, once he'd spoken to Simone and the dust had settled, he'd head to his parents for the weekend. But was that guilt because his workload had kept him from seeing them for almost three months, or a reaction to him feeling shunned by the Lacaille clan, left out? He should have known from the start that seeing in Jean-Paul some sort of replacement father figure to make up for his father's shortcomings had the potential for disaster, would only complicate his deep-rooted feelings about family: fear now that once again he was being deserted, the backs of those he held fond were again turning away, just when –

The ringing phone crashed abruptly into his thoughts. He crossed the room hurriedly and grabbed the receiver before the second ring. 'Yes?'

'Georges . . . Simone. I got your message.' Background clatter of voices, plates and cutlery, muted music. Simone was struggling to be heard above it. 'They're deep into the thank-you speeches now – hopefully nobody will miss me for a few moments. What's the problem?'

'I've got to see you. Something's happened, and I need to talk to you about it urgently. Can you come by here afterwards?'

'I . . . I don't know. I've got a real splitter here . . .' Her voice faded for a second, the clatter taking over. 'Can't you tell me over the phone?'

'No. This isn't the sort of thing that can be done over the phone. We need to sit face to face.'

A moment's pause, then Simone's voice came hesitantly: 'Not a problem with me . . . with us, is it, Georges?'

'No, no . . . nothing like that. It's a problem I might have with your father and Roman.'

Less marked pause this time. 'Let's meet tomorrow, please . . . I couldn't hack it tonight. If I make it through this, all I'm looking forward to is some hot cocoa and bed.'

'Yeah, okay . . . okay. Tomorrow, then.' Simone only had a half-hour free at lunch, and Georges was sure it would take longer than that, so they agreed on dinner at Thursday's on Rue Crescent. 'Eight-thirty table. I'll book it and pick you up at eight.'

'Yeah, great . . . see you then. Love you.' A light-blown kiss quickly swallowed by the clatter, and she was gone.

174

Georges let out a slow, tired exhalation as he hung up. So, he'd have to wait twenty-four hours. He'd waited a year to finally bare his soul; given that perspective it hardly seemed to matter. Nothing much was going to happen between now and then.

'Georges . . . Simone. I got your message. They're deep into the thank-you speeches now – hopefully nobody will miss me for a few moments. What's the problem?'

'I've got to see you. Something's happened, and I need to talk to you about it urgently. Can you come by here afterwards?'

Funicelli sat forward with the urgency in Donatien's voice as the tape rolled. Donatien sounded troubled. Funicelli had to tweak the sound up to fully hear Simone's voice above the background clatter. He hoped that the problem might be explained, especially when Donatien commented that it was to do with her father and Roman – but everything ended abruptly with their arranging to meet. All he could do was pass it on. Maybe Roman would know what was troubling Donatien.

Roman got the tape by messenger at 8.12 a.m. the next morning, and wished that Funicelli had phoned him immediately the evening before. Funicelli's covering note mentioned the call from Simone and Donatien sounding worried: *'Maybe you know what might be worrying him?'* But obviously any attached urgency hadn't immediately dawned on Funicelli. The one drawback of always making sure the people around you only had half the picture.

And while Roman knew all too well what was troubling Donatien, with his meeting with Simone taking place in a restaurant, there was no chance of finding out exactly what was going to be said. He'd just have to fill in the gaps himself.

He remembered a maid that his mother Lillian had shortly after his father died. She would move objects around in the room as she cleaned, and some of them would get progressively closer to the door. Then, next thing, they would disappear completely. It was as if the maid wasn't quite bold enough to steal them straight away, but once they got closer to the door they became *almost* hers; the next step wasn't so bold.

That's what Donatien was doing: moving his story closer to the door. He hadn't wanted to tell all to Jean-Paul, perhaps hoping naively that yours truly, Roman, would meanwhile have a sudden stab of conscience and do it all for him. But first and foremost, no doubt, was the awkwardness of Donatien admitting at the drop of a hat that he'd been lying to Jean-Paul for the past year. All trust went out the window either way, and coming hot on the heels of him keeping quiet about meeting Chenouda as well, there were high chances Jean-Paul would have had doubts about both stories. No, he'd read Georges well.

He had little doubt now that Georges was going to tell all to Simone, unburden all the messy details he'd been unable to reveal to her father and use her as go-between. She would be able to explain all the subtle reasons why Georges had lied for so long, in a way that would be difficult for Georges himself to do directly.

Roman closed his eyes for a second and bit at his lip. A faint sheen of sweat glistened on his forehead as he opened them again and glanced at his watch: just over an hour to know the outcome of Jean-Paul's deliberations; twelve hours before Donatien passed the ticking bomb to Simone. How long before Simone in turn passed it to her father? A day, two days at most. He'd have to move quickly.

If Jean-Paul didn't sanction a move on Donatien straight away, he'd have to make his own plans before the day was out. And he knew now that those plans would have to include Simone as well, or he'd have to think of a way whereby her voice would be ignored, would have no potency.

14

'I'm sorry, so sorry . . . I just didn't know how to tell you at the time.' Elena shook her head. There were no tears left now: she'd cried them all out during the day, ruined two sets of make-up.

'But you could have told me.' Gordon held one hand out, as if clutching for an invisible explanation in the air. 'I thought we could admit anything, confess anything to each other. I thought we had that sort of relationship. Obviously I was wrong.' He hovered the wine glass in his other hand close to his lips, then he put it down firmly. He'd drunk four glasses during dinner and the hour while waiting for the kids to go to bed, and was now most of the way through a fifth. Although it had adequately dulled and mellowed his mood, which is what he'd wanted, he sensed that it was starting to make him confrontational: not what he wanted. After twelve years of secrets and silence over this, the last thing he needed was for Elena to become defensive and clam up, retreat back into her shell. 'I'm sorry . . . I didn't mean that. I just need to know, that's all . . . I just need to know.'

Elena was stung by the pathetic plea in his voice. She'd run an emotional sword straight through the man who most loved and trusted her, a sword she'd worked inch by inch through his guts the past twelve years without him knowing, and all he wanted to know was *why?*

Gordon's only retaliation had been to leave her alone all day to dwell on the bombshell problem. He'd received the folder in the early-morning post and dumped it in front of her half an hour later. 'I've already read through it. I'm going out now to see clients. Perhaps you'd like to explain it all to me when I get back.' His tone and his sharp stare made her realize immediately that it was no light problem. But Gordon hadn't returned until the kids came home from school, Elena thought on purpose, so they'd moved around each other like two awkward bantam cocks, avoiding eye contact and with conversation kept to curt, abrupt comment when absolutely unavoidable – until after the children had gone to bed. Hardly a virulent payback: a day's awkwardness to compensate for twelve years of deception. And already there was no fight left in him. He just wanted to know.

She started with what Gordon did know about her background and her past rift with her father: the years in Marrakesh and in hippie communes and squats when she returned to England, the drug busts, the demonstration marches. The years of rebelliousness not just against her father, but all he stood for. 'That was all that appeared on the surface. The visible symptoms of the root problem.'

Gordon looked at her aslant. 'Are you saying that perhaps I should have known – or guessed – that something else was wrong from all of that?'

'No . . . no.' She shook her head vehemently. 'How were you to know? I wouldn't have been the first rich kid to rebel against establishment parents. In the sixties, it was practically mandatory.' She forced a wan smile. But she sensed she wasn't going to get far fluffing around the edges: the only way she was going to get through this was by going back to the beginning. Back to her pregnancy at fifteen and how she'd come close to death twice within a month.

'His name was Michael Tierney. We were very much in love – such as love is when you're only fifteen. At the time it seemed all-consuming. He was all I cared about. He had wavy dark hair and the most incredible blue eyes, and at nineteen he seemed to me so adult and masterful, so in control.' *Greeting her at the door for their second date with a single white rose and a Theodorakis instrumental of 'The White Rose of Athens'.* 'He was caring, romantic – rare, I suppose, for that age, looking back now – and had one of those easy smiles that made you feel warm, alive.

'My father hated him on sight. Too smooth, too smarmy by half. When pressed, my father said that he just didn't trust him, "didn't think his intentions were good". Though I suspected – and probably my mother too if you could *ever* have got her to speak out against my father on anything – that it was more to do with Michael's family background. Only two things counted for my father: serious money and status within British society. Michael's father had a successful landscape gardening business, but it fell far short of where my father had set his sights by then, and his nationality too was a drawback.'

Elena noticed Gordon look quizzical for a moment, not fully grasping, and she went on to explain about her father's early days in England and the discrimination he'd suffered, both shielded and overt.

How even at the stage he'd built up a successful import trading business, he was still refused membership of the local golf club. 'Don't forget it was the fifties, and minds were narrower then. But those memories rankled deeply with my father; that's why later he completely anglicized his name and buried his Greek Cypriot background: to feel accepted, part of British society. Apart from the transformation into Anthony George, he wore tweed and herringbone, tried to play the perfect English gent as seen on a Pearl & Dean advert.' Elena smiled wryly. 'And because Michael's family were Irish, my father saw them as only one rung above the Cypriots in British societal acceptance. It just wasn't enough for him by then.'

Gordon still looked vaguely puzzled. 'But why was that all so important? You were only fifteen – you could have been looking ahead to scores of different boyfriends over the years before getting close to finding the right one.'

'The pregnancy. The pregnancy was what made it so important right there and then. If Michael had fitted the bill more, my father might have pressed him to marry me, do the right thing. But instead it quickly became I-told-you-so time: "I told you he was no good."'

Gordon nodded knowingly. 'So that was the abortion?'

'Yes. But I lied about everything else about it – not only to you, but everyone else at the time. Which is what caused most of the problems. You see, it was nine weeks before my sixteenth birthday when my period didn't come, and I hoped first of all that it was something else. Then the second month, and still I didn't say anything. I was desperately fearful of my father's reaction not just for myself, but by then for Michael as well: I knew that if my father discovered I'd conceived under-age, he'd have been blind with fury, would have probably called the police and had Michael locked up. So I bluffed and kept quiet about it until after my sixteenth birthday – though the first point I could have worried I was pregnant then from missing my period wasn't until about seven weeks after. The earliest date of possible conception I proposed was ten days after my sixteenth birthday – which was when I claimed I'd first had sex with Michael. I said that we'd been together only twice since. But instead of trying to get the "poor girl has just been unlucky" sympathy vote, I should have been more concerned about that three-month lie – because it almost ended up costing me my life.'

Elena watched Gordon's eyes cloud and glance down for a moment:

some sympathy at last, thirty years later. Elena took a hasty gulp of wine and shook her head.

'You know, nobody actually asked me if I wanted an abortion. I've never seen a family rally round so fast – all of them talking and arguing about what to do as if I wasn't there, had no say in the matter. Only Uncle Christos boldly ventured that I should be asked what I wanted, but he was shouted down – mainly by my father, with everyone else just numbly going along, too afraid to go against him. Single mothers were social lepers in those days, Michael wasn't suitable, so it was the only remaining option: a quick, quiet abortion. The whole matter quickly swept away and forgotten.' Elena waved one hand as if she was swatting a fly, her eyes filling. She closed them tight for a second.

'Oh God, I was so frightened. I knew nothing, read nothing, was so young and naive – and even my closest girlfriends I didn't confide in because I feared the secret would get out. And for the same reason my father didn't have any tests done that might have revealed that I was lying about the date I conceived. All he did was arrange a back-street Kilburn butcher – and lead me there by the hand a month later.' *Looking across and recalling that the last time her father had held her hand like that was five years earlier at a fairground, leading her safely on to one of the rides.* The welling tears spilt over, started running down Elena's cheeks. She dabbed at them with the back of one hand. 'He thought I was only two and a half, three months pregnant – but I was already almost six months gone.'

She glanced at the light glinting off a lone knife and spoon left on the table after dinner. *Instruments glinting on a white cloth. The cold press of the Formica table against her back. Staring up at a bright fluorescent striplight that washed in and out of focus.* 'It was all decided in those twenty minutes: the die cast on practically my whole life. I remember the doctor giving the abortion – if indeed he was a doctor – had a faint Irish lilt. And I remember wondering, looking back on it all, if that was all part of my father's cruel humour: "an Irishman to give it to you, another to take it away".'

Elena smiled crookedly, but Gordon could see that it was just a weak attempt at relief from the descent into hell at play behind her eyes.

She shook her head. 'But at the time I was too numbed, too frightened to think anything. The abortionist realized halfway through that he was dealing with a fully developed baby rather than something hardly beyond a foetus – but by then it was already too late, the damage was done. My water had broken and I was bleeding heavily from a ruptured womb.' *Blood running off the table, droplets starting to splatter rapidly against the linoleum floor. The doctor shouting frantic instructions to her father for fresh instruments, swabs, fresh towels, water.*

'There was a suspended moment between my father and the doctor when my father said, "Do something with him." And after a moment the doctor very slowly and deliberately stated that he merely stopped babies being born, he didn't kill them. The main problem by then was with me, the doctor reminded him: if I didn't get urgent attention, I could die. And perhaps to appease what he thought was a dire concern of my father's, he added that born so prematurely it was unlikely the baby would survive in any case. We couldn't go to a hospital, too many questions would be asked – so he rang ahead to a colleague in Swiss Cottage, a doctor with a fully equipped surgery who dealt with a lot of "quiet" pregnancies for Arab and foreign clients.'

Elena closed her eyes for a moment. Her voice trembled with the effort of biting back the tears to get the words out. 'You know, that was the first moment, holding him in my arms on that four-mile drive, that it hit me what I'd done.' *Streetlights flashing in rapid bars across his tiny, bloodied body, his eyes struggling to open and see against the piercing strobe effect.* 'Call that moment maternal bonding or what you will – but it hit me then that it was a life. A life that was a part of me and I'd tried to get rid of. My life-blood was fast flowing away over the seat of my father's new Mercedes –' That crooked smile again which didn't quite make it – 'But all I could think of in that instant was him. Willing him with every ounce of me to stay alive, and too numbed, beaten up and washed out to care about myself any more.

'And as I hugged him close, my father fired me a strange look that I just couldn't read: anger at the nightmare I'd caused, still wishing my baby dead, or anger at seeing me so close to someone else? A closeness I'd never really had with him? But I remember thinking: thank God it's not me driving and him holding the baby. A horrible, creepy feeling that he might have smothered or strangled it en route.

'Four days in an incubator and little Christos – that's what I'd decided to call him by then – survived, as did I.' Elena waved an arm dismissively and shivered, as if someone had laid a cold hand on the back of her neck. 'Except for that part of me that would never again be able to have children.

'I wanted to keep him . . . Oh God, I wanted to keep him – but again I was given no voice in the matter. I was too young, had my whole life ahead of me, didn't have a husband. My father made the running, and the rest of the family quickly supported him: he was going for adoption. I was still too numbed with it all – and in any case felt it would have done little good – to even trouble to fight back. But as those plans became set in stone, that feeling of powerlessness and a terrible sense of loss and desolation at what I'd done gripped me hard. I felt totally worthless: that with him gone, there could be nothing good ahead anyway, even if I could face another day, or myself, with what I'd done. I tried to take my life, emptied half a bottle of aspirins from a bathroom cabinet down my throat. My mother found me, my stomach was pumped . . . once again I made it.' Elena tapped her chest and fired a brief sardonic smile. 'Either God was watching over me . . . or more likely he wanted to keep me alive because he had a much longer, more fitting punishment in store. That would have been too easy a way out.'

Elena cradled her forehead for a second before running her hand roughly through her hair. She took a quick sip of wine. 'But at least when I came around, I'd found my voice: I wanted to keep him! My father fought me every inch: papers are already done, cut and dried. Then he brought up the suicide to get a court ruling that I was unstable, unfit to be a mother. Finally, he said that if I fought him any more over it, he'd have Michael charged with having sex with a minor and put away. I dropped it, didn't even trouble to turn up for the final ruling – I knew already what it would say. But having seen the fight I'd put up, and perhaps fearing that I'd change my mind again in a few months, my father vowed that he'd bury him out of reach and out of sight. I'd never find him.' She traced one finger absently across the tablecloth. 'And looks like he was right. I never could win the day against my father . . . and now it's much the same with Ryall. Powerful men: blight of my life.' Elena grimaced tightly and looked down for a second before looking back directly at Gordon. 'But at least you now know why there was such antipathy between me and my father. Why I rebelled against him so all those years.'

Silence as she finished, crushing silence: she could practically hear Gordon swallow as he tried to marshal his thoughts and some composure in order to meet her gaze with equal steadiness.

After a moment, she added pensively: 'I suppose there might have been some sort of tame reconciliation later if it wasn't for Andreos' suicide. I blamed my father mostly for that too – always pushing towards this perfect picture of what *he* thought everyone should be doing with their lives. But nothing was ever good enough for him.' She bit at her bottom lip and lightly shook her head. 'After all, who could live up to the great Anthony George?'

Gordon merely nodded, the stifling silence returning. 'You could have told me,' he said at length. 'I'd have understood.'

'Could I? . . . *Could I?*' She saw him flinch under the feverish intensity of her stare and look away again, suddenly not so sure. 'This wasn't just about *you* not knowing, Gordon, it was about everyone not knowing – but most especially me. Because if I had to admit what had happened to anyone, I'd have also had to admit it to myself. And before you know it, I'd have been back in the bathroom, swallowing another bottle of pills. And so I buried it: buried the thought, buried the memory, buried *everything*. It never happened.'

She rubbed her left temple, her brow furrowing. 'The years in Marrakesh and in hippie communes weren't just to seriously piss off my father – it was all part of the oblivion, the forgetting. Then eleven years later I woke up in a Camden Town squat lying partly in somebody else's vomit, having lost a flatmate just the month before from an OD, and trying to fight my way through an LSD haze to work out if the pattern on the wall ahead was wallpaper or just in my mind – and finally said enough. *Enough!* I realized then that I was punishing myself more than my father – he'd probably given up caring long ago. And meanwhile I wasn't making good on what I'd done: no amends were being made. That's when I cleaned up my act and started working with Uncle Christos. Then a few years later we met, married and started adopting – which was how I felt I could possibly make amends.'

'Uncle Christos to the rescue again.' Gordon raised his glass, but it lacked any exuberance: the mire of abortions, attempted suicides, lost children and lost years, clung too heavy in the air for even a trace of a smile. 'Was it always him that helped you?' Gordon remembered her telling him that during the years in the hippie wilderness, Uncle Christos sent bits and pieces of money. Her father had set up a trust fund for her, but she refused to touch it on principle – so Uncle Christos had stepped in.

'Yes, pretty much. You know, my father was annoyed even that I wanted to name the baby Christos. He protested: "You only name children after dead relatives."' A fleeting wry grin curled her mouth. 'There was always this rivalry between them, mostly coming from my father's side: "If Christos had done this, if Christos had done that – he could have been as successful as me." But my father seemed to have missed the point completely. Uncle Christos was too laid back to be bothered to compete. He didn't want to be a big shot like my father, didn't have the first inclination to be ruthless or determined like him. And when I saw those qualities as endearing, started to see Uncle Christos as a father figure – that incensed my father even further. He couldn't stomach it – or maybe he truly couldn't comprehend it – but he used to rub the salt in all the more about Uncle Christos being a failure.'

She looked at her glass and tapped its rim, as if prompting herself. 'So making amends became the thing. We adopted, named him Christos, and though for a while everything was fine – it still wasn't enough. So when he was old enough, I joined the agency . . . to see how many children I could make happy after the child's life I might have destroyed – my *own* child's.' Elena gripped the stem of her glass tight. Her eyes were watering again.

Gordon wanted to reach across to grip her hand, assure her that everything was all right. He understood. But her other hand was clenched tight against her, and with her still caught up in the throes of her confession, her body trembling slightly, his reaching all the way across would have felt like he was imposing, invading her space. He felt frustrated, inadequate. A decade of secrets stripped away between them, and he couldn't reach across to bridge that final gap of the tabletop.

Elena shrugged helplessly. 'But still it wasn't enough. I had to save one of those children myself . . . so we adopted young Katine. Still something missing, a need there – and the only thing that helped fill it was each child I saw successfully placed with a happy family. Because each one told me that the son I'd given up had probably gone to a good family somewhere: he'd been happy, had had a good life. And I was doing fine . . .' Elena smiled awkwardly. She was suddenly reminded of a line from an old Bill Cosby routine about doin' fine, only then his eyeballs started bleeding. The thought seemed so ridiculously out of place that she burst out with a nervous laugh; but it went awry, became a half-laugh, half-cry, her muttered 'until . . .' on a fractured breath barely out before her face contorted, the build-up of her emotions in the end too much. Her shoulders sagged as if a load had been laid across them and her head dipped as she sank into uncontrollable sobbing.

That brought Gordon around to hug and console her, though still he felt inadequate: it had taken the submission of his wife's tears for him to be able to cross that last distance between them: it wasn't that noble.

He held her a moment more, trying to savour the fact that now, finally, there were no more secrets between them; but apart from her body quaking with crushing emotional distress, it felt no different from all the other times he'd embraced her.

He made fresh coffee for them both – always Gordon's solution in times of trouble, Elena thought wryly, wiping back her tears: make tea or coffee – poured a Bailey's for her and a Glenfiddich for himself, and she told him the rest: how Lorena's problems with Ryall had broken down the wall she'd long built up and set her on her search of the past ten days which now too, like her help mission for Lorena, had hit a dead end.

'Until Ryall, I'd always told myself that my son was probably in a good home somewhere, happy. And each child I saw successfully placed reaffirmed that. Then with Ryall it hit me that no matter how secure and happy-looking that home might be on the surface, all kinds of horrors could be lurking beneath. And suddenly I had to know. I had to know what kind of life he'd had. Whether he *had* been happy, or whether I'd abandoned him to a wolves' den, a living hell.'

Gordon thought of venturing how that might help: if he'd had a bad life, how she'd even begin to make up for it. But that basic desire to find a long-lost son he knew rose above all else: rationalizing wouldn't help. And besides, the possibility of ever finding him now seemed gone, chapter closed – so in the end all he said was, 'I understand . . .' Then after a moment he shook his head. 'You know, I should have known . . . should have at least guessed. All the signs were there.' The depth of antipathy towards her father, the lame story – now in retrospect – of her not being able to have children due to an early horse-riding accident, the aid agency, the adoptions . . . She'd held up a giant route map in front of his face, and he'd hardly noticed.

'How could you have known?' She raised an eyebrow, sensing that he was just saying it to make her feel good, to take the brunt off the fact that she'd held all of this secret throughout their marriage, deceived him. 'I'd buried it even from myself, so everyone else was a step further removed. They couldn't get there until I got there first.' As she saw the acceptance slowly filter through in Gordon's eyes, she looked away again, fixing blankly, distantly ahead.

Gordon came and snuggled close again. He felt her breath against the hollow of his neck and slowly closed his eyes. She'd finally got there, and now didn't know where to head next. The route map had finished in two dead ends. And he wished he could think of some bright, snappy answer to buoy her spirits.

Because while the barrier of twelve years of secrets between them had suddenly gone, the son that she would now never be able to find again had as quickly taken its place. While that stayed unresolved, he knew that a part of her would remain distant, out of reach. The barrier would continue, having lifted only briefly for those few moments of her pouring out her heart to him – before crashing back down again. Like some cruel magician's trick.

15

'You just don't seem to grasp the seriousness of this.' Roman threw his right hand towards Jean-Paul as if he was tossing dice. His hand gestures had become increasingly volatile as their arguing hit fever pitch.

'Yes, I do.' Jean-Paul's eyes stayed fixed hard on Roman, had only shifted at moments as their voices rose, as if concerned others might hear beyond his office walls. 'More than obviously you appreciate. But what I don't want to do is throw everything away, everything we've worked long and hard towards these past three years – over a two-minute panic.'

'He could destroy us, Jean-Paul. And yeah, that's all it takes – two minutes. Two minutes with the wrong thing said. But he was there fucking hours, and he lied to you about it. And that might be just the tip of the iceberg, who knows what else . . .'

'Enough . . . *Enough!*' Jean-Paul held one hand up. 'We went through this chapter and verse yesterday. I thought hard on it over-night, and I've made my decision. I'm not going to rake over the same ground now.' Jean-Paul moved the letter-opener used for that morning's mail to one side. 'Besides, this isn't just about you, me and the remnants of our past activities. Georges is practically family. There's Simone to consider, and our mother too holds great fondness for him. There'd be a lot of people hurt if we made the wrong move on this.'

'I know.' Roman looked down, bracing his right hand on his thigh as if to forcibly stop it from gesturing wildly. 'But that could be part of the problem right there. You know, that was always our father's main worry with you: that when it came to the crunch, you might shy away from strong action. That the more reasonable, diplomatic route would one day not be the right route to go. This could be that crunch time now, Jean-Paul, and you're too blindsided with Simone and family to be able to make the right move.'

'That's as may be.' Jean-Paul shrugged: impatient, as if he'd only half-registered the remark or wished to give it scant relevance. 'We just can't be sure yet – which is my main point. And why for the moment I think we should –'

'I mean, if you've got a problem with that, you don't need to say it straight out. The fact that it's *your* daughter puts you in a predicament, but not necessarily the rest of us. Just silently nod or close your eyes for a second – and I'll take it as understood that you just don't want to know about the problem any more, and I'll take care of it. I'll take it off your hands.'

Jean-Paul visibly jolted with what Roman was suggesting. He blinked as if he might have picked up the wrong signal. But seeing the intent in Roman's eyes, his body arched slightly forward, little doubt remained. Jean-Paul contemplated Roman stonily. 'You know, that's the other thing father said – that you were far too rash, impulsive, hot-headed. That's why in the end he left the final decisions with me, not you.' His tone was cutting, acid. 'And make that decision I will – *when* the time is right and we have all the facts.'

Roman met Jean-Paul's glare challengingly, his jaw setting tight; then finally his eyes flickered down uncomfortably. Hopefully he'd given the intended impression: suitably cowed. 'Yeah, sure . . . sorry. I, uh . . . it's just there's a lot for us to lose, that's all.' He'd feared just this reaction from Jean-Paul, which was why he'd already started sowing the seeds of his other plan. He'd gone as far as he could pushing Jean-Paul conventionally. 'And maybe too some rumours I heard about Donatien at the club, and I'm putting two and two together and coming up with five.'

'What sort of rumours?'

'Well, you know, it's probably nothing.' Roman tried to shrug it off, but Jean-Paul was looking at him keenly. *God*, he knew how to play them: Leduc, Georges, Venegas and now Jean-Paul. And they all thought he was so dumb. 'Just talk that when Georges does the take at the club, he's a bit overfriendly with a couple of the girls. But, as I say – it's probably nothing. Only me getting paranoid in face of all this other shit now.'

As Roman watched the cogs turn in Jean-Paul's mind, he wondered what was most prominent: that *if* the rumours had substance, Georges cheating on Simone would make it a stronger bet that he was also cheating on them; that it would then be easier to make a move on Donatien vis-à-vis family; or simple, straightforward concern for his daughter's emotional welfare.

'Still, looks like it warrants watching, following up.' Jean-Paul's hands had clasped tight together on the desk top. He freed one and gestured to Roman. 'Which brings me back to what I think we should do for now. He should be watched closely – I want to know his *every* move. And anything new from the club about Georges, I want to know immediately – not like with this other thing, a month or two later. Right?'

'Sure . . . sure.' Roman struggled hard to keep deadpan, conceal his inner mirth. *Watched closely!* He'd had a bug up Georges' ass the last month without anyone knowing, and now Jean-Paul was personally sanctioning the club sting he'd already set into motion. Which was just how Roman had hoped it would go. *Played so well.*

And for one of the first times he didn't feel intimidated in Jean-Paul's study, with its tomes and diplomas; for once, *he* was in control. He talked about Frank and who else he might need to keep an eye on Donatien, glancing at his watch as if considering when he might be able to get hold of them. But in reality his thoughts were already shifting to timing the final parts of his sting plan and to just how much longer Donatien had to live.

The full impact of Georges' story hit Simone halfway through her Plaice Florentine. Her fork hovered, suspended, above her plate. She shook her head and closed her eyes for a second. 'God, what a mess. You should have said something earlier.'

'I know . . . I know.' Georges said it like a penance. 'But I was fresh on the scene and so afraid of coming between your father and Roman by telling tales out of school. And by the time I'd waited, hoping meanwhile Roman would say something himself, it was already too late for me to come clean and make good.'

'But still . . . Roman . . . *Roman.*' She shook her head again. 'If the situation was reversed, he'd have been pretty quick to speak out against you.'

'I know.' More penance. 'But I wasn't aware of that so much then: that I was such a thorn in his side and he didn't totally agree with Jean-Paul's new moves with the business. And it was still early days for those moves; I just wasn't sure how much the old rules of staying silent and not ratting on one to the other still applied.'

Simone looked at him levelly and shrugged, as if she only half accepted his rationale. Her fork finally dipped down again to her plate.

Georges continued. 'Okay, now it's easy to see I made the wrong decision. But it wasn't made lightly, I can tell you.' He picked at an Alaska King Crab claw. His favourite, but he wished now he'd chosen something else. It had been difficult enough getting through this with Simone, and at times the cracking of the claws grated, added an extra flinch. 'I agonized long and hard over it, and more than a few times came close to telling your father.'

'So, fine. You've got good reason not to say anything early on. But when you were hauled in by this guy Chenouda – why didn't you say something straight away then?'

'There was so much to weigh up. Too much. If Chenouda knew from Savard's statement that Leduc didn't have a gun that night, was he aiming for a murder rap? If so, I felt that was unfair. Because however hasty or stupid, it was an honest mistake by Roman: he *thought* Leduc had a gun.' Georges leant forward, keeping his voice low, practically a whisper. 'Also, would that then make me and your father accomplices: me for being there, your father for ordering the meeting? And what about Savard? Did Roman have him killed to cover his tracks, or was Chenouda just pushing that angle for leverage? And again it would have felt odd just blurting out to your father that I'd been lying all that time. It was all bubbling away: all I wanted was a week or two for it to settle and decide what to do. But meanwhile I started to worry that your father might have heard or at least suspect something – and then, with our meeting the other day, I knew for sure.'

'Did he mention directly that he knew?'

'No. You know your father – he's far too subtle for that. He started talking about confiding and commitment, particularly how important this whole change in the business was after Pascal's death; and how even Art Giacomelli had shown a keen interest because of his own son.' Georges saw Simone's brow furrow slightly. He filled in the details.

As he finished, Simone eased out her breath and sat back. 'I thought you said "subtle". He tells you that America's leading mobster is keen too that you perform well. But don't feel the pressure any!' She forced a trite smile, but heavier shadows shifted behind her eyes. She paused for a second, as if deciding whether to reveal them. 'But with Pascal's death, my father's not pulling any punches. It ripped the family apart. You know that my grandma is very religious?'

'Yes . . . I do.' Georges decided finally to crack a fresh claw.

'Well, she always kept a statue of St Antoine in her room: he's the one you pray to when you want things made right. Things that have already gone wrong, or that you fear might do. But as kids, every now and then we'd see St Antoine turn up in the fridge. And we then discovered that when things went wrong and St Antoine hadn't answered her prayers – she'd stick him in the fridge. So we always knew when things weren't going right in the family, because there was St Antoine – out in the cold alongside the milk and butter.' She smiled briefly, but the shadows were quickly back. 'With Pascal, she prayed and prayed – you know, there was this period of three days when he clung on in a coma and there was a slim hope – and when he died, we expected to see St Antoine back in the fridge. But he wasn't there, nor in her room. She'd smashed him, given up all faith in him, or God, for that matter. At least for a while.' She pulled a stray strand of hair back behind one ear. 'St Antoine didn't show up in the house again until fifteen months later, and she didn't even go to church for nine months after Pascal's death.'

Georges looked to one side for a moment as the bustle of the restaurant intruded, a waiter showing a party of three to a table close by. Miguel, their usual waiter, smiled over from the bar. It was strange: all the other times they'd come here, their conversation had been so light, carefree. Two young socialites high on the city's grace list among the throng of yuppies that regularly crowded Thursday's restaurant, three bars and basement disco, with Miguel invariably leading them straight from their table and past the usual disco queue at weekends. On occasion some of her friends from the agency would be there, or they'd meet up with his old friend Mike Landry and his latest date, but most of the time they'd be alone. They would talk about the week's triumphs: her new accounts at the agency; fresh business ground he'd broken for her father; or where they might take their vacations that summer or ski that winter; or, more recently, wedding plans. Now he was worried not just about his status in the Lacaille family, but also, if Chenouda was right, about the threat to his life – and he was dumping on her twenty-three-year-old shoulders the pressure of bailing him out. It was no light burden, far removed from her normal concerns of what colour to choose for the next sports car her father was buying her, and she was rising to the challenge by filling in the poignant mosaics of her family background that might shed some light on this problem now.

'Is that why your father chose Santoine International for the company name?' he asked.

'Yes. It seemed to sit right for him: new hope despite the odds he saw stacked against.' She waved her fork. 'But certainly my father wasn't just playing on your emotions by mentioning Pascal. So much else changed in the family then, like a house of cards tumbling down: grandpa dying soon after, grandma turning her back on religion for a while . . . and my father finally deciding to move away from the old ways.'

Pascal. Despite the odds. It gripped Georges all the harder just what a heartfelt quest this had been for Jean-Paul, and how much he'd let him down; it felt almost a cheek, a final insult, that now he was getting his own daughter to bail him out, make good. Now he had her tiptoeing through the same minefield, using terms like 'old ways' instead of 'crime' in case someone was listening in.

He shook his head. 'I shouldn't be asking you to do this.'

'No, no . . . it's okay. I want to help.' She smiled and shrugged. 'Besides, I don't know if there's anyone else who *can* help you with this. So looks like I'm stuck with it.'

He knew she was making light of it mainly for his sake, to make him feel that he wasn't burdening her too much. He reached out and clasped her hand across the table, closing his eyes for a second as if in final penance. 'Thanks.'

She leant across and planted a warm and lingering kiss on his lips, as if she somehow sensed that he needed an extra touch of comfort, reassurance. But it brought a few glances from nearby tables. *God*, how he loved her. *Both* sides of her: fun, flippant Simone with hardly a care in the world, which was all that most people saw; and the little girl who'd grown up before her time under the shroud of a crime family, seeing St Antoine in the fridge next to her milkshake and flapjacks each time her father or grandfather came out the wrong side of a turf war. The first, Georges was sure, was just a camouflage for the second.

He clung on to her hand a second longer, telling himself that his depth of feeling in that moment had little to do with dependency; even though throughout his life – from when his mother had died and the subsequent years of abandonment in an orphanage, or even the times his adoptive father had let the family down financially – his concept of love had often been forged through dependency. He couldn't face being left out in the cold again: it would be almost as bad as having Roman's death threat hanging over him. A tingling chill washed through his shoulderblades and the nape of his neck and as his hand started to tremble, he let go of Simone's. *Almost.*

But little doubt remained now that he was dependent on her – and as she began to talk about how best to tackle the subject with her father, he realized just how much so. She stressed that it was important she didn't come across just as the concerned girlfriend doing her duty: she had to sell herself as the right and only person to deal with the problem, given the circumstances.

And it struck Georges that for her father to take her seriously and her to pull it off, impassioned, old-before-her-time Simone was needed; yet he didn't know, nor had he ever troubled to find out, how Jean-Paul viewed his daughter. If, like most people, he saw her simply as a carefree, happy-go-lucky twenty-three-year-old, then he was sunk.

Roman was in heaven. He'd watched Viana writhe in the club half the night, and now she was writhing on top of him.

He held his hands by her waist as if to guide her, but her body had a rhythm and purpose all of its own. He tried to match his thrusts to it, but more often than not he'd be a beat out, so would just relax and let her do it all. It was as if she mimed to screwing all evening, just building up to the real thing so that she could let it all go with one final, virtuoso performance.

That's why he liked to show up half an hour early for the take when he was planning to head home with her. He could look at her dancing and gloat: *you guys are just getting the play-acting, I'll be getting the real thing.* The anticipation added to his excitement: that was *his* build-up.

She'd already had one orgasm, and the second was even more tumultuous, bringing him to a finish at the same time – quicker than he'd have liked. He was trying to draw it out, savour the experience longer. She shuddered with a last few strangled gasps and then lay on top of him, her breath hot in his ear, her chest rising and falling hard as she clawed back to normality.

Her gasps and screams had been loud enough to make neighbours think she was being murdered – except that his nearest Mount Royal neighbours were at least a Cadillac length away behind thick brown-stone walls.

Her breathing gradually settled, but he could still feel her heart racing hard. Her body poured out heat like a steam blanket against him, and he could feel her still moist and pressing against his thigh. Another moment to savour – but there was no point in delaying any longer. He'd not wanted to broach the topic before sex; it would have spoilt the mood. Now that was over and time was tight: he still had to get back to the club later with Funicelli. He rolled her off gently, but the jolt in the mood still registered faintly in her eyes. He touched her face with the back of one hand: reassurance.

'Babe, I've got this little problem . . . but I think you might just be ideal to help me out with it.'

'What sort of problem?' Curiosity rather than suspicion: he'd never before asked anything of her besides sex.

Roman ran through the story he'd constructed: Georges was fooling around, it was threatening all sorts of problems with Simone and the rest of the family, but the problem was he didn't have proof. So the only choice left was to set him up and take a few photos, and that was where Viana and an escort-agency girl he'd arranged came in. She looked perplexed, doubt starting to set in, so he jumped quickly to the money.

'This is important to me, so I'm paying top dollar. Eight grand – and don't worry none about paying for supplies the next four, five months.' He gently touched her nose. 'The treat's on me.'

Her smile slowly emerged. 'That's good of you, Roman. Thanks.' Her eyes flickered, searching his fleetingly. 'This must be important to you.'

'Yeah, yeah, as I said . . . it is.' He knew he'd have to be generous: she earned fifteen hundred dollars some weeks. But probably the nose candy was enticing her most.

A sly twinkle suddenly came to her eyes. 'Anyway, *Georges* – I always thought he was quite a cutie. Would hardly seem like work.'

Roman sat up, bristling. He reached out and pinched her cheek. 'Look – this is just play-acting. You're not there to fuck him for real. Besides, he's gonna be zonked from what you put in his drink back at your place, so this'll just be look-good stuff for the camera.' He gave one last hard pinch and pushed her face away in disgust.

She came sidling up against him after a second, stroking the nape of his neck. 'Come on . . . I was just teasing, Roman. But I didn't know you cared so.'

'That's where you got that wrong. I don't care . . . that's why I'm fuckin' paying you.' He remained rigid a moment more before finally giving in to her insistent stroking. He shrugged and smiled reluctantly. 'Well, maybe when you've just fucked my brains out like now, I do care just a little.' Her hand froze on his neck, and he gripped it and pushed her back on the bed, straddling her. She glared back at him for a moment before realizing from his smile that he was teasing too. But he was glad in a way that she'd chosen to rib him over Georges: it would make what was coming easier.

The tension gone between them, he ran through the rest: someone from the club that she'd made the mistake of dating. He'd become a bit freaky and possessive, was waiting outside her place the night before, and they'd ended up having a fight. Could Georges run her home, see her safely into her apartment? She was afraid the guy might be waiting for her again that night.

She grasped the plan clearly after only a couple of minor questions, except for one point. 'A fight? Would it be enough just that I'm rattled, afraid?'

'No, I think we're going to have to be a little more convincing.'

'What? I put on some make-up for it to look like bruising or something?'

'No . . . I don't think so. He might pick up that it's just make-up, get suspicious.' This was the best part, watching that gradual dawning of realization on her face. He was still stradding her, and her eyes darted uncomprehendingly for a moment before fixing on him.

'No, Roman . . . no way. My face is my work, my money.'

'Sorry, doll . . . I just don't see any other way round.' Fear settled in her eyes and she flailed around frantically to push him away. He wrestled one arm back easily with his left hand and pinned the other under his right knee. 'The bruising will be gone in just a week – back to normal.'

'No, Romy . . . please . . . *please.*' She writhed and bucked to try and shake him loose, but he had her pinned too tight. Her breath came short with the effort, verging into tears and gasping sobs as she realized the futility. She wasn't going to get free. 'Noooo . . . *please!*'

'I'll round it off to ten grand – and just think of all that nose candy.' He cocked his right fist above her face.

'No, Roman . . . don't do this to me, I'm begging you . . . *nooooo!*' She shook her head wildly, tears streaming down her face. She let out a piercing scream that went straight through him, and he dug his knee harder into her left arm.

'Shut the fuck up and keep your head still – unless you want to get your fucking nose broken as well.'

Her head stopped shaking and she stared straight up at him, her pupils dark and dilated, full of terror. He drank in that terror for a moment, wallowing in the heady sense of power. Combined with her body's trembling, it told him that finally he was in control, all her resistance had burnt out. But there was a plea beneath her eyes that he found disturbing.

'Or maybe turn your head a little so that I can be sure of a clear shot.'

She slowly, reluctantly, turned her head to one side, tears trailing down her face. Her body trembled beneath him like a trapped humming bird, her only sound a muted whimper as she bit tautly at her bottom lip; and with his whispered 'Sorry, babe' her eyes fluttered gently shut a second before his fist came down.

Roman let Carlo Funicelli into the club less than an hour later.

Funicelli perched up at the bar, Roman poured them a couple of beers, and they started talking. Aimless chatter, it was all for the sake of the security cameras: if Jean-Paul got sight of the tapes, he'd say that he met Funicelli at the club after hours to talk over the surveillance of Donatien.

After a moment, Roman pointed something out along the rows of bottles behind, and Funicelli came around the bar. They moved along, but as soon as they were out of security camera view – Roman knew the exact position – Funicelli ducked to one side towards the cash register.

Roman had already given him the key, and in just over a minute Funicelli was finished: two sets of codes keyed-in that he knew would disrupt the club's four linked registers handling both cash and automatic stock ordering.

They moved back into the view of the security camera, with Roman pointing out some *sambuca* on a high shelf as Funicelli nodded.

Azy would call in a panic soon after they opened that night, and ever-efficient Donatien would come running: the new system had been his recommendation. Roman knew that he couldn't wait for Donatien's normal monthly till check and reconciliation – he had to somehow get him there quickly.

Funicelli noticed Roman's right hand clenching and unclenching and asked, 'Something wrong?'

'It's nothing.' Roman shrugged. 'You know, for every bit of love there's always some pain.'

Funicelli didn't pursue it; he went back to silently sipping at his beer as Roman glanced at his watch: forty-eight hours left for Donatien to live, and counting.

16

Five days since baring her soul to Gordon: five days of searching with nothing but fruitless dead ends, and now practically Elena's last hope lay with these two old steamer trunks, going through her father's memorabilia and keepsakes. All that remained: sixty-two years of life neatly packed away. She was so absorbed with their contents that she hardly registered the footsteps behind her.

'Come on . . . Enough, Elena. You can go through the rest later. If we don't get ready, we're going to be late for the restaurant.'

'Yes, I suppose so.' Elena was kneeling down, her breath short from raking and sifting through. She lifted her head and half turned towards Uncle Christos. 'Just five minutes more, and then I'll jump into the shower. Get some of this dust off. Okay?'

After a second, a reluctant 'Okay' from Uncle Christos. 'I'll make us another coffee meanwhile.' Then the sound of his footsteps shuffling back down the stairs.

The first three days had been spent searching through UK credit reference agencies for the Stevens, previously Stephanou, family, mostly at Gordon's instigation: she'd all but given up, felt that she had no fight left in her to continue. But Gordon insisted it wasn't the sort of thing she could give up on lightly; it would only come back later to haunt her. He offered to help with his knowledge of credit-reference tracking, and the next forty-eight hours they burnt up the phone lines between Terry, Megan's trace man, and seven reference agencies from Gordon's card file. But they found nothing linking back to their previous Canterbury address with either Stevens or Stephanou. They concluded that the Stevenses had miraculously survived without any credit for three years after moving or had lied about their previous address, or, more likely, that they'd left the country.

They were stuck at first as to how to find out where they might have gone – then Gordon hit on the possibility of her father's old passport providing clues. If her father had had a hand in spiriting the Stevenses away, then he might well have visited their destination around the time of their moving. Elena thought it worth pursuing, but the only problem was that her father's belongings were still stored at her mother's, and Elena didn't want to see her: especially not for this purpose. She'd had little or no contact with her mother while her father was alive, and with Elena not turning up for her father's funeral five years before, things had become even more strained between them: they'd only spoken briefly once on the phone since, after Uncle Christos had informed Elena that her mother was ill.

So it was Uncle Christos to the rescue again, phoning her mother with an excuse about trying to find some old business papers. 'I'll pick the trunks up and have them back to you within a few days.' Then, straight after he got the trunks, he phoned Elena back and she jumped on a train to London to start her search.

She'd received a call from Barbara Edelston the day after her heart-to-heart with Gordon, and halfway through a predictable dressing-down about her being desperately out of order to still be interfering in the Ryalls' affairs – 'especially given your background' – Elena had finally snapped and given Edelston a piece of her mind. 'One day you'll wake up to the fact that Ryall is a control freak, and a dangerous one at that. He's been controlling young Lorena all along. He controlled Nadine's inquiry by taping our meeting; me by getting a secret report done; and you by sending you both the tape and the report. And just like the mug he hoped you'd be, you fell for it all and responded strictly by the rule book. If all of that doesn't look the tiniest bit suspicious to you, then I'm afraid I can't help you.' She slammed down the phone before Edelston could respond, and dialled straight out to Shelley McGurran. Shelley too would no doubt have received Ryall's poisonous file, and she didn't want Shelley to have to phone first to get an explanation.

After a strained half-hour on the line with a condensed version of her soul-baring to Gordon, with Shelley voicing her sore disappointment that Elena hadn't felt they were close enough to be able to share this earlier, Shelley finally rallied behind her. 'I agree. You have to find him, Elena. *And* try and help young Lorena, if you can. That is, if you've got either the time or the inclination to handle both.' Elena wondered if that was Shelley's polite way of saying that she no longer had a job with the aid agency, but Shelley was quick to reassure: 'God, no. Devoted workers like you are hard to find. I'm disappointed, and I only *half* accept your reasoning – but not enough to boot you out. And especially not at the bidding of that prick, Ryall. Take a month off, or whatever it takes to sort out your life, then give me a call. Your place will still be here. And give that Ryall's arse an extra kick for me. Promise?'

Elena was close to tears when she came off the phone: Shelley's ready understanding made it all the harder. Another who so loved and trusted her, and her repayment to them had been so poor over the years; so lacking in trust.

And it was those close to her, like Gordon and Shelley, who were now firing her up into action: after twelve days of searching with Megan and Terry that had ended nowhere, and Ryall rallying half of Chelborne against her and sending his damning report, she'd all but given up, felt she had nothing left to give. Until her father's two trunks were in front of her. Then suddenly she was on overdrive again, frantically sifting through: dusty plans for their old house; GCE results for her and Andreos; her communion prayer book; her first school photo; Andreos at nineteen standing proudly by a new Suzuki bike he'd just bought; the family all together raising glasses in a Cyprus beach bar when she was just nine.

She'd found her father's passport covering 1970 near the bottom of the first trunk, but still she kept going. Poignant nostalgia of the years she was there, the family all together, plus filling the gaps on the years she wasn't. She was totally absorbed, found it impossible to break away. It was strange: looking through photos of herself and Andreos as children and some old birthday cards, one from her at the age of seven to her father with a pressed flower inside, it was as if a soft and vulnerable side of her father, which she'd never witnessed while he was alive, had been exposed. When she'd aired that thought to Uncle Christos, he mentioned that her mother too had packed away some old family memorabilia in the same trunks. So again her father remained an enigma: she couldn't be sure of a chink in his emotional armour.

The agreement had been that as soon as she found her father's passport, Uncle Christos would book a table for them at Beoty's, his favourite Cypriot restaurant: a small celebration. There were five entry stamps in the few months either side of the time the Stevenses had disappeared; hopefully one of them would prove fruitful.

She'd made the excuse of continuing her search in case there were other papers which might give some clue, but when over an hour later Uncle Christos found her still on her knees busily raking through, now half covered in dust from the trunks' contents, he became concerned. He reminded her that time could be tight for the restaurant, but she was sure his main worry was that she was getting too wrapped up in the trunks' contents: some of them might be too emotionally painful for her.

So when he returned with coffee, she immediately stood up and dusted herself down, took a few rushed gulps and knocked back the rest after showering – and within fifteen minutes they were in a taxi wending through the remnants of rush hour traffic between Queensway and the West End. Street-lamp light bars playing across one arm. *The small face looking up at her, struggling to see.* She closed her eyes for a second, shaking off a faint shudder. Perhaps going through her father's things for so long hadn't been such a good idea.

The face across from her now, thirty years on, wasn't far different to her father's: the resemblance was mainly around the eyes and nose and they both had the same thick hair, which had turned from black to stone grey in their early fifties; but it was a slightly more rounded face, with a readier, easier smile, the edges softer. The clownish, compassionate foil to her father's stern, all-business manner. It was no wonder that she'd warmed more to Uncle Christos as a child; and before she was old enough to discover if she would ever break the barrier of how she felt about her father – somewhere between cool remoteness and open fear – the rest had been written in abortion blood and sealed with court adoption papers. Never to be reversed.

'You don't rate Athens, Hamburg or Rome too highly, do you?' Uncle Christos commented.

'No, I don't.' Three of the five stamps in her father's passport around the time of the Stephanous' disappearance. 'I think that to anglicize their name and then turn up somewhere where that name would stand out would be pointless. Whereas in Chicago the name Stevens would be commonplace, and almost half of Montreal's population is Anglophone.'

'You're working on the assumption that your father had it all planned out?'

'Do you know of any time that he didn't plan everything to the last?'

Uncle Christos shrugged a tame accord, and they sat silently for a second.

'Anyway, we'll know soon enough,' she said. They'd used Terry to put in trace requests with both the American and Canadian embassies for visa or emigration applications in the name of Stevens or Stephanou around the time the family disappeared. Terry had been asked to call back the next day.

Uncle Christos merely nodded. She could tell that something else was on his mind, and finally he turned to her, his expression slightly drawn, concerned.

'Elena. You really should see her sometime. I know with picking up the trunks it could have been difficult – she might have asked too many questions. But before you leave London, you should make the effort. Maybe when I return the trunks tomorrow, you could come along at the same time?'

'No, no . . . It would be too painful – for *both* of us. Too much has gone before.' Uncle Christos' pet beef: reconciliation with her mother. She watched his expression change from hopeful to questioning and added, 'Especially not now with everything else I've got on my plate.'

Uncle Christos grimaced with reluctant understanding and turned to stare blankly ahead again. Night-time London rolled by their taxi windows, the lights from an oncoming car making his profile shadow more pronounced for a second. She could practically read his mind: every time an excuse. Whenever he broached the subject, she'd usually raise how her mother had always taken her father's side, was practically a silent conspirator: she found that difficult to forgive. Or, the last time he'd asked, she'd said that it was too close to her not showing up at her father's funeral: her mother wouldn't have forgiven her yet. Now it was the search for her son.

'You know, she's not getting any younger, Elena.'

'I know.' Elena bit lightly at her lip, guilt worming deeper. Then after a silence: 'She's not ill again, is she?'

'No, she's not.' Christos shot her a look of tired reproach. 'But that shouldn't be the only reason you feel you must make contact again – because you fear she might be on her deathbed. Besides . . .' His eyes flickered down slightly; direct eye contact was suddenly difficult. 'Has it ever struck you that she was just as afraid of your father as you? That alone, apart from the fact that she's your mother, is something you have in common: you were both on the same side of the fence more than you probably appreciated.'

'But I was barely more than a child, Uncle Christos. Only fifteen! At least at her age she had a voice; she should have said *something*, she might have been able to –' She stopped herself, realizing she was launching again into a diatribe about how much more her mother could have done. She didn't want to spoil the mood for the restaurant, and she hated to see Uncle Christos' face darken: the lighter, jovial side would suddenly be gone; he would remind her too much of her father. Despite her own feelings, she understood why Uncle Christos was so deeply grieved by the split in the family: Andreos and her father long dead, her years apart from all of them, and now the thought that her mother might die after years of being alone without any reconciliation between them – all this was too much for Uncle Christos to take. She reached across and gripped his hand.

'You're right. I should make the effort sometime. And perhaps when I'm through all this will be that time. I can show up at her door with my son for a big reunion. She'll know then that I have back what I want – there'd be no reason for me to still hold any resentment. I'm there at her door because I want to be there, not because I feel I *have* to be there.'

Uncle Christos smiled tightly and patted her hand. But as he looked away again, she could tell that he was only half reassured: it could be just another excuse, her meeting her mother pushed out of reach again by being tied to something that might never happen. She had so many hopes and desires riding upon finding her son; and now Uncle Christos' hopes that one day their shattered family would be patched back, she'd strapped to the same possibly doomed ship.

At least they didn't have to wait long to know. Two calls the next day could decide it: Montreal or Chicago.

But when the next morning Terry called with the good news that the Canadian embassy had confirmed they had a Stevens family listed in October 1970 for immigration to Montreal, 'father, mother and a young baby', Elena had other problems: two calls late the night before from young Lorena.

Gordon'd phoned her about the calls not long after she'd had the news from Terry. 'They came through to your studio, so I didn't even hear the phone ringing last night and didn't play the answerphone back until just now.'

'I see.' She swallowed, then asked Gordon to play them. 'I should hear them.'

'Okay, one second.' But Gordon sounded hesitant, as if worried about the effect the messages might have on her. A rustling and clicking as he set the answerphone up, then Lorena's frail, uncertain voice:

'*Elena . . . Elena . . . I thought you were going to help me. Since you came to the house . . . I . . . I've heard nothing . . . and Mr Ryall is still coming to my room. Please,* please . . . *if you can hear me, pick up the phone* . . .' A moment's silence, then the sound of soft whimpering before the line went dead. A short beep, then her voice again.

'*He* . . . *he doesn't touch me when he visits* . . . *maybe he's frightened to since you visited. But he does touch me in the dreams* . . . *and they're so real* . . . *sooo* . . . *I* . . . *I don't know what to do.*' A pause, a sniffle as she battled to control her tears. '*Please* . . . *if there's anything you can do, Elena. I'm sorry to call you like this* . . . *but I don't know who else to call. If you're there* . . .' The tears had stopped; only shallow breathing as Lorena waited on expectantly for the phone to be picked up before finally she gave up.

Elena took a second to compose herself as Gordon lifted the receiver away from the answer machine. She pictured again Lorena reaching out her hand to the back window of Nicola Ryall's Range Rover; but nobody was there to grip on to that hand, to help her.

She took a fresh breath. 'How did you get on with Mikaya?'

'I finally found someone in the village ready and willing to speak up: Joe Hawley at the garage. He had a run-in with Ryall over a bill last year. Apparently, Mikaya's at Durham University – hardly anyone down here sees anything of her any more. I've phoned the university twice now and left messages, but no return call as yet.'

Elena sighed. 'Might still prove fruitful, but I'm not sure we've got the time to wait now.' They'd agreed that the best way to help Lorena was to find out more about what had happened with Mikaya. Gordon had offered to start digging while Elena was in London looking through her father's things. But having heard Lorena sounding so distressed, she began to reassess: Mikaya might well decide not to speak to them now or at any time, and they had to do something quickly. She outlined her new plan.

'You're crazy,' Gordon said after a pause, as if unsure for a second that she was serious. 'It's far too risky.'

'Maybe so. But look where I am now because of not taking risks, not standing up to my father. Twenty-nine years without seeing my own son, and too afraid to admit that I've even got a son to anyone – just so that I don't have to face it myself. Pathetic. If something is happening with Ryall and I do nothing, I'd never forgive myself. Lorena could end up in a few years' time where I found myself – so screwed up that she empties a bottle of pills down her throat as the only way out. And Ryall's just like my father: the only way is to make a stand, push back. Otherwise they just steamroller straight over you.'

204

'I still don't like it.' There were only a few ways Gordon could see it going right, and far too many of it all going horribly wrong. But he could tell that her mind was made up: he might as well start thinking of how to help her, try and reduce the risk. Whichever way the cards fell, one thing looked certain: from this point on, their lives were going to be very different.

17

Viana wore a mask covering her bruise for her dancing that night: bright turquoise feathers with cream tinges, it covered one eye and swept in a semi-circle down one side of her nose and across just under her left cheekbone. She'd had it made specially by a friend who made costumes for the annual Caribbean carnival.

She'd felt self-conscious at first, as if people could somehow see the ugliness of the swelling on her face behind the mask, or guess that she was covering something. But as she realized people were none the wiser, and that with some the mask even heightened her mystique, her allure – made her stand out from the other girls – she relaxed back into her normal rhythm.

She saw Georges turn up an hour after opening, but she didn't want to rush over. Roman had assured her that he would be staying for the evening, or, if he did leave for a while to eat, he was going to be back to do the take at closing. She bided her time, kept half an eye on him between dances. For the first fifty minutes he was busy with a technical guy checking all the cash registers, just as Roman had said would happen. She waited until about fifteen minutes after the technician left before sidling over. Georges was sat at the bar nursing a beer while Azy was at the far end serving another customer.

'Hi, Georges.' She perched on the bar stool next to him. 'You should come by more often. We always get stuck with that goon Roman.'

'Trouble with the cash registers.' He waved his beer towards the bar register and smiled back. He wasn't sure what was more important: her paying him a compliment, or her taking a swipe at Roman while he wasn't there.

'Ah . . . and we thought it was because you couldn't keep yourself away from us all here.' She mimicked a hurt expression.

'Yep, that's it.' He raised his glass in acknowledgement and took a quick slug. 'Couldn't keep away from that smile, Viana.' He remembered all of the girls' names, even though he came to the club at most twice a month. He thought it was important in a trade where they were usually treated impersonally: pieces of meat to just gawk at. He often talked with the girls, and Viana had been as free and easy with the smiles and talk as any of them. But what had stayed with him most was that, as with another girl who was sending money back to her family in Costa Rica, noble aims lay behind her work: Viana was saving for surgery to help her mother's crippling arthritis. 'How's your mother now? Closer to having the money together?'

'Yeah. Quite close now. Thanks.' She flinched slightly at the mention. This sting tonight would go a long way towards helping pay. Nor did Georges have any idea that if it wasn't for her habit, she'd have probably had the money together months back. She was touched also that he remembered: Roman *never* asked about her mother. She hoped that this was all, as Roman said, just to split Georges from Simone because he was fooling around; that Roman wasn't thinking of harming him. With the still tingling ache behind her mask to remind her of what Roman might do if she let him down, she pushed the worry from her mind: as with so much else in her life, what choice or control did she have? His fleeting concern at least seemed to have set the right tone. 'Georges . . . there was something else I wanted to talk to you about. A little problem that I . . .' She raised her eyes as Azy started down the bar towards them. Roman had stressed to keep it all out of earshot of Azy. She looked to one side. 'Can we go over there maybe and talk?'

Georges nodded with a tame smile: he could see that she looked troubled, was conscious of prying ears. They moved two booths away from the bar.

She ran through the story exactly as Roman had coached: a club visitor who she'd made the mistake of dating; he'd become difficult and possessive, started shouting that he didn't want her working at the club any more while she was going out with him. She'd tried to break it off the night before '. . . and we ended up arguing. Things went from bad to worse, and that's when he hit out. Gave me this.' She lifted up her face mask. She was careful to keep her back to Azy, who was no doubt keeping half an eye on them, although Azy would have clearly seen Georges' pained flinch as the ugly bruise was exposed. She bit lightly at her lip as Georges sucked in his breath. 'I was worried that he might be waiting by my place again tonight. So I was wondering if . . . if you might be able to run me home after work . . . see me safely to my door.' The right emotions were easy to turn on: seeing Georges' reaction to her bruise brought home just what a mess

Roman had made of her; she was close to tears again. 'If it's not putting you out any . . . You see, normally I would –'

Georges clasped her hand. 'No, no . . . it's okay. I can run you home.' Georges' eyes searched hers a moment longer. Her fear was genuine, and if her intention was to hit on him she would have chosen another time: with her face half mashed up, she wasn't at her most alluring. 'But what about the other nights I'm not here? What will you do – get Roman to run you back?' He looked past her shoulder. 'Or Azy maybe?'

She held up one hand. 'No, I don't want either of them to know about it. You know what Roman'd be like if he found out – he'd half kill the guy. And Azy's real strict on us dating clients because of past problems: he'd feel that he had to tell Gérard or Roman. I've laid on my cousin to pick me up most nights . . . It's just that he couldn't make it tonight.'

'No, it's okay – I'll run you.' Georges gave her hand one last reassuring pat before pulling his away. 'I've got to nip out for something to eat, but I'll be back later to do the take.'

'Roman's not doing it this evening?'

'No. Because of the problem with the registers, I wanted to do the tally tonight: no point in us both being here. I phoned him an hour back.'

Viana let out a slow breath as if a burden had been eased. 'That was another thing I was worried about, having to cover with Roman. If he asked about the mask, I was going to have to lie to him, tell him I fell down some stairs.' She forced a nervous smile. Everything was going how Roman'd planned, and hopefully she'd feigned her side well: Georges seemed convinced, settled. But as she turned slightly, she was aware in her side vision of Azy looking over at them. 'I'd better get back now. Thanks again, Georges. See you later.' She touched his sleeve and headed off towards the far side of the room, quickly slipping back into her normal seductive sway as she roamed for fresh dance clients.

She hooked a client after only a minute, but as she started to dance her nervousness began to build. She noticed Georges was back at the bar talking to Azy; she was sure Georges wouldn't say anything, but what if Azy read between the lines? Azy looked up at her for a moment before moving along the bar to serve another customer. She closed her eyes, tried to absorb herself in the mood of the music and her dancing.

Twenty minutes later, straight after another check with Azy of the bar cash register, Georges left. Viana waited ten minutes more, then went to the mobile in her handbag and put through the prearranged call to Roman.

'It's done. He's gone now – but he's coming back to pick me up later.'

'Okay. Good stuff. We'll be sitting outside. See you later.'

But wondering if Azy suspected something each time he looked over and thinking ahead to what she'd have to do, didn't help her growing agitation. Her hand was shaking as she tucked the mobile back in her handbag.

The passing hours made it worse. She took a shot of vodka in each of the three cokes she had after 11 p.m., but still her hands were shaking, her stomach in knots. She even took a quick snort of coke in a washroom cubicle, but all that did was sharpen her focus, her sense of apprehension: Georges was one of the nice guys, one of the few that took the time to show some interest in her welfare, what might lie beneath her skin. What if Roman did intend to harm him?

When they were getting near closing and Georges still hadn't returned, she started to hope that he wouldn't show up; that he'd had second thoughts about them being alone together, worried that she might come on to him. As far as Roman was concerned, she'd have done her bit: it wouldn't be her fault if Georges didn't show up. Surely Roman wouldn't take it out on her?

The pros and cons tugged at her, but any clarity seemed out of reach beyond the pounding of the music and a buzzing in her head: she wished now she'd laid off the drink and cocaine, and registering the slight frown from the client before her, she realized that her preoccupation had made her pause for a second in her dancing. She picked up the rhythm again, and halfway through a second dance for the same client, Georges walked in. By that time her nerves were so out of control that all she could manage was a small wave and a tight, anxious smile.

She became even more concerned that Azy might have sensed something was wrong when, after wiping down the bar and just before leaving, he came over to her and another girl, Lucy.

'Everything okay, girls?'

'Yeah, my boyfriend's coming by to pick me up,' Lucy answered.

'I'm waiting on my cousin,' Viana said quickly.

Azy nodded and said smiling goodbyes to them and Georges, who was busy finishing the register tallies; but Viana couldn't help noticing that Azy's eyes lingered on her a moment longer than on Lucy.

Viana arranged with Georges that just as a precaution she'd leave a minute earlier and wait a block down for him to pick her up.

Georges too noticed her nervousness, seeing her hand shake as she slid in the car and shut the door – though he put this down to her worry that her boyfriend might be waiting for her.

'Don't worry,' he assured. 'He sees me roll up with you – and even if he *is* there he's going to disappear pretty sharp.'

'Can you stay inside with me maybe fifteen, twenty minutes, just to make sure?' Viana asked. Her nerves put a faint croaky tremble to her voice: just the right touch. She looked at him expectantly: with this last cog in place, the die would be cast: no turning back. 'A few nights back he rang my bell five or ten minutes after I showed up.'

Georges paused only for a second. 'Yeah, sure.' He glanced at her briefly. He could see that she was deeply perturbed, which made him feel safe: romance was the last thing on the girl's mind.

WALMERTON SCHOOL
Founded 1894

The school plaque was discreet, gold lettering on a small, black-printed board by the main playground double gates. A smaller school than Chelvale Primary where Katine went, though nothing between them academically: perhaps the school's longer heritage had attracted Ryall. Elena had visited it only once before, five years ago when deciding where to send Katine.

But she was far more nervous now than she was then, even though that meeting had been terrifying: the school's atmosphere austere, stuffy, and the interviewing headmaster no less so, with the accent on rules and tradition more than any ambient needs of the pupils.

Now, crossing the school playground, it was deathly silent apart from faint birdsong from some nearby trees: the quiet before the storm of the lunchtime bell and the playground being filled with a mass of shrill voices suddenly let loose. But now all Elena was conscious of was the fall of her own footsteps beyond her heavy heartbeat. For a second they fell in unison, sounding ominous, like marching soldiers, and she changed pace slightly . . . Through the main door, into the corridor. A faint echo for ominous effect now: Elena could hear her own laboured breathing above the muted murmur of voices straining through the pale cream walls.

The classroom doors were all marked with types of tree: Oak, Ash, Beech . . . Elena found Lorena's classroom four along: Elm. She didn't want to hover by the small glass look-through and possibly gain the teacher's attention too early – so she went a few yards past and sat on the nearest bench seat.

She pondered over her plans. She'd chosen the regular weekly time when Nicola Ryall went to the hairdresser's and then had a long lunch with her newly acquired charity-circle friends; gin and tonic do-gooders whose nearest appreciation of the gritty reality of children starving was through a Catherine Cookson novel. Mrs Ryall would be indisposed two and a half hours, maybe three, and normally switched her mobile off. Elena had tried just twenty minutes earlier: she'd been put straight through to a 'caller unavailable' recorded message.

Then she'd phoned the school and, posing as Mrs Ryall, had left a message that Lorena had to go to a dentist's appointment at 1 p.m. 'Our housekeeper will come and pick her up at lunchtime.'

Elena hoped and prayed she'd managed a reasonable approximation of Mrs Ryall's voice; but then how many times in the year would Mrs Ryall have phoned and spoken to the school? Maybe two or three at most. Mrs Truett, the school secretary, merely asked if Lorena would be back for class later in the afternoon or the next day?

'Tomorrow now, I think,' Elena answered. 'Though if she can make it back in time for the last lesson today, I'll make sure she returns.'

Judging from Mrs Truett's reaction, nothing seemed to have jarred, to be untoward. But what if someone else from the school was now looking out and knew what Mrs Ryall's housekeeper looked like? Or what if they'd managed to raise Mrs Ryall on her mobile to check, or . . .

The ringing bell crashed into her thoughts. On impulse she stood up, looking around expectantly. A door at the far end of the corridor was the first to open. A few children emerged, a teacher's voice booming from beyond – but as the main mass appeared, the other doors too were opening and spilling out pupils. Within seconds, the corridor was awash with a cacophony of small voices and movement.

Eight or ten children had so far emerged from Elm. Elena moved closer to the door so that she could watch out for Lorena, and as she picked her out she caught the teacher's eye practically at the same time. A quizzical frown crossed Lorena's face. She'd have to move in quick.

'I've come to take Lorena to the dentist. Mrs Ryall phoned earlier.'

The teacher, a thirty-something redhead with a strained smile as she tried to bark some calm into the exiting class, looked in turn at Elena and Lorena. 'Nobody told me anything.'

'Uh . . . it would have been only about forty minutes ago.' Elena had affected a slight foreign lilt, sounding like some of her Cypriot relatives speaking English, to distinguish her voice from Mrs Ryall's on the phone. Instant domestic: speak with a foreign accent. She forced an apologetic smile, and Lorena finally cottoned on to the game and came across and took her hand. Elena swallowed hard against her hammering pulse. 'Mrs Ryall forgot earlier.'

The teacher gave them one last look. 'Okay, fine . . . I'll –' Then her attention was gone as she called out to two children jostling each other towards the back.

'She'll be back tomorrow,' Elena said, but the teacher only turned towards them briefly with another 'That's fine' before continuing the shepherding of her pupils' exit.

Elena led Lorena out by the hand before she had more time to think about it. Her mouth was dry, her legs leaden as they wended their way through the crowded corridor. She gripped Lorena's hand tighter in reassurance, but partly it was to quell the trembling in her own hand. The shrill voices echoing from the walls seemed to merge with a solid pounding at her temples . . . only a few paces more to the main doors.

The call of 'One minute!' from behind barely broke through it all. It had to be repeated – 'Hold on a minute!' – before she finally halted and turned.

An older, matronly woman approached, with Lorena's teacher alongside her. Elena's heart sank. She wasn't going to get away with it after all. Someone had managed to raise Nicola Ryall on her mobile, or maybe this woman knew the Ryalls, knew full well that she wasn't their housekeeper.

The matronly woman pointed a thumb over her shoulder. 'If Lorena's not coming back later – she'll need her satchel from her locker.'

'Oh . . . of course.' Elena smiled and patted Lorena's shoulder. She recognized the voice from her earlier call: Mrs Truett, the school secretary. 'Yes, go on.'

They stood as an awkward triangle for a moment as Lorena scurried off, a stream of children milling past them. Then Mrs Truett commented, 'Nothing too serious, I hope.'

It took a second for the penny to drop. 'Uh, uh . . . no. Hopefully just some fillings.'

Elena felt exposed standing in the corridor with all the children passing. Katine had a friend who went to this school. What if she came past and spotted her? *Mrs Waldren, what are you doing here?* She pushed a taut smile to cover her nervousness at Mrs Truett – who looked about to say something before deciding against it, given the level of noise around them.

Elena silently screamed for Lorena to hurry and return. If the noise abated, Mrs Truett might well decide to pipe up again, and she wasn't sure her nerves could take it. Already she could feel her blouse sticking to her spine with sweat, and her legs were close to crumpling.

Lorena appeared only seconds later, though already the numbers in the corridor were thinning. But at that moment another teacher came to talk to Mrs Truett, and with a quick wave and 'Thanks!' Elena made good her escape with Lorena.

Through the main doors, across the playground, a slight weave to avoid a group playing ball . . . through the entrance gates, into the car. Elena didn't speak to Lorena throughout. Nor did she dare look back in case someone else was trying to attract her attention.

As they got in the car, Lorena asked, 'Where are we going?'

But still Elena didn't speak. She kept her eyes resolutely ahead until they were over five hundred yards down the road, well clear of the school. Only then did she finally let out a long breath and turn to Lorena.

'I got your message, Lorena. So I'm going to help you. That is, if you want me to help you?'

'Yes . . . of course.' Lorena seemed vaguely puzzled. 'That's why I called.'

Elena looked at her sharply. 'No, it's more than that I need, Lorena. I could get into a lot of trouble for what I'm doing now. You're going to be away from home two or maybe three days. The police will start looking for us, trying to track us down. This isn't a game any more.' But from the light in Lorena's eyes at the mention of police and tracking, she realized that that was exactly what Lorena thought this suddenly was: an exciting game. 'So I need to know for sure – cross-your-heart sure – that this is what you want.'

'Yes, I'm sure. Sure, sure.' Her clipped accent added vehemence.

'Okay . . . okay.' Elena's eyes flicked to her rear-view mirror. No cars visible behind – but they were still too close to the school. Elena took the second turning on the left and went half a mile down before stopping at the first pull-in by a farm gate. 'But I can't be seen to be abducting you, Lorena. So it has to be clear also to others that this is all totally of your own free will. Something that *you* want rather than me.' Elena took the half-page she'd typed earlier from her inside pocket. 'If you'd like to read that. And if you're happy with it, we'll put it on tape.'

Elena felt guilty watching Lorena's consternation as she read. Only seconds with her out of Ryall's clutches, and here she was acting like a big city lawyer whose first thought was to cover her back. But she had to do it to have any hope of avoiding a jail sentence, and it might also help take some of the steam from the police pursuit of them.

'Yes, it's okay,' Lorena said finally.

'Are you sure?' Elena pressed. Lorena was probably so relieved at being helped that she'd have said yes to anything; but Elena didn't want her answer to be guided by force or lack of choice: Lorena had had enough of that with Ryall.

'Yes, I'm sure.' Lorena smiled hesitantly. 'Sure, sure.'

Elena took the cassette recorder from the back seat. There was a falter at one point and they had to redo the last two sentences, but the whole thing was wrapped up within a couple of minutes.

Elena's nerves had bristled with the two cars that had passed them in that time, and now she was hawkishly alert as she rejoined the main road, her eyes jumping to the rear-view mirror whenever a car appeared. She dropped the tape off at home, gave Gordon a quick peck on the cheek and a 'Call you later' – they'd said their main goodbyes earlier – and hit the road again.

She didn't want to take the Sandbanks ferry and risk getting stuck in a queue where she could be easily apprehended – so she'd decided to head through Wareham, which would add an extra fifteen miles. She glanced at her watch: three hours to Eurotunnel or the ferries, and by then Nicola Ryall would know that Lorena was missing. Then she'd probably lose half-an-hour or even an hour waiting for the next departure and boarding. How long before Mrs Ryall raised the alert with the police: fifteen, twenty minutes? It was going to be tight.

Perhaps picking up on the worry and strain in her face, Lorena clutched at her left arm and nestled close. 'Thank you, Elena. Thank you.'

Elena gave her a little hug and ruffled her hair. She felt like adding, 'Don't thank me yet', but she didn't want to dull the light in Lorena's eyes: the first light of hope that had probably been there for a while.

And she was equally concerned now about her own state of mind. The last half-hour of tension had totally drained her: her nerves were still as tight as piano wire, leaping wildly with each car that came close. She could feel her body's gentle trembling as she held Lorena. With forty-eight hours or more of the same ahead, she wasn't sure she'd be able to cope.

'Do you want coffee or something stronger? Or maybe something soft?' Viana posed the question just how Roman had suggested: try not to leave the option of Donatien *not* having a drink.

'Just a coke, thanks.' Georges' voice sailed through from the lounge.

'Okay.' Viana felt some of the weight lift from her shoulders, though still she found the shaking of her hands impossible to control as she reached for a glass and took the coke from the fridge. She pondered for a second what to have for herself before deciding on coffee: more time pottering around in the kitchen, more movement to provide cover for her slipping the two pills into Georges' drink.

While the coffee was percolating, she went to her handbag and took out the tablets wrapped in tissue. Then with a quick look back, checking out that he wasn't moving and about to walk in on her any second, she put them into his drink. They fizzed a bit while she was pouring her coffee. She stirred cream into her coffee and gave the coke a quick stir too, just to make sure the pills had dissolved, and walked back into the lounge with both drinks, easing a smile.

'There you are.' She handed Georges the coke and set her cup down on a coffee table between them. 'I really appreciate you helping me out like this. Thanks.'

'That's okay. It's nothing.' Georges took a quick sip of coke. 'What's this guy's name, the one giving you all the trouble?'

'Oh . . . uh . . .' She stumbled for a second. That was one thing they'd never thought about. She grabbed quickly for a client's name she recalled. 'Barry. Barry Picard.'

Georges just nodded and took another sip.

Viana became concerned that he was drinking too slowly. Five minutes, Roman had said; but that was probably from when he'd finished it all. What if he sipped his way slowly through, then knocked back the rest only seconds before leaving? She looked away as Georges met her eye, worried that her preoccupation might have shown.

'You're obviously still anxious,' Georges said. 'But stop worrying. Even if he was waiting outside, he'd have probably left by now – or certainly within a few minutes, max. I don't see him waiting beyond that. It's cold out there.'

'You're probably right.' She fired back a hesitant smile. Her guilt weighed heavier with the reassurance: how many had ever taken the time to give any thought to her welfare? 'But you'll stay the extra ten or fifteen minutes, just to make sure. Right?'

'Yeah, sure. No problem.' He took a longer gulp this time. He could tell that she was deeply agitated; it was going to take more than just off-pat reassurance to calm her. Seeing the fear in her face made him think for a moment of his own problems: Jean-Paul was on a quick loop trip to New York and Boston; Simone wouldn't be able to see him till the morning. He just hoped that Jean-Paul wasn't delayed; he was near the end of his tether, his nerves shot with waiting on the outcome.

Viana took the first sips of her coffee. She could sense the awkward-ness, the tension between them growing more with each beat of silence. Georges still had only drunk a third of his coke, and would be more likely to leave prematurely if he felt uncomfortable. She tried to lighten the mood, smiling wryly as she launched into petty politics at the club between Azy, Roman and Gérard. Telling him how, because Gérard as floating manager was there only one or two nights a week, Azy seemed to assume responsibility the rest of the time.

'Often he'll talk straight to Roman about something serious without bothering to consult Gérard, and a few times it's caused problems. Gérard feels he's losing his authority.' Viana shook her head, watching keenly Georges take another few sips. 'And there's no rhyme or reason to what Azy might pick up on to complain about. One time, Amy, you know – well, she took too many hits of dope before going on, then she slipped a Quaalude and topped up by sneaking some large whisky shots into her orange juice from a flask in her hand-bag. An hour into dancing and she was on cloud nine. She started laughing uncontrollably when her ass brushed too close and knocked a client's toupee out of place. The client complained, and Azy was all apologies and offered the client a drink on the house – but Azy didn't say nothing to Roman or Gérard about it.' Viana's smile broadened.

'Fact is, as soon as the client left, Azy too was wetting himself over it.'

Georges grinned. He could just imagine Azy's fawning, wide-eyed 'yes, bossman, sorry, bossman' act until the client was gone. He felt himself relax a bit, but maybe that was because Viana was relaxing and smiling for the first time – her fear and tension were easing a notch. But he could definitely feel his body mellowing; no, more than that, his senses were floating slightly, which struck him as strange: he could only remember having one glass of wine with dinner and a beer earlier while checking the tills. And it was also hot in here, his throat was dry. He loosened his collar a little and took a couple of gulps of coke.

Viana followed the glass anxiously: *two-thirds down*. 'But then other times, Azy will be as strict as hell, won't budge an inch. Particularly when it comes to dating clients. Perhaps it's because we had a lot of trouble with that Michelle last year dating one, some real nasty scenes and shouting matches in the club before Gérard and Roman got rid of her. And then Azy too had that problem with dating Janine last year. He got a real roasting over that – so perhaps that's why he's so strict on it with others.'

'Yeah, I can see that.' *God*, it was hot. He took another slug, felt it cut through the chalk in his throat. And he felt dizzy . . . with a dull ringing in his ears. Perhaps the beer he'd had earlier was off, or maybe it was something he ate.

'That's why I didn't want anything said to Azy about this guy bugging me. For sure he'd have said something to Gérard or Roman.'

'Yeah, yeah.' Georges held out one hand. 'I understand. No problem. Look, I . . . I . . . I'm afraid I'm not feeling that well. I think I'd better go.' The ringing had turned to a solid ache at his temples, and everything was becoming hazy, more distant. He got uncertainly to his feet.

'Oh . . . right. Can't you stay just a few minutes more? He could still be waiting outside.' Her concern, she hoped, came over as real: inside she was panicking. At this rate, Georges was going to flake out halfway along the building corridor or in the lift for all her neighbours to see; or, worse still, while he was driving home.

'Stay longer? Uh . . . I . . . I don't know.' His legs seemed to hardly hold him. He took a step, but they felt like numb jelly and buckled quickly. He grabbed on to the coffee table for support. The room shifted and swayed, Viana's voice little more than a dull echo. And suddenly all the other signals gelled in that instant: her insisting on him staying longer, her pause recalling the boyfriend's name . . . her watching his glass keenly as he drank. '*Viana* . . . what have you done to me? . . . What have you –'

'Nothing, Georges . . . nothing! Are you okay? You're frightening me.'

Georges tried to look at her directly, to see from her eyes whether she was lying – but at that moment his legs gave way completely, his right shoulder and arm crashing into the table before his face hit the carpet. Perhaps he'd got it wrong, it *was* just some bad food or beer: her plea that she was frightened had sounded heartfelt, real. And he could feel her now shaking his shoulder, her voice frantic.

'Georges . . . *Georges!*'

But there was a moment before everything faded when Viana obviously thought he was already unconscious and couldn't hear anything. She started gently sobbing and then he felt the soft press of her lips against one cheek, the moistness of a single teardrop against his temple as she muttered, 'I'm sorry, Georges . . . so sorry.' He began to fear the worst.

18

Elena was a little breathless as she jumped back in the car and waved the tickets. 'Great. I've got them.'

She started up and headed off. Judging from Lorena's uncertain smile, the significance of the triumph was obviously lost on her. Elena had become rigid with tension when the clerk seemed slow at processing everything on screen, filled with sudden panic that an alert might have already reached the ticket desk. First hurdle down: two more to go. As she wended her way around and got her first view of the Eurotunnel check-in kiosks eighty yards ahead, she could see that there were about three or four cars in each queue.

'Don't forget, if anyone asks – you're my daughter, Katine.' Elena stared the message home for a second to Lorena. She'd already mentioned it on the long drive, but it was crucial now that they were coming up to customs. One of the key parts of her plan: Katine was still on her passport, and with Lorena only a year older, they should sail through with no problem. 'I don't think they will ask – but just in case.'

'Okay.' Lorena nodded and fixed her eyes straight ahead again as they veered over a lane to join a queue that had just reduced to two cars.

Each car seemed to be taking about a minute. Elena tapped her fingers on the steering wheel as the one in front started to take longer. The ticket-desk clerk had informed her that she could go to the duty-free shopping area for the twenty minutes before boarding, but she wanted to get through straight away. If there was no alert at the ticket desk, then probably one wouldn't have reached the check-in kiosk yet either. But each extra minute increased the likelihood. The car at the kiosk finally moved off: just one ahead now.

Elena's body ran hot and cold. She stopped tapping, tried to look relaxed, calm. Nicola Ryall would have discovered Lorena was missing fifteen minutes earlier. How long before it hit Nicola that it wasn't just some innocent mix-up with Lorena getting a lift from a friend's mother and she called the police: five minutes, ten minutes? Then how long for them to arrive, start questioning and get to the stage where they realized that Elena had taken Lorena? Another twenty, twenty-five minutes at most. But would they put out an alert straight away, or head to her home first and listen to the tape left with Gordon? The car ahead moved off. Elena pulled forward to the kiosk.

The clerk, a man in his early twenties, smiled cursorily at her. She stiffened her arm as she handed over the ticket folder to temper the visible shaking of her hand.

He flicked through the tickets for a second before looking up. 'One adult and a child?'

'Yes.'

The clerk studied the screen ahead and keyed in some details. After a second his brow furrowed and Elena's heart froze. Then as quickly his face relaxed and he made a quick note as he tore off part of the tickets. 'Board at Gate 8 and wait for the green signal there. Thank you.' He handed back the tickets with a boarding card.

Elena was a second slow pulling away, caught off guard at getting passed through so quickly. But the most difficult part lay only sixty yards ahead: customs. Any alert put out would have probably gone straight there, not to the ticket desks.

She felt a rush of guilt when she thought of the crushing shock that must have hit Nicola Ryall when she realized Lorena was missing – reflecting for a moment on how she'd feel upon discovering that Katine had disappeared from school with a stranger. To abate that panic, she wanted Nicola to get to Gordon and the tape as quickly as possible to know that Lorena was safe and wouldn't be harmed. But her wishes were seriously at odds with each other: to allow her time to get away, she was hoping that there'd be some delay.

Two cars ahead in the shortest queue at customs, one by the time she'd slowed and pulled in – people were being passed through quickly. She took her passport out of her side-pocket, her heart beating wildly. If an alert had come through, it would all be over now. Brief nod as the guard handed the passport back to the driver in front, and Elena edged up to the kiosk.

The customs officer fired a curt smile, hardly looking at her as he asked for her passport. His only direct stare into the car, as he flicked through its pages, was towards Lorena. 'Your daughter?'

'Yes.' Elena tried to keep her voice flat, calm, but she could have sworn she could hear a few nervous modulations just in that one word.

The officer looked again at Lorena and then at her, and handed the passport back. 'Okay. Thank you.'

Elena kept her return smile as curt and controlled as his had been, tried not to let him see the relief and elation that swept through her in that moment. She pulled away, but not too hurriedly. So, no alert as yet; at least not one that had reached customs.

But her elation faded quickly in the first minutes of waiting in the queue for a green light: fifteen minutes more to go to boarding. Her name and car registration were now on the computer, and an alert could come through at any time. She found her eyes drifting anxiously to the rear-view mirror. What would they do: run out of the customs kiosk to catch up with her? Or would they just contact the guard controlling boarding with a walkie-talkie? Then the half-hour journey itself: more than enough time for the police to visit Gordon, hear the tape and alert customs. They'd simply phone ahead and stop her as she rolled off the train at Calais. Her mouth was suddenly dry and it was hard to swallow.

Lorena picked up on her consternation. 'We're through now, no? Everything's okay?' Her tone was questioning with a hint of plea.

'Yes, yes. Everything's okay.' Elena took her eyes from the rear-view mirror and let out her breath. By necessity she'd put Lorena on her mettle approaching Customs, but there was no point keeping her on a knife-edge for the next forty minutes. After what she'd probably suffered with Ryall, Elena didn't want this trip to be yet another nightmare. She'd just have to weather the brunt of that alone. She forced a reassuring smile as she ruffled Lorena's hair. 'France, here we come.'

'I'm sorry to phone again so late. It's starting to become a habit.' The good humour in Azy's voice stopped short of a chuckle: it was way too late for open jibing. 'But I thought you'd want to know this straight away.'

Michel blinked and rubbed his eyes as he focused on his bedside clock: 3.08 a.m. this time. 'That's okay. What's up?'

Azy related how he'd seen one of the club girls, Viana, get a lift home with Georges Donatien. 'She told me she was getting a lift home with a cousin, but I was suspicious – so I hung about a block up from the club and saw her get into Donatien's car. What made me suspicious was she was talking earlier to him, and it all looked pretty sensitive, private. They moved away from the bar, didn't want to be overheard.'

Michel didn't see anything overly worrying, at least not warranting a 3 a.m. call. 'Doesn't Donatien talk to the other girls or sometimes give them a lift home?'

'Yeah, he talks to 'em, he's friendly enough, all right. But it's all at arm's length, he never usually leaves the bar. As for him giving them lifts home, I don't think so – he hardly ever hangs around that late.' Azy's gravel voice hushed a shade, as if he was concerned about listeners-in, as he came to the crunch point. 'But the problem with this girl, Viana, is that she's also Roman's girl on the side. That's why I called.'

Michel sat bolt upright, a sharp tingle running up his spine. 'Are you sure?'

'Uh huh. As sure as can be. They tried to keep it quiet, low key – but I've had my suspicions for a while. Then a few nights back – the last time I called, in fact – they had a scene in the club and it all came out. Roman blurts out about her riding his dick like it was going out of style – embarrassed the hell out of her.'

The pieces were all tumbling into place for Michel. 'So this was the girl Roman gave a hard time to the night he finally materialized after Venegas disappeared?'

'Yep, one and the same.'

Michel fell silent. The tingle in his spine had grown into a solid tense knot at the back of his neck. He massaged the taut muscles with his free hand. Faint traffic sounds from beyond his window were starker, more pronounced through the phone. Azy was obviously calling from a downtown booth. 'And you think they were headed for her place, not his?'

'Yeah. They went east on Sherbrooke, and her place is in the Latin Quarter, a couple of blocks beyond St-Denis.'

Michel was sure it was some sort of set-up, but how would it pan out? His brain was still too addled with sleep to apply clear thought to it. He realized he'd left another long pause and brought his attention back to Azy. 'You were right to call. Thanks.' Then, having got confirmation that the same girl was on the next night, he asked Azy to call him again then: 'I want to know her every movement and who she sees – but, just as important, her mood, how she acts.'

Michel contemplated the phone thoughtfully for a moment after hanging up. Another early-hours call tomorrow, but he needed to know straight away; in fact, it might already be too late by then. Michel ruffled his hair brusquely as he ran through likely scenarios: some photos of Georges and the girl together, for sure. But would that be enough on its own, or would Roman want something more torrid, graphic? More graphic, knowing Roman. He'd have to build his case strongly with Jean-Paul, a set-up that left nothing to chance, no other possible interpretations. Which would mean that unless Georges was tempted and the camera was concealed, they'd have to drug him . . . and once he was drugged . . .

He got up, started pacing. His hand was back quickly at his head, but now clutching lightly in exasperation as he ruffled. But would Roman be bold enough to take advantage while Georges was drugged and take him out straight away, with the photos then purely to cover his tail with Jean-Paul, or would he play by the book and use the photos to get Jean-Paul's sanction for a hit?

Michel stood by his apartment window, looking out. The floodlit flank of Notre-Dame was the strongest light outside and made a faint silhouette of his body against the dark room behind. That was the problem with Roman: you never knew. Option two might be the most sensible, but if time was pressing he'd take whatever rash action suited him best. But it hardly mattered: even if Roman waited for Jean-Paul's final nod, that would delay things one or two days at most, and there was little or nothing Michel could do in the meantime anyway. He'd already hauled Georges in on the premiss that his life was threatened and held him hours on a technicality: Georges wouldn't even give him the time of day a second time.

Michel regarded the rough stone walls of Notre-Dame with a wry, sour grimace. So, no fanfare wedding there in a few months' time; not even a burial there. Georges' family were middle class and suburban, from out in Beaconsfield, as Michel recalled from his files. They'd probably arrange a quiet burial and service for him somewhere out there. He'd be forgotten quickly by the Lacailles.

He found his eyes watering slightly: unsure for a moment if it was sorrow for Georges, anger and frustration, or the floodlight glare on the basilica walls. His hands had unconsciously balled tight at his sides, and he took a deep breath as he loosened them, tried to ease the tension from his body. It felt wrong sitting by when he knew with such certainty that Georges was about to die, the final condemnation that showed just how pathetically hand-tied they'd been throughout with the Lacailles – but then what could he do? What could he do?

'. . . but most important is that you should know I've gone with Mrs Waldren of my own free will. I've not been abducted. I phoned Mrs Waldren only a *few nights back and asked for her help – to arrange for me to see a psychiatric counsellor to know if my experiences with my father are just dreams, my imagination . . . or whether they might be real. Counselling which my parents and the local social services have refused. That is why I asked for Mrs Waldren's help.'* Faint swallow, hesitation from Lorena. The sound of a passing car drifting through the small cassette speaker. *'But when we'd left my school, Mrs Waldren asked me again if I was sure that I wanted to go ahead with seeing a counsellor. If not, she'd return me straight away to school. I said that I did want to go ahead.'* Another brief pause as Lorena took fresh breath. *'So I want you all to know that I'm safe, well and in good hands and will remain so. I don't want Mrs Waldren, Elena, to get into trouble for this. She's my friend, she's helping me, and there's nothing to worry about. I'll be back home safe and well in only two or three days.'*

Gordon left only a second's silence before stopping the tape. The lead police officer, DS Barry Crowley, was slow in breaking his gaze from the recorder. An assisting detective to his side had a notepad out, but so far had only scrawled two sentences. A uniformed constable stood sentry at the lounge door, as though wary that Gordon might make a sudden break for it, and another sat in the car outside, probably to start putting through traces on Elena's car.

Crowley had announced on introduction that they knew Elena had Lorena, and asked Gordon where she was. 'I don't know, not here,' he'd said. 'But she left me a tape to play you.' Crowley then asked what car she was driving, and after another 'Don't know', which Crowley had serious doubts about, judging by his return glare, he'd sent one constable back to his car. Gordon heard some radio squawk filter through from outside as he stopped the tape. They'd probably have Elena's car registration within minutes. Perhaps saying he didn't know had come across as pointlessly obstructive, but then the leeway Elena needed might be just those few extra minutes.

Crowley was looking at him sharply. 'So, if we're to believe this tape and she's not been abducted – then why the secrecy with you not knowing where your wife is or what car she's driving?'

'I'm aware that the Ryalls probably wouldn't share that view. They'd want Lorena back straight away. Particularly Mr Ryall . . .' Gordon nodded towards the tape, but Crowley held his gaze with worn indifference. 'He wouldn't be keen on Lorena receiving counselling. But Lorena desperately needs those two or three days for a few sessions to be put in.'

Crowley nodded thoughtfully. 'You seem eager to tell me, so it might as well be now: why wouldn't Mr Ryall be keen on Lorena receiving counselling? What's the supposed problem between him and Lorena?'

'Well, uh . . .' Gordon was caught momentarily off balance being asked straight out. 'Lorena's afraid that her father might be interfering with her.' The statement still sounded lame, unable to carry the weight of all the connected horrors it mentally ignited, even with the pause for emphasis.

'I see.' Crowley pursed his lips and looked down. He'd in fact heard a part of this already from Nicola Ryall, in one of the few moments he'd been able to get any sense from her amid her panic and screaming to please find her daughter, *please!* Halfway through his interviews at the school, news winged in that a pupil had seen Lorena leaving the playground and thought she recognized the woman with her: *'Mrs Waldren, lives up the top of Chelborne Chine.'* Mrs Ryall seemed relieved at first at this news: at least some mad stranger didn't have her child. But then panic quickly set in again, as if other consequences had suddenly dawned on her. Crowley asked if she had any idea why Mrs Waldren might take Lorena, and she'd told him about the two visits from social services with Mrs Waldren in tow. 'Mrs Waldren has some crazy, misguided notion that there's a problem between my husband and Lorena.'

Crowley contemplated Gordon steadily. 'You said that Lorena was *afraid* something might be happening with her father . . . Doesn't she know for sure? Has the girl said nothing directly in that respect?'

'No . . . it was all mainly from her dreams, she couldn't be totally sure.' Gordon realized then that Crowley had probably heard something already from the Ryalls. He tried to add ballast so that the claim didn't come across as so tenuous. 'Hence the recommendation for psychiatric counselling – to try and make sure one way or the other.'

'I see. Only in her dreams.' Crowley's tone was vaguely mocking. 'And what did social services say?'

Gordon sighed heavily. Crowley seemed intent on throwing out the ballast, making his explanation not just tenuous but almost laughable. 'The social worker who interviewed Lorena on two occasions along with my wife in fact herself recommended counselling. But her supervisor apparently had other ideas – mainly courtesy of Mr Ryall trapping the officer and my wife by taping their last interview with Lorena.' Gordon forced a tight 'I bet the Ryalls didn't tell you that' smile.

Crowley's eyes flickered only fractionally before recovering. He leant forward, resting his hands resolutely on his knees. 'But the upshot is that social services saw no reason for Lorena to have counselling. Lorena herself has made no direct accusations, it's all just in her dreams . . . so in the end your wife decides to take the law into her own hands and abduct the girl.'

Gordon shook his head firmly. 'No, no . . . it wasn't like that. For God's sake, you've listened to the tape. If Lorena hadn't wanted help, my wife wouldn't have –' Gordon faltered, realizing his voice had risen, he was almost shouting. Crowley's soft Dorset brogue had a lulling effect, as if this was all just a cosy fireside chat. And his appearance – pressing forty with fast-thinning blond hair, a rumpled brown suit which had seen better days – made him seem worn, tired, almost past caring. But his sharp, pale blue eyes warned of stronger mettle beneath, and as he met them steadily now, it dawned on Gordon that the sharp about-turn with pressure was purposeful: Crowley was getting the rise out of him he wanted. He was obviously going to be a stronger adversary than he'd first judged, but there'd be more than enough to raise Crowley's hackles over the coming hours: no point in going head-on with him now. Gordon tempered his voice. 'Well, my wife simply wouldn't have taken Lorena if it wasn't something the girl wanted, that's all. That's why the tape was made, so that not only my wife was sure of that – but you also.'

Crowley looked back at the cassette recorder. The tape certainly muddied the chances of any clear-cut procedural line. Minutes before he'd arrived to confront Gordon Waldren, his immediate boss, Inspector Turton, had raised him on the radio to advise that he'd just had Cameron Ryall on the phone ranting and demanding fast and firm action. Turton had assured that he was taking full personal control of the investigation, but privately to Crowley he admitted that he had no intention of getting hands-on unless or until it was clear that the girl had been abducted or was in danger. This was going to be an interesting conundrum for Turton: Ryall would no doubt scream that she *had* been abducted, whereas the Waldrens, supported by Lorena on tape, would claim that she hadn't. The only saving grace was that Ryall would be unlikely to scream too hard and push things to a press appeal, given that the reason for the girl being taken would also no doubt come out. Innocent or not, some mud was bound to stick. And what if the Waldrens were right? His own daughter was only a couple of years younger than that now. The thought made him shudder. He decided to give the soft approach one more try.

'I can sympathize completely with your wife's reasons for doing this – that is, *if* her suspicions are right. But if she's wrong, just think of what she's putting the Ryalls through now. And unfortunately it's not our job to judge whether or not her action might be justified: either way, she's broken the law. And so the quicker we can talk to her and sort this all out, the better. So again I urge you, Mr Waldren, to tell us your wife's whereabouts and what car she's driving.'

'I'm sorry, it's more than my life's worth . . . I gave my wife my promise. In any case, I don't know exactly where she is right now.' Which was partly true: he wasn't sure if she was still in England or would have crossed to France by now. Would Crowley have already put out an alert? If so and Elena hadn't yet hit customs, that'd probably be the furthest she'd get. Maybe that was what the constable outside was waiting for news on. Gordon felt suddenly hot, a faint film of sweat rising on his forehead. He resisted the temptation to check his watch and forced an apologetic smile as he looked towards the window and the intermittent radio squawks outside. 'Still, I'm sure that won't hold you back long from finding out what car she's driving.'

Crowley grimaced tautly and looked down for a second. He didn't want to revert again to a hard line, so he decided to go in between. At least it would put Gordon Waldren on a tight time leash. 'Look – you've obviously given me the tape to argue the case that your wife hasn't abducted Lorena. To try and keep your wife clear of a jail term for this. And while right now that argument might just wash, as the hours pass with the Ryalls worried sick and screaming for action, that's going to quickly fade and attitudes will harden. So I'm going to cut a deal with you, Mr Waldren, one that hopefully I can sell to both my superior and the Ryalls: if your wife can get Lorena Ryall back by, say –' Crowley glanced at his watch – 'midnight tonight, I'll recommend that charges for abduction not be pursued, and that we put this all down to an unfortunate mix-up. But if not . . .'

Gordon was shaking his head. 'I'm not sure that my wife will be in touch at any point tonight for me to pass on that message . . . even if she might agree to returning Lorena straight away.'

Crowley held Gordon's eye for a moment. He seemed to be sincere. At length a reluctant nod. 'Okay – I'll stretch that to 10.30 a.m. tomorrow, eighteen hours from now. But already I'm pushing things to the very limit, so try not to let me down. If you can sell that to your wife, you have my word that I'll do everything I can to make it stick my end. But after that time, I'm afraid, a nationwide alert will go out and your wife will be tracked down as a common criminal.'

Gordon closed his eyes for a second and nodded. 'Yes, okay. I'll do my best.' He was trembling from the confrontation. It was clear now that after tomorrow morning Elena was facing a jail term, and he was pretty sure already that she wouldn't be able to make it back by then.

'Well, at least we have hopefully reached some understanding on this, Mr Waldren.' Crowley left his direct-line number, and with a final curt nod departed with his assisting detective and the constable manning the door.

As they pulled away, the constable he'd left in the car informed him that vehicle registration had two cars listed for the Waldrens. 'And I've already eliminated the Suzuki jeep parked in their drive. Which leaves a Saab 900 – three years old from the registration. What do you want me to do?'

Crowley eased back in his seat and let out a faint sigh. He paused for only a moment. 'Ask Central to put out an all-points alert, county and nationwide, including customs points.' Turton's directive had been to wait until he'd visited the Waldrens' home before doing this, just in case they had Lorena tucked away in a bedroom. Crowley felt a stab of guilt that he had lied to Gordon Waldren, but then everyone else was lying: Turton to Cameron Ryall and no doubt Waldren in turn to him. Gordon Waldren probably knew exactly where his wife was right now. But at least it was only a low-level alert for now – missing persons instead of abduction and kidnapping. Turton had advised initial caution. And if they apprehended Elena Waldren before tomorrow morning, Crowley had every intention of keeping his promise about charges not being pressed – *if* he could convince Turton and Ryall. He'd said only that he'd try his best, no more.

The camera clicked repeatedly as the two naked girls slithered and writhed over Georges laid out flat on the bed.

Viana and the other girl, a luscious green-eyed blonde escort called Eve, started at opposite ends: Viana took him in her mouth while Eve licked his nipples, then they changed position for a moment before Viana slid on top of him, Eve guiding him slowly home. Looking on from the back of the room, Roman found himself getting excited

228

despite the fact that it was Viana. The drug was working as per the recommendation: Georges could still hold an erection, in the same way as a sleeping man having a wet dream, but was out cold, would remember nothing. Roman was probably getting more sensation from just watching than anything Georges might be enjoying.

The photographer had to set up some of the shots: placing Georges' hands on Viana's and then Eve's hips as they rode him, pulling his eyelids open for some shots so that it looked like he was staring up at them. For the rest he made do either with profiles or with angles where Georges' eyes appeared to be closed in abandon. Viana had taken off her face mask, and at Roman's instruction the photographer was careful to keep her just in profile, her bruised side concealed.

When they had finished, something in the way Roman surveyed Georges' body on the bed, as if gloating in the control he had over him, made Viana ask what he planned to do with Georges. 'You promised that you wouldn't harm him. I wouldn't have had anything to do with this if I thought you were. You said that it was just to make a clean cut with Simone.'

'That's right, that's right. It's just a spoiler 'cause he's doing the dirty on Simone. But I don't remember saying nothing about not harming him.' That teasing, mocking smile which now she knew so well, then his face suddenly became deadpan, stern. He reached out and lightly pinched her cheek, her bruised side. 'Don't worry your head none about what I'm going to do with him. Whatever it is, it ain't going to happen here. We'll have him dressed and out of your place in no time.' One last pinch, harder, which made her gasp in pain. 'You did good, that's all you need to think about.'

The sign flashed by: Béthune 8 km. A ballad in French played on the radio, the sound on low. Elena would turn it up when songs came on in English, particularly those Lorena recognized and liked.

She looked thoughtfully towards Lorena. They'd stealthily avoided the subject so far, their conversation had been light, incidental, but Elena found her mind turning to it more and more, particularly in the silent lulls.

'You know, if you did want to say anything more about what happened with Mr Ryall – we're away from there now. You don't have to worry any more about what you say because he's hovering in the next room.'

Elena watched Lorena's expression keenly. Weak sunlight flickered through the trees, Lorena's light-brown hair intermittently strobe-lit silver, translucent. Lorena bit lightly at her bottom lip, pausing for a second.

'I was nervous in the interviews, yes . . . thinking about what he'd say or do afterwards. But that wasn't why I said nothing then.' She shook her head. 'I just couldn't remember being awake when anything happened . . . not for sure at least.'

'It's okay . . . you don't need to explain.' Watching Lorena's small face tense, grapple for images that were out of reach, pushed deep into her psyche for her own protection, Elena wished she hadn't asked. But Lorena simply shook her head again; she appeared too wrapped up in her own thoughts to take heed.

'It seemed so real, him touching me, his voice in my ear . . . I imagined I could almost feel his breath against my cheek. But then when I woke up in the morning, I just couldn't remember having been awake in the night. And the dreams too had seemed so real . . . you remember?' Lorena looked directly at Elena.

'Yes . . . I remember.' Elena's throat tightened. How could she forget? Lorena's recurring nightmare was that she was back in the sewers and the waters were rapidly rising. When she couldn't lift the manhole cover to get free and was about to drown, she'd awake screaming, her body bathed in sweat. Elena recalled two such nights at the Cerneit orphanage during Lorena's ten months there after her sewer days, when she'd hugged Lorena tight and reassured her that she was no longer in the sewers, she was safe. And there had apparently been many more nights with similar nightmares when Elena hadn't been present. One of the Cerneit wardens had voiced concerns about Lorena's state of mind when after a nightmare Lorena had pressed whether the warden was sure that she hadn't sneaked off in the night back to the sewers 'Maybe to look for Patrika.' Patrika was her closest friend from the sewers and he'd drowned one night when the waters had risen: the main event, they suspected, that had triggered the nightmares. The line between the dreams and reality had often been thin in Lorena's mind, and perhaps Lorena was flagging that now because she was worried that, for all the trouble Elena was going to, her fears might end up as nothing: her suspicions of Ryall proven unfounded, all of it just in her dreams. Elena felt suddenly guilty: that wasn't why she'd asked.

She reached out a hand to touch Lorena's shoulder. 'It doesn't matter . . . that's what the psychiatrist is meant to sort out. If nothing is happening, at least then you'll know that for sure.' Elena pushed a smile that she hoped rose above her uncertainty. 'And hopefully be able to sleep easy.'

'Okay. I understand.' But seeing the faint shadows that lingered in Lorena's face as she took her eyes from Elena to look stolidly at the road ahead, Elena wondered if she did.

A couple of songs later All Saints' 'Never Ever' came on the radio, and Elena turned it up a notch, noticing after a moment Lorena hum along at intervals, the shadows receding. But Elena's guilt and uncertainty remained. She'd brought up the subject because between their lightweight, inconsequential conversation and the awkward lulls, it felt almost as if they were purposefully tiptoeing around the issue: it was starting to rise as an awkward barrier between them.

But she wondered if she had pressed in part for her own ends. She'd been tongue-tied with nerves practically throughout the shuttle crossing and Lorena had done most of the talking. Then with the relief of getting clear on the open road in France, in contrast she'd been more animated, taking over the conversation – until they'd passed a police car travelling in the opposite direction: a reminder that they were still far from home and dry. An alert could be out with the French police at any moment.

They'd encountered only one more police car since, but again it made her pulse race triple time and put her stomach in knots – and perhaps she was hoping for a quick admission from Lorena so that the nightmare could end here and now. She wasn't sure she could face many more hours of this assault on her nervous system, a constant trembling that rose spasmodically to an intense hot rush, her hands at times shaking so hard on the steering wheel that the muscles in her arms ached. But even if there had been a sudden admission and she'd stopped the car and put it on tape, it probably wouldn't have helped: she'd no doubt have needed the recording to be redone under the guidance of a psychiatrist for it to hold up with social services.

And what if those sessions revealed nothing conclusive either way? Or, worse still, if they leant towards the likelihood that Ryall was molesting Lorena, but without providing enough to support that claim with social services. Despite Elena's frayed nerves, at least Lorena saw it as an adventure and a hopeful escape to freedom? But how on earth would she be able to return her to the Ryalls if she knew with all certainty what fate awaited her?

★

The first real break in the case came through just after 7.30 p.m.

Within an hour of interviewing Gordon Waldren, Crowley had a team of five working on tracking down Elena Waldren and Lorena. In addition to an all-points police and customs alert, they'd traced all cash cards and credit cards in her name, and news had finally come in that one of her cash cards had been used fifty minutes beforehand, at 19.38 in France. Crowley went through immediately to Inspector Turton's office.

'Where?' Turton asked breathlessly.

'At a Crédit Lyonnais branch in Bonneval, about fifty miles south-west of Paris.'

'Where does it look like she's headed?'

'At present she's on a direct line for the south-west coast: Bordeaux or Biarritz.' Crowley shrugged. 'But she could easily veer off sharp and head to Brittany, or direct south to Provence or even Spain.'

'Okay.' Turton brooded only for a second. 'Contact Interpol and ask them to put out an alert for her and her car, with special emphasis on the areas you think she might now be travelling through.'

'Will do.' Crowley nodded curtly and headed back into the harried activity of the squad room – hectic at the best of times, but the Waldren case had added an edge of urgency: it wasn't often they got a child abduction, particularly one that started to blaze a trail across Europe.

He had to look up the Interpol number; the last time he'd contacted them had been over eight months ago. As it started ringing, Crowley glanced at his watch: forty minutes or so to process everything through Interpol, and then Elena Waldren would be hunted down in earnest. A British-plated car travelling out of season, it probably wouldn't be that hard to track down. The bonus would come if she used her credit card to pay for a meal or a hotel that night. Either way, Crowley was confident that within hours Elena Waldren would be apprehended.

19

Jean-Paul swam with more vigour than in his regular pre-breakfast sessions; not faster, but with more determined, cutting strokes, as if he might somehow thrash away the lethargy and pent-up frustration tying up his muscles and joints.

Roman had interrupted his normal time for a swim, was hot on his doorstep at first light with news of Donatien, eagerly waving a brown envelope in his right hand. They spent a sober half-hour over breakfast with Roman going through the details as he laid out the photos in the envelope before him: last night Donatien had slid himself in a private corner with this club girl, Viana, for quite some time. Roman used the opportunity to get his guy into Donatien's apartment to place some bugs and, while there, he'd done a search. 'And look what he found tucked away in a drawer . . .' While Jean-Paul was still frantically making some sense of the tangle of naked bodies, Roman went on to tell him that Donatien had given the same girl a lift home: 'Didn't leave her place for over two hours.'

Jean-Paul picked at his breakfast: the body blow of the photos and the revelations about Georges had suddenly taken his appetite. Their meeting ended soon after with him begging a few hours in which to make his final decision; though he could see from the keenness in Roman's eyes that only one decision was expected now: there was little room to manoeuvre. He would have taken his swim then – immerse and hopefully swill away all his problems, ease some of the aching burden from his shoulders. But his meeting with Simone was only twenty-five minutes away, and he needed every second of that time, if not more, to get clear in his mind how on earth he would present all of this to her.

He paced agitatedly, fuelled by two more coffees, for most of that time, mulling over possible scenarios. But when she arrived, most of them went straight out of the window: he'd planned to broach the subject immediately, but she'd clearly arrived on some sort of mission with something pressing to get off her chest, so he let her speak first, still gathering his thoughts.

He hadn't intended to actually show her the photos, his initial plan was just to say that he had strong, reliable information that Georges was seeing another girl; and, combined with the fact that he had lied about the circumstances of his questioning by the RCMP, she should steer clear of him until they decided what to do.

But as Simone ran through Georges' account of events that fateful night with Roman and Leduc, and why supposedly he'd said nothing then or since, his anger began to grow uncontrollably. Obviously Georges had somehow realized they were on to him about the club girl, so he'd primed Simone to throw in this ridiculous story at the last hour to try and save his neck. Georges didn't even have the courage to face him personally; he'd chosen to hide behind his daughter's skirts! He cut in halfway through and voiced his thoughts in a fierce volley, and within minutes they were arguing.

No, she didn't accept it. Georges wouldn't do that. 'It's just something made up by Roman because he knew Georges was going to come clean.'

'I don't think so. I had my doubts too initially when Roman claimed something was going on with this girl – but now he's brought me proof.'

'Proof, *proof*? What proof?' And as he hesitated, not wanting to cause her pain by actually showing her the photos, she sensed the advantage, sneering: 'And what girl is this supposed to be?'

'One of the girls from the Sherbrooke club.'

'Oh, right. *Right!* One of Roman's pet harem slipped some money to say she's got a thing going with Georges – and you're ready to just accept it.'

'No, no . . . of course not.'

'Georges always feared that when it came to the crunch, you'd take Roman's side . . . and he was right. That's why he was so nervous about telling you this all along.'

He recalled just closing his eyes then and holding up one hand, willing her to stop as his anger bubbled over. Though it wasn't directed at her, more at the way Georges had her wrapped so much in his control. But she was on automatic, unable to stop now that Georges had wound her up and sent her in.

'Roman's playing both you and Georges for mugs, has been for a while . . . but you're just too blind to –'

He flung the photos across the table in that moment. Flipped open the envelope and just emptied it out from a foot up, a half-dozen of the twenty falling face-down, then scrunched his eyes tight shut again and shook his head. 'I'm sorry. So sorry.'

Jean-Paul rested one elbow against the pool edge as he came to the end of his third lap, his laboured breath showing in the humid air. Across the courtyard through the glass, the breath and body heat of the stable horses rose in the cold morning air, as if competing with the vapours drifting from the pool's heat-exchange vents.

He remembered his father crossing the courtyard the year before he died, one cold February morning. His father and Lillian had moved into the separate wing at the end – which Jean-Paul's growing family had previously occupied – when Raphaël was born and Simone was just seven, seeing Jean-Paul's need for space as greater than their own. Security became more of an issue with the advent of their battle with the Cacchiones, and so the pool block and gymnasium were added: the house, they felt, was too vulnerable with the courtyard open to their rear gardens, which in turn were open to the St Lawrence only two hundred yards away. The pool block squared it off, made it more of a compound. Not that any of that made a difference, Pascal was picked off leaving a Rue St-Gabriel restaurant before the pool block was even finished.

Jean-Paul had been in the main dining room looking out when his father ventured out for the first time after Pascal's funeral: shoulders sagging, breath heavy on the air as he trudged across the courtyard snow, raising only a weak acknowledging hand to the builders finishing off the pool block. Jean-Paul should have known then that his father might not have long to live. He seemed to have aged ten years in the past ten days, defeated, all spirit gone.

But he could have done with his father's sage, years-worn advice now. He felt so alone with the decision he now faced, undoubtedly the toughest call he'd ever had to make.

He regretted immediately showing Simone the photos, even though in the heat of the moment there appeared no other solution. Her eyes darted uncomprehendingly between them for a long moment before she finally looked back up again. He could see clearly the hatred aimed at him beyond the hurt, anger and her fast-welling tears. He reached out a hand to her – there was so much else he wanted to say in that moment – but all that came out was another weak 'Sorry' as she flinched back from his touch, turned and stormed from the room.

He knew that he risked losing his daughter over this; it wouldn't be the complete loss his father and the family had suffered with Pascal, but with Simone's love for him fading and its place taken by nothing but recrimination, would be like a death of sorts. Jean-Paul didn't think he could face that, but he just couldn't see any other possible choice.

Crowley leapt across the squad room as one of his team of five, DC Denny Hobbs, raised one hand, frantically waving.

'More news just in! Cash card used again.' Hobbs cradled the phone tight in his shoulder as he covered the mouthpiece with one hand.

'Where?'

'A small town called Montrichard. Banque Nationale de Paris cash machine this time.' Hobbs lifted his hand from the mouthpiece and started scrawling with his pen. 'Yeah, yeah . . . okay. Thanks.' He hung up, tore the top sheet from his pad and handed it to Crowley. 'Fifteen-hundred francs taken out at 21.27, French time. And the street location of the machine.'

The second breakthrough in only fifteen minutes. The first had been that an Elena Waldren and child had been ticketed through to catch the 4.10 p.m. shuttle.

Crowley went back to his desk and leafed again through the Routiers guide that he'd pored over on and off for the past hour, trying to work out the likely pace and direction of Elena Waldren's journey. Montrichard. Population: 15,870. One hundred and sixty-four km south-west of Paris; 9.27 p.m., dark for over two hours, the next town, Loches, not much larger and almost 30 km away, and getting late to check into a hotel. It was worth a try, at least: no other leads or sightings of her car as yet.

He went over to Sally, the only one of his team with reasonable French, and asked her to raise the gendarmerie at Montrichard. 'Get the number from Interpol or the main Gendarmerie Nationale number in Paris.'

Sally pushed a prim smile and clutched lightly at her hair as she tapped and brought up a fresh screen on her PC, scrolled down and dialled out. She'd been under more pressure and more harried than most of his team, had borne the brunt of their liaison with Interpol and putting out a French police alert on Waldren. Introductory burst in French, and then a more generous smile from Sally. *'Oui. Oui. Angleterre.'* She looked back at Crowley. 'Okay, I've got them. What do you want to know?'

Crowley got her to ask how many hotels there were in town. Five:

four in and around the centre, one just a kilometre outside. Then which hotels were closest to the Banque Nationale de Paris on Rue Pétupliers. The Richault was the closest, only thirty metres away on the same road; then the Chateauville, a hundred and fifty metres around the corner. Crowley got Sally to explain their current situation with Elena Waldren: Interpol had already been advised and a French National Police search was out for her. Sally quoted the Interpol reference number she'd been given and the liaising inspector's name at Lyon Central, if they wished for verification – then Crowley got to what he wanted: two or three gendarmes, or whatever they could spare, to visit both the Richault and the Chateauville to check for Elena Waldren or her car. Crowley had to wait patiently while Sally spelt out the name and car registration. As for the other three hotels, just a call to their receptions would suffice.

A last flurry of translation tennis, which at one point appeared to overstrain Sally's vocabulary grasp, and she conveyed to Crowley that Captain Lacombe, head of station, assured that he would take personal charge of the situation and do all he could to assist. 'He'll dispatch some men straight away.'

Crowley passed on descriptions of Elena and the girl, in case Elena had given a false name, and they waited.

The return call came through seventy-eight minutes later.

Lacombe's men descended on the Montrichard hotels as if they were searching for one of France's most wanted criminals. Montrichard rarely got foreign or Interpol inquiries, six years since the last if Lacombe remembered right, and he was eager to prove that the Montrichard gendarmerie was nothing if not efficient.

He visited the Richault himself, assisted by two gendarmes, sent a team of two simultaneously to the Chateauville, and one man to each of the other three hotels, taking all but two men from the gendarmerie. Lacombe personally saw and, with the help of the receptionist, questioned the only two British residents at the Richault – a single man and a family of four. His other men ran through the same exercise at the remaining four hotels: seven British registrations, but only one close to the description passed on of a forty-something woman and a child of ten. But the interviewing gendarme who had sight of them said that the mother was blonde, no more than 1 metre 55, and was quite plump, probably close to 70 kilos.

Crowley did some quick mental arithmetic: four inches shorter and twenty pounds or so heavier than Elena Waldren, even if she had dyed her hair.

Lacombe had liaised with all his other men while still at the Richault and as a precaution had asked for the passports of all British guests to be photocopied.

Almost as an afterthought, Crowley asked where the two British registrations at the Richault were from. 'A clue is the last page of their passports, emergency contact addresses.'

'It's okay, I know from my interview notes where they're from,' Lacombe proudly announced back through Sally. 'The family of four are from Maidstone in Kent and the man on his own is from Poole, Dorset.'

Poole. A tingle ran through Crowley. Practically on the Waldrens' doorstep. 'What age is the man on his own?'

'Forty-five, maybe fifty.'

Crowley was pretty sure he knew what had happened: the Waldrens had got a friend to run decoy with her cash card. He thought of sending Lacombe back to question him, but there was little point: he probably wouldn't admit it or give any clue to where she'd gone, even if they had been stupid enough to tell him, and using someone else's cash card with consent was no crime. But at least Crowley had a clearer view now of where she'd probably headed: three or four main options, as far as he could see.

He made use of Lacombe's eagerness to ensure that Elena Waldren hadn't continued on to the next town, Loches, by having him check by phone with their hotels. And when Lacombe phoned back twenty-five minutes later with a blank there also, he asked Sally to recontact Interpol to urge them to concentrate their focus on border posts with Belgium, Germany and Switzerland, and Paris airports: Orly and Charles de Gaulle.

Elena was frantic within half an hour of waiting at the airport.

Gordon's elaborate plans might have worked – the train journey for the last stretch so that her car wasn't visible on the road for too long, the decoy run with her cash card – if it wasn't for their flight being delayed by almost two hours. More than enough time for the police to work out possible alternatives and start circling in on her.

She heard the news first at the check-in desk and it made her head spin. Walking away, she felt nauseous, faint, as if her legs could hardly carry her. The blaring airport tannoy echoed and reverberated inside her head, making it all the worse. She feared she was going to black out at any second and eased herself down on the first bank of seats only twenty paces from the check-in. Lorena asked if she was okay.

'Yes, I'm fine. Just tired from driving and all the rush.' Elena didn't want to let on how frightened she was, her nerves at breaking point. Every police car they'd passed, the ticket guard on the train, another man not far behind who looked from side to side, seemed to be observing everyone as he walked down the aisle – each incident had raised her tension another notch. 'And now I've just heard that we've got a bit of a wait for our flight. Let's grab a coffee.'

She smiled and went to take Lorena's hand, then realized that her own shaking hand would give away her panic – so in the end she just draped her arm over Lorena's shoulder.

But her hands were now shaking openly on her coffee cup, and seeing the concern in Lorena's eyes she felt she had to explain. 'I'm worried that the people who'll have been looking for you – probably now for the past few hours – might be able to catch up and find us because of this delay with our flight.' Elena kept her voice low so that nobody nearby could overhear, but as an extra precaution said 'people' instead of 'police'.

'But we left that tape to tell them that there was nothing to worry about. I was okay.'

Elena shook her head and smiled. The naivety of children. If only she could take the same simplistic view to stop the combined-harvester of nerves churning her stomach. 'I know. But I think they'll still come looking for you – for us.'

Lorena's brow knitted. 'But even if they find us – nothing will happen to you, will it?'

'Well, I'm not so . . .' Elena's eyes flickered past Lorena's shoulder, to a uniformed policeman shifting into view at the back of the room, going over to talk to a man in a grey suit with a walkie-talkie in hand. They seemed to be paying little attention to anyone in the coffee area, but still Elena felt uncomfortable with them so close. 'I'm more concerned about you.' She reached over and gently patted Lorena's hand. 'Come on, let's go.'

They spent the next twenty minutes browsing in airport shops, picking up a Walkman and three tapes and a Harry Potter from a section with English books to keep Lorena occupied during the flight. Or was it equally for herself, so that she didn't have to brave out any more awkward questions from Lorena: where are we going? How long will it take? How long will we stay there? Two or three days . . . It seems a long way to go just for that. Lorena was animated, excited; to her this trip was an adventure. Whereas Elena felt like a condemned prisoner, too preoccupied with her impending doom to waste her last moments with idle chat.

At least she felt less conspicuous rummaging in the back of airport shops, away from open concourses and everybody's eyes. But still the occasional policeman or airport security guard would pass and make her heart leap. And as they finally came back out into the main throng of activity, Elena's nerves were back to hammering intensity: more policemen, security men with walkie-talkies, customs officials, anti-terrorist guards with sub-machine guns. Just passing the occasional policeman every forty minutes or so on the way to the airport had put her nerves on edge – now she was surrounded by them! Having to spend two whole hours trapped here was Elena's worst nightmare come true.

She glanced at her watch: still one hour and eighteen minutes to go. The question was whether to go through customs now and wait out the remaining time airside, or whether to go through at the last moment. If any alert had come through, that's where the main check would be. The longer she waited, the more likely the chances of something coming through. But if she went through early and the alert came afterwards, would her name then be down so that she was just a sitting duck trapped airside for them to stop upon boarding?

'It's okay, don't worry. I'm sure everything will be all right.' Lorena reached out and slipped her hand into hers, lightly clasping.

'Thanks. You're probably right.' *Oh God.* She bit at her lip, suddenly guilty: she should be the one consoling, reassuring. But it suddenly struck her that this ten-year-old girl had practically seen it all: abandonment at only three, shuffled from orphanage to hell-hole orphanage where the mad and infirm were strapped to cots and simply left to cry and scream the nights away, with often only death finally bringing silence; her horrifying sewer days and seeing more of her friends die; and now her struggling to unscramble the nightmare images in her mind to know if her father was molesting her or not. She was old beyond her years, probably far tougher, far better equipped to deal with this than Elena would ever be.

Elena dragged Lorena into a gift shop to grab another moment's clear thought away from the hustle-bustle – before finally deciding to go through customs straight away. Not just because she felt she should be putting on a braver face for Lorena, but because, given her growing panic, if she waited any longer she feared she might not be able to face going through at all.

'Okay. Let's go.' She gave Lorena's hand a reassuring squeeze, though as much to comfort herself.

But within minutes in the customs queue, she was having second thoughts. She was shaking and her legs were weak again, the echo of the airport announcements making her feel slightly dizzy – she could hardly understand a word, for all she knew they could be rallying all guards to apprehend her immediately. And at that moment she noticed the plain-clothed guard with earpiece and walkie-talkie a few yards behind the three customs desks ahead, watching hawkishly each person that went through.

But it was too late to leave the queue and turn back – eight or ten people now behind them – they'd be spotted by the guard, singled out. And so she just continued shuffling numbly forward like a condemned person, almost certain now that there would be no last-minute reprieve.

Simone drove blindly for the first twenty minutes, the passing buildings and oncoming traffic blurred with her streaming tears. She was headed downtown, but with no idea where she wanted to go. Certainly not to the office: she'd already begged the morning off with an excuse, and the way she felt she'd probably take the afternoon off as well.

She didn't want to see or speak to anyone, or even be near people for a while, so decided in the end to head for Mount Royal Park. She wound her way to the far side of the hillside park and pulled into the parking for the look-outs over East Montreal and towards the north. In the summer, there would always be two or three coaches and several cars. But now, mid-week and barely out of winter, it was deserted but for two cars and an elderly couple at the last telescope in line. Simone purposely parked furthest away from them.

She took deep breaths, trying to claw back some composure, but her anger still burned red-raw and her eyes kept filling; she could barely pick out any detail from the blurry landscape ahead. The photos and the deception had been bad enough, but what hurt all the more, what she could never forgive Georges for, was how he'd played her for such a patsy with her father. She felt foolish, used; it made the betrayal far more bitter.

The elderly couple were ambling back to their car, so she decided to get out. She wiped her tears and walked across to the rail edge, looking out. There was faint spring warmth in the air from the mid-morning sun, but at the rail a biting wind hit her, making her eyes water again. Snow had all but gone from the city and surrounds; only patches of white could be seen in the distance, towards the totally white Laurentides mountain range on the horizon. She took a deep breath. The isolation was what she wanted to clear her head, but the Laurentides suddenly reminded her of skiing with Georges, and the images on the photos were quickly back, searing through. She needed a drink or three.

She didn't want to bump into anyone she knew, so picked out a bar at random on her way through Outremont. She started with a couple of Brandy Collins, but with the effects slow in washing through she went on to tequilas. Two quick shots later and she felt the first glow, her senses mellowing, swimming pleasantly. But she started to feel self-conscious drinking alone among strangers, a few eyes drifting her way and wondering why she was knocking them back so quickly.

She headed for Thursday's. It was more of an evening haunt with her crowd, so she wouldn't bump into any friends, but at least the barman Miguel would be company and good for some advice.

She went back on to Brandy Collins, was halfway through the first as she looked up thoughtfully and asked him, 'Could you go for someone like me, Miguel?'

'Yes, I . . . I suppose so.' He was cautious, given the possible implications: come on to a Mob girl one week, end up in the river the next.

'I mean . . .' She toyed with her swizzle stick. 'Do you find me attractive?'

'Yes, of course . . . You're a real pretty girl. But you've already got someone – Georges. I've got strict rules about things like that.' Not necessarily true – he'd fooled around with a couple of married women – but he thought it was the right thing to say, would keep him clear of the river.

'Yeah, sure.' She pulled a face and looked down into her drink. 'Shame he's not got the same rule book.'

They were silent for a second. Miguel could see that she'd been drinking heavily, but her maudlin mood was the main signal that she wanted him to ask, 'Something wrong?'

'Yeah.' She slowly nodded and pushed a rueful smile. 'I just found out that Georges has been . . .' She stopped herself short; they saw Miguel every other week, but still she didn't really know him well enough to share something like this. 'Well, we've . . . we've got our problems right now.'

'I'm sorry to hear that.' He reached out and lightly touched her arm; the closest to consolation he dared get. He flushed slightly; he could tell from her suddenly downcast expression that it was no light problem. He was probably better off not knowing: another step away from the river. 'I . . . I just hope it all works out okay.'

'Thanks.' Simone patted Miguel's hand for a second before it was pulled away. 'I –' her mobile started ringing – 'I hope so too.'

Miguel broke away with a pained smile and went to serve some customers at the far end of the bar. She looked at the display: Georges' office number. She'd promised to phone him at midday to let him know how it went. 1.12 p.m. now: obviously he was curious and wondering why she hadn't called. Let him stew. She let it ring out, then as soon as it had stopped she switched it off.

Miguel started to get busy with the lunchtime crowd, so she decided to leave. She didn't feel like going on about her problems with others close and, besides, what else was there to say? She knocked back her Brandy Collins and lifted one hand to Miguel, who volleyed, 'Take care now, Simone', as he served a fresh customer. The same pained smile. He was concerned about her.

She ambled down Rue Ste-Catherine, aimlessly window-shopping – her thoughts were still elsewhere – then dived into Eaton's shopping centre. But some of the shops reminded her of days out with Georges: the boutique where on impulse he'd bought her a dress she liked, the jewellers for her engagement ring . . . The tears were quickly back again, and she began to feel uncomfortable with so many people milling close, some of them looking at her curiously. She headed out to the street again. She was far too drunk to drive, so hailed a cab to the Latin Quarter. It should be quieter there.

She dived into an Italian restaurant at the start of Rue St-Denis – maybe she'd feel better if she ate something – but could manage only three mouthfuls of lasagne before pushing it away; though she made good work of the half-carafe of red she'd ordered with it, finishing it all. Two calls had come through to her mobile message board since she'd left Thursday's. She played them as she ambled away from the restaurant.

The first was her father: *'I'm sorry everything went the way it did earlier.*

But I don't want things just left on that note. Call me back as soon as you can.'

The second was Georges: *'I tried to get you an hour ago, but it didn't answer. How did it go? Please, if you have any news . . . I'm getting frantic here, Simone. You know how important it . . .'*

His wheedling tone pushed her over the edge: she smashed her mobile against a lamp-post before the message had finished – then gave it three sharp stomps with her right heel. Fragments of plastic and circuit board splayed across the pavement. A waiter from a Vietnamese restaurant to one side was staring at her, and a group of three further down who weren't quite in focus. She stepped back as if to detach herself from the mess, but her legs felt suddenly weak, unsteady, and she buckled slightly before righting herself. She fixed her gaze finally on a Labbatt's sign twenty yards away and headed for it; she had enough of her senses left to know that she probably wouldn't make it much further than that.

Her hands were still shaking with rage as she wrapped them around her glass, another Brandy Collins. She closed her eyes as she took the first few slugs. Bastard. Bastard. *Bastard!* And as she opened them again, she noticed for the first time the guy looking over from the end of the bar: late twenties, ponytail, black T-shirt cut high on his shoulders – totally inappropriate for the weather, but it showed off his biceps and the small tattoo high on his right arm. Why was it men had some homing device to pick out drunken women who might be easy targets? She looked away, tried not to encourage him. Though maybe that's what she should be doing: pick up some hunk and get him to fuck her stupid, then send Georges the photos. Let *him* see how it felt.

It put the first smile of the day on her face – but a sudden worry, one thing she hadn't thought of before, gripped her then: her father's uncharacteristic anger as he'd hit back about Georges, his comment about Roman providing proof, no doubt the photos, and their concern about Georges giving information to the RCMP. As much as she despised what Georges had done and probably never wanted to see him again, that was a far stretch from wanting to see him in any way harmed. She reached to her pocket, then remembered she no longer had her mobile. She paid and made her way uncertainly out of the bar, looking for the first phone booth.

'They've got her!' Sally beckoned Crowley excitedly and covered the phone mouthpiece with her other hand.

'Where?'

'Paris, Orly Airport. They stopped her at Customs just ten minutes ago.' She lifted her hand free and turned her attention back to the phone. '*Oui . . . oui. D'accord.* Yes . . . I see. We'll wait for your call back then.' She let out a tired breath as she hung up. 'They're just getting someone to question her officially. They've got a fair few English speakers at customs, but apparently they had to wait for a National Police officer with sufficient rank and good enough English for the purpose.'

'And she's got the girl with her?'

'Sounds like it from their description. Girl with long brown hair of ten or eleven.'

'Great!' Crowley clutched the air by his shoulder into a fist. He decided to use the lull to phone Turton, who'd called just twenty minutes before to complain that he'd had Ryall on grilling him again.

Turton agreed that it was good news. 'I didn't even mention the Montrichard hotels fiasco when he called. Just said that we had some good leads in from France and were confident that she'd be apprehended soon.'

'Yes, well at least it finally looks like we're . . .' He faltered. Across the room Sally answered her phone again. Her face rapidly clouded. She glared towards him and waved urgently. '. . . we're there. But, uh . . . perhaps best not to say anything to Ryall until we have the interview confirmation through. We're waiting for that now. Yes . . . Should be no more than ten or fifteen minutes.' Sally's expression told him he'd need that time to unravel whatever this new problem was. He hung up and darted across. 'What now?'

Sally exhaled heavily as she dropped the bombshell: close call, but not her. The woman's name was Walden, not Waldren. Janet Walden. 'Apparently the alert went out just on the surname, the customs officer misread it on the passport, and everything trickled down wrong from there . . . until the police officer went to interview her in the detention room.'

'Middle name?'

Sally glanced at her notes. 'Emily. Oh . . . and the girl with her is twelve, not ten.'

Crowley grimaced tensely. It wasn't her. This time it was an error rather than a deliberate foil, but he was starting to develop a healthy respect for Elena Waldren: obviously she hadn't just leapt for the first border post and airport options; she'd planned things through. He went back to his maps and tried to put himself in her position. If he'd had a false trail blazed through the middle of France, where in reality would he have headed? He'd better come up with at least some sensible suggestions before he phoned Turton back.

The two men in the black Econoline held eighty yards back from the St-Laurent bar, practically the last clear view that could be had of its entrance. A discreet distance, with the van's tinted windows adding extra discretion.

The man in the passenger seat was on his mobile. 'They've been inside almost two hours now.'

'Still hang on. They can't be much longer, and this might be the best shot we'll get.'

'Yeah, okay. Will do.'

'Wait till he's heading home, or at least the two of them are parted and well clear of each other – then make your move. And make sure you grab Monsieur D, not the friend.' A lighter tone to the voice, but falling short of a chuckle. The line was digital and hopefully secure, but still he was careful not to say Donatien's name.

'Not much chance of that. We've got the photo right in front of us.'

'And make sure you're not seen.'

'Don't worry. We'll have ski-masks on and we'll pick a quiet spot. And we'll have the hood over his head before he has a chance to even turn around.'

20

Eight beers and half a bottle of Kentucky bourbon between them and they'd put half of Georges' and the world's problems to rights, but still hadn't come up with any answer to his dilemma with Jean-Paul. Georges stared miserably into his tumbler and rattled his ice.

'For God's sake, why doesn't she call?'

'Perhaps she still will.' Mike Landry knew it sounded lame at this stage: according to Georges, Simone was meant to have called over six hours ago. But Mike had already spun through most of the options: perhaps she got tied up at work; perhaps things got delayed and she wasn't able to see her father till later; perhaps she tried to get hold of him and missed him; perhaps, perhaps, perhaps. But Georges was adamant: no, she'd have made sure to get hold of him one way or the other. She knew how important this was to him. Something was wrong.

'No, I don't think she'll call now.' Georges chewed at his bottom lip. After trying her countless times, late afternoon he'd phoned Mike Landry. Landry was an old friend from university and they'd also worked together at Banque du Québec: the only person he could think of turning to with this dilemma. They arranged to meet at 5.30 p.m. at the Gypsy, one of the new wave of bars on St-Laurent. 'I think I was right about last night being some sort of set-up.'

'Can't you remember *anything* that happened after blacking out at this girl's place?'

'Almost nothing until I was in the foyer back at my place with the lobby guard fishing through my pockets for my keys.' The guard had informed him that a taxi had dropped him off just ten minutes beforehand. No, the taxi driver hadn't said where he'd been picked up from. *'Don't you know yourself?'*

'And a gap of almost two hours lost in between?'

'Yeah. But as I said, all I can recall are hazy fragments.' *Viana naked on top of him, but then the feel of someone else's slow tongue licking him, someone lower down just out of view. And a man's voice . . . Yeah, that's it . . . That position. Hold it for a second.* Then nothing until the foyer.

247

But it all had a dreamlike, surreal quality, and when he'd fallen asleep later in his own bed it was Simone naked on top of him, writhing. But the heat and sweat from her body suddenly became Leduc's blood, an expanding pool spreading across his stomach, his thighs . . . and it was Roman's voice from the side, taunting: *Yeah, that's it . . . You do it. You kill him for me.* He awoke abruptly and made strong coffee. He'd had barely three hours' sleep and his nerves were ragged. As he'd told Mike after going through everything over their first drinks, he just couldn't be sure now whether the earlier images were real or just another dream. He shook his head. 'Then as the hours passed with still no call from Simone, that's when I began to fear the worst about last night.'

Landry pulled a tight grimace as he looked at his friend. Georges' hands were shaking, his eyes bloodshot and unfocused from drink and lack of sleep. He was a wreck. But they'd already raked over everything twice over, and now there was little for him to offer as encouragement or sound advice. Georges was practically beyond consolation.

When Georges had first aired the problem, Landry had felt uncomfortable with the burden and commented flippantly, 'I thought it must be something pretty serious for you to phone me out of the blue.' But it quickly went the wrong way, descended into heated banter. Well, just that I haven't heard from you for over three months. He'd been busy. Busy? 'When's the last time you saw your parents?'

'I was planning to go out and see them this weekend or next, as soon as this all blew over.'

"Yeah. But when's the last time?'

'Christmas time.' Georges closed his eyes solemnly, accepting the point: early on in his relationship with Simone when he'd been lauding Jean-Paul, Landry had aired that he should be careful not to see Jean-Paul as a surrogate father, a larger-than-life figure to make up for his adoptive father's shortcomings and ups and downs over the years. Georges'd hit back that it wasn't all one-way, things hadn't been made any easier with his father in turn putting down Jean-Paul because of his criminal background. 'And to my old chums at Banque du Québec, I was suddenly a total no-go area. They daren't be seen near me in case word got around that they were associating with a supposed money launderer. Always one eye on that next promotion, huh? It was only you that didn't give a shit, because we went all the way back to university.'

Landry agreed that that was the case with a lot of their colleagues at the bank. 'But not everyone. People like Gerry Marchant, for instance – he couldn't have given a shit either. In fact, he found the whole thing quite glamorous. But you put up the barriers just as much, Georges. As soon as you got in deep with the Lacailles –'

Georges gripped Landry's hand tight on the bar counter at that moment. 'Look – this isn't just about social ostracizing because I'm worried about being cast out of the Lacaille precious golden circle. I'm afraid for my life, Mike. But if you don't want to help . . .' Georges got up from his bar stool, but Landry clutched at his shoulder, sitting him back down.

Yes, of course, he wanted to help. What were friends for? 'Just that it would be nice to see you now and then outside of the latest hot problem.'

But now there was little help Landry could offer and few consoling words beyond 'maybe you're jumping to conclusions' and 'maybe she'll still call'. He felt redundant, merely along for the ride while Georges steadily drowned and spilled his woes; no more use than a confessional priest, except that instead of three Hail Marys he was telling Georges that perhaps he'd drunk enough and should think of heading home. A few hours' rest and he'd probably feel better, get a clearer view of things.

'Come on, let's get you out of here.'

Georges wasn't so drunk that he needed support, but he definitely needed encouragement up from his bar stool. In his morose state, and with a finger of bourbon still in his glass, he seemed reluctant to leave. Finally he knocked his drink back as Landry paid, and they ambled out.

The two men in the Econoline saw them as soon as they were a yard beyond the giant gypsy dancing figures that marked the bar's entrance.

'*Okay. Which way they headed?*'

'*Looks like towards Donatien's car.*' They'd agreed at the outset that a good spot to snatch Donatien would be the side street where he'd parked. It was quiet, not much activity. The friend was parked further up on the opposite side of St-Laurent.

'*Shit . . . Looks like the friend's staying with him.*'

'*They're stopping. Maybe they're going to split up now. Oh, great. Choose now to give the fucking Gettysburg Address.*'

The fresh air on St-Laurent had cleared Landry's thoughts a bit. 'I think you should tell Jean-Paul everything. Bare all to him in the same way that you have to me.'

'Yeah, sure. I'm here to rat on your brother because maybe your daughter didn't put the point across properly. Oh, and whatever happened with that club girl last night, if anything – I don't remember a thing. I was drugged and out of it.'

'I know. But it's probably your only chance. And maybe something in your account will strike a chord, throw some doubt on whatever Roman's spun about it all. Enough at least for Jean-Paul to hold back until he's checked it out.'

Georges met Landry's gaze evenly. He was serious. 'So when am I meant to spill all of this to Jean-Paul?'

'Come on. Come on. Move it!'

'Not tonight. You're in no fit shape. And besides, Simone might still call and clear up the whole mess.' Still trying to sell the hope of her calling. 'Or maybe meanwhile you'll get hold of her. If not, go see him first thing tomorrow morning.'

A keen wind along St-Laurent stung Georges' face, made his eyes water. Landry was practically the only thing in focus among a blur of café signs, streetlights and the streaming tail-lights of passing cars. He started shaking, though he wasn't sure if it was with cold, or exhaustion and nerves. Only half a day with Simone's back perhaps turned to him, and he felt so alone, deserted. At least the drink helped numb the pain a little; he could feel its effect more now with the cold air, and swayed uncertainly in the wind. 'Maybe you're right.'

Landry reached towards him. 'Look, I don't think you should be driving. Let me run you home.'

Georges put one foot back, steadying himself before the hand connected. 'What, you? You're almost as bad as me.'

Landry shrugged as Georges smiled incredulously at him. Not exactly true: Georges had drunk at least three to his two; he'd felt it his duty to keep a clear head so that he could throw a sharp light on Georges' problem. Not that it had helped. 'Then at least grab a cab.'

'No, no.' Georges held one hand up. 'I leave my Lexus in that side street and by midnight the wheels and the radio will be gone . . . if not the whole car. Maybe that'd be the best thing: thrown in a cell for the night for drunk driving. Safest place for me.' He smiled crookedly and swallowed down the tail end of a belch, holding up his hand again at Landry's concerned expression. 'Don't worry, I'll take it easy. Can't be more than a dozen blocks.'

'That's it . . . come on.' They watched the friend step back, a few more words spoken between them, then with a parting half-salute the friend turned to cross St-Laurent. Donatien continued on the same side towards the turning where he'd parked thirty yards away.

The driver fired up the engine and looked in his wing mirror. Two cars passing, then a gap – but the next car was approaching fast. He waited for it to pass.

Donatien was pacing briskly, only eight yards from the turning as they pulled out.

Their every move from this point on had been pre-choreographed. The passenger went into the back of the van and picked up a ski-mask and a black-cloth hood. He slipped on the ski-mask and crouched expectantly by the van's back doors, ready for the signal to jump out.

The driver moved slowly for the first ten yards until Donatien turned into the side street, then he sped up the last distance. He eased over to the centre line for the left turn and waited for a passing car . . . but just as he started to turn, had edged forward a yard, a parked car five down pulled out. It beeped and both vehicles stood uncertainly nose to nose for a moment before the car swung lazily around the Econoline.

'Shit!' The driver clutched the wheel hard as he finally made the turn. Donatien's friend further up had looked around briefly, but his eyes didn't seem to dwell on them. He was already at his car, had the door half open to get in.

Donatien hadn't looked round, but the problem was that he had gained eight or nine yards meanwhile. They'd agreed that the best time to grab him was just before he got in his car – but now he was only yards from it, bleeping it open.

The driver accelerated down the street, his pulse racing as Donatien reached out, opening the car door. The driver kept in close to the parked cars, hoping that at the last minute Donatien would push the door back and stay pinned tight by his car until they'd passed, afraid of getting his door creamed: they'd brake sharp just past, swing the back doors open, and . . .

But Donatien went for the second option of jumping in swiftly and shutting the door before they reached him.

The driver slowed and finally screeched to a halt ten yards past, his breath falling hard with the adrenalin rush of the near-miss.

'What now?' Ski-mask asked anxiously. Through the back window, he saw Donatien starting up.

But the driver stayed frozen with indecision a second more before suddenly slamming the van into reverse. 'We block him in! Duck down out of sight!'

The van sped back and stopped sharp with its back four feet beyond Donatien's front bumper.

The driver watched in his wing mirror Donatien quickly check if there was enough room behind to reverse and still swing out. There wasn't: only two or three feet's leeway at most. Donatien's lips pursed tight as he pressed his horn.

A curtain was pulled back briefly from a window four houses along, but other than that, no one was paying attention: there was nobody out walking on the side street and the few passing on St-Laurent thirty yards behind didn't look over. A trickle of sweat ran down the driver's forehead. Hold tight. *Hold tight.*

The horn blared again, and Donatien's head came out of the window. 'Come on! Shift it!'

Ski-mask hissed from behind, 'Yeah, come on. Let's get out of here. He'll wake half the fucking neighbourhood!'

'Just a second more. Just keep out of sight.' The curtain four along stayed still, and there was no other movement that the driver could see. But now he was sweating profusely, his nerves close to snapping, and he was ready to accelerate hard away as soon as the next beep sounded. He saw Donatien's hand rise again – but this time it was to swing the door open as he came out shouting.

'Come on . . . move, will you? Move! I can't get . . .'

'Okay . . . *Now!*'

Ski-mask burst the back doors open and had the hood over Donatien's head before he'd finished the sentence, one hand clamping hard over his mouth. The driver leapt out and they bundled him quickly into the back and sped off.

No other curtains moved in the street and nobody looked from St-Laurent. Seconds later it was as if they'd never been there.

Elena's nerves didn't start settling back until three hours into the flight.

Dinner had been cleared away an hour and a half before and most of the cabin shutters were down, the lights subdued. *End of Days* was playing on three pop-down screens above the centre aisle, with a choice of German, English or Flemish dialogue through her headphones. But she paid the film little attention; her headphones were tucked into the seat-back ahead, her eyes flickering lazily in the semi-dark as she willed on sleep. She felt exhausted, completely burnt out by her Niagara-rush of nervous energy of the past hours. But still some residual nervousness, as she turned over in her mind things that might yet go wrong, kept her from slipping completely under.

Lorena was beside her in the window seat and had decided to watch the movie, only to doze off halfway through. Elena gently removed her headphones. Lorena looked so serene and untroubled sleeping: no hint of concern that she was probably by now on police wires across half of Europe.

Elena returned the prim smile of a passing stewardess, then leant her head back, trying to let the last of her tension wash away. Gordon's plan seemed to be working, at least so far: dumping the car at Lille so that she wasn't on the road too long, then the train to Brussels to catch the second leg of a Frankfurt–Brussels–Toronto–Edmonton flight. She'd booked to board at Frankfurt to foil early ticket searches at Brussels, and originally they were ticketed to go all the way to Edmonton. But they'd changed at the last second to Toronto and would catch the train up to Montreal. Even if they were finally traced as catching the flight, the police would hopefully start looking for them in and around Edmonton. Gordon had carefully mapped out every move, and revelled in it. Seeing his 'cat's got the cream' grin as he put the final embellishments to her route, she'd ribbed him that he'd missed his vocation: he should have gone into the secret service, not banking.

She'd decided to tell Lorena the other reason why they were travelling so far as soon as they were airborne – but the first good opportunity had been when dinner was cleared away. 'I'm also hoping to see someone I haven't seen for quite some time.'

'Who's that?'

'My son. We got split up some time ago, so I haven't seen him much, you see.' She swallowed back the lump in her throat; she was unable to bring herself to say that she hadn't seen him since he was born.

Lorena's expression was quizzical. 'Why did you get split up? What happened?'

'Well, it's a long story . . . It goes all the way back to when my father was alive and . . .' Elena suddenly stopped herself. She couldn't go into the horrors of the story with Lorena; and, regardless of the reasons, this girl whose life had been so scarred by abandonment since infancy would never understand how anyone could possibly abandon their own child. Especially someone like her, whom Lorena no doubt looked up to as a saviour of abandoned children. One light of hope among the gloom and confusion: Lorena had had enough of her hopes and dreams torn down by Ryall not to have to bear any more disillusionment. She smiled with that indulgent reassurance grown-ups often present to children when they suddenly realize they're not old enough to know something. 'As I say . . . it's a long story. Maybe if I do finally catch up with him, I can tell you it all then.'

She couldn't resist another smile to herself at the irony. She should be as excited as Lorena by this adventure: she might soon meet the son she hadn't seen since birth! It wasn't enough that she probably had an army of police tracking her to take the edge off that – now she'd also be playing shell-games with her constant companion. But having lied to Gordon and everyone else for half her life, that part at least should be easy: now all she had to do was deceive a ten-year-old child.

She closed her eyes, shut out the faint flickering light from the changing screen images, and willed on sleep to envelop her nervous exhaustion. But her mind kept churning: what if they did track their tickets while they were in flight? What would they do: radio ahead to the pilot, or simply have a police welcoming committee with handcuffs for when she alighted?

Her eyes flicked suddenly open again, watching keenly the move-ments of the stewardesses, trying to judge if they were glancing her way at all anxiously or guardedly. She might as well forget it: sleep was impossible.

Georges was still gasping for breath minutes after the hood had been put on; not just because it was tight around his head and face, but from the exertion of the struggle as he was bundled in and tied up. And his breath was hot: he felt as if his head was boiling, his pulse pounding like a jackhammer at his temples.

'What the ffffuck . . . isss this? . . .' Two tremulous, breathless bursts. 'What's this about?' Though in his rapidly sinking heart, he knew exactly what it was about; he'd worried about little else for days.

No answer.

As he regained more breath, he ventured: 'This is about Roman, isn't it?'

Still no answer. Only the drone of the van and its vibrations against his side as it sped through the city. He was laid flat in a half-coiled position, found it difficult to sit up with his hands tied behind his back and his legs also bound.

Georges tuned in to the city sounds beyond the fall of his own breathing, trying to work out where they were headed. Two turns already, a left then a right. Or had it been a right then a left? He was so filled with panic that he'd hardly paid attention. He felt them slowing and finally halting: a junction or traffic lights. Indicator ticking for ten or twelve seconds, then they swung left.

A long stretch this time: their speed picked up more than before and seemed to be staying constant. The rush of other traffic close by was also stronger, as if on occasion they were being overtaken. After a few moments, a voice finally from the front.

'So, what did you tell the Mounties when you were in with them?'

'Nothing . . . I didn't tell them anything.'

'You were in there quite some time. Whadya do? Talk about the weather, conditions on the ski slopes?'

'No, they put me in a holding cell for a while to cool my heels because meanwhile they were tracking some guy called Venegas, and they . . .' Georges found it hard to talk with the hood tight on his face. He spoke in bursts between fractured breaths, raising his voice because of its muffling effect, and could instantly feel the strain to his throat. It made his explanation sound all the more like a desperate plea. 'They were worried that if they let me out straight away I might warn Roman and spoil their operation.'

'Yeah, sure.' Heavy doubt in the voice. 'And nothing else?'

'No . . . that was it.' *The tape!* He'd mentioned Chenouda playing the tape to Jean-Paul. If Jean-Paul hadn't in turn told Roman, no point in mentioning it now. If he had, then it put an extra dark edge on what was happening now: they'd know that he was aware he was about to die.

The thought made him feel suddenly queasy. He wished he hadn't drunk so much: his thoughts were spinning frantically with fear-induced adrenalin, but he couldn't focus clearly on what to say that might save his neck. It felt as if two sets of nerves were at play in his stomach: one clutching so tight he could feel the ache, the other skittering wildly around the edges – and with the van's swaying and bobbing, he started to feel sick.

'I don't think he's going to say anything.'

'Nah. Doesn't look like it.' The driver speaking for the first time.

'So . . . where are we going to do this?'

'There's a multi-storey a few blocks beyond the bus terminal. I thought there'd be good.'

'What's the drop?'

'Six floors . . . but it'll be enough. He won't survive it.'

Georges' nerves hit fever pitch. His whole body was racked by cold-sweat trembling, his pulse a pounding ache at his temples as he felt himself spinning close to black-out. Raw bile swirled up without warning and he let out a couple of weak liquid belches before swallowing back, tasting the sourness as he fought for even breaths and some control. Almost surreal, as if it wasn't actually happening to him, their conversation now mirroring the tape – but he was sure now from the tease in their voices that it was purposeful: they *knew* he'd listened to the tape. It was just the sort of sick move that would appeal to Roman.

Was that why Simone hadn't phoned? But even if she did know about whatever happened in the two hours he'd lost at Viana's place – while he could imagine her angry and beating his chest with her fists or not wanting to speak to him for weeks, maybe months or ever – he couldn't picture her just simply turning away while her father said that he'd have to 'take care of it now', or whatever tame euphemism he used when he had to order someone's death.

The van rattled and swayed. He felt it turning, but more of a veering off than a sharp turn this time. He remembered meeting Simone that first time: her warm open smile with its sly teasing challenge. Fired at him so often when he'd catch her eye after meetings with her father at the house – yet it'd taken him almost a year to get up the courage to ask her for a date. Maybe her beauty, maybe who she was and how it might affect his relationship with her father. And now, finally, that smile was turned from him, she was walking from the room.

He lunged after her, desperate to explain that the girl last night was a set-up, it had probably all been Roman's doing . . . but as he touched her shoulder, he felt the stiffening in it, the power and muscle – the same raw tensing he'd felt in Roman's thigh beside him the night he pulled the gun on Leduc . . . and as she turned it was her familiar sly, challenging smile, but Roman's face. *'Yeah, fooled you, didn't we . . . foooo . . .'*

He snapped to with a jolt as he felt the van hit a bump and rise up sharply. He realized that he'd blacked out for a while, lost some seconds, maybe minutes. He had no idea where they were, how far they'd gone. The van was winding, circling – then came another bump and rise. *Ramps!* They were at the multi-storey the driver had mentioned – or maybe, as with Savard out in some field with snow-pack ramps. Roman would no doubt have enjoyed this part too: after hearing the tape, him not knowing, not being sure.

His eyes were stinging: part tears at Simone's betrayal, her letting him die like this, part sweat from fear and the pressure-cooker heat inside the hood. Another ramp, more winding round. He was tilted back, had to press himself forward to compensate. How many floors now: four, five?

He listened hard, tried to pick out the background sound of city traffic or the van's engine reverberating off concrete, or was it just the silence of an open field? But the engine revs were high, whining, and his own pounding heartbeat now filled his head, drowned out anything else.

Another bump and rise and the passenger said, 'Quite a few empty slots over the far end there.'

'Right. Looks as good a spot as any.'

The van straightened, slowed, and Georges felt them turn in and stop.

'*Jesssus*, guys . . . you don't have to do this.' Georges was hyperventilating so hard he could barely get the words out.

No answer. Their doors opened, closed, then a second later the back doors swung open. He felt himself being lifted, carried out.

'For fuck's sake, don't do this. I'm begging you. *Don't do this!*' Georges shouted out the last. Maybe someone would hear him. But the quiver and tremble in his voice robbed its strength; muffled by the hood, it probably hadn't carried far.

'One last chance, Georges.' He was still being carried; they were shuffling him into position as they spoke. 'What did you tell the police?'

'Nothing, nothing . . . *Pleassse*, you've got to believe me.'

They stopped. He felt the cool whip of the wind around his body. Six floors up or an open field? Probably the field: everything else had followed the tape so far.

'He ain't gonna talk, so we might as well do it. On the count of three, right?'

'Right.'

As Georges felt them start swinging him, suddenly he wasn't so sure – this was just the sort of warped last twist that Roman would love: to have him think that he'd just be dropped in a field, as in the tape, and then the cruel last-second surprise as he started sailing down a six-floor drop.

'*One . . .* big drop down there, Georges . . .'

'No, please . . . No! . . . *God, no!*' Georges screamed at the top of his voice. He'd hoped to rob them of the last-minute satisfaction of mirroring *everything* that had happened with Savard; but in the end instinctive fear overrode, he was blubbering and yelling for his life just the same as Savard.

'*Two . . .*'

Georges felt himself swinging higher. 'No . . . *No!*'

His stomach suddenly surged again, though this time he couldn't hold it back. He retched violently, sour vomit clogging his mouth, his nostrils; he started choking, could hardly breathe with most of it trapped inside the hood.

'*Three . . .*'

Georges prayed for another black-out so that he wouldn't have to feel the sensation of falling, but it didn't come. And he saw Simone finally turn to him and reach out – her sly smile was gone, she looked concerned, tender, as if there was something troubling her which she couldn't quite bring herself to say – but her hand missed gripping his, and he started falling. *Falling.* It felt like a lifetime, but it was probably only two seconds before he felt the solid thud of earth against his back. Shock exhalation: combination of relief and getting winded.

A suspended moment to allow adjustment, then, 'We lied, Georges. You see, we're really quite generous guys . . . because you have in fact got a second chance. Now, what did you tell the police, Georges?'

Georges was coughing, spluttering, fighting for breath. After a second a weak garbled 'Nothing . . . I promise, *nothing.*'

'He's not going to say anything.'

'Looks like you're right.' Resigned sigh. 'Shame.'

Faint rustle of movement, then the sound of gun safeties being clicked off. Georges pictured them positioning themselves and pointing their guns.

'No . . . *no . . . please!*' Georges' mind frantically spun for something apart from pleading that might stop them; but there was nothing, *nothing,* and facing the inevitable seemed to sap what little clear thought was left along with his resolve: he felt washed out, desolate, no more than a hollow shell.

'Sorry, Georges. Roman wanted us to tell you that he never liked you. Always thought you were a smarmy shit. He said it would give him great satisfaction to know that was the last thing you were thinking about. But for us, Georges, it's nothing personal. Just sorry.'

And at that moment Georges did finally black out, his psyche thankfully protecting him from what he knew from Savard's tape was coming next: two bullets to the body, one to the head.

21

'As I say, listen to the tape, then call me later on if you have any questions or particular points you want me to put across at tomorrow's session. Oh, my notes are towards the end of the tape.'

'Right.' Elena glanced at the cassettes in her hand in acknowledgement. 'Yes, yes, I will. Thank you, Dr Lowndes.' She turned with Lorena to the door. A twenty-something auburn receptionist to the side smiled with a silently mouthed goodbye aimed more at Lorena than at her.

'If I don't hear from you, I'll see you in any case at eleven tomorrow.' Dr Lowndes looked keenly at them both.

A hulk of a man with wild, grey-tinged blond hair, John Lowndes looked more like an ageing lumberjack than a psychiatrist. The only hint of erudition, apart from the diplomas on his walls, were pince-nez glasses which looked all the more out of place given his size. But he came well recommended by one of the local Dorset psychiatrists in Nadine Moore's file: apparently, one of Montreal's better Anglophone child psychiatrists. From his fifteen-minute introduction before the one-hour session, he seemed very capable, and, though the only clue was his parting smile now, he was obviously also eager to get to grips with Lorena's problem, *if* there was one.

'Yes, see you then. Thanks again.' Elena headed out with Lorena and took the lift four floors down to Rue Drummond. They walked a block and a half down to the car park where she'd left the hire car, paid the ticket, and headed east along Rue Ste-Catherine as she slotted Lowndes' tape into the cassette player.

The first moments were taken up with settling Lorena in and getting her general background, nothing of any relevance, so she tweaked the volume down a bit as she asked Lorena, 'Did it all go okay?'

'Yes, I suppose so.' Lorena grimaced and shook her head. 'But I still couldn't remember anything.' She sounded annoyed with herself.

Elena reached out and clutched her hand. 'Don't worry. It's only the first session. We didn't expect alarming breakthroughs straight away.' But she had at least hoped, and she *was* silently worried: they didn't have weeks for endless sessions. Two or three might be all they could cram in before the police finally closed in on them.

Worrying news from Gordon on that front when she'd phoned the Chelborne call box they'd prearranged. He'd told her about the swoop search in France, related to him by the friend who'd run as decoy; her name had obviously been out on the wire with Interpol practically from the word go. They'd originally hoped that the tape would give them at least twenty-four hours or possibly avert a police search altogether.

How long before they traced the Frankfurt–Brussels–Toronto–Edmonton flight? Gordon's bet was at least another twelve or eighteen hours, and they'd probably start trawling Edmonton first. Canada was a big country but, she'd speculated, 'What if they always put alerts out nationwide as a matter of course?' Gordon fell silent, and his 'Unlikely' a few seconds later sounded uncertain. And when she pressed him, he admitted that of course he couldn't be sure that they hadn't already traced her flight and put her name out on the RCMP network, or might do so in only a few hours. Another 'But unlikely'.

And so her nerves were still on edge with every police car that passed; she found it impossible to relax. The clock was fast ticking on her getting to the root of Lorena's problem *and* finding her son. She'd visited three of the Stevenses with initials N, M or G listed in the phone book, all she could fit in before Lorena's session, but no matches or even remotely hopeful leads there: twenty-six more to go plus the two unlisted Terry had given her, *if* they were still in Montreal. She shook her head. She must have been crazy thinking she could do both at the same time under this set of circumstances. The pressure was stifling.

The lack of sleep on top of everything hadn't helped. She hadn't slept at all on the flight, and had grabbed barely an hour on the train up from Toronto before the blaring train klaxon as they crossed a series of level crossings had woken her abruptly.

'I was trapped, couldn't lift the cover, couldn't breathe.'

Elena turned the volume up again.

'And this was a recurring dream during your time in the orphanage?'

'Yes . . . and for a while afterwards.'

'How long afterwards?'

'Well . . . a few months at least.'

'I see. But by this time you were settled in with your adoptive parents, the Waldrens?'

'Yes . . . yes. I was.'

Elena picked up on Lorena's beat of hesitation as she mentally prompted herself about the false name and story. Elena had presented herself as Lorena's adoptive mother concerned about abuse from her husband. It was the only thing she could think of to get Lowndes to handle the case. Elena smiled conspiratorially at Lorena.

'But then the dreams started to become different,' Lorena continued.

'In what way?'

'Well . . . in the last two, I was able to get the manhole cover open. Get free.'

'I see. And you felt relaxed then? No problems or concerns with Mr Waldren coming to your room at night?'

'No.'

As Lowndes' questions rolled on and it became clear that nothing dramatic was being revealed, Lorena looked at the tape player and then at Elena with an 'I told you so' expression. The only small triumph was Lowndes establishing that the return of the bad dreams coincided with Ryall (Mr Waldren) starting to visit her bedroom late at night. And this time the nightmares had come back in their original, more worrying form. The manhole cover was once again immovable. Lorena was trapped.

'And when you dreamt that your father was touching you – was that part of the same dreams, or separate?'

'Separate.'

'The same nights – or different nights?'

'Different nights. Oh, I . . . I think one was on the same night.'

Longer pause this time from Lowndes. 'Now, I'd like you to think about this question a bit more carefully, Lorena. When you wake up and remember the dreams with your father touching you – do you also ever remember actually being awake when he touched you?'

'No, I can't . . . I'm sorry.' Faint rustling, as if Lorena was moving or shaking her head. 'The dreams seem so real at times, but . . . but I don't think I am ever awake.'

'Don't think? Is it possible that you might have in fact been awake, but the sleep either side has muddied your memory?'

'I don't know . . . I'm not sure. I can't remember.' Lorena sounded flustered.

'Well' – for a moment it seemed Lowndes was going to press more, but then he decided against it – 'That's okay. That's okay.' Gently soothing tone.

As Lowndes recapped on some of the circumstances when the dreams first started – the real sewer floods they'd suffered and the death of Patrika – Elena turned the volume down again. It was background she knew all too well, *too painfully*, and one that she wished she didn't have to drag Lorena through again now.

Lorena looked wistfully at the tape player and bit lightly at her bottom lip as she cast her eyes down, as if concerned she might have let everyone down.

Elena turned into Rue St-Denis, heading towards their hotel. 'Don't worry,' she reassured. 'It's early days yet. Tomorrow might be a completely different story.'

But she could read the frank questioning in Lorena's eyes as she looked at her: if she didn't remember, she didn't remember. How were these sessions going to help?

Jean-Paul picked up the message from Simone on his answerphone.

'*Pa, I know that I'm angry at Georges,* verrry *angry. And I know you've got your own problems with him, and I don't want you to read into this that I'm trying to interferrre in your business – never have done. But I don't want Georges in any way harmed.*' Brief pause, the sound of traffic in the background. '*Oh, and I'm sorry that things were left the way they were earlier. I'll be back at my place in half an hour. Call me there.*'

Breathless, the words punched out as if she was afraid that if she hesitated she'd forget them completely, with a slight slurring on some words. Jean-Paul wasn't sure if she'd been drinking or it was just due to distress, or both.

He kept the tape rolling: two business calls in between, and then another call from Simone.

'*With you not calling back, I decided to phone Georges' apartment. No answer. I tried his mobile, but that just rang out too. I've tried five more times in the last two hours – still no answer. I'm starting to get worried. You promise that nothing's happened to him?*' A heavy pause, as if she expected him to offer reassurance in the gap, then with a 'Speak to you later' she hung up.

Jean-Paul anxiously checked his watch: 10.14 p.m. After leaving a message on Simone's mobile, he'd got wrapped up in a meeting with Jon Larsen at their tax lawyer's office the rest of the afternoon, then had gone for an early dinner with Larsen, the purpose of which was in part to delicately explain that they might have some problems with Georges. Larsen should shy away from sharing any possibly sensitive business information with him, 'at least for the time being'. Until they'd finally worked out how to play everything.

He dialled Simone's number. She answered on the second ring.

'Hi, Simone. I've just come in now and got your messages. Have you managed to get hold of Georges yet?'

'No, no. I tried him again just ten minutes ago – but still no answer. Not at home or on his mobile.'

A moment's tense silence between them as Jean-Paul's concerns edged towards panic.

'Please tell me that he's all right. That nothing's happened to him.' Simone's voice broke with the plea. 'I know that you've had some concerns about him seeing the police, but –'

'No, *no*! . . . Of course I've done nothing like that. Do you think I'd be calling back now if I had?' He sounded more annoyed than he'd intended; but his anger wasn't aimed at her, it stemmed mainly from his rising worries about Roman. 'Look, let me make some calls – then I'll phone you back.'

'When?'

'Give me an hour or so to sort it out. And if Georges turns up meanwhile, call me straight away.'

He hung up and dialled straight out to Roman. No answer at home, so he raised him on his mobile.

'Roman. We've got a problem. Georges has apparently disappeared.' Jean-Paul homed in intently on the silence and the intonation of Roman's response.

'When . . . *Where?* How do you know?'

Little indication either way. 'Simone phoned. She's been trying frantically to get hold of him the past few hours, can't find him anywhere. I want you to come to the house right now so that we can sort this out.' Maybe he could pick up more face to face, from Roman's eyes and body language.

'Well . . . I was planning to go to the Sherbrooke club to –'

'I said *right now*! See you here in twenty minutes.' Jean-Paul slammed the phone down before Roman could draw breath, let alone answer.

Roman made it to the door at Cartier-Ville in seventeen minutes, visibly agitated, obviously half-expecting a confrontation: Jean-Paul rarely lost his temper.

Jean-Paul rounded on him as soon as they'd entered his study. 'I'm going to ask you the difficult question first, Roman. Have you done anything to Georges?' He held one hand up, forefinger and thumb close together. 'Harmed even a hair on his head?'

Roman looked shocked at the suggestion. 'No, no . . . of course not.'

Either he hadn't or a very good act. But then he'd probably had a few hours to prepare. Jean-Paul shook his head. 'You know, because it's just the sort of thing you'd do. You've been pressing and pressing for me to do something about Georges, telling me what a danger he could be. But in the end, you just couldn't wait for the final nod, could you?'

'No, *no* . . . I'm telling you. I ain't done *shit* to him.' Roman held his hands out in exasperation, his face redder still, fit to burst.

'As father said, always the bull-head. Barging in before you've had a chance to put your brain in gear.'

Roman moved a step closer to Jean-Paul, his eyes fixing hard on him. 'Look – I haven't touched the fucking creep. *Okay?* Much as I might have liked to.' He appeared ready to strike out.

Jean-Paul paced to one side, looking away uncomfortably. 'I don't know. I come back home to find nothing but frantic messages on my answerphone from Simone. She can't find him anywhere, is worried sick about him.' He ran one hand through his hair and sighed. 'I just don't know what to think.'

Roman found more confidence with Jean-Paul easing off. He raised a quizzical eyebrow. 'I don't quite see the panic – even if I *had* done something, which I haven't. Surely having him taken out is what you'd have decided yourself in the end anyway? Bleeding hearts from Simone or not?'

Jean-Paul looked back sharply at Roman. Was this an attempt at rationalization because he had in fact done something? With Roman protesting his innocence so vehemently, any further push to unearth the truth was probably pointless. Jean-Paul exhaled tiredly.

'I was actually thinking more in terms of sending Georges to Cuba to run our business interests there and in Mexico until things cooled down. Not only out of respect for Simone, but, in case you've forgotten, because we're meant to have moved away from crime. Respectable businessmen don't go around killing people.'

'Yeah, and mugs who get ratted on end up spending twenty in Orsainville.' Roman smiled drily. 'I told you the transition wouldn't be easy, Jean-Paul. Cuba might be a good short-term solution, but in the long –'

'Whatever!' Jean-Paul held one hand up abruptly as he felt his anger rising again. 'That would be my call, not yours.' He watched Roman flicker his eyes down and shrug with a subdued 'Yeah, yeah. Sure'. Jean-Paul took fresh breath. 'But that's not the main problem right now. Hopefully Georges will materialize later tonight, but if he still hasn't shown up by tomorrow, if he doesn't turn up at the office – then I think we've got to face the fact that we could have a real problem. Georges suspects that we might be rallying against him, because he sent Simone in with some wild story to try and turn the tide at the last minute. And if he fears that he's out in the cold, that's when he presents the strongest danger to us: he might go to ground for a day or two until he's worked out what the hell to do, but there's strong chances he'll prove our worst fears and end up in the arms of the RCMP. And then solutions like Cuba *would* be out of the window – I'd have to leave things in your hands.'

'Right. I see.' Roman noticed how Jean-Paul couldn't even look at him straight, let alone say it – just the tame wave of one hand to signal that Georges might, after all, have to be taken out. He thought it pathetic – deathbed promises to their father over Pascal or not – Jean-Paul used to be so direct, unflinching, someone to respect. This new Jean-Paul, trapped between a recently found social conscience and what he needed to do to take care of business, he found hard to stomach. His conviction that he should be the one taking the reins of their business couldn't have been stronger than in that moment. But it was important to keep up the image of acquiescence just a little longer: until the final elements of his double game were in place. He held out his palms. 'So what do you want me to do?'

'If Georges doesn't show in the office tomorrow, then I want you to find him – and find him *fast*. Work every street contact you know.'

'And if and when I do?'

'Bring him to me so that I can decide what to do.'

But again that tell-tale flinch in Jean-Paul's eyes which told Roman that that final decision would be difficult, if not impossible, for Jean-Paul to take. He'd read things right all along.

'You will probably notice, Mrs Waldren, that although I pushed a bit on the subject of whether Lorena remembered anything happening with your husband while awake, rather than just in her dreams, I wasn't insistent. I didn't push too hard. There was a specific reason for this.'

Elena was in her hotel room playing the end-of-tape notes from John Lowndes. He'd advised that Lorena shouldn't hear them, so she'd sent Lorena down to the hotel bar to have a coke and some crisps with the promise that she'd join her in 'eight or ten minutes'.

Pause as Lowndes drew fresh breath. He was obviously measuring his words carefully. *'We have a slight dilemma here. If the problem with Lorena not remembering is that she's blotted something out because it's simply too terrible to remember, then the only way for us to break that protective barrier and draw the memory out is to push. But then if we push too hard and it starts to look as if we might have suggested a particular scenario to Lorena, unfortunately we get into the muddy area of FMS – False Memory Syndrome. Is it a real memory, or one we've planted there?'*

Half-defeated sigh from Lowndes. *'Though there's nothing conclusive either way at this stage, I'm afraid I am very concerned that your suspicions might indeed be well founded. The main clue to this is that so many of the horrors Lorena has suffered in Romania have in fact been transposed to her dreams. She sees that as safer ground than direct recall. It might also follow, therefore, that any horrors she feels she can't face now she also stashes away there. A safe haven to protect her psyche, if you will. But that's a long way from tangible proof. Let's hope we have a better day tomorrow.'*

She stopped the tape and let her thoughts settle for a second. She was sat on the edge of a kingsize bed with a tape player borrowed from the hotel owner, Alphonse 'Just call me Al' something. The decor made an attempt at French Regency with fake wood beams, mock fireplaces and fleur-de-lis wallpaper, but overall was too garish, heavy-handed. Even the dressing table was mock Louis XV, with the bed a matching four-poster with red velvet trim. The only modern things in the room were the TV and Lorena's sofabed.

But it was just what she wanted: a small and faceless establishment, just one of many bow-window-fronted B&Bs in the Latin Quarter. She'd decided to avoid the larger hotels which might register their clients with a central computer as a matter of course. The only problem was that Alphonse, a small rotund man with dark Brylcreamed hair and a thick bristling moustache, who also doubled as the hotel barman and receptionist, was discomfortingly gregarious and friendly. He seemed to want to tell them everything about the city – while at the same time drawing out snippets about them: 'Dorset, huh? Sounds nice' – practically on sight. Given their situation, she'd have preferred one of those mousy, indifferent desk clerks that barely looked up when you came in or left.

She drummed her fingers lightly against the cassette player. Great start, she thought ruefully. They needed desperately to push, but their hands could be tied from the word go.

She went down to see Lorena. She'd finished her coke, but was nibbling at some peanuts Alphonse had put before her.

'She was just telling me all about England, the house you have there,' Alphonse commented.

'Oh, right.' Elena went on alarm. Which house had Lorena mentioned: hers or Ryall's?

'Sounds like a palace.'

'Well, not quite. But getting there.' Probably Ryall's: their place wasn't quite so ostentatious. But she was nervous about what else Lorena might have talked about, worried that she could get caught out. She was eager to leave. 'Look, sorry. Got to dash now. Long-lost relatives to track down, and not much time left.'

'What you mentioned earlier?'

'That's right.' She fished her hire-car keys out of her bag, Lorena got up, and they hustled out. 'See you later.'

They headed towards Avenue du Parc. If Alphonse was going to show willing, then she might as well use him to advantage. So she'd spun a story about looking for long-lost cousins, 'the Stevenses, previously Stephanous – Greek Cypriot relatives, from my father's side'. She'd shown him the list of addresses she'd written down, and he'd given her a quick guided tour of the city: French to the east, English to the west, with St-Laurent as the main dividing line. 'Except for Outremont just north-west of St-Laurent, which is decidedly upmarket and almost exclusively French. Then we've got the Jewish community around Main and St-Laurent, the Italians, of course, in Little Italy around St-Joseph and Laurier, and the Greeks and Hispanics spread mostly in between. Westmount is the main upmarket Anglophone area, and the few blocks wedged between St-Laurent and du Parc thirty years ago used to be a predominantly Greek area – but now the new immigrants are mostly Portuguese.'

Elena turned off du Parc into Rue Milton, then took the second left – the street that Terry had given her as the Stevenses' first address in Montreal – and started counting down: 467, 465 . . .

She pulled in as the house came into view and turned to Lorena. 'Will you be okay here for a little while?' She didn't just mean the few minutes she'd be now, but for the five or six calls she hoped to get in before dinnertime. 'You've got the radio, or the Walkman if you like.' She glanced towards the back seat where Lorena had left it from her earlier calls.

'Uh huh. I'll be okay.'

Elena patted her hand and got out. The pavement was wide, then three yards of approach path and five steps before the house. Two bells. She rang the bottom one.

A narrow brownstone with a half-basement, orange-painted window frames on the ground and lower-ground floors, neutral cream on the top two floors. It was obviously now divided into two apartments – but twenty-eight years ago it could well have been all one house.

A small, swarthy woman in dark-grey track suit and floral headscarf opened the door. She looked Elena up and down curiously. *'Oui?'* Then glanced over Elena's shoulder towards her car.

'I was looking for some old relatives of mine that used to live here, and I wondered if you might have known them or know where they might have gone. How long have you lived here?'

'Four year now. Why? What their name?'

'Stevens. But it was a long time ago – over twenty years.'

The woman considered for a moment. 'No. No know any Steven. Sorry.'

From her appearance and her accent, Elena thought she was probably Arab or North African rather than Greek or Portuguese. The woman kept her gaze over Elena's shoulder, looking towards the car and Lorena, rather than meeting her eye directly. But then Elena too was looking over the woman's shoulder, taking in the decor in the hallway and what little she could see of a room halfway along through a half-open door.

Elena pointed to the top buzzer. 'And how long have your neighbours been here?'

'Just over a year. No longer.'

'Right.' *Twenty-eight years?* There'd probably been a dozen or more occupants since then. Elena glanced around: a bike against the railings leading down to the basement, an infant's blue plastic tricycle on the six yard square of front lawn. And it suddenly struck her what had drawn her here, despite knowing that the Stevenses would probably have left long ago – what was making her look keenly around and try to get glimpses of the inside.

She was following in his footsteps, trying to see what life he might have had after she'd given him up: good environment? Bad? Well cared for or neglected? Happy? Sad? She snapped to as she noticed the woman's eyes on her quizzically.

'Sorry. Thanks for your help, anyway.' There was no way she could know the answers from this postage-stamp of a garden and a glimpse of a half-lit hallway almost thirty years on.

The next few hours became an increasingly wearying blur. Practically the same pitch each time: Stevens, previously Stephanou; Nicholas and Maria and baby of only eighteen months, George. Twenty-eight years ago, 'relatives that my family lost contact with'. A lot of head-shaking, shrugs and hastily closed doors. And when it had been dark for over an hour and she was still knocking on fresh doors, Lorena started to become agitated.

'Still more? You haven't found him yet?'

'I haven't seen him in years now: we lost contact completely. It could take a while more.' Elena smiled sheepishly. After the long flight, and perhaps because she was nervous about the impending sessions with the psychiatrist, Lorena had been quieter than normal, more subdued; now she was obviously getting alert and bright-eyed again, and impatient with it. 'Just a few more, then we'll go grab a pizza. *Promise.*'

She managed to talk to two more people before deciding finally to call it a night. It was getting too late to keep on knocking on doors and they were both hungry, with Lorena bordering on cranky, complaining that she'd listened to all three tapes on the Walkman and there was hardly anything on the radio. 'Most of the stations are in French.' She sounded bemused.

Elena now realized that her search was going to take a lot longer than she'd first envisaged: there where three households to call back on out of the ten Stevenses so far canvassed, plus eighteen more fresh calls to make. It was going to take her all of the next day, if not spill over into the day after, especially since five of the addresses were in far-flung suburbs.

The only brief respite – a fleeting flash of hope that had made her catch her breath in her throat – had been a man in his twenties swinging open a door to greet her. Dark brown hair, quite tall . . . but as she looked closer, she could tell that he was probably closer to twenty-two or -three than to twenty-nine. And she quickly discovered that his name was Guy, parents Charles and Madeleine.

It suddenly struck her then that that was easily how it might happen: the right door swinging open, and suddenly he'd be there.

Twenty-nine years melting away in an instant: all the years she'd turned her back on him and tried not to think about him, although in actuality he'd hardly left her thoughts for a second; and she'd clutch at him and embrace him . . . or perhaps stand trembling uncertainly for a second before bursting into tears . . .

But then she was quickly back to the harsh reality of the head-shakes, shrugs and hastily closed doors, with her father's voice ringing incessantly in her ears: *'I'll bury him out of sight and out of reach. You won't find him.'*

22

Maurice Roubilliard pulled up in front of the Bar Rodéo with his
normal trademark show and flourish: one Harley taking the lead of
his gleaming silver four-wheeler, two more bringing up the rear. His
attempt at a presidential cavalcade: at least in terms of drug-dealing
at street and club level in Quebec, Roubilliard was omnipotent,
all-powerful.

At six foot three and two-forty pounds he cut an imposing figure,
with immaculate black leather trousers and matching jacket which
was closer to a waistcoat with its arms cut out and a four-inch silver
chain linking it at the front. It looked as if it had been purposely
tailored to show off his biceps and pecs. His age he'd frozen at
thirty-eight, but most put it closer to forty-six, with the main sign
evident in his fast-thinning shoulder-length rust hair. He sported the
green and gold Mohawk headband he'd always worn, but now it was
pushed further back on his crown to shield his receding hairline. He
was on his fourth hair transplant to cure the problem, but any of his
inner circle caught tattle-taling about his problem put their health at
risk: vanity went against the ruthless hard-man image he carefully
nurtured, boosted years back by him beating a murder rap with only
manslaughter; he'd served five out of the seven-year sentence, had
continued running his drug network from inside Leferge Prison, and
been out now nearly four years.

The four-wheeler was heavily customized, with tinted glass – bullet-
proof, rumour had it – an oversized chrome exhaust snaking up one
side like a trucker's funnel, and big wheels that pushed it ten inches
higher off the ground. The two girls with Roubilliard stepped down
carefully in their high heels. A blonde and a brunette, both stunning
and leggy, close to six foot, if more than a little tarty in their dress:
matching black leather trenchcoats open at the front to show tight
silver hot pants and bubble-gum-pink tank-top on the blonde, a black
leather mini, black see-through blouse and black lace bra on the
brunette – who looked about nineteen. But the blonde looked disturb-
ingly young, no more than fifteen.

At a table by the front window of the Rodéo, Roman nudged Frank Massenat and smiled as Roubilliard's entourage approached. 'Would you get this fucking guy. Makes you wonder if we're doing something wrong; we should be flauntin' it too.' They'd parked the Beamer discreetly round the corner and had entered quietly. But in their suits and Crombies, they couldn't help feeling nevertheless as if they'd made some sort of grand entrance: the bar was awash with check shirts, jeans and leathers, and more than a few eyes had turned to them curiously.

Roman noticed a hooker outside intermittently stepping a yard into the road to attract passing drivers, wearing hot pants not dissimilar to Roubilliard's blonde's, but with black nylons and a grey fake fur. He couldn't resist the jibe as Roubilliard burst through the Rodéo swing doors. He stood up theatrically, holding his arms out.

'Hey, hey. Maurissse, Maurissse.' He clamped his arms around Roubilliard's bulk in an embrace, then gestured towards the girls as he pulled back. 'These two come with you, or did you just pick them up outside?'

Massenat guffawed as the two girls scowled, the brunette perching one hand on her hip challengingly.

Only one corner of Roubilliard's mouth curled slightly, making it clear he thought the humour value was scant. 'Let me tell you, my friend, these girls are a cut above.'

'What – you mean they're ten years younger?'

'Yeah, yeah. I suppose you could say.' Roubilliard levered himself down into the seat opposite Roman with a faint grunt as Roman sat down again. He nodded towards the window. 'I didn't know you liked your girls street-worn like those tired pussies out there.'

'I just like them to at least finish their schooling so that they pick up on the finer points of my fucking humour.' Roman eased into a ready smile. 'Still, enough of my pussy preferences. To business.' No point in riding Roubilliard too hard. The regular drug shipments Roman was middle-managing for Medeiros guaranteed Roubilliard dancing to his tune; but this was a side issue on which he wanted Roubilliard's cooperation.

Roubilliard peeled off a twenty-dollar bill and told the two girls to perch up at the bar, he'd join them in a while, and, breaking off only to order a fresh jug of beer, Roman ran through his new dilemma with Donatien: nobody had seen him in the last twenty-four hours. He hadn't shown up at the office, wasn't contactable on his mobile and hadn't left messages with anyone. 'And we've checked every likely place he could be. He's completely disappeared. And we need to find him. *Fast!*'

Roubilliard nodded knowingly and sipped at his beer. 'Knows too much, huh?'

'Yeah, well, we're starting to get worried about him. He had a little run-in with the RCMP recently, and we need to talk to him, that's all.'

'Right.' Roubilliard took another slug of beer and fixed his eyes keenly on Roman, a slow leer rising. 'Rumour has it that he's been a problem to you for some while. So maybe this disappearance now means that you finally decided to do something about it: he's already keeping Venegas company at the bottom of some lake or river, waiting for the spring thaw.'

Roman sneered and chuckled nervously. 'Don't be ridiculous. Why would I be sitting here' – he waved his arm towards Roubilliard's henchmen at the table behind and the bar at large – 'surrounded by a bunch of assholes who look like they've been stuck in a fucking time warp ever since *Easy Rider*, asking you to find him?'

Roubilliard shrugged. 'Maybe 'cause, like everything else with our drug deals and Leduc and Venegas, you haven't told Jean-Paul. He doesn't know you've already offed Donatien. And so you need to go through the motions now with me to keep up the pretence.'

Roman reached across and gripped Roubilliard's arm hard. 'Look – you're just arms and legs in this. Someone with the right street connections to find this fucker – *if* he's still in Quebec. I'm not paying you to think.'

Roubilliard gave a more philosophical shrug, as if accepting the comment as a compliment: if his connections weren't second to none, they wouldn't both be sitting here now. By necessity, his drug distribution network touched every club, clip-joint, neighbourhood café or bar dealer in the province, and his contacts with fences and counterfeiters were also excellent. If Donatien had gone to ground anywhere, or wanted a false-plated car or false identity and credit cards to be able to disappear discreetly out of Quebec, Roubilliard would soon know about it.

'Matters not to me if you've already taken out Donatien – I'm hardly likely to let on to Jean-Paul. We don't exactly mix in the same circles: he's only interested in being seen around politicians and city

274

movers and shakers these days, not ex-con bikers.' Roubilliard raised his glass towards Roman. 'If you say try and find Donatien, I'll try and find him.'

But Roman held the same poker face with just a hint of ingratiating smile: Roubilliard couldn't tell either way whether he'd already taken care of Donatien or not.

Session 2

'. . . The tragic incident with your friend Patrika drowning in the sewers was something that intensely upset you? Something you found hard to forget?'

'Yes . . . yes, it was.'

'And what were your feelings about the rest of your time in the sewers outside of that tragedy? Did you feel vulnerable and uneasy, frightened, even?'

'Yes, we did . . . very much so. There were always noises: the rush of water, strange echoes . . . rats running about. We never slept much – it was just somewhere to escape from the cold at night.'

Elena sat in a small annexe seven-foot square listening in on headphones to Lorena's session in the adjoining room. No window between the two rooms: in front of her was a Nova Scotia Tourist Board poster with a rugged coastline vista. The headphone leads snaked out of a cassette player rolling to one side, and there was also a microphone before her. Lowndes dealt with many children's cases and the room was for parents who might need reassurance that their offspring weren't being unduly pressured. The microphone was only for necessary prompts or, in extreme cases, for parents to call a halt to the session. Lowndes had urged her only to use it if absolutely necessary, as it tended to interrupt the flow.

During a ten-minute briefing beforehand, Lowndes had voiced that, having reflected on the first session, he had strong doubts he'd get anywhere trying to draw directly from Lorena that she might have blotted out unsettling events with her father: his aim therefore was to start with other events and edge in.

'And how long did you keep on using the sewers as a refuge after Patrika died?'

'Three months, I think . . . maybe four.'

'And were you even more frightened then, knowing what had happened with Patrika?'

'Yes . . . yes.' Lorena was a little breathless, obviously agitated by the memory. 'It was even harder then to sleep each night. We would all huddle together and listen . . . and the slightest rush of water would wake us. The fear of it maybe rising again, trapping or sweeping us away.'

'I see. But this didn't in the end happen, did it? You were merely scared of it happening . . . and this replayed mainly through your later dreams?'

'That's right . . . it was only really in the dreams.'

Edging. Elena's hands clasped tight and worked together. She'd have done anything to avoid Lorena now being dragged back through those dark days – but Lowndes was insistent that there could be a vital link there, a key to the protective barriers in Lorena's psyche.

'And it's the same with what happened with Patrika. His death, and all the fear and anxiety that came as a result – all of that came up only in your dreams, did it not? Did you spend much time thinking about those events at all while you were awake?'

'No, no . . . I didn't. Not much, anyway – it was mainly in my dreams.'

'So, your recall of this period – possibly one of the worst in your life – would it be true to say that to a large extent you pushed it away at arm's length into your dreams?'

'Yes, I . . . I did push it away, I suppose.' A long pause, faint rustling, the sound of Lorena swallowing. 'It was very tough for me to think about, you know.'

'I know. I understand.' Soothing tone.

Elena closed her eyes. She could hear the tremor in Lorena's voice as she finally admitted to 'pushing' events away, her East European accent more evident. The breakthrough Lowndes had no doubt been seeking, but at what price? Elena too found herself trembling with the stifling pressure of Lowndes' questioning. Lowndes had warned that unless they tried a fresh angle and had a breakthrough soon, he had strong reservations about continuing with the sessions. 'We could find ourselves just going around in circles, hitting the same brick wall.' And so she'd finally relented and allowed him free rein. It was either that or risk having to throw in the towel: the thought of sending Lorena back to Ryall, possibly even later that same day, made her shudder.

'And so with other terrible incidents in your life that you don't wish to remember – do you think it's possible or even likely that you might want to push them away too?'

'I . . . I don't know.' Lorena sounded uncertain, or perhaps she hadn't quite picked up the link.

The prompt from Lowndes came quickly: 'Push them away into your dreams, where perhaps they're easier for you to deal with?'

'I . . . I suppose so. I hadn't really thought about it.'

Slow exhalation from Lowndes – Elena pictured him summoning up fresh reserves – then he continued on relentlessly, as if afraid that if he eased off the pressure, the thread would be lost. With a few more questions, he drew out of Lorena that if indeed something was happening with her father, that too would probably be too painful for her to remember. He finished with a flourish: 'Something you might wish to blot out, perhaps again – as with your terrible sewer days and what happened with Patrika – push to the safety of your dreams?'

There was a suspended moment as Lorena contemplated this: it was as if the realization of where Lowndes had been heading hadn't really hit her until that final connection was made.

Tentatively: 'It . . . it could be that, yes. I see now. I just didn't know what might be happening because I didn't really think about it before, I –'

'It's okay,' Lowndes cut in, perhaps sensing that this would be the most he'd get at this stage and that Lorena was once again drifting towards more uncertain ground. 'You don't need to think about that fully now. That would be unfair: after all, this is probably the first time you've even looked at such a possibility. But I do want you to stay looking at it for a moment, letting it settle more, as I ask you to consider something else . . .'

Elena had to admit, Lowndes was good. Before he'd voiced his concerns prior to the session, she'd begun to worry that even if they did manage to get Lorena to unlock her memories it might not be enough on its own, and in her call to Gordon late the night before she'd asked how he was getting on with Mikaya: they'd agreed that as soon as she'd reached Canada, he'd try and make contact with her. 'I've left two more messages, but no return call as yet. I'll try twice more tonight and if there's still no luck, I'll drive up to Durham University first light tomorrow.'

'One of the most beautiful Oriental girls I've ever seen.' If there were darker secrets behind Mikaya's earlier pregnancy and she pointed the finger at Ryall, they'd have enough for a social services order to get Lorena away: a few months' respite if not longer for more considered sessions to discover if the same thing had been happening with Lorena, rather than this madness now of trying to cram in everything in a few days in the hope of a breakthrough.

'What do you think would happen if you did speak out against your father and say that these terrible things that you picture only in your dreams were in fact occurring? That they were real?'

'I'm not sure . . . In what way?'

'Well, we're only talking hypothetically – what if – for now. But what do you think would happen to you, Lorena? You obviously wouldn't be able to stay in the same house as Mr Waldren any more, so where do you think you would go?'

'I don't know . . . I haven't really thought about that.'

'I see. I truly don't think you have.' Heavy pause, then a fresh breath from Lowndes. 'But have you considered that perhaps part of your mind has, and that part might fear that you'd have to return to what you knew before – the horrors of the orphanages and your days and nights in the sewers.'

'I . . . I don't know.'

'But apart from the dreams and your concerns about Mr Waldren, you're happy there at the house? It's comfortable and secure and you have everything else you need?'

'Yes, I think so . . . it's a very nice house.'

Elena held her breath as Lowndes teased out of Lorena that in fact this was a level of comfort and security that she'd *never* experienced at any time in her life before: there was a tremendous gulf between her current lifestyle and the deprivation and horrors of her past existence.

'Something you'd probably wish to avoid going back to at any cost?' A marked pause, as if Lowndes perhaps expected an answer or was intently studying Lorena for her reaction. 'Now that may or may not also be causing something of a block. But it's never that easy just to say, "Now that I know there's a block, I'll just remove it." So I'm going to ask you, Lorena, to relax and imagine that if you did have to leave Mr Waldren's house, you'd go somewhere equally nice and warm and secure. Somewhere with your mother, obviously the first choice, but if not perhaps some friends. Do you have some other friends perhaps you'd like to stay with?'

'Yes . . . There's my aid worker who first saw me in Romania. She doesn't live far away.'

'What's her name?'

'Elen . . . er . . . Ei . . . Eileen.'

Elena closed her eyes and swallowed hard. The warm rush at being

Lorena's first choice of alternative haven was swiftly quashed by guilt about what she was putting Lorena through: just when Lorena was meant to be opening up her mind to discover the truth about her own life, she was forced to hopscotch around lies as to who everybody else was.

'And is it a nice house?'

'Yes. It overlooks a wooded ravine . . . and at the end is the sea.'

'There. See. At least one good option, and no doubt there're others.' Lowndes let out a relaxed, soothing sigh. 'Now I want you to think about those nice places that you'd go to . . . just as comfortable and secure as where you are now. Because for sure your mother or your friend, Eileen, aren't going to let you go anywhere that's not nice or safe. And if you're worried about your father being angry and ranting and shouting at you – don't. He won't be allowed near you. You'll have nothing to fear from him . . . and absolutely nothing to fear concerning where you might go or what might happen to you. Is that perfectly clear now? You're settled about that and understand that you have no worries at all in that regard?'

'Yes . . . I understand.'

'And I want you now to draw on that, feel relaxed . . . feel calm. Feel the pressure gone of perhaps being afraid to speak out because of how your father might react or what might happen to you. But I also want you to be cautious: if you still can't remember anything happening with your father, even with all that pressure now gone – and I mean clearly remember – then we want to hear that too.'

'I . . . I'm not sure. Like I said before, some of it seemed so real . . . as if it couldn't possibly be a dream. But I just can't remember any time when I was awake.'

Elena's palms sweated as she clutched unconsciously at the headphone leads: she could feel the clawing pressure on Lorena with each fall of her breath, swallow or faint cough. Lowndes had edged in so deftly, purposefully: it reminded her of the carefully layered brush strokes of her painting. But then it was as if he'd suddenly remembered False Memory Syndrome and gone back and wiped out a stroke, worried that he might have painted her too much into a corner. He needed to push hard to break any block, but then he didn't want it possibly viewed that the memory had come about merely as a result of that pressure – because Lorena thought that that was what he wanted to hear.

'And when you were thinking back, trying to recall if it was real or just a dream – this was already the morning, the first moments of waking?'

'Yes.'

Lowndes confirmed with Lorena that her father wasn't usually there when she awoke. 'But have there been times in the night when he was at your bedside when you awoke?'

'Yes . . . sometimes when I had the bad dreams.'

'About Patrika and the sewers?'

'Yes.'

'But in any of those dreams, was your father touching you . . . and then you'd awake to find him there at your bedside?'

'Only one . . . I . . . I . . .' Faltering pause, Lorena's breathing fractured, laboured.

Gentle prompt from Lowndes: 'It's okay . . . go on.'

'I dreamt that he was stroking me, soothing me, telling me that it was okay. Then it became the water of the sewer washing over me . . . but it was somehow warm, strange . . . and as it came up to my mouth, I was choking and spluttering for breath . . . but still he was stroking me, telling me everything was okay . . . *okay* . . .'

'And when you woke up, was he touching you?'

'Yes . . . yes. But only my forehead . . . and he was saying the same words, that everything was okay.' Lorena swallowed hard, trying to regain her breath and her composure. 'He said that I'd been screaming . . . had woken him up.'

'Did you think he'd just run in from his room, or did you get the feeling he'd been there all along?'

'I . . . I don't know . . . I couldn't tell. I'm sorry.'

Lowndes paused and took a deep breath. Elena couldn't help sensing that he'd reached a crossroads of sorts – uncertain where to head next, or perhaps, with only a few minutes of the session remaining, not sure he would have time to fully explore where he wanted to go. Elena looked down to see her hands shaking noticeably: Lowndes' questioning, or all the other panics she was frantically juggling at that moment?

Crossroads. In their call the previous night, Gordon had warned her that by now they might have traced her flight to Canada and she should be doubly wary the following morning. She'd squeezed in three more door calls before the session with Lowndes, and as she was heading down St-Denis a squad car had come out of a side street and pulled up two cars behind her at the Avenue du Mont Royal crossroads. She'd tried not to look too pointedly or repeatedly in her mirror

– but it'd stayed behind her all the way to Sherbrooke before turning off, by which time she was completely frazzled. She'd pulled over immediately afterwards: her stomach was still somersaulting and for a second she thought she was going to vomit.

'You don't need to be sorry, Lorena. As I said, if nothing is happening, then that's fine too. And if this is still a question of your memory being blocked in some way, I don't expect it to suddenly be freed within minutes; it could take time. But what I do want you to do is continue thinking about what we have just covered: you mustn't feel under pressure or worry about what might happen to you as a result of speaking out – *if* you finally remember anything. And maybe, once that thought has had time to settle, it will help us in your next session.' Lowndes' voice lowered, becoming soft, almost conspiratorial. 'Would you do that for me, Lorena?'

'Yes . . . I will.'

With a perfunctory but equally soft-mannered 'Good, see you tomorrow then', Lowndes closed the session. He let Lorena go on ahead to the reception area as he held back a moment to speak to Elena. He looked at her thoughtfully.

'You realize that if there's no breakthrough early on in the session tomorrow, it could all be over quickly? There might be nowhere else we can go with this?'

'Yes, I realize that,' she agreed sombrely. As much as she wanted the nightmare to be over quickly – the only acceptable way was *with* a solution. She didn't think she could bring herself to send Lorena back to Ryall in the knowledge that he might be molesting her.

'Oh, one more thing. This Eileen . . . Lorena's friend. The aid worker. Are they very close?'

'Yes, fairly. She helped Lorena a lot in Romania.' Suddenly realizing she should distance herself more, she added: 'So I suppose so.'

'And does she know about this new problem now with Lorena?'

'I . . . I'm not sure,' she stuttered, her heart suddenly in her mouth. But as all the possible pitfalls flashed through her mind – she'd already mentioned the social services visits to Lowndes – she decided to at least partly tell the truth. 'Yes – she must know now. She came along with the social worker on her second visit. But probably she didn't know at the beginning.'

'Right. I see,' Lowndes mumbled.

She could see that he was still lost in thought, and quickly added: 'Any problem?'

'No . . . no. Not at all.' He looked at her directly, forcing a smile. 'Just it's always useful to have as much background as possible.'

But fifteen minutes later, grabbing a quick beefburger lunch with Lorena, she couldn't help dwelling on whether Lowndes had some deeper concerns regarding Lorena's mention of Eileen the aid worker. As Lorena reached across for more ketchup, the hustle and bustle of the restaurant crashed back in and she pushed it from her mind. She had enough to worry about, and it was probably nothing: just her paranoia because she knew they were lying.

The telephone lines had burned red hot the last twenty-four hours between Cameron Ryall, Inspector Turton and DS Crowley, and in turn between Crowley, Interpol and an ever-widening net of airports and customs posts halfway across Europe. And as the likelihood of a quick breakthrough diminished, Inspector Turton decided that rather than try and kid-glove the increasingly heated calls from Ryall, he'd pull himself out of the loop and suggest that in future Ryall should contact Crowley directly to be kept up to date on progress.

'I've been told I should now speak to you about this. Apparently you're doing all the *leg work*.' Ryall made the emphasis as if it was the lowest form of activity. The message was patently clear: he was only talking to Crowley through sufferance, and his patience was already long gone. 'Now what the hell's going on?'

Crowley clarified for Ryall the information Turton had already passed on, then picked up from there. 'The cash-card trail seems to have petered out in the middle of France. We've had no other notification of its use there, or indeed anywhere else.'

'And any sightings of her car in France?'

'No. Nor anywhere else for that matter. I don't want us to get stuck on the fact that she might still be in France. So we've got alerts out not only with most airports in northern France, but also with border posts with Belgium, Switzerland, Holland and Germany – not to mention the airports that she could have by now reached in those countries. We're also going through airline passenger records at those airports, plus we mustn't rule out that she could still be in England. The shuttle ticket and the cash card might have all been just a diversion.' He didn't add that he'd soon have to widen the net to cover Italy and Spain as it became possible that she'd reached that far: it made the search sound all the more tenuous, underlined that they really had *no* idea where she'd gone. He tried to sound confident. 'Believe me, we're doing everything we can. Wherever she is, we'll find her.'

'What about Mr Waldren?'

Turton had already told Ryall about them putting Mr Waldren on a tight time leash the first twelve hours by promising to hold back on pressing charges till then – so Crowley jumped to what had happened since. They'd piled on the pressure by extending the deadline by a few hours, but that too now was well past. They'd applied for a telephone tap on the Waldrens' line as well as for a record of all calls made the past thirty-six hours, and both had been granted the previous day.

'But nothing interesting from the record or from the monitoring so far. Though that might be because Mr Waldren seems to make a habit of travelling out to call boxes, usually late at night. Which is the other thing we're doing – following his movements. He uses different boxes each time: two in Chelborne and one on the way to Wareham. And every time he appears to be receiving the calls rather than making them.' The way it came across, Crowley couldn't help thinking their efforts sounded quite impressive. 'As you can see, sir, we're not sitting on our haunches on this. We're covering every possible option.'

'Is that right?' Ryall quickly killed his exuberance. 'But the end result of all this marvellous activity is that you've found absolutely *nothing* concrete?'

'Yes, well, I . . . I'm not sure what else you'd expect us to be doing.'

'I thought that was *your* job to work out.' Mix of bristling impatience and sarcasm. 'But if I think of anything, I'll make sure to phone you.' Ryall hung up abruptly.

Child molester or not – Crowley didn't want to go near the dangerous area of even attempting to think about it – Cameron Ryall was certainly not a nice person.

Ryall's intimation that he might not be doing his job properly had particularly stung him; he felt a strong urge to redress the balance, score back some points. And when forty minutes later the two DCs trailing Gordon Waldren patched in to say that he was on the move – 'heading out of the area this time, obviously not seeing local clients' – he thought he might just have something. Though he waited for another hour to receive the news that Waldren was on the A421 approaching Northampton before he called Ryall.

'It could be that he's going to meet up with his wife – or at least where he's headed could give some clue to her whereabouts. Certainly it's a change to his normal routine so far.'

'Yes . . . I see. Some activity, I suppose, rather than nothing. Thank you for phoning. Keep me posted.'

Crowley's next call wasn't for over two hours. 'He's gone to Durham, it appears. My men have just watched him park.'

'Which street?' Ryall asked pointedly.

'What?' Crowley was fazed for a second, then got on to his other line to ask. 'Elvet Hill Road.'

'That's where my other daughter is, you oaf.'

'Your *other* daughter?'

'Yes, my eldest daughter, Mikaya. She's at Durham University.'

'And what would Gordon Waldren be doing seeing her?'

'I don't know, for God's sake,' Ryall blustered. 'Maybe abducting her as well. A full bloody house!' Though he *did* know. An icy finger ran up his spine, made his whole body rigid. At his raised voice his secretary had looked up concernedly through the glass office partition. He cast his eyes down, lowered his voice to an urgent rasp. 'Look – you've got to stop him seeing her.'

'I . . . I don't know if we can do that. It's not our job to deal with crime prevention management, just because you *think* something might happen.' Now it was Crowley's turn to be condescending. 'Besides, Waldren's not even meant to know we're tailing him. And he's not exactly going to get far with anyone with my two men sitting right over his car.'

'But you've got to do *something*. I don't want him speaking to her – is that clear?'

No it wasn't, not really; but given that his other daughter had now been missing for over forty hours, Crowley conceded that Ryall's reasoning powers were probably heavily bruised. 'As I say, I don't think there's much we can do. But you could, of course, phone her yourself – warn her against meeting him. *If* that's what he's got in mind.'

'Thanks. You've been a big help.'

For the second time with Ryall, Crowley found himself left holding a dead line.

Ryall tried Mikaya first in her dorm room: no answer. Then he tried to find her through her tutor, but still no luck. All he was left with was the Registrar secretary's consolation: 'We've got messages out for her with the note that it's urgent. I'm sure she'll call you back as soon as she's able.'

'Yes . . . Thank you. I'm sure she will.'

By then it would probably be too late. Waldren could already be with her in a study room or quiet corner, questioning her. Ryall started trembling, a tingling heat rising up through his neck to his face. His secretary looked away as he looked up sharply.

Turton had revealed that the main reason given for Lorena's abduction was that she needed to have psychiatric counselling, and now Gordon Waldren was about to confront Mikaya: it was like a one-family all-out assault! He doubted that conventional child psychiatry would uncover much straight away – but with repeated sessions the odds against him could rise rapidly. Who knew for sure? Each extra hour with no news, the tourniquet on his nerves seemed to tighten, made him want to scream out loud: part anxiety and fear, part exasperation at the lack of control – *so* alien to him.

Mikaya too probably wouldn't recall anything – but what worried him most with her was the time that had since elapsed. How long did something like that stay buried at the back of the mind before it would finally emerge?

23

Elena observed her hand shaking as she put her cup of herbal tea back on its saucer. The shaking was less now, but still evident.

Another three squad cars she'd passed that afternoon with her nerves on a knife-edge until they'd finally gone from view. She should have known that trawling door to door across half of Montreal, the chances of crossing the path of the police would be greatly increased – but the rationalization did little to ease the tightrope pressure. She didn't know how much more she could take of this.

She'd dived into a local chemist after squad car number two – which had slowed for a second while the passenger officer gave her the once-over as she delivered her by now standard doorstep pitch to Stevens family sixteen or seventeen, she'd lost count – and grabbed a bottle of natural nerve-calming tablets. Their main ingredient was something called valerian, and the label advised to take two tablets at four-hour intervals. She swilled down four straight away with an orange juice from a *dépanneur*.

Then she started to recall the advice given to Gordon by his doctor on how to combat stress and high blood pressure and stave off another heart attack. Avoid fatty foods, dairy produce and high sugar intake; avoid stimulants such as coffee and coke; brandy and vodka were a definite no-no, but beer was okay in moderation and whisky was actually good for him. 'It has a calming effect and also thins the blood, actually improves the circulation.' But again in moderation.

She'd missed the kick-start of her normal five or six cups of caffeine a day, and already the craving for it was excruciating – she badly needed the energy to plod around yet another six or seven doors that evening before finally calling it a day. The herbal tea was a poor substitute.

She'd picked up three whisky miniatures at the same *dépanneur* and had downed the first just before her next door call; but she'd held herself in check since, hadn't taken any more. She hadn't slept well the night before, and with her eyes slightly bloodshot and her nerves frayed, she was beginning to look like a woman on the edge: she couldn't help noticing that doors were being opened more cautiously, tentatively, some people talking through only foot gaps. If she started enveloping them in whisky fumes, she'd be given even less of a welcome.

The thought put a faint ironic smile on her face, and from the side of the café she noticed Lorena now smiling back at her, as though in sympathy. Elena smiled more openly. Lorena was zap-crashing her way through Tomb Raider on a game machine, for the moment seemed happy, untroubled: brief respite from the pressure of the sessions and the tedium of reading Harry Potter or listening to cassettes to help pass the car-waiting time while Elena continued with her door-to-door search – each time hopefully the last door; the one where someone would suddenly smile and invite her in rather than the succession of knit brows and shaking heads.

I'll bury him out of sight and out of reach . . . Who was she kidding? Two days, and she didn't even have the faintest sniff of a lead. And the way the sessions with Lorena were going, it didn't seem likely that anything would be uncovered there either. Her father had got the better of her, and now Ryall too. Dominant men, story of her life: why should she be so surprised? Her hand gripped tight on her teacup as she took another sip. At least she was consistent. And when she returned to England defeated, maybe even as soon as tomorrow – she was facing a jail term for this. Gordon had made that clear during their last phone conversation: the deadline for no charges being pressed was now almost twelve hours past. No possible reprieve. Don't pass GO, don't collect £200, go straight . . .

A plump woman in a thick quilted parka brushed past her heading for her table, broke her maudlin train of thought. Middle-aged, Afro-Caribbean. This area of east Montreal around Rue Hochelaga had a heavy Caribbean population, both French- and English-speaking, with an equal number of French Canadians and a wider ethnic mix than probably any other area of the city. Halal butchers jostled next to Greek steak houses, burrito bars and *dépanneurs* selling yams and cassava, and every so often shops that were boarded up and covered with posters and graffiti.

There were actually some areas of the city where Elena hoped she *wouldn't* find him: she didn't want to face the added guilt that his life might have been tough, underprivileged.

She decided to try and buoy her spirits with some calls in a better area. She paid, hung over Lorena's shoulder a moment while she finished her game, then they headed north to the block between Rues Beaubien and d'Iberville – a Stephanou this time.

Halfway through the day it had suddenly struck her that her line of enquiry was incomplete. She'd ask if there was a Nicholas, Maria or George Stevens in the house, give respective ages and some background – then that was it. There was nowhere else to go. She couldn't ask if they might be relatives, because Stevens was their new name. And she began to wonder too about the choice of Montreal: if the sole purpose of the change to Stevens had been to help bury themselves deeper in a city – then why not Chicago or New York, where the population was almost completely Anglophone? Maybe they'd chosen Montreal because they had relatives there. She checked the phone book: eight Stephanous. It added to her door-calling burden, but at least she was sure that she was covering all the bases. She'd called on two earlier, and this now was Stephanou number three.

The street was wider and tree-lined, and her hopes rose for a second when the elderly man that answered said there was a Maria in the family. But the age was wrong, thirty-four, and she'd moved to Montreal only nine years ago.

Elena's shoulders slumped and she closed her eyes for a moment as she sat back in the car. 6.40 p.m. She'd hoped to squeeze in three or four more before calling it a night, but the way she felt now she didn't think she could face it. Washed out, dejected, her nerves in shreds, she was hardly able to raise an ounce of spirit or energy for anything.

'I'm sorry you haven't been able to find him yet,' Lorena said thoughtfully, almost worriedly.

'That's okay.' Elena was about to add mechanically 'It's not your fault', but instead chewed at her lip for a second before commenting: 'I'm sorry too to trail you around so much like this.' She reached across and gave Lorena's hand a gentle squeeze. 'You've been very good. Very patient.'

Elena looked again at her list and checked the map: one Stevens only five blocks away, another within a mile. She should at least check these two while she was here, then see how she felt.

She could sense that Lorena wanted to say something else. It finally came as she started up the car and pulled out.

'You know what the doctor asked – about where I might go? Was it wrong that I mentioned perhaps staying with you?'

'No, no . . . not at all, I –'

'I mean, is that something that *could* happen . . . if I had to leave the

Ryalls? Maybe I could keep your Katine company and play with her – be like a sister?'

She'd jumbled it all together before Elena had a chance to see it coming. Elena reminded herself that Lorena could at times be cute to get what she wanted – left over from her having had to become streetwise beyond her years to survive in Bucharest – but it was the raw plea in Lorena's voice that came through strongest. Lorena was obviously deeply concerned about what might happen to her. Elena's throat tightened. To her shame, she'd spared little thought to where Lorena might go after the Ryalls: a good family somewhere, yes, without saying; but not necessarily hers.

'Yes, of course – you know that I'd love to have you.' Her voice was laden with assurance. She pushed from her mind the chain of procedural nightmares that might make it impossible: the whole mess of having given up her own child and the fact that she now was an abductor no longer made her exactly ideal adoptive parent material. But she sensed that right now it was more important to keep up Lorena's hopes of a familiar, welcome alternative to the Ryalls to help ease the block in her mind.

Yet another deceit to add to the heap, albeit well-meaning. She tried not to dwell on the ludicrousness of it all: making promises to Lorena when, with the jail term probably awaiting her, she wouldn't even be able to take care of the two children she already had.

As she slowed to a stop at the next junction, she noticed her hands were shaking again on the steering wheel. But at least the valerian pills had helped in one respect: they made the lying easier and numbed some of the crushing problems she faced; she felt oddly distanced from reality, driving through the night-time streets of a strange city with more purpose and more at stake than she'd ever had before, yet feeling totally aimless, lost.

'So, what sort of problem is it with my father?' Mikaya Ryall arched an eyebrow.

'As I said, nothing serious.' Gordon had already assured her on first approach that her father wasn't ill or anything. Looking agitatedly around him in the bustling university corridor, he'd added that all the same it was something he'd prefer not to discuss too openly. Guarded nod from Mikaya after a second, and they'd headed to a nearby café. 'Has he phoned you in the last couple of days?'

'No, why?'

Strange, thought Gordon. Either the Ryalls' panic had kept them from phoning her, or it was an indication of some distance and barrier between them and Mikaya. He'd introduced himself as Donald Benham, one of his clients, because he hadn't wanted her blurting out *'Waldren?* Aren't you the people who've abducted Lorena?' She'd have refused to speak to him. They'd taken a seat by the far wall of the small café, which with about a dozen people interspersed, was only a third full. The smell of frying bacon was thick in the air, but there was a no-smoking policy so there was only one pollutant to cope with. Gordon held one hand out and made an expression of strained apology.

'Well, it's young Lorena, you see . . . She's been abducted. Your parents know the person who has taken her, so there's absolutely nothing to fear for her safety. But it is the reason why I'm here.'

That eyebrow again and a slight exhalation as she absorbed the blow of the news. 'Are you with the police?'

'No, nothing like that. I know both Lorena and the person who has taken her – but it's more the reason *why* Lorena's been taken that's brought me here.' Gordon launched into the dramatic chain of events, interrupted only by their coffees being brought to the table: Lorena and the two social services visits, her father blocking psychiatric counselling, and then the abduction. All the while he watched Mikaya's expression, especially her eyes: large, dark-brown with only a slight slant, but he was looking more for the shadows, her reaction as he spoke. Five-six, slim with sleek dark hair almost to her waist and a warm if cautious smile, she was stunning. It was hard to get away from the thought that Ryall chose his adoptive daughters primarily for their beauty. Heavier shadows as he mentioned the possibility of Lorena being interfered with – but that could have been just the shock reaction most people would have to such news.

'Are you with the social services?' she asked.

'No – let us just say I'm a family friend who knows everyone involved, including the aid worker who has taken her for counselling – and I sympathize with the reasons why she did this.' Gordon took the first sip of his coffee. Now for the difficult part. 'But, you know, I wondered if there was anything from your own past experiences with your father that would lead you to think that Lorena's fears might be valid.' More delicate than just asking straight out if her father might have molested her as well – but the only effect was a second's delay before the shock realization hit Mikaya.

She stood up abruptly, shaking her head. 'I really don't think this is a good idea . . . us talking.'

'Please, I . . . I've come a long way.' He half got up, clutching her arm, his eyes imploring. 'The woman who has taken Lorena has done so with nothing but good intentions, only because she didn't see any other option and couldn't bear the thought of just leaving Lorena at your father's mercy – *if* something is happening. But she could be in a lot of trouble for what's she's done. And she happens to be a very nice person, someone I care a lot about.'

Uncertainty, the shadows in Mikaya's eyes darker. Gordon was sure in that moment that she knew something: it surfaced only fleetingly, then was pushed back as she pulled her arm away.

'I'm sorry, I can't talk to you.' She half turned, found it hard to meet the plea in his eyes. 'Anyway, nothing happened to talk about.' She hitched her bag hastily back on her shoulder.

She was flustered, the bravado unconvincing: Gordon could tell that she was lying. Whatever had happened, the thought of it suddenly resurfacing was making her intensely anxious. He observed her hand shaking on her bag. He clutched back at her arm.

'I know it's difficult, but please – if you can help, if you can think of anything. The woman who's taken Lorena could face prison if she's got it wrong about her.' Gordon's tone was urgent but low so that others in the café wouldn't hear. Still, a few were starting to look at them: an older man clutching at the arm of a beautiful young girl, the girl agitated and eager to get away. A lovers' tiff that looked like it might develop interestingly.

'I'm sorry . . . *I'm sorry*.' Mikaya shook her head again and looked close to tears. She kept her eyes stoically averted from his, as if afraid of what he might see there. 'I just can't help you.' She pulled her arm back and turned away.

'*Please* . . . What about the pregnancy? *Anything* you can tell me.'

Gordon had to raise his voice because she was already a couple of paces away. Others in the café did hear this time, confirming their suspicions. But Mikaya was head down, shoulderbag clutched tight to her along with her secrets, and didn't look back as she walked out.

Elena didn't look round at first when the policeman walked in the shop; she was too busy trying to watch and direct what Lorena picked up from the shelves: left to her own devices she'd pick up an armful of sweets, pop magazines and CDs, when all they'd come in for was some soft drinks and a chocolate bar. It was quite a large *dépanneur*, almost a small supermarket.

She only half turned as she felt the presence of the figure a couple of paces behind: black leather jacket and dark navy trousers, motorcycle boots, wide black belt with baton and gun, French writing arched over an insignia on his jacket epaulette. A tall, rangy man, at least six-three, with his crash helmet making him look even taller. She looked away hastily, her heart thudding wildly, returned her gaze to Lorena as the policeman shuffled closer behind, browsing along the newspaper and magazine shelf displays to one side.

'Look, they've got the Spice Girls – but I think it's in French.' Lorena was looking down a rack of CDs. 'They've got Billie too, and this one's in English. Do you think I could have it?' She lifted it out of the rack with a hopeful smile.

'Yes, fine. Fine.' The last thing Elena wanted to do was protest and lengthen the conversation. If Lorena had held up ten CDs she'd have just nodded dumbly: right. Great. She didn't want to hiss 'Let's go', which was her first inclination; the policeman might notice the tremor and haste in her voice, tune in to some problem. So she just glared at Lorena and shifted her eyes slightly to indicate the problem behind. But Lorena couldn't see the policeman because of her height and the shelf rack in between, and before Elena could catch her eye she'd turned her attention again to the CDs before moving further down: pop posters, cards, chocolates.

Lorena picked up a chocolate bar and a bag of toffees. 'Do you think they might have *J-17*?'

'No, I don't think so. The magazines are mostly in French.' *Come on*, Elena silently screamed. The policeman was now just two feet away, she could almost feel his breath on her left shoulder. She'd injected a slight American lilt into her speech, tried not to sound so English, and she hadn't wanted to say straight out that the shop wouldn't have magazines from England. Her pulse was racing. She could feel it pumping a vein in her neck and her throat felt tight; she could hardly swallow. They could easily have traced her by now: a dispatch alert rattling around in the back of the policeman's mind about an Englishwoman with a young girl, and then as he hears them talking it all finally gels.

The policeman approached the counter with a newspaper and magazine, said something in French, and handed across a note. The boy at the counter, pimply and barely out of his teens, cashed it on the register and held out the change. But the policeman seemed to remember something else at the last moment and pointed behind the boy. *'Et un paquet de Winston.'*

Elena cast a sideways glance towards the till counter and the boy; she didn't trust herself to look straight at the policeman now directly at her side. She stood there clutching a bottle of orange juice and a coke, and felt his eyes on her for the first time as the boy reached behind for some cigarettes.

'Cinquante-cinq cents de plus.'

The policeman handed some coins over, and at that moment Lorena emerged from behind the shelves.

'Maybe they'll have *Sug –*' She stopped as she saw the policeman and her eyes went wide. Her hands suddenly seemed to lose their grip on the items she was holding and she fumbled and dropped the bag of toffees. Her face flushed as she bent to pick them up.

Elena stepped forward quickly and got there before her: she could just see Lorena dropping everything else in panic as she stooped.

'Okay. That's everything now.' A statement so that Lorena didn't have to respond.

As she straightened, she saw the policeman smiling lightly at Lorena: hopefully thinking that she'd simply been startled by seeing someone so large in uniform. Elena gave a tentative smile back as she put everything on the counter. She pressed her hands against its surface so that he wouldn't notice them shaking. But with a brief nod – Elena wasn't sure if it was at them or the counter-boy, she'd looked swiftly away – he turned and left.

The heavy tread of his motorcycle boots receded almost in time with her pounding heart, and she thought: never again. She couldn't stand another minute of this, let alone hours or days.

'We're looking. Believe me, we're looking.' Jean-Paul closed his eyes for a second and held out one hand. That's all he seemed to have done these past long hours: make excuses, make penance.

Simone shook her head. 'It's almost two days now with no sign of him. Nothing. I know something's wrong, seriously wrong. I can *feel* it.'

They were in Jean-Paul's study. Raphaël had been talking to Francesca the housemaid in the corridor outside, asking whether two of his favourite sweatshirts were in the laundry, and they'd shut the door for privacy. Simone looked worse than when she'd first confronted him after her furious drinking binge. Two nights of fitful sleep and her worst fears mounting with each hour had put dark circles under her eyes; her hair was lank, unwashed, her usually immaculate make-up scrappy. She chewed nervously at the side of one nail.

'How do you know Roman's not done something to him already?'

'I can't be sure, I know.' His eyes closed briefly again: more contrition. 'I'm stuck with taking his word. But if it's a bluff, it's a good bluff. Don't forget it's Roman that right now has got half of Montreal looking for him.'

She'd switched off from what he was saying halfway through, was lost again in her own thoughts. 'It's just what Georges feared – why he asked me to talk to you.'

'Like I said before, Simone, I just don't think Roman would do something like that without my sanction. He might be hot-headed and irrational at times, but he's not completely suicidal.' Her first screams of accusation, at first light the day after Georges' disappearance, had been directed at Jean-Paul, with Roman merely doing his dirty work. Jean-Paul had fired back that a six-month cooling-off period in Cuba or Mexico was all he'd had in mind. 'That's not how I do things any more, and you more than anyone else should know that.' His reprimand, carrying with it Pascal and all he'd fought so hard for since to make amends, made her flush and softly say she was sorry, and they'd turned their thoughts to Roman possibly acting on his own. Jean-Paul had pointed out that there would have been little point in Roman investing so much time in convincing him that there was a problem with Georges, if he was going to then suddenly jump the gun and take action himself. 'Even if he was of a mind to do it himself, he could have done it long before. He didn't need to waste breath on me.'

'Yeah, you're probably right,' Simone agreed dolefully, looking down. She stopped nibbling her nail and pulled a strand of hair behind one ear. The photos were back before them as the only reasonable explanation for his disappearance. He knew that they'd been found and was embarrassed as hell, knew that she'd be furious and so he'd gone to ground for a few days until she cooled off. He was right on that count: she'd phoned his two numbers at least thirty times, each time ready to slam the phone straight down. *Good, now that I've got you – this is just to say fuck off and never phone me again!*

'Maybe he's looked up an old friend up-province or out of Quebec or headed to a ski cabin for a while to rethink and re-evaluate.'

Jean-Paul didn't add that the main reason he had Roman trawling half of Quebec wasn't to find her lost albeit fallen-from-grace love, but because Georges going to ground could be the final signal that he was about to talk to the RCMP. Roman could have been right all along. 'Or maybe even he's gone on a short hop to Mexico. He's got a lot of friends and contacts down there now.'

'Yeah. He'll probably surface later tonight or tomorrow and call me.' She eased a tentative smile, the first in nearly forty-eight hours. 'And then *I* can kill him.'

The policeman was a bad start to the day, seemed to have sapped all of Elena's energy barely a half hour into her door calls. Or maybe it was the build-up of nerves, the lack of sleep and the valerian pills and whisky – she'd downed the two remaining miniatures the previous night, then nursed two tumblers at the hotel bar with Alphonse after Lorena had gone to bed.

She'd sunk another three valerian pills straight after leaving the *dépanneur* with the policeman to steady her nerves. She was a quivering jelly, frantic. Her trembling was clearly visible, and as she looked in the car's vanity mirror she noticed a small muscle spasm below her left, very bloodshot eye: she looked almost like a hard-line heroin case.

The spasm eased after twenty minutes and her nerves settled; she just felt numb. But the problem was that the numbness was all over her body, and her steps felt heavy, laboured, as she made her way towards the front door of her second call of the day. Her legs felt leaden, as if they were weighted with loads. She'd hoped to squeeze in three or four calls before Lowndes' session in just under an hour – but the way she felt now this would probably be the last.

Or maybe it was the repetitive nature of the calls, the endless chain of head-shakes, frowns and 'sorry's, that was responsible for her lethargy, steadily grinding her down so that now she didn't feel the faintest spark of hope or enthusiasm as she approached a fresh door. It just wouldn't be any different. More head-shakes and frowns with nothing to do but trudge on to the next. And the next. And the . . .

She felt dizzy, disorientated, felt herself sway slightly, her step unsteady.

She was deep inside the chine and, with dusk approaching, the light at its end was fast dying. She started to head back up the slope to home, but her legs felt heavy – the same weight and lethargy she felt now as she made her way up the four steps to a cream front door – progress was slow; she started to fear that she might not make it back up before the light died completely. She wouldn't be able to find her way any more: the darkness of the chine was intense, no trace of moonlight or starlight filtering through the thick blanket of trees above. And it suddenly hit her that the light at the end didn't just represent hope, but that without it she wouldn't be able to find her way at all. She was totally lost.

She rang the bell. Its chime lingered in her head for a second after she pulled her finger away.

But didn't she know her way in and out of the chine practically blindfold? – she'd been there so many times. Muted sound of footsteps approaching the other side of the door. Suddenly she wasn't so sure – she wasn't sure of anything any more.

And when after her standard pitch the man before her, a Stephanou in his late fifties, nodded and with a strained grimace opened the door wide – 'You'd better come in' – she was still grappling with reality, slightly lost. It took her a moment to finally respond and walk into his house and realize that the light at the end of the chine was suddenly back again.

24

'*Pardon. Bell Canada, madame.*'

'*Oui, oui. Vous êtes rapide.*' Odette Donatien opened the door wider to let the man in. 'We noticed the line was dead – but we haven't even reported it yet. I was just about to go to my neighbours and phone in.'

Carlo Funicelli shrugged and smiled amiably. 'We found a junction box burnt out with a short that affects you and three other houses. Which means that one of you has a problem with too much resistance on the line.' He followed her down the hallway. Slightly broad in the beam, but still a good figure for what he'd heard from Roman was a mid-fifty-year-old: the grey tracksuit and trainers maybe helped her look more youthful and there was only a touch of salt in her auburn hair. 'So we thought we'd better check.'

'Oh, right.' She could see him scanning each side of the lounge. She pointed. 'It's over there.'

'Thanks.' Funicelli smiled at her again as he reached the phone, as if to say 'It's okay now', hoping that she'd disappear for a while and leave him to it. But she just stood there looking at him as he undid the phone cradle casing. 'Could take a little while.'

She stood there a moment more looking blankly on, then prompted, 'Oh, sorry. Would you like coffee or something?'

'Yes, thanks. That would be very nice, madame.'

'Black, white?'

'White, no sugar. Thanks.'

Funicelli breathed a sigh of relief as she finally disappeared. At a push he might have got away with the phone bug with her still watching, but the other two would have been more difficult. He had both in place – one under the sofa and another behind a sideboard – within forty seconds of her turning away, then started on the phone bug. He'd have to hurry: the last thing he wanted was her coming back in and asking, 'What's that?' Or why he was tampering with the handset rather than the cradle. As it was, he'd been nervous about the few minutes he'd had to spend up a telegraph pole outside to disconnect her line. If she'd seen him through the window, fine, that tied in with his story now. But he was more worried about a real Bell engineer passing and seeing him. His uniform looked authentic enough, but a van with logo had been impossible to arrange: he'd parked his plain white van twenty yards along so that it was obscured from the Donatiens' view by some trees.

His hand shook a bit as he positioned the bug behind the earpiece and connected it. Sound of footsteps starting back along the hallway. He clipped back the handset cover and tightened its one connecting screw, then quickly shifted to putting the phone cradle casing back on as she walked in. He gave the cradle a few more screwdriver turns as she put his coffee on a side table.

'Thanks. There were a couple of wires touching that could have caused a problem, so I've separated them. I'll just check the socket, then I'm done.' He busied himself undoing the socket and checking connections with a meter between sips of coffee while Odette Donatien talked aimlessly.

'Lot brighter today for a change. I might go out and do some gardening later.'

'Yeah, yeah. Looks like it could turn out nice.' He screwed the socket back together and knocked back the last of his coffee. 'That should be okay now. I'll just reconnect on the junction box outside – and you're ready to go.'

She thanked him and showed him out, and after another three anxious minutes on the telegraph pole outside – hoping again that no Bell engineers would pass and that none of the neighbours would think something was suspicious and decide to phone in – Funicelli drove away.

Roman was probably right: if anyone, Donatien was bound to contact his parents at some stage. But the word on the streets was that Roman had already taken Donatien out, and all of this frantic search activity was merely a smokescreen for Jean-Paul's benefit. Funicelli had no firm thoughts on it either way: if Roman wanted to waste time with planting bugs that he knew wouldn't bear any fruit, it was his money.

Viana couldn't help looking around as she stood in the boarding gate queue for her flight to Haiti at New York's JFK, afraid that Roman or one of his goons would appear at the last minute and stop her escape. She'd done the same at ticket check-in just an hour before and at check-in and boarding for her flight from Montreal to New York at 5.14 a.m. that morning.

Only five people ahead of her in the queue now. She could hardly believe her luck that she might actually get away.

The first warning sign had been Azy early on the previous night. 'You know that Georges has disappeared? What happened with you two the other night?' Azy looked deeply concerned and kept his voice low, even though he'd chosen a moment when there was nobody at the bar. He obviously saw her answer as potential dynamite, not for anyone else's ears.

'Nothing. I don't know what you mean.' She acted nonchalant.

He leant closer as he gave the bar a couple more wipes. 'Look, Viana. What you get up to in private is your own business. But the thing is I saw you get in his car. And then the very next day he disappears. Gives you plenty to think about, no?'

'It was nothing. He just gave me a lift home, that's all.' She shook her head and got up from the bar. 'How should I know what's happened to him?'

But she could tell by Azy's eyes following her as she went back to dance that he'd picked up on her nervousness, was suspicious.

Then Roman came by the club two hours later with the same thing. 'He disappeared the night after your place. Not a trace since. Hasn't been on to you, has he? If nothing else, to ask what'd happened at your place that night?'

'No, no. Nothing.' She tried to read the bluff in Roman's eyes, but as usual she just couldn't tell: poker face, poker heart. Then she recalled his gloating at Georges' powerlessness on the bed and his pinching her cheek and telling her not to worry about what was going to happen to Georges. She felt certain in that moment that Roman had killed Georges: he'd been dumped at the bottom of a river or chopped into two or three sacks for a garbage-truck mangle or incinerator, never to be found again. And all of this was just a pretence to throw her off the scent. He didn't want anything possibly linking back to his involvement.

But how long was that going to last? At some stage he was going to panic that, as she knew about the sex sting with Georges, she could provide a lead back. And that would come sooner rather than later if Azy let slip to Roman that he'd seen her get in Georges' car that night. She'd be next for the garbage sacks and incinerator!

Roman kept her dancing for him for four records in a row, and it was one of the hardest things she'd ever done. She was desperately afraid that he'd notice how nervous she was – a couple of times she'd had to lithely snake away from his hand in case he connected and felt her trembling – or how hard it was for her to force a smile and keep the small talk going. He stayed another twenty minutes nursing a brandy at the bar with Azy – all the time with her panicking that Azy might mention her getting in Donatien's car. Then, as soon as he'd gone, she'd headed for the toilet and emptied her stomach.

She resolved then to leave that night: she couldn't face Roman another minute, let alone night after night like a caged bird, waiting on when he'd finally decide to kill her.

She got clear of the club at 2.18 a.m. and forty minutes later she was packed and heading back out of her apartment to Mirabelle Airport. New York, Atlanta and New Orleans were the best hubs for Haiti: the earliest flight she could get on was the 5.14 a.m. to New York. And now the 12.10 p.m. from JFK to Haiti.

A smiling stewardess held out one hand for her boarding card and welcomed her on board.

Viana couldn't resist one last glance back to make sure that she'd actually made it before returning the smile. 'Thank you.'

Elena found her eyes drifting to different objects in the room as Sotiris Stephanou talked: a decorative plate with five different harbour and city views of Limassol; photos of a boy and two girls at what looked like their first communions; a horribly syrupy wedding portrait in sepia with its edges fading into misty, heart-shaped clouds. Elena could see in Sotiris the likeness of the young man he had been, but it was harder to relate her past image to his wife Nana, now a good fifty pounds heavier, ferrying in halva and cakes and a pot of thick strong coffee – both to show good as a host and, presumably, to provide the fuel to help her beloved recall events from almost thirty years ago.

Sotiris shook his head. 'A tragedy. A real tragedy.'

Elena found it hard to follow, assimilate it all. She'd been starved of details for so long: twenty-nine years trying to blank it all out, then the forced drought of the last days and weeks, and suddenly there was a torrent of information hitting her all at once. A car accident over twenty years ago, the boy's adoptive mother Maria killed, his adoptive father Nicholas – Sotiris' younger brother by three years – gravely injured, the boy surviving with only minor injuries.

When Sotiris' eyes had clouded with the first mention of tragedy and accident in the same breath, her heart had sunk like a stone as she thought for a moment that her son was dead. She quickly masked her look of relief as Sotiris filled in the details, nodding in sympathy as he remarked what a terrible ordeal it had been for his brother and how he'd never really recovered from it.

'Believe me, the last thing he wanted to do was let the child go. If he could have possibly avoided that, he would. But he just couldn't cope.'

Her heart sank again. 'What – you mean let him go to another family?' Elena's voice was high-pitched, strained.

'No, that would have taken eight or nine months, even if at that age – little Georgiou was almost four by then – he could have been placed anywhere. When the problems hit Nicholas they hit hard and quick. He felt he couldn't cope another day, let alone months.' Sotiris cast his eyes down, found it hard to meet her searching stare directly. 'I'm afraid the only choice in the end was an orphanage.'

This time the stab of pain went deeper, made her feel emptier and number inside than a whole bottle of valerian pills. Her eyes shifted inadvertently to the window and Lorena sat in the car outside. *Oh God*, how she'd fooled herself. She'd clung to the false hope all those years that at least he might have had a good life somewhere, but in reality it had been little more than a living hell: one adoptive parent dead and then the other giving him away to an orphanage when he was barely four. Her eyes started brimming with tears and she kept her gaze averted as she bit at her lip for more composure.

But Sotiris clearly saw her distress and tried to lighten the impact. 'It was a very good orphanage – run by Grey nuns, if I remember right. Nicholas went a couple of times to sort out the initial papers and it was a nice place, apparently. They were very kind, very caring.'

'I don't doubt that. But what I don't understand is why your brother didn't keep him.' She'd managed to push back the tears, but still her voice was strained. 'Why he didn't at least try to make more of –' Elena broke off. *Lorena in the car outside!* With her explaining the reason for her visit and then Sotiris talking, she'd got carried away with time; at least half an hour had gone. She checked her watch: she should leave now for the session with Lowndes, but there was so much more she wanted to find out. 'Look, I'm sorry about this – but my young daughter is in the car outside and she needs to be downtown urgently. Do you know of a good, reliable cab firm?'

Sotiris looked genuinely relieved at the shift to more comfortable ground, where he could also be more helpful: his cousin worked as a cabbie. 'I'll make sure it's either him personally or one of his close friends that he knows he can trust.' You didn't want a ten-year-old girl jumping in any old cab.

Because it was a quiet time of day, they were able to get his cousin Dimitrios. He arrived in only four minutes and Sotiris gave him instructions that he was to walk the girl right to this doctor's door and she wasn't to be left on her own for a minute.

Elena told Lorena that she'd be there as soon as she could, twenty minutes or half an hour. 'But if I'm late, stay right there at the doctor's. Don't go anywhere.'

During the wait for Dimitrios, Sotiris had explained that his brother had been crippled by the accident. He wasn't wheelchair-bound – otherwise he might have got permanent help – but one leg was affected, so he was allocated a home help two half-days a week to take care of washing and chores. The rest of the time though, he was on his own. He tried to cope, but what got him in the end was self-pity because, with half a leg lost, he felt that both his job prospects and his chances of finding another woman were slight. He felt that Georgiou needed a woman's touch and love. And so he hit the bottle, decided to drown out what he'd lost and what he felt he could no longer provide for the boy. 'Within two months he was a hopeless case, and the orphanage became practically the only option.'

Sotiris waved one hand towards the photos on the side cabinet as they sat down in the room again. 'We would have gladly had him ourselves – but we already had three of our own, and money was tight. Very tight. I'm sorry.'

'No, I understand. I . . . I suppose I'm just looking for others to point the finger at because of my own guilt.' She hadn't told Sotiris that her baby had been practically ripped from her arms. She just said that she'd been under-age, there'd been a bit of family pressure and it had all been very awkward at the time. In the end she'd made the decision to let him go – the wrong decision, she now felt, with the benefit of hindsight. But she'd mainly blanked it from her mind since, and hadn't troubled to look for her son until now.

Her eyes stayed on the cabinet for a second: it was stuffed with silver and silver-framed photos, with decorative plates dotted in between, mostly from Cyprus and Greece. She saw only one from Canada: Niagara Falls. The cabinet was the main divider from the dining room beyond: dark-wood furniture and still more decorative plates, an oil painting of a terraced olive grove and a dark-velvet and silver-thread embroidery of the Acropolis. The only modern items were the beige leather sofa they were sat on and an abstract print on the far wall.

And she suddenly realized why she was so interested, sucking in every small detail: Sotiris had mentioned that his brother hadn't lived that far away then, only eight blocks: she was trying to get some measure of what Georgiou's environment might have been like those few years. She stopped the chain of thought abruptly, chiding herself. Only eight blocks, but a million miles in heart and spirit: mother dead and a father intent on blotting out what little life he felt was left with drink. The only hope was that Georgiou would have been too young to remember it all, that the scars wouldn't have been too long-lasting.

'We wondered at the time, didn't we?' Sotiris directed his comment towards his wife rather than Elena.

Nana just nodded as she nibbled at some halva.

'There was all this talk about some problem with them having children and getting fertility treatment from some doctor in London . . .'

'Dr Maniatis?' Elena prompted.

'I . . . I don't remember. I'm not even sure they mentioned a name at the time.'

Maniatis was the only likely middleman Elena could put between her father and the childless Stephanous. She nodded and Sotiris continued.

'Well, anyway . . . suddenly there was a child. But the gap seemed too short, and we thought we would have heard something as soon as she was pregnant.' Sotiris ran one hand through his thinning hair. 'We guessed that they'd probably adopted, but we never stuck our noses in and pushed them on it. We thought maybe Nick had heard the problem was down to him and they were embarrassed to talk about it. You know, male pride and all that. Especially Greek male pride.' Sotiris forced a weak smile.

'And the new name, Stevens – my God, we argued over that.' The smile quickly died. 'I told him he should be proud of the name Stephanou like I was, not try and bury his roots and his heritage. But he said that he wanted to make a fresh start, didn't want to be seen as ethnic and possibly suffer discrimination that might hold him back – or his new son for that matter. We didn't see eye to eye on that one, I can tell you: things were strained between us for quite a while.'

They were silent for a second.

'What happened to your brother?' Elena asked.

'He met someone else eventually – about five years later. And a few years after that they ended up going to Cyprus to settle there. Too many bad memories here, I suppose.' Sotiris' eyes drifted slightly: melancholy at the lost years or something that would have been best left unrecalled? 'I think he felt a lot of guilt later about giving up Georgiou, but by then it was too late.'

'Why – what happened?' Elena's interest was piqued, though the last thing she wanted was to empathize with Nicholas Stephanou, especially not on the guilt front. She surely had the market cornered there.

'Well, not long after meeting this woman and finally getting his act together, clean of the drink once and for all, he went to the orphanage hoping to see Georgiou. But he was too late: he'd already left and been placed with a family.'

'How long before?' Elena's spirits lifted a fraction: maybe he'd had a more settled and happy family life the second time around.

'Fifteen, eighteen months, I think.' Sotiris shrugged. 'I'm not totally sure.'

Elena calculated: three and a half years in the orphanage, almost eight years old before he was finally picked off the shelf again. She reminded herself that it would have been a far cry from the orphanages she was used to in Romania. If it wasn't too austere or cool an environment, hopefully the experience wouldn't have been . . . then quickly stopped herself again, realizing she was just rationalizing to ease the weight of guilt she'd felt settling heavier as Sotiris talked.

She checked her watch again: she'd covered practically everything, and Lorena would already be over halfway through her session by the time she'd get there. 'Do you remember the name of this orphanage?'

'I don't remember exactly, but it's in a small town about seventy miles up province . . . Baie de something.' Sotiris pulled at the air with his fingers for the exact memory.

'Baie du Febvre,' Nana prompted.

'Yes, that's it . . . du Febvre. And it's the only orphanage there run by nuns, I would think – so it shouldn't be difficult to find.'

Elena thanked them for the help and the coffee and cake, said that she'd better go. 'Catch up with my daughter.'

As they were walking along the hallway, Sotiris commented, 'You know, it's funny, we had a man phone from England way back asking exactly the same thing about where young Georgiou had gone.'

'When was this? Did he give a name?' Elena turned by the door.

'Oh, Georgiou was only in his teens at the time. He didn't give a full name – just said he was Tony, an old friend of Nick's. Said he was curious about what had happened to the boy, that's all.'

Tony. *Tony*. Her nerves tingled, the name spinning in her head as she drove to Lowndes' office . . . but she finally discarded it as a coincidence. Why bury the boy out of sight only to try and find him again years later? It made no sense. No, it was obviously just some other friend of the Stephanous.

Lorena was forty minutes into her session when Elena arrived and she couldn't go through to the adjoining monitoring room without disturbing them. Lowndes would speak to her after the session and she could listen to the tape then, the receptionist informed her. So she decided to use the wait to find out the name of the orphanage in Baie du Febvre. Eight minutes of leafing through Quebec telephone directories and two calls later and she had the name: Couvent de Ste-Marguerite. She phoned and made an appointment: 4.00 p.m. that afternoon.

Hanging up, she tapped the details she'd scrawled on a piece of paper thoughtfully with one finger. After the nightmare saga related by Sotiris, she was now regretting embarking on this odyssey: her son's real life was so different from the glossy image she'd fixed in her mind to help ease her guilt. She wasn't sure she could face any more nightmare tales.

Michel Chenouda sat quietly as the three men the other side of the conference table flicked through the thick file before them, identical copies for each of them. He let out a quiet cough muffled with one hand, then there was heavy silence again: only the sound of turning pages and the faint air rush of the heating vents below the tinted-glass windows behind the men. The view was over Ottawa's McArthur Avenue seven floors down.

The man in the middle, Superintendent Neil Mundy, silver-haired with sharp blue eyes in an otherwise nondescript rotund and ruddy face, was the first to look up.

'So, your claim is that the Lacaille family set up this hit on Georges Donatien, who apparently worked as a money man for their organization?'

'Yes, that's right. It's all there: dates, times, movements.' Michel pointed across at the file. 'How they set it up is almost identical to a hit on Tony Savard back in February, part of which was monitored by us during a surveillance operation.'

'Yeah, I can see that.' Mundy flicked back a couple of pages before returning to the place he held with one finger in Chenouda's summary notes. 'Pretty cheeky, huh? Right under your noses.' Wry, awkward grimace from Chenouda, but Mundy rolled straight on without waiting for a response. 'And your reason for coming to us here is that you're afraid there's a leak in your department?'

'Yes, I . . . I think it was how the Lacailles knew about the set-up with Savard, and perhaps also how they knew they'd have to jump quick with Donatien.'

Mundy arched one eyebrow almost doubtingly and, as if to add support to what he was thinking at that moment, Inspector Kaufman to his right commented: 'That's quite a serious charge.'

'I know.' Michel nodded and cast his eyes down for a second. 'Otherwise I wouldn't be here troubling your department with it.'

S-18. The Ottawa-based RCMP department you went to when you suspected internal corruption or an information leak and there was nowhere else left to go. Ultra-secret and the ultimate sanction over every other RCMP department. To Mundy's left was Inspector Bob Welch, his first point of contact when he'd approached them.

'You didn't think this was something you could go to your department head with?' Mundy checked the file for the name. 'Chief Inspector Pelletier? Surely you don't suspect he's in on it too?'

'No, I . . . Well, I just don't know. It could be anywhere up or down the chain from him, or sideways . . . I just didn't want to take the risk.'

Mundy nodded thoughtfully. The questions continued for a while, mainly clarifying details already in the file – then Michel was asked to wait in the adjoining room while the three discussed his request privately for a moment. Michel waited almost twenty minutes before Mundy finally reappeared with the good news: request approved. Michel's smile was slow in rising as he shook Mundy's hand, the uncertainties that had settled during the wait finally slipping away. His first judgement had been right after all: the combination of such a large organized crime strike and internal corruption S-18 would find impossible to resist.

Mundy passed him a sheaf from a notepad. 'Phone this man at three this afternoon, Inspector Steven Graydon right here in Ottawa. I'll have already spoken to him by then, so he'll have been fully primed to provide the men and the back-up you need from this point on.' Mundy patted his shoulder and perfunctorily checked his watch. 'And if we can move everything along as fast as I hope – perhaps we can aim to make an official announcement by say . . . ten or eleven tomorrow. Okay?'

Michel's step was light for the first time in weeks as he left the building. No more leaks or interdepartmental wrangling to stop him from now finally nailing the Lacailles. His only regret was that things might have been different with Donatien; but with a game of chess this big, there were always pawns that ended up having to be sacrificed.

25

'I think we've had a breakthrough at last.' Lowndes had ushered Elena into his office straight after the session, leaving Lorena for a moment with the receptionist. He glanced briefly towards the closed door, as if worried she might still hear. 'Or at least with what is probably the key to the Lorena's problem.'

'Oh, right.' Elena sat forward slightly: one bit of hopeful news at last, though it took a moment to seep through her valerian haze and the day's ups and downs with Sotiris and the orphanage. Her mind was mostly on what might await her there.

'There was one thing that troubled me at one point . . . but once again I'm afraid we didn't get that far with Lorena actually remembering anything happening with your husband. My ploy of easing up any subliminal pressure on her psyche didn't quite work as I'd hoped – and I'm now convinced there's simply no such memory there.'

'I see.' Elena was suddenly adrift: Lowndes' two comments were completely at odds with each other.

'But tell me more about this Eileen – the aid worker.' Lowndes opened out his hands. 'I think we might have hit on something there.'

'Why, I . . . I don't understand,' Elena stuttered, frantically trying to gather her thoughts. Further adrift: what on earth had Lorena said in the session? She cursed herself now for not being there and listening in. 'She's very competent and cares a lot about Lorena, but I don't see what –'

'I think that's the problem right there, Mrs Waldren – she possibly cares too much. Or rather Lorena has tuned in to the fact that she does and might have purposely played on her emotions with this situation now. You'll see what I mean when you listen to the tape. Now, did Lorena insist that Eileen was told about this possible problem with your husband early on?'

Panic gripped Elena: she couldn't even remember what she'd said last time. 'I think so, maybe . . . but I'm just not sure now.'

'Lorena says that she was told about the problem almost straight away.'

'I see, right. Probably, yes.' Elena felt her whole body flush hot; her palms were suddenly clammy. This was a nightmare: all she could think of was getting away from Lowndes' clutches and listening to the tape before she said anything and possibly put her foot in it.

'This Eileen, I understand, was the main one to help Lorena through her tough orphanage days, particularly after her time living rough in the sewers . . . and she also helped a lot, I believe, in getting her placed in England with you – smoothing the way?'

'Yes, yes . . . she did.' One safe foothold.

'And when this new problem came up and Lorena wanted her to mediate with social services – was Eileen keen to get involved? Did she rally to help quickly?'

'I . . . I'm not sure.' She was desperately searching again for where to put her feet. She began to panic that Lorena had let slip that she had been abducted, or at least had made Lowndes suspicious; and now he was testing, trying to draw her out. 'I . . . I suppose so.'

'Because I'm beginning to fear that all of this might be just a cry for help. Mainly for this Eileen's benefit, to get her attention . . . but at the same time you've got sucked in too.'

Elena's head was spinning with it all. She started trembling. She just had to get away and listen to the tape. She stood up abruptly, glancing at her watch. 'Look – I'm sorry. There's somewhere else I'm meant to be now . . . and all of this has caught me a bit by surprise. I'd rather us talk when I've had a chance to listen to the tape – soak it all in.'

'I understand.' Lowndes got up to open the door, but kept one hand flat against it for a second. 'In a nutshell, what I'm trying to say is that this Eileen has been there to help Lorena with all the main dramas of her life. And through all of that they've formed an attachment. Probably closer than we appreciate. Then Lorena is with you and your husband and everything's hunky-dory and suddenly there're no dramas any more . . . and therefore also no Eileen. Lorena craves that attention again and the close bond she had with Eileen as a result – so she creates her own new drama.'

'Yes, I . . . I suppose it makes some sense.' Lowndes' words touched a raw nerve deep inside her. Her world had already been tilted ninety degrees with Sotiris that morning, now it was being turned completely upside down. Nothing was what it had seemed any more. Or was it just the valerian pills and the lack of sleep making her feel so adrift, detached from reality? Her pulse stabbed at her temples and a grey film washed behind her eyes. She feared that if Lowndes didn't hurry and open the door she was going to black out right there.

'Oh, one word of warning: some parts of the tape are probably best not played in Lorena's presence . . . She gets quite distressed at points. And, as before, certainly don't play my notes at the end while she's listening.'

'Right, right.' All Elena could focus on was the door ahead. The trembling reached her legs, she felt them weakening, threatening to crumple . . . then suddenly the door was open and she was walking into the reception area. She hoped that she wasn't swaying or looking unsteady. Small smile from Lorena as she stood up. Elena gave her a light embrace with one arm – something to steady her at least – as she turned to Lowndes. 'I'll call you later,' she said, and swiftly led Lorena out.

Elena was still trembling twenty miles north of Montreal on the open highway heading for Baie du Febvre.

On the outskirts of Montreal she'd stopped at a Radio Shack and picked up a set of headphones to plug into the car's cassette player. She was going to be with Lorena all day, and she couldn't bear waiting till that night to hear what was on tape. The salesman had at first offered her an impressive, studio-quality set with bulbous cushioned earpieces. But in the end she'd gone for the most discreet set with thin black leads and small black earpieces that would be mostly hidden by her hair. It would be an ironic twist of fate to be stopped by the police for wearing headphones while driving. But still she was careful not to put them on and start listening to the tape until she was well clear of Montreal and driving with open fields each side, not a police car in sight.

Lorena had said that she was sorry as soon as they'd jumped in the car. 'He asked a lot of questions about this Eileen . . . well, *you*. And I just didn't know what to say half the time.' Lorena looked disconsolate, close to tears, perhaps partly out of sympathy because Elena seemed shaken and upset

'That's all right. It wasn't your fault. I should have been there.' She was sure Lowndes hadn't imparted his suspicions to Lorena, and there wasn't much more she could say herself until she'd listened to the tape, gauged the extent of the damage.

It was getting worse by the minute: Lorena lying to Lowndes, Lowndes lying to Lorena, and her in the middle – half-zonked with valerian, whisky and sleep deprivation – pathetically trying to juggle it all when she already had a full set of balls in the air from her own lies of the past twenty-nine years. And this was proving to be the day when the balls were finally starting to slip from her grasp, hit the ground with a thud of reality.

Still she felt awkward playing the tape with Lorena looking over at intervals, so after the first eight minutes she stopped it and didn't press Play again until Lorena dozed off thirty-odd miles into the drive.

'He was standing by the bedside, saying that it was okay . . . that I was very tired, couldn't remember.'

'And you're sure you were asleep at that point . . . that you were only dreaming?'

'Yes, yes . . . I'm pretty sure. And he was saying some numbers . . . seven . . . eight.'

The first event of any significance – the first minutes on tape had been spent mostly re-establishing the ground of the previous session and probably what had 'troubled' Lowndes. She could see where Lowndes was coming from: it was the sort of conversation that happened when you were awake, it wasn't particularly dreamlike.

'Some numbers? Was that part of a story perhaps, something from school? Or was he saying that you couldn't remember the numbers?'

'I . . . I don't remember now. It wasn't clear.'

'And did you talk back to him at any point? Did you say anything in return to your father?'

'No, no . . . I didn't. It was just him talking all the time.'

Which then was more dreamlike, Elena reflected: one voice talking, no two-way conversation. Lowndes asked if her father touching her was part of the same dream.

'Yes, but later.'

'Later?'

'There seemed to be a gap in between, as if I'd slept a bit in the middle without dreaming . . . and it was a second dream.' Lorena's breathing was laboured and unsettled. 'I . . . I didn't like it.'

'I know. That's why you're here.' Calming tone from Lowndes. 'But I don't need to know about the specifics of him touching you in the dream – it's just enough for you to say that it was where it shouldn't have been . . . lower down?'

'Yes, yes . . . it was.' Even that simple admission seemed difficult for Lorena to make, her breathing becoming more laboured, staccato.

'But what I'm more interested in is whether you did talk to your father then, say or shout back anything in protest, ask him to stop?'

'I wanted to . . . I tried. But it was as if my voice was trapped in my throat and I couldn't make any noise, however much I tried. I felt I couldn't breathe . . . and then I was back in the sewers again with the waters rising. It went up quickly above my head, started to fill my mouth and nose, and I was trying hard to scream out for help, but . . . I . . . I just couldn't . . . I –'

'It's okay . . . it's okay.' Placating tone with an edge of concern. 'It's just to get clear that you didn't at any time speak to your father while all this was happening.'

'No, no . . . I didn't.'

Elena could tell that for Lowndes that practically sealed it: he saw it as hardly conceivable that Lorena would have said nothing if she'd been awake. He moved on to the subject of Eileen. The questions were relaxed and conversational at first, no edge: when did you first meet her? Did you see her a lot while you were at the orphanages? So, she helped you quite a bit through those days – you became quite close. 'And when you arrived in England – did you see her much then?'

Lorena answered calmly, casually; she obviously felt she could talk freely, without worry, about the period before her problem with Ryall. But Elena felt the tension building with each question because she knew already that a trap was being set up.

Lowndes gradually circled in.

'So with you not seeing much of Eileen once you were in England – you must have missed her.'

'Yes . . . I suppose I did a little.' The first hesitation from Lorena.

'I mean, you'd become so close before. She'd become one of your closest friends . . . and practically the only person you felt you could confide in.'

'Yes, I . . . I suppose she had.' The hesitation was marked now: Lorena probably didn't see where Lowndes was heading yet, but she was obviously becoming unsettled about so many questions concerning Eileen.

'Is that why you confided in Eileen about your problem with your father?'

'Yes . . . but I told my mother first.' Lorena was suddenly more alert, wary, starting to fight back. 'I only told Eileen because my mother couldn't be in the interviews with me, and I didn't want to be on my own with someone I didn't know from social services. I wanted someone there I knew.'

'I appreciate that.' Slow exhalation from Lowndes, as if he was slightly peeved at getting dragged away from his target. 'But without this new drama now with your father – it's unlikely you'd have even seen Eileen again. There would have been no reason for you to see her.'

'I . . . I don't know. I haven't thought about it.' Lorena was on uncertain ground again.

'And that would have made you very sad, wouldn't it? Because you like Eileen – in fact, before your adoptive mother she was the person you felt closest to.'

Elena bit at her lip: what Lowndes didn't know – and which made it all the more poignant – was that in Lorena's mind at that moment Eileen and her mother were one and the same. Lorena paused for a moment, only the shallow fall of her breath coming over on tape. Finally:

'Yes, that's true. That would have made me sad.'

Elena glanced over at Lorena curled away in sleep, and suddenly felt like swinging the car in and hugging her tight. One simple sentence that somehow made all the long years of her work in the orphanages worthwhile – despite the dilemma it had now led to.

'And so this problem with your father at least gave you something you'd long missed and craved – seeing Eileen again. Being close to her again and sharing a problem with her . . . like the good old bad old days in Romania.'

'Yes, that's so. I like Eileen a lot and I –' Lorena faltered with an uneven intake of breath, almost a gasp. She'd seen where Lowndes was heading. A suspended second, then as she let her breath free: 'But I wouldn't have done anything like that to Eileen. She took a very great risk taking me away and –' She stopped herself again, suddenly realizing.

'Taking you away?'

Oh God. She should have been there. The pressure on Lorena must have been insufferable. Elena would have probably decided to throw in the towel and bare all to Lowndes, felt that it was all too much for Lorena to face alone. But once again she'd put her own quest first and left Lorena forgotten.

'Yes, my . . . my mother asked Eileen to take me away one day to see her house and the nearby chine and beach – but in fact it was to talk about my problem with my father. My father found out and was very angry about it, told on Eileen to the social services.'

Elena couldn't resist hissing 'yes' under her breath: Lorena's Bucharest streetwiseness obviously had its uses.

'Right . . . I see.' Lowndes had little choice but to accept it, but the lingering doubt was evident in his voice.

He went back for a moment to the dreams and her father, as if seeking one last affirmation that she remembered absolutely nothing on that front while awake – then he closed the session.

Lowndes' summary notes merely went through in more detail the concern he'd voiced earlier, now using the tape for almost point-by-point illustration. But listening to Lowndes, Elena couldn't help wondering as she looked across at Lorena – so innocent while asleep, but perhaps her life so far had made her wily and complex rather than just confused and vulnerable – whether Lowndes' assessment might be right: after all, her bond with Lorena was far more acute than he even realized. Lorena's bond with Nicola Ryall was almost non-existent, so even long before this makeshift role-play now, Elena had been filling both roles: mother *and* helper. *Saviour.* It was a powerful combination.

Ste-Marguerite's became progressively quieter, the atmosphere heavier, as Elena started along the cloister-style corridor away from the main building – a flat-fronted gothic stone edifice three storeys high. Elena suspected that the children's dormitories took up the top two floors, and the classrooms and playrooms the ground floor.

She'd spotted a playground area to the side of the building as she'd parked, and at 4 p.m. it was active and noisy. Beyond the play area was farmland, with the warehouse units and sawmills on the edge of Baie du Febvre visible half a mile away. Elena had stood for a moment taking it all in: not too bad an environment and view, and possibly the warehouse units had only appeared in the last ten or twenty years. When little George had been here, probably the . . . She shook her head and turned abruptly to head in. No more mental compensating after the event.

To the left of the cloister corridor were four arched windows looking on to a small courtyard with a statue of St Marguerite at its centre. Elena could see a Grey nun reading on a bench under St Marguerite's outstretched palm.

Elena and Lorena were following Sister Bernardine, who two-thirds along the corridor indicated towards three upright chairs to the side. 'If you'd like to wait there. I won't be a moment.'

Sister Bernardine walked to a door a few yards further along, and with a light knock and a small tight smile back at them, went inside.

The silence was intense as they waited. The sound of the children in the playground outside was muted and distant, barely audible. This section wrapping around the courtyard was two-storeys on one side and single-storey the remaining two. Elena got the impression that this was the nuns' private quarters, cut off from the noise of children so that they could concentrate on administrative paperwork and prayer.

Elena glanced towards the door. Bernardine at least appeared helpful, keen to please, and had a ready smile. Elena knew that orphanages could be strict about passing on information; hopefully Bernardine's seeming compliance was an encouraging sign.

But moments later, as she left Lorena in the corridor with a 'Shouldn't be long' and Bernardine ushered her into the room, Elena's hopes waned a bit upon sight of the woman behind the large oak desk ahead: small, no more than four-eleven, mid-fifties – about twenty years older than Bernardine – and wearing thick glasses that gave her an owlish, stern countenance, not aided by her scant, economical smile upon greeting.

Bernardine introduced her as Sister Thérèse. 'Her English is not perfect – so I'll translate where necessary.'

Elena eased herself down into the proffered seat, another old-wood upright with faded red velvet seat covering. Her spirits sagged another notch: language was a possible extra barrier between her and Sister Thérèse. But with a fresh breath she launched into her story as best she could. She was careful not to mention she'd become pregnant under-age – a bad start with nuns – she just said that she was sixteen at the time, very young, and her family and her had made a joint decision because of her studies and college plans. Vocational aims seemed a better bet to get their understanding. She admitted, though, that she'd suffered guilt years later about what she'd done, and this had led to her working with orphaned children in Romania. Vocation *and* guilt: raising the empathy stakes. She avoided too the problems with Lorena, she said that her involvement in a heartfelt reunion between one of the Romanian children and her family had finally made her realize that an important part of her life was missing.

'. . . and would probably remain so until I find him.' Despite the lies, just talking about it brought the pain of the separation and the lost years to the surface, and Elena felt tears beginning to well up. She cast her eyes down for a second. 'That's why the special trip now all the way from England. I was given the name of your orphanage just this morning by my son's uncle at the time – Sotiris Stephanou. I phoned straight after for this appointment now.'

Elena had aimed her set speech at Sister Thérèse, with only occasional glances towards Bernardine, and hopefully had come across as appropriately humbled and beseeching. It was difficult to tell with the translation at intervals from Sister Bernardine: she translated only selected segments, so she was either relying on Sister Thérèse's rudimentary English or heavily editing.

Sister Thérèse then asked a few basic questions herself in English. Elena clarified that Stephanou was the family name before the change to Stevens, then gave the approximate dates when young George had arrived at Ste-Marguerite's and then later left for a new family.

Sister Thérèse spent a moment more checking through two files and a large register book on her desk. 'Yes. George Stevens. I see it now.' She traced along with one finger for a second before looking up. 'I'm sorry. I don't think we can help.'

'I . . . I don't understand.' Elena looked at the register accusingly, incredulous that it might lead to such a blunt assertion so quickly. 'Don't you have the information I want?'

'No, no. We have it all here. It's not that . . .' Sister Thérèse turned to Bernardine and spoke in rapid French; her English had apparently gone as far as it could. Bernardine explained.

'In the register we make note of any children who later get in touch with us and express the desire to have contact with their parents. If the parents have also contacted us, or later do so – we then pass that information on to the child. It's the only criterion we have for putting the two parties together.'

Elena nodded thoughtfully. Similar to the Adoption Contact Register and, for that matter, most orphanages. She more than anyone knew that the child had to make the running. But she'd come too far, overcome too many obstacles and dangers to entertain possible failure at this final hurdle now.

'But now that I've made contact, you could pass this on to my son and still leave the decision with him as to whether he wanted direct contact with me or not. I know he would; I'm quite sure there wouldn't be any problem with that.' Just the delay: she'd have to wait on in Quebec another two or three days for his response.

Another burst of French between Thérèse and Bernardine. Sister Thérèse spoke this time. 'I'm sorry. I'm afraid there's nothing we can do. The system we've set up is the only one through which contact can be made.'

Elena couldn't help wondering if they'd done this before; it looked almost a routine: Thérèse for blank refusals, Bernardine if any elaboration was necessary. The three-way nature of the conversation put up an extra obstacle – but having battled so hard to get this far, she was damned if she was going to let herself be defeated by two nuns.

Elena smiled wanly. 'I'm sorry too. Because I know from my own work that there's a legal principle according to which you're duty bound to notify my son that I've made contact.' It was a bluff: the principle held only for the ACR, the rules differed between orphanages. But it was the only thing she could think of.

Sister Thérèse frowned as Bernardine translated. She fired back sternly in French without looking at Elena: suddenly Elena was invisible, and Thérèse was showing her indignation by not gracing her with any more English.

With a fresh breath – awkwardness at getting caught in the crossfire more than impatience – Bernardine translated: 'Sister Thérèse says that unfortunately we have our own strict rules. Rules that are explained to both the parents leaving children with us and adopting parents. These become part of our contract with them – the right to bring up that child without later harassment or interference – and we dare not breach that. If your son hasn't told us of his desire to make contact with his parents, I'm afraid there's nothing we can do. Sister Thérèse really is truly sorry.'

Elena was sure that Sister Thérèse hadn't offered any apology: her expression was too severe, unyielding, and she hadn't spoken for that long. Bernardine was obviously edge-softening now as well as elaborating. Regardless, it was all slipping away. The light at the end of the chine was more distant, dull again – and when Elena listened for the sound of the children in the play area, she could no longer hear them. Either playtime was over or Sister Thérèse's office was too remote from the children for the sound to carry. *Remote from any emotional involvement.*

Elena had a sudden image of young George as he might have been then scurrying in the playground or through the corridors and classrooms of Ste-Marguerite's along with the other children. And then when he might have fallen from grace, he was suddenly cut off from them and brought along this same cloister, the noise of his friends receding with each step until he reached this deathly silent, foreboding office to face some predecessor of Sister Thérèse and know his fate.

She wished she'd been there to hold his hand but, pathetically, she couldn't even put a face to that lone figure. She hadn't asked Sotiris for any photos, nor had he offered any: probably he had none. She had no idea what her son had looked like at *any* age.

She felt a tight knot in her chest – anger, frustration and her sinking spirits as it dawned on her that a whole lifetime of images and memories was lost to her. But the rest of her just felt numb: it seemed so unreal, unjust that it could all possibly end here, now.

'You have no idea what I've been through to get here.' She started scrambling wildly in the hope of striking a more poignant chord. 'I've even brought my daughter with me all the way from England to see him. How do you think she's going to feel when I tell her she can't see her older brother? The brother she's never seen? She's so built up this moment in her mind, looking forward to finally meeting him.'

The tears were suddenly welling again, threatening to brim over this time. Of course the lost hope was all hers – but that was almost too painful to voice, would probably have made her break down in racking sobs on the spot: much easier and more likely to evoke sympathy to transpose it all to a ten-year-old girl.

Sister Thérèse and Sister Bernardine looked more concerned at this, and some more rapid French flew between them. Absolutely everything hung by a thread on what was said next, Elena realized. Her hands started to shake and she pressed them firmly into her lap. On the drive, when her mind had drifted to how to approach every-thing and how she might handle the unthinkable of them saying no, she'd found herself becoming nervous. She'd tried to blank her mind to the possibility, but still a trace of nerves remained; so half an hour before the meeting she'd downed two more valerian pills. Now those were beginning to wear off, or the intensity of the moment was pushing her agitation beyond even their effect.

'Sister Thérèse says that she's truly sorry.' Bernardine cast her eyes down, as if she was consoling over bereavement or found it difficult to meet the plea in Elena's eyes. 'She fully appreciates the time and trouble you've put in coming here now. But there really is nothing we can do to help. Our hands are tied.'

The finality of the words, the brick wall she'd ultimately run into, jolted Elena. It was as if the pressure had been quietly building up for the past twenty-nine years, then as it had eventually become too much, she'd been shot like a champagne cork through the drama of the past days: search agencies, abducting Lorena, customs, ducking the police, her grinding door-calls, the pilgrimage through the seemingly endless succession of frowns and head-shakes, her diet of valerian and whisky just to keep going, and finally the breakthrough with Sotiris –

but she'd been gathering momentum all along, not seeing, not preparing herself for the possible dead end ahead. And as it came now it took her breath away, and its surreality made her slightly dizzy: surely she couldn't have gone through all of that only to hit this brick wall now? She *had* to fight back. But she felt tired, oh so tired, and her scrambled mind couldn't clutch on to what might be left to fight back with. Nothing left but to beg.

She leant across the desk. 'Please . . . *please.*' She slid one hand across to make contact with Sister Thérèse's, to add weight to her imploring; but Thérèse's hands were almost out of reach, and she pulled them tighter into herself and looked alarmed. 'If you have an ounce of compassion left in your heart.'

Elena felt her tears brimming over, running cool down her cheeks, and her trembling ran deeper, now gripping her whole body. It was visible in her hand reaching across the desk – and from the shock on Sister Thérèse's face she knew she probably did in that moment look like the half-crazed heroin addict she'd viewed earlier in the mirror.

Some more words between Sisters Thérèse and Bernardine before they turned to her again: a defensive tone, but it was suddenly quieter, more distant, she could hardly tell if French or English was being spoken. Their figures too were now more distant, like two apparitions in the last fading light at the end of the chine. And as the greyness behind her eyes washed through, she watched their figures slowly tilt as the floor rushed up to meet her.

Voices. Remote voices, high-pitched, excitable. The voices from the playground were back again. Then suddenly they were closer: Elena could hear the clatter of footsteps at the end of the cloister corridor. A group of children were looking on at her, their voices now muted to hushed whispers.

Young George was among them, and he broke free and ran towards her. He put one hand on her shoulder, gently shaking.

'Are you okay now . . . are you okay?'

Then another voice: 'I've brought you coffee. *Coffee.*'

And as it all finally fell into focus, Elena saw that it was Lorena shaking her shoulder.

'Are you okay now, Elena? Are you awake?' And Sister Bernardine was standing to one side looking equally concerned as she held out a cup.

She was back sitting next to Lorena in the cloister corridor. She shook the last woolliness from her head and took the proffered cup.

'Thanks.' She noticed her hand still shaking as she held the cup, but the aroma and the warm liquid cutting the dryness in her throat felt good. She closed her eyes for a second in appreciation. As she opened them she noticed a group of small children looking on from where the cloisters joined the classroom corridors. They were quickly ushered away by a Grey nun following behind.

She was sure she saw one of them smile; probably things hadn't been so bad here – but the fact was she was never going to see her son again. The emptiness she felt inside at that realization was overwhelming, but at least there was one compensation: she didn't have to battle on any more to try and find him. She felt she hardly had the energy left to continue anyway, she was so battle-worn and weary; so as a result, perversely, she felt a strange sense of serenity: a feeling that she could finally breathe easy, let it all wash away from her and say, 'It's over.' No more door calls, obstinate nuns and ducking from the police. Just home with Gordon, Christos and Katine, her warm and familiar bed, her studio and paintings, the chine and the fresh sea breezes, and life as it was before the nightmare started.

And as for Lorena . . . *Oh Jesus.* She bit lightly at her bottom lip between coffee sips at the thought of what might happen there. Lorena so concerned about her, as if she was the only person in this world she felt close to or cared about – which sadly was probably true – and yet even if the nuns had told her where George had gone, she was about to betray Lorena, send her packing back to England.

Everything Lowndes had said in his last session had begun to stack up in her mind as uncomfortably true. All the signals were there: her close attachment to Lorena going back all the way to Romania; Lorena's distance not only from her father but also Nicola Ryall; her being the first person Lorena had called for help; Lorena's ready agreement to the abduction and her excitement at times on the trip, almost as if it was some sort of holiday; then finally Lorena asking if she could stay with her permanently. *'Maybe I could keep your Katine company and play with her – be like a sister.'*

Even if the mosaic didn't slot together so well and Lowndes had somehow got it wrong – there was nowhere left for her to go with it. They'd tried their damnedest to uncover something with Ryall and still no light in sight: further sessions would just hit the same stone wall. And she couldn't possibly return to Lowndes: now that he felt he had the right bone in his mouth, he'd just continue gnawing at Lorena's attachment to Eileen. Lorena would either crumble under the pressure or her abduction would finally be uncovered. No, she'd decided just before going in to see the nuns, there was no option left but to put Lorena on the first flight back to England.

'Are you feeling better now, Elena? I was very worried about you.'

That gentle angel's wings touch of fingers on her shoulder. Elena shuddered at the thought of what she had planned for her: Lorena would no doubt see it as a form of betrayal, or at the least think that she was once again being discarded, given up on. But there was no choice. *No choice!*

'Yes, I'm fine now . . . fine.' She nodded and closed her eyes again for a second. At least that might now help soften the blow: she could tell Lorena that they'd be flying back to England together. Nothing left here for either of them.

Elena sensed Sister Bernardine hovering to her side as if she wanted to say something. The nun glanced anxiously back towards the door of Sister Thérèse's office, then slipped a piece of paper from the folds of her habit and pressed it into Elena's hand.

Elena looked at the piece of paper almost indignantly. 'What is this?' Ticket perhaps to the convent fête as an apology for giving her such a hard time? She unfolded it: two names, Claude and Odette Donatien, and a Montreal address.

Sister Bernardine leant over, whispering conspiratorially. 'That's where he's gone. But I haven't given it to you, okay?' Another nervous glance back towards Sister Thérèse's office.

'Okay.' Barely audible mumble. Elena stared at it blankly a moment more. She should have felt elated and leapt up and hugged Sister Bernardine until she turned blue. But clearly Bernardine wanted her to stay subdued, secretive, and a part of her still felt numb: just when she'd let go of the last thread, it was back in her grasp again.

'I should have told that man too when he came all those years ago. He was sat exactly where you are now, head in hands, when he found out he wouldn't be able to see the boy.'

'What man?' Elena was still in shock, reeling from the ever-changing turn of events.

But as Sister Bernardine sat down next to her and explained, nothing could have prepared her for this one final change, pulled out of the hat as if Bernardine was some cruel magician. Elena felt her whole world turn upside down, its very foundations shaken to the core. She felt herself close to fainting again and shook her head, refusing to accept. But all she could think of was rushing to the first phone box to speak to the only two people who could possibly explain, set her world to rights again: Uncle Christos and her mother.

26

Roman had insisted he be urgently told of any developments on tape, so Carlo Funicelli checked them twice a day – lunchtime and early evening – with sometimes an extra check at midnight or in the early hours if he was downtown late.

For the early evening session he usually stayed the longest, forty minutes or sometimes an hour, and he'd grab a sandwich and an espresso on the way in if he wasn't heading later to a restaurant. The tapes were all on sound-activate, so the one fed from the bugs in Donatien's penthouse would usually play through in eight or ten minutes: the only sounds so far had been the increasingly frantic messages left by Simone, plus the occasional social or business-related call, all seemingly innocent.

But now that there were also bugs at Donatien's parents in Beaconsfield, the tape for there was running longer. A lot longer: the house was a hive of activity, with Odette there most of the day, her husband and her talking, dining or watching TV in the evening, and then the various calls from friends, neighbours and Claude Donatien's business partner or his golfing buddies.

Funicelli quickly became bored. He started fast-forwarding for more interesting soundbites, and almost missed the one conversation that didn't quite fit the pattern. He wound the tape quickly back to the beginning of the call.

'*My name's Waldren. Elena Waldren. I'm sorry to trouble you like this, but I've just come from Ste-Marguerite's, and they gave me your number. It's regarding your adopted son, George. I . . . I really need to see you and talk to you about him.*'

'*Why . . . what's happened?*'

'*Nothing . . . nothing. But it is nevertheless a bit delicate, personal. Something I'd rather discuss with you and your husband in person rather than just over the phone.*'

'*I see.*' Long pause, static over the line.

'*And I have come quite a long way for this – all the way from England, in fact.*'

Funicelli picked up on the caller's agitation. She sounded anxious, very anxious that Odette Donatien might not agree to see her. Whatever it was, it was important. The prawn salad roll held poised by his mouth the last ten seconds, he finally took a bite out of. Maybe that was where Donatien was holed up: England.

'Well . . . I suppose so. But, you know, sometimes we don't see him from one month to the next, so I don't know how much help we'll be. You're sure there's nothing wrong – he's not in trouble or anything?'

'No, no . . . really. Nothing like that. This is just a catching-up exercise from someone he hasn't seen in a long, long while.'

Funicelli munched steadily. Odette Donatien still sounded uncertain, but it was difficult to tell which was paramount: her concern due to the secrecy, or her curiosity not being immediately sated. She obviously wanted to know more than her caller was willing to tell her at that moment.

The caller said that she'd just left Ste-Marguerite's and was still fifty miles up-province. Odette Donatien said that she and her husband were planning to go out that night – so in the end they arranged that Mrs Waldren should come to their house at 1 p.m. the next day.

'My husband more often than not stops by for lunch – so I'll make sure he's around tomorrow when you call.'

Funicelli stopped the tape and phoned Roman straight away.

'Sounds promising. Could be the break we've been looking for,' Roman agreed. He was thoughtful for a second. 'Look – you stay there and listen to the tape live tomorrow. And I'll make sure to get someone parked looking on at the house for when she shows.'

'There was no conspiracy, no collusion between me and your mother to keep things from you. Believe me, Elena, it just wasn't like that.'

'Then tell me, Uncle Christos – what was it like?' Elena could practically hear the swallow, the catching of breath at the other end of the line in London.

'Well – all I know is that your father tried to find young Christos, George as he was then, not long before he died. But I'd been sworn to secrecy by your mother, and in any case I had no idea where he'd gone to try and find him. There was nothing useful I could have told you, and by then you'd already narrowed things down to Montreal or Chicago. Why do you think I was urging you so hard to go and see your mother? She said she'd in turn been sworn to secrecy by your father, but I just had the feeling that if you told her that you'd finally

324

decided to try and find your son, that you were at that moment desperately searching, she'd have opened up and told you what she knew.'

'Right.' Now it was Elena's turn to swallow hard. She'd almost lost a part of it, had to strain her hearing with the noise of a long trailer passing on the highway close by. She was still at the service station where she'd leafed through directories to get the Donatiens' current address and number and bought a global call card to phone England straight after her call to them. The phone kiosk was halfway between the service station building and the road, and at intervals the traffic noise interfered. 'I . . . I thought that was just you banging the same old drum. Trying to patch up old family differences, get us all back together again.'

'I began to tire of banging that drum long ago, Elena. Or hadn't you noticed I'd hardly mentioned it the past year or so? Maybe in the back of my mind I saw it as an opportunity for some of the old wounds to be healed – but my first thought was that your mother might be able to help. Have you spoken to her yet?'

'No, not yet. I wanted to speak to you first.' The shaking was more pronounced in her legs. Build-up of the emotional helter-skelter of the past days and the final twist in the tale at Ste-Marguerite's, or the fact that she'd now been standing for almost twenty minutes on the same phone? She noticed the cashier starting to look out of the window at her. 'Why did he suddenly decide he wanted to find him after all those years?'

'Because he was dying, Elena. Don't forget, he'd known about the cancer for a good three years. In fact, the doctors only gave him eighteen months, two years. As I say, your mother hasn't really shared the details with me – but I think he saw it as a last chance to make some amends.'

A lump suddenly rose in her throat; she found it hard to swallow. But in the end he hadn't been successful. *He was sat exactly where you are now, head in hands, when he found out he wouldn't be able to see the boy.* The wave of empathy that hit her felt so strange, alien, that it made her shudder. She hadn't felt that way about her father since . . . well, since almost the age young George had been when he left Ste-Marguerite's.

'There's something else, Elena. Something I do know more about, and I think should tell you now. You know that money I used to send you now and then?'

'Yes.' She'd blankly refused to touch the money left in trust for her or take any money from her father. Then when she'd run into problems – which was probably more often than she'd have liked on the hippie trail – Uncle Christos would send money. It wasn't a fortune, but given the dire circumstances, it was practically a lifesaver each time. Then, in addition, he'd send generous sums for her birthday, Christmas, her patron's name day, Buddhist New Year – whatever excuse he could think of. She was sure she'd never have survived those years without Uncle Christos' help.

'Most of that money was from your father. I'd send a bit for your birthday, thirty, forty pounds, whatever – but he'd insist on sending the other two-sixty or -seventy. Or when you had problems, a lot more. And he'd swear me to secrecy each time: he knew that if I said it was from him, you'd refuse it.'

Elena felt as if her life was like a set of plates in a Greek restaurant. Just when she had the table set again – 'Right. Okay. That's what my life was like' – some mad waiter would come along and spin the plates into the air, sending them smashing to the ground. She found it hard to find her voice; she sounded frail, tremulous. 'But, why . . . why didn't he say something later? Tell me what he'd done?'

'You know your father. Proud to the end. Proud and obstinate.'

'I know. I know.' She leant against the kiosk and closed her eyes, sighing deeply. Suddenly it wasn't just a problem with her tired, trembling legs; her whole body and mind felt weary, not a spark of energy or clear thought left.

'I think he'd have seen it as admitting that he'd made a mistake with you. And you know your father was never very good at that – admitting he was wrong. It was the cause of probably ninety per cent of the arguments I used to have with him.' Uncle Christos risked a small chuckle.

'Is that it? Or is there something else maybe I should know – like perhaps he wasn't a hot-shot businessman after all but secretly head of the Hampstead Hare Krishnas? Or, surprise, surprise, he's not dead, but living in some commune in the Himalayas along with Elvis and Lord Lucan?' She'd aimed for humour as an escape valve, but the acid, tremulous edge in her voice left little doubt: she was angry. Angry and confused.

'I'm sorry, Elena. I know how you must feel. But, no – that's it, that's as much as I know. As to why your father made that last trip to try and see George and what happened when he was there, only your mother knows the details. When are you going to phone her?'

'Well . . . straight away, I suppose.' It seemed a stupid question given how much she desperately needed to know what had happened – but she picked up the concern in Uncle Christos' tone. He was afraid things would follow the same pattern as in the past with her mother: she'd put off contacting her and in the end would never do it. 'I'll call her as soon as I put the phone down now.'

'That's good. I'll . . . I'll leave you to it, then. And once again I'm sorry, Elena . . . It was just how your father wanted it.' Small resigned sigh, smothered by the air rush of a passing truck. 'Good luck with your mother.'

But, having said her thanks and signed off, hearing the dialling tone again, she noticed Lorena starting to look around expectantly from the car only a few yards ahead, and suddenly she wasn't so sure. She didn't feel she could take any more shock revelations right now. Each one had been like a body blow and she felt like a punch-drunk boxer, sagging against the side of the kiosk for support under the relentless rain of blows; her legs were aching from trembling and now her hands shaking too as she gripped the receiver. One more blow and she was down.

She stood uncertainly a moment more, wondering whether to ring then or wait till later and meanwhile hopefully summon more reserves and nerve to face the call. Lorena looking over anxiously also reminded her that she still had to decide what to do with her.

The delay hardly helped. Elena was going to wait until they were back at the hotel to make the call, but with each passing mile back to Montreal on Highway 30 her anxiousness to know pressed harder. It was like a tightening coil at the back of her neck, and as she started to get a headache and could barely summon a clear thought, she swung the car into the next available stop, a roadside diner seventeen miles from Montreal.

It was busy and, judging from the car park, popular with truckers. She ordered a mineral water at the counter for herself and directed the waitress over to Lorena for her coke and blueberry muffin. She swilled back two aspirins quickly followed by another valerian tablet with the mineral water on the way to the phone by the washrooms at the back. She'd gained a bit more resolve and energy since speaking to Uncle Christos, but still her nerves were shot: how best to start a conversation with the mother you've hardly spoken to in half a lifetime?

The ringing tone seemed slow with a slight echo to it. As a hesitant voice finally answered 'Hello', Elena put her other hand by her ear, fading out the clatter of plates and voices and the hiss of the short-order grill.

'Mum, is that you? It's Elena . . . Elena!' She began by enquiring about her mother's health, then quickly lurched into not being able to even think of how to start apologizing for not being in touch for so long. 'I'm sorry, Mum, so –'

But her mother cut in halfway through. 'You're there now, in Montreal?'

'Yes . . . yes, I am.'

'Uncle Christos said you might phone. And it's okay, Elena – you don't need to apologize. You had every good reason to stay away and not see me. I understand.'

Oh God. Elena closed her eyes and wished the floor could open up. The ready, almost fatalistic acceptance made it all the worse, made the guilt worm deeper. But then her mother too rambled for a moment about how was Gordon and her two young ones Christos and Katine, before returning to the main purpose of Elena's call: her father's trip to Montreal the year before he died.

'Uncle Christos is right that him knowing that he was dying provided the final push. But it's not as simple as that – it had been building up for a while. Many years, in fact . . . Going all the way back to when you discovered you could no longer have children, and then later Andreos' suicide.'

Elena felt the years being stripped away, pictured herself again in her late teens in Andreos' room telling him how upset she was with their father, how she felt like just running away. And him saying 'Don't leave', but never explaining why she shouldn't: too shy to admit that he wanted her to stick around as his own emotional bolster. 'But . . . but all those years. How come I never knew, or at least guessed?'

'Your father was very secretive, very guarded. He felt the guilt straight away – I saw it in him where probably others didn't – but it didn't surface fully until years later. One of his secretaries had a messy miscarriage and couldn't have children any more. She cried on his shoulder that it was the worst thing she'd ever endured or could imagine happening to *any* woman – and days later he was on the phone to the Stephanous asking about young George. Nick Stephanou had given the boy up to the orphanage two years before, but he didn't have the stomach to admit that to your father. Maybe he feared your father would ask back for the money he'd paid them. So he didn't mention the accident, didn't mention any problems. Just said George was growing tall and doing well at school and both he and Maria were very happy and very proud. Your father would phone every year or so and get the same story – 'Yeah, fine, at high school now, you know' – and it wasn't until eight years later that he finally got to know the truth, when he was having trouble contacting Nick and ended up phoning his brother Sotiris. George would have been fifteen then – but what could your father do? He phoned the orphanage and they told him George had gone to a new family at the age of eight and their rule was not to pass on any details – so all he could do was just shrug his shoulders and hope that he'd gone to a good family somewhere, that he was having a good life and hadn't suffered.'

Good family somewhere. Good life. Elena felt a shiver run up her spine. All the years she'd thought how different she was to her father, how opposite their views were, particularly regarding her son: that her father had given him away purely to punish her and hadn't spent a minute since wasting an ounce of emotion on what he'd done or worrying about the boy's welfare; yet all the while his thoughts had been almost exactly the same as hers.

'Your father, as he did with most things, put on a brave face, on the surface shouldered it well – but I could see the pain and guilt beneath the surface. And he was missing you too, regretted what he'd done. He used to send you money through Uncle Christos and asked that you weren't told – thought you'd probably refuse it.'

'I know. Uncle Christos told me.' She looked up to see their waitress heading back to the counter. Lorena was taking the first sips of her coke.

'And so practically the whole focus of his life, all his ambitions and hopes got poured into your brother Andreos. "Andreos is going to be a great successor in my business." Andreos is going to do this, Andreos is going to do that. There seemed no limits to what Andreos might achieve in your father's eyes. Then, with Andreos' suicide, particularly when it looked like the main reason was that he felt he couldn't cope, couldn't live up to your father's expectations – all hope there too was lost and again your father blamed himself. He drunk himself silly for weeks and one night I caught him gently weeping in his sleep –

probably one of many times he'd done so without me knowing – and he turned to me tearfully and asked what was wrong with him. "What is it about me that drives people away or pushes them into the ground? Am I such a monster?" '

Tears welled in Elena's eyes, the café scene ahead suddenly blurred, distorted. She'd never before seen that soft, emotional side of her father; it was so totally out of sync with the image she'd long held true of him. And all she'd done was add to his guilt and suffering: her brother's funeral had been the last time she'd seen her father; she'd stood stoically by her mother's side as Andreos' body was lowered into the ground and the priest said the prayers; then when her father had finally summoned the courage and spirit to speak to her, she'd turned abruptly and stormed off, berating him: *'This is all your fault too. You're to blame for this.'* 'I'm sorry. I . . . I had no idea.' Her own voice sounded distant, lost among the hustle and clatter of the restaurant. She had to shift slightly to one side as two men in blue overalls came past her from the washroom behind.

'How could you? He never showed that side to anyone. When I suggested to him that maybe that was part of the problem and he should try and show his emotions more, he said that I was being ridiculous. If he wore his heart on his sleeve, he wouldn't last a minute in business. His competitors would have him for breakfast. And besides, it just wasn't him. So the defences would quickly come up again, that tough skin he saw as his protection from the world outside. I remember him once saying to me that that sort of thing was for "old Greek widows, wailing and gnashing their teeth". I think with the prejudice he experienced early on, he'd fixed this strange notion in his mind that not showing his emotions would somehow make him more English and less Cypriot. Stiff upper lip and all that rubbish.'

Elena wiped her eyes with the back of one hand and looked towards Lorena. How could she have got it so wrong? *So wrong?* Her thoughts about her father had guided practically everything in her life – the rebellion, her hippie years, her staying away from home, and now they'd been the foundation of her suspicions over Ryall. Another dominant man. Very likely Lowndes was right, nothing was happening there, it was just Lorena's over-attachment to her. Full house. She'd been wrong about everything. *Everything.*

'Then with the cancer, he probably did look at me and imagine an old Greek widow in a few years, and everything else crashed back in at the same time. He started to dwell on his life and things past and think of all the mistakes he'd made. He started to think that it had all been a waste: devoting so much of his life to money, building up an empire. What was it all for when you didn't have family and loved ones around you? It wasn't only the son he'd lost with Andreos, or with you the daughter he'd driven away – it was the fact that you could no longer have children and Andreos had died before he'd even started a family that brought it all home to him. There was no continuing bloodline – and the only grandchild he'd ever had, he'd given away. That was when he resolved to try and find George.'

The tears brimmed over, streaming down Elena's cheeks, and the trembling was back in her legs. They felt ready to crumple at any second. She half turned and put one hand flat on the wall for support as a truck driver in a red check shirt approached, heading for the washroom. But he'd already noticed her distress and mumbled something in French, then, with her blank look, switched quickly to English.

'Are you okay, lady? Everything all right?'

'Yes, it's . . . it's okay. Just someone I haven't spoken to in a while.'

Her mother's voice crashed in halfway: 'Elena? Is there someone there with you?'

The truck driver nodded with a tight smile as he went past her, and she assured her mother that it was all right, she was in a restaurant and 'it was just someone passing by the phone'. Her emotions wanted to scream: 'No, no, it's not all right. Stop. *Stop!* I can't bear it any more, can't take more of my life's foundations ripped apart, any more illusions on which I've based almost every principle the past thirty years destroyed.' But her mind was curious, thirsty, wanted desperately to know every last detail, however painful.

'Trouble was, your father never was able to succeed in that final quest. He hoped that maybe if he visited personally . . . but in the end the nuns wouldn't relent, wouldn't pass on where George had gone. That final blow hit him hard, Elena. He died a very sad and lonely man.'

'He was sat exactly where you are now . . .' Elena couldn't hold it back any longer: racking sobs convulsed her whole body, and she turned to face the wall so that people in the diner wouldn't see her tears and distress. She hadn't even shown up for the funeral, if nothing else to support her mother in her moment of grief; nor troubled to phone at any point to offer her condolences. And in the years since she'd never visited; they'd only spoken once briefly on the phone. Her mother

had buried the man she loved knowing that he'd died with a heart heavy with a lifetime of regrets, and purely because of her own past battles with her father she'd left her mother alone for all those years with that terrible pain and burden. No wonder Uncle Christos had kept urging her to see her mother. How could her mother possibly ever forgive her?

She clenched her hand in a fist against the wall, her eyes scrunched tight to stem the flow of tears, and finally found some composure to speak. 'But *why* . . . why didn't he say something earlier? Or maybe you . . . Why didn't you call me and tell me?'

'What was there to say? That he tried to find your son that he'd given away twenty-odd years ago – but in the end failed? And before he died, he swore me to secrecy. He said there was little point in telling you if there couldn't possibly be a good final resolution. It would just build up your hopes only to dash them again, and, besides, you'd probably blanked it all from your mind long ago. Too painful to think about.'

'Yes . . . that was partly true, I suppose.' Elena rubbed her nose with the back of her hand, sniffed back the remnants of tears. She felt uncomfortable admitting that it was spot-on, that her father knew her so well; and just like her father she'd kept the truth and her real emotions buried from everyone, going one better by keeping them even from her own husband. *Oh Jesus*, she was her father's daughter more than she realized.

'He said that only if you decided to find him – when you were finally sure you wanted to fill that gap in your life – should I tell you.'

'I see.' Still her voice was uncertain, she feared she might collapse again into tears at any time. She felt nothing but empty inside, as if a team of emotional burglars had stormed through her and upended every drawer: love, hate, family closeness, hopes, ambitions. *There, now you try and sort it all out.* And she was left to pick through the ransacked mess, one hand braced against the wall of a diner full of strangers, keeping her head turned from them so that they wouldn't see how destroyed she was, or see the tears streaming down her face, or notice that her whole body was shaking uncontrollably with her legs threatening to buckle; and meanwhile her mother at the end of a crackly line three thousand miles away had, in the space of less than fifteen minutes, told her that nothing in her life so far had been quite what it seemed.

But there was only one possible silver lining she could see now, one way to repay how she'd unknowingly betrayed her father's memory and left her mother to grieve alone these years past. 'One good thing, Mum . . . partly why I was phoning now. I think I might have found him: one of the nuns ended up giving me the details of the family that took George in. I'm seeing them tomorrow.' She didn't add that the one quirk of fate that had led Sister Bernardine to give her the address had been her father sat in the same spot six years before, head in hands. If he hadn't have visited, she probably would never have got the address. It was as if an invisible hand was reaching out: *'I tried to make good while I was alive . . . but at least you might now be able to succeed where I failed.'* 'When I catch up with George, I'll try and convince him to come to England sometime, and we can all have a big reunion.'

'That would be nice, Elena. But, you know, you don't need to make promises just to make me feel good. I'd be happy enough just to see more of you when you get back. But you need to find him for yourself, Elena. To fill that gap in your heart and soul that your father was never able to fill.'

27

'You know, you're quite a little girl for your age.' Alphonse beamed and reached across the bar, playfully pinching Lorena's cheek. He looked towards Elena perched on the bar stool next to her, seeking confirmation.

'She certainly is.' Elena nodded with a rueful smile and took another sip of her champagne. 'Particularly on holiday. You get twice the questions – so of course you need twice the energy just to keep up.' She hardly looked at Lorena as she spoke; she found it hard to meet her gaze directly knowing what was coming – very likely packing her off back to England in the morning, or at the latest soon after she'd seen the Donatiens.

They'd grabbed a quick pizza on the outskirts of Montreal, then headed back to the hotel. Alphonse was all smiles, asking how their day had been. Elena didn't want to get into the rollercoaster dramas of the day, just said that they'd finally tracked down these long-lost relatives and were seeing them tomorrow – 'So maybe a celebratory drink is in order.' She ordered a bottle of Moët and mixed Lorena's with orange juice. Lorena wasn't sure she liked it at first, only warming to it after a few sips; then at the start of her second glass, she became more talkative.

Alphonse was originally from northern Yugoslavia, 'the part that is now Slovenia', and had been in Montreal fourteen years. But rather than him swap notes with Lorena on the one experience they had in common – the hardship of life in the old Eastern Bloc – Lorena wanted to know all about Canada. How deep does the snow get in winter? How cold does it get? Do you go hunting? Are there a lot of bears?

'I remember a dancing bear once in Bucharest,' Lorena commented thoughtfully. 'He looked so sad. His owner was getting him to dance and hit a tambourine and act like he was happy – but all the time his eyes were so sad.'

So sad. Elena should have been pleased seeing Lorena come out of her shell, become more lively, animated. Except for the sessions with Lowndes, when her problems would weigh heavy again, Lorena had

334

been getting better every day since leaving England. But Elena was now worried that talking so openly, excitedly, Lorena would suddenly say the wrong thing and give the game away. She herself sometimes forgot who they were meant to be each time: Elena Waldren and daughter Lorena for Lowndes; daughter Katine for customs and the police, and now Alphonse as well because she'd had to show her passport on registration.

Perhaps Lorena's liveliness and change of spirit confirmed Lowndes' finding that her claims had all been just a ruse to get Elena's attention: Lorena had got almost nothing but attention these past days, no wonder she was happy. But what if she was wrong? What if the smiles were coming back to Lorena's face purely because she was free of Ryall's clutches – and tomorrow she'd be sending her back to England to . . .

'Are you okay?'

'Yes, fine . . . bit tired, that's all.' She gripped her champagne glass firmer. She was still far from recovered from the day's slings and arrows, and her nagging doubts about Lorena weren't helping.

Alphonse repeated the bit of conversation Elena had faded out: 'What Lorena says is true – you *do* share the same first name with Ceauçescu's wife.'

'I know.' Elena grimaced tautly. The late Romanian dictator and his wife were blamed for most of the country's orphan problems because they'd encouraged couples to have large families. Elena reached across and pulled Lorena to her for a second, but still she avoided direct eye contact. 'One Elena to cause the problems, another as saviour. Hopefully she's forgiven me by now.' Her driver Nick used to joke about her name whenever they got a difficult border guard or policeman. 'Just tell them your name, and they'll quickly do the sign of the cross and wave us on.' But she was careful not to air this: right now she was Elena the mother, not the aid worker.

She decided in the end to delay her decision about Lorena until her call to Gordon later that evening – by which time, 1 a.m. in England, Gordon had said he'd be back from seeing Mikaya Ryall in Durham.

When she made the call – using a booth at the end of Rue Berri – she started with the day's ups and downs and the elation of at last getting an address. She didn't go into the whole messy drama of her father visiting the orphanage or her phoning her mother – that was going to take another heart-to-heart: her secret life, Part Two, when she returned – she just said that one of the nuns had suddenly changed her mind about passing on the address. Gordon was full of bonhomie and good wishes for her meeting with the Donatiens the next day, then finally they got to how it had gone with Mikaya Ryall. No great revelations – except that Gordon was almost sure Mikaya was hiding something.

'. . . something which made her very uncomfortable, very quickly. She practically ran from the café halfway through.'

Elena agreed that it was suspicious, but she'd practically reached the end of the rope with sessions. 'There's nowhere left for me to go with this, and it's just not enough for me to be able to hang on to Lorena. I can hardly walk back into Lowndes' and say that he's got to probe deeper because Lorena's sister too is now having panic attacks at the mention of possible sexual interference by their adoptive father.'

'I know. I know you need something more concrete, and I'm already one step ahead of you.' Gordon had been uneasy after the meeting, so on the way back he'd put through a call to an old contact, an investigator who worked for the banks and insurance companies. 'I thought, if Ryall can dish the dirt on you, then maybe we should try turning the tables on him. I gave him everything I knew, and told him to dig particularly deep around the time of Mikaya Ryall's pregnancy.'

'When's he coming back to you?'

'I told him it was urgent, and he's already been on it half a day. He said he'd try and get back to me with as much as he could by close of play tomorrow.'

Lunchtime by then in Montreal. About the time she was seeing the Donatiens. Elena liked the idea of turning the tables on Ryall, giving him a run for his money – but overall she couldn't help feeling that they were clutching at straws. On the one hand the delay made her nervous: having to keep running the gauntlet with the police; yet on the other she was relieved to have an excuse to put off breaking the bad news to Lorena.

'Okay – let's wait till then to decide what to do.' And having said it, she felt as if a weight had been lifted: it was no longer inevitable, a foregone conclusion, that Lorena was going back to Ryall. There was still some hope left, however slim.

Or was it mainly for herself that she didn't want to dwell on the problem? To keep her mind clear for the big day ahead: meeting the Donatiens and then hopefully later her son. Once again pushing Lorena into the background because her own score card was full.

Twenty-nine years! Her mouth was suddenly dry at the thought. What would she say? How would she even begin to explain? The prospect was far more daunting than finally having to let down Lorena.

Elena didn't sleep well that night. She thought she might, given that she'd at last reached the end of her search and was utterly worn out from the nervous anxiety and lack of sleep of the past days.

But the excitement of the day to come kept her mind churning over how she might broach everything and how it might go. Then there was some commotion with sirens not too far away that seemed to go on for ever: in the end it was over two hours before she finally drifted off.

And suddenly the sirens were coming for her. They were all around and policemen were pounding up the stairs – she couldn't escape. Then she was outside in chains on the pavement with a crowd of people looking on, pointing. Lorena was also standing there in chains – though it was Ryall who was holding her captive, not a policeman. He was smiling crookedly at Elena. 'I've got her back now, and she'll never get free again. Now dance and clap your hands and try and look happy – there's people looking.'

And she thought: Yes, I should be happy, I'm seeing my son tomorrow. But all she could see was her father as she'd left him by Andreos' graveside, when everyone had turned their backs and left him alone. She rushed over to comfort him, to say sorry for having deserted him for all those years. But as she got closer, it wasn't Andreos' name her father was muttering as he looked down at the grave: *'George . . . I tried to find you, really I tried.'*

And she shouted out breathlessly to her father that she'd found him, pointing to his figure at the end of the chine. 'Look, he's there! *There!* I found him, I found him!' – though still George was like the young boy she'd pictured in the orphanage, not a grown man; and in that moment George turned and she was afraid that he'd move away before her father looked up and saw him. But the chains were still on her legs, and she didn't seem to be getting any closer to be able to attract her father's attention . . . and as George finally turned away again, the light at the end of the chine faded, leaving her in darkness.

The darkness was total, a black shroud. She couldn't see her father or George any more, could only guide her way by grappling branches and feeling for trees where she remembered them. Then suddenly there were other footsteps behind her in the pitch darkness, the fall of somebody's breath competing with her own in the new silence, and getting closer, *closer* . . . bearing down quickly, the breathing more rapid with each step and so close now she could feel it against the back of her neck, making her shiver . . . and she wasn't sure if it was Ryall or the police or . . .

She woke up, her breathing ragged. She went over to the mini-bar and opened a bottle of mineral water, felt the first few slugs cut through the dryness. *Oh Jesus, Jesus, Jesus.* She let out a heavy exhalation to ease the tightness in her chest. Hopefully after tomorrow she'd no longer need the sanctuary of the chine to try and bury the ghosts of what she'd done.

The man in the back of Roubilliard's four-wheeler shrank back a few inches as the heavy bulldog face suddenly appeared at the front side window, peering in.

'What do you think?' Roubilliard half turned round from the driver's seat, joining Frank Massenat in his appraisal of the back-seat passenger.

Massenat wrinkled his nose questioningly. 'Take off his glasses?'

Roubilliard's henchman, sitting beside the passenger, obliged. The passenger now seemed more anxious than at any time during the fifty-minute wait, his eyes dilating wide and his breathing falling hard: from what he remembered from his schooldays, this was what usually preceded a fist landing on your nose.

Massenat squinted doubtfully a moment more. 'Nah, not him. Close, but no cigar.'

'Sure?'

'Sure.' Massenat straightened up and turned away, taking out his mobile.

Roubilliard pulled out a twenty-dollar note and held it in front of the passenger. 'Some guy who owes our friend money – you could be his twin brother. Now lose yourself and make sure to lose your memory too about all this. Okay?'

The passenger looked at the note and Roubilliard, hardly believing he was being let go, there must be some last-minute surprise in store; then with a hasty nod – 'Okay' – he took the note and was out of the car, practically breaking into a run as he passed Massenat on his mobile to Roman.

Roman nodded knowingly at the other end. 'Yeah, thought it was too good to be true. Finding him in less than thirty-six hours – and right on our fucking doorstep in Lavalle. Yeah, yeah. Catch yer later.'

Roman kept on staring at the phone for a moment afterwards, cracking his knuckles. The third false alarm already – but this was the first time Roubilliard hadn't been able to rule them out himself. At least it meant that Roubilliard was busy, and in a few hours there'd be news too from Funicelli on just why this woman all the way from England was visiting Donatien's parents out in Beaconsfield.

The news item came on at 11.32 a.m. Female newscaster against the backdrop of a faint grey map of Canada with Quebec highlighted in yellow, talking about an RCMP breakthrough in their investigation into Montreal's Lacaille family. She glanced to one corner as prompt, and the news-clip about Neil Mundy's press conference just half an hour beforehand began. Mundy sat in the centre flanked by Michel Chenouda and Inspector Pelletier as cameras repeatedly flashed.

The television was at the end of a counter-style deli, the sound on low. One of the three sandwich servers closest to the screen looked up for a moment with interest, and two of his customers seemed engrossed, but hardly anyone else, including Elena and Lorena at the other end sharing a large french-stick sandwich, paid it any attention.

Elena had woken up late, so she decided that they should grab a quick brunch before heading off to see the Donatiens. Alphonse had told her it should only take thirty-five, forty minutes to get to Beaconsfield, but she wanted to leave some leeway to be safe.

Talk was stilted on the drive, she was far too preoccupied with what lay ahead to give anything more than brief responses to Lorena, and didn't instigate any conversation herself. She got there seventeen minutes early, so cruised around the area for a while: a small lake two blocks over with a park on one side bordered by a pine forest, a parade of shops three blocks in the other direction. They'd passed some messy industrial stretches on the outskirts of Montreal on the way there – grain silos, dilapidated warehouses and car dumps – but this was a nice area. A good place to bring up a child. George would have . . . She shook her head. She was doing it again. For all she knew, the directory listing for this address was recent, the Donatiens might have moved several times since they'd taken George from the orphanage.

They spent the last few minutes parked a hundred yards along the road from the house, Elena checking her hair and make-up and that she still didn't look like a half-crazed heroin addict – then drove up the last distance and pulled up outside. She didn't notice the man in the green Oldsmobile saloon parked thirty yards back, his gaze following her and Lorena intently as they walked up the path to the front door.

She tried to control her breathing as she approached the door, tried to relax – her nerves had mostly settled since the previous night – but all that pent-up tension was suddenly back in her body as she rang the bell and in the anxious few seconds' lull before the door opened. Then she was on automatic pilot, her senses bombarded: smiles, handshakes. Claude. Odette. Yes . . . and this is my daughter, Katine. Come through, come through. Odette was compact and well-presented, and Claude, dwarfing her, was heavy-set, but with his broadness and height carried it well. He had a shock of stone-grey hair and a ready smile, and Elena immediately warmed to them. Odette offered freshly made coffee, and Elena asked if her daughter could perhaps wait in another room or play in their garden.

'Some of what I've come to talk about could be a bit sensitive.' She'd explained away the orphanage to Lorena, claiming that her son had some schooling there, and that the Donatiens now were 'sort of godparents' – but if Lorena sat in on their conversation, she'd know the truth. 'I didn't want to leave her in the car outside, you see.'

Claude Donatien nodded knowingly, his expression suddenly more sombre. Odette took over and led Lorena down the hall, asking her what she would like to drink. Claude looked up at Elena in the moment they were left alone and forced a smile; but its openness had gone, he was obviously nervous, concerned – and that same mood prevailed when Odette returned with coffee and Elena launched into the reason for her visit.

Claude and Odette exchanged glances at intervals as her story unfolded, and looked increasingly troubled and uneasy. They asked few questions and sat mainly with their eyes cast down, their heads nodding slowly and solemnly, an occasional awkward glance between them. At first Elena thought it was just a reaction to the poignancy and drama of her story, but after a while she got the impression that there was something else troubling them, some unspoken worry that she'd triggered in their minds. And before she even reached the end of her story, Claude Donatien was shaking his head, his lips pursed tight together.

'I'm sorry . . . I thought you knew. Haven't you heard the news?' Again those downcast eyes; he could no longer bring himself to look at her directly.

'What news?'

'You shouldn't be so surprised, Claude – it was only on a few hours ago.' Odette rallied to her defence: 'She could easily have missed it.'

'I know.' Claude looked up briefly at Elena. 'It's just that before you explained, I thought your visit might have something to do with what's happened – that you somehow had advance notice, or maybe even had links with the RCMP.' He ran one hand through his hair and let out a slow sigh. 'It's just the timing threw us . . . the two things happening at the same time, you understand.' He shook his head. 'And . . . and after all you've been through now.'

'Why – what's happened?' Elena looked keenly at them both, and her heart sank. Their faces said it all before Claude Donatien had finally gathered the composure to explain.

28

'Sorry, Georges. Roman wanted us to tell you that he never liked you. Always thought you were a smarmy shit. He said it would give him great satisfaction to know that was the last thing you were thinking about. But for us, Georges, it's nothing personal. Just sorry.'

Georges felt everything tilt and slip away into darkness. He wasn't sure initially how long he'd blacked out. The first thing he was aware of was the rapid shuffling of footsteps; then, as two bangs sounded, for a second he thought they were the shots he'd been expecting – before realizing it was the sound of the Econoline's doors closing. He'd probably lost less than a minute. The engine was revved high and there was a sharp squeal of tyres as the van sped away. Then the sound of another engine, headlamps playing across his body – the approaching vehicle had obviously disturbed his two abductors.

The sharp slam of two more car doors, then after a second another car pulling up, and more lights: the stark beam of a torch swung haphazardly on the ground close by before finally settling on his body. And voices: frantic, jumbled. He found it hard to pick out what was said at first, but as they came close he recognized Chenouda's voice.

'Is he okay? Did we make it in time?'

Georges was given fresh coffee and doughnuts and left to rest for almost two hours before his first debriefing by Chenouda, which lasted only forty minutes. Georges discovered in that session that Chenouda knew from a source close to the Lacailles – Chenouda didn't elaborate – about him being lured away the night before by one of the Sherbrooke club girls, Viana. They had suspected he was being set up by Roman, so started closely following his movements. Two of his men had seen the abduction take place and radioed straight through to Chenouda. They'd lost the van at one point and there was a scramble to catch up, which was why Chenouda had arrived almost at the same time as them.

'And none too soon by the looks of it. Thirty seconds more and we wouldn't be sitting here talking now. Your body would have been tagged in the morgue.'

Michel Chenouda made no demands on him that first session, asked no questions: he ran through the events of the past twenty-four hours almost dispassionately, except for that final emphasis that Georges was lucky, very lucky, to still be alive, and that he had the RCMP to thank for that. Then he was left alone for the night to sleep. Chac, one of the men from the car tailing his abductors, stayed to keep guard. That was the first thing to strike Georges as strange: they were in some nondescript three-star hotel near Dorval Airport, not at Dorchester Boulevard or another police station. Upon leaving, Chenouda had instructed that there should be no calls, strictly no calls, and Chac reminded him of this just before they bedded down for the night.

'If room service calls or the phone goes at all, let me get it. You're incommunicado, for the moment don't exist.'

The session with Chenouda the next day was more intensive and lasted over two hours. Chenouda made it clear within the first minutes that he wanted Georges to testify against the Lacailles. Georges refused, sticking to his ground from their last confrontation, saying that despite what Roman had done, he wouldn't betray Jean-Paul.

Chenouda fired back: 'Then just who do you think ordered that little number last night? Because if you think Roman acted on his own, think again. He went to the trouble of setting you up with the girl purely to get Jean-Paul's final go-ahead. If he was going to take you out on his own, he'd have done it weeks back.'

It made sense, Georges knew, but still he refused to accept that Jean-Paul, whom he so admired and trusted, would have ordered his death.

Chenouda paced, cajoled and waved his arms as he threw across every possible rationale in his armoury, and at one point his patience finally ran out. 'Fine. Okay – you go back out there and take your chances. Let's see how long Roman is willing to let you live. I won't have to waste my time beating my head against a brick wall with you – and we can even have some fun in the squad room making bets on just how long you'll last. Three days, a week maybe?'

Finally, after almost an hour, they reached the bones of a deal. Georges agreed to testify against Roman about the night with Leduc, but nothing beyond that. He wouldn't talk about any of the inner financial workings of the Lacaille enterprises; besides, they'd just support what he'd been saying all along, that Jean-Paul had moved away from crime these past few years. And he could only confirm that Jean-Paul had sanctioned the meeting with Leduc, not that he had arranged or had prior knowledge that Leduc was to be murdered – because Georges himself hadn't known; the attack on Leduc had come as a complete surprise, looked at first like an attempt at self-defence gone wrong. Georges ran through the mix-up with the notebook and the gun and then Roman flipping his own second gun on to the floor before Savard had reached the car.

'But that's as far as I'll go. If you want to get some sharp prosecutor to fill in the gaps and try and show a link to Jean-Paul, then that's up to you. But I'm not testifying directly against him – because there's nothing I really *can* say. That's it, take it or leave it.'

Michel spent another twenty minutes fleshing out the details, and took it. With Savard's murder and now the attempt on Donatien's life, a pattern could be shown. Donatien confirmed that he'd speak openly about his abduction and the set-up with the girl, and Michel's mind went briefly on overdrive: hopefully with some persuasion he could get Azy to spill about the girl being Roman's pet favourite, and maybe even get something from the girl herself. But when he pushed his luck, asking whether Donatien thought that the night with Leduc had also been a set-up by Roman – 'He probably knew damn well Leduc didn't have a gun, but he needed it to look like self-defence for your benefit, and maybe for Jean-Paul's too, *if* he wasn't already in on it' – Georges' reluctance resurfaced.

'With what's happened since, I can see how that probably makes sense. But I can't really say anything beyond what I saw that night. Again, that's going to be down to your prosecutor earning his pay by trying to make the connections.'

Michel quit while he was ahead. He spent some time going back over and making notes on what they'd agreed, skeleton structure for Donatien's later statement – then called S-18 and explained his dilemma: a hot informant in his grasp and concerns about leaks within his own department.

Each RCMP regional office had their own section operating a Witness Protection Programme and Internal Affairs department for investigating police corruption. But when that corruption could lead to a leak and endanger the person in the programme, very often the only option was S-18, the special service that had been set up in Ottawa.

The next morning he was sitting before an S-18 review board chaired by Superintendent Neil Mundy, and from there everything moved rapidly: that same night Donatien was escorted by two S-18 officers out of Montreal to a safe house, where he would stay until the trial. Then he would go fully into the WPP and be given a new identity. Chenouda himself didn't even know the location of the safe house; only Donatien's escorting officers and an 'eyes only' handful within S-18 had the details. At 11 a.m. the following morning, by which time Donatien had already been ensconced in the safe house for over twelve hours, Mundy called a press conference to announce their breakthrough with the Lacaille investigation, with Inspector Pelletier also present to dampen any speculation about inter-departmental wrangling. It was hailed as a joint operation between Montreal's Criminal Intelligence division and S-18.

The whole process from Donatien's abduction to final announcement had taken two and a half days. For that time Donatien's whereabouts had been a complete mystery; and now with him in a safe house until the trial, six or seven months of the same lay ahead. Then he would disappear completely, never to surface again as Georges Donatien.

29

'*Witness Protection Programme . . . never to be seen again.*'

Elena drove back from Beaconsfield in a daze. Claude Donatien's words spun through her head like some mad mantra; though he hadn't directly said the second part, she'd read that between the lines while he fluffed around and tried to soften the blow: 'We're not sure even when we'll be able to see him . . . if at all. We're going to phone later and find out. Maybe there'll be a loophole and we'll be allowed to see him and, if so, hopefully you'll be able to as well at some time.'

Loopholes. Hopefully. At some time. Claude Donatien just didn't want to say it straight out – 'Look – I just don't think you're going to be able to get to see him now' – especially not right on the heels of the heart-rending saga of ups and downs that had finally brought her to their door. It would have seemed cruel to push the trapdoor lever straight away, much kinder to send her down in the express lift: she'd get there almost as fast, but she'd hardly feel the motion and she could listen to piped music on the way. Sugar-coat the pill.

She'd spent over an hour at the Donatiens after the bombshell, getting all the background she'd hoped for originally: what was he like? Had they lived here long? Where did they live before? His home-life, schooling . . . then later college, girlfriends and work. And every small trait and nuance and what he'd had for breakfast the past twenty odd years – if she'd been able to keep them on the subject long enough.

Odette brought out some photo albums as guide posts to the passage of time and events since they'd taken Georges from Ste-Marguerite's. *Georges.* Odette explained that the minor name change was because they were a French Canadian family; his school had been Francophone, and they hadn't wanted it too obvious that he was adopted.

Elena found herself reaching out and gently touching some of the photos as she leafed through: his ninth birthday party; a school photo from when he was twelve; throwing a frisbee in a park for a red setter; Odette with one arm around him at a woodland picnic table; a family group photo from a Florida holiday, with Georges as a teenager against a marina backdrop . . . his twenty-first with some college friends spraying him with a just-shaken champagne bottle. Until then she'd just felt numb, the shock of the news had stripped her of any emotion, but at that moment the tears started to come – though she quickly wiped and sniffed them back, embarrassed. It wasn't only due to all those lost years coming home more poignantly with the sight and feel of something tangible, a face to finally put to him – but also because she then realized that this might be as close as she'd *ever* get to him.

It was all too much for her to bear at one point, with Claude and Odette looking on concernedly and Lorena by that time back with them from playing in the garden, and she got up and went over to the back window, looking out. She'd managed to stop herself bursting into sobs, but still her eyes were welling and she was having trouble keeping her tears from flowing. The land sloped away at the back and there was a partial view of the lake two hundred yards away between the trees. Claude Donatien left her alone for a moment before coming to stand alongside her.

'We used to bring Georges to the park by the lake to play when he was younger, and it became something of a dream for us to one day live in this area. We managed to grab one of the last plots with a lake view going.' Claude was a builder and, between the lines, Elena gathered there had been a few ups and downs through the years, their previous homes hadn't been quite as plush – though Claude was eager to point out that they had been comfortable, in pleasant neighbourhoods, Georges' schooling had been excellent and he'd been well provided and cared for and always loved. But business had been good the past six or seven years, partly thanks to some money from Georges and his financial savvy, Claude conceded. 'And so we finally built our dream home.'

Elena had the sense in that moment that Claude had somehow displeased Georges, or maybe it was just the awkwardness of their roles changing: Georges suddenly grown up, adult and organized, the hot-shot financier, and Claude then the errant dependant. It wasn't in anything actually said, more implied in between the lines or in the timing of when Claude fell silent or quickly changed the subject. But perhaps, having spent a lifetime shadow-dancing around the truth in her own life, that was where she saw everything now: in between the lines and in the silences.

Then came the more awkward topic of how Georges had gone

from successful banker to involvement with a crime family. Elena never asked directly, but Claude seemed keen to make clear that Georges wasn't in the least criminally inclined. 'He had a good position, was very solid with Banque du Québec before joining the Lacailles. That's why I find this now so hard to take, let alone understand.' He pointed accusingly to the TV, which had been switched off since she arrived. 'He always said that the only reason he'd joined them was because they'd moved away from crime. And it was a challenge. He was very strict about things like that . . . Strong principles. The only problem he ever hinted at was the two Lacaille brothers not always seeing eye to eye – but he said he worked only for Jean-Paul, who he insisted was clean as a whistle and equally as principled. Maybe it will all turn out to be nothing.' Again he was back to trying to make light of it, lessen the blow for her.

She shook her head, her eyes blurring with tears. *Never to be seen again . . .*

The express lift was still falling, an abyss of dark despair sucking her inexorably down since she'd left the Donatiens. She'd skirted dangerously around the edges at times during her door-call search and at Ste-Marguerite's – but now the depths of that despair, the gut-wrenching emptiness she felt inside, overwhelmed her. And after her battles of the past days, her diet of pills and whisky, her lack of sleep and her nerves almost constantly on a tightrope, she felt completely drained, no reserves left to claw her way back up again.

Besides, it was all over . . . *Never to be seen again.* What could she do? Claude Donatien'd said he'd phone later, when he'd spoken to the police – but what was the point of deluding herself and still clinging to hope? From the little that she knew, the whole point of witness protection was to keep the subjects away from family and friends – because that was the first place criminals would try to track them.

Never to be seen again . . .

She gripped tight at the steering wheel and tensed her jaw against it, but still she was falling, the dark edges of the abyss washing in. Traffic was heavier now approaching the centre of Montreal and she had to concentrate. But her eyes were welling faster than she could blink them clear or dab away the tears with the back of one hand . . . And through her blurred, pastel-wash vision a car appeared out of nowhere and veered in front of her – or had she swerved over slightly as she wiped at her tears? The car's horn blared, and she braked and swung the wheel . . . then suddenly a squeal of tyres and two sharp beeps from the other side, one after the other – and she realized that she'd cut in on something on the inside.

'Elena . . . watch out!' Lorena hit the stop button on her Walkman, looking worriedly over her shoulder. 'There's a . . .'

Oh God. Oh God. Elena was shaking uncontrollably, still falling, a kaleidoscope blur of cars and road and buildings, tilting, slipping sideways; she thought for a second she was going to black out right there with the traffic streaming all around her. She slowed, waiting for the car on her inside to pass – its driver fired her a last stony look – then she pulled across and took the first turn on the left, stopping twenty yards in.

She gave into the abyss totally in that moment, sank down into its darkness as if it were a feather-down duvet. The near-accident had jolted away her tears; all that remained was her shaking and a tight, aching knot in her stomach, the only sensation left in the overwhelming emptiness she felt.

The night before, struggling to get back to sleep after her dreams, she'd vowed silently to her father that she would find Georges to make good on how she'd betrayed his memory all these years – thinking in that moment that she'd never felt closer to him, and how ironic it was that finally now, after all this time, she'd found some common ground with him – and already she'd struck out. Pathetic, really; almost as pathetic as the sham that had been her life so far.

'Are you okay?'

And now Lorena's voice full of concern to remind Elena that in a couple of hours she'd phone Gordon and then let her down too. Another failure.

'Yes . . . I just need a minute. I'll be fine.' *A minute?* She probably needed twice as long in therapy as even poor young Lorena to sort out the mess of her mind. But only after she'd slept for a week to shake off this tiredness sapping every last ounce of energy; that was her first promise to herself.

She remained head down on the wheel, eyes shut a moment more, listening to the steady rise and fall of her own breathing against the ebb and flow of city traffic, like a metronome rhythm that might guide her when it was all right to start driving again.

She was slow in shaking off her dark mood, finally lifting her head – but the urgency in Lorena's muttered 'Ele!' and her sudden awareness of a figure by the car made her look up sharper: brown uniform, one hand by the holster, the other reaching out.

The RCMP officer tapped at her window, signalling her to wind it down. Though now she no longer felt afraid but strangely relieved that it was finally all over. She could get the sleep she needed and she wouldn't have to break any bad news to Lorena: they'd both been victims.

'You just couldn't wait, could you? Just couldn't wait!'

'No, Jean-Paul, I tell you – you got it wrong. What they put on the news about Donatien has got *nothing* to do with me.'

'Oh, yeah. Really?' Jean-Paul glared back stonily.

Roman flinched under the intensity of his gaze. Jean-Paul's jaw was set rigid and Roman noticed a small muscle pumping in his neck. Jean-Paul had started shouting before his study door was shut behind them, and for a moment Roman thought he might break with character and start pushing and shoving him for an explanation; what he himself might do if the situation was reversed. Roman couldn't remember Jean-Paul ever angrier; and he had to admit things looked bad, real bad, whichever way he might try to explain them away. He was still pondering whether to keep protesting or to stay silent and leave Jean-Paul to let off steam, when Jean-Paul continued: 'I mean, we sat in this room not forty-eight hours ago and you swore blind that you had nothing to do with his disappearance, and now this . . . *This!*'

'You gotta believe, Jean-Paul – it wasn't me. Wasn't me.' Roman was shaking his head vigorously. 'Don't know shit about it.'

Jean-Paul rolled on as if Roman hadn't spoken. 'I've been assuring Simone all along that you hadn't done anything . . . *wouldn't* do anything without my sanction. Don't worry, *don't worry* . . .' Jean-Paul closed his eyes for a second and appeared to almost shudder. 'All that time lying to her.'

Roman leant forward and slapped the flat of his palm on the desk. 'You're not listening, Jean-Paul. I didn't do it – know *nothing* about it.'

Jean-Paul flinched only slightly, then he slapped his own hand twice as hard on the desktop. 'You're right, I'm not listening! Because that's what I did before – fell for every word and the same fucking outraged act you're throwing at me now. So this time you're going to have to explain yourself, Roman, and maybe you can start with just who did this if not you? *Who?*'

The doubt in Jean-Paul's voice had now reached incredulity. Roman had rarely heard him swear. It made him more hesitant about his first and most obvious explanation; the second, and what he thought had really happened, would sound even more incredible. 'I . . . I suppose it must have been the Cacchiones.'

'The Cacchiones . . . the Cacchiones,' Jean-Paul mimicked. 'To blame for Pascal's death and now conveniently every family problem since: Leduc, Savard . . . now Georges. Don't you think they'd have given up on us by now? Realized that we're out of crime and no longer pose a threat to them?'

Roman leapt for the opportunity to build his case. 'I think you're right; they probably do realize that. But this isn't about us and continuing old vendettas – this is more about Medeiros. The Cacchiones are still dealing drugs for sure – but Medeiros thinks he's blocked their supplies and pushed them out for good.' Roman chose his words carefully. He was skirting uncomfortably close to the truth, and didn't want to inadvertently give away that he knew more than he should. 'The other way that the supplies could still be getting out there is through *us* – so Cacchione is keen to jump on anything, such as this RCMP investigation right now, to keep us in the frame as still involved in crime and still dealing. It throws Medeiros off of the scent.'

Jean-Paul mulled it over, but looked far from convinced. 'I suppose there's *some* sense to it – but how would they know to pick on Georges? Know that he was our weak spot?'

Roman felt himself getting cornered. 'They could have known from Savard, or maybe that's my fault: I have at times complained, to Frank and maybe one or two others, that Georges worries me. Things like that can too easily get out.' All he could think of: concede to a lesser crime. Perhaps it would also give Jean-Paul somewhere to direct his anger.

'I don't know, I don't know.' Jean-Paul swayed for a second before doubt again took grip. 'And the timing too: how would the Cacchiones know about the problem with the girl – that at this moment of all moments Georges would automatically think that any attempted hit must be down to us, because he feared he was out in the cold?'

Roman's collar was suddenly tight and he felt hot. Finding a clear way through Jean-Paul's maze of doubt was getting more complicated with each step. 'Maybe the girl. When I called the club last night, Azy said she hadn't shown. Maybe she knew something had gone down.' Originally, he was going to keep that under his hat until he'd found

351

out more; of all people, she knew too much, could prove a problem. But he'd grabbed at the first thing in desperation: right now he needed everything he could possibly throw at Jean-Paul to break down his wall of doubt.

Jean-Paul found himself swaying again. But then Roman had been just as convincing the last time, then only forty-eight hours later he'd been left feeling like a mug, Simone's words ringing in his ears – *'How do you know Roman's not done something to him already?'* This time around he'd make Roman sweat, and as credible as Roman might be he'd pass his comments on to Simone dispassionately, with a healthy reserve of doubt. Safer stance. He studied Roman levelly. 'A lot of maybes, Roman – but you're the only one who knew for sure about Georges' problem with the girl.'

'Yeah – so why would I go to all the trouble of telling you about it, only to try and take him out myself?'

'Because you started to worry that I might not deal with it the way you hoped and have Georges hit. That I was inclining more towards getting him away to Cuba until things had settled down.'

Roman leant across the desk. His patience was fast evaporating: he'd thrown across every good argument he could think of and still Jean-Paul appeared entrenched. 'I didn't know that was the way you were thinking until the last time we were in this same fucking room shouting at each other – *after* Georges had disappeared.'

That was true, thought Jean-Paul: the only tangible fact Roman had so far thrown at him among a sea of maybes.

Roman swept one arm away dismissively. 'Besides, if I was going to take the fucker out, I'd have made sure to do the job properly. Not left him for the Mounties just so he could testify against us. The only person that sort of scenario benefits is Cacchione.'

Jean-Paul nodded and cast his eyes down: truth number two, but he was damned if he was going to leave himself vulnerable again. And he was tiring of the argument; they were just going round in circles. The most he'd move to was a mid-ground, reluctant concession. 'Regardless of whether it's Cacchione or not – if it wasn't for your little political background battle with Georges, the opportunity for Cacchione to take advantage wouldn't have existed, or for Georges to even think it might be us and end up in the lap of the RCMP giving evidence. So whichever way, this falls down to you, Roman – with the onus on you finding him now stronger than ever. What news on that front?'

Roman wasn't comfortable ending on that note, but his nerves were shot from fencing with Jean-Paul and perhaps it was the best he could hope for. He brought Jean-Paul up to date: nothing yet from the streets, and now it was pretty obvious why not. No call yet from Georges to his parents – but some Englishwoman had turned up out of the blue wanting to speak to them urgently; sounded real cagey, concerned. Could be something, could be nothing. His guy Funicelli was monitoring their conversation right now – he'd know more in an hour or so.

And for the first time since they'd entered the room they were pulling in the same direction. But their differences through the years, both aired and left unspoken – and now more than ever to remain so – still hung heavy in the air. The gulf between them had never been wider.

Of course Roman knew that it wasn't Cacchione; he knew that because he'd been working closely with Cacchione for the past three years.

When Jean-Paul had first announced that they were moving away from crime, he'd thought that he was joking. Then, when he realized that he was serious, his first protest was that that would simply leave the whole pie to Cacchione: 'How's that going to pay him back for what he did to Pascal?'

Jean-Paul, almost as if enlightening a naive child, calmly explained that it was no longer a matter of payback or getting even: that would simply continue the cycle and Pascal's death would have been for nothing; that if that was the cost, then Cacchione was welcome to 'the pie'. He had made a solemn promise to their father and he wasn't about to budge. That same condescending tone every time Roman'd tentatively raised the issue over the following twelve months, as if Jean-Paul's new quest was based on moral principles beyond his grasp; and whenever that wasn't enough Jean-Paul would raise the subject of Pascal or their father as final moralistic tombstones to end the argument.

No care or consideration or even a minute's thought that Roman might not be happy with their new direction. That as muscleman and enforcer, the guy who took care of all the messy details nobody else wanted to get their hands dirty with, what place was there for him in a set-up without crime? Head of security? Made to sound important, but in reality he'd been relegated to checking the takings from their pussy clubs and restaurants, with the occasional excitement on the rare occasions someone got drunk or out of order. And meanwhile golden boy Georges was in the hot seat, the Lacaille family money spread like monopoly confetti on stocks and shares or marina and hotel developments across Mexico and Cuba: all eyes suddenly on him to secure their future fortunes.

And, as he'd warned, Cacchione did take 'the pie', fill the vacuum they'd left – until the run-in with Medeiros. It was then that Roman had seen his big opportunity. Cacchione's business had died as quickly as it had expanded over the previous eighteen months. Cacchione tried a couple of times to establish himself with other suppliers – but two middlemen at the bottom of the St Lawrence later, Medeiros' message was clear: Cacchione was a no-go area, under no circumstances to be supplied. And with Jean-Paul out of crime, the vacuum was once again there.

Roman contacted Medeiros. His story was that he and Jean-Paul had split the business: Jean-Paul would continue solely with legitimate business and, now that their 'cooling off' period had achieved its aim of suitably diverting attention, Roman would quietly revive some of their past enterprises. With the accent on 'quietly': officially they were still out of crime. Jean-Paul therefore wouldn't at any time contact Medeiros or talk to him about that side of the business; all dealings would be with Roman. And for the same reason absolute discretion was demanded: no mention whatsoever on either side that Medeiros was supplying to them.

Medeiros agreed, but Roman knew that for the other part of the equation he'd need Gianni Cacchione's cooperation: Cacchione wasn't just going to sit back and let him freely take over his old territory and contacts; they'd have to work together.

Drug distribution in Quebec and Eastern Canada was organized as a strict hierarchy: the Colombians and Mexicans provided the raw shipments and the import and business arrangements were handled by the local Sicilian, Neapolitan or Union Corse Mafia, who then used the bikers for distribution. The Colombians wouldn't deal with the bikers directly: they saw them as renegade and volatile, and at times indiscreet. That was why Medeiros had warmed to his approach, in particular the discretion.

Roman checked his watch as he crossed Avenue Jean-Talon. He was driving faster than normal, one finger tapping on the steering wheel; he was still wound tight as a coil from the session with

Jean-Paul. Twenty minutes before his arranged call to Funicelli, but he wanted to squeeze in another call beforehand: he couldn't go a second longer without getting an inside track on the current state of play at Dorchester Boulevard.

Discretion was also at the heart of his partnership with Gianni Cacchione, and the tightrope nature of their duplicity seemed to appeal to Cacchione as much as him: Medeiros thought it was the Lacailles, Jean-Paul the Cacchiones; in reality they worked together and split the proceeds 50/50. And they used independents such as Leduc, who'd previously worked for the Lacailles, or some of Cacchiones' old fold who'd also gone freelance since Medeiros shut them down. But apart from the strong insistence on discretion that was passed down the line – 'You don't want to end up like the last two dealers that fell foul of Medeiros, do you?' – these were mid-level soldiers with no contact with Medeiros and Jean-Paul: their secret was safe.

Until the problem with Leduc and Jean-Paul's suspicion. He'd spent hours briefing Leduc beforehand, getting him to painstakingly fill in details in a little black book. They'd made sure it would give nothing away, would just send Jean-Paul on a few wild-goose chases. 'You don't give the book up too easy, though – that would look suspect. Wait until I interrupt and start pressing hard, then finally you pull it out of your ankle sock.'

Roman knew all along that he was going to blast Leduc as soon as he pulled it out. They might have put Jean-Paul off with a smokescreen for a few weeks, but he'd have kept pushing and eventually Leduc would have cracked. Roman was close to breaking out laughing by the third time Leduc wanted to run through the sequence and timing with the notebook, as if it was a dress rehearsal for his big moment. Bigger than he realized.

Then Tremblay, then Savard . . . now Donatien. Maybe there should be a definition in Mob handbooks. Felucci's theorem: the size of the fuck-up minus the number of people involved, times the money and gain squared, shall determine how many finally need to be wasted.

His wry smile quickly faded. Fifteen months now he'd sweated that one problem with an iron fist and muscle and blood – how it used to be in the old days before Jean-Paul developed a conscience. And he was good at this double game. What he savoured most was that everyone thought he was so dumb, the bone-headed muscleman, a

Neanderthal Moustache Pete symbol of the years they'd left behind; and meanwhile he was playing them all like a string quartet.

But now there was another player in town. One just as sharp at this double game as him – and, from what had happened with Donatien, equally as willing to bend the rules. Because if neither he nor Cacchione was behind the attempted hit on Donatien, there was only one remaining option.

DS Crowley decided to give Gordon Waldren one last push. He called at the house without announcement, having been told by his men keeping watch that Waldren was in: he wanted this to be eye-to-eye, to see Waldren's reaction.

Crowley started by just asking straightforwardly if Gordon Waldren had had any contact with his wife or knew where she was. 'No' to each, and Crowley grimaced as if he'd bitten into sour fruit. He'd stayed standing, saying he wouldn't be long, and started pacing as he turned the screw.

'You know that when I saw you last time, I said that we'd have to put out a general alert on your wife and Lorena. Well, that was eventually done.' Crowley didn't elaborate that he'd put it out practically the moment he'd left Waldren: at least the next part was the truth. 'That was just a missing persons alert, not a criminal one. Our idea was to pile on the pressure if we received a specific lead.' Crowley didn't feel like going into the fiasco in France either; he didn't want to give Waldren the satisfaction of knowing that the false trail they'd set up there had worked. 'But we are now coming to the point where we will have to put out that criminal alert, unless you cooperate.'

Gordon shrugged. 'I'm not sure I see the difference. I thought an alert was an alert, and you'd have either put one out by now or not.' He hoped that his anxiety wasn't obvious. He was meant to leave any minute, and his pad with notes was still by the phone along with a fax from the private investigator he'd put on Ryall. He made sure not to even glance in that direction and possibly bring Crowley's attention to them.

'The difference is that it will suddenly be shifted to grade-one priority. Right now it will be on most police computers courtesy of Interpol. But they get a lot of "missing person" enquiries – enough as it is from their own neck of the woods. So often they're not given priority. All of that will change by, say' – Crowley theatrically checked his watch – 'five p.m. tomorrow, twenty hours from now, if your wife either hasn't returned Lorena or made firm, verifiable arrangements to do so. That gives you more than enough time to make contact and convince her. After that, she'll be hunted down in earnest. She'll be top priority on computers worldwide.'

'I see.' Gordon gazed thoughtfully towards the window. Taking Crowley's warnings at face value, he was concerned. But he couldn't help wondering if it was all just a ruse for Crowley to be able to set another pressure deadline after the first hadn't worked: a second bite at the cherry. But Gordon didn't have time to banter and perhaps draw him out. Crowley had caught him seriously on the hop: in order to be able to make his next arranged call to Elena, he needed to wrap this up quickly.

'Well, if and when she does make contact – I'll be sure to pass that on.' Gordon gave a tight smile. A 'we're finished here' look. But Crowley's reaction was to take a seat and Gordon's heart sank: he was settling in!

Crowley's expression clouded, his forehead furrowing. 'I don't think you appreciate the seriousness of this, Mr Waldren. First of all you're insulting my intelligence by insisting that your wife so far hasn't made any contact with you – at least to check on the welfare of her own children. But this now means that she'll be hunted as a criminal. And the reason that she hasn't been listed as such to date is down to me – mainly because of the tape and your insistence that your wife was not a kidnapper. I decided to take you at your word on that, Mr Waldren.' Crowley looked at him keenly: Waldren was trying to brush the whole thing quickly off, act offhand, but Crowley could tell that beneath the surface he was agitated, off balance. What Crowley hadn't mentioned was that the alert status had been mainly for their benefit, not Waldren's. The tape had been one factor for not listing Mrs Waldren as a 'kidnapper', because of possible later problems with the Crown Prosecution Service. But the main reason had been a recent Metropolitan Police case where an estranged father had abducted his eight-year-old son and taken him to Italy. They'd listed the alert as a kidnapping, which rang major alarm bells with the *carabinieri*. In the resultant storm-trooper style siege, the father had been shot and seriously wounded. The size of the financial claim was only surpassed by the dent to police reputation. Turton had advised caution, at least for the first alert put out. 'Given that I've gone out on a limb for you, I don't think insulting my intelligence is really a fitting repayment – do you?'

Gordon nodded solemnly, looking down. 'No, no . . . you're right. I'm sorry.' He had less doubt now; Crowley was probably telling the truth. But he had to get rid of him *quickly*: already a minute over when he should have left, and he'd have to wait at least another two after Crowley's departure. But no point in trying to make light of things or act indifferent, that was just raising Crowley's hackles and making him dig in his toes. He'd have to indulge him. 'Look, my wife *has* called – but I just can't say where she is. It really is up to her to decide what to do now. But I will, I promise, pass on what you've said and try and convince her to return Lorena.'

Crowley kept his eyes fixed on him, trying to gauge his sincerity. After a second: 'I think that would be very wise, Mr Waldren. Because some countries adopt a very serious and aggressive stance with kidnapping. And once the alert has gone out, from that point on charges for kidnapping will almost automatically follow. At this stage while it's still "missing person" status, we still have the chance of stepping back from the brink.'

'Yes, yes . . . I understand. Really, as soon as I speak to her, I'll pass that on.' Two minutes over, and counting. His brain was screaming: *Go! Go! For God's sake, just fucking go!*

'It would also greatly help your case if your wife gave herself up *before* we traced her: once we have, I think it will be that much harder not to press full charges.' They'd been able to check scheduled flights from all major airports in France and Belgium, but charters were proving more difficult; due to the sheer volume they were only halfway through and still had some way to go.

'I understand.' Gordon cast his eyes down again for a second: hopefully showing contrition. *Go! Go! Go!*

'Right.' Crowley nodded thoughtfully. He'd probably piled on the pressure as much as he could. He thought originally Waldren was trying to brush it all off with indifference – but now, as Waldren stood up, he noticed one of his hands shaking. He'd struck a chord: Waldren was so panicked he couldn't bear to stay on the subject a second longer.

Gordon felt a pang of relief as Crowley finally took his cue and stood up – then quickly tensed again as Crowley looked towards the phone.

'So – five p.m., no later. You'll phone me by then and let me know one way or the other.'

'Yes, yes, I will. Don't worry.' Gordon quickly came round, blocking Crowley's view of the phone and the papers there as he ushered him out.

Crowley stopped just before the front door. 'Oh, and another thing. You're doing your wife's cause no favours by bothering Ryall's other daughter at university. He called us to complain.' Brief strained smile. He didn't want to give away that they'd been following Waldren.

'Right, right . . . I'm sorry.' He opened the door. Three minutes over, two minutes still to wait. He wasn't going to make it! His heart was hammering out of control, and for a moment he feared Crowley was going to bring up another last-second issue – but then he appeared to think better of it, and with another curt smile and nod – 'Five p.m. tomorrow, then' – he left.

Gordon's breathing was laboured, heavy, as he shut the door; he had to strain to hear Crowley's receding footsteps, his car door closing, the car finally starting and heading away. He'd aimed to leave a full two-minute gap, but in the end he counted only fifty seconds before he grabbed the fax and notes by the phone and rushed from the house.

He put his foot down hard. Six-mile drive to the phone box: hopefully he would be able to claw back a minute or so. Crowley would probably have gone in the opposite direction towards Poole; the last thing he wanted was to race past him.

He screeched to a halt and leapt out. The telephone box was on the opposite side of the road, but he could hear the phone ringing as soon as he was out of the car. He had to wait for one passing car, then bolted across. But within a yard of the box, it stopped ringing.

'What do you mean, you don't know what's going on? It's your job to fucking know what's going on.'

'I tell you, now it's gone to S-18, there's a complete shut-down on information on Donatien here. Not a whisper's being passed round – everything is being handled by Mundy's team out of Ottawa.'

Roman clutched the receiver tighter on hearing Campion's wheedling tone. He'd phoned through ten minutes before as a clerk of the court chasing a file – their usual prearranged alert. Campion then left Dorchester Boulevard and headed to a phone kiosk two blocks away to receive Roman's call. 'Someone must know something. Chenouda is still right at the heart of this, I know. And he can't possibly be working this alone.'

'No, he's not alone. But it's a tight-knit group. Only two of his team, Chac Patoine and Maury Legault, know anything – because they were apparently handling surveillance on Donatien when he was snatched. But then Chenouda went straight to S-18. He hasn't shared anything with the rest of his team, and I don't even know if Patoine and Legault are still in the information loop now that it's gone to S-18.'

'Great. Fucking great.' Roman's jaw clenched. Just when he needed Campion most, he was ineffectual, useless. Hopefully the bombshell about Chenouda would shake him up. 'When I say Chenouda's at the heart of this with Donatien . . . it's more than you probably realize.' He told Campion his theory that Chenouda had arranged for Donatien to be snatched to apply the final pressure to get him to testify. 'Certainly it wasn't me, and I know for sure it wasn't Cacchione either – so you tell me. From where I stand, I don't see any other option left.'

Only the fall of Campion's breathing at the other end for a second. 'You're joking?'

'No. Deadly fucking serious.'

'Are you sure? I mean, I know he was desperately trying to get Donatien to testify, but going to those lengths . . .'

'Sure? Sure I'm sure. If it wasn't me or Cacchione, then who the fuck do you think it was? Boy Scouts practising rope-ties for Canada Day?'

'I know. I know. I'm not doubting what you say: it's just that it seems so . . . well, so extreme. Chenouda's whole career would be at risk for a stunt like that – not to mention a healthy jail term on top.'

'So, the Indian's got big balls – it was him, no doubt. But what I'm getting to is Chenouda couldn't have pulled something like this alone. He had help, and there must be clues and an information trail there somewhere. If you dig and push some, you'll find them.'

Campion sighed. 'You don't get it, do you? It's with S-18 now – it's not within my jurisdiction to push or even ask a single question about this case any more. And the reason it's with S-18 is that Chenouda said he suspected an internal leak at Dorchester Boulevard – so the heat on that front is going to be intense. I'll be keeping my head low and holding my breath as it is: if I start asking questions and probing, who do you think is going to be first in the spotlight?'

They both fell silent for a second. It hit Roman then just how clever Chenouda had been: he probably suspected a leak and needed S-18's help in any case to put Donatien in the Witness Protection Programme. Yet, at the same time, putting everything in S-18's hands out of reach of his own department put an extra camouflage over him arranging Donatien's abduction. But Roman just couldn't leave things on that note; there was too much now at stake.

'Then you're going to have to take a leaf out of Chenouda's book. He managed to organize snatching Donatien without anyone knowing – you're just going to have to dig without anyone knowing.'

'I'm sorry. It's just too risky.'

Roman felt his blood boil. He'd first got his hooks into Campion, an assistant Crown attorney under Tom Maitland, when he'd learned about his gambling and high-life tastes. He'd have preferred someone in Chenouda's own department because there were always delays with information filtering through to Maitland's office, but it was the closest option going. Now he was beginning to feel even further short-changed.

'You know what pilots always say. They say that nowadays the computers and automatic pilots do everything. That they really only need to concentrate for the few moments of take-off and landing; for the rest of the time they just watch the instruments and read a book, whatever. And that ninety per cent of their training and the justification for their pay packets is to do with how they might react in an emergency; if, God forbid, something should go wrong. Well, the plane is going down *now*, Campion – this is when we fucking need you! Otherwise, what's been the point of the money I've paid you these past two years?'

'It's not that I don't want to help.' Campion was suddenly more hesitant, his voice tremulous. 'It's just that I don't know what I *can* do now with S-18 involved.'

'Well, you work that out and come up with something more positive next time we speak. And if you're worried about attracting too much attention from S-18, then just think on one thing: if Donatien testifies against me and I go down – what do you think I'm going to tell them when they ask about my internal contact, if there's the chance of five or seven off my sentence?' Roman bathed in the warm glow of the stunned silence at the other end for a few seconds, then hung up.

30

'What are you going to do?' Gordon asked.

'I don't know. I don't know.'

When Gordon hadn't answered the first time, Elena'd tried again after a minute or so – thinking that maybe he'd been held up in traffic or had car problems – and on the third try, he'd answered. They'd spent a while swapping respective tribulations and dramas – his with Crowley were almost insultingly trivial compared to hers: now it was decision time.

Elena was relieved to hear that her flight hadn't been traced yet, and the level of alert explained why she hadn't been flagged down by the first squad car. The policeman who'd approached her had seen her near-miss and was merely enquiring if she was okay to drive on or if she needed assistance. But that would all change in only twelve hours: the next one to approach her would be with handcuffs and his gun drawn.

She was on a phone in the Eaton Centre with Lorena at a table eight paces away in an open food hall area. The clatter and bustle of people eating echoed slightly; she had to cover her other ear at moments to hear Gordon clearly.

She didn't notice the man at a far table watching her every move between cappuccino sips.

'If you're not heading back yourself, will you at least send back Lorena?' Gordon prompted. 'As much as I know you'd like to keep trying – it's probably the only sensible option left now.'

'I know.' *Sensible?* Nothing she'd done so far had been sensible; most of her life in fact, though she'd only discovered it these past few days, had been a nonsense. How was she suddenly going to gain 20/20 vision now?

Dead ends at every turn, all her options fast closing down; and now she'd reached the stage of inaction through fear, almost fatalistically certain that whichever one she chose it would be wrong. Crowley's deadline, little chance now of seeing her son, and nothing helpful in the investigative report on Ryall: nothing suspicious about the adoptions or around the time of Mikaya's pregnancy; the only other link with children was him apparently doing magic tricks at parties to pay his way through university.

But the bombshell news from the Donatiens about Georges hung like a heavy cloud over most of their conversation. At first all Gordon could manage was 'Oh Elena', followed by a weighty, defeated sigh. Then after a second: 'I just don't know what to say.' That was all she seemed to get these days: silent empathy. The Donatiens so awkward they could hardly meet her eye, and now Gordon winded and lost for words. Only Lorena seemed to be bold enough to talk openly about it, ask her what was wrong; and she'd either fluff around it or lie. So in the end there was really nobody she was fully sharing the burden with.

And she felt tired, so tired: the endless search and chase of the past days only to hit the brick wall of the Donatiens' calamitous news, then the jolt of the policeman by her car immediately after. She felt totally drained, no reserves left to struggle on.

She leant against the wall by the phone and exhaled softly. 'I think you're right. I should send Lorena back. With nothing on Ryall and the sessions heading nowhere, no point in holding on to her here any more.'

Gordon said sorry, he hadn't caught the last part, and Elena turned into the wall to cut off the echoing bustle behind and repeated herself. Gordon asked when, and she said, 'Probably first thing tomorrow. I think it's too late to arrange anything tonight.' Then after a second another thought struck her: 'The only problem is that as soon as I send her back, Crowley will know where I am and alert the Canadian police.' She felt unsettled having voiced it: that the only reason she might keep Lorena there was to serve her own aims, once again she was putting those first.

'Well, if you don't send her back till tomorrow morning – you'll probably get a good twenty-four hours' grace overall, what with the flight and then time for Crowley to make contact.'

'I probably need a hell of a lot more than that to sort out this mess with Georges: several days or even weeks, that is *if* I'm going to be able to get to see him at all.' Elena glanced around to see Lorena heading back towards their table from her direction. She must have gone to the food counter again for something or to the toilets to Elena's side.

'When will you know for sure?' Gordon asked.

'I've arranged to call Claude Donatien in just over an hour. He said he'd have phoned the police by then and got their initial reaction – found out not only if it would be possible for me to see Georges, but if and when *they* might be able to see him.'

'I know it sounds trite – but good luck.'

'Thanks.'

'But if you are able to see him, you appreciate the risk you're running – because you're certainly on police computers *somewhere*.'

'I realize.' She'd thought of little else since leaving the Donatiens and then hearing about Crowley's new deadline. Originally, her fear was that as soon as she made contact with the police about Georges, her name would come up on the RCMP's computer. Now it was like Russian roulette: it might come up, it might not. But if she didn't make contact now, before Crowley's deadline, even that chance would be gone: the gun would once again be loaded with six bullets.

'There's also the possibility that Crowley was bluffing just to create an extra pressure deadline: he might have put out a grade-one alert immediately.'

'I see.' And now a factor she hadn't considered: the gun could already be fully loaded. In that moment, doubt once again seized her: she was crazy to think she could go through with it, she turned into a quivering jelly just at the sight of a passing squad car – she'd never be able to brave contacting the police about Georges. She should just throw in the towel and head back to England with Lorena. 'Well, maybe Claude Donatien will just say it's a no-go, so it's not something I'll even have to –' Elena broke off as she looked around: Lorena wasn't at their table. Her eyes darted like a pin-ball: not at the food counters, not by the toilets, not by the shops to one side. Then she surveyed quickly the other tables and the crowds milling around. She was nowhere to be seen! *'Oh Jesus!'*

'What's wrong?'

'It's Lorena. I left her at a table . . . and now she's gone. I can't see her!' Her breath was coming hard and fast. 'Sorry, Gordon – I've got to go now. Got to find her.'

She hung up halfway through Gordon replying 'I understand, we'll –' and started working her way through the tables, trying to see if Lorena was perhaps obscured by some of the plants and pillars. *Nothing.* She then recalled Lorena heading back to their table as if from her direction: Lorena had probably heard her talking, heard her mention sending her back to England and Ryall!

Oh God, that's what this was all about. She became more frantic, her step quickening and her breath staccato as she scanned furtively through the crowds, then rushed and checked the toilets and the shops in both directions, finally stopping at the fourteenth checked: Lorena surely wouldn't have gone this far and she'd no longer be able to see her if she suddenly appeared and returned to their table. Still nothing, *nothing*. Elena returned to where she'd started by the phone, frantically scanning all around. Her breath was laboured and heavy with exertion and panic, and her chest ached as if a nail had been hammered home dead centre. She'd asked herself what else could possibly go wrong on the way from the Donatiens, a whimsical escape valve from the ludicrous, impossible problems with Georges: now she had her answer.

She stood in the same position as before, her breath easing and her heart sinking deeper with each passing minute, until finally, after almost fifteen minutes, she felt nauseous, the rest of her body little more than an empty, numb shell, with the realization that Lorena probably wasn't returning. She'd lost her.

Grey-blue water iced over, white in patches where the snow had settled from the previous night. A ring of pines encircled the lake in an oval half a mile away, and extended into the distance as far as one could see.

Right now the snow and ice gave the lake a hostile, barren feel, but Georges imagined that in a month or so they would melt and it would be almost idyllic. Azure blue water and rich green pines stretching endlessly, straight out of a 'Canada Wilds' vacation brochure. Difficult for Georges to think of it in terms of it being his prison for the next six or seven months, maybe longer.

He guessed from the ice on the lake and the dusting of snow overnight that they were somewhere further north: northern Quebec or Ontario, perhaps even Manitoba. The ice and snow had mostly gone around Montreal, but further north it took longer to melt.

That, apart from the two-hour small plane journey and following twenty-minute car ride, was the only clue to where they were. He'd had to put on a headset with blacked-out visor the minute they were airborne and wasn't allowed to remove it until they'd arrived. Chac, Chenouda's sidekick assigned to guard him for the first two weeks, wore the same, as would Chenouda, apparently, when he came out for his first briefing in a couple of weeks. S-18 were taking no risks. It wasn't a matter of trust, Chenouda'd explained when they'd initially run through the procedure; just the fact that the three of them, by necessity, would have contact with other RCMP staff over the investigation and might inadvertently give away clues as to his location. Any such contact by Georges would obviously only be by phone: secure line, Chenouda was eager to add.

The others on the plane out, the pilot and two detective constables, were all S-18 and travelling without headsets: the safe house was already well known to them and they'd stay with Georges one month on, one off, swapping duty with another three S-18 guards. Chenouda went to great lengths to explain how they were a clandestine elite, cut off from all other RCMP and barred from discussing their movements even with their families. 'The secrets of the Kingdom have got to rest with someone, and their record is second to none. They've never lost anyone yet.'

Georges knew that Chenouda meant well, but it was going to take a while for his unease to abate; and the danger he was in was only part of it. This level of remoteness, being cut off from all other human contact, was totally alien to him; he was a city dweller, used to the hustle and bustle of downtown Montreal and a crammed, stopwatch-timed business day. This lakeside retreat with nothing but empty hours on his hands was going to take some getting used to and, probably due to the time he'd had to dwell on it, already he was starting to miss Simone.

What hadn't helped was his phone conversation with Chenouda the day before. The mention of the secure line they were on led him to raise the subject of Simone and that he'd like to phone her. 'One last call, a sort of goodbye, if you will. I never did get to say goodbye to her, as you know. And also to tell her that I'm sorry and reassure her that I wouldn't testify directly against her father – that this is all just about Roman.'

Chenouda was vehemently against the idea. Simone would be one of the first they'd expect him to phone, along with his parents. 'We can use whatever scrambling and encryption codes we like – but a skilled guy the other end can always crack it.' And under no circum-stances did he want Georges giving away what he might or might not say in testimony. 'It'll just give the Lacailles' defence lawyer ammunition to use against us.'

His three S-18 guards – Clive, Steve and Russell, he'd been told only their first names – had done everything to make him feel at home, and the house was spacious and comfortable enough to stave off claustrophobia: a stunning wood-and-glass contemporary design with five bedrooms, family and games room with a snooker table and even a small gym and jacuzzi. A first-floor veranda stretched the entire length of the house facing the lake, and on his first look around from it in daylight he could easily see why this particular house had been chosen: the lake then separated into two channels which joined again a hundred yards behind the house, so that effectively it was on an island with only a bridge connecting it to the mainland. And the study was apparently crammed with monitoring equipment, with the guards taking it in turn to watch its screens: views over the lake and the bridge from all directions, plus motion and weight sensors on the bridge and dotted around the first five yards of land in from the lake.

This was a fortress; and as much as that made him feel more assured about his safety, he couldn't escape the final key-turn that gave to his sense of isolation. He was kept apart from the world outside as much as it was kept from him. A gilded and comfortable prison, but a prison nevertheless.

He shuddered, recalling his feelings as he'd first approached the house. With the blackened visor and the bumpiness of the last stretch of track before the bridge, suddenly he was back in the van with the hood on. He wasn't sure what upset him most recalling his kidnapping now: that he'd faced death and given up all hope, or that now it represented his first moment of imprisonment. The pivotal event after which his life could never be the same again.

Lorena's pulse pounded inside her head as she paced determinedly down Rue Ste-Catherine away from the shopping mall.

'. . . you're right. I should send Lorena back. With nothing on Ryall and the sessions heading nowhere, no point in holding on to her here any more.'

She'd trusted Elena. She'd been the only one left she felt she could turn to, and now Elena too had turned her back on her, betrayed her.

And everyone seemed to blame her, look at her oddly when she told her story: Elena, the girl from the social services, Nadine, and now the psychiatrist. All asking the same questions with that same doubting expressions only half believing her, wanting her to recall her father actually touching her while she was awake, when she'd already told them ten times over she couldn't. Just *couldn't*.

All of those faces staring at her dubiously. Maybe all of them were right and she was wrong; maybe it was all just in her dreams and there'd been nothing happening after all. Maybe there was something wrong with her – that's why the psychiatrist – but they were all holding back, afraid to tell her the truth.

'*Pardon!*'

Lorena felt the jolt to her arm and side as the man bumped into her, or more her into him, and as she turned his eyes contemplated her with concern.

'Are you okay?'

She just nodded dumbly and looked hastily away, picking up her rapid pace straight ahead again, her vision blurred and unclear with tears. A couple of other people turned to stare at the same time and she could feel their eyes on her back, and now others in front of her were also staring curiously. More people looking at her concernedly, doubting! Wondering whether she was okay, but afraid to say anything.

Where was she going? As far from Elena as possible, but where? All these stares now were from strangers, she didn't know anyone. The traffic and the voices around started to spin in her head, she suddenly felt as if she was floating. Her determined step faltered a bit.

The night after the second session with the psychiatrist, she'd had another dream about Patrika. The sewer waters were rising, and as they had come up to her face, clogging her mouth and nostrils, and still she couldn't push the manhole cover open to escape, her father had been shaking her and telling her that it was all right . . . *All right!* The waters had magically receded, but his hand had kept stroking her body; then she'd suddenly realized that it wasn't the sewer waters against her cheek, but his kisses . . . and as she felt his hot breath and the moistness of his lips against hers, she'd awoken in revulsion and horror.

Maybe it was the mention of Patrika and Ryall in the session that had brought on her dream; or maybe it was just that she'd got hot and clammy sleeping – but she hadn't woken Elena or told her anything. She was afraid that Elena might say, 'Maybe it's all just happening in your dreams, your imagination.'

After all, isn't that what everyone thought? Isn't that why Elena had finally decided to send her back to England tomorrow?

She slowed, came almost to a halt. But where to go now?

It had taken her ages to build up the courage to ask Elena the other day if she could stay with her and keep Katine company, *if* she left the Ryalls. And although Elena had said, 'Yes, of course', she'd sensed a reluctance, something held back. And now she knew why: Elena didn't believe her!

She stopped and stood stock still as she closed her eyes tight, trying to blot out the blurred confusion of people passing – practically all of them now staring! – and the hubbub of traffic, voices and milling footsteps. But the noise stayed with her in the darkness, and she felt herself sway uncertainly for a second. What to do now . . . *Where to go?*

Now that Elena no longer believed her, there was no one left to turn to.

Roman sat with Funicelli in his car forty yards back from Elena Waldren's hotel on Rue Berri. He'd instructed Funicelli not to break off from watching her for a second, so the only option had been for him to come and collect what Funicelli had on tape so far.

Roman couldn't resist a faint smile as the cassette tape rolled. Funicelli had related the substance of this woman's conversation with the Donatiens when they'd spoken almost two hours ago, and Roman'd immediately relayed it to Jean-Paul – but hearing the conversation at first hand, its significance hit him stronger, tugged at the heart-strings. Separated at birth, the son she hadn't seen in twenty-nine years. Pure gold-dust. If anyone was going to have a shot at seeing Donatien, it would be her.

The light was fading fast as Roman listened, and Funicelli found himself squinting slightly, wondering if the street light was enough to see if Elena Waldren came out of the hotel or whether he'd have to pull up closer.

'The strangest thing was with the girl,' Funicelli commented absently. 'I saw everything from where I was . . . saw *exactly* where she'd gone. But I couldn't say nothing. Makes you wonder what was going on there.'

'Yeah, strange.' Roman was too absorbed with the tape to shift his concentration much.

When the Donatiens started talking about family background and how long they'd lived in their current house, Roman fast-forwarded. On the second wind-on, as Claude Donatien's voice on the phone came across, Funicelli prompted, 'This is where he phones the police to find out the lay of the land.'

Roman rewound a fraction. After some preambles with another RCMP officer, Roman recognized Chenouda's voice: he was saying that he was glad of the call, because they were in fact about to get in touch with the family anyway to brief them about the current situation.

'We've instructed your son not under any circumstances to make contact with you, because you'd be one of the first places the Lacailles would look. So if anyone approaches you and asks questions, anything suspicious at all – you're to let us know. Anything like that already?'

Roman held his breath and looked sharply at Funicelli; but Funicelli seemed relaxed, having already heard the tape.

'No . . . not that I can think of,' Claude Donatien answered.

Probably his wife hadn't even mentioned the telephone engineer calling; or if she had, he didn't see it as suspicious.

'Well, that's good. Good. It's probably too early yet for them to react; they're still scrambling for what to do.'

Roman nodded and smiled at Funicelli. 'Always said he had big balls . . . but they sure ain't fucking crystal.'

'But you'll let me know the moment anything changes?'

'Yes, certainly – I will.' Then Claude Donatien went on to the main reason for his call: if and when they might be able to see their son. He sounded hesitant; Chenouda's opening about Georges being instructed not to contact them had obviously put him off his stride, boded the worst.

But Chenouda listened patiently and didn't entirely pour cold water on the request. He explained that the idea of the programme was that their son was to have no contact with family or friends. *'But that's not to say that a meeting couldn't be arranged at a later stage – if we can put the right safeguards in place.'*

It was difficult to tell if Chenouda meant what he was saying or was letting the Donatiens down softly, didn't want to tackle right now the thorny truth that they might *never* get to see their son again.

Roman sat forward as Claude Donatien came to the topic of the woman who'd visited them. Chenouda was off balance at first and it took a couple of questions for him to get things clear in his mind. Then he was circumspect, pointing at the coincidence of the timing.

'Surely this comes under what I mentioned initially – things out of the ordinary, suspicious. People making contact out of the blue and asking questions.'

'No . . . no, I don't think so. She came across as very genuine, and she showed us some papers from England. Birth certificate, something too from a search agency. She's been looking for him for a month or so . . . way before any of this happened.'

Chenouda fell silent for a second. *'Well, whether or not she's genuine, I suggest you leave to me to decide – after I've had her checked out and seen for myself what papers she's got.'* Faint resigned sigh as Chenouda asked and made note of her name and where she was staying. *'I'll speak to her.'*

Roman glanced up at the hotel ahead. Perhaps she was talking to Chenouda right now: if only they could get a bug inside there as well. The uncertainty, not knowing for sure, was stifling, had his nerves on a razor's edge.

He told Funicelli to phone him the minute anything new broke or she left the hotel, then took the tapes and headed off to see Jean-Paul.

Jean-Paul looked up thoughtfully as the tapes finished playing. 'What do you think?'

Roman shrugged. 'I think that if she lays it on thick like she did with Claude Donatien, we've got a chance. Thing is, it's our best and only chance right now.'

Jean-Paul nodded. 'Maybe so. But this Chenouda sounds more than a little reticent, was very non-committal.'

'Yeah, true. It's all in the balance – could go either way.' But Roman was more confident than he made out, because what Jean-Paul couldn't take into account was how Chenouda arranging Donatien's abduction could now be a vital card in their favour. Cutting Donatien off from his family, friends and past was bad enough – but being responsible for him never being able to meet his natural mother added an all the more poignant, crushing burden; hopefully the straw to break the camel's back.

Roman had been blind with fury when Chenouda's involvement had first dawned on him. It hadn't just been the sheer cheek of it, or that someone else apart from him was suddenly playing under the table with an extra deck, but the fact that he'd been first to fall in the frame – which Chenouda would have known all too well. He'd been made to look a fool and a liar to Jean-Paul. Despite his protestations at the time and making good now, Roman was sure Jean-Paul still harboured doubts. Chenouda had probably had a good laugh up his sleeve at that: getting Donatien to testify and at the same time putting him and Jean-Paul at each other's throats. But now hopefully there'd be some divine pay-back in store for Chenouda.

Roman grimaced tightly at Jean-Paul. 'We'll just have to wait and see which way he finally jumps.'

'If there was any way to avoid sending you back, I would, Lorena. But there's nowhere left for me to go with this. Can't you see that?'

'Yes, I . . . I suppose I can.' Lorena's eyes flickered down and she bit lightly at her bottom lip.

The first acceptance, perhaps even a shade of guilt at the trouble she'd caused. But it had been a tough few hours to get there, Elena contemplated.

After hearing Elena on the phone, Lorena had apparently got halfway down Rue Ste-Catherine before panic had seized her at the realization that she was in a strange city, and she'd returned to the mall. She'd stood inside a shop doorway, trembling, trying to frantic-ally think of what else she might do. She could just see Elena from where she was, but was careful to duck inside the shop when Elena turned towards her. Then, as Elena appeared about to give up and go, she'd rushed over and clung on to her and burst into tears, saying she was sorry, sorry, *sorry*. Between the sobs she'd explained what had happened and begged and pleaded for Elena not to send her back the following day.

The display took all the steam out of Elena's anger. All she did was wipe away Lorena's tears, order a coffee for each of them and sit Lorena down, trying calmly to explain her dilemma.

But Lorena was practically beyond consolation. 'Mr Ryall will be angry with me . . . much worse than before. I *can't* go back now.'

Elena reasoned and cajoled, but Lorena clung to her ground obstin-ately, still pleading, panicked at the thought of having to face Ryall again. And in the end all Elena could think of to get through to her was to be dramatic.

'You don't understand, Lorena. If I don't send you back to England tomorrow, I'm going to jail for this.'

'But that tape, I thought that was to help you . . . so that you wouldn't get into trouble.'

'Yes, that helped us for the last few days. But after tomorrow, that won't help any more. And they could send me to jail for a long while, Lorena. You wouldn't want that, would you?'

'No . . . no, I wouldn't.'

Watching the shadows in Lorena's eyes as she looked away awk-wardly – torn between her own very real fear and the worry of getting Elena into such serious trouble – Elena felt immediately guilty that she'd resorted to such a tactic. But she hadn't seen much choice.

She'd had to break off to make her call to Claude Donatien. Claude said that the officer he'd spoken to, Michel Chenouda, was non-committal, but at least had said he'd contact her; he hadn't closed the door straight away.

Claude said he'd passed on her details and Elena was suddenly apprehensive. She'd hoped to just be given a number, to have the option of making contact or not. Now that had been taken from her control. Probably best: she might have balked and never made that final move. But she was worried that, now the police had her name and address, they would be checking her out. She might return to the hotel to find it ringed by police cars with their beacons flashing.

Both she and Lorena were silent heading back to the hotel: Elena anxious about impending arrest, Lorena about returning to Ryall.

There'd been no flashing lights at the hotel, but Elena had been too tense waiting for Chenouda's call to talk much about Lorena's concerns. She'd just placated that Lorena shouldn't worry so, they'd sort something out.

'We'll go for something to eat and talk then.'

Chenouda's call had been a non-event after the level of anticipation and panic she'd worked herself up to: all he'd done was confirm with her the details Claude Donatien had passed on to him, then suggest that they should meet and discuss things more fully at eleven-thirty the next day. He gave her an address on Dorchester Boulevard and asked that she bring her passport and all relevant paperwork regarding her son.

But soon after putting down the phone she began to panic: how on earth was she going to face walking into a police station, right into the lion's den?

They found a restaurant on St-Denis that had a special on lobsters, and Elena talked Lorena into trying one as a change from pizza.

'If this meeting doesn't work out tomorrow, I'll be heading back with you.' Elena was still throwing across everything she could to reassure. Earlier Lorena had looked concerned when she'd explained that if she was staying on, all she could do was walk Lorena to the nearest British embassy and give them the Ryalls' details; they'd have to arrange transport back for her. Anything to meet the deadline. 'I don't think much will come of it, so you'll probably end up in my company.'

The shadows only eased from Lorena's eyes a fraction. Elena once again opted for dramatics to divert Lorena's worries. She decided to open up more about her son, explain why tomorrow was so important to her.

'I said that I hadn't seen him in a while, but I lied. Truth is, I've *never* seen him since he was born. I was very young when I became pregnant . . . and my father gave him away to another family. I was left no choice in the matter.'

'I'm sorry,' Lorena said, appearing confused for a second as to how to respond. 'You missed him a lot?'

'Yes . . . very much.' *And now I don't know if I'll ever get to see him again.* She blinked slowly, but suddenly there were no more welling tears: the see-saw events of the past forty-eight hours, the valerian pills and her mounting tiredness had battered her senses numb. Sometimes she felt completely empty of emotions, little more than a hollow shell. Or was it simply a protective barrier so that any new shock wouldn't send her reeling and rip her insides out? She was finally battle-hardened for the worst.

'Was he cruel, your father?'

'No. Just very strict. Impossibly strict.'

'So he wasn't someone for you to be afraid of – like Mr Ryall?'

'No, I suppose not.' Elena smiled wanly as she made the concession. She'd raised her own problems as trump cards, but Lorena had deftly slipped them back in the deck where they belonged. Of course, she *had* been afraid of her father, but that suddenly put it all in perspective: if Lorena's claims had substance, Lorena had a *real* fear to face.

Suddenly Lorena was once again the frightened little girl reaching out for help from the back of Nicola Ryall's Range Rover. And whatever rationale Elena threw across, she knew that she could never shift the lingering fear in Lorena's eyes. Jail sentence or not, in the end she just didn't think she could face sending Lorena back to Ryall tomorrow.

Another restless night.

Elena had been hoping finally to get a good night's sleep. She was so exhausted and so keen to make the right impression for her big day tomorrow. Get rid of the blood shots in her eyes and steady her nerves, not come across how she felt: haggard, desperate, at her wits' end. *There's no way this half-crazed woman is getting to see him.*

But, perversely, her anxiety about how the day might go kept her mind alert; she was unable to drift off; and now she still had Lorena to worry about. She'd hoped at least to put that to rest, but all she'd said in the end was for Lorena not to fret, she didn't think that she could send her back. 'We'll try and sort something out tomorrow.'

Left that small gap open in case in the end there was no choice. Sometimes she wished that she had been arrested so that she didn't have to make the decision. It was frustrating. She'd set her mind on a plan of action, had almost managed to convince Lorena, got her to accept – then suddenly she'd been slam-dunked at the last moment.

The problem was, who was the real Lorena? Had Lorena hit the right note about her father purely out of naive bluntness, or had she purposely aimed for it, her street-wiliness showing through? Was Lowndes right in saying that Lorena had formed an unnatural attachment to her and this was all just a cry for attention, to re-establish some of their old bond? If so, Lorena must have planned everything practically from the start.

Except for one thing: the fear Elena had seen in Lorena's eyes in the restaurant. That was difficult to fake. She herself was full of concern and panic for what the next day held, but what she'd seen in Lorena in that moment went far beyond that. Whether something was happening with Ryall or not, it was certainly real in Lorena's mind. So why after all these sessions couldn't she recall anything?

The thought had a loop effect: there was no real answer and so it just went around, and Elena let it because it was soporific, pushed her closer towards sleep. She finally dozed off after almost an hour, her last thoughts on what she might wear for her meeting tomorrow. Something clean-cut and respectable but at the same time not too cool and formal: it should be soft-edged, maternal. She'd glanced at the weather forecast before getting into bed to help her decide.

Overnight lows of 4 or 5, 10 or 11°C by mid-morning, rising to highs of 13 or 14.

For some reason she found the numbers replaying in her mind halfway through the night, jumbling with a segment from one of Lowndes' sessions: *'And he was saying some numbers . . . seven . . . eight.'*

Elena was suddenly wide awake, her breath falling sharp and fast. *Magic tricks!* She sat up and looked at the bedside clock: 3.26 a.m. Barely two hours' sleep.

She felt like waking Lorena, screaming out loud that she thought she'd found the key, and they'd both jump up and down excitedly and wake the rest of the hotel. But she needed to know for sure – so she threw on some clothes, grabbed her bag and headed for the nearest phone box. She used her global call card and dialled her home number.

Gordon, initially pleasantly surprised, almost relieved to hear her voice – perhaps he'd been half expecting another call from Crowley – berated her for breaking their call policy.

'This couldn't wait,' Elena said, still slightly breathless from the rush to the booth. 'Besides, I've used a global call card. It'll be scrambled through some faceless exchange in Virginia. I could be calling from anywhere in the world.' She told Gordon what she needed to know – Ryall's stints as a children's magician – and why. 'Where did your investigator get that from?'

'From some old newspaper clipping, I believe.' No, he hadn't sent them through; but, yes, Gordon could get hold of him now. 'He works from home. Phone me back in fifteen minutes and I'll see what he's got.'

Six minutes later Gordon had the fax through: three newspaper clippings in total. He scanned them rapidly, his blood running cold as he came to the reference two-thirds of the way into the second article. Elena's hunch had been right! He tapped his fingers on the table by the phone and read more thoroughly as he waited on Elena's call back.

Elena's nerves had been wound too tight to do anything more than pace agitatedly back and forth ten yards either side of the call box to kill time; once again she was slightly breathless. All she could manage was 'Oh God! *Oh God!*' when Gordon told her. She'd hoped that she'd be right; but another part of her had hoped desperately that she'd be wrong. She sighed heavily. 'The rest, I suppose, will have to be sorted out on the psychiatrist's couch.'

Gordon wished her good luck for tomorrow as they signed off. 'Thanks.' Hopelessly inadequate for one of the biggest days of her life: decision day now on *two* fronts. But she felt too numbed and shell-shocked to say anything else.

She stood for a moment by Lorena's bed before getting back into bed herself: Lorena didn't appear to have stirred or even noticed that she'd been gone. She realized then that she couldn't mention anything: it might later be said that Lorena had merely filled in the gaps to suit. She'd only be able to tell Lowndes, then they'd just have to hold their breath to see if events followed the nightmare path she suspected. But the strongest emotion she felt looking at Lorena gently sleeping was that she was sorry, so sorry for ever having doubted her.

31

Funicelli located a telephone junction box in a service slipway fifteen yards along from the Hôtel Montclair, the hotel where the English-woman was staying. The box also appeared to service three or four other buildings in the first stretch of Rue Berri.

He picked through and found the wires and switches for the Montclair, then started making the connections. Four minutes, five tops, he estimated. But four or five minutes in the open by a busy street was a lifetime. He'd been uneasy just in the couple of minutes up the telegraph pole outside the Donatiens. But that had been Beaconsfield, peaceful suburbia; now he was in one of the busiest parts of Montreal. The hustle-bustle and the sheer number of things he had to watch out for made this an entirely different proposition.

He'd chosen to do it early: 8.08 a.m. Telephone engineers often started at 8.00 a.m, but by the time their rosters were done and they were clear of the depots, the earliest calls were usually after 8.30 a.m. So he shouldn't have to worry about a Bell Canada engineer passing and asking what he was doing.

But the rest of the city was rapidly coming to life: the flow of traffic and people passing was increasing, the occasional passer-by throwing him a glance. An East Indian by the *dépanneur* on the corner, possibly its owner, studied him thoughtfully for almost thirty seconds before going back inside the shop.

Funicelli was sweating profusely, his hands trembling on the wires. This was a nightmare. But Roman had been insistent that they get a bug on the woman's line.

'We've got to know what progress she makes with Chenouda. If anything's going down, it'll probably be decided within the next few days.'

That was the other thing Funicelli had to worry about. That no faults were reported on any lines within that time to make engineers open up the junction box and discover his bug. They couldn't risk leaving something like that inside the box for any length of time.

For the final minute he hardly paid attention to who might be passing or looking at him, his concentration was focused intently on securing the last few wires in place.

He glanced at his watch as he slammed shut and locked the box. Four minutes twenty-two. Not bad. He let out a slow sigh as he walked down to his white van parked round the corner, but still his hands were shaking slightly as he opened its back doors and threw his tools inside.

He nodded briefly to Frank Massenat parked ten yards back on the far side as he jumped in the driver's seat. Funicelli had kept look-out on the hotel until 10 p.m., then Massenat had taken over for the night.

Take the van back, change, breakfast, coffee and check his cousin hadn't burnt down his shop while he was away, then he'd return to replace Massenat at 10 a.m.

'Nothing, nothing,' Massenat commented as they changed over. 'Except that at half three she suddenly comes out and makes a call from that booth over there. Then she paces up and down as if her ass was on fire before making another call. Then back to the excitement of watching people sleep.' Massenat shrugged. 'And no signs of life yet this morning.'

But just over an hour later that changed as Funicelli watched the woman leave the hotel, girl in tow. She made a quick call from the booth Massenat had seen her use, then hailed a taxi. Funicelli followed through the mid-morning traffic, two or three cars behind. A light drizzle started falling halfway along René Lévesque and he put the wipers on intermittent. He'd already phoned Roman two hours before to tell him that the bug had been successfully placed, but as he saw the taxi pull up outside RCMP HQ on Dorchester Boulevard, he took out his mobile to call again. Roman would want to know this news straight away.

The first half-hour of questioning was mostly mundane and low key. Apart from a couple of jump-backs to fill in small details at first overlooked, Elena ran through everything in historical and hopefully – to Staff Sergeant Michel Chenouda patiently listening – logical sequence: her father, Dr Maniatis with the birth certificate, the Stephanous, the orphanage at Baie du Febvre, and finally the Donatiens.

Michel Chenouda sat directly opposite her at an oval table and the papers she'd produced were spread between them. At one end of the table a tape ran while another officer at its side made brief notes. For the most part Chenouda stayed silent with the occasional thoughtful nod as she ran through her background; on the surface at least he appeared to accept her story. But she couldn't help sensing that underneath he was uneasy, harboured doubts. And then the questions started to reflect those doubts, became more intent; the pressure was turned up a notch.

Chenouda shook his head. 'But what I don't understand is why you left it until now to try and make contact.'

'Well, for a long while I blanked it from my mind. Then I adopted two children of my own and I started working with children in need in orphanages in Eastern Europe, mainly Romania. I think part of that was to push away the guilt that I'd given away my own child.' Elena looked down, then towards the corridor outside. Three doors along, Lorena aka Katine waited in an open-plan RCMP general office. 'It was in fact a problem with one of the Romanian children, not much older than my own daughter, Katine, that started me thinking again about my son. I'd told myself all along that he'd have been all right, he'd have gone to a good home somewhere. And suddenly it hit me that that wasn't always true.'

'What sort of problem?' Chenouda looked at her keenly.

Elena felt the intensity of his stare like a blowtorch on her cheek, and her heart skipped a beat. He'd probably already seen an alert and so known about her all along, and the chain of seemingly innocuous questions had all been leading to this *coup de grâce*. She tried to cling again to the steely nerve that had made her able to walk into the building in the first place. She'd paused just before its wide glass doors, taking a deep breath. She thought she was okay, but walking along all she'd been able to hear was the pounding of her heart; she couldn't even hear her own footsteps or any of the movement or activity around. Now, again, the pounding was drowning out all else: the officer at the end of the table was scrawling in his notepad, but she couldn't hear it. She swallowed hard in an attempt to clear her ears. Perhaps Chenouda was just being thorough, didn't know anything after all.

'Well, it turns out her father was molesting her.'

'I see.' Michel's eyes flickered down awkwardly for a second and he pursed his lips. 'And what happened to the girl in the end?'

Elena watched Chenouda's gaze slowly rise to meet hers, and again her resolve slipped away. They'd probably found her on the computer hours ago, and were now busily matching Lorena on screen in the office down the corridor. Her left hand started to shake on the table and she pulled it down and clenched it tight in her lap. The other officer looked up keenly from his notes for a moment; she hoped he hadn't noticed.

'She, uh . . . she's gone to a foster home while the court case is pending. And meanwhile she's also undergoing psychiatric assessment.' Pretty much the scenario she anticipated with Lorena moving things on a couple of months. She'd phoned Lowndes to try and get an early-morning appointment, but the earliest he could fit her in was 2 p.m. She'd called Gordon upon leaving to see if he could delay Crowley's alert; if not, it would be going out about now. Maybe Chenouda's people hadn't found anything yet on the computer, but someone would walk in at any second. Or Lorena would slip up and forget that her name was meant to be Katine. *Too many possibilities.* She felt them tugging her in all directions at the same time. She must have been crazy to walk in here, *crazy.*

'Right.' Chenouda's gaze stayed on her steadily, and for a moment she half expected him to suddenly stand up and announce: 'But that's not what we in fact know to be the case, Mrs Waldren.' And signal to his assistant to handcuff her. But in the end all he said was: 'It must have been very tough on you.'

'Yes . . . yes, it was.' She let out a tired breath. As quickly as the pressure had been turned on, it was off again.

Michel contemplated the papers on the table. It would have made everything so much easier if this was a hoax, a predictable try-on from Roman. But it all seemed so real, far too intricate and detailed to be a scam: the English connection, the court order and birth certificate . . . the orphanage. Roman was devious, but even he couldn't have gone to these lengths.

Michel had already checked her out on the computer for any criminal record an hour before she arrived: nothing. Now he had some new names and details to check, but his gut feeling was that this Englishwoman, Elena Waldren, was telling the truth. She was Georges Donatien's birth mother.

The coincidence of the timing he'd been uneasy about the most, but her explanation there too had come across as real. Heartfelt, emotional – her voice had been close to breaking at points: if she wasn't telling the truth, then Roman had found one of the best actresses Michel had ever come across. The other possibility was that Roman had at some stage discovered that she was Georges' real mother and pulled her out of the woodwork now when he needed her.

But her initial enquiries with the search agency were weeks ago, when Roman still had Georges firmly in his sights and high hopes of soon removing him. And from her passport, her flight over had been three days ago, eighteen hours before Georges' abduction. Even her visit to the orphanage was the day before their TV appearance, so Roman couldn't possibly have known then that he might need her as an ace card.

Though still Michel sensed an underlying anxiety and nervousness that he couldn't quite fathom. He looked at her contemplatively for a second as he forced a weak smile.

'I'm sorry, but we can't be too careful.' Maybe it was more shell-shock than nerves: she'd obviously been through the mill, and now on top had to face the third degree from him and the worry that, having got this far, she might fall at the final hurdle. She might never get to see her son. And all of her hopes now rested in his hands. It was enough to make anyone nervous, and that realization also pressed the weight heavier on his own shoulders: just how was he going to wend his way through this, explain? 'These people threatening your son are highly dangerous and probably by now also desperate. They'd go to any lengths to use others to try and get to him.' Michel held out a palm. 'Others such as yourself.'

'Oh, I . . . I understand.' Though it had taken a second for the penny to drop. They'd been at crossed purposes all the time! With the questioning starting to have an edge, she'd become convinced that he'd seen something on the computer, but all the time he'd been thinking that she might be a Mafia plant! She almost couldn't resist smiling – partly release of tension, partly at the ludicrous thought – but bit it back: out of step with the mood. What had brought her to this room, and the fact that the outcome balanced on a knife's edge, hung heavy in the air, smothered all else.

Now for the difficult part, thought Michel. He felt her eyes on him expectantly, full of hope that he'd say she'd be able to see her son. *The son he'd made sure was hidden away from everyone, possibly never for her to see again.* He felt the pressure of it like a dull ache at the back of his neck.

He remembered his mother saying that if you tell a lie, it'll come out somehow. 'Don't know how, but it always does.' He'd convinced himself before the meeting that the woman's quest must be a ruse from Roman. It had his trademark all over it, was the perfect extra pressure to bring into play: 'You want to hide him away for ever:

there, I've trumped you. The mother he's never seen. Get out of that one.' He'd become so convinced that it was false that he didn't expect to have to face this moment now. Tell this woman who'd already been through hell that the chances of her getting to see her son were slim.

'The problem is, Mrs Waldren, as I told Claude Donatien and he no doubt passed on to you – this programme is very strict. The idea is that your son sees no one – and I mean *no one* – from his past. Now that's not to say that that rule can't be bent given very special circumstances, and then again only *if* we can put the right safeguards in place. The first thing to happen is that we tell your son – because it's certainly not in the programme's charter that we should withhold vital personal information from him. Now if he doesn't want to see you for whatever reason, then that's the end of the road right there. If he does, then it has to be put before the department that set up the programme in Ottawa. Then we have to . . .' Michel broke off. She'd been through enough for her to be spared hearing him bury the likelihood of seeing her son under a chain of procedural details. It was the least he owed her. 'Well, put it this way – we have to measure the strength and need of your request against the risk taken by granting it.'

'What are my chances?'

Michel looked slightly down to one side. She'd wasted no time, cut right to the core. Now the spotlight had swung round on him, and he found the plea in her eyes unsettling, difficult to meet head-on. His first instinct was to bluff, buoy her spirits, if nothing else then to ease that searching stare. But he'd already played enough shadow games; he didn't want to also be responsible for leading her on.

'They're no better than even.' His voice was level, matter-of-fact. 'Your reason and need are strong, couldn't be stronger – but the risks a meeting would subject your son to are equally strong. In the end it won't be up to me to decide – S-18 in Ottawa will have the final say.' Another truth: Mundy would decide. Michel wasn't just passing the buck so that he could side-step the pitiful plea in her eyes. Right now he was the *only* focus for what she wanted.

But her eyes stayed steadily on him, and she reached one hand across the table and gently gripped his. 'But you'll do your best to help me? To try and convince them?'

Michel wished she hadn't made that final physical contact: he'd saved a last gap for himself in case he needed to shield within it, stay remote from her dilemma. And now she'd bridged it: he'd felt her hand trembling like a trapped bird, felt all the hopes and desires of a lifetime built up and now passed on to him with that single touch.

'Yes . . . yes, I will.' His voice wavered slightly, though once again he was telling the truth.

But what he couldn't explain was that he'd plead her case strongly as much for himself as for her: having trawled his conscience long and hard before ultimately going ahead with Georges' faked abduction, what he couldn't bear was an ounce more doubt or guilt over it. And if she finally got to see her son, there was no harm done. Things would be back to how they were before she'd made contact.

'I think we can trace her.'

Crowley was hit with the claim as soon as he walked in the squad room that morning. DC Proctor, one of the more technically attuned of his team, invariably took pole position whenever things drifted sufficiently into cyberspace to make eyes in the squad room start to glaze over.

'Really?' Crowley prepared himself for an onslaught of techno-babble as he took off his jacket and looped it over the back of his chair. He might have shown more enthusiasm if Proctor hadn't broken the golden rule that it was best not to speak to him before he'd downed his first coffee.

Proctor continued undeterred. Crowley blinked at him twice, yawned and halfway through headed to the coffee machine with Proctor's voice trailing behind him. It was about the call Elena Waldren had made with a call card. Yes, central exchange, but the cards were usually all numbered. 'If we give them the number called and the time, they should be able to tell us which card was used for that call.' Proctor paused for emphasis. 'And also where that card was sold.'

Crowley took his first sip, but the last words had already got him fully awake. His eyes were wide above the cup. 'You're sure?'

'Sure as can be.'

Crowley gave Proctor the green light to start chasing it. A stream of secrecy and liability disclaimer forms faxed back and forth between them and the global call company took up much of the day, and mid-afternoon Gordon Waldren was on the line about his wife's deadline. Could Crowley extend it? His wife had a session planned with a psychiatrist and she fully expected to come out of it with proof positive that Ryall was molesting Lorena. 'But I won't know for sure until my next contact with her at eight-thirty tonight.'

'I don't know.' Crowley clasped at his hair and looked across at Proctor. At any other time he might have said yes, but if they found a firm trace Turton would probably be reluctant to delay any longer. 'I'll make a call to the powers that be and let you know in an hour or two.'

Proctor had the information in only another forty minutes that the card used was in a batch that had gone through a distributor for Eastern Canada.

'Eastern Canada?' Crowley confirmed. 'They can't narrow it down closer than that?'

'No, that's the closest. They supply to the distributor, and from there have no track of exactly which cities which cards go to.'

Great, Crowley thought: they'd narrowed it to an area geographically five times larger than the half of Western Europe they'd originally thought she might be. But at least they were down to a population of 14 million rather than 200 million and the number of cities and towns was far less. He phoned Inspector Turton and explained the state of play.

'Could be just a delaying tactic from Gordon Waldren,' Turton commented, sucking in his breath: added weight to his deliberations. 'He knows that she's made a mistake with the call card, knows that we could well be close to tracing her. So he's trying to buy some time. But he could be telling the truth, and either way I don't want a heavy-handed arrest or her cut down in a hail of bullets. So alert the RCMP, but just keep it lightweight for now. Arrange to speak to Waldren at, say, nine tonight, straight after he's spoken to his wife. And if it appears he's mucking us around, get straight back to the RCMP with a grade-one abduction alert.'

'Jerry! Jerry! . . . Jerry!'

As Georges walked into the lounge after having grabbed a coffee in the kitchen, Clive and Steve were on their feet watching *Jerry Springer*, chanting along with the audience as two scraggy blondes tried to tear each other's hair out. Chac sat to one side smiling. Russell was downstairs in the study watching monitors.

'Don't tell me you're into this shit?' Georges raised an eyebrow as he sipped his coffee.

'Yeah, we're into this shit,' Clive said defensively. 'It's one of our top-bet shows. You never know how many times that bleeper's going to go.'

As the show wound down and Clive and Steve exchanged some money – Steve apparently held Russell's stake money – Clive explained: to kill the boredom on safe-house assignments, they'd started betting at first on sporting events: ice hockey, football, boxing, whatever. Then they'd stretched it to popular TV shows, with *Springer* one of the first candidates.

'We've been running bets now for over a year on just how many bleeps and fights there are in one show – closest call wins. The record so far is eighty-four bleeps and twenty-two fights.'

They bet on how many times the dog appeared or the brother called at the door in *Frasier*, how many tunes were played in *Ali McBeal* and how often the record needle scratched off halfway through, or whether Kenny would get killed or Chef would sing in *South Park*. For them the soap-opera day suddenly took on a new excitement.

Georges shook his head with a wry smile and went out to the terrace as *Friends* came on. The running bet was apparently how many times Joey said 'Hey'. The sun was strong enough by midday that you could sit out wearing a thick sweat shirt, but still it was crisp. Georges' breath showed on the air.

Chac joined him after a minute. 'You okay?'

'Just starting to worry that this is what my life holds from here on: watching ice melt and putting bets on the number of F-words on *Springer*.' Georges went back to staring out blankly across the frozen lake.

'I know.' Chac shrugged. 'But don't worry – it's just the first months up until the trial. After, you'll be relocated with a new identity – you'll be playing golf in the Carolinas or fishing in the Florida Keys with some Jennifer Lopez lookalike on your arm. Or maybe, with the language thing, they'll buy you a new life in the South of France. Things will be looking up again.'

'Yeah, sounds good.' Georges nodded dolefully. He confided in Chac more than anyone else. Perhaps because Chac had been with him throughout since the abduction, or maybe it was just his size: broad shoulders and soft edges to cushion problems. 'But the thing is, Chac, I'm missing her. I'm missing her like hell.'

'Did you speak to Michel about it?'

'Yeah. But he says no go. They'll be watching her too closely, and whatever I said would probably only be used against us at trial.'

Chac joined him in staring out across the frozen lake. Georges had probably explained it better to him than he'd got a chance to over the phone to Michel: just why he was unhappy leaving things on this note with Simone. And it made sense: he needed a sort of closure on that part of his life so that he could get on with this new chapter now. But Chac could also see the risk from Michel's viewpoint.

'I'll try and talk to him about it next time he calls,' Chac said. 'Maybe there's a different angle to play it.'

Crowley's call came through to RCMP Central in Ottawa at precisely 11.08 a.m.

'No, we can't narrow it down more than that, I'm afraid.' And, no, she wasn't armed and dangerous. 'In fact, they know each other quite well, so the girl is in no immediate danger. But it is urgent we have contact with them and that the girl is returned to her parents.'

Within the hour the alert was logged and put out on the network for the attention of all stations in Eastern Canada, which included Dorchester Boulevard. But Michel Chenouda had already done his checking for Elena Waldren on the system over an hour before.

Then at 12.52 p.m., Ottawa received another call from Crowley.

'We've narrowed it down! They've gone to Toronto.'

'You're sure of that now? Before I make the final change?'

'Yes, yes . . . positive. We just got the confirmation through from the airline.'

'Okay.' A few key taps, and the alert was amended solely for Toronto and Ontario police. It had been on the Quebec network for less than two hours before vanishing like a dying radar blip.

Hanging up, Crowley was bursting with excess adrenalin and energy. They'd finally traced the flight, a charter from Brussels to Toronto and Edmonton: she'd booked all the way to Edmonton, then changed at the last moment.

Two days with nothing, and suddenly the breaks were all hitting at the same time, the squad room was once again buzzing with it. Often the way.

The squad room was like a morgue.

A hubbub of activity only seconds before, each time Michel Chenouda walked in it fell quiet. This was the pay-back for having put his colleagues under suspicion with S-18. Michel felt like picking out individuals and saying I don't think it's you or you, or 'Come on, we've worked together years now: I'm not pointing the finger at you; it's others here I'm not so sure about'. And then those others would stare at him blankly. Chac and Maury were getting the treatment too, because they were the ones he'd singled out to trust. He'd had to trust somebody, and they were his longest standing partners. But nobody had any idea just *how much* he'd trusted them, that they shared his secret about Donatien's abduction.

Maury had taken notes during his interview with Elena Waldren, and the squad room had predictably fallen silent as they'd walked back in. Chac thought he'd drawn the short straw getting the main guard duty with Donatien: unlike Michel and Maury, he didn't have kids to see, a failed marriage to try and make good on after the event. But Chac was better off out of it, Michel reflected: at least his isolation was real, tangible. This kind of isolation, being surrounded by people you knew so well, yet made to feel so apart from, out in the cold, in a way was much harder to take.

He felt guilty about having roped Chac and Maury in on his little scheme, subjected them as well to this icy departmental blast. As much as needing their help, he'd wanted them as sounding boards to convince himself he was doing the right thing: 'If we just leave Donatien, Roman's going to take him out for sure. All we're doing is bringing forward what Roman's going to do to him in a few days. And at the same time we get our witness.' Chac and Maury had been full of doubt and concern at first. There'd been a lot of frowns and forehead-cradling at the awful risk to their careers, so Michel'd moved in swiftly with the clincher. 'What's the alternative? We know he's about to die – yet we just sit around and let it happen?'

He'd wanted their honest input, but in the end had shamelessly cornered them, left them little choice: how could they put their precious careers before a man's life? The reverse of that same coin, once the battle banners had been raised, suddenly made their actions seem terribly noble. They'd put their necks on the line to save Donatien's. Michel clung to that, recited the same headline justification each time the guilt seeped back.

Because what Michel didn't want to have to face was that his obsession with the Lacailles might have finally made him step too far. He'd known all along that he was going to corner Chac and Maury, because he couldn't have done it without them. He didn't just want tame head-nods confirming that he was doing the right thing. Chac had in fact helped him choose the two abductors and set things up, then he'd assigned Chac and Maury to watch over Donatien, allowing just the right leeway for his abductors to get away – until the last moment. Every detail had been painstakingly pre-choreographed and timed.

And now Maury was alongside him in a small back office at Dorchester Boulevard with Chac and Georges at the other end of the line in the safe house. Russell had set up the scrambler and watched a monitor for a second to ensure the signal kept shifting and the line was secure, then left them to it. Their small circle of conspiracy was once again complete.

Chac spoke only briefly and said that he wanted another word when Michel had finished, then passed him over to Georges.

Michel swallowed hard. This wasn't going to be easy.

Georges had at first been defensive and incredulous. It was impossible. His real mother had died when he was only three in a car accident: Maria Stephanou. And his father had been too spineless to bring him up on his own.

'That's *how* I ended up in the orphanage. And that's why I've never troubled to see him since, or even tried to make contact.'

'I'm sorry, Georges. I've seen her papers and heard her story. And I think she's for real.' Michel ran through everything as it had been presented to him: early pregnancy, dominating father, the court order, the birth registration with the same doctor also finding the Stephanous. He didn't want to pull any punches, so his tone was straightforward, almost matter-of-fact; belied the emotional weight of the subject.

It would have made everything so much easier if Donatien'd just said, 'I don't want to see her.' Washed away all the guilt and the difficult decisions yet to come in one. And it would have been easy to put a spin on the information now to lead to that response. But Michel already carried enough on his shoulders through influencing events, moulding them the way he wanted. It was unlikely enough that Donatien would ever be able to see his birth mother; he didn't want to be responsible for plunging home the final knife, manipulating to ensure they'd never meet just to save complications. That would be a step too far. This one he'd have to play straight down the line.

Georges still clung on to disbelief defensively, much of it covering ground that Michel had tossed around a dozen times over the past hours. Surely it was all just a scam dreamt up by Roman? No, first thing Michel had thought of: no possible link and her search had started ten days before Georges had even been abducted. Then why had she left it until now to try and make contact? And Michel had told him the rest: her cutting herself off from her father and trying to blot it from her mind; her work with orphaned children to salve the guilt.

'Telling herself all along that you'd have gone to a good family somewhere. And everything was going well until she suddenly hit the problem of a child placed with a family where everything wasn't so fine.'

Georges let go reluctantly: it was almost half an hour before his anger and defensiveness finally wound down. Silently submissive. *Too* silent after the earlier outbursts, stiflingly awkward: Michel could still sense a hundred questions bubbling beneath. But it was probably as close to acceptance as Georges would come until all the pieces had sunk in and finally settled.

There was a moment towards the end when Georges had suddenly blurted out: 'What would you do in my position?'

'Well, I don't know. I suppose I –'

But Georges butted in. 'Oh, I forgot. You couldn't possibly have any idea of my position or know how I feel. Cut off from everyone I know and love, and now one more added to the pot.' He eased an awkward, muted chuckle. 'Are you sure this isn't one of Roman's warped games?'

'Yeah, I'm sure. As I say, we checked it every which way.' As if countering the barb, after a second he added that Georges didn't exactly have the exclusive on isolation. 'Since I went out on a limb for you by bringing in S-18, a lot of backs have turned here. I might as well –' Then it was his turn to cut short. His situation paled in comparison. The closest he'd come to knowing how Georges felt was the situation with his own family. Following his wife from Toronto to Montreal because he couldn't bear being away from his children. When they'd left it had been like a stab to the heart, grinding month by month deeper: the ten months before he'd finally got his transfer and followed were the hardest of his life. Because of the squad room giving him the cold shoulder now and his role winding down as S-18 took over, he'd thrown himself more into his family, arranged a couple of days out with Benjamin and Angèle; absorbed as he had been with the case, all too often they'd taken a back seat. Being snubbed by work colleagues was one thing – uncomfortable, a pain in the ass – but separation from family was in an entirely different league. 'Well, if it's any consolation, I know how you must feel – I was separated from my own children for a while.' Though he didn't have the time or inclination to explain just how and why. He took a fresh breath. 'This might not be a decision you can make right now. But she has flown all the way from England and can't stay indefinitely on the off-chance – so I promised to let her know one way or the other within twenty-four hours. If you're not ready now, fine; we can just tell her that and when you are ready – three months, six months, whatever – she can be contacted again.'

Georges sighed nonchalantly. 'What's the point? Even if I decide I want to see her, it'll probably just be the same as with Simone: no go.'

'I can't say one way or the other. I'm just the messenger here. I passed on what she said – and if you decide you want to see her, I'll pass that on to S-18. In the end it's up to them to decide. One thing in her favour is that, unlike Simone, she's not someone Roman and Jean-Paul will be keeping watch over. She's new on the scene – they won't even know about her.'

Michel was pleased with the way he'd handled it: no edge or influence. If Georges decided he didn't want to see his birth mother, he couldn't possibly be held to blame. But with what Chac had to say as he came back on the line – pausing momentarily as Georges left the room – Michel began to wonder whether perhaps he should have tried to influence Georges, mould him, push him where he wanted. Things hadn't changed: each time he feared the Lacailles might slip from his grasp, everything else quickly went to the wind.

32

'You feel completely relaxed . . . feel yourself drifting deeper, deeper . . .'

Elena was in the small room listening in, breath held as Lowndes pulled Lorena down through the final stages. This would be the first acid test of whether Ryall might have hypnotized Lorena: not everyone was susceptible.

'But you're still aware of my voice. You're able to follow my instructions, do what I ask. Deeper . . . deeper . . .' Silence for a few seconds, only the sound of Lorena's steady breathing. 'You're in a deep sleep now. But can you still hear my voice, Lorena?'

No answer from Lorena, but Elena imagined that she'd nodded, because Lowndes immediately said, 'Good. Good.'

Longer pause this time, then: 'Now let us go back to one of the nights your father came to your bedside – any night – did he at any time do what I've done now: talk you into a deep sleep?'

'I . . . I don't know. I can't remember.'

'Can't remember?' Lowndes was doubting, disbelieving. 'But you'd surely remember clearly something like that, Lorena. Or is it that your father *told you* not to remember?'

'I don't know . . . I can't say.' Lorena was flustered, her breathing rapid and fractured.

'Can't say? I think more like won't say.' This time it was a statement. Lowndes decided to head abruptly in another direction for questioning. 'Last time we spoke, you mentioned Mr Waldren counting some numbers – seven . . . eight . . . Is that when he was counting you down into sleep or bringing you awake again?'

Elena's heart was in her mouth. Waldren? But there was merely silence, Lorena's breathing slightly laboured, uneven. Lorena didn't seem to have picked up on it. But Elena could sense her uncertainty: the misuse of the name might have thrown her, or maybe, as Lowndes feared, Ryall still held her in check.

Seven . . . eight . . . Lorena recalling the counting had given Elena the first clue, then Gordon's private investigator had mentioned that

Ryall had performed on and off as a magician at children's parties to pay his way through university. One of the clippings he'd faxed Gordon revealed that part of his act sometimes involved hypnotizing the parents and getting them to do all manner of silly things. No doubt a great hit with the children; though not so popular when used against them, Elena thought sourly.

'It's okay, Lorena, we're your friends,' Lowndes prompted, trying to ease her from the dead end, her uncertainty about where to head next. 'And it's okay to tell us. Your father only said that you shouldn't tell anyone else *after* he'd counted you back awake, didn't he?'

No answer. A heavy swallow, then the steady, rapid fall of Lorena's breathing returned.

'And we're still there with you – he hasn't counted you back awake yet. So it's okay . . .'

Another swallow, then: 'Are you sure?'

Lowndes seized the advantage. 'Of course I'm sure. We're your friends . . . Your father would *want* you to tell us. We're still with you now just the same as he would be, waiting for his countdown . . .'

Silence again, back to Lorena's fractured breathing, her uncertainty. Elena's hands were clenched tight together with expectancy. Lowndes had mentioned that Ryall had probably built something in to protect himself: that would be the second breakthrough stage.

'He'd *want* you to tell us, Lorena,' Lowndes repeated. Brief pause, then: 'So let's move on to when your father has already put you in a deep sleep, like now.' Lowndes had obviously decided to take the initiative to break the deadlock; or maybe he felt that part of Lorena's uncertainty was that she didn't know where to start her story. He'd have to lead her by the hand. 'What happened next?'

Still silence from Lorena. Elena counted up with one finger against the table. One. Two. Three. Almost in time with Lorena's breathing.

'He's already soothed your brow . . . told you everything was okay. Is that what he continues to do – stroke and soothe your brow?'

Five. Six. Finally, hesitantly: 'Yes, he . . . he continues stroking me, but gently on my cheek now, saying everything's okay, okay . . . we're all alone now. Nobody else around to disturb us.'

Lowndes eased a deep breath. He'd told Elena that one of his worries was that the protective key could be quite complex, involving an unusual word to be repeated: it could take them hours to hit on it. Though that method had drawbacks too in that a subject could stumble on the word in real life, or what they thought was that word, and suddenly start talking. He'd hoped that there'd simply be a 'no one else once awake' key.

Back to the silence. 'This is *your* story, Lorena – so you have to lead us through it, tell us what happens next.'

Elena sensed Lowndes' reluctance to continue prompting. He'd had strong reservations about hypnotizing Lorena initially: it was outmoded, something he rarely practised any more, but also it was viewed as strongly suggestive. False Memory Syndrome could all too easily be claimed, especially if it was seen that he'd in any way led her.

After a second. 'He . . . he continued stroking me. My neck, my shoulders . . . then lower . . .' Lorena swallowed hard.

'Where was he touching you then?' The most Lowndes dared prompt.

Another long pause. 'On . . . on my breasts.' Then, as if uncomfortable with what she'd just said, she moved quickly on. 'And all the time he was saying it's okay . . . it's okay. It's our little secret. Nobody else will ever know.'

Elena closed her eyes and felt herself sucked back down into the darkness of the chine. Ryall had probably been molesting her practically from day one, back even to when Lorena'd first visited her that day and they'd gone down into the chine. And all the time he'd been dragging her into his own private darkness every other night. Straight from the hell of the sewers and orphanages to Ryall's personal magic-show hell-hole.

Elena shuddered, could hardly bear to listen as Lowndes wrenched Lorena through the rest: her father's hand travelling lower, lower, until it was between her legs. Ryall gloating, telling her it was okay to enjoy it, to feel excited. It was their secret, remember. He wasn't going to tell anyone.

It was a difficult passage for Lorena. She paused frequently, her breathing laboured, staccato, her voice often pushed out in bursts in between breaths. And it was also difficult for Lowndes. Several times he sighed deeply; it was evident that he'd rather she didn't have to relive these memories. His awkwardness, his frustration with not being able to openly prompt her came across clearly at moments. Elena could sense him wanting to reach out, guide her through the more difficult parts, help her wrap her tongue around words and descriptions she thought she'd never have to speak.

And all the time Elena had harboured doubts, sometimes small, sometimes large – but practically all the way through she'd had *some* reservations about Lorena's claims. And Lowndes too only forty-eight hours before had doubted Lorena, and once again Elena had been swayed. Anger, frustration, just wanting to hug Lorena tight and say again that she was sorry, sorry, sorry for ever having doubted her. And tell her that now it really was okay; she was finally safe. Elena suddenly pictured herself showing up at Ryall's door before the police had even arrived to tell him personally the news that Lorena would *never* be coming back, and as he registered surprise she'd swing a punch flat on . . . Elena was distracted. Lowndes' questioning had changed direction.

'Don't you mean *Eileen* the aid worker? She's the one you contacted for help.'

'No, Elena – that's her name. She's the one I phoned. She visited originally with someone else, a local social worker, before she finally got me away.'

Oh no! Elena's heart sank like a stone. The realization had first hit her when Lowndes said 'Mr Waldren' in reference to Ryall: the whole idea of hypnosis was to uncover buried secrets, get to the truth. But that worked equally for *all* buried secrets. She felt like bursting in and screaming *'Stop! Stop! We've already got what we want.'* But it was too late: Lowndes had picked up the thread.

'Got you away?' He tried to sound casual, mask his astonishment.

'Yes. Got me away from England and the problems with my father, Mr Ryall. She's here with me now.'

'What – here as in here in the next room? Waiting for you?'

'Yes.' Questioning tone, faint surprise that he didn't know this already.

Elena's heart was pounding hard and her mouth was dry as Lowndes wound the session down. Still she waited in the room rather than walk straight in; as if she was an errant schoolchild hiding in the stock cupboard in the hope that the teacher wouldn't find her.

Sound of a door opening and closing as Lorena went through to the reception area, then seconds later Lowndes swung open the door to her room.

'I think we need to talk.'

'Yes. I think we do.'

Within two hours of putting down the phone on Georges and Chac, Michel decided to phone Mundy.

He'd spent the time deep in thought in his office or pacing up and down the squad room, frantically turning over all the possibilities. One advantage of being out in the cold: nobody called out to disturb him, spoil his train of thought.

Could Chac's reading of the situation be right? He started to work on angles as soon as he was off the line; suddenly he felt he should be back in the fray, pushing, moulding things how he wanted. A possible ace card to play occurred to him after only half an hour; but if Donatien said that he didn't want to see her, he wouldn't get the chance to play it. There wouldn't even be any reason for him to contact Mundy. They'd all just have to sit tight on the rollercoaster and wait and see if it derailed, as Chac suspected it might.

But with all that had gone before, everything they'd risked to get to this stage – Michel saw that as an unacceptable final chapter. He couldn't leave anything to chance. He decided to phone Mundy straight away, before he'd even received Georges' return call.

Mundy listened patiently as Michel explained the latest developments. He sighed long and hard as Michel finished. 'Strong, heartfelt case. Couldn't be stronger. But you know the rules with this type of programme. Absolutely *no* contact with outside.'

'I thought that with the emotional stakes in this case and the fact that it's so unusual, there might be an exception. We could cut some slack.'

'Nothing could be worse emotionally than not to be able to turn up at a loved one's funeral – but we never let them go. A case a couple of years back with Pepe Aquilana. His mother died while he was on the programme. And, believe me, he loved his mother, doted on her – *and* she was around all of his life. But we couldn't let him go.'

'I know.' Michel had half expected this response, had his game plan prepared. 'But that's mostly because funerals are the first place they look. They expect the mark to come back for a loved one's funeral, and they're waiting. That's why you didn't let him go. But this is different – she's new on the scene, nobody has even a sniff of her. Until the other day, not even Georges or the Donatien family – so certainly not the Lacailles. She could see him and they wouldn't know the first thing about it.'

'I don't know. I don't know.' Mundy said it more to himself. Then after a second: 'No doubt Georges Donatien says he wants to see her?'

Michel sensed Mundy was starting to waver; just a touch more. 'From our earlier conversation, I think he'll want to. He's going to get back to me later.'

'Then why don't we just wait for his confirmation. He might say no, he doesn't want to see her.'

'I . . . I wanted to make sure of the ground first: where S-18 stood.' Michel purposely appeared hesitant. 'I didn't want to build his hopes up only to let him down. He's already had one let-down with not being able to speak to his fiancée. And . . . well, we've got another problem.'

'What's that?'

Mundy was where he wanted. Teed up and ready for the swing through. 'I'm worried that Donatien isn't going to last through the programme. Only three days in, and he's missing his fiancée like hell. The fact that he isn't allowed to speak to her has hit him hard.'

'Withdrawal symptoms – happens a lot. He'll probably get over it in a week or two.'

'I don't think so. Him wanting to speak to her is all tied in to a sort of guilt complex over what he's done. He feels he needs to explain that this has nothing to do with her father; that it's all just about Roman and survival. He feels that her father was good to him, and he doesn't want it seen that he's let her and her father down, betrayed them. And for good measure he wants to throw in that he still loves her. Maybe he sees that as the final noble gesture: "I still love you, but look what I'm sacrificing for it." And if he's not going to get the chance to pass that on, get closure on the whole caboodle with her and her father, then I think the guilt's just going to work deeper. We'll end up with a problem – he won't last the course.' Michel's voice was doom-laden as he hit the last words. Part of it had been passed on earlier by Chac, part was him filling in and embellishing – but hopefully the whole was seamless. Only twenty-four hours sitting on the fence and once again he was back to steering events where he wanted them to go. The fear of losing grip on the Lacailles was again running through him like raw voltage.

'So, what's the solution?'

'I think there's a way of using the situation now with his birth mother to our advantage. Killing two birds with one stone.' Michel explained his thinking and Mundy stayed mostly silent, confirming only a couple of small points. At the end he was back again to 'I don't know', but Michel sensed that Mundy was warming to the idea, his earlier reservations were fast dying. He was eighty per cent there.

'As soon as you hear from Donatien whether or not he wants to see his birth mother, let me know.' Mundy exhaled like a deflating tyre. 'I'll give you my decision then.'

Except for a couple of times when Lowndes looked down and shook his head, his eyes hardly left Elena's as she ran through the whole sorry saga of the past weeks.

'You mean the police are seeking you now, as we speak?'

'Yes. The last four days – since we left England.'

'*Oh boy.*' Lowndes ruffled his hair, clutching at it. 'Some mess.'

'I'm sorry.' Seeing the weight of problems she'd carried with Lorena suddenly shift to Lowndes' shoulders, she felt the need to apologize. 'But I just didn't see any other way through it. Ryall had blocked all the routes – if I'd turned my back, she'd have been trapped there. And if I hadn't made out I was Lorena's mother, you probably wouldn't have seen her. She's the only one you'd take authority from.'

'Right.' Lowndes looked at her levelly. 'One truth at least.'

Elena glanced away awkwardly for a second, then gestured towards the session couch. 'And as things turned out, in the end I was right to take that action. Vindicated.'

'Yeah, yeah. Vindicated.' Lowndes chuckled nervously. He was quickly back to ruffling, trying to clear his thoughts. Then stopped abruptly, looking up again. 'Look – what you've just told me, you never told me. Right? Otherwise it might be seen that I've been an accomplice in this too.'

Elena raised a quizzical eyebrow. 'I don't see how that's such a problem now. I've got to contact the police in any case, hand Lorena over and tell all about Ryall. Given that my reasons for taking her were well founded, I don't see that they're going to pursue it. And certainly Ryall won't be in any position to press charges.'

'True. But . . . but that's not the main problem now. This really all goes back to my first concerns about False Memory Syndrome.'

'What sort of problem?' With Lowndes' hesitation and his eyes suddenly having trouble meeting hers directly, Elena got the first warning signs that this was no light problem. One last hair-ruffle and Lowndes leant forward with forearms rested on his knees to explain.

He'd mentioned False Memory Syndrome at the outset of the sessions with Lorena, and particularly before this last session now involving hypnosis.

'The reason that I raised the subject again is that under hypnosis the

397

patient is considered as highly prone to suggestion. That's why I was reluctant to employ it, particularly in a potential child abuse case. But, as you pointed out, it was probably the only way to draw Lorena out. And you were proven right on that front. We succeeded there, and we have every right to feel happy with that success.'

Lowndes paused and drew a long breath. 'But unfortunately it could all too easily end up a hollow victory.' Lowndes went on to explain a case a couple of years back involving a close colleague in Montreal. A similar child abuse claim where the main evidence was gained on the psychiatrist's couch. The father screamed 'False Memory Syndrome', said that the psychiatrist had planted the idea in the child's mind, and he got off. 'There's been a half-dozen or more such cases nationwide the past five years, and all of those just involved conventional therapy. With hypnosis, where suggestion is already seen as a possibly strong factor – one of the reasons in fact why it has become outmoded – the chances of the FMS flag being raised are even higher. It depends how on the ball the adoptive father is – this Mr Ryall?'

'He's a pretty high-profile businessman,' Elena said vacantly. It probably came across as a surrender flag, but all Elena felt was numb. She was still assimilating what Lowndes was saying: no clear thoughts yet. Then she remembered something from the adoption files: 'Oh, and he used to be a barrister.'

'Oh.' The single exclamation was like a pistol shot, echoing and ricocheting round the room: *No chance, no chance, no chance.*

In the following silence, as the prospects of a doomed case against Ryall settled like a grey shroud where only moments before Elena had seen nothing but bright hope, it suddenly dawned on Elena that Ryall had probably been aware of this contingency from the outset. The chances of his secret being discovered were slim enough, but this was the final safeguard: even if it was, he'd known all along that FMS would be his get-out. All of her efforts and the dramas of the past weeks had in the end been for nothing. He'd covered every possible option. Controlling men. Story of her life.

'No, no!' She shook her head. That couldn't be the final note; she couldn't let it be. 'Surely Lorena can't just go back to him. The police can't possibly let that happen.'

'No. But you probably know how these things work as much as me. Lorena will go to foster parents for a while until this whole wrangle is sorted out. But I wouldn't hold your breath on this one going against Ryall. She'll probably end up having to go back to him

– and the best you can do is try and complicate the legal process as much as possible to delay that inevitability.'

'Delay?' Elena jumped in. Only moments before Lorena in her mind's eye had been free of Ryall for ever, and now she was reduced to desperate bargaining for time. 'How long do you think we could play things along?'

'A good lawyer should be able to spin things out for a year, eighteen months. But don't forget Ryall is going to be pushing just as hard to cut that time back, short-circuit things. And I don't think you'll have helped your case any by taking Lorena from her home in order to bring her here. Abduction, probably arguing that the evidence shouldn't even be considered because it was gained under forced, criminal circumstances – if Ryall's lawyer pushes all the right buttons, they could get it thrown out in a preliminary hearing within only a few months.'

'Right. I see.' Elena blinked slowly. The abduction she recognized as an obvious strike against her, but she hadn't realized that it might also get the main evidence thrown out. The chances of nailing Ryall were slipping further away by the minute. She'd hardly had a chance from the start, let alone as the half-crazed woman she was now: her nerves shot from the stream of valerian pills, the pressure-cooker anxiety of playing hide-and-seek with the police, and only a few hours' sleep grabbed in days. She felt strangely pathetic, that somehow she could no longer get anything right: wrong about her father, and while she'd been right overall about Ryall, she'd read everything else wrong; in the end she'd been ineffectual, unable to change anything. Michel Chenouda would probably phone her that night and tell her 'no go' on that front as well. Dead ends at every turn.

Maybe they should be glad of small mercies: six months' respite, perhaps even a year or more. But to have Lorena go back to Ryall after that time, fully knowing that he was molesting her, was somehow even crueller, more unacceptable. She voiced that thought. 'I couldn't possibly let her go back knowing that. I'd do again what I've done now – abduct her.'

Lowndes shrugged awkwardly, glancing towards the reception room where Lorena waited for them. 'The thing is, she doesn't know what's happened yet. She was speaking under hypnosis. And if the tapes were entered in camera, she never would get to know. Unless of course you won the case.'

Elena considered the option for only a second before discarding it.

She shook her head, cradling it with her left hand as she gently massaged her right temple. Another secret hidden, more shadow games; she'd spent too much of her life playing them already.

Seeing her so forlorn, the storm clouds settling in her face, Lowndes felt the need to reach a hand out. She thought she'd cleared the last hurdle, and now he'd suddenly put another half dozen in front of her. 'Maybe I've painted too dark a picture, but I didn't want you to get carried away with false hope. And that's only how I see it from the Canadian perspective; things might be completely different in England. When you speak to the police, the best thing is to get their view. They might well see a brighter and better way through.'

Curiosity. In the end that's what won the day.

Everything else all but cancelled out. On the one hand the fact that she'd left him alone without any attempt at contact for all these years; on the other that she'd obviously gone to considerable trouble to make contact now: search agencies, the trip from England, finally the orphanage. She'd let him be given away, unforgivable; but then she'd been so young, the father domineering. Perhaps a couple of years older, she wouldn't have let him go.

Chenouda said that she'd blotted it out, too painful. What did that mean? That she thought of him frequently but blotted it out? Or that she blotted it out from the start and rarely thought of him? How much thought, how much blotting out? Given her work with the aid agency, it certainly looked like the guilt had stayed with her. Thought, blotting out, guilt? With each passing minute that Georges pondered and paced on the safe-house veranda, the questions multiplied. He'd only get so far quizzing Chenouda; probably he'd passed on most of what he knew. For the rest, the only way would be to meet her face to face.

Then there were the many gaps to be filled in his own life. One that already sat comfortably was knowing that Nicholas Stephanou wasn't his real father. He'd always found it hard to accept that that spineless wonder, consumed only with burying his own misery at the bottom of a whisky bottle, selfishly and heartlessly giving him away to an orphanage so young – when he too was blinded by grief over the loss of his mother – could possibly be the same blood.

His mother? But at the same time he'd revered what he thought was his mother: so beautiful, died so young. She was a victim, just like him. He'd touch her photos longingly in the dark days in the orphanage and dream about her. Think how nice it would be to feel her hug and hold him tight, feel the soft press of her lips against his cheek. Now those fond memories would be sacrificed, and *that* he didn't feel so comfortable about. In the balance. It was difficult.

But the action of Nicholas Stephanou and the orphanage had left by far the biggest shadow on his life. His memory of Maria Stephanou had been little more than a fragment, fading fast with the years: in the end it was more what he hoped or imagined her to be like from her photos that had stayed with him, rather than the brief reality he recalled from before the car accident.

Shadows that plagued him for years with his second family – or was it now the third? – the Donatiens, Claude and Odette. They loved him, doted on him, but Claude Donatien's business ups and downs through the years had meant that often things had to be cut lean. He was a jobbing builder, and whenever there was a property slide their own home fortunes slid with it.

They weren't able to have children of their own and there'd been another adoption planned, a baby sister for him, but in the end tight finances had put paid to that too. But despite the see-saw problems, Claude Donatien always managed to bravely smile his way through. He never let them drag him down, in any way overshadow his affection for him as a child, nor did he hide in a bottle like Nicholas Stephanou; or at least he never showed it. Odette too was amazingly supportive throughout. She never balked at anything or strayed from Claude's side.

Though it was many years before he'd seen those attributes as in any way positive. When the problems hit, his predominant fear was that once again he'd be given away. The financial pressure would crush Claude, or Odette would leave him because it was finally one crisis too many, and in the mêlée he'd be given away.

Nicholas Stephanou and the orphanage had left him with deep-rooted insecurities that had hung over him most of his life. Even in his teens, when abandonment no longer held the same threat, he still harboured resentment, viewed his adoptive parents' problems with disdain. Probably what had made him so driven to end up in finance and banking. He wouldn't make the same mistakes.

That didn't change until he'd been through his first yuppie years in banking and had a bellyful of shallow people who chased money to the exclusion of all else – including loved ones and family. Possibly they even viewed him as one of them, didn't realize that to him family was vitally important, with money mostly a means to that end. It was only then that he finally started to appreciate the Donatiens: despite their financial problems, they'd always put him first, kept the family bond strong. Now he'd seen the other side of the coin: money dividing families. Battles over estates and wills; money all too often taking pole position over a child's welfare in divorce battles, or children cast aside and forgotten in the rush as one partner found a better financial match somewhere else.

In comparison Claude and Odette had suddenly shone through as heroes. Champions of how to survive business crises and still cling on, hold body and soul and family together. Most other men would have long ago been trampled under, but Claude had this amazing bounce-back quality; he'd have probably made a good spokesman at a small-business survival conference. And with a little financial help and guidance from Georges, business had been good the past five years; perhaps that gentle touch on the rudder had been all that Claude needed all along.

But still on occasions it was laid at his door that his attraction to the Lacailles was because of his own past family insecurities: that he saw in Jean-Paul a strength and security that had been lacking in both Nicholas Stephanou and Claude Donatien.

And all of that as a result of *one* abandonment – now there was meant to be two. Maybe that's why the insecurity had wormed so deep: a part of him had always known that it had happened twice.

Elena Waldren. He uttered her name on a slow breath, watched thoughtfully the vapour drift and disperse in the cool air. She could probably fill in a lot of the gaps in his life, shades that had never been fully clear. But having spent so long coming to terms with what he thought was his life to date, he wasn't sure he was ready to have it upended yet again. He was curious, curious as hell. But was he ready for the Pandora's box that might be opened up?

He was still pacing and rolling the pros and cons on his vapoured breath when Chac knocked on the glass behind him.

Chac waved him in as he slid back the veranda door. 'Michel on the line for you.'

33

John Lowndes leant forward and stopped the tape as it came to the end.

At the other end of the line, DS Crowley stayed silent a moment longer before he asked whether that was it. The wavering in his voice was discernible. The tape had unsettled him. 'Is that all of the session?'

'Yes. Yes, that's it.'

Elena had asked Lowndes to set up a conference call to play the tape, so that he was there for confirmation and any psychiatric-related questions she couldn't answer. Crowley merely wanted a few points clarified about the total number of sessions and the dates; asked if he, Dr Lowndes, could confirm that what he'd just played was an accurate recording of his last session with Lorena Ryall – then asked to be put back on to Elena.

Elena had already flagged Lowndes' concerns with FMS, and now spent a moment more filling in detail. 'Now I don't know how that sits with you, Sergeant Crowley – but it sits very badly with me. In fact, it makes my flesh crawl thinking that in the end Lorena might have to go back to Ryall. So please tell me some good news.'

'I don't know. In a way what Dr Lowndes says is right, and things run pretty much the same here as in Canada – there's at least a couple of similar cases that I can recall. But that by no means makes this an impossible or hopeless case – it's just that the chances of successful prosecution might only be thirty per cent or so. If we could get anything else – say, like Mikaya Ryall coming forward; some extra testimony that wasn't gained under hypnosis – that could increase the chances.'

'My husband went to see her.' Elena sighed heavily. 'She was a stone wall, didn't want to even talk about it. And she might be just the same as Lorena – not be able to recall anything while awake.'

'True.' Crowley was at the same time filling in some of his own gaps: he'd been curious about what had happened when Gordon Waldren had met Mikaya. 'But an official visit from us and some extra pressure might just open her up. It's worth a try.'

'Yes, I suppose so.' It felt strange, having run like a crazed rabbit from the police these past days, to suddenly have them on her side, calmly discussing how they might work together to nail Ryall.

Crowley felt guilty building up her hopes, but then she'd asked for good news and that was the best he could give. With the abduction, their chances were probably far less than thirty per cent, and with odds so low it was doubtful the CPS would even take the case on. But he didn't have the heart to tell her that, make everything appear so hopeless at the first strike.

And also he didn't want to have to face that himself. She'd only just played the tape and broken the news, but already he felt his blood boiling. It was bad enough that Ryall was molesting the girl, but he'd been so arrogant and condescending with pushing them to trace her. Crowley recalled the way Ryall had spoken to him, and he felt like putting Ryall on a spit roast. But how? From what Elena Waldren had told him, without a doubt it looked like Ryall was going to walk.

Flesh crawl. He couldn't have put it better, but his position stopped him voicing it, being forthright. By the book. Sometimes it was frustrating. The seed of an idea started to form at the back of his mind, but it wasn't exactly something he'd want to discuss on an open police line.

'Look – you've just broken all of this to me. And there's a score of things I'd like to check internally before I give you a final opinion. Is there a number I can get you on in an hour or so?'

Elena was back at the hotel to take Crowley's return call, and by then he had the whole game plan worked out. She was almost breathless at its audacity.

'Do you really think it could work?'

'I certainly hope so. The thing is, what other choice is there?' Crowley was calling from an outside booth, having already primed the man whose name he'd passed on to Elena. 'We could contact him and run this, we've used him before – but it could take ten days or so to get the paperwork through, with also the chance that it won't get approved. Concerns about police entrapment and all that. You contact him directly and he could have it all up and running by tomorrow. You don't want to leave Lorena exposed to Ryall any longer than you have to.'

The mention of Lorena's exposure made Elena consider again what she saw as the main problem. 'The trouble is, to pull this off Lorena's going to have to be in on it. She's going to have to be told that Ryall's been molesting her. Knowing that, I'm not sure she'll be able to face going back to him – even if it is only for a matter of days.'

'That's the one question I can't answer for you. Whether or not she'll be strong enough to go through with this. But that *is* the choice right there: nail-biting worry for a few days, but if it works she's rid of him for ever. Or taking chances with a court case in the knowledge that there's a seventy per cent probability of her going back to Ryall in six months or a year.' Crowley suddenly felt he should mention his concerns about the CPS, so that she had the full weight of the options. 'With the odds so low there's even the chance of them deciding not to pursue the case at all. She could end up back with him in only weeks.'

There was silence at both ends of the line for a moment. Another blow. Elena sensed that Crowley wanted her to take the leap, but she just wasn't sure Lorena was up to it. She'd braved the worst that the Bucharest streets and orphanages could throw at her, but playing this knife-edge game with a wily old fox like Ryall was something else again. She moved on to other issues to give herself a moment more to think.

Crowley told her not to worry; Ryall wouldn't give her any trouble with abduction charges. His plan was to remind Ryall of the tape she'd left with Gordon, which made it clear that Lorena had consented, then comment that one of the sessions in Canada could be seen as damaging in regard to the claim that he'd molested Lorena – though in the end they'd decided it was inconclusive. 'But of course if he was to press for your prosecution, you'd no doubt bring all of that out in your defence. That should be enough to warn him off.'

When they came to travel arrangements, Elena said that she didn't know yet if she could travel back with Lorena. 'There's something very important that I might have to stay for.' She paused only for a second before adding, 'I'm hoping to meet up with the son I haven't seen in twenty-nine years. He was taken from me at birth.' She originally wasn't going to explain to Crowley, but it struck her that he might think it odd that she'd let Lorena travel back alone, especially given what Lorena might have to face.

They arranged that if she was staying she'd take Lorena to the British embassy. Crowley would make the necessary arrangements directly with them from that point. 'Either they'll send someone or we will. Quite honestly, I'd fly over myself and hold her hand all the way if it was going to make her brave enough to go through with this and help us nail Ryall.'

Elena got the first hint of antipathy between Crowley and Ryall; or maybe it was just the tape she'd played. But, everything else filed and sorted, the problem was back before them: whether a ten-year-old girl could help them succeed where the system had failed.

Ryall had probably been molesting her for years, dragging her down into a deep hypnotic sleep so that he could do what he liked with her. His eager hands travelling all over as her small body lay inert; her steady breathing suddenly fractured, more hesitant, but only part of her subconscious registering what he was doing. And he'd probably done the same with Mikaya for years before that. Elena shuddered with revulsion at the thought. And now when they finally revealed to Lorena what her subconscious had kept trapped for so long, they wanted her to lay inert for Ryall one more night so that they could get the proof to nail him.

Elena rubbed her forehead and glanced towards her hotel-room door. Lorena was downstairs, no doubt still swapping stories over the bar with Alphonse. In the end only Lorena could decide if she could possibly face that. Throw the decision back to a ten-year-old girl. The rest of them were hopeless: the system, Crowley and, most of all, herself – strung out from pills, stress and lack of sleep – she was the last one balanced enough to decide. 'I'll talk to Lorena and see what she thinks.'

Elena was still in the same position minutes later, hands clasped anxiously together, chewing lightly at her knuckles, wondering how on earth she was even going to begin to broach this topic with Lorena – 'I've got some good news and some bad' – when the phone rang again. It was Staff Sergeant Michel Chenouda.

'Mrs Waldren, I've got some good news.'

'I was planning this all for tonight. If we're going to do this, we should move quickly. One thing I stressed in your favour is that you've just arrived – nobody knows about you. As time goes on, that advantage could be lost. I was thinking, say . . . ten o'clock tonight. Is that okay?'

'Yes, yes . . . I think so.'

'You'll have to come on your own . . . So can you make arrangements for your daughter by then? You won't be returning till tomorrow morning.'

'Yes, uh . . . I have a friend she can stay with.'

'Fine. Now it's a few hours' run. A two-hour flight by small plane, and *the car drive each end. And as soon as you start heading out of the city, you'll have to wear a blacked-out visor and a headset. Secrecy is absolute on this — nobody's to know where he is.'*

Funicelli listened to them go through the last of the arrangements, then phoned Roman. Fourteen minutes later Roman was alongside him in his car as he replayed the tape. They were five blocks away from the Montclair on Rue Berri. No point in keeping up the look-out: the police might run a sweep before coming by to pick her up. They'd return later and start following.

Roman checked his watch as the tape ran to an end. 'Just over four hours, huh. We're going to have to move fast.'

Funicelli nodded thoughtfully. He hit Stop and rewound. 'You should listen to the conversation she had just before.'

'Right.' Roman was still thinking about the tight schedule and the flight. Particularly the flight: that could give them problems tracking and following. It took him a moment to switch to what was happening on tape. He smirked almost as slyly as when he first heard Chenouda had given her the green light. 'Sounds like she's a bit of a player herself.' Some scam with the young girl and the British police, and she'd told Chenouda it was her daughter. But he didn't have the mind space to throw it around much, his thoughts were quickly back on his own problems. Maybe Roubilliard would be able to help with this flight dilemma. In half of Roubilliard's distribution territory in the northern reaches of Quebec, light aircraft were one of the main modes of transport.

Roman raised Roubilliard on the phone. He knew at least half a dozen guys with small planes. 'But probably the best bet is a guy I know with a farm up near Chibougamau — mainly because right now he's here in Montreal for a couple of days. Flew down yesterday.'

'Is he someone you'd trust? Some heavy stuff could go down.'

'Yeah. He's run more than a few kilos for me in with the seed packets and farm supplies.'

'Okay. Get back to you.' Roman was on the phone almost constantly the next hour: Jean-Paul, Frank Massenat and twice more to Roubilliard, who by then had in turn confirmed arrangements with their pilot for that night, Mel Desmarais.

Only ninety-four minutes since Chenouda's call to the hotel and they'd worked out every last detail. Two and a half hours left until she was picked up at the hotel. Roman met up with Massenat forty minutes later and they grabbed some kebabs and falafels from a takeaway on St-Laurent and sat eating them in a side street in Roman's BMW, waiting. Funicelli had gone to hire a car for them to follow Waldren – no familiar registrations in sight – and would join them again at 9.15 p.m.

Roman made one last call just before Massenat arrived, to Gianni Cacchione. It was a call that he knew one day he'd have to make, but events had brought things forward. Once Georges was hit, the genie was out of the bottle. He felt strangely empty, morose, after putting down the phone. He'd weighed this from every side so many times that he thought he'd worked the guilt through long ago. Jean-Paul had cast him aside, showed little thought for him while pursuing his foolhardy plans; he'd brought this on himself. Maybe it was just that with Jean-Paul gone, there would be no more challenge, nothing more to strive for; he'd miss the banter and confrontation, playing in the shadows which he did so well. From now on, *he'd* be in the spotlight.

'You think everything's going to go okay?' Massenat asked.

'Yeah, it's not that.' Heavy rain slanted against the windscreen, and Roman broke off from the repeated tapping of one finger against the steering wheel as he peered up at the night sky. 'Just not the best night to be flying. So go easy on the falafel and the hot salsa; I ain't brought a change of suit.'

'Art. It's Jean-Paul. I need a favour.'

Art Giacomelli in Chicago listened thoughtfully as Jean-Paul explained his dilemma. 'Things got that bad between you, huh?'

'Well – it's just I don't know whether I can trust him with this or not. There's always been some bad feeling between him and Georges, and I'm afraid that in the heat of the moment he might do something rash. It's important to me that this is done right.' Jean-Paul could hear the slow draw and exhalation of a cigar or cigarette being smoked Giacomelli's end.

Faint smacking of the lips as Giacomelli chewed it over a second longer. 'I can help, Jean-Paul, no problem there. But it's very short notice – three and a half hours. I'm not going to be able to send one of my own guys. The closest that could make it is a guy I know works out of Toronto – Dave Santagata – "Santa Dave" as he's known.'

'Is he good? Can he handle something like this?'

'Yeah, one of the best. I've used him a lot. Young, keen, but not hot-headed. Cool professional all the way – he ain't earned the catchphrase "Santa always delivers" for nothing. Don't worry, he'll keep Roman in check.'

They made the arrangements. 'Santa Dave' would catch the next shuttle flight from Toronto and arrive with half an hour to spare. He'd call Jean-Paul directly from the airport, by which time Jean-Paul said he'd have phoned Roman and told him he had one more along for the ride.

Jean-Paul looked up at Simone as he hung up, his mouth slightly skewed. 'Is that okay? Do you feel better now about things?'

Simone ruffled her hair. 'I don't know. I don't know.' She thought again of Georges' panic about Roman that night in the restaurant, then the abduction; and now it was Roman being sent to get Georges out of the clutches of the RCMP. Perhaps someone else riding shotgun like this would make it okay, but still she felt uneasy. She shook her head. 'Can't we use someone else instead of Roman?'

'Who, *who*?' Jean-Paul held out both hands. 'I can't go myself. Even when the family was more involved with crime, I never got involved with such things – with security. Let alone now. And Massenat on his own without Roman's direction would be useless. Like sending in a sheepdog without its owner.'

Simone didn't answer. She cast her eyes down, shaking her head. Jean-Paul could tell that she was distraught, anxious, but he didn't know what else he could do. She looked better than in the panicky first hours after Georges' disappearance, but not much. Her hair was tidier but still lank, her mascara smudged where she'd rubbed at her left eye, and her face was taut with tension.

He wished he could just reach out to her as he used to when she was a young girl, gently stroke her hair and say, 'It's okay, it's okay.' And she'd look up at him with big eyes and immediately trust, and that would be the end of it. But she was older now, time had moved on and passed him without him noticing – or had he just been too busy taking care of business? It seemed only yesterday she was a little girl. Still he might have been able to get away with reaching out to her, but these problems with Roman and Georges seemed to have put an extra barrier between them that was difficult to reach across.

He felt a sudden pang of fear again, a heavy constriction in his chest, at the thought that he might lose her over this. In a way he had as much to lose as her if it all went wrong.

Before the call to Art Giacomelli, he'd laid out clearly how he saw everything. They *both* desperately needed Georges back to talk to him:

409

Jean-Paul felt sure that Georges going into the WPP was purely as a result of the abduction. He wanted to reassure that he'd had nothing to do with that, and hopefully then go ahead with his original plans of getting Georges away to Cuba for a while. And Simone no doubt wanted to let Georges know her feelings, see whether their relationship had any future – which Jean-Paul sensed she hadn't even got clear yet in her own mind. He'd batted on Georges' behalf at least in one area: she felt stung that she'd received no call, considered it a clear indication of how Georges felt – and he'd defended that it was probably more to do with the rigours of the programme. 'They wouldn't allow him to call – no matter the excuse.'

Jean-Paul shook his head in sympathy with her. 'I don't think Roman would dare play renegade on this one. He wouldn't be able to face me if he did. He swears blind that he had nothing to do with the abduction, that it was down to Gianni Cacchione. But even if it was Roman, he was playing under the table where nobody would know and he could get away with blaming Cacchione. Now he's out in the open with nobody else to blame: he wouldn't dare take the risk. And with Giacomelli's man looking over his shoulder, he won't even get the chance.'

Simone looked up slowly. 'I hope so. I hope you're right.'

And for a moment, with her eyes fixed on his, it was easy to believe she was a child again, blindly trusting. Things hadn't really changed that much, Jean-Paul reflected: just with each passing year everything became more complex, the explanations to maintain that same trust longer.

Elena looked down at the street-lamp light bars playing across her lap as the squad car made its way through the city, and she recalled Uncle Christos in the taxi the day before she'd flown out. Streetlight and shadow playing alternately across his face as he'd told her only half the truth about her father. And she'd in turn told everyone else only half the truth. Now you see it, now you don't.

Shadow games. And now Ryall with Lorena. *Close your eyes . . . trust me.* Elena closed her eyes and bit at her lip. She wished she could be as brave as Lorena. She'd left her at the British embassy over two hours ago, and the parting had been emotional, tearful.

At first Lorena had been in shock and very reluctant when Elena told her what had been revealed at Lowndes' last session, then explained Crowley's plan. She'd agreed with Lowndes and Crowley to spare Lorena from actually hearing the tape, she just told her that some things in the session pointed to her being right about suspecting that Ryall was molesting her. But very quickly their roles had become reversed and it was Lorena telling *her* not to worry, she could handle it. 'If that's how it has to be, I can do it. Don't worry.' Once again one of those Kodak moments when Lorena was suddenly old beyond her years, drawing from some deep inner resolve that had helped her endure the dark days of the orphanages and sewers. She'd survived a thousand rats down there; this was just one more rat.

Returning from the embassy after leaving Lorena, Elena nursed a Scotch up at the bar with Alphonse to steady her nerves, and after a while felt she had everything under control again. But gradually images started to bombard her: baring her soul to Gordon, fainting in the orphanage, Uncle Christos and her mother on the phone turning her world upside down about her father, the Donatiens telling her that they didn't think she'd be able to see her son. 'I thought you knew. Haven't you heard the news?' And it was all going to end here, now, in only a few hours.

Within half an hour of the squad car coming to pick her up, she was in pieces again. A few hours' meeting to explain away a lifetime. She was back again to frantically working out what she would say. Where would she even start? Would she open with how sorry she was or just plough into explaining, then apologize later? Would she hug him first, or again wait till later and the moment was right? Or, if she felt the same as right now, would she just stare at him dumbly with her whole body shaking – too numb to put into words the nightmare she'd been through to finally get to see him – then break down into tears and weep out her catharsis on his shoulder before she could even utter a single word?

Elena kept her eyes closed for a moment and listened to her own breathing as she sank deeper down into her own solitary darkness, trying to keep it even, get her nerves steady again. They'd be hitting the city outskirts soon and she'd have to put on the blacked-out visor and the headset: she'd have a couple more hours then for her own private contemplation. *Wished she could be so brave.* She thought she might get some images from the chine to guide her, tell her what to do, but there was no longer anything there. Only darkness. She was on her own.

★

411

'Fuck you! Fuck you! *Fuck you!*' Roman hissed into his mobile. He'd already pressed 'End call' after speaking to Jean-Paul. He gave the phone one last clench before tucking it back in his inside pocket.

'We got company,' he said in a flat tone to Massenat.

'Yeah, I gathered. Either it's Maria's mother or someone else you're not too keen on.'

'Look, Frank – leave the fucking jokes to me, okay?' Roman was slow in pulling his stare from Massenat to look blankly ahead through the windscreen. His temples ached with tension and he wiped a bead of sweat from his forehead with the back of one hand. 'Some fucking bright torpedo from Toronto Jean-Paul wants to ride along with us. Santa-fucking-something, one of Giacomelli's golden boys.'

'Oh, right.'

The silence following said it all. They had a problem. Roman cursed Jean-Paul: he either suspected something or just wanted to make doubly sure everything went right. All these years of being pushed deeper into the background, but this was the final insult: when it came to something important, one of Giacomelli's pet school monitors sent along to keep tabs on him.

Roman had protested, but not too strongly – that would have made Jean-Paul all the more suspicious. He'd said that he already had one of Roubilliard's best along to fill the last place on the plane. Jean-Paul fired back that they didn't come any better than this guy and, besides, they were relying on Roubilliard too much as it was: the pilot plus a few more of Roubilliard's men at the other end when the plane's destination became known. Anyway, it was all cut and dried. 'Art has already agreed to send him – and I wouldn't want to let him down. He'd be upset.'

Let down. Upset. Roman felt the extra pressure like a leaden shoulder yoke. Giacomelli wasn't the sort of person you upset. Jean-Paul probably thought he was being clever, the perfect dilemma to keep him in check: *don't think of stepping out of line, because now you'll not only be putting my nose out of joint but Art Giacomelli's as well.* But Jean-Paul had no idea of the extent of that dilemma. Jean-Paul's death would be bad news as it was to Giacomelli, though he'd put that down to Cacchione. But one of Giacomelli's own going down was quite another thing, and Giacomelli would no doubt then also link the two and point the finger at Roman.

Roman was careful to shield his worries when forty minutes later he greeted 'Santa Dave', but with each passing minute weighing up his options, his nerves had pulled tauter. One more thing to worry about just when he didn't need it, and no simple solution that he could see. If he had any remaining doubt or guilt about what he was doing, it went in that moment: once Jean-Paul was gone, he wouldn't have to worry any more about dancing to his tune.

Thirty-five minutes later they were rolling, following an unmarked RCMP grey Buick Century with Elena Waldren accompanied by two plain-clothes officers Roman didn't recognize. No Michel Chenouda visible.

As they took the turn-off for the Pont Victoria, Funicelli realized the Buick was probably heading for St-Hubert Airport. It took just under thirty minutes to get there. Funicelli was happy that it wasn't one of the major airports: better and closer access to the perimeter fence and less aircraft activity. He observed patiently through night-sight binoculars for a while before he saw them emerge and head towards a plane: a Piper Saratoga.

'Okay, gotya. Number is SXR35467.'

Roman relayed the number immediately to Guy Campion, waiting for the last half-hour in a phone kiosk two blocks from Dorchester Boulevard. Campion made a note of the number and type of aircraft, but had to return to his office to make the enquiry. An access code number had to be given by computer to get the information from the Air Traffic Control central database, but it was generic for the main server at Dorchester Boulevard. Campion was confident that it couldn't be traced.

He keyed in the aircraft type, registration number and place and time of departure, and asked for its destination. Thirty seconds later it came up on screen: Cochrane, Northern Ontario. Campion left the building to make the return call, said only those few words and hung up. The whole exercise since Roman's first call had taken only twelve minutes.

Roman phoned Roubilliard with the destination. After a moment consulting a map, the closest chapter Roubilliard could see were the Lightning Bars, based in Timmins, about fifty minutes' bike ride away. 'I've done a bit of business with them before, but best thing is I phone and see if they're up for it. The other option is a team I know well based in La Sarre, but it's almost two hours away.'

'Mmmm. Cutting it too fine,' Roman replied, having mulled it over. 'Let me know how you go with the Timmins guys.'

They were close to meeting up with Mel Desmarais at Point aux Trembles airfield by the time Roubilliard called back with the news that he had a green light from the Lightning Bars. 'Their head honcho, a guy called Jake Kirkham, says that he'll go himself with two men. Sounded keen: don't think they get too much excitement up there in Timmins. They'll watch for the aircraft landing and follow from there. So maybe a couple of hours to get back to you with where they've gone.'

'Yeah, looks like it.' Roman checked his watch. Their own flight would probably be about fifty minutes to an hour behind, so they'd learn the final destination halfway through. Forty minutes or so to check the lie of the land and prepare, then they'd move in. 'Catch you later.'

With the quick-fire volley of calls back and forth, Roman's adrenalin was racing: he was back in control, in the hot seat. His left hand tapped on his thigh, beating out the rhythm of the mounting nervous tension in his body. They swung into the Point aux Trembles airfield and a figure waved as the car's headlamps fell on him. Trenchcoat with fur collar, wild wavy red hair and beard, and a large silver crucifix dangling from one ear.

'All we need – the fucking Red Baron,' Roman remarked, bringing a chuckle from inside the car to help ease the tension. The plane behind Desmarais looked hardly big enough to carry the five of them and the wind was still sharp, flurrying tree branches and Desmarais' hair.

There was only one thing left to make that control complete, Roman thought, looking at 'Santa Dave' ahead of him as they got in the small plane. There'd been too much else going on for them to exchange anything more than a few words, but now he needed to draw 'Santa Dave' out more, get him to open up: like an undertaker measuring a client, try and weigh up whether or not he could get away with taking out 'Santa Dave' without at the same time making a coffin for himself courtesy of Giacomelli. There wasn't much time left now for Roman to decide what to do.

Barry Crowley sent Sally to escort Lorena from Montreal. She had the best French in his department and he felt it was a task more suited to a woman.

But apart from light, incidental conversation about what food or drinks Lorena wanted or the in-flight movie, Sally felt stuck for conversation.

Normally with an abduction or missing person, she'd have asked if they were looking forward to returning home. Although Crowley hadn't gone into detail, he'd shared enough for her to know that there was a problem with things at home. Crowley had a plan afoot to tackle it, which also involved sending a couple of officers to see Lorena's sister at Durham University. Home was a subject to be avoided.

So all that was left was to ask Lorena a few tame questions about what she'd seen in Montreal and whether she liked the big brown bear in Mountie uniform Sally had bought for her at the airport during the two-hour wait for the return flight.

'Yes, he's very nice. And very big – probably the biggest teddy bear I've ever had.' Lorena looked down wistfully for a second. 'Though I haven't had one for a couple of years now.'

'Right.' Sally nodded and smiled. The measure of how much Crowley knew about ten-year-old girls' tastes: his own daughter was only seven and he probably thought the fluffy-toy stage lasted until they were young teenagers. But he had insisted that Lorena be bought one, and also that it should be large. 'Something that could have been given to her by the Canadian police rather than Mrs Waldren and could take pride of place in her bedroom.' A bear in Mountie uniform was ideal. Crowley was worried that if Ryall thought it was from Elena Waldren, he wouldn't let Lorena keep it.

But while Sally tiptoed around whether Lorena was looking forward to returning home, she suddenly realized that the mention of the bear was a reminder of what the girl had yet to confront. Lorena was doing a good job of putting on a brave face, but as she looked ahead towards the movie screen, Sally could clearly see the shadows working beneath the surface. The girl was petrified.

Sally didn't know what else to say, so after a moment just reached across and gently clasped Lorena's hand. 'Don't worry. I'm sure everything will be okay.'

34

'And she's already left?' Claude Donatien asked.

'Yes, just about forty minutes ago.' Michel Chenouda glanced through his office window to the squad-room clock. Seventy per cent of the staff had already left, but a faint hubbub rose from those remaining. With the numerous calls he'd made and returned in the past few hours, some of the activity had spilled over to them. 'She's staying overnight and returning tomorrow.'

'And you're sure that she'll bring a message back for us.'

'Yes, sure. That was the deal made. Messages for both you and his fiancée.' Michel had been more concerned with Georges' worsening withdrawal symptoms over Simone, but he'd had his parents in mind too. In only a few months Georges might start to feel the same way about them. The ideal halfway house: Georges gets both to meet his long-lost mother and to send messages to his loved ones. Two birds with one stone, and who better to add poignancy to the messages. Michel dropped his voice a note. 'There was just too much danger attached to either yourselves or Simone seeing Georges. This was the best compromise I felt we could make. I hope you understand our position.'

'Yes, I . . . I understand. I just hope she keeps to what was agreed and brings back messages.'

'I'm sure she will.' Listening to the strain in Claude Donatien's voice, Michel wondered how much he really did understand, and whether any parent could. After the message, nothing. No contact at all. It was a pretty poor substitute: a single written note to fill the space of the long years they'd never see him. Again Michel felt a twinge in his chest at what he'd done, but then what other option had there been? Georges dead, the loss would have been even more final and heart-rending. 'I've already spoken to Georges about the messages, and they're very important to him. And I've also got one of my men there to remind him. I'm sure they won't get forgotten.'

There was a faint buzz and crackle on the line towards the end, and Claude said, 'Sorry, I didn't quite catch that last part. We had a

416

telephone engineer call a couple of days back about a fault, but the line seems worse than ever.'

'I said I've got one of my men there as well, so I'm sure the messages won't –' Michel stopped mid-track, a lightning bolt running through him. 'What was that you said? A telephone engineer?' His voice was suddenly high and strained.

'Yes . . . uh, called a couple of days back. Maybe three.' Claude stammered at the new sharpness in Michel's tone.

'I thought I told you to let me know if anything unusual happened. *Anyone* called to your house out of the blue.' Michel was almost shouting. A couple of heads turned in the squad room.

'Yes, but . . . but this happened *before* you told us. Before it had even been announced about Georges' attempted abduction and him testifying.'

'How long before?'

'Well, uh, the day before . . . maybe two days.'

The lightning bolt hit the pit of his stomach. Michel felt physically sick, and his hands were shaking so hard that for a moment he feared he might drop the receiver. He should have realized! He'd marked the announcement of Georges testifying as the pivotal point, but Georges had already been missing two days and his parents' home was one of the first places he might phone. Michel slowly closed his eyes. There was still a chance he might be wrong.

He answered 'I don't know yet' to Claude's 'What's wrong?' 'I've got a few calls to make.' He signed off hastily, looked up Bell Canada's number, and dialled straight out, giving them the Beaconsfield address and approximate time to check their records for an engineer calling. They said it would take five minutes or so. They'd phone him right back.

Michel burst out of his office like a whirlwind. He spotted Maury in the corner and signalled to him. 'Grab a guy from Denault's department who knows anything remotely about electronics and head out with him to this address in Beaconsfield.' He hastily wrote down the Donatiens' address. 'And if he's got anyone else to spare, they should at the same time head here to check.' Michel wrote down the Montclair Hotel address underneath and ripped the page from the notepad. 'I'm looking for telephone bugs planted at each – like now! *Pronto!* So separate cars to each if Denault can spare anyone.'

Maury grabbed his jacket from his chair-back as Michel whirled away. One of his office lines was ringing. Michel grabbed it on the third ring. It was Bell Canada. No, they had no record of a call made at that address, or indeed in that street, in the last week.

'Last noted service call in that street was eighteen days ago, at number 1426.'

Michel's stomach sank like an express lift, and for a moment he felt dizzy, his legs unsteady. His own voice sounded distant as he said 'Thanks' and hung up. Maury was only halfway down the corridor, and already he knew what to expect. But he had enough to make S-18 stop Elena Waldren reaching her destination, or get a message to the safe house. If he waited for Maury to confirm there was a phone bug, he might be too late.

But when he got hold of the S-18 control-room operator, she advised him that she didn't have any of the safe-house details on her computer, the only people who had that information or could authorize contact were Superintendent Mundy and Inspector Graydon.

'Then put me through to one of them.'

'They're not available right now. Inspector Graydon's on a week's break, but I might be able to get a message to Superintendent Mundy later on tonight if it's urgent.'

Michel ascertained what she meant by 'later', then asked for her name. He eased a weary sigh. 'Look, Constable Fuller – or Melanie, whatever you'd prefer. In two hours it will be too late. It's that simple. The mark that Mundy and your department have gone to so much trouble to protect will be dead! *Unless* you can somehow get a message to Mundy right now, or find some other way to contact the safe house or the team heading out there now to warn them.'

She started stuttering under the pressure. 'I . . . I'm sorry. I'm doing the best I can with what I have. The operation is top-security coded, and there's just no other information on screen.'

'I know. I know.' Michel backed off a step, clutching at his hair. He'd simply got the stone-wall protection he wanted, and there wasn't a single frame of reference he could think of to guide her. Two S-18 men who apparently made up the following month's guard shift had flown up from Ottawa to pick Elena Waldren up from her hotel and escort her all the way. No idea where they were flying from and no names; nor were any exchanged in the few conversations he'd had with the safe house. That was the whole point of the operation.

Constable Fuller drew fresh breath. 'All I can do is try and raise Mundy. He says that he's not available – but I don't whether that means he simply can't be contacted, or whether he just doesn't want to be. If he starts shouting, I'll blame you.'

'Thanks. But quick, huh. Every second counts on this.'

'I think I've got that clear. I'll phone you back in ten minutes if I can't raise him on his phone or bleeper – sooner if I can.'

'So just the four jobs, huh?'

'Yeah.' Santagata shrugged. 'And then this one now.'

Roman's mind was racing. Four contracts? Didn't show much of an allegiance. But then if they were key contracts, 'Santa Dave' could be one of Giacomelli's stars.

'All pretty much the same as this?'

'One the same, backing up. The other three hits.'

They fell silent again. Roman kept his gaze straight ahead, watching wisps of mist drift past the plane's window as they battled through the night sky. He'd asked the questions nonchalantly, as if it was only of passing interest; and he didn't want to press too hard or ask too much – Santagata might latch on that he was angling at something. Guys like him usually had natural antennae for warning signs: it's what kept them alive. He could feel 'Santa Dave''s eyes on him for a moment.

Roman tried to ease the tension in his body. Massenat was wedged between him and Santagata at the back of the aircraft with Funicelli in the front with Desmarais, but for a moment Roman worried that the nervous tapping of his heel and hand might give him away – that Santagata might pick up that it was more than just due to the rough flight and what lay ahead of them.

The questions had been sporadic, not only to make them not so obvious, but because for the first half-hour the flight had been very bumpy. On the worst parts, as the plane lurched and tossed and rattled, they all fell deadly silent. Nobody felt like talking. Except for Desmarais, who whooped excitedly, 'Just like riding a wild bronco at Calgary.' The sight of four tough guys gripped with white-knuckle fever seemed to tickle Desmarais. Roman felt like saving an extra bullet for him.

Then the weather settled a little; there was still the occasional bumpy flurry, but not so violent.

'It was mainly cross-border jobs in Canada,' Santagata added after a moment. 'Art was always worried about me flying back out or crossing the border straight after a hit, especially as I became known. I think otherwise he'd have used me more.'

'Right.' Roman nodded solemnly. He felt a tingle rise up through his body until it reached his fingertips. Santagata had said it as if to explain why Giacomelli hadn't used him more, but at the same time he'd signed his own death warrant. Roman knew every hit Giacomelli had made in Canada, and none of them were major! 'Santa Dave' was dispensable. Giacomelli wouldn't stretch that far to make amends, especially not with himself and Cacchione later declared as a team. Giacomelli wouldn't risk that level of confrontation over a lone hitman.

But having made the decision, the only question was when? He'd originally planned to do it later: he could claim that Santagata simply got caught in the cross-fire with the police. But there'd be too much going on then, too much else to think about. Roman chewed at his lip and felt Santagata's eyes on him again briefly, glancing sideways and meeting them only for a second: dark, almost black eyes, even more impenetrable now with the weak cabin light. Difficult to read into.

Had Santagata picked up on something? On some invisible electrical signal running between them? – *He's planning to kill you, so make sure to take him out first.* Or had it been a double-bluff all along? Santagata at the same time measuring him for a drop? Jean-Paul had never really believed him about not abducting and trying to kill Georges – and this was the payoff. After all, that's what Santagata did most: hits, not playing chaperone.

He felt the sudden pressure of it all like a powder keg: the bumpy flight, Santagata's eyes on him intermittently, what lay ahead and the contingencies yet to cover – his nerves wound so tight with it all that his whole body was shaking almost in time with this tin-can rattling through the night. And all because he couldn't bear living in his brother's shadow a day longer. If he didn't make the . . .

'*Jesus!*' The bottom dropped out of his stomach as the plane fell abruptly. A sharp shudder as it hit the end of the air pocket, followed by some heavy tilting and swaying – then it rose again as swiftly until Roman's stomach was in his throat.

'Here goes again,' Desmarais commented, wrestling with the joystick.

They saw sheet lightning out to their right, about five miles away. The small plane bobbed and jolted, but just before the next sharp drop Roman noticed one advantage: Santagata was no longer paying him any attention, his eyes were fixed stonily ahead.

The drop was longer this time, the shudder so hard as it bottomed out that the cabin lights flickered off. Roman decided in that instant to take his chance: he simply might not get as good an opportunity later! In the darkness he leant forward; and as the lights came back on he already had the .22 out of his ankle strap and pointed at Santagata's face.

Santagata took a second to focus on the gun. Distant lightning flickered against one side of his face. 'What the fuck is this?'

Massenat between them eased back with his hands held by his shoulders. A 'this ain't nothing to do with me' gesture.

Roman smiled slowly. 'You know those Bond films where he's got a gun pointed at the bad guy, but he daren't fire it in case one of them gets sucked out of the plane?' Roman steadied the .22. 'That's the one advantage of these low-flying shit-heaps. We don't have that to worry about.'

Roman squeezed the trigger as Santagata lurched and reached across. Still he would have got the shot off cleanly, but at that second came another sharp drop, the cabin lights flickering off again.

Then Santagata's hand was on his arm, pushing it away. Roman struggled to point back at Santagata's face. But Santagata was strong, straining hard, and Roman had to bring his left arm up to get any movement back towards him. He daren't risk another shot on the off-chance: too many danger points it could hit.

The cabin lights flickered back on and he saw a patch of Santagata's hair matted with blood, a trickle running down his forehead. He'd grazed the skull with the first shot.

Santagata reached for his own gun with his other hand; Roman didn't notice but Massenat did. He pinned down the gun arm, then whipped his elbow sharply back into Santagata's stomach. Santagata keeled forward with the blow, heavily winded.

All the strength went from Santagata's body in that same instant, and Roman wrenched his arm free as Santagata's grip loosened.

Roman grabbed Santagata's hair and pulled his face back up straight. 'So it's goodbye, Mr Chips.' Santagata's eyes had barely refocused on him as he put the gun by his left eye socket and pulled the trigger.

Santagata's head flew back with the impact and Roman was left with some hair in his hand. He wiped it disdainfully on his seat.

Desmarais half turned, his face as red as his hair. 'You guys wanna pull stunts like that – least you could do is fucking warn me.'

Roman smiled drolly, his breathing still ragged. 'Just imagine it's still the fucking Calgary stampede – but now the cowboys are shooting in the air.' Roman was glad that something could rattle Desmarais; it was his turn to gloat at the fear in Desmarais' face.

They sat out the rest of the turbulence in silence, Santagata's body intermittently double-lit by bursts of lightning. Then Desmarais dropped two thousand feet so that Roman and Massenat could risk opening the door to get rid of the body.

'Never did like paying fucking excess baggage,' Roman remarked as it sailed out.

Massenat chuckled briefly, but the silence was quickly back. They'd weathered one storm, but there was a tougher one yet ahead. And now they were one man down.

Eight minutes later Jake Kirkham called. They'd seen the plane land, and the car had just left the airfield. 'Two men and a woman inside. I'll call again when they've reached the safe house. Let us know what you want us to do then.'

When S-18's Melanie Fuller phoned back after only seven minutes, Michel thought she had good news. But no, Mundy hadn't responded to his bleeper message yet.

'It was something else I thought I should pass on straight away. One of the guys here with a high clearance pass was able to access a bit more information. He says that it's a Sector 14 operation, three-man monthly rotation guard team. Still pretty basic info, I'm afraid – but it might help.'

'Sector 14? Where's that?'

'Northern Ontario. An oblong block stretching between Hearst, James Bay and Iroquois Falls, sixty miles from the Quebec border.'

'Okay.' All Michel wanted to do was race to a map, but it was immaterial: he'd already decided that if they didn't raise Mundy fast, he was heading to the area.

'I'll call you back as soon as I've got something on Mundy. If he doesn't phone within the next few minutes, we'll start trawling his regular haunts.'

Michel said that he'd probably be on the move soon. 'At least make a start on heading to Sector 14.' He gave his mobile number and signed off.

He'd spent the last few minutes pacing the floor of his office and the squad room like a caged lion, the door left open between the two, and spent only another minute continuing pacing before diving for the phone to make the arrangements for his flight.

Sea King helicopter would be the fastest way. One could be brought up from the RCMP and army air-base on Montreal Island within minutes. 'All that's needed is a nearby roof pad.'

Michel got Christine Hébert to arrange the roof pad and liaise back with the air base, and two minutes later she confirmed that she'd laid everything on with the West-Laurent Towers just three blocks away. 'And the chopper's already left. Said they should land there in about six minutes.'

Michel managed to get everything together with a minute to spare. Breakneck run along the Dorchester Boulevard corridors and down the three blocks with an ERT* of four – with him still shouting and filling in details as they went. He was breathless as they rose in the lift to the roof pad. His heart pounded hard and heavy. Still no call back on Mundy's whereabouts.

He glanced at his watch. They wouldn't get there for at least an hour and a half after Elena Waldren's arrival. He shook his head. They'd probably be too late: raising Mundy and phoning the safe house to warn them was still the best bet.

Art Giacomelli looked at the numbers on the computer screen. They hadn't moved for the last fifty minutes. Something was wrong, seriously wrong.

He phoned Jean-Paul and said that he had concerns about 'Santa Dave'. He didn't explain exactly why, just asked Jean-Paul to phone Roman and find out where they were at that moment, and then ask to speak to Santagata.

'Maybe it's nothing. But I'll know for sure from what Roman tells you. Phone me straight back.'

Jean-Paul made the call. Roman answered after the second ring, and Jean-Paul asked how it was going.

'Fine. Everything running to plan. We just landed ten minutes back.' Roman sounded slightly out of breath, agitated.

'And you found out the location?'

'Yeah, it's about a half-hour run away.'

'Where did you end up? Where are you now?'

'Some dead-and-alive place called Cochrane, Northern Ontario.'

It meant nothing to Jean-Paul. 'One advantage of Canada's wilds, I suppose. *If* you want to hide someone away.' A second's pause, then

---

* Emergency Response Team

Jean-Paul asked for Santagata to be put on. 'There's just a small thing I need to clarify with him.'

'He, uh . . . He can't come to the phone right now. He's taking a leak in the bushes. Long flight and too much coffee.' Roman chuckled hesitantly.

Apart from the hesitation, Jean-Paul could clearly hear the engine noise and the rush of them on the move; they weren't stopped by the roadside. Roman was lying.

'I really need to speak to him, Roman,' Jean-Paul pressed.

'As soon as he's finished taking a leak, I'll get him to phone you.' Roman didn't trouble to mask his annoyance. 'That is, if he gets a chance with all we've got on.'

The line clicked off abruptly.

Jean-Paul dialled straight back to Giacomelli and relayed how the call had gone.

'Bad news,' Giacomelli said on the back of a heavy sigh. He explained why. Four years ago Santagata had a hit contract on someone he knew. Problem was the guy was always on the move, but Santagata knew him well enough to be able to buy him a present without making him suspicious. 'So he buys him one of those satellite watches. You know, the ones where you can move from one country to the next and it always shows the right time 'cause it's linked to a satellite. But it also tells you exactly where you are, within ten fucking yards! It's that accurate. And if you know the watch's serial number – which "Santa Dave" did – there's a website where you can find out exactly where it is. So he knew where the mark was, made the hit, then took the watch back.' Giacomelli drew hard on his cigar. 'So tonight he arranged to phone me every couple of hours to bring me up to date – which he's now twenty minutes late in doing – and he wore the watch and gave me its serial number. And for the last fifty minutes it hasn't moved from near a place called Holtyre, a good hundred and fifty miles from where Roman says he is now. So either "Santa Dave"'s thrown the watch out of the plane window in disgust 'cause the battery's flat, or he's gone with it.'

'Let us know if you can remember anything?'

The two police officers had left over an hour ago, but still the words bounced around in Mikaya Ryall's mind. *Remember?* That was half the problem: she'd never been able to remember a single thing clearly enough so that she could say, yes, my adoptive father molested me.

424

He came to my room on this night and touched me here, here and here. It was all just shadows, dreamlike fragments.

But those shadows had haunted every other moment of her life since. It all seemed so real, but when she tried to recall she could only remember it happening in her dreams: nothing she could pass on or tell to anyone else. They'd think her mad. But the shadows leapt out and became all so vivid and real again each time a boy touched her or tried to kiss her. She'd shiver and shrink away in panic, terrified. She'd been called frigid and cold and weird, and a couple of times a lesbian. A few of the boys she'd really liked, and she'd reach out to them tearfully and want to explain: but how could she when the images were only in her dreams?

The tears streamed down her face as she cut through the bed sheet with the scissors, trying to make sure she kept the strip even as she went.

And now young Lorena as well. Mikaya kicked herself: maybe she should have been bolder earlier and said he was molesting her, then try and fill in the gaps later. But each time she ran it all over in her mind, there were always too many questions she wouldn't be able to answer: which nights? Where did he touch you? What did he say? Why didn't you say anything, try and stop him? She shook her head. Even now that they knew why she and Lorena weren't able to respond and fight back, they still weren't able to do anything concrete. They were still trying to get her and Lorena to recall something happening while they'd been awake, from real life rather than dreams. 'Sorry, I just can't help you. I wish I could.' Nothing was going to stop him now.

She wiped at her tears with the back of one hand and started cutting the second strip.

Even if she could remember anything, it was too late. *Too late*. She would never be the same again. She wanted children, loved children. But what would she do? Lie there with teeth gritted, her whole body trembling, until the boy had finished? And if she wanted more children, a proper marriage – night after night of the same? It was unthinkable, a living hell.

And now she'd let Lorena down too by not speaking out. Lorena was suffering the same. Probably it would be too late for Lorena as well – she'd go the same way as her. All Lorena had to cling to was the hope that one day the dreams would fade. Maybe she'd be luckier; for Mikaya they hadn't, and she knew now with certainty that they never would.

Her vision blurred with tears, she looked up thoughtfully to the handle of the high latch window, wondering if it would hold her weight. She'd have to be quick. Her dorm friends had gone to the Student Union bar to give her time alone with the policemen, but they'd be back soon.

Neil Mundy regularly had eight to nine hours a week to himself that were sacrosanct, off-limits to any contact from his department, no matter how urgent: his regular card game, golf round and going to watch the Senators play. But the last two months, since he started dating Suzie Harrigan, he'd added another few weekly off-limit hours.

Twelve years his junior and class all the way. Long auburn hair and large hazel eyes with sweeping lashes that could melt Greenland. Audrey Hepburn and then some. Mundy was in love. But this would be the third time up to bat for him; he wanted to put in the time to make sure that she was the right one. He didn't want to spend his early retirement in lawyers' offices sorting out yet more alimony.

So, when he was with her, his mobile and pager were switched off; she had his undivided attention. Not that it would have made much difference where they'd gone tonight: the Clair de Lune. A popular venue with high-flyers and government ministers, it had banned the use of mobiles and pagers. Otherwise the restaurant would have been a cacophony of endless bleeps and rings. What few were brought along and kept switched on bleeped and rang without anyone paying them attention behind the closed door of a cloakroom.

As they left the restaurant, the air was brisk. Mundy wrapped Suzie's coat around her. In his own coat pocket his bleeper light flashed, but he hadn't yet looked at it nor had he any intention of doing so. Mundy was strict with his time alone with Suzie: nothing like being dragged away on emergencies every other date to give a taste of things to come and kill all hopes of a future relationship.

'Where do you fancy tonight?' he asked. 'The Glue Pot or the Laurier?' They usually went to one or the other after dinner: short night-cap at the Hotel Laurier piano lounge or a longer session listening to live blues.

She mulled it over for only a second. 'Mmmm, the Glue Pot.' She pecked him on the cheek.

Melanie Fuller was still on switchboard, so most of the calls to track down Mundy had fallen to her S-18 colleague, Brian Cole. He called

Clair de Lune twenty-five minutes into his roster, fourteenth on his list.

'Yes, he was here earlier. But I'm sorry – you've just missed him.' An effete, faintly French accent that sounded faked.

'When did he leave?' Cole pressed.

'About ten minutes ago.'

'Do you know where he might have gone?'

'I'm sorry. We make a habit of not chasing after our clients to ask where they might be going.' Mocking tone, the accent more exaggerated. The phone was put down abruptly.

Cole turned and passed the news to Melanie.

She sighed heavily and ran one hand through her hair. 'Keep trying. Keep trying.' She checked her watch. 'It could take him fifteen or twenty minutes to get home, so it'd be worth another try there soon. If not, start working through bars and clubs.'

'If Roman's going to make a move, it'll probably be tonight. Once all of this has gone down, he knows he'll have you to face. Do you want me to send someone over?'

'No, it's okay. I doubt there'd be time anyway.'

'True. But take my advice, Jean-Paul. Either get some protection there fast, or leave the house. Don't just stay there like a sitting duck.'

Jean-Paul said 'Okay' to put Giacomelli's mind at rest, but hanging up he couldn't think of anyone he could call in fast – Roman always took care of that side of things – and the last thing he felt like doing was running scared from his own house. It would feel too much like defeat, like waving the white flag at Roman. Admission that when it came to the crunch the old ways held sway, all of his new aspirations amounted to nothing.

But then he started to became uneasy, agitated. Was that the pool filtration system, some pigeons alighting on the roof, or something else? Raphaël's footsteps upstairs, or were they coming from another part of the house? He suddenly began to feel the isolation of the big house, to feel vulnerable.

He went into his study and took out the SIG-Sauer 9 mm from the top drawer. He was aware of his own breathing falling heavy, but kept his listening honed beyond it for out-of-place sounds. Some faint music now he could pick up drifting from Raphaël's room. Looking out across the dining room and through the windows, he saw a light was on in his mother Lillian's apartment at the end of the courtyard.

He closed his eyes and gripped the gun tight. His hands were shaking, his pulse racing hard. Some flight away from crime this was. A hitman probably moving in, and he hoped to brave it out when he hadn't fired a gun in years. And he wasn't alone in the house. A fine epitaph that would be to all his noble hopes and aspirations: Raphaël walking in to see his father or his adversary in a pool of blood, the other with their gun still smoking. Maybe his father had been right all along: 'As much as you might wish to escape the past, the past will never allow you that escape.'

Maybe that's how it was meant to end, his punishment for being so naive, blindly foolish. Roman had probably been playing him along all the time, and now he'd won the game. With Roman already closing in, nothing he could do to save Georges. Probably Georges could have been trusted after all – Georges who had looked up to and trusted him – and he'd repaid him by turning his back. He might as well have fed Georges to Roman with his own hands. He'd lose Simone without question: she'd *never* forgive him. And if he tried now to stand this last bit of feeble ground, at the same time he turned his back on everything he'd aimed for. He lost either way. Game, set, match.

He snapped himself quickly out. The thought of Raphaël and his mother being there when anything happened overrode all else. He raced up the stairs and rapped sharply on Raphaël's door, swinging it open. Loud wave of techno with a faint beep-beep backdrop.

'Raphaël! We've got to go – leave the house!'

'What? I'll just finish this game, and –'

'Now, Raphaël! This *second!*'

Raphaël saw a look of panic on his father's face he hadn't seen before, then he noticed the gun. He swiftly turned off the game and the music, grabbed his coat and fell in step behind Jean-Paul down the corridor. By the time they hit the stairs, they were at a run.

'We'll just pick up your grandma and head off.'

'What's happening?'

'Long story. Long story.' Jean-Paul said it almost in time with his laboured breathing. 'We'll grab a cappuccino somewhere and then I can explain.'

Lillian was slower, more reluctant to leave without explanation, and Jean-Paul had to blurt out that their lives could be in danger to finally light a fire under her. He gestured with his gun as if to say, *'Why in hell do you think I'm carrying this?'* 'We must leave this second!'

428

He grabbed the keys to the Cadillac on the way out – more space, more protection than his new sports Jag – and seconds later they were swinging out of the driveway. Brief pause to open the electronic gates, and then Jean-Paul turned right on Boulevard Gouin, heading for the city.

Cacchione's men, Lorenzo and Nunzio Petrilli – 'Lorry' and 'High Noon' – weren't Cacchione's first choice, but they were all he could get at short notice. They'd been competent enough on a couple of past jobs and there were two of them. If one fucked up, hopefully the other would cover.

The Petrillis had arrived outside the Boulevard Gouin mansion just eight minutes before, and were still checking out the perimeter railings and the house beyond to finalize their plan when the double gates opened and Jean-Paul's Cadillac pulled out.

They were startled, and it took a second for them to kick into action. Lorenzo fumbled before finally firing up the car, then swung around and started to close some of the long gap that Jean-Paul's car had opened up.

Two hundred yards along, Jean-Paul turned left into Avenue Christophe-Colomb. He was oblivious to the car lights trailing a steady fifty yards behind as he took out his mobile. Suddenly he'd thought of how he might be able to help Georges. The most unlikely of calls, but it was all he could think of.

He tapped out the number and a woman's voice answered. 'Royal Canadian Mounted Police. Dorchester Boulevard.'

'Staff Sergeant Michel Chenouda, please.'

35

Lorena held her breath for a moment, listening.

The faint, muffled voices she'd heard downstairs had stopped. Her parents had stopped talking. Sound of footsteps on the stairs now. Mr Ryall or Mrs Ryall? After a second she could pick up that the step was lighter: Mrs Ryall.

She settled back again and eased out her breath. Probably Mr Ryall wouldn't come to her room this first night; he'd wait a few days. But the waiting would be almost as bad as the fear that he might come in at any minute.

She was tired, very tired. She'd slept on the flight, but only a couple of hours. And now it was three or four in the morning. She'd lost track. But she felt almost too afraid to fall asleep in case Mr Ryall *did* come to her room.

Maybe once she'd heard his footsteps come up the stairs and head for his room, she could relax a little. But then several times he'd come out of his room without warning an hour or two later to see her. It was almost like he knew instinctively the best time to visit, when she was at her most drowsy, her defences weak.

But what would she do? She couldn't stay awake every night, waiting. She remembered what'd happened in the sewers after Patrika had died: for several nights they'd laid awake for hours listening out in case the waters rose again. But after a few nights they were exhausted and would have slept through anything.

What had Dr Lowndes said? 'When he starts counting down, put other numbers and thoughts in your head. Act as if you're succumbing, falling under, but all the time keep your mind alert, resist.' If she didn't get sleep, then her mind simply wouldn't be alert enough to be able to resist.

She held her breath again for a second, listening. Footsteps starting up the stairs, heavier this time. Mr Ryall!

She swallowed hard, looking over at the large Mountie bear. She'd positioned it where they told her, looking straight at her and the bed. Perhaps it would have been better if they hadn't told her anything about it all. They'd tried to put her mind at rest: 'Don't worry, as soon as he starts touching you, we'll be there. That's the whole idea: to stop him touching you once and for all.'

She said she could do it. But now, as the moment was upon her, her heart was racing out of control. Her whole body had broken out in a sweat. Mr Ryall was bound to notice her fear, her body's trembling.

Footsteps moving nearer, creaking some boards among the top steps.

She closed her eyes, feigning sleep. The darkness felt welcoming, her tiredness threatening to suck her under. Maybe she should just sleep through it all, wake up when it was over. If he came in and started counting down, just let herself sink under. Let it all stay in the darkness and shadows, like every other night. Where it belonged! She just didn't think she could bear being awake for a second while his hands moved over her body.

Her breath froze, suspended, as the footsteps reached the top of the stairs; then was released again as she heard them start moving away towards his bedroom. But after a few paces they paused, turned and started heading towards her.

Derek Bell watched the blue-grey images on a monitor less than a mile from the Ryalls.

He adjusted the dials. With the directional mike, he had to work hard to cut down the background hiss. Finally the sound was clear: the fall of Lorena's breathing, the faint rustle of bedsheets.

Rush job, but that was often how he liked them. More of a challenge. He'd only had forty minutes turn-around to get everything planted and the bear sewn up again. The lens was in the cap band, the mike in the belt.

He noticed Lorena look over directly for a moment, and silently prompted: *Get used to not looking. Act as if I'm not here.*

Her eyes shifted towards the door after a second, then finally flickered shut. Faint sound of footsteps from the corridor. The steps receding for a moment before turning and becoming louder again. Bell watched Lorena's eyes open again fleetingly, then shut again.

The footsteps were now in the room, moving closer, closer . . . and Bell clearly saw Ryall – his back at first, then more of his profile. Bell adjusted the focus slightly, his hand staying expectantly by the dials.

Ryall leant over and touched Lorena's hair, starting to stroke it lightly. Bell's pulse was suddenly in his throat. He thought he'd be in for a few long nights, but now he began to wonder.

'You poor girl,' Ryall mumbled under his breath. 'You've been through so much.'

Bell tweaked the volume up a bit.

'So much. Such an ordeal.' The hand continued stroking, now gently tracing across Lorena's brow as Ryall sat on the side of the bed.

Lorena's eyes stayed closed, though Bell knew that she was feigning sleep. Only as Ryall's hands traced down and started gently stroking one cheek and her neck, did she finally flicker her eyes slowly open, probably sensing that it was too much for her to sleep through.

Good girl, good girl, Bell thought. Keep this up and we'll get the bastard. He was leant forward, intently following each small movement, beads of sweat shiny on his forehead in the glow from the screen.

But as Lorena's eyes looked up, Ryall's hand suddenly paused, hovering an inch above her cheek. Had he sensed something was wrong, seen something in her eyes to alert him? Or was he just deciding: count her down into a deep sleep so that his hand could continue its journey, or return another night?

The heavy rotor blades cut through the night sky.

Michel felt their rhythm driving him on, pumping his adrenalin. The energy of the motion and the four men sat with him, rifles and automatics at the ready, were the only things to make him feel positive.

He found it hard to escape the feeling that they were heading there after the event; it would all be for nothing. The cavalry turning up after the last Indian arrow had hit Custer. They must be at least an hour behind Roman and his men. Roman might spend some time checking the lie of the land and finalizing a plan, but an hour?

Michel slowly closed his eyes, the dull thud of the rotor pumping almost in time with his pulse. And there was no doubt now that Roman was on his way. He'd had Maury on the radio phone only minutes ago: phone bugs both at the Donatiens' and in a switching box outside the Montclair. Roman knew every last detail!

'Ontario border ten miles ahead!' the pilot announced.

'Okay.' Michel opened his eyes, nodding. He'd purposely asked for the alert: they'd hit Sector 14 only twenty-five minutes after the border. And if there was still nothing from Mundy, they'd have to start circling. More time lost to Roman.

Michel asked to be patched through again to Melanie Fuller – he'd already spoken to her twice in the eighty minutes they'd been airborne.

No, she confirmed, she still hadn't heard anything from Mundy. 'We just missed him at a restaurant by minutes, but he didn't head home – so now it's down to bars and clubs. But it's more difficult: no check-in reservations. We've either got to eyeball him or find his car. So there's a team out there checking every possible dive, and every patrol car's alerted.'

'We'll be crossing the border any minute, so time's tight now.' Michel had to raise his voice to be heard above the rotor.

'I know, I know. Don't worry, the second I've located Mundy, I'll be back to you.'

Michel's gloom, his sense of despondency, settled like a cloak in the following silence.

'Four miles now to the border,' the pilot announced. 'We'll be crossing any minute.'

But the cloak was heavy, difficult to shake off this time. Six men on a hell-bent mission – *to nowhere.* Probably he'd known all along they'd be too late, but he needed all of this activity so that he could reassure himself later that he'd done everything he could. Because, unlike the men with him, he knew that he was mostly to blame. The set-up so that he could push Donatien into the Witness Protection Programme. Making sure that Donatien's birth mother could see him and take a message to Simone to keep him there. *If you tell a lie . . .*

At every stage he'd pushed things to the limit, and now this was the payback! They'd get there and there'd be nothing left to do but pick through the bodies, see first hand the result of –

Michel visibly jolted as the radio phone went again, thinking it was news of Mundy – but it was Phil Reeves at Dorchester Boulevard.

'Strangest call just come in, Michel.'

'Why? What is it?'

'Jean-Paul Lacaille has just phoned. He's on the other line right now – wants to speak to you.'

Michel was stunned into silence, and after a second Reeves prompted, 'Do you want me to tell him you're too busy to talk right now?'

Michel snapped himself out of it. 'No, no, it's okay. I'll take it.'

Darkness. Constant, all-enveloping darkness.

Elena tried to think of it as the solitude she'd sought in the chine, an escape from all the madness outside – God knows she'd seen more than her fair share these past days – and for a while that worked. She could retreat into her own thoughts, continue spinning around what she might say to Georges. But the bumpy flight did little to help her already ragged nerves. And as the darkness continued, the long minutes stretching into hours – the journey seemed to be taking for ever – her unease returned. This was different! This was a forced darkness, an imposed solitude. In the chine she was always free to make her way back up to the light.

In that moment it struck her why Lorena had run in panic from the chine – she'd spent half her life in forced darkness in the sewers and the orphanages, and now with Ryall. Eyes clenched tight shut behind the visor, Elena silently prayed that it would all go well with Crowley. And she was suddenly piqued at her own rising paranoia: all she risked was rejection, non-acceptance if she said the wrong thing. Probably all she deserved having mostly blanked Georges from her mind for a lifetime. It paled in comparison to what Lorena faced.

She should be rejoicing, not chewing her fingernails – she'd finally got what she wanted. Isn't that what the whole nightmare had been about? Perhaps her anxiety was due as much to that passage as to what was to come. A sense of a lifetime's odyssey coming to a close. She'd get her few hours in the spotlight with Georges to try and make good, and then that was it. And she wasn't just performing for herself: she couldn't help sense her father riding along with her. He'd been unable to track Georges down, make amends before he died: now it was up to her to make amends for both of them.

Forced darkness. But as they hit the last stage of their journey driving from the plane, the chilling account from her last conversation with Michel Chenouda was suddenly back with her: how Georges had been blindfolded in the back of a van and would have been killed if they hadn't intervened.

Probably that journey wouldn't have felt far different from this, Elena thought, settling back for a moment into the darkness and the thrum of the wheels on the road. She shuddered at what it must have been like: going through this same forced solitude thinking that at any second you were about to die.

But as it struck her that in part she was grappling for an empathy link with her son – a reminder of the chasm she now faced with little idea of how to even start crossing it – she pushed the thought away.

★

Brian Cole weaved through the tables of the busy jazz club.

On the small stage, a trio were running through a passable instrumental rendition of Jobim's 'Girl from Ipanema'. He thought for a moment he could see Mundy in the far corner, but as he got closer and could get a clearer view, realized it wasn't him.

Only nine clubs they thought Mundy could get away with visiting at his age, but each one took time to search. They'd split the list between two of them: this was now the third on Cole's list. Bars and cocktail lounges presented more of a problem: they'd made a list of twenty, but there were probably a dozen more they could have added. The other two in their team were busy working through them. The only advantage was that they could rush in, a quick scan, and rush out again.

It wasn't until Cole started down the steps of his next club that his mobile rang. His colleague Tim had found Mundy at The Glue Pot.

'He's here with me now. I'll pass you over.' Tim was almost shouting to be heard above the noise of the club.

Mundy came on with a gruff 'What is this?' – clearly irritated at the intrusion – and Cole sneaked a quick glance at his watch as he explained the problem. Almost an hour and a half into their search: he wondered whether they'd still be in time.

'Come on, come on!' Roman rubbed his hands together and stomped his feet to fight off the cold.

He wore a lined bomber jacket – it was still bitter at night in Montreal, but where they were now felt a good ten degrees colder. And with the waiting around, it was starting to cut through more to his bones.

Funicelli studied the house through the night-sight binoculars: two lights on that he could see. One at the side upstairs which also shone through at the front on to the veranda – probably the main lounge – and the other downstairs at the back. They hadn't been able to check the far side of the house; although the lake all around was iced over, they'd have been too visible. But they couldn't see any reflected glow on the lake surface.

Thirty-five minutes now they'd been waiting for the two men escorting the Englishwoman to leave – an hour and twenty minutes since Jake Kirkham had followed them there. Maybe Roman was wrong. He thought they'd be heading off to a local hotel or, if it was a brief meeting, heading back with the woman – but maybe they were staying the night. The house looked big, but was it big enough to take them all? These places usually had a tight spec: enough room for the guards and the main subject, with not a lot to spare. And already they might have to make room for the woman.

Funicelli had placated that maybe it didn't matter. With the gas he was using, it was going to knock all of them out anyway.

But it was the panicky few minutes between them cutting the telephone and power lines and putting in the gas that Roman was worried about. With only three or four men, one would see to the generator and they wouldn't dream of leaving less than two guarding Georges or risk sending someone out alone on reconnaissance. But with another two, they'd have the extra manpower to check for anything suspicious.

Roman had decided to wait, but now the cold and his impatience were getting the better of him.

'Maybe you're right,' he muttered under his breath. 'Maybe we should take all the fuckers out at the same time.'

'Yeah.' Funicelli nodded mechanically, still looking through the binoculars.

Massenat was to Roman's side, with Desmarais and Jake Kirkham hanging a couple of yards back as if they were only peripherally involved with whatever the three decided.

Roman had quickly set the tone on first greeting Kirkham: Kirkham had glanced at the blood splatters on his shoulder and arm and asked what happened. 'I cut myself shaving.' As Kirkham's eyes shifted to the heavier splatters on Massenat's collar and chest, Roman added with the same wry smile, 'He's got the same razor.' The message was clear: don't pry. We're here to get a job done, not answer twenty fucking questions.

Kirkham's other two goons they'd left over a mile away at the start of the dirt track leading to the lakeside. Funicelli had given them simple instructions on exactly where and how to cut the electricity and telephone wires to the house: one advantage in the wilds, everything ran overhead. But they looked like two rejects from *Wayne's World*; Roman seriously wondered if they could manage that without frying themselves.

'Wait!' Funicelli announced breathlessly, adjusting the sights. Shadows of figures moving across, but as the car interior light flicked on with one door opening, they became clearer. 'Looks like they're leaving after all.'

'Great.' Roman stomped his feet again, but now it was more to mark time: four or five minutes to let them get down the track and clear, then they could cut the lines and move in.

'I know this call is going to seem strange to you – but I didn't know what else to do.'

Michel listened as Jean-Paul explained that his original plan had been to spirit Georges away somewhere, possibly Cuba – but he'd suddenly discovered that Roman had other plans. 'That's why I'm phoning now.'

'I know. That's where I'm heading now,' Michel said, and the line fell silent for a moment. Before Jean-Paul got the impression that his call might have been wasted, Michel added, 'But the one thing I don't know is *exactly* where the safe house is – I know only the general area. Did Roman mention anything to you?'

Jean-Paul was fazed for a second that Chenouda didn't know the location. 'Uuh . . . just some place called Cochrane, Northern Ontario. But no exact address.'

'Cochrane, Cochrane,' Michel repeated, gesturing towards Stephan, the ERT constable with the map.

A moment while Stephan traced one finger about on the map, and then as it settled on one spot he held the map up towards Michel.

'Okay, we've got it. We've got it!' Such was his long-ingrained suspicion of the Lacailles that for a second it struck him that Jean-Paul could be giving him a false location. But he could see clearly that Cochrane was in Sector 14. Another awkward pause, then, 'Thanks. I know it couldn't have been easy for you to call. I owe you a drink for this.'

'Yes, you do,' Jean-Paul agreed, adding drily, 'And lifting the threat of a jail sentence from my head wouldn't be a bad idea either.'

The line clicked off and Michel looked towards the pilot. 'Time estimate for Cochrane?'

The pilot glanced at the map, skewing his mouth as he mulled it over. 'Fifteen, sixteen minutes.'

Michel tried to shake off his earlier despondency that they'd be too late. They still needed to raise Mundy to know the exact location. That call finally came through ten minutes later.

Michel breathlessly explained their dilemma and Mundy said that he'd phone the safe house to warn them and call straight back. But when Mundy's return call came, he had crushing news: subdued,

437

defeated tone as he told Michel that the line was dead. He couldn't get through.

Michel's heart sank like a stone, his hopes fading again.

'What about mobiles?' he asked frantically.

'We don't use them – for security reasons. Too easily tracked and monitored. The secure line is the only line in and out, and it's already dead.'

Michel closed his eyes. This time the image of them picking through the bodies was more vivid, difficult to shake off. But the hardest part, Michel knew already, would be him living with what he'd been responsible for.

Ascending the stairs, Cameron Ryall had been in two minds as to what to do.

It had been one of those days. Three days of being on the police's back every other hour over Lorena with little or no positive feedback, then suddenly out of the blue they'd phoned mid-afternoon to say she was on her way. From Canada!

Ryall shook his head. Most of the police search had been centred on Europe; no wonder they hadn't found her. And now they were fluffing about whether or not to press charges.

'She did give Lorena up voluntarily in the end. And then we've got the problem of that original tape and why she says she took Lorena: what she thought might be happening with her. Mrs Waldren took her to see a psychiatrist in Canada, but nothing conclusive came out of that in the end – which is why she's now returning her. But if we did press charges, no doubt all of that would come out in her defence.'

The call had come through from Crowley. Obviously Turton found it all too awkward to tackle himself. It was left to Crowley to carefully tiptoe round words like 'molested' or 'interfered with'.

Nothing conclusive. Ryall wondered just what had happened at those sessions in Canada. He'd have thought that pressing charges against Elena Waldren would normally have been automatic. Maybe more had come out than they were making out; enough at least for them to harbour strong doubts about proceeding against her.

His step was measured as he made his way up. The thought was starting to rankle: what *had* come out of those sessions, what did they know? Probably now he'd never know, and did it really matter? If it had been that serious or suspicious, *he'd* have been the one the police would be charging, or at the least asking some very pointed questions.

438

His step was a shade lighter as he reached the top. He'd been in two minds, but finally decided not to go to Lorena's room. Let her rest for a few days, settle in. But a few paces along he suddenly paused, having second thoughts. He listened out. Faint shuffle of movement from Nicola in their bedroom. She'd hit the gin and pills even heavier with the nervous anticipation of Lorena's return. She'd be zonked out within minutes. Besides, she'd never interfered, had never dared in all of the eleven years since he'd discovered *her* secret. He remembered the one time she'd caught him by accident with Mikaya; she just turned from the doorway after a second without saying anything. The mounting neurosis of her carrying the burden of his secret on top of her own showed mainly with her increasing diet of pills and alcohol. It was all that kept her going. Pathetic, but Ryall was long past caring. The most important thing was that she wouldn't disturb him.

And Lorena's first night back after such an ordeal! – it was just the time that any father would brow-soothe, reassure. He turned and started towards Lorena's room, his mouth suddenly dry with expectation. And he'd desperately missed her: missed the gentle feel of her skin at his fingertips; the soft, even fall of her breath on his cheek as he'd lean over, lightly trace one finger across her closed eyelids just before he counted her back awake. She was totally his in that moment; he had control over practically her every breath.

He stood stock-still for a second, controlling his own breathing now as he looked down at Lorena; then, his hand visibly trembling, he reached out and gently touched her hair. And in that moment it suddenly occurred to him how he might find out what had happened in the sessions in Canada.

Bell's every nerve was as taut as piano-wire as he watched the images on screen.

And as Ryall started to talk and count Lorena down into a hypnotic sleep, he punched the air with a fist. 'Yes, *yes!* Got you, you bastard! First night back, but you just couldn't wait.'

'*Seven . . . eight . . . Feeling drowsier now, every limb in your body feeling totally relaxed. Drifting deeper . . . deeper . . .*'

Bell was on the edge of his seat as Ryall hit nine and ten, then reached out and lightly stroked Lorena's cheek and passed the same hand twice only inches in front of her eyes.

Then silence. Stone silence.

Bell couldn't tell whether Lorena was in a real sleep or not. Had

Lowndes' advice about mentally counting down other numbers worked?

Bell watched Ryall's hand. It had made contact again at her shoulder and traced down her arm a few inches, then stopped.

Some trivia about the trip and Canada and the rough time she'd been through to which Bell didn't pay much attention – he was too busy watching where Ryall's hand might travel next. Then suddenly he tuned in to where the conversation was heading.

'And when you were there you saw a doctor. A psychiatrist. What did you talk to him about?'

Bell's whole body went rigid. Ryall was digging for what had happened in the sessions! If Lorena was really under, she'd spill the beans any second. The whole operation would be over before it had started!

'About my time at the orphanages . . . the sewers and Patrika. And about my family.'

'I see. Your family. So what did he ask you about them?'

Oh Jesus! Bell swallowed hard. He tapped one finger on the desk by the screen, could hardly bear the tension of everything hanging on what Lorena said next. His eyes were back on Ryall's hand. It had moved a fraction lower on her arm, the thumb spread and touching the side of her breast. But was it enough? Probably not. Could be construed as innocent.

'Come on!' Bell hissed. 'Move that hand lower and –' Then he suddenly stopped, could hardly believe he was egging Ryall on because he feared they might only have seconds left. And it suddenly hit him that if Ryall uncovered their game, realized that they were trying to entrap him – Lorena could be in danger. He glanced anxiously at the phone, wondering whether to call Crowley and stop it all now – except that they wouldn't get there in time. If the game was up, Ryall would know *everything* within the next couple of minutes.

'Different things. He . . . he wanted to know if I was happy with them.'

'Happy with them . . . happy with them? But what did he ask you in particular about them?'

Crunch time. Bell's stomach sank. Their only hope was that Lorena wasn't really under, that she would be able to bluff and lie her way through. Ryall's hand was on the move again: it traced tantalizingly down her arm and across, coming to rest on her stomach. Still not enough.

'He . . . he asked me if anything bad was happening to me. Anything I didn't like.'

440

'What sort of bad things? What did he –' Ryall suddenly broke off, looking towards the door as the telephone started ringing.

Late for anyone to be calling, but then this was the night his daughter had returned: maybe a relative or well-wisher? Bell's pulse raced double-time. Was Lorena awake and fending Ryall off, or relating accurately how the sessions had gone? With the danger of FMS, Lowndes would probably have avoided direct prompts about Ryall molesting her. But within a few questions, Ryall would unearth the truth. The telephone stopped ringing: either they'd given up or Nicola Ryall had answered.

And as Ryall looked down again at Lorena and finished his question, Bell leant closer to the screen, his eyes only inches away, following every small movement: the delicate flicker behind her closed eyes, her gentle moistening with her tongue as she spoke. His hands were balled tight in fists, and he unclenched one and lightly touched the screen. 'Come on, little angel, be awake. Be awake.' But he couldn't tell either way.

Jean-Paul noticed the car trailing him in his rear-view mirror soon after hanging up on Chenouda. Two cars behind, a steady fifty yards. But he was sure it was the same car he'd seen follow him into Avenue Papineau from Gouin. He'd since taken two more turns, and it was still with him a mile further on along St-Denis.

Just to make sure, Jean-Paul took the next right at Rue Jarry, then left again on to St-Laurent heading towards the city centre. It stayed with him at each turn, the same steady distance behind – except for the last turn when almost a hundred yards grew between them when they had to wait for a car to pass before pulling out. No doubt left: they were following him!

'Why are we driving around like this?' Raphaël asked from the back. 'I thought we were going to Le Piémontais?'

'Yes, we are. We are.' Jean-Paul wrenched his eyes from the mirror. He'd frightened them to get them out of the house, but he didn't want to panic them now. He'd told Lillian where they were heading when she'd impatiently asked as soon as they'd started moving.

But his eyes couldn't help being drawn back to the car as he noticed it swing out and overtake the two cars in between, closing the gap again to fifty yards.

As Lorenzo Petrilli cut back in from overtaking the last car, Nunzio asked, 'Do you think he's on to us?'

'I don't know, I . . .' Then, as he noticed Jean-Paul glance once more in the mirror. 'Yeah, yeah – looks like it. I think he must have had some kind of warning. The way he left the house like his ass was on fire . . . and he made us too easily.'

Nunzio looked at his brother for a second, not sure if he was just making excuses for following so obviously; but what he said made sense. He shrugged. 'Whatever. We're going to have to make our move sooner rather than later. Closer to downtown it's going to get more difficult.'

Lorenzo nodded. Right now they could make the hit, swing on to one of the cross highways and get away easily. Downtown there'd be more junctions before they could get clear, and more police cars. Lorenzo put his foot down, closing the gap towards Jean-Paul's car.

Jean-Paul's palms were damp on the steering wheel as he watched the car get closer behind. Surely they weren't going to make a move with his son and mother with him? They'd wait until he was alone? But as he watched the car edge nearer still, that hope began to fade.

With his repeated glances in the mirror, this time Raphaël picked up on his consternation. 'What's wrong?'

Your uncle has sent someone to have me killed. Lillian would be even more distressed when she discovered this Cain-and-Abel drama between her two beloved sons. All he said was, 'What I was worried about earlier.' Then, towards Lillian beside him in the front, he hissed under his breath: 'Cacchione!' The name meant something to her, but not to the boy. That's what it had been about all along: changing their lives so that his son didn't have to live in the shadows like he'd had to. But now his son was in the middle of it all; in the end the shadows had reached out to him anyway.

Jean-Paul's jaw worked tight as he cursed Roman: he'd been so eager that everything else had quickly gone to the wind; he'd broken the golden rule: *never involve other family.*

Jean-Paul took the gun out of his jacket and held it in his lap as the car edged closer – only twenty yards behind now – feeling Raphaël's eyes on him anxiously. His father the great protector. In reality he hadn't fired a gun in years, and Roman knew that too: he'd be an easy target.

The car moved closer – twelve yards, ten – and at that moment its full beam came on, washing them in light. Sudden flash image of him and Roman together as children, playing in the garden on a sunny day as their father called out to them. Happier days. But it faded quickly to the raw reality of the car pressing close behind; he could almost imagine Roman in the back seat goading them on.

Jean-Paul put his foot down, trying to put some distance between them. Streetlights and neons flickered past more rapidly. He had to concentrate hard on the road ahead. A car pulled out suddenly at a turning just ahead, and he blared his horn and swerved around it. He gained some distance, but it was short-lived; checking his mirror, he saw they were rapidly closing the gap again: fifteen yards, then back to twelve again. He checked his speedo: seventy, and creeping up.

Jean-Paul was shaking hard, his palms clammy on the wheel. If they pulled alongside, what was he going to do? If he wound the window down to get a shot at them, he'd be all the more vulnerable. And he wasn't even sure he could get in a good shot and control the car with one hand at this speed.

The lights ahead changed to orange, but he kept his foot down hard, screaming through as it turned to red. The car behind stayed with him, a couple of cars beeping at it as they started across the intersection.

'Watch out!' Lillian shouted as a bike with a weak tail-light loomed suddenly on the inside.

She'd been remarkably restrained so far: normally she complained if he was doing 10 mph over on a downtown shopping trip. Jean-Paul swung a yard out to clear the bike and felt the back drift slightly.

At this speed he risked killing them all anyway. The Cadillac was heavy, difficult to control if he had to swerve or make last-second adjustments. He wished now he'd brought the Jag: they'd have been cramped and had less protection, but he could have weaved in and out easier and sped away and probably lost them. *Heavy*. It suddenly gave him the spark of an idea.

As the car started to close the gap again, this time Jean-Paul let them; he didn't speed up to try and gain distance. But at the same time he had one eye on the car lights coming towards them.

'Okay, I think we've got him now,' Lorenzo announced as he closed the distance down to only five yards. He tapped one finger on the steering wheel as he waited for an oncoming car to pass, then swung quickly out and accelerated. The next approaching lights were some distance away, and they didn't seem to be moving that fast.

Nunzio opened the side window and the air rush filled the car. He levelled his gun: the Cadillac glass was only slightly tinted, he could pick Jean-Paul out clearly. He thought he had him with a clean shot when the Cadillac suddenly surged forward a few yards.

Nunzio looked across as Lorenzo frantically pulled level again, eyes darting between the Cadillac and the traffic ahead. And suddenly the shot was there again. Clean. *Clear.* Nunzio levelled his gun at Jean-Paul's head and eased the trigger.

A heavy kick and the Cadillac seemed to swing away a fraction with the impact. But as Nunzio focused on the starburst where the bullet had hit, he saw that it hadn't penetrated. Bullet-proof glass! The side of Jean-Paul's mouth curled in a smile. Nunzio levelled his gun again.

'Come on! *Come on!*' Lorenzo screamed, glancing across and suddenly registering what had happened.

'A couple more in the same spot should do it!'

'But quick, huh!' Lorenzo's eyes were fixed back on the lights ahead, faint sweat beads popping on his forehead. He could see now that it was a large truck. But they'd still be able to swing back in time.

Nunzio got his aim square-on again, but then the Cadillac suddenly swung in towards them at the last second, startling him – it swerving away or pulling forward again would have been the natural reaction. He squeezed off the shots anyway, saw two more star bursts appear to the right of the first just before Jean-Paul's face loomed inches away and the Cadillac crunched against them.

They drifted away a few yards, and Lorenzo juggled frantically with the wheel, pulling them back in. His eyes opened wider. The truck was bearing down hard, its air-horn blaring – but they should still make it in time. He accelerated to cut in front of Jean-Paul, but at that instant the Cadillac swerved towards them again. Another shot squeezed off by Nunzio, and Lorenzo had anticipated this time by turning his wheel back in just before impact.

But it was no contest – the Cadillac was almost twice their car's weight, and the shunt was much harder this time. They careened wildly towards the truck as Lorenzo tried to make a last-second compensation with the wheel.

Too sharp. 'What the . . .' The back swung around and they slewed totally out of control.

The screeching of tyres and air brakes filled the air. The truck driver had expected them to cut in, or even that if they pulled over slightly there'd still be room for him to pass – so he was late braking. The car fish-tailed at the last moment and he hit it broadside, staving in the driver's side and carrying it along for ten yards before the momentum rolled it over: it turned over 180 degrees, coming to rest on its roof.

The driver finally managed to come to a halt five yards short of the mangled wreck. He jumped out, not sure whether to advance closer or get clear. The driver he could see had been killed instantly, but he was trying to judge whether there was any movement from the passenger when the spilt petrol igniting made the decision for him. The flames quickly leapt higher, and he was only eight paces into his sprint away when the whole thing blew up.

Jean-Paul had pulled over fifty yards down on the far side and they'd got out of the car. He braced one hand on the Cadillac roof as they looked on. His father had bought the car in the midst of their battles with the Cacchiones: it hadn't been able to save Pascal, but his father would have been smiling upon them now if he could see the good use it had been put to. Something from the past to allow them to escape to the future: somehow fitting.

As the explosion came, he could see for a second the excitement reflected in Raphaël's eyes – the stock reaction of the video-game generation – then as it dawned on the boy how close they'd come to death themselves, his face crumpled and he pulled in close as his father hugged him tight. Lillian gently clasped Jean-Paul's hand over Raphaël's shoulder – but still the circle wasn't complete, Jean-Paul reminded himself. If Roman got to Georges, Simone never would be reaching out for his hand.

36

So many emotions.

Elena knew already what he looked like from photos at the Donatiens, so she found herself studying other things: the way he moved, the inflection in his voice, the way he looked at her and smiled – what few smiles there were.

She'd spun so much around in her head about what to say that now she was tongue-tied. She just stood there stuttering, 'How are you?' Then, realizing she'd already said that on greeting, added hastily, 'It's so good to see you at last.' And she wasn't even sure whether to hug him or not – whether that would be too bold, presumptuous.

So in the end she was rooted to the spot, blinking like an idiot – she was still adjusting after her hours in the darkness. And as he'd finally advanced a step, smiling hesitantly – possibly in response to how awkward and nervous she must have looked – they embraced. But it was slightly stiff, almost formal – far from the emotional catharsis she'd envisioned. She could feel the barriers of three decades without contact with that first touch. They wouldn't be torn down in the first minutes, or even in the few hours she had.

But as they sat down and someone called Russell offered her coffee, at least they started to make progress. She hesitatingly started to explain, but as she faltered at one point, not sure where to head next, the questions started coming: my father, what was he like? And *your* father? How old did you say you were when it all happened? Where did you live then? Were you long at the orphanage – did you look around much? So you found out through my adoptive father's brother: I haven't seen him since I was a child – what's he like now?

At first she was glad of the questions, she no longer had to think of what to say next to explain. But after a while they started to feel a bit mechanical, as if she was at a job interview: Georges gauging if she was good enough material to actually be his mother, or if she would score enough points for him ever to be able to forgive her; she could clearly pick up the anger in his undertone on some words. And she was already becoming uncertain again, fumbling for words, her hand trembling on her coffee cup as she sipped at it – when the crunch question came:

'You having to give me away, I can understand – you were so young. But why didn't you try and find me in the years since?' He shook his head and looked down morosely, his eyes slowly lifting again to meet hers challengingly. 'All those years. *Why?*'

And she started to stumble through the rest: her blanking it from her mind; her work with orphaned children to try and bury the guilt, telling herself all along that he'd have gone to a good home somewhere – until Ryall and Lorena. But as she got to that point and her thoughts turned again to what Lorena was now facing and the nightmare odyssey that had brought her here: the search agency in England, the Stephanous, the orphanage, her tears when her mother had told her the truth about her father – *all those years* wasted not only with her son lost from her, but harbouring a grudge that had long ago become misguided – her eyes started filling. She'd got so much wrong for so long. That was a loss that she'd never make good on, let alone in these few hours now.

As her body began softly quaking and she dabbed at the tears with the back of one hand, Georges moved closer and hugged her again.

'I'm sorry. I'm sorry to push you so.' He gently patted her back. 'It's just . . . just that I felt I needed to know.'

'No, no . . . it's okay.' She sniffed back her tears, got more control. 'You have every right to know.' And this embrace, she felt, was suddenly different from their first: more open, welcoming. Maybe there was hope yet that she'd be able to break down the barriers.

As they freed from the embrace and Georges surveyed her face – saw the shadows of the years of pain and guilt in her eyes – that was the first moment he could truly say he warmed to her. He'd spent the first forty minutes clinging too tight to his own long-built-up resentment for anything else to filter through. But the change came more through admiration than any emotional bond or love – maybe that would come later. In that moment he appreciated and admired what she'd gone through to try and see him. She could so easily have just shrugged and turned her back on him for the rest of her life, saved herself the grief.

He smiled ruefully. 'Explains one thing. Your father being a hot-shot banker.' He'd always had trouble relating to Nicholas Stephanou's weak-spirited defeatism, wondering how he could possibly be of the same blood. But he wondered now if that too was what had made him look up so to Jean-Paul: the image of the proper patriarch in his mind inescapably entwined with money and power.

'Oh, I see.' Elena was a second late catching on. She remembered the Donatiens telling her that Georges was in banking.

Their hands were the last thing to part, and there was an awkward lull for a moment. Elena glanced towards the glass sliding doors and the veranda: inky blackness beyond, only a faint moon picking out part of the lake and the ring of trees beyond. Her eyes had been naturally drawn there upon first walking in, a relief from the stark light of the room after her hours in the dark.

'Well, now you know a bit about me. Such as it is.' She chewed her bottom lip, turning back towards Georges. 'I heard quite a bit about you from your adoptive parents, the Donatiens. They're very proud. But there was a lot we –' She suddenly froze. At that moment all the lights went out: all-enveloping blackness, the distant moonlight on the lake the only visible light.

Almost like being back behind the blackened visor, except that now she could hear her son's uncertain breathing along with her own.

Faint sound of footsteps and movement from deeper in the house, and after five seconds some weak emergency lights came on and Russell's voice trailed from near the top of the stairs:

'Looks like a general power outage. The lights on a minute ago at a cabin to the west seem to have gone too. Steve's just sorting out the generator – should be up and running in a few minutes.'

Behind them, Chac's head had peeped out of the kitchen. 'Okay. Keep us posted.' Then with a brief nod towards them he went back in.

She relaxed again. But as she continued talking, she could see that Georges was still on edge, eyes darting, listening out for every small noise downstairs – he was hardly listening to what she was saying.

'What was that?' he asked at one point, tuning back in.

'I was just saying how difficult it must be for you now with your fiancée, Simone. You obviously still have strong feelings for her. Sergeant Chenouda mentioned a note that –'

More alarming noises suddenly broke out: heavy scuffling footsteps and muffled shouting, then a bang that at first they thought might be connected with the generator starting until Russell's repeated shouts rang up the stairs.

'Gas . . . *gas!* Get out . . . oouuu . . .' His pounding footsteps petered out halfway up, stumbling.

448

Georges jumped up, his eyes narrowing. 'You brought them here, didn't you? You brought them here!'

Chac was already three steps out of the kitchen, gun drawn. 'Come on! We gotta go!'

'What?' She was disorientated for a second. Then suddenly her heart was in her throat as it dawned on her what Georges meant. The threat that was upon them. 'No . . . *no*,' she pleaded, reaching out to him. But as she rose, she felt her knees buckle, something sweet in her nostrils and at the back of her mouth, her head suddenly light. And Georges was already out of reach, heading towards the veranda doors.

She wondered for a moment whether this was like the day at the Baie du Febvre convent, and she was just fainting with the upset; or maybe she was still lying on the convent floor waiting to come around and everything that had happened in between had been a cruel nightmare.

But as she saw Chac crumple only two yards away, choking for breath, and Georges sink to his knees as he opened the terrace doors, she knew different. The house was rapidly filling with gas. She saw him get the door half open and partially raise himself to try and stagger out – but at that moment she felt the solid punch of the carpet on one cheek and everything spun into blackness. She didn't see whether he made it.

Nicola Ryall's hand was shaking as she put down the phone, a shaking that became more pronounced as she reached for the bedside drawer and the gun.

'I'm sorry to call so late. It's about your daughter, Mikaya . . .'

It was an antique gun, a pre-Second World War Luger. She tried to remember how the barrel plug, put there to make it look like a replica and avoid licensing problems, worked: unscrewed or pulled out like a stopper?

'She's okay now, stable. But if her roommates had returned a minute later, it would have been too late.'

She fumbled for a second and in the end pulled it out. She checked it for ammunition, almost dropping it at one point with her hand shaking so much: it was fully loaded. He'd always said it was, in case of burglars. And she remembered him mentioning that he'd test-fired it in the fields at the back last summer.

'Still, we're sure that it was a genuine suicide attempt – not just a cry for help. Your daughter had no idea her friends would be arriving back so soon.'

The call was from one of Mikaya's tutors, who'd gone to the hospital with her. Mikaya was heavily sedated and asleep now, but there might be the chance to talk with her in four or five hours' time.

Suicide. Nicola thought of all those years she could have done something, at least tried to stand up to him. But at every turn she'd pushed it away – taken another pill or shot of gin.

My God! She'd even seen him with Mikaya one night, but still tried to convince herself that nothing was really happening. What with the heavy shadows, she just thought she'd seen more than she really had.

She raised the gun slowly towards her face.

All the time the veiled threat that he'd spill her little secret. 'We'll just live our own lives, do our own things from now on. No questions asked.' He'd stopped sleeping with her soon after he'd discovered she couldn't have children – but still it must have been a shock to him coming home a day early from a business trip to find her in bed with another woman. A strange, sly smile had crossed his face, though she wasn't to fully fathom why until later when they adopted Mikaya. Among her village knitting circle of church fête organizers and charity do-gooders, he knew a lesbian scandal would be like a napalm bomb: he had the hold over her he wanted.

She blinked for a second at the gun barrel as it came to eye level, then moved it and held it out by her head.

Still she should have said something. Should have done something. Her precious village reputation in exchange for what had now happened with Mikaya? She closed her eyes, shaking her head. All those years Mikaya must have suffered in silence. A feeble, pathetic trade-off. And poor Lorena was no doubt now suffering the same. Each time the pain wormed deeper: the pills and gin needed to numb it increased. She was at her limit: she couldn't face the pain or guilt a second longer.

She levelled the gun by her right temple, her hand shaking so wildly that she was worried she might miss even at those few inches.

She remembered hearing about a famous political couple with the wife developing lesbian preferences later in their marriage. They'd stayed married for the sake of image, and the husband had responded by playing away from home – except that, unlike his wife's sexuality, this surfaced and hit the headlines. For a while that had made Nicola feel better about herself, not such a freak – but it was little consolation now. And the husband's playing away had been with twenty-somethings, not little girls!

A slow tear trailed at the corner of one eye, and she scrunched her eyes tighter shut as she tensed her finger against the trigger, her pulse pumping a wild tattoo. No other way out. *No other! Too much pain.* Gently squeezing, thinking how poor Mikaya must have felt in that same moment . . . but at the last second she suddenly eased her finger, her held breath rushing out in one. Her eyes blinked slowly open again. She'd been a coward all the way through, and now this was the coward's way out!

If she pulled the trigger, she still wouldn't be doing anything: she'd be making a pathetic gesture, not a stand! He'd just look at her body and sneer, seeing the final proof that she never had the guts to stand up to him. Worse still, poor Lorena would be left alone with him: there'd be nothing left then to stop him.

She lowered the gun. And where was he now? Lorena's first night back, and still he hadn't been able to resist sneaking along to her room.

She got to her feet, her legs trembling and her head so light that she thought she might topple over; then with a brief pause to get her mind clear and a last swallow of resolve, she started her way uncertainly towards Lorena's room.

Roman's breath rasped as he ran around to the front of the house, echoing back at him within the gas mask. The night-sight vision also took some getting used to: a strange grey-green with a slight blur left in the wake of any movement. With the jolting as he ran, almost everything ahead had a blurred edge.

All had gone well at first. They'd got to the back of the house before the power came back on. Funicelli had cut a hole in the back-door glass pane, slipped the latch and slid three gas pellets into the downstairs corridor.

The gas should have hit the S-18 guards in the rooms each side and seeped upstairs about the same time. But a guard from one of the rooms came out only seconds after the pellets had been thrown – perhaps he'd heard their faint skittering along the floor even through the closed door – and instantly he was running for the stairs and shouting.

A door opened the other side with another two guards who started to head in their direction at the back but didn't make it far: one collapsed halfway along the corridor, and the other, staggering, managed to get one hand on the door before Roman decided it was too close for comfort. He stepped from the shadows and shot the guard through the face from two foot away.

Immediately the guard fell, Roman's ears were honed sharply to catch movement upstairs: footsteps at the front of the house, the sound of a door sliding open. And when he heard the faint creaking of boards on the front deck, he started sprinting around. The rest followed five or six yards behind.

By the time he'd got around to the front of the house and could pick out shapes clearly from his jerky grey-green vision, the running figure was at least seven yards clear of the bottom of the veranda steps on the far side, heading towards the nearby trees and bushes: Donatien! At any second he'd be lost among them.

Roman steadied himself, levelled and fired – and saw Georges duck down and disappear among the foliage. Roman wasn't sure whether he had been hit, or was ducking to weave through the branches.

Roman ran on. His breath fell hard, almost deafening inside the gas mask; and as he realized it was smothering practically every other sound, he ripped the mask off and threw it. No danger of gas this far from the house, and listening out for Georges' movements was now the best guide: the tree foliage was too thick for him to see much.

No fallen body in sight as Roman reached the trees: he'd either missed or only clipped Georges. But as he started pushing and weaving his way through, it suddenly struck him that it was immaterial. Georges wasn't going anywhere! The trees stretched for no more than forty yards before hitting the edge of the lake. Then there were at least a hundred yards of frozen lake before the next landfall.

As soon as Georges started to cross it, Roman would have a clear shot at him. He wouldn't be able to get away.

Georges struggled to get his head clear.

He'd been close to black-out by the veranda door and had taken deep breaths in the cold night air, finally managing to get up and stagger out. He gradually picked up pace, but still his head was fuzzy, his step uncertain. He'd stumbled and almost fallen down the last few veranda steps in his haste – then at the edge of the trees, when he heard someone behind and a shot zipped through the leaves only a foot away, he almost stumbled again as fear made his legs turn to jelly.

A nightmare race: he desperately needed to gain more distance from his pursuer, but the more his lungs gaspingly pumped his run rather than cleared his head, still hazy and spinning from the gas, the closer he came to blacking out.

He thrashed his way wildly through the branches and shrubs. As another shot zipped nearby, he realized that his pursuer was either firing blind towards the sound of his movements or catching momentary glimpses of him.

He stumbled on, saw the clearing ahead. But as he burst through and came to the edge of the frozen lake, he stopped. It was too long a distance for him to be in the open, vulnerable. It was then that he noticed the small jetty with a power boat and snowmobile thirty yards to his right. Sound of rapid footsteps, tree branches flailing behind him. He bolted towards the jetty.

He was rasping heavily; he had to strain his hearing to pick up the position of his pursuer. His chest ached from running and his legs threatened to give out again in the last few yards; he practically fell on the snowmobile, frantically fumbling: button dead centre on the handle bars, pull-chord to the right.

Sound of his pursuer rustling through the last few bushes. Georges pressed the button and pulled the chord, but it didn't start.

His pursuer appeared through the bushes, and with the gas mask now removed Georges could recognize him: Roman! There was a suspended moment between them, Georges watching through his breath vapour as Roman orientated himself and finally fixed on him.

Georges pulled again, and this time the engine roared to life. But Roman was already raising his gun, aiming.

Georges revved quickly, leapt on and started speeding away. The first bullet whistled close by when he'd gone barely five yards, but the second hit: Georges felt it like a mule kick to his left shoulder, spinning his steering off for a second before he straightened again. The third came quickly afterwards, hitting the metal at the back of the snowmobile, and the fourth whistled clear again – by which time he prayed he was too distant for a clear shot.

Still he kept in the same hunched-forward position for at least another seventy yards, teeth gritted against the pain of his shattered shoulder, before he straightened up and risked a look back at Roman's position.

It took him a moment to pick out the figure in the weak moonlight: gun held limply at his side, breath heavy on the air as Roman stared bemusedly towards him. Georges couldn't resist smiling, then laughing, and as he sped along on the ice in no time it became a raucous whoop for joy with the sudden release of tension.

Over half a mile to the far ring of trees, and by then . . .

Georges thought nothing of the slight jolt at first, but it was the crack and heavier tilting as the snowmobile landed from the bump he'd hit – snow-covered tree branch or whatever – that was more worrying.

Then, as one of the skis caught against the edge of the ice, suddenly everything was spinning and Georges felt the solid thud of the ice against his side and the snowmobile jamming against his left leg. He lay there for a second, breathless, trying to get his bearings. But as he felt his trapped leg getting wet and saw the snowmobile tilt further and start to slide away from him, he suddenly realized with panic what had happened: the ice had cracked and he was sinking through it!

He desperately tried to scramble away as the snowmobile slipped deeper into the water – but its sheer weight tilted the severed ice block to a sharper angle, and Georges felt himself sliding inexorably with it. The water was like an icy hatchet hitting his groin. Georges clawed hard at the ice, but it was like trying to grip on to wet glass.

The water rose swiftly, taking Georges' breath away, and at the last moment he thrashed his arms against the water to stay buoyant – but the suction of the snowmobile sinking seemed to draw him under as well, and he felt the water fill his mouth and lap over his head for a second before his flailing arms were able to bring him back up again.

He spluttered and spat, grappling blindly for the first solid ice edge. He grabbed on to one block, but it moved. He bobbed down again for a bit, only just managing to keep his mouth clear of the water, eyes frantically scanning as he thrashed around. He could feel his body rapidly numbing, all sensation going from his nerve-ends. If he didn't get out fast, he wouldn't make it.

He gripped on to one more loose chunk before finally connecting with a solid mass. But as he started to lever himself out, his spirits sank. He could see that Roman was only fifty yards away, and fast closing in. He'd obviously started his sprint as soon as he'd seen the snow-mobile get into trouble.

If he didn't hurry, he'd get clear only to be a sitting target! The pain of his wounded shoulder was excruciating; he had to lever and slither mostly on his right side, was breathless from the strain before finally sliding his torso on to the ice like a landed seal. But as soon as he stood up and put weight on his left leg, he felt it buckle and the pain shoot up through his body – then remembered it getting jammed under the snowmobile.

Georges felt any last hope slip away in that second. And as he hobbled pathetically away and heard Roman's footfall rapidly approaching, he wished he hadn't bothered. He should have just let himself sink back below the icy water: at least he'd have robbed Roman of the satisfaction of shooting him.

37

Faint flicker of the eyes. Just for a second.

Ryall leant in closer. 'Are you awake, Lorena?'

After a moment, uncertainly: 'No.' The eyes perfectly still again, no movement.

But Ryall wasn't totally satisfied. Her answers had started to become evasive, weren't really telling him anything, and as he straightened up from leaning over and let out a sigh, he was sure her eyes had flicked open. And she'd had to think before answering his question.

But her eyes hadn't opened to look at him, more at something on the other side of the room. He turned, following where she'd been looking: the Mountie bear from Canada.

He studied it for a moment perched on a dressing table at the far end of the room, then started moving closer towards it: it was difficult to pick out much of its detail with it obscured in heavy shadow.

At his end, Bell tensed as he watched Ryall peer towards him, edging nearer. 'Oh, shit!'

He glanced again towards the phone, wondering whether to call and abort. But he felt rooted to the screen, afraid to move even for a second in case he missed something. Ryall came to within two yards, then suddenly turned back again.

Ryall was sure he'd seen Lorena's eyes shut just as he turned; as if she'd been curious as to where he was heading, what he was looking at.

'What's the game, Lorena?' he asked, moving back towards her. No response. Her body and her eyelids suddenly frozen, deadly still. 'I know you're awake, so we can stop playing now, Lorena . . .'

Bell leapt for the phone, punched out the numbers. It rang once, twice. 'For God's sake . . . *Come on!*' He banged his fist against the phone table.

'All that's left now is for you to tell me.' Ryall leant over Lorena's inert body. He trailed a finger gently up her neck and moved close until he was only inches away, could feel her soft breath against his face. And for a second it would have been easy to believe she really was under his control, like every other night. His voice lowered to a chilling whisper. 'Tell me . . . *tell me*. What's the game?'

Lorena's closed eyelids pulsed, a moment's trembling uncertainty which Ryall could feel too through her body; then he watched in satisfaction as her eyes finally snapped open.

'It wasn't my idea . . . wasn't my idea!'

The phone was answered halfway through the third ring, and Bell was immediately passed on to a duty sergeant. He frantically outlined the problem, his eyes still fixed on the screen six feet away: Lorena now sitting up, eyes wide, her head shaking as she pointed straight ahead at the camera lens.

The sergeant said that Crowley had gone off duty over two hours ago. 'But we'll phone him at home straight away and mobilize at the same time.'

Ryall had now joined Lorena in staring at the camera, this time with undisguised hostility. Then his voice came over strongly as he gripped her by the shoulders, shaking her. 'What have you done? . . . What have you done?'

'But for God's sake, hurry! There's probably not much time left.'

'We should have a squad car there in no more than six or seven minutes.'

Bell leapt back in front of the monitor the second he hung up, his hand trembling wildly as he reached out to the screen, as if to touch Lorena. 'Hold on, angel. Hold on! We'll be there soon.'

But he felt totally powerless. It was strange: able to watch every small movement, but unable to do anything. Like watching a sepia horror film which had suddenly headed in the wrong direction, and he'd had to phone someone else to stop the reels.

And as he saw Ryall throw Lorena back against the bed and move towards the camera, his face a mask of fury, he realized they'd probably be too late. He knew what was coming next: Ryall would rip the bear apart and destroy the camera, and it would be lights out: he wouldn't see what happened when Ryall turned his rage back towards Lorena.

But two paces away from the camera, his hand distorted as he reached out, Ryall suddenly stopped, turning to one side.

'*What?* . . . What the hell are you doing?'

'*What have you done? . . . What have you done?*'

The first sound that Nicola Ryall heard as she reached for the door handle. As she swung the door open, he was moving rapidly away from the bed, seemed to be interested in something at the far end of the room – then stopped as he noticed her, eyes falling quickly to the gun as he asked her what the hell she was doing. A condescending, indignant sneer.

She raised the gun a fraction higher and pointed it at him. 'Just don't move!' It sounded good in the movies, but coming from her, particularly with the tremor in her voice, it sounded lame, pathetic.

Ryall greeted it with the derision it deserved. 'What, are you going to shoot me? *You?*' One eyebrow raised, his mouth curled into a smile. 'Anyway, that thing doesn't even work.'

She hesitated only for a second; she was sure it was a bluff. 'Yes it does. I tried it out only a few months back,' she lied. And as she saw his face drop, she knew that it *did* work. She decided to pile it on. 'I'm getting quite good with it now.'

Now he looked seriously worried and raised his hands a bit. She relished the moment, the unfamiliar sense of power over him making her slightly giddy. She should have tried this earlier. She'd hardly ever been able to take control over her own life, let alone anyone else's.

Ryall met her gaze stonily and shifted a foot back towards Lorena, and Nicola waggled the gun at him more intently. 'I said don't move.' A frozen moment between them, then: 'The phone ringing just then. It was about Mikaya. She tried to take her own life.'

'*What?*' His brow knitted. 'Is she okay?'

'She is now.' Heavy sigh that quickly turned to a sneer. 'As if you should care. You're the cause of it.' She shook her head, her hand tensing on the gun. 'I let you get away with it with Mikaya for all those years. But not now with Lorena. Not any longer.'

His eyes fixed back on the gun. He leered nervously. 'You don't have the guts.'

'I wouldn't bank on it.' She moved a step closer.

Ryall could still pick up the tremor in her voice. He was sure that when it came to the crunch, she'd bottle out; but he wasn't sure enough to take the risk. He desperately needed a distraction. His eyes darted around uncertainly, sweat beads rising on his forehead. *The bear!*

He forced a strained smile. 'Anyhow, you shoot me – they'll get it all on film. They'll know it wasn't self-defence.' He pointed. 'They've got a camera in the bear.'

'*What?*' Nicola glanced towards it incredulously. *Camera in the bear?* She was the one meant to be on pills and alcohol. 'Can't you think of a better bluff than that?' But as soon as she said it, she realized it was almost too ridiculous to be a bluff.

'No, no – *really*. What do you think I was doing when you walked in? I was going to rip the bear apart and smash the camera.'

He was insistent, sounded convincing, and Nicola glanced towards Lorena for confirmation. Lorena just numbly nodded, and looking at her, wide-eyed and fearful as this drama unfolded, Nicola suddenly had something else to give her pause for thought. As much as her adoptive father was a monster, Lorena seeing him shot right in front of her was quite another thing.

'So why don't I just finish the job now and destroy the camera,' he said. 'Or better still, since you're such a good shot – why don't you shoot it, then.'

Nicola looked at him and at the bear. He was sneering challengingly, as if this was some kind of test between them. If she backed down, once again he'd have the edge.

'Go on,' he taunted. 'You're the crack shot after all.'

She levelled the gun at the bear; but as the shaking of her gun hand became more pronounced, almost out of control, the game was all but over. He could see through the bluff in that second, see her for the sham she was; the pathetic, quivering wreck she'd become. Fifteen seconds of control in fifteen years: in the end all he'd allowed her.

His leer became wider. 'You haven't even got the stomach to shoot a toy bear, let alone me.'

She gritted her teeth hard, struggling to control her trembling, determined to prove him wrong.

As Ryall saw her focus her aim and tense to squeeze the trigger, he made his move, lunging towards Lorena.

The gun swung sharply around, the shot zipping above him and smashing through the window behind. He'd crouched down low, most of his body shielded by the bed as he scrambled along the floor and clutched Lorena from behind.

As he got up again, he had her pinned tight against him: a complete body shield. His eyes jousted with Nicola's for a second, as if pressing home who was in control now.

'Move away from the door or I'll snap her neck.' He pulled his forearm tighter around Lorena's throat to demonstrate.

At the other end of the camera, Bell was on a knife's edge, his heart like a jackhammer as he watched events unfold. As the gun had pointed at the camera, he'd been screaming, 'No, *no*! It's a trick, a trick! If you're going to shoot anything, shoot *him*!' Now he was muttering under his breath, 'Be careful . . . be careful. Just hold him off – don't try anything. The cavalry will be there any minute.'

Bell watched Nicola hesitate, then finally move aside a couple of feet as Ryall edged half a step at a time towards the door with Lorena gripped tight against him. As Nicola followed, they were gone from camera vision; all Bell was left with was sound.

Nicola had moved aside almost mechanically. Afraid that he might harm Lorena, or just following his command the way she'd become programmed to all these years? Only as he edged towards the top of the stairs did the thought hit her.

'Where are you going with her?'

'I don't know yet. I'll decide that once I'm in the car.' Ryall's eyes shifted nervously downstairs. They'd know about the hypnosis from the tape, but had he touched Lorena anywhere he shouldn't? He'd got so used to touching Lorena where he liked when she was under that he just couldn't recall. 'They'll be here soon.'

'Here? *Who?*' She squinted as if she was having trouble focusing.

He nodded towards Lorena's bedroom. 'The bear. They've been taping.' Tired tone: tedium of the long years of having to explain every last detail to cut through her drink and pills stupor.

For Nicola, everything suddenly gelled in that instant. All she had to do was hold him up a couple of minutes. She raised the gun more confidently. 'Then you're not leaving.'

That condescending sneer again. 'You hardly had the stomach to shoot the bear . . . and both you and I know that you're not a good enough shot to get me without also hitting Lorena.' His eyes fixed on her gun hand, which started to shake more under his stare.

She found his confidence infuriating: a few words and she felt her own confidence blow to the wind like dandelion seeds. Exactly why he'd got away with everything for so long with Mikaya, and now Lorena. She'd let them down; and now even with a gun in her hand there was nothing she could do to stop him.

She put her other arm up, trying to steady the gun with both hands. But still it shook and wavered wildly.

'You're pathetic!' Ryall grinned at the spectacle. 'Go back and practise shooting at the bear – then when you're ready in a couple of years, let me know.'

She tried to face him off a moment longer, but finally crumbled, lowering the gun. He was right: she was pathetic. A hopeless wreck of a woman on the edge. She'd been crazy to even think she had the strength to –

But as he turned to the stairs with a last indignant 'Pathetic' and she caught the pleading look in Lorena's eyes, a fresh spark suddenly rose. A red-raw anger that made her eyes sting. Anger and disgust at the shell of a woman she'd become, at what he'd made of her. She'd done nothing to help Mikaya – but she couldn't let him go off now with Lorena! If she didn't do something now, she never would: one last chance of redemption! And in that moment, there was a window of opportunity: he turned slightly to take the first step down the stairs, his guard down fleetingly as he thought she'd given up the ghost.

She raised the gun and fired in the same motion, before his eyes could settle on her and steal her confidence away again.

But at the last second he'd half-turned towards her – perhaps catching the gun rising in the corner of his eye – and as she saw the splay of red on his side and at the same time on Lorena's night-dress, it looked like she'd caught Lorena as well.

Then she watched in horror as they were thrown down the stairs, Lorena almost directly under him as they tumbled down. They landed with a sickening thud at the bottom, and Nicola closed her eyes for a second, hardly daring to look, before finally rushing down.

She knelt a yard away from the tangle of their bodies: Lorena blood-soaked, half-trapped under his chest. No movement from either of them.

She tentatively reached out, then retracted her hand halfway. Her nerve had suddenly gone again. And so she just stayed in the same position, chewing at the knuckles of her gun hand and rocking back and forth on her haunches as she looked on at their bodies.

At the monitor's end, Bell had been listening out for every small sound after the gunshot, praying that he might hear Lorena's voice. Nothing but silence for a full minute; then, as he homed in closer, his ear less than an inch from the speaker, he finally picked up something: Nicola Ryall muttering 'What have I done? . . . What have I done?', punctuated by gentle weeping.

The search-beam of the helicopter raced across the landscape ahead of them.

'How far now?' Michel asked. They knew from Mundy that the exact location was halfway between Cochrane and a place called Fraserdale.

461

'Two or three miles, no more.'

Trees, lakes. Trees, lakes. They knew the house was on the edge of a lake, but Michel couldn't tell one from another. Hundreds of miles of the same vista stretching out across Northern Quebec and Ontario.

'I think that's it,' the pilot said after a moment, nodding to one side. He tilted the helicopter, starting to circle in.

And then as they straightened, the search-beam hit the house: no signs of life at first, not even any lights on. Michel's hands clenched tight. Again the image of picking through the bodies.

Then Michel spotted a figure in front of the house and another running along the lakeside. 'There! Something there!' He pointed.

The man by the house looked up at them anxiously as he was caught in the beam, but the man at the lakeside seemed to have half his attention on something deeper out on the lake.

'Where is *he* heading?' Michel pondered aloud.

'Don't know. Let's look see.' The pilot swung back and pointed the beam towards the lake.

At first they didn't see anything, and he had to tilt the beam to reach further out before it finally picked up the two figures facing each other at the centre of the frozen lake.

'So what now?' Georges gasped for breath.

'I think you know.' Roman smiled as he levelled the gun. 'Oh, but one thing just before you go. I had nothing to do with that abduction and attempted hit on you. That's not to say I didn't plan to kill you – but I think your friend and mine Chenouda knew that, and decided to try and get you into the programme.'

Georges shook his head. His first reaction was to disbelieve Roman, but then why would he bother to lie at this moment? So many side-games that he'd never been aware of; but there was one that did now prey on his mind.

'I can't believe that Jean-Paul is responsible for this now, has ordered you to kill me. It goes against everything he believes in.'

'Yep, you're right there. His idea was to get you away to Cuba. Soft fool that he is.'

Georges glared hard. 'He'll have you for breakfast when you get back.'

'I don't think so. As we speak now, he's being taken out. He won't be having any more breakfasts.'

'What, I . . . I don't –' But as he saw the gloating satisfaction on

Roman's face, he knew that it wasn't a bluff. His stomach dipped sickeningly, but his first thought was for Simone. Jean-Paul dead, and now him. She'd never be able to face it. He closed his eyes for a second and shuddered. Maybe they'd been wrong all along, wasting their time. In the end, Roman's ways held sway.

But if he was going to die, he might at least have one last swipe back. 'Jean-Paul was right about you all along. No fucking brain! The bullet the answer to everything.' Roman glared back intensely, his jaw set tight, but Georges met his stare evenly. 'So if you're going to shoot me, shoot me! Prove us all right what an absolute no-brainer you are.'

Roman's smile rose slowly as he remembered Venegas. 'That's where you got it wrong, college boy. I ain't going to shoot you.' Roman wallowed in the quizzical look on Georges' face for a moment before lowering the gun to Georges' feet. 'Sometimes I'm a little more subtle than you might appreciate. Or for that matter Jean-Paul.'

He fired and the ice cracked a foot to Georges' side, but the block didn't sever. And as the echo of the shot died, they suddenly heard the whirl of the helicopter.

Roman looked over his shoulder, momentarily distracted. But it was hovering over the house – one shot more and the block would break off. He fired again, but Georges had anticipated and leapt a yard to one side as the ice block severed and sailed free.

Roman aimed again at the ice, then suddenly his eyes shifted uncertainly. The engine tone of the helicopter had changed. It was moving towards them, bearing down fast.

Roman raised the gun towards Georges. Brief apologetic smile. 'Sometimes subtleties have to be thrown to the wind.'

In the helicopter, Michel had put a sniper called Gilles on alert by the open side door as soon as they started moving towards the two figures. Within a short distance, Michel could make out that the far figure was Georges, but with the other wearing night goggles he couldn't make him out clearly. But they could see the gun, and they were close enough by then for the sound of the second shot to reach them.

'*Oh God!* Are we too late?' Michel shouted. 'Try a shot! Try a shot!'

'He's shooting at the ice for some reason.' Gilles tried to steady the rifle against the movement of the helicopter, get the figure central in his night-sight. 'But we're still too distant.'

Then, as Gilles saw the gun being raised, he realized there was little choice. The figure moved wildly in his cross-hairs with the vibrations: it would be pot luck. But if he didn't try, it would be too late anyway!

Gilles squeezed off the shot, saw the figure jolt; not sure if it had fallen or if it was the kick of the rifle.

'You've got him!' Michel announced excitedly, seeing the figure sprawl a second before Gilles could pick it up again in his sights.

But as Gilles trailed the cross-hairs back across the figure, he could see that he'd only clipped him, a shoulder wound: the hand was rising again with the gun. Though this time they were closer, the shot cleaner. He pumped two bullets in quick succession through the back.

Clenched fist *'Yes!'* from Michel, but the elation was short-lived.

A high-powered .308 calibre, the bullets had gone straight through the body, shattering the ice beneath. A large ice block had broken free, the body sliding into the water as it tilted. But at the far end of the block was Georges. He tottered unsteadily for a second before falling on his side, and Michel watched in horror as he too slid in with the tilt of the ice block.

'Get us down. *Fast!*' he screamed.

'We can't land on the ice. It won't take us,' the pilot shouted back. He pointed with his thumb. 'Someone will have to go down on the winch.'

Michel assessed the situation for only a second before moving forward. 'Okay.'

Gilles leant back from the side door as a colleague hooked in Michel and they started to winch him down.

The winch rope swayed and spun wildly with the wind from the rotors, and Michel's view of Georges below came and went. A third of the way down he caught a glimpse of Georges thrashing around in the dark water, trying to grab on to a solid ice edge. He was still there halfway down, but as Michel straightened from a half-spin close to the ground, Georges had completely disappeared. His heart sank. No. *No!* He hadn't come all this way for it to end like this.

He frantically waved to the helicopter to bring him down closer. There was still a good five yards between the end of the rope and the ground. As more winch rope was fed out, its swing became even wider. Michel had to be careful where he landed in case he hit the broken ice and fell in as well.

And in the last few feet, just before he finally made contact, with a jolt, he was sure he saw the brief bob of a head and part of an arm appear above the water.

He quickly unhooked, ran breathlessly towards it. But by the time he got to the edge of the broken block, Georges had gone again. Michel scanned frantically for movement, bubbles. *Anything*. But there was nothing but still black water.

'No. *No!*' he screamed, falling to his knees. Knowing in that moment that if Georges died, he'd never be able to forgive himself for what he'd done. He started hurriedly brushing away the snow to see through the ice. Still only blackness: too dark to see through! He waved to the helicopter to bring the searchlight in closer.

Colleagues would pat him on the back, console him that he'd done his best. But all the time he'd know the dark truth; know that if it wasn't for his obsession, this would never have happened. He might as well have pushed Georges under with his own hands!

He clawed desperately at the snow, his hands red-raw and numb. 'Can't end like this . . . *can't –*' And suddenly he thought he saw something, a couple of feet to his right. He clawed away more snow, shrinking back slightly in shock as it finally became clear: Georges' face only inches beneath the ice, ghostly in the searchlight beam.

Michel let out a gasp of relief. Though he wondered whether he was already too late: Georges had probably been under almost two minutes. He banged on the ice, but it didn't break. He tried again, but still it didn't budge.

'Oh, Jesus, no . . . *No!*' Salt tears stung his eyes as he realized he couldn't get to Georges. Getting so close but still not able to save him! Having to watch from only inches away as Georges drowned before his eyes: maybe that was his punishment!

And he noticed something else then: Georges' body was shifting beneath the ice with a slight current. He tried another smash with his fist with no luck, then he had to clear more snow to see Georges clearly again.

Three more strikes in rapid succession, Michel grunting and screaming with each, putting all his strength into it. And with the last, with still no ice-break, Michel felt the last of his strength go with it, was about to roll over on to his back and give up, give one last cry of frustration and . . . then suddenly he remembered the sniper's bullets.

Michel took out his gun, measuring. He'd have to be careful with Georges' body shifting with the current. A few inches out and he'd hit him. But no time to clear away more snow!

He fired once, twice, just ahead of where he thought Georges would be. A crack appeared, and he fired a third shot to break the block free.

He scrambled down, reaching into the icy water. Nothing, *nothing*! He was frantic. Try another shot or clear some snow to see where Georges was? He started to clear with his other hand – a glimpse of something, though not very clear, and a second later Georges' body connected. He grappled on and yanked up hard, pulling Georges' head and shoulders above the water. A quick breath, and then he yanked again, putting all his weight into it until he had most of Georges' body solidly on the ice.

His breath vapour billowed hard in the freezing air as he leant over to resuscitate Georges – but at that moment he could see the ice block they were on cracking with the weight. He had to desperately grab and slide the body again, this time almost a full two yards – before collapsing in a heap at Georges' side, exhausted, as only a foot away the ice block gave way.

He was almost too out of breath to give mouth-to-mouth, he had to furiously pull in every breath he gave out, muttering repeatedly 'Don't die on me now . . . Don't die on me!' as he intermittently lifted off and pressed against Georges' stomach.

And as the first coughs and splutters finally came from Georges' mouth, Michel rolled on to his back and let out a great whooping victory cry towards the night sky and the swaying beam of the helicopter above.

Epilogue

July 8th, Montreal, Canada

Jean-Paul slowly surveyed the large reception room from the head table. The only one standing among the almost two hundred wedding guests.

'It's good to see the whole family together. Old friends, some that I haven't seen for a while.' His gaze fell on Art Giacomelli, who puffed on his cigar and nodded in recognition. 'And new-found friends.' Jean-Paul briefly acknowledged Michel Chenouda at the far table, then looked more pointedly towards Elena Waldren only a few places away at his table.

The reception was in the Hôtel de Ville, a spreading colonial-style five-star dating from the 1860s overlooking Place Jacques Cartier. The six-course dinner was finished, the telegrams read, and the only background sounds to Jean-Paul's speech were the unwrapping of truffles and chocolates, the hovering waiters replenishing brandy and liqueur glasses, and the gentle puff of cigar smoke sent twirling around rococo columns towards the high ceiling.

Jean-Paul spoke about his joy at Simone's birth, his eyes cast down for a second in memory of Claire, her mother, and Stephanie, whom she'd treated as a mother. Then he quickly lightened again with a few anecdotes from Simone's childhood and early teens before getting to the subject of Georges.

'I've trusted him with my business affairs these past few years, and now with my daughter. I'm not sure which I should be more worried about.'

Murmur of laughter from the guests. Jean-Paul held one hand up, changing the mood again. 'But not to make light of Georges' help. What we've tried to achieve since he joined us hasn't been easy – some said all along that it was impossible. And during that transition, there's been some changes and transitions too in the family, some of them painful. There was the loss of my brother' – Jean-Paul left a significant pause – 'Pascal. My father. And there's been some other close calls too . . .'

As he looked towards Georges and Simone, Simone's eyes watered.

He could have meant Georges' near-death, or the fear of losing her that he'd told her about soon after. The ambiguity of the way he'd mentioned his brother Pascal wasn't lost on her either. He'd vowed that he'd never speak Roman's name again, but to those not in the know he might have been referring to him as well as to Pascal.

'No, my friends. That transition has at times not been easy.' Jean-Paul pursed his lips tight and looked down for a second before looking up again to pick out Giacomelli and Chenouda. 'But hopefully we got there in the end.'

Michel solemnly nodded his accord. *Not been easy*. The understatement no doubt to pay homage without overshadowing the day.

Their entire RCMP game plan had changed in the aftermath of Roman's death, Michel reflected. Frank Massenat had turned Crown's evidence and spilt everything he knew about Roman's side game with Gianni Cacchione, and they'd also found out who was their internal leak: Guy Campion, now facing three to five for corruption. Michel was relieved that it wasn't anyone in his own department.

Massenat would get a lighter sentence, even though what he'd passed on probably wouldn't be enough to successfully prosecute Cacchione. But apparently Art Giacomelli had spoken at length with Carlos Medeiros. Now that Medeiros knew that Cacchione had been duping him the past three years, bets were being made that Cacchione wouldn't last the year.

Strange, after all these years of pursuit of the Lacailles, but Michel had felt a sense of gratification when he'd finally closed the investigation against Jean-Paul Lacaille. In a last meeting, Pelletier and Maitland had piped up about a few minor infractions that Jean-Paul could probably still be nailed over, but Michel was quick to remind them that if it wasn't for that last-minute call from Jean-Paul, they'd have lost their main witness anyway. And with the final rub of salt in Maitland's wounds about the damage caused by his boy Campion, the issue was closed.

Jean-Paul was quick to offer his thanks when he heard, but Michel brushed it off. 'You did nothing wrong. You were telling the truth all along – just that with Roman running interference in the middle, it took us a while to realize it.' Michel felt almost embarrassed at how close to the edge his obsession had taken him. If only Jean-Paul knew.

When Michel had gone to visit Georges in hospital, Georges had squinted up at him quizzically at one point. 'You know, Roman said the strangest thing just before he died. He said he had nothing to do

468

with my abduction and planned hit; he was trying to make out that you had something to do with it.'

'Strange.' Michel shrugged. 'Roman certainly was losing it towards the end.'

'He said that you probably knew he was about to kill me, so did it to get me away to a safe house and save my life.'

Michel smiled tightly back. 'I already saved your life once – so let's not get too carried away.'

From the way Georges' stare lingered on him a second longer with a challenging wry smile, he could see that Georges wasn't convinced. But that was probably as far as it would ever go: an ambiguous secret held just between the two of them.

Everything had settled back to normal at the Sherbrooke club. Azy had phoned him to say that Viana had returned from Haiti within a week of Roman's death. And hearing her account of events through Azy, his suspicion that Roman had been about to kill Georges was confirmed: no more lingering doubt or guilt whether he'd done the right thing getting Georges away.

At Michel's side, Sandra gently squeezed his hand as Jean-Paul came to the end of his speech.

The day had hopefully been as much a joy for his guests as it had been for him. There would be a firework display in forty minutes, Jean-Paul announced, and he hoped that they would enjoy the rest of the evening. 'And if you see anyone reaching nervously inside their jackets with the first bangs, they're nothing to do with me.' As a muted chuckle rose, he closed his eyes briefly, as if in penance. 'Not any more. From now on, there's only the future to look forward to. A future that belongs to Simone and Georges . . .'

Michel squeezed back. Sandra and he had started seeing each other socially outside of just when he went to pick the kids up. Nothing too serious, just a dinner date now and then and functions like this – but the kids lived in great hope. It was almost as if his obsession had crowded out everything else in his life, left no space for her and the children. And now that he'd finally let it go, she'd somehow sensed it: perhaps there was room for them again.

One step at a time – and while his future looked far less bright and certain than Simone and Georges' on this day, as almost two hundred strong rose to join Jean-Paul in toasting them, maybe there was some hope for him too.

★

The star-burst firework lit up the night sky over the St Lawrence.

Elena watched it fade out in raindrop tears of light, then another two dazzling bursts exploded in quick succession to its side. Bright sparks of hope among the darkness.

Some guests had clustered two deep on the open balcony, and the rest had gone downstairs in front of the hotel for a clear view. Elena had managed to get a front position on the balcony next to Georges and Simone.

The fireworks were being set off from a barge moored to the jetty. On Elena's first night back in Montreal two nights before, she'd sat only fifty yards away on the terrace of the La Marée restaurant having dinner with Georges and Simone. They'd taken a horse-drawn buggy ride there, and on the way Georges had pointed out the Basilica of Notre-Dame where the wedding would take place, the hotel for the reception, then the river as he mentioned Jean-Paul's firework plans. 'He got the idea apparently from the Jean-Baptiste Day displays.'

Now, as they looked on wide-eyed at the spectacular display, Georges commented, 'Looks like Jean-Paul's keeping to his promise of trying to outdo them.' Then, in a brief lull, he smiled warmly and reached out and clasped Elena's hand. 'I'm so glad you could make it, Mom.'

'That's okay.' She felt her eyes mist and flickered them down slightly in acknowledgement. She was about to say not half as glad as she was, but it would have sounded trite. 'I'm just sorry that it took me so long to get here.'

Georges grimaced tightly and gave one last reassuring squeeze before letting go, as if to say, 'It doesn't matter. You're here now.'

Mom. Only the second time now he'd said it. The first time had been at the end of the dinner at La Marée, as if she'd finally earned the spurs to the term, enough had now passed between them.

The Donatiens were a few people away from them, not close enough for Odette to have heard, though she probably wouldn't have minded. She'd spoken to them at length earlier, and from the brief acknowledging smile now as she caught their eye, they seemed to approve of this new-found affection between her and Georges. It had been a while in coming, and while the main push had come initially from her, in the end Georges had worked equally towards it.

Though this was only her first time back to Montreal since the nightmare night of their first meeting, she'd stayed on an extra five days then while Georges was in hospital, and there'd been hours on the telephone and a chain of letters between them since.

He'd asked everything they hadn't covered at that first meeting: more about her father, her mother, Gordon, her children – which by then also included Lorena, the *other* new-found member of her family.

Lorena had looked worse than she actually was when Crowley's men first arrived. All of the blood was Ryall's and she was unconscious from the fall; but it was only mild concussion, no skull fractures, and the most serious result of the fall was a broken arm.

Nicola Ryall would face a manslaughter charge, but with the mitigating circumstances would probably only get three years. With the prosecution and the disclosure of her lesbianism, there'd been no hope of her keeping Lorena. Elena and Gordon had been granted fostering rights, with the final adoption order expected within six months.

Elena had visited Nicola Ryall twice since with Lorena to assure her that she was free to come and see Lorena whenever she liked, and Nicola had freely admitted that even without the obstacles she wouldn't have made the bid to keep Lorena: she lacked the mental strength and ability to even cope with herself, let alone anyone else. It would take some time for those scars to heal.

Georges seemed to take a special interest in Lorena's progress. Maybe because what she'd been through had also been so tumultuous, or perhaps because he shared with her being a new-found family member.

Elena had seen her mother practically every other weekend since returning to England – catching up on lost time – and the first couple of meetings had been tearful. She'd gleaned the full story of how painful her father's final years had been, how deep his regrets had run. She'd reached over and consoled her mother at that point.

'Well, at least I finally found him. Hopefully for both of us.' Then they'd hit the Metaxas that Uncle Christos had brought with him harder, and started to laugh out loud as they dredged through fonder family memories and anecdotes. They moved on: the subject of her father's last years wasn't raised again between them.

Georges and Simone were honeymooning in France, and Elena's promise to her mother that one day she'd bring Georges to her door for a reunion would be made good when they visited Elena in only three weeks' time on their way back. Maybe then the circle broken thirty years ago would once again be complete, though there was nothing Elena could do to make good on all those lost years. Not just with Georges, but with her father too. That still left an empty gap inside her, and probably always would.

A warm summer breeze wafted against Elena's skin. Stark contrast to the cold when she'd last been here. And the mayhem she'd been through then also seemed a million miles away from this occasion now. Difficult to correlate the two.

But as the last of the fireworks died, she found her eyes drawn into the darkness, a momentary chill running through her as she recalled that night trapped within the darkened visor, going to see Georges. She pushed the thought abruptly away, tried to think of it like the warm and welcoming darkness of the chine.

On her last visit to the chine only a week ago, Lorena had asked to join her. Elena had been anxious at first that Lorena would be nervous, would run in panic from the smothering darkness as before. But after an initial trembling that Elena had felt in Lorena's hand, she'd been fine; maybe the ghosts that Lorena always feared would come for her as darkness settled – the sewers and Patrika and then later Ryall – had finally gone from her mind.

For Elena, though, while the chine still felt warm and welcoming, a place where she could escape from the madness and pressures of the world outside, most of its magic had somehow gone. And only now did she realize why: she had no more secrets to share with the darkness.